GRIEVOUS

Grievous

H. S. CROSS

FARRAR, STRAUS AND GIROUX

NEW YORK

Farrar, Straus and Giroux
175 Varick Street, New York 10014

Copyright © 2019 by H. S. Cross
All rights reserved
Printed in the United States of America
First edition, 2019

Library of Congress Cataloging-in-Publication Data
Names: Cross, H. S., 1968– author.
Title: Grievous / H. S. Cross.
Description: First edition. | New York : Farrar, Straus and Giroux, 2019.
Identifiers: LCCN 2018042816 | ISBN 9780374279950 (hardcover)
Subjects: | GSAFD: Bildungsromans.
Classification: LCC PS3603.R6739 G75 2019 | DDC 813/.6—dc23
LC record available at https://lccn.loc.gov/2018042816

Designed by Jonathan D. Lippincott

Our books may be purchased in bulk for promotional, educational, or business use.
Please contact your local bookseller or the Macmillan Corporate and Premium
Sales Department at 1-800-221-7945, extension 5442, or by e-mail at
MacmillanSpecialMarkets@macmillan.com.

www.fsgbooks.com
www.twitter.com/fsgbooks • www.facebook.com/fsgbooks

1   3   5   7   9   10   8   6   4   2

For my parents and my godmother

Dramatis Personae

Time: March–December 1931

At St. Stephen's Academy, Yorkshire
    Forms: Third, Fourth, Remove, Fifth, Lower Sixth, Upper Sixth
    Houses: Grieves's, Burton-Lee's, Lockett-Egan's, Henri's
    Terms: Lent, Trinity, Michaelmas
    The Senior Common Room and staff
        James Sebastian, Headmaster, Divinity
            his wife, Marion
        John Grieves (Grievous), History
        Robert Burton-Lee (The Flea), Latin and Greek, Dean of
            Upper School
        Lockett-Egan (The Eagle), English
        Henri (Ennui), French
        Kardleigh, choirmaster and school physician
        Palford, Mathematics
        Lewis, secretary to the Headmaster (Capt. ret.)
        Fardley (Fardles), porter
        Mrs. Firth, Grieves's matron
    Boys (at start)
        The Third: Timothy (Infant) Halton, Malcolm minor, White,
            Fletcher
        The Remove: Thomas Gray (Brains) Riding, Trevor Mainwaring,
            Leslie, Prout, Ives, Whittaker

The Fifth: Tighe (Legs), McCandless
The Lower Sixth: (Pious) Pearce, Moss, Crighton,
  MacCready (Mac)
The Upper Sixth: Carter, Swinton
Grieves's Prefects / Junior Common Room (at start)
  Carter, Head of House (Head Boy)
  Swinton, Captain of Games
  Moss, Prefect of Chapel
  Pearce, sub-prefect (replacing Austin, Prefect of Hall)

In Saffron Walden: The Líohts—Cordelia, Owain, Margaret (Meg) neé Drayton; Mrs. Kneesworth

In London: The Woodlings—Alec, Bea (née Ousley), Nicholas, Claire, Tony, Arabella, Rory

Elsewhere in England: Jamie's father, Bishop Sebastian; Gray's mother, Elsa Riding (née Ousley); his godfather, Peter Andersen; Morgan Wilberforce; Merewether; the Audsleys

On the Continent: M. Chose, Julia and Randall Vandam, Miss Murgatroyd, Zoltan Zarday

The Dead: Gray's father, Tom Riding; Peter's wife, Masha; John's parents and his wife, Delia

LENT

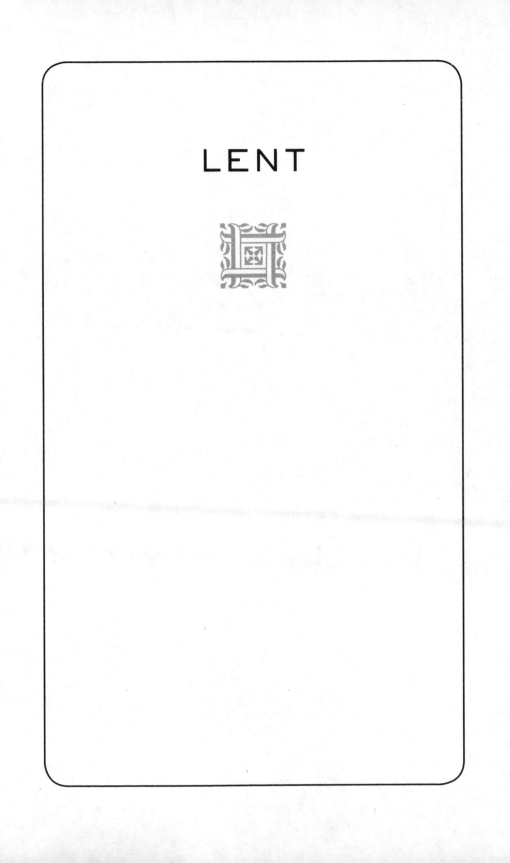

Ewes, lambs, pocked lanes, ivy—rain, raining, rained upon.

Third row of the Remove's History lesson, Gray Riding slouched as much as discipline would allow, pen, exercise book: *Weds. half hol, nothing worth changing shoes. Rain last five, rain today.*

Everything in sight had succumbed to the damp. Towels never dried. Walls perspired. Games kit hung clammy in the changing room, where mildew grew with abandon.

Fifty-seventh day, Lenten Term, boredom chronic, boredom acute, the most dismal day in the year of our Lord 1931.

Then—in an instant?—paper brightened, silence fell. Mr. Grieves left his lecture and drifted to the window. Gray lifted his pen. Could everyone feel it on their skin, colors blooming warm and sharp? Even the back of his throat had a taste, like what you smelled when spring came to wake up the ground and banish winter in a night.

Gray wiped his spectacles. The rain had stopped, leaving only drips from the gutter. The Remove saw it, too, and when the bell rang, they cheered. Gray screwed the cap onto his pen, but the ink had run, pooling on the page and then smearing when he closed the book on the mess.

✦

After lunch there was a wire. John took it from his matron and fumbled with the seal. Urgent notes never brought good news, but in this day and age what hazard? He tore it in frustration, *Mr. John Grieves, St. Stephen's Academy, nr. Fridaythorpe, Yorkshire.*

The tides at Lancaster came faster than a racing horse. If the drowning didn't get you, the quicksands would. He was a grown man and a Housemaster; he was seven years old and his mother was dead all over again.

✦

Where did it come from, all that water? Cordelia opened the window in the alcove off the ward, but when she stuck out her head, the rain was gone. She knew about weather systems, trade winds, the Gulf Stream. Perhaps the Atlantic had dried up at last. Perhaps the spires of the lost city were poking through the seabed while England and the Emerald Isle drowned.

When she was small, the rain had made her think of Heaven.
—The angels are crying, Uncle John would tell her.
—Why?
—The sins of the world.
—What's that?
Her godfather would open his mouth but say nothing.
—Where do angels come from?
—God made them.
—Where does God come from?

✦

They were one missed call-over away from the cane. Gray hadn't been caned since the beginning of last term (a prank of Trevor's—egg, saltpeter, chimney), but despite the recent rocky patch, he thought he could make it to Easter. He put only 35 percent on Trevor's avoiding the Junior Common Room, but bets on Trevor, even with himself, were notoriously unpredictable.

Gray wasn't a coward, he hoped. He'd survived as many as six from the JCR. But as a punishment, the cane contaminated days. You couldn't look the JCR prefects in the eye afterwards. The physical effects lingered. It was all unendurably personal. Lines at least could be done with an air of sarcasm, chores completed as Jean Valjean in prison, and even punishment runs might offer an interval with their Captain of Games when Swinton might speak to him with something other than the scorn due a boy hopeless at sport. All punishment brought shame, but the cane left him feeling ill, even after it was over.

In *Stalky* they didn't care. They took just punishment in their stride and exacted revenge for anything else. Valarious, likewise. Marks were a badge of honor to him, as they essentially were to Trevor.

Trevor emerged from the washroom and led him through the post-luncheon throng. They might be on tight terms with the Absence Book, but they were, Trevor reminded him as they passed the school porter, no longer gated. Sun was breaking through the clouds, hours of half holiday stretched before them, and there was no reason they oughtn't spend the afternoon at the Keep and make it back well in time for call-over. Ninety-eight percent (though you couldn't forget the standard deviation for Trevor himself).

They strolled nonchalant past the juniors diving in the mud, past their compatriots in the Remove heading to the fives courts for battle, past upper schoolers choosing sides for ad hoc football. They walked without urgency, as if on routine ramble of their wide, wet bounds. *Beyond the jousting fields of Castle Noire stands Grindalythe Woods, alluring and entirely out-of-bounds.* Their boots squelched as they circumnavigated the puddle-cum-lake that divided the upper and the lower pitch. *Beyond the woods, even more alluring and even farther out-of-bounds, stands McKay's Bothy.* They slid down the ditch that marked a boundary in cricket season. *There is, in bards' lore, a third route, through the woods, past the keeper, Grendles módor, the details of which have evaporated like mead at the bottom of a barrel.* Slipping from sight, they dashed for the old lodge. *For three years, it has been widely suspected that Valarious holds the keys to that byway. Did he not squire for the Great Wilberforce? The Great Wilberforce, who, it is known, often took leave of Castle Noire to cavort with his men at the tavern in Fridaythorpe?* Inside the ruined hut, they hauled up the stone—*None of the men told how they were able to disappear from castle grounds*—crawled down the chute—*and then return, listing, hours after the watch*—wriggled through mildewed, pitch-black—*If none of Wilberforce's men had told*—tickling, hopefully not spiders—*who else could know but Valarious? Of course, the knights of Castle Noire find it difficult to imagine that young Valarious could hold the keys to such a fortress, but even as they resent the possibility,*

5

they hope for it—every creeping thing—*If secrets are not passed on, they pass away, into dead knowledge.*

The ground sloped up, and they emerged into the woods, into air, light, and freedom. Their confinement at the Academy, some from rain, some from gating, had lasted three weeks, and now as Trevor led them up the path, Gray saw that streams had colonized the woods, presenting muddy ravines and newly fallen branches. He half-expected to find the Keep washed away, but as he and Trevor arrived at the wall above the barn, there it stood, stalwart and loyal.

On the heels of his relief, fear flashed, like being told his name was on the notice board. What if the barn actually were to wash away, or collapse? Inside the hollow wall, beyond the ledge that sheltered their books and cigarettes, beyond sight of anyone who looked without knowing what to look for, there in the heart of the barn, if such a place could have a pumping organ or seat of feeling, there, though he hadn't touched it or looked at it in years, though most of the time he let himself forget it was there, there in the smoldering ashes or the rain-soaked splinters, however it happened, there someone would find it.

Sometimes he dreamed of the box. In his dreams, there was no fear. In his dreams, he swam through Grindalythe Woods, slid down the slope behind the barn, and reached into the rat-nesty walls for his father's medicine box, the silver nameplate, *T. Riding*, untarnished. The box had no latch, the treasure his for the taking, and in the dream it was treasure inside, rich beyond measure, known to no one, power and luck and blessing all his, nearly forgotten but not.

 Mrs. Kneesworth disapproved of her reading, but Cordelia pretended not to notice. That black tome was full of air to breathe. She'd waited nearly six weeks for it at the library, and because things always came in threes, it had arrived the same day that she'd recited, without forgetting, the poem for the last meeting of term and the same day that she'd won the geography prize, a brilliant gold-edged volume. A triple good, which ought to have told her a triple bad was on its way. If she'd been paying attention, she would have noticed two of the three bad things already arrived, her parents' quarrel on the way back from the school concert and her father's case missing from the corridor in the morning, but she had been so filled with anticipation about the recitation and the prize that she'd let the two bads pass before her eyes. Not until the third bad did she see how blind she'd been.

Mrs. Kneesworth plied her with childish books, *How about Miss Nesbit? Mr. Milne? Oh, Mr. Louis Stevenson!* She worried, Cordelia knew, about children her age. She'd confided to Cordelia's mother some malarkey about children conceived in the turmoil of war. They'd been shaken in the womb, Mrs. Kneesworth said, and there was something not quite right about them. Cordelia told Mrs. K the black book was for school, an important bit of holiday work her teacher had flattered her by assigning. She could tell Mrs. K didn't approve of that either, but at least the woman kept her peace.

There inside those pages she boarded the research schooner Poseidon and sailed west with its crew, past Ireland and into the wide Atlantic. No matter what shoes clacked across the ward, what doctors and Sisters whispered and wrote, she stood with salt wind in her hair, looking through the glass for that floating seaweed jungle, their quarry, the great Sargasso Sea.

✦

When they finally reached the barn, Gray was sweating, though thankfully it hadn't marked the book he carried under his shirt, the new copy of *Stalky & Co.* He'd first encountered *Stalky* in Wilberforce's study; he'd been subjected to Kipling before and never cared for it—who could make sense of India?—but the little red book on Wilberforce's shelf spoke one imagination to another. Here were Stalky, McTurk, and Beetle, three schoolboy crusaders against stupidity, self-importance, and boredom. Inside those pages and inside the Kipling avatar, Beetle, he found himself as he would like to be. When Wilberforce left the Academy, a legend in his time, he gave the book to Gray, and while Gray wanted to refuse Wilberforce's gifts, he didn't. Couldn't.

Gray had turned fourteen last month, and his godfather had sent a fresh copy of *Stalky.* At first Gray had been disappointed at the duplicate, but then he'd noticed the title: *The Complete Stalky & Co.*, an expanded volume containing stories Kipling had omitted from the original. No one at the Academy had such a book. No one else had read these tales. No one else knew how Stalky had earned his nickname, how there had been a day when Corcoran (Stalky-to-be), McTurk, and Beetle had gone on a cattle raid with some other boys, an excursion Corcoran disparaged as not *stalky* enough for them. Since his birthday, Gray had read the story enough to have it nearly memorized. He could see it, even dream it, but wasn't there a power that could transport him inside it to inhabit with his body the stories whose every word was written on his heart?

He and Trevor had agreed it was prudent to keep the *Complete* at the barn, safe with the original *Stalky*, their cigarettes, and their penny dreadfuls. These they collected from the cache in the wall before mounting the ladder to the loft. The afternoon passed in desultory conversation, cigarettes shared, Trevor reading the *Complete*, Gray running his eyes across a penny dreadful as the barn sheltered him from the wind, the Academy, and the person he was there . . .

It was possible that Valarious had at some point been sent, by exasperated guardians, to an academy for knights (not an academy per se, but dispatched to some école or chivalric crammer) where he met two friends, an Irishman and a scholar, and one day embarked on a cattle raid (he would have been fourteen at most) with assorted other knights-in-training, manor-born, knowing not their right hands from their left. Valarious would have scorned the venture, not valarious enough for him, but along he'd gone, and when the manor-borns had been captured, Valarious & Co. had engineered the rescue, trapping manor-borns and captors together in a barn and—

—Listen, Trevor said, you've got to face facts.

Gray opened his eyes and closed his mouth. Trevor closed his book:

—At the end of the day, Grieves is a beast. He must be Cadified.

The day's task, determining which of their associates were foul enough to deserve the title Cad-with-a-capital-C, an exercise dubbed Cadification.

—You can't drag Grievous back into it. Once off, off, we said.

—We didn't strike him off, Trevor replied. We passed him over temporarily.

They'd struck their Housemaster off, early and firmly.

—You've got to be impartial, Brains. If we get this wrong, Cadification will mean nothing!

—It'll mean nothing if you chuck Grievous in the same boat with the Flea and Pearce.

Trevor began to roll a cigarette with the last of the good tobacco:

—Exhibit one, his sense-of-humor failure Monday night.

Grieves had looked a storm as they stood on his carpet, dockets in hand. Official charge: insolence at call-over. Unofficial: toying with Pious Pearce, a sub-prefect freshly minted, too keen for the genuine article, too pi for good taste. Less than a fortnight into his post, Pearce had earned the resentment of the lower forms, the scorn of the Upper School, and from the Remove, a burning hatred at his heavy-handed brass. His pomposity at call-over could not be borne. The plan was Trevor's, the text Gray's.

—Mainwaring? Pearce had read haughtily.

—Here am I! Trevor had replied.

Snickers in houseroom at the deviation from *sum*. When Pearce had hectored, Gray had called from the crowd:

—Saul! Saul! Why persecutest thou me?

Grieves's House had found it droll, and the rest of the alphabet had replied with *Here am I* or, *Here am I, Saul*. But Mr. Grieves had found their dockets unamusing. He had told them to knock it off. He had more pressing matters than their restlessness. He was tired of them, Gray saw, and when Grieves gave the imposition, there was no ironic look, just fifty lines and *This will stop*. The next night, they'd answered properly, but those who'd persisted with *Here am I*, Grieves had sent to the JCR, which dealt them two apiece.

—It was only fifty lines, Gray said.

Trevor lit the cigarette and flicked the match over the edge of the loft.

—I don't know if it's blindness or love, he said, but you're missing the point, Brains.

—For the last time, I do not love him.

—*Oh moon of love*, Trevor crooned.

—How can you Cadify the only master who doesn't whack?

—*High up above* . . . That's what makes him Cad Royale. He doesn't have the nerve to do it himself, so he passes it off to the JCR and closes his eyes to their megalomania.

—It's not as though he's a coward.

—Worse, Trevor said, he's a pacifist. Everyone knows they're more vicious than the rest.

Gray began to collect their things, wrapping their books in the oilcloth.

—The bare fact, Trevor continued, and you'd know it if you paid any attention to *Stalky*, is that Grieves is afraid to wield the cane because he's afraid of the influence it might have over him.

9

—Got that from your idea shelf, did you?

—He's scared to death he'll enjoy it.

—One, that's vile.

—But true.

—Two, why hasn't anyone checked the time?

He fished Trevor's watch from the cigarette tin as Trevor's foot kept patter time:

—*Oh what the deuce, do you suppose we care to hear the silly stuff you have to spill about the moon?*

Gray looked at the watch and shook it.

—*Of course the moon is high above, for everybody saw the guy who hung it up this afternoon.*

It hadn't stopped. It still ticked, its minute hand inching towards twelve, and its hour—he threw it at Trevor's head—

—Oi!

. . . but missed.

—It's five!

—Don't be stupid.

—Five o'clock!

—It's still light.

—You swore—

Trevor consulted the watch:

—If you hadn't kept me jawing—

—Just this afternoon, you *swore* we'd be back!

—And if you shut up, we still will.

They dashed to their tasks. Trevor scoured the hay for cigarette stubs as Gray climbed down to stash their things in the wall (and lift the lid of the box long enough to snatch the letter he'd meant to—)

—Cave! Trevor called.

Gray froze on the ladder and then crawled back up to where Trevor was crouching. The window's cracked glass broadcast news from the common: four figures, school togs, two from their own House, two from another. Four fags out-of-bounds, approaching, identifying, entering—

—And this is where Fletchy and me bunked to last week, said a white-haired fag.

—Plummy, said Malcolm minor.

The white-haired fag was from Burton-Lee's House, as was the one called Fletchy, or Fletcher. Of the two from Grieves's House, Gray knew Malcolm minor from the dorm. Despite having an elder brother with a bold reputation, Malcolm minor ran his gaze across the barn as one viewing pin-ups for the first time. The white-haired fag, whose name proved actually to be White, bragged about his and Fletcher's exploit, their escape last week from farmers, their refuge in the barn, the hours they passed there, hours they proposed to pass there again, regularly, having claimed it for their own.

—Is this where that chap got killed? asked the last fag.

Newly arrived that term, lowest in Grieves's House, lowest in the school, his name was Halton.

—Is this *McKay's* barn?

A horrified pause in which the other three absorbed Halton's speaking the unspeakable. Then, they tackled him:

—Shut up, Infant.

—Shut up, you little sod.

—Shut up or we'll shut you up.

—First, White lectured, there were two chaps, not one. Second, the chap who died didn't get killed. He killed himself.

The kicking stopped. Halton caught his breath:

—That isn't what Pearce said.

The kicking resumed.

—First, White said, Pearce is a cretin. Second, he's an idiot.

—Third, Malcolm minor continued, if he'd quit wanking over the Bible, he might get a notion.

Not that Malcolm had a notion, but Gray supposed that compared with Halton, the others were fountains of notions.

Fourth, White said, they were in our House, not yours, so we ought to know.

Wilberforce had known what happened, but he'd always refused to speak of it, even to Gray. If Gray didn't know the truth, then without a doubt neither did these pip-squeaks from Burton-Lee's. They needed taking down a peg. Or three.

—You need taking down a peg, White told Halton.

That was how it went, how it always went. Gray wasn't sure where Halton had come from or why his mother should have shipped him off to the Academy in cold February when everyone else had been fighting their way through the Third Form since September. As a citizen of the Remove, Gray naturally made it a point not to notice the Third, but Halton, friendless save Malcolm minor, bottom of his form (Gray read the notice boards), fagging for the odious Pearce—

—What'd he kill himself for?

Halton, though balled on the ground, would not shut up.

—And what happened to the other chap?

Fletcher and Malcolm minor hauled him up until he hung, toes just off the floor, for White's inquisition.

—What's the Natural History Society?

—Bug and ticks, Halton answered.

And on it went, pinch for yes, punch for no, slap across the face for hesitation.

—Kit and Caboodle?

—Choir. Ow!

—A kitten indeed, Fletcher remarked.

—Never fear, Fletchy, we shall educate!

Fletcher took the lead: to expel (dispose), vegetables (grass), roast mutton—Halton hesitated. A ringing—

—Dead Man's Leg?

A chorus of *No!*

—You *absolute* shag-rag. It's Cat's Head.

—Cat's Head!

—He's a half-wit, Fletch concluded. And an infant, and a snot. I shan't bother with him any longer.

—One, White announced, grasping Halton's ears, you have no brain in your putrid head. Two, if you want to assist us any longer, you'll shut up and go stand guard.

An emphatic yank and he let Halton go.

—*Cave canem*, Halton muttered, moving gingerly towards the door.

—Infant!

—What?

—What did I just say?

—To shut up and guard the door.

—And what are you doing right now?

—Going to the—

—*What* are you doing *right now*, Infant?

—Talking to you?

—Thank you. Now if, Infant, you are talking to me, would you kindly tell me how you can be shutting up?

Fletcher seized him again as White applied a penalty.

—I do believe he's blubbing, Fletcher said. Are you blubbing, Infant?

—I'm bloody not.

—There he goes, Malcolm said, not shutting up again.

Gray began whispered conference above:

—It won't take them long to monkey it up here.

—Keep your hair on, Trevor said. I'm thinking.

As the hour of call-over approached, they watched from their Olympus, gods trapped by human affairs. Halton went outside, White began tearing planks from the walls, and Malcolm attempted acrobatics from one of the stalls. Intruders in the Keep, not one or two but four, savages all, nothing to lose. As with all bad things, time raced, and just as one disaster had made itself at home, another arrived.

—Bloody . . . *Saul*, Trevor breathed.

Gray peered through the window where Trevor gazed in disbelief. Tramping up the slope, a fifth party, mackintosh, cap, prefect's badge affixed to the front, Pious Pearce incarnate out-of-bounds, trudging with purpose towards the barn, around it . . .

—What's all this?

Pearce threw open the door, dangling Halton by the collar like some music-hall bobby with public school accent. The juniors froze.

—Malcolm, White, Fletcher, and Halton. *Very* good.

White recovered first:

—Hullo, Pearce. What brings you out this way?

His bravado did not impress Grieves's sub-prefect. Pearce informed them that he would be asking the questions.

—What was the question? Halton piped.

Pearce half smiled as the barn door fell closed behind him.

—I don't know where you get your cheek, he told Halton. You must be either a dolt or an adamant sinner.

(—Oh, Saul, Gray whispered.)

—You may as well out with it, Pearce told them. You're already done for bounds. And trespassing at McKay's barn.

—McKay's barn! White cried. Is that what this is?

—Save it for someone less credulous than me, Pearce said.

(—*More credulous*, surely?)

(—*Will* you shut up? Trevor hissed.)

—Honestly, Pearce, we'd no idea we were out-of-bounds. But the mist came in, and we ducked in here, and—

—Where did you think you were when you crawled through the hedgerow?

White looked to his companions:

—Hedgerow? We didn't see any hedgerow, did we?

The juniors professed no knowledge of hedgerows.

—The one that runs across the entire south bounds. Ever heard the term *flagrante delicto*?

Trevor snorted.

—Why compound it all by lying transparently?

The juniors replied with silence. Pearce dropped Halton and commenced a tour of the barn. (Satisfying his own curiosity about the forbidden?) Passing under the loft, he stopped.

—*What's* that smell?

—Smell? White protested.

—Oh, you're in it now, Pearce said. Bounds, trespassing, *smoking*.

He snatched Malcolm minor up to his toes:

—Do you know the penalty *just* for smoking?

—Hic! Yes.

—Do you know *why* this place is out-of-bounds?

—Yes. Hic!

—Why are you making that revolting noise? Pearce demanded.

—I—hic—have the hiccups, Malcolm said.

Pearce dropped Malcolm and summoned his own fag. Halton approached.

—I must say, Pearce opined, this does not look good. The Head is going to take a dim view. The dimmest.

—But we *weren't* smoking, Halton said. I swear.

—Don't perjure yourself in the bargain! I'm trying to help, don't you see?

He twisted Halton's collar:

—Do you know the root of the word *worry*?

Halton did not.

—It's *worien*, to strangle. I want you to feel the worry I have for you. For your soul.

Halton appeared to feel it.

—Uncle Stalky's had a flash, Trevor breathed. Wait for the signal, crawl across the ledge under the eaves, down that shaft, and bunk.

—I'm not jumping off the roof! Gray protested.

—Do it. Unless you want to wait for this lot to morris off.

And he was gone, across the ledge and out of sight. Trevor hadn't, of course, said what the signal would be or where to look for it, but below,

14

Pearce continued to badger Halton, Halton continued to resist, and Malcolm minor's hiccups continued to strain their nerves.

—I worry, Pearce said, not what will happen if you do wrong, but what will happen if you carry on doing wrong.

Gray felt it before he saw it. Could fear make things true? Or had all his errors rolled at last into this ball, festering, unguarded, until now when the rain had stopped—started, stopped, started again—it had been found, as all shame was found.

—At least stop lying, Pearce said. At least do that.

Halton—again off his feet, again at the wall, only hurt before him—Halton stared over Pearce's shoulder, stared as if seeing, as if his gaze had o'erlept the desperate present and landed there in that gaping, fatal cleft where Gray would have placed, if allowed, their books and cigarettes, that chasm where still lodged, to any who would see—

A ringing crack and Halton's hand flashed to his face.

—You make me sick, Pearce said. You deserve everything coming your way.

Halton's gaze was still in the wall, but he made no sound.

—Right, Pearce announced, back to the Academy, all of you.

He strode past them to the door and with an impatient thrust of the arm lifted the latch. The portal did not budge. He applied his shoulder, but the door held firm.

Gray's heart began to race before his brain could understand—the how and why beyond power of thought—but Trevor's signal was undeniable, clear as an icy lake, chapter one, page fifteen, *Stalky* manifest.

—Is this your idea of a joke? Pearce demanded.

—Hic.

—Malcolm!

He didn't wait for the rest. As Pearce rattled the door, Gray crawled along the ledge under the eaves and landed hard below.

—Bottled 'em in there jolly tight, Trevor said.

—You wouldn't care if I killed myself!

Trevor hoisted him to his feet:

—Life's perilous, Pauline, and that door won't keep Pearce happy long.

They slipped down the slope and through the hedgerow to the road. The rain, having spared them, began to fall in earnest as they ran. If they made call-over (5 percent, names in the second half of the alphabet) they'd be soaked, and yet, wasn't there a story in there somewhere . . . ?

The bells of Fridaythorpe rang then, not five but quarter past, the hour of call-over. Gray staggered to a stop and bent over, panting. Trevor rummaged in his pocket, spilling coins, nibs, sheep bones:

—Bloody sodding excuse for a ticker.

—Only works when you look at it.

—*Bloody* hell.

—You're so Stalky, Gray gasped, did you know that? You're a whole Stalky and—

—Shut *up*.

They'd escaped the barn but would not escape punishment. They never should have gone, except they should have been weeks ago, before White & Co. tramped their nosy feet inside, before they conquered it, they thought, as their own, before Pearce, before Halton, before hungry eyes looked and took—

—This will never do, Trevor declared.

—We can appeal to Grieves. Maybe he'll only gate us.

Trevor had been tapping the surface of a puddle, and now he plunged his foot in.

—If we hoof it now, we'll still make lock-up, Gray continued.

But Trevor wasn't listening. No longer scowling, his face was calm, alert.

—Hold on a tic, Trevor said. I think I hear something.

Dread fell with the rain. Not only was Trevor's expression one Gray had seen countless times before; not only had Trevor retreated from the twilight and taken refuge in *Stalky*; not only was Trevor, in their hour of doom, persisting with Stalky's far-fetched adventure—

—I believe someone is calling for help!

—You can never admit you're wrong, can you? You've always got to take things—

—Riding, do you or do you not hear voices crying from yonder hillock?

—I hear our docket in tonight's prefect meeting!

Not only was Trevor beyond reason—

—You're narrow-minded. That's your trouble. All you think about is your own skin when there are people in need, and we—we have happened by!

Not only that, but Trevor's lunacy was the only logical course of action.

And they were off, jogging back up the common to McKay's barn, out-of-bounds, Strictly Forbidden, occupied by the enemy, Gray's spectacles pointless in the rain, that blurry, dripping frontier—was that how it would be, if he could ever travel inside, inside *Stalky*, inside Valarious, to be the kind of creator who could take on flesh inside his creation and touch with his skin the people he had made?

They arrived, as Kipling would have phrased it, bellowing halloos of rescue. Two more perplexed boys the March rain never wetted. And they were so difficult to enlighten.

—Who's there? Pearce called.

—Who's *there?*

—We're from the Academy!

—The Academy?

—St. Stephen's!

—So are we!

—You are?

—Are *you?*

—Who the devil is that? Pearce thundered.

—Mainwaring. Who the deuce is that?

—Mainwaring, Pearce here!

—Pearce? Trevor exclaimed. What are you playing at?

—We're stuck.

—You're *stuck?*

—The door's stuck.

Trevor rattled the latch:

—It's jammed *jolly* tight, Pearce. It'll take us at least half an hour to knock it open.

—Unless we go to McKay's for an ax? Gray suggested.

Pearce implored them to do their best without troubling Farmer McKay, but Trevor was troubled by something else, specifically by having missed call-over tramping o'er moor and fen after yon hideous baying. If they stopped to break into the barn, they'd miss lock-up as well, and they didn't want to worry Mr. Grieves.

—He'll worry a heap if we don't come back.

—He'll *what* a heap? Gray shouted.

—Worry! He'll *worry.*

Gray collapsed, stifling laughter in the grass as Trevor resumed parlay with Pious Pearce. The sub-prefect vowed not only to clear their names but also to burnish their reputations with their Housemaster. The rain was beginning to pelt. Trevor accepted the terms and commenced worrying the crossbar. It was one thing to read of Stalky's japes but quite another to stand cold and itching until Trevor at long last released the door—not a door of poetry or song, but theirs, unheroic yet instrument of metamorphosis. It swung aside for Pious Pearce, red of face, turning wrath away from his slanderers-cum-rescuers and towards his captives, recently so confident and brutish, now silent, dejected, small.

 Stalking the school like leopards. There was no other way for John to think about the unseen, unknown, ultimately rapacious forces that toyed with his fate. He understood ancient prohibitions against displaying joy. One made oneself a target for jealous gods. He himself had not revealed so much as a bright face in anticipation of their holiday, but the leopards had found him all the same.

Paris hadn't become a concrete reality—tickets bought, pension booked—until just before Christmas, but hadn't he and Meg talked for years of going, for Cordelia's thirteenth birthday, they said. Of course, Owain would come as well, but John thought it not too much to hope that the man's business would take him away for at least part of the time. And indeed it did not prove too much to hope, for Owain claimed the calling of some professional gathering, leaving John, Meg, and Cordelia a fortnight to themselves.

He'd told no one of his plans, a concealment designed specifically to protect against the very beasts that stalked him now. The entire term had been brighter than Lent had a right to be, because each morning as he shaved, he imagined himself crossing out another box in the calendar with red china pencil, as he'd done when a boy hoping for the holidays. This crossing out, let it be repeated, had never trespassed into the physical realm; it had remained always and only in his imagination. But now on the day of fifteen-sleeps-to-Paris, now, after hunting him through the corridors, the classrooms, the cloisters, the bath, now had come the telegram. Not bringing news of the maiden aunts but of Meg, née Drayton now Líoht, wick of his hope.

She often fell ill, but never had telegrams disturbed the break after luncheon. He'd spent the afternoon telephoning round to the hospital in Cambridge, endeavoring to learn facts, trying repeatedly to reach Mrs. Kneesworth, working himself into indigestion. Then, just as he'd managed to get Mrs. K's voice in his telephone receiver, he found she had nothing helpful to tell him, and he realized like a blow that his hope, that shining good thing that had consoled him for so long, could possibly, would probably be ravaged, bones flung broken aside.

He'd just put down the telephone when knocking commenced, not in his chest but at the study door. His Prefect of Chapel had come to report several boys missing from call-over and now lock-up. One or two truants were a perennial problem, but five? Including a sub-prefect? Leopards, not single spies, but battalions—mixing his metaphors, but if such a day didn't allow it . . .

✦

At one end of the changing room, Trevor and Gray peeled off wet clothes, while at the other, Halton and Malcolm minor shivered. Pearce berated the juniors pointlessly, unless the point was to vent his ire at the fact that the porter, Fardley, had stopped them at the gates and, rather than hail Pearce's triumphant return, had treated him as a common criminal: *All to Housemasters directly, them's orders!* Trevor revealed no glee then and looked none now as he straightened his tie and ran a comb through his hair:

—Fardles looked *jolly* put out.

—You were detained, came a voice across the room, on an errand of mercy.

Trevor looked into the glass and then at Gray. Were they or were they not being addressed by cheeky Halton? Halton, who, even if Grieves did not hand him over to the JCR, would come to grief later with his fagmaster, none other than gentle Pearce? Showing off was one thing, rank disregard of school practice another.

Gray turned on the taps to rinse their things, but Pearce emerged from the drying cupboard to rustle them along, making them leave their wet clothes where they lay, hauling all four of them through the House, past hungry onlookers (told by Pearce to nose out), to Grieves's study. Filing in, lining up, nothing to distinguish their guilt, Grieves's voice cut to the quick:

—Right.

It wasn't like the classroom. Gray knew that man, what he wanted and hated, but here in the study, on the carpet, Grieves's glare unfiltered—a churning, horrible realness.

—Pearce! Come in here and close that door.

The other Mr. Grieves, arctic and rigid.

—An *hour* late for call-over, three quarters of an hour late for lock-up. You can wipe that smirk off your face, Riding.

Gray's mouth opened, then closed.

—You realize, of course, that we'd phoned the constabulary?

His gaze lingered with his question on Gray, as though he could see inside, not only to his mind but further, Stalky, Valarious, the place in the barn with the box and its edge.

—Sir, I can explain, Pearce said.

The sub-prefect launched into a faithful account of events as he had witnessed them, including his deliverance by Stalky & Co. Grieves leaned against the front of his desk, arms crossed, but at mention of McKay's barn, he stood as if Pearce were confessing depravity. Gray avoided looking at Trevor, but he could feel from Trevor's posture that Stalky was preparing to enter the arena.

Mr. Grieves declared his astonishment and gall. He truly could not believe his ears. There were several matters he was entirely failing to follow. How, for instance, had Trevor and Gray—innocents both—found themselves in proximity to McKay's barn without violating school bounds themselves? Had they perhaps glimpsed the site before?

Stalky went to work, warming to his subject, holding that gaze. No, sir, he avowed, they did not. They knew as well as the next fellow that the barn was strictly forbidden, and dangerous, as Pearce's mishap proved. No, sir, they had been . . . tracking a badger near the south-bounds hedgerow when the pitiful cries had reached their ears.

Mr. Grieves professed himself perplexed, for how had the heroes heard voices when the barn stood almost a mile from the south hedgerow (over Abbot's Common, in fact)? Well, sir, they wondered that themselves. Perhaps the wind? Mr. Grieves had never heard of such an amplifying breeze. Well, at the time, sir, they didn't know where the voices hailed from. They were merely intent on helping, sir, as any Christian would.

—Don't overdo it, Grieves said.

But honestly, Trevor rejoined, if Mr. Grieves had himself heard the woeful baying, he would have rushed after it forthwith. And considering the fog, not to mention the approaching night—

And what about the approaching night? Surely they were aware of the impending call-over? Well, yes, sir, the thought did cross their minds, but they hoped Mr. Grieves would understand, especially considering the Head's recent lecture on fostering neighborly relations with the local husbandry.

—Your intentions are touching.

Sarcasm like nettles. Gray looked to Trevor—*Stalky, leash; exit, now.*

—Thank you, sir. Will that be all?

But no, that was not all. There was another matter troubling their Housemaster, and that was the matter of the barn door. (Grieves hadn't read *The Complete Stalky*—had he?) Just how, exactly, did it jam? Jam so that no effort from inside could budge it? Mr. Grieves demanded to know how, in what condition, Trevor and Gray found the barn door upon arrival.

Shut up, shut up.

Well, sir, it was jammed stubbornly. It seemed the cross timber had fallen and, rotten and treacherous as old barns are—*shut up!*—had somehow wedged itself into the latch and refused to budge. Stalky could not say how this had transpired. He could only elaborate on the hammering, chipping, and digging necessary to free Pearce & Co., all the while mindful of their Housemaster's worried clock. At which point Pearce reiterated his support, for that clock was still ticking busily and Mr. Burton-Lee, Housemaster of the other fags, would soon be on his way to tea, White and Fletcher perhaps already dismissed.

Mr. Grieves opened the docket book and consulted its ledger. Mistake, monumental. Books were not real, and maneuvers only worked within the pages of—

—Very well, you two may go, Grieves said.

Too easy, too quick, but they took their leave, stepping around the remaining defendants—

Just one more thing, Mr. Grieves recalled. On the topic of the smoke Pearce had smelled, did they know anything about it? Nearly escaped, they turned back to the room. No, sir, quoth Stalky, they were afraid they could be of no assistance in that matter.

The fifteen-minute bell rang for tea.

—Sir, Pearce began.

Grieves snapped a finger at Pearce and consigned Stalky to outer darkness. They escaped before Trevor's mouth broke into celebration.

◆

John was too discombobulated to give them the dressing-down they deserved, and it only got worse when Pearce let slip—as if immaterial!—that two of Burton-Lee's fags had been apprehended as well. The leopards had him by the thigh. Of course things were going in the worst possible way.

But he pulled himself together. He wrote the docket, instructing the JCR to deal with Malcolm minor and Halton in the strongest terms. Furthermore, he informed the miscreants, they were gated for the rest of term. Pearce herded them mercifully away, and John went to stand by the fire, as if its flame could purge the chill.

He had to stop jumping to dire conclusions. Boys transgressed every bound; it was their nature and their duty. Just because the barn hadn't come to John's attention of late did not mean boys hadn't been trespassing there. And, actually, a minor scandal might deflate curiosity about the place. The short, sharp shock would haul the juniors back into line, and if John heard anything else from either of them, he was prepared to chuck them into extra tuition as well. Burton would deal with his own, and whatever illicit romance McKay's barn had stirred up would end in exemplary fashion. Later, after Prep and Prayers or perhaps tomorrow, John would have a chat with his Head Boy, Carter. Of course they had Pearce to thank for reporting the escapade, but couldn't Pearce have apprehended them before they reached that barn? At any rate, John trusted Carter to temper Pearce's zeal. The whole affair was typical school discipline from start to finish, now decidedly finished.

Except for Mainwaring and Riding. They'd been trading in mischief for weeks. If not for Pearce's unambiguous witness, John would have accused them of lying to his face, Riding anyhow. Mainwaring was generally frank and direct, but his companion positively smirked. John knew they disliked Pearce, and there had been that business with call-over, but now they were indebted to Pearce. Whatever they had been pursuing—and if it was a badger then John was a Dutchman—their crime had been interrupted by Pearce's predicament, which had ultimately led to rapprochement. If Pearce would maintain his gratitude and if they would refrain from overdoing it, then perhaps the House could be persuaded to give Pearce a chance. Mainwaring, at least, seemed bent on reconciliation, so hopefully he could influence his sidekick before Pearce quite realized he was being laughed at.

Burton of course would be furious and would remonstrate with John. Burton would have thrashed Mainwaring and Riding along with the rest,

22

would have informed them that he cared not if they'd rescued the Prince of Wales, he wasn't having it with that barn, and he'd tell Pearce the same thing in private and threaten to thrash him as well if he ever heard of his going there again—but Burton would never have realized the truth about the debacle, that it was a rare chance to advance the cause of peace in the House by encouraging détente between his sub-prefect and two blue-tongued members of the Remove.

The fire was going out, but the disaster had been turned to advantage, the leopards given a kick in the eye. He had to corner the Headmaster later, and it would not be about this.

 She shouldn't have looked away from what she'd seen: her mother's tight mouth, her father's outsize humor, the sounds down the corridor in the night. She should never have left her mother sleeping and gone to school through the rain, shouldn't have laughed in the courtyard under the awning, shouldn't have swept all concerns from her mind during the recitation.

O Thou, with dewy locks, who lookest down
Thro' the clear windows of the morning, turn
Thine angel eyes upon our western isle,
Which in full choir hails thy approach, O Spring!

When dismissed for the holidays, she shouldn't have gone with the girls from 7b to buy fish and chips, shouldn't have squelched across the village green to the Free Library to ask the librarian what she could have waited to know:

—Who won, Mr. R? Who won the geography prize?

If she hadn't so disturbed the normal order of time and menu of activities, she never would have let down her guard as the librarian slid the golden prize book across the desk: *The Earth, with Maps and Illustrations.*

It was wrong to hunger so fervently and for places beyond her ken. There was a word for such overmastering desire, and although she would never speak such a word aloud, she knew that it was lust that brought her week after week to the Free Library to pore over photographs of Britain's wide empire. Lust made her long for the snows of Antarctica and its elusive, guarded Pole. Lust waylaid her when she should have rushed home that afternoon, lust for the color plates inside her prize book, for the icy ridges of Tierra del Fuego, that sensational archipelago where travelers could in a moment of failed vigilance succumb to vertigo and be sucked down to the polar regions.

She'd called to her mother while kicking off her wellington boots, but the silence failed to touch her because madness had taken, as it did when she let it. Bedroom door closed, she surveyed her treasures. Poseidon's black tome she set aside for the prize book. Plate one: Map of the World, hydrological basins without outlet to the sea tinted gray. Plate seventeen: Delta of the Ganges. Plate twenty-two: Upheavals and depressions; plate twenty-three: Atoll Ari. Before scruples could speak, she unlatched pencil box and with slash of knife freed plates from binding. Putty, step stool, they joined the maps on the walls and ceiling. She lay across the bed and felt her heart pound in her ears: Atlantic, Doldrums, Horse Latitudes—

—Cordelia?

Downstairs, a voice not her mother's. Mrs. Kneesworth, gray and wobbly:

—Dear?

 Outside the refectory, Trevor held court with the Fourth, the Remove, and those of the Fifth who could not maintain their indifference.

—But who did you think was inside?

—We'd no idea, Trevor said. Sounded like a cross between a slaughterhouse and some Methodist revival, what with the fags blubbing and Pearce saying his prayers.

—His prayers!

—Never would have guessed who it was.

It was the Stalkiest thing they'd ever done (Stalkiest thing they'd ever cribbed?), and this was their hour of triumph. The truth, though, was that it was far more strenuous to do things than to read about them.

—Thought he'd had one or two from the sounds of it, Trevor confided.

—Come off it!

—Pearce tight?

—Bet a bob he's secretly a mackerel snapper, Trevor said. They slosh it up every chance they get.

—What happened to the Flea's fags?

—Oh, Trevor said, I think we can be fairly certain.

Guffaws from the crowd.

—As for the others, Pious hauled 'em into JCR, and I don't think *they'll* be amused.

—Old Carter'll have a heart attack.

—The fags'll get something to remember anyhow, Trevor concluded.

Chants of *six* began amongst the Remove, only to be disputed by the juniors, who reminded everyone who would listen that four strokes of the school cane was the limit for the Lower School.

—Six, six, six!

Those beyond the House joined the ruckus, not even knowing why, until two of Henri's prefects appeared to hector them into queues. Trevor bantered with the Remove, and Gray scanned the cloisters for their own JCR, which had not arrived.

—I say.

Someone cut into the queue beside them, someone shorter—Halton:

—It was jolly lucky you turned up this afternoon.

Trevor for once seemed incapable of reply.

—I can't think *what* would've happened, Halton continued, if you hadn't come by.

Trevor lifted the brat physically from the queue.

—Am I hearing things, he asked Gray, or are we being addressed?

—I think it's talking to us, Gray replied.

—Look, toe-rag, someone ought to have told you that fags do not address the Upper School.

The Remove was not the Upper School, as the nearby Fifth Formers would normally have reminded Trevor, but Stalky's spell had so entranced them that they replied with *Hear-hear.*

—My name's Halton.

—Congratulations.

—Jolly clever, the way you jinked the door.

If Halton thought he would get anywhere with nerve, he had another think coming. Public opinion had little sympathy for fags, and none for those who allowed themselves to be tracked by Pious Pearce.

—The whole thing was just plain Stalky, Halton concluded.

Trevor turned to him:

—How's your arse, Halton? Get a taste of Swinton's wrist?

The mob guffawed.

—Little brutes like you, I don't see how four would cover it, Trevor opined.

The crowd agreed.

—Something to remember, that's what you deserve.

Several bystanders seized Halton as if to administer civil justice, but the arrival of the bell fag began the queue moving. Halton shouldered past Trevor and Gray, treading with force on Gray's foot.

—We got six, he muttered. And it was Pearce.

✦

Pearce always had to overdo things, and if anyone should know, it was Moss. In their first term, Pearce lacked all proportion. When he and Moss were bloodying each other's noses, Pearce always took it too far. Even when Wilberforce pulled them apart, Pearce always made as if he could escape Morgan's grip and somehow destroy Moss in the moments before recapture.

Pearce may have mellowed in the intervening five years, but Moss had been warning Carter and Swinton all week that their fellow prefect was headed for some melodramatic mess. Carter had accused Moss of pessimism and pointed out that they were all benefitting from Pearce's help as sub-prefect. Moss conceded that if Pearce could confine himself to bureaucratic tasks, he'd save the rest of them a year of boredom, but who imagined Pearce would be confined?

—He's got more earnest ambition than the Salvation Army, Moss complained.

Swinton, for his part, didn't much care what Pearce did so long as he kept order in the changing rooms and relieved Swinton of dorm rounds. But Swinton and Carter were a year ahead and so hadn't had to go up the school with Pearce; they didn't know him as Moss did, and Moss knew, the moment they learned that Pearce was missing, that the going-overboard was at hand. Although Carter, as Head Boy, ought to have gone to alert Grieves, Moss volunteered. He'd not been able to stop Grieves ringing the constable, but he had talked him out of rousting Fardley to search for the missing boys. Moss left his Housemaster pacing the study and returned to the JCR, where Carter and Swinton had begun on the evening's dockets. They put a stop to whatever rumors they encountered (that the five had run away, had drowned in a ditch, been shot on the moors, had—).

—Thank you, touch your toes.

They were just finishing the register when in walked Pearce, hair still wet, brandishing a docket. The miscreants Carter sent to the corridor while they debriefed Pearce and discovered for themselves his Grand Bag. (Tracking fags? Would he covet a deerstalker next? And McKay's barn? *Honestly?*)

When Pearce wound himself up, you were lucky to get a word in for the next half hour, but Carter thankfully cut it short:

—All right, Pearce, you can go ahead.

Moss and Swinton had to work to conceal their surprise—that Carter was not only extending Pearce the privilege, not typically granted sub-prefects, of wielding the cane, but also doing so in the midst of Pearce's batty caper. The fags looked equally shocked and not a little intimidated, whether by Carter's sentence of six or by an informal acquaintance with Pearce's arm, Moss couldn't say.

When it came to it, Pearce did them proud. Even Swinton looked impressed. Pious, it seemed, had a bit of an eye. Well, the fags more than deserved it, and when word got round, the JCR might finally get a day's peace.

The trouble, of course, was that Pearce never knew when to stop. At tea, he bruited his adventures up and down the Sixth Form table. Moss had to physically restrain him from leaving his seat to petition Burton-Lee about the other fags mixed up in the business. Once the Head dismissed them, however, there was nothing to stop Pearce buttonholing the Dean of the Upper School, dizzying Burton-Lee with overwrought blathering. Moss soon lost sight of them, but he knew well enough what was happening. He didn't need to be present in Burton-Lee's study to smell the cherry tobacco and to see Pearce perched on the edge of the rust leather wing-chair, pawning his nauseously earnest tale. Moss had no doubt Burton-Lee would summon and execute his fags on the spot, likely with Pearce in attendance to cut short any equivocating from the little worms, but Burton was also likely to take more interest in Mainwaring and Riding than Grieves had done. (Whoever trusted Mainwaring two inches needed his head examined.) Moss didn't especially care what became of those two, but if the business stirred up animosity between Grieves and Burton-Lee . . . Swinton offered Moss their flask and advised him to contemplate soothing things. Their Housemaster was ever a trial; their duty as JCR was to run the House and keep Grievous on a more or less even keel. It had ever been so and would yet be so to-morrow. And tomorrow and tomorrow . . .

 John did not have prep duty that evening, but he felt it would have been better if he did. One hundred and five minutes confronted him, and although he had composi-tions to mark, not to mention the ever-reproachful bas-ket of correspondence, he felt at a loss. His study door had no lock, though in damp weather, which was to say most days, it was swollen enough to require heavy pushing. He gathered up the pa-pers from the armchair and piled them on the mail table. After shoul-dering the door fully into its frame, he collapsed into the seat and allowed his head to fall onto his hand.

Meg had never asked anything of him. There were the thousand things that weren't really things, all unspoken when he was with them, but nothing like this. He had thought the request was simply Mrs. K's loopy notion. There was no reason for him to *Take Cordelia*, as if his god-daughter were a puppy that required minding while its owner attended urgent business. The girl had friends and neighbors, including Mrs. K herself; Meg was nearly family to the Meeting in Saffron Walden. Only a harried woman such as Mrs. K could commit to telegram the sugges-tion that John summon his twelve-year-old goddaughter hundreds of miles north to St. Stephen's Academy, a male society undisturbed by the opposite sex, notwithstanding matrons and a pair of staff daughters under the age of three.

Besides which, Owain was bound to turn up.

But Mrs. K had made it clear that Owain's premises were locked and that no one could locate him or the young lady he employed. Mrs. K her-self would gladly *keep* Cordelia except that her son expected her on a long-ago-booked holiday and Meg insisted she depart as planned. As for the myriad friends and neighbors, Meg had given Mrs. K a verbatim mes-sage, which the woman read to John down the telephone. *Darling, will explain, believe me no alternative, please.* Those words illuminated little but quickened John's pulse. Mrs. K whispered a gloss into the receiver—

Margaret was desperate that nobody know. —Her illness or her husband's disappearance? —Surely both, Mrs. K avowed. No alternative would Meg entertain. She drifted in and out of consciousness, and whenever she regained herself, she repeated the same plea: *John.*

It was not humanly possible to refuse her. John had given Mrs. K the train details. It would have been better for the Headmaster to decide to allow the girl to come. A better man than John would be able to conduct the conversation so that Jamie believed her arrival was not a fait accompli, but everything John imagined saying spun off incoherently as he prepared for Jamie's reaction. He needed sleep, a full night's rest untroubled by dreams or heartburn or noises or restless legs. He needed a clear mind, an invigorated body, a supple will, and charm.

Someone had turned up the gravity and his body stuck in the chair. Meg had asked for him. Now, in this year—sixteen after he'd lost her to Owain—she was summoning him, message bound to a prize-winning bird, one lost in the winds but now come home, feathers warm in his palm. *We must go back to the book and ink out our errors,* Moss was telling him. Moss needed the docket book from his desk. There had been mistakes, things done in salt water when they should have been done in fresh. But John told Moss, *You are Prefect of Chapel and mistakes are all part of it. The book has never been changed as long as we've kept it. Let the errors stand.* Moss had departed, and the Bishop had joined John in his study, pouring them each a brandy and soda, and John was explaining that he took only soda with no more than half a splash of brandy, less than a drop of blood, not so much as the Bishop had poured him, but the Bishop was telling John what he'd come to say, that all this time he'd been working for John's promotion. Every position he'd held, the Bishop had engineered. The ambulance corps? The Bishop had gone to Parliament to keep John out of prison. St. Stephen's? He'd told the previous Headmaster to engage him. Housemaster? Everything. John was filled with remorse that he had so long considered himself passed over, when in fact this man, who he thought had abandoned him, had been moving pieces around the board to his advantage. And now the Bishop refilled his glass and asked if he was certain he wanted to adopt this child. All these years he had not wanted a child, and now was he certain? John told him yes, yes, he was certain. It was true children took your time, devoured it, and he had so little, all these boys— Yes, the Bishop asked, weren't they enough? But John, heart full, told him no. Children took everything, your freedom and your hours, but what was he doing with all his hours? Children gave shape to time, gave it purpose. And if he could find Meg, wherever she had gone, they could do just that. Somehow, someone ought to be able to find her, Margaret Drayton, Margaret Líoht—no one could hide forever if you looked hard enough. The world was enormous, but it was finite.

Except then he remembered the body and the funeral, and he thought it was possible—no, true—that she had died. He had found her dead in their bed, and there had been a burial, and now she was nowhere to be found anywhere in this world. And he fell on the floor sobbing, *Lord, have mercy,* and then the bell was ringing, far then near, that clang for the end of something, metal alarm, Prep, and he was clutching his forehead in the chair by the door, sobbing without tears, salt or fresh, his mother dead these twenty-seven years, his wife twelve, Meg in hospital, the school seething outside, rain splatting his windows, the chapel bells jangling and calling them to Prayers.

At Cambridge, John used to slip into King's to hear evensong from time to time. Of course, he'd thought he didn't believe any of it, that the church, its creeds, and even great swathes of the Bible failed to convince him and quite possibly, if he had taken the time to examine them, offended. But evensong at King's was a thing that drew him as a bucket drew water from the bottom of a long well. *You'd have to be a stone not to be moved by the beauty,* he would say to anyone who discovered him there.

Now, he was obliged by contract and custom to kneel each morning and night on the tamped-down kneelers, to recite the creed, the confession, the responses, to listen to the lectionary, and to sing, as this evening, from the hymn books whose spines had let go their bindings.

Dear Lord and Father of mankind,
Forgive our foolish ways;
Reclothe us in our rightful minds,
In purer lives thy service find . . .

A hymn, after all, written by a Friend sometime in the shadows of another century, when they walked and sought and waited on the light.

Nothing had physically changed since Jamie had become the Academy's Headmaster, yet anyone could see that it was a different school than it had been. The blind turmoil of Jamie's first year; the large-scale removal of boys, masters, and staff—called in popular mythology the

Great Clear-Out; the transformation of arbitrary justice into a system of dockets, sorted each night by Housemaster and JCR, addressed with a cool head after the offense, with firm limits on the coarser forms of discipline; Kardleigh's arrival and resurrection of the choir; all combined with a re-cultivation of beauty and purpose in their daily gatherings. Jamie wasn't moralistic, at least not compared to his predecessor, but he quickly and with few words projected a seriousness towards matters that had been allowed to atrophy.

John was still a Quaker, but on evenings such as this—*Lighten our darkness, we beseech thee, O Lord, and by thy great mercy defend us from all perils*—on such a night he found little to offend him and much to comfort. He even, behind the veil of the confession, unburdened himself to whatever ear would listen.

We have left undone those things which we ought to have done, and we have done those things which we ought not to have done—we have hoped for those we ought not to have hoped for—*there is no health in us.*

He needed to catch Jamie directly after Prayers. After that, marital duties rendered the Headmaster unavailable save emergencies, and John did not want this to be an emergency. On the way out of the chapel, though, John encountered Lockett-Egan and followed him back to his House for a quick Soda & B. He told the Eagle about the boys and the barn. The Eagle listened and at the end asked if John had informed the Head. John got up and announced his intention to do just that, but rather than proceed to the Headmaster's house, John stopped by his own House and dropped in on dorm rounds. Pearce he found corralling the Lower School, patience short. John's appearance awed them. He told the juniors to get into bed. He proceeded to the washroom and exercised the same chilling influence over the Remove, but when in the corridor Pearce thanked him, John realized that he had undone whatever advances Pearce had won that day.

He headed to the Tower, where he found Kardleigh at his desk, having just turned the lights out on the ward, which, Kardleigh reported, was nearly empty after the outbreak of vomiting earlier that week. Kardleigh, too, listened to John's tale of the barn, though unlike the Eagle, he hadn't yet heard it. He was displeased to find Halton mixed up in it.

—I shouldn't worry, John said, he should be back on form for choir practice tomorrow.

But it was Halton's company the choirmaster disliked, not his misadventures. Kardleigh did not think Halton needed friends like White, certainly not with the Stanford coming up Sunday. John expressed his baffled admiration that Kardleigh had managed to train Halton to the choral repertoire given the boy's near illiteracy in the classroom.

—I've no idea what they tried to teach him in the colonies, John said, but none of it stuck. He's thick as two planks.

But Kardleigh found Halton bright enough, though he suspected the boy couldn't read much music and got it mostly by ear. And so they talked about the choir and about the boys, as usual, and by the time they left off, it was too late to see Jamie. It was also too late to see his JCR about Pearce. So John returned to the Eagle, who took one look at him and told him he'd better come in. The drop in John's soda was rather larger than usual, and the Eagle confessed that Burton-Lee had been by; the man was wound up, he wanted the barn torn down, and he planned to speak to Jamie in the morning. John agreed about the barn, but, he wondered aloud, if Farmer McKay hadn't torn it down yet, why would he now? And as for the Headmaster, John didn't see why a case of Third Formers trying it on, duly thwarted by a prefect, ought to be blown out of proportion.

—Burton doesn't see it that way.

After midnight John took his leave, not having mentioned the thing that was making his stomach burn.

But the Lord sometimes had a way of blowing a curtain aside, a napkin off the table, an exercise book open when John had ceased hoping; and now, as he crossed the quad to return to his House and face an adversarial night with his bed, now a light came on, literally, in the window of Jamie's study where it had not been. And so, trembling with relief and awe and also dread, John turned into the cloisters and towards Jamie's door.

 Someone had shouted in his sleep, and now Gray lay heart-poundingly awake.

Things hadn't seemed bad at lights-out. They were heroes in the Remove, not only because of the exploit itself, which Trevor had embroidered to suggest that they had rescued the fags from the predations of Pious Pearce, but also because of their cool indifference in the face of the lines Burton-Lee gave them for disseminating said embroidery at Prep.

Trevor had done his lines, but Gray had advanced Valarious two days' journey on his quest, through Magnus Marsh, where dwelt hags who told him lies disguised as fortune, into the mists of Fulsom Fell, whose stones bedeviled his compass, leading him farther and farther astray until he collapsed in a thicket of heather, his gabardine pulled tight against the rain.

His own lines would have to be done tomorrow during French or just before tea. He should have done them at Prep, but after Valarious, an idea had come to him about Napoleon, a parallel between Napoleonic Code and Dr. Sebastian's regime at the Academy. Grieves would demand more evidence than Gray could provide, but that was precisely why he'd presented it as *some might say*. Grieves, as a rule, did not stand for some-might-say, but if the notion intrigued him—*Wipe that smirk off your face*. In the study, Grieves had treated him like a magsman whose trick was known. (What smirk even?) Trevor said Grievous had believed them, or at any rate he'd let them go, which Trevor deemed a top-hole outcome. But Trevor was native to *Stalky*, not an imposter like Gray. What kind of book could ever revolve around Gray? He was failed material for a character.

Halton had got six and then had the nerve to bait them, his elders and betters, before half the school. He'd got it from Pearce, of unknown reputation, but bets on vindictive. Gray had only taken six once, and not until this year. The difference between four and six had not been trivial. Halton clearly had a grudge against them, or at least against him. Whose foot had he trod?

A mind like Trevor's would press him to say what he'd actually observed from the loft of the barn. What could he swear to in a court of law? Squeezed by Pearce, Halton had turned his head in the direction of their cache. He was close enough to see inside, m'lord. The expression on his face had changed. Oh, he could hear the barristers cross-questioning him—Were there not any number of things to change the expression of a boy in hot water?—but given Halton's remarks in the changing room, in the cloisters, could Gray ever allow himself to imagine they were safe?

If he were the writer rather than merely an observer from above, of course Halton would have seen not only the worn spines and tattered covers of Gray's penny dreadfuls (testifying to a regular occupancy of the barn), not only their original *Stalky* (the *Complete* was above in the loft), but seen also deep into the crevice, where light from the sun, having broken through cloud—except it had started raining again by then, hadn't it?—light from the sun, filtered through cloud, passing on express purpose through the dirty windows of the barn, straight into that crevice until it collided with the silver nameplate, which would reflect the light and send it out again until it met the next object, the cornea of Halton's eye. It was simply too inefficient for Halton to find himself in the Keep, to be threatened almost beyond endurance by cruel and wicked Pearce, and for him *not* to see the treasure. Enemy hands, enemy eyes, the thing he ought to have burned years ago.

Halton would have stood cold and hungry before the JCR. An inquisition more probing than their Housemaster's would have rolled forth: the barn, their habits, the smoke. Whatever Halton had said, it had not caused Trevor and Gray to be summoned, but it had inspired the JCR to the maximum penalty. Had Holton gone first, according to school practice that saw boys dealt with in order of seniority, or had he been made to wait in the corridor? Gray knew the churning fear, the slowing and speeding of time. Halton would be told to bend over. He'd remove his jacket and lean across the back of the JCR chair until his head touched the seat. Feeling a stretch in the back of his legs, he'd lock his knees. One of the prefects would take up the cane—Carter if he was lucky, Swinton if he wasn't, but, right, in this case Pearce, still hot with anger. He'd do what they always did, flex it as he paced, building suspense, working the nerves. When he saw a sufficient trembling, Pearce would back away from his target, raise the cane, and cut through the air with a swish-and-crack.

Halton would gasp. He wouldn't be able to help it, and as his breath returned he'd feel the burning, stinging ache. Nothing for him in the world besides this bottled breath, this room upside down between chair rungs. If Pearce had learned anything over the past five years, he would strut back to the mantel, giving Halton time to think. Halton might wonder how many he could take without yelping; he might decide the exploit hadn't been worth it; he might reconsider silence for no cause. Pearce might not know what Halton was thinking, but he would certainly know what he was feeling when he delivered the second cut with a force and precision equal to the first. Halton would gasp again and brace himself for the third, already slicing through the air. With it no thought, just pain, more pain, three to go.

If Moss was giving it, or Swinton in a mood, you'd know they wanted you to stick it; and even if later the shame bit, in that window when it was happening, they might if they were decent (most weren't, but if they were) make you feel they were on your side. But with one who hated you, one who kept going—and then afterwards, no matter who had given it, you'd be altered. It was grafted to you, whatever you might pretend, like the marks that changed color, reminding you, even after it hardly hurt anymore.

But all that had happened to Halton, not to them. He oughtn't be lying awake to demented hours. They had got away with it. There was no reason for Grieves to have done anything but thank them for rescuing Pearce. Instead, their Housemaster had released them under a cloud. It would have been one thing if he'd made them return on their own, dragged them formally over the coals, told them to their faces that he didn't believe them, but to send them away with an air of disgust? *You must remember to use your eyes*, his father said. *If you close your eyes, it grows bigger, stronger, monstrous.* What if Grieves didn't suspect him of anything? What if he simply didn't care? Grieves had liked Wilberforce, at least Gray remembered Grieves treating Wilberforce with a warmth he showed no one else. Was the man incapable of loving, or was it merely that no one could ever love—

 John knew he had slept because he had no memory of lying awake, but he couldn't say he had rested. Conversations had too late at night always colored sleep, and each of the evening's chats had coated his mind in its own way. Kardleigh's smelled medicinal but had the quietly frenetic character of a physician-cum-choirmaster. The Eagle's were like the chintz fabrics that he had, over the years, brought back from continental holidays and used to upholster his furniture. The last conversation, with Jamie, though conducted in Jamie's austerely tidy study, had filled his mind with capacious disorder.

Jamie had been sitting at his desk in dressing gown and slippers. He had listened without interruption to John's account of Meg, Cordelia, Owain, and the very singular nature of the circumstances. John had paced, mouth tasting of metal. Then had come the sword, that stroke cutting life before from life to come: Jamie had looked at him and said,

35

Bring her. Said, *Let me explain it to the SCR.* John had been so shocked, so physically dizzy and pattering and incapable of thought that he'd— what? He'd gone back to the House, he'd devoured the rest of the biscuits from the Christmas tin—had he cleaned his teeth?—he'd fallen asleep across the bed and had to get under the covers when he woke later, frozen. Evidently, he'd forgot to set his alarm, so he was wakened by Mrs. Firth just before breakfast. There was a wire on his desk, she announced. John fetched it before dressing, but his fear faded upon discovering only his goddaughter's train details. No one was dead. Meg hadn't even got worse. The night's mercy persisted, with the minor annoyance that Mrs. Kneesworth had for some indefensible reason put Cordelia on a train bound for York rather than the local stop at Sledmere and Fimber. John asked his matron for tea in lieu of breakfast, dressed calmly, and then began to sort out arrangements for Cordelia's retrieval and accommodation.

This was the way sane people went about living, one snag at a time, panics refused, mercies acknowledged, daily bread.

✦

The bell rang just as he'd fallen back to sleep. Now, nearly dizzy, Gray was being hauled from bed by Trevor, who clipped him round the ear and told him to hurry. The bell was the second. Breakfast shortly, very shortly. The tap water ached but chased away the fog. In the changer, Trevor beat reveille on the bench as Gray threaded his collar.

—Brains, Trevor said in his avuncular voice, about Grievous's little comp . . .

—If you haven't done it, it's too late now.

—I did it, Trevor said, but it needs something more.

He produced an exercise book and prepared to take dictation.

—You didn't, actually, did you? Gray said.

—I had more lines than you.

Gray gave an aggrieved sigh and combed his hair into place:

—Thesis, Napoleon wasn't conquering for the sake of it—

—Like hell he wasn't.

—But to spread enlightenment through Europe.

—That's Rousseau and his nancy friends.

—Code Civil, end of feudalism, legal reforms.

The breakfast bell rang. Trevor cursed. They dashed to the refectory, where scorched porridge and cold toast awaited them.

✦

John arrived to chapel late and sat in the back. A congregation of half-asleep boys held down the pews as Jamie led Morning Prayer. And the Lord gave the commandments to Moses again, after they had broken, and Moses' face shone, because he spoke with God face-to-face.

✦

Concordat. Consular. The Remove humored Mr. Grieves by supplying dates for his time line.

—And when was the marriage of lovers, famous in story and song, Napoleon and Josephine?

Incorrect answers were earning marks in the corner of the black-board, and since the tally stood three short of a group penalty, they were reluctant to guess. Except, after a pause, Trevor:

—Isn't it true, sir, that Josephine was in the Bastille during the revolution?

The sparkle came off Mr. Grieves's mood. He would not, he told them, be misdirected today. He was well aware that the exam for their Upper School Remove beckoned them from the far-off land of summer, but, he informed them, they would not revisit Napoleon again. He raised the chalk to the corner box and asked Trevor if he'd anything relevant to contribute.

—Well, sir, isn't it true that Josephine sucked up to the Bastille guards so she'd get off being guillotined, and then she met Napoleon and thought it would be clever to marry him, but then he divorced her when she couldn't give him a son, so they weren't really lovers in story and song?

Grateful as he was for tidbits from the Bastille, Mr. Grieves was determined to learn the date of the nuptial event. He moved chalk to time line: *marriage of Nap & Jo (lovers??)*.

—1810, sir.

—Guessing, Grieves said. Sit.

A slash to the box.

—Someone redirect us. Riding.

—Sir?

—Stand up. Wake up. Pull your weight.

—The marriage, sir?

Throat, phlegm.

—Wasn't it sometime in their youth?

Another slash to the box, to the ribs—

—I had supposed, Riding, that you were reasonably informed of Monsieur Bonaparte, but evidently I was mistaken.

They'd never covered it! How could he—

—Paper, pens, questions. Thirty things you truly do not know concerning Bonaparte, five minutes.

—But, sir!

—Go.

◆

He couldn't be that stupid. Unless he was cracking up? Jamie had said, *Bring her.* He'd given his blessing. They'd talked face-to-face. John had left, he'd walked, he'd eaten, he'd slept. The relief had lasted through the second telegram, through Moses, through the Fifth on Crimea, through the lazy Remove on the dates that would, he knew, figure heavily in their summer exam. Then Riding was smirking, as he had the night before, and the leopards were tearing the back of his neck.

But they were writing now; he needed to calm down. No one was dead. They'd talked face-to-face, Jamie had given his blessing, John had left, had walked, had eaten, had—had he actually not told Jamie the other thing, the thing he most certainly had owed Jamie to say? Had the mercy towards his goddaughter been so absorbing, so deceptive that he'd gone derelict of his duty?

—Two minutes. Chop-chop.

He had to have mentioned the business with the barn. Jamie had heard of it already, surely? They must have discussed it briefly, John scarcely paying attention in his anxiety about the other matter. Jamie must have considered it unimportant, or a thing put away. It must have happened like that.

—Leslie, put it away. Now!

Except it didn't.

His heart wasn't slowing, it was picking up pace. He hadn't mentioned

38

it. He'd petitioned Jamie about his goddaughter and failed to warn him about the barn. And now, soon, Burton-Lee would be telling him.

✦

Gray felt almost happy. He was good at Questions. Grieves sprang it on them regularly, and Gray knew what he liked. *What stories and songs were written about Napoleon and Josephine?* Actually, he'd say that was cheeky. *How long did he have that awful rash? Did he treat his men decently? Why did the English hate him so much when his ideas were good? And what about Josephine? What were her ideas? What did he imagine he'd be when he grew up? What kind of education did he have? What did he do when locked away in prison? Did the weather there help his rash?*

—One minute.

Bonaparte, in truth, was a bore and a boar. There were so many more interesting things to know! Valarious had a tutor when he was younger, a crotchety mage who lived in a mildewed cottage. Valarious had been too young when they sent him to the man. He hadn't wanted to do anything except the things they told him not to. The mage tried to teach him, and later, much later when it was too late and the mage had been killed and the cottage burned to the ground and Valarious had fled to the place beyond the mountains, then he would remember all the books, which had seemed so deadly boring then, not even written in a language he could read (had Valarious even been able to read then?—*work this out!*), but later Valarious would think of the books, how far back their knowledge had gone, now ground to grit by the feet of marauding—

—Riding!

—Sir?

—Stop trying my patience. Pen down.

Were they going to have to pass it in?

—Marks for number, marks for insight. Leslie, you're first.

Leslie, Whittaker, Ives. Grieves was not liking their questions.

—Prout, our hopes hinge on you!

—What is the significance of the year 1815? Prout offered.

—I hope you're jesting.

—Sir?

—You have plunged us into the abyss. Things you *do not know?* Of all people, Prout, I'd have thought we could rely on you for dates.

—Thank you, sir—

—Absent sense, of course, not to mention wit, style, or interest. Sit down.

Grieves attacked blackboard with duster. When he swept the corner box, signaling a group imposition, protest erupted. Grieves, back turned, invited them to continue if they wanted fifty lines each in addition to the extra prep they had just earned. The room went silent. Numbers appeared down the board, and beside them, Grieves began to write questions. Free time vanished, time Gray needed to finish his lines from the Flea.

—Sir?

Gray froze. Grieves froze. Trevor was on his feet.

—Please, sir?

The man turned, chalk in one hand, duster in the other.

—Fifty lines . . . Mainwaring.

—Sir, Trevor said firmly, it's impossible for us to answer the first question—

—Sit down, boy.

—Impossible because there's no way to explain the significance of 1815 without bringing in the Germans.

Grieves hurled the duster at Trevor, who dodged.

—The Germans, Grieves enunciated, who didn't exist as a nation in 1815?

—The Germans in 1914, sir.

Grieves dropped the chalk on his desk.

—Go on. If you can.

Trevor stood as before the firing squad.

—It's only that in 1815 you've got everyone uniting to stop Napoleon, and in 1914 everyone's uniting to stop the Kaiser.

—Everyone except Austria-Hungary, you mean.

—Yes, sir.

—And the Ottomans. Bulgaria, the sultanate of Darfur, the Dervish state, the Democratic Republic of Georgia.

—Exactly, Trevor replied. The only people on the German side were ridiculous countries no one's ever heard of.

Mr. Grieves crossed his arms.

—Is there a point, at all? he said acidly.

—The point, sir, is that unlike the Kaiser, Napoleon wasn't conquering Europe for his own benefit.

Grieves raised his brow. It was time for Trevor to shut up. Grieves wasn't going to revoke the prep, and the best move was silence so they could start work now.

—Setting aside for the moment your staggeringly shallow understanding of the recent war, it's an interesting question.

An interesting question, the words you hoped to see in your exercise book, the words you hoped to hear but seldom did.

—Should Napoleon have been stopped from conquering Europe? Grieves asked. Or should his project have been allowed to flourish?

The room stared, baffled.

—No one? You're breaking my heart.

✦

Mainwaring was chomping at the bit, but John couldn't play favorites. He stepped down from the dais and invaded the classroom. Riding had likely turned in a worthwhile composition, and his questions, if they pertained to Napoleon (one could never count on his classwork being quite relevant unless something new was being presented) appeared to have filled two sides. John strolled down the aisles and perused their questions. Some pages he tore out, wadded up, and tossed across the room. To some he issued marks with the nearest pen. Some he rolled up and used as a weapon against the author's thick skull. Riding's he squinted to decipher—the handwriting, the spelling . . . the flight of fancy. The boy buried his face in his arms like some lunatic ostrich. John closed the book and told him to sit up. The boy obeyed with an air of betrayal, as if John had read out his secrets. No other questions called for debate. There was not enough time to start on Poland.

—All right, he said, Mainwaring.

✦

Grieves was going to kill him, but first, apparently, he meant to draw Trevor into combat. Trevor, too eager, took the bait:

—Napoleon ought to have been allowed to govern for at least six years.

—Monsieur Bonaparte, Christendom's saving grace? Perhaps you will be good enough to support your assertion with fact?

Trevor mounted his steed, visor down, lance balanced.

41

—He wasn't trying to conquer Europe. He was trying to spread Enlightenment.

—Specifics?

Trevor cantered ahead. Gray began to write.

—The Code Napoleon was based on the French model, of course.

—Ye-es, Grieves allowed. And what's so spectacular about that?

Relig Tol East, Gray wrote.

—He spread religious toleration in the eastern nations, Trevor said.

Grieves nodded.

Serfs-feud-guilds.

—Then he abolished serfdom, and that ended feudalism in Europe.

—He abolished all serfdom?

Trevor hesitated. A hand across the aisle.

—Ives?

—Except in Russia, sir.

—Of course, except Russia, Trevor snapped. But even more, he abolished the guilds, so careers were open to talent.

—So?

Gray was still writing, but Trevor had eyes only for his mark.

—So you take that, and you take the end of feudal manorial rights, and what do you get?

—Modernization! called Leslie.

—And then, Trevor persisted, industrialization.

—I thought industrialization began as early as 1780, Grieves said.

Another voice from the crowd:

—That was in England, sir.

—Modernization on the continent didn't get going until there was general equality under the law, Trevor said.

—And, Leslie continued, there were all the Napoleonic codes all over the place so people *could* be equal under the law—

—Modernization!

—Industrialization!

—But then Napoleon had to overdo it, Prout said, so Nelson went over and sorted him out, in 1815.

Four boys were on their feet. The civilized joust had become a riot, but Grieves, rather than kill Trevor and then kill them all, crossed his arms indulgently:

—Why six years?

—Sir?

—Why should Napoleon have been allowed to rule six years?

The others sat, leaving Trevor in the fire.

—It's a generation, isn't it, sir? Look at the Academy. It takes six years to get an entirely new set of boys. Take Dr. Sebastian.

—What about him?

—Next summer, it'll be six years since he came to the Academy. That's when we'll know for sure if he's a success or a failure.

—I'll be sure to let him know.

—It's all a bit like Napoleon, sir. More than a bit! Dr. Sebastian came in, he sacked the ancien régime. The docket system's the same as the Code Napoleon.

—But did he end serfdom? Leslie murmured.

The class erupted. Prout said it was rubbish. Trevor said the Head had ended serfdom everywhere but Russia. Gray closed his notebook and capped his pen.

—That will do, Grieves said at last.

He returned to the board and erased it. Cheers. The bell rang for break, and Grieves lingered near Trevor, now more than bemused. Trevor was dropping names, the *Lettres inédites, deuxième édition*, and Grieves was looking pleased, believing Trevor had read Napoleon's letters, read and comprehended, when in truth it had been Gray who'd found the volume in a remote corner of the library, found and partly read, though it was too difficult to read much. Gray, who'd been thumped by Trevor just two days earlier for reading too much, reading *it* too much. Gray, who—

✦

There were days, and this was one, when the forces of chaos toyed with him like a dog that shook a half-dead bird and then dropped it to pursue a squirrel. After the morning's unspeakable realizations, to end an unpromising lesson so perfectly! John had no idea how he'd roused the jaded Remove, but even lunks like Prout had hurled evidence into the fray, and once Mainwaring had introduced the fascinating parallel with Jamie's regime, the whole room had fallen to argument, citing points like city barristers, more facts than he'd seen them recall about Napoleon and more than he thought they knew about the school. If only his colleagues could have seen the tide turn, they'd know his methods bore fruit. Know he bore fruit.

They would have carried Trevor on their shoulders if they could. Instead, they bought him kill-me-quicks at break. Trevor, dazed by fame and food, abandoned shrewdness and approached their Latin master, Gray's elbow in fist. Burton-Lee regarded them:

—*Salvete, legirupae.*

Trevor bowed and presented his lines. The Flea inquired as to Gray's. Gray, he was displeased to hear, did not have them.

—Not in hand, or not complete?

The latter, sir. The Dean of the Upper School professed himself baffled. He hoped that Gray's career as locksmith would not interfere with the fulfillment of a simple imposition.

—No, sir.

—Don't take tones with me, young man, unless you prefer a docket.

Gray stared at the gravel.

—Sir, Trevor assayed, about that business in the barn.

But the Flea had no intention of discussing the matter with them, and he quickly rang the curtain on Trevor's performance (though not before Trevor had voiced concern about Pearce lingering in barns with Third Formers). The boys of his House had been thoroughly dealt with, Burton declared, which was more than could be said for Trevor and his sullen companion. How, for instance, did the cries for help—

As much as Trevor longed to examine this most absorbing affair, he did still have his Latin prep to review. At any rate, he'd already told Mr. Grieves everything he knew, and—lo!—there was his Housemaster now. Perhaps Mr. Grieves could answer any questions that troubled the Flea.

Mr. Grieves nibbled a ginger nut:

—What might I be able to do?

Trevor flashed a smile. Gray turned to leave.

—Answer one or two questions, Burton growled, about this wretched barn.

They melted into the crowd, which was filtering back to the classrooms block.

—Do you think, Gray said, that you could tone it down just a cosine or two?

—*Audentes fortuna iuvat*, Brains. We've got Grievous buttered to the crust. Now for the giddy toast.

Whatever Trevor meant by that, it appeared to require nonstop ban-ter during Trig, which in normal circumstances would have been a wel-come diversion from Mr. Palford's nonsense re: angles, adjacencies, waves, and the like. Today, though, the chatter recalled the rumble of tumbrils, the ring of sharpened blades. What about the pallor that had come over their Housemaster when confronted by the Flea? Was it, as Trevor insisted, evidence of a Stalky victory? Or was it the return again of the arctic man, dour and impenetrable?

✦

—It didn't seem important! John said. They'd been stopped, dealt with, done.

The memory of ginger nut ashes in his mouth, John stood before Jamie's desk like a boy on the carpet.

—You should have told me, Jamie said. I thought we were past this.

✦

At the end of lunch, during which Trevor massaged his reputation near to lion tamer, the Headmaster announced that Mr. Grieves wished to see his House directly following grace. Gray had hoped to use the twenty-minute interval to start his lines; instead, he crowded into the houseroom, where everyone was muttering in consternation, even prefects.

Grieves swept in and silenced them. There had been too much idle chat, he declared, concerning Farmer McKay's property. He appealed to their sense of decency to stop rumors flying. Leslie nudged Trevor, who stood pillar-straight.

—Second, Grieves continued, until an inspection can be conducted and the site secured from injury, the entire House is gated. Prefects included.

Sharp intake of breath, murmurs, then protests.

—This is a precaution, Grieves snapped, not a punishment.

—But, sir!

—How long, sir?

—Are the other Houses gated as well?

—I'll see the JCR in my study after Games, Grieves declared.

And he left, in a swish of soutane and a hush of disbelief.

45

Gray felt ill all through English. Lockett-Egan tried to entice them with *A Tale of Two Cities*, but despite Gray's having read it before, he couldn't enjoy the Eagle's performance. When they got to the third chapter, his heart started beating in his gums. *Buried how long? Almost eighteen years. You had abandoned all hope of being dug out? Long ago.* Unlike Dr. Manette, his father could never be recalled to life, whereas the thing now imprisoned in the barn—*Buried how long?*

—What's up your nose? Trevor demanded after the lesson.

—This beastly gating.

Trevor sighed, as if it were folly to expect better of their rulers.

—If they search the Keep, they'll find our stash, Gray said.

—No, they won't. They'll find a heap of books and cheroots in a tin. *Stalky*'s a loss, but there's nothing for it.

—They'll find the box.

Trevor implored him to speak sense.

—There's a box with my name on it.

—There isn't.

—There is. I hid it there when you were in the Tower with appendicitis.

Trevor, flabbergasted:

—That was two years ago.

Gray bit the inside of his lip. Trevor put his hands in his pockets:

—That was phenomenally stupid, and now you're in a phenomenal mess.

—Inside is a record of all our campaigns since we found the Keep.

Trevor's eyes widened, and Gray felt heady at the lie, the most bald he'd ever told his friend.

At French, Monsieur Henri announced a discussion of their *grand tour de Paris en printemps*. Gray volunteered to go first, and after praising *les musées, les parques, les cafés, les salles de danse,* and *les bibliothèques* all visited with his *mère, tante,* and *jeunes cousines*, he was permitted to take his seat and discreetly write lines.

Buried how long? Almost eighteen years. I hope you care to live. He wouldn't get anywhere by panicking. The thing with panics was to see them for what they were, a kind of vice. He didn't think Dr. Sebastian understood vice this way. With him it was all self-will and conduct degrading to character, but didn't vice lead to ruin? If so, then panic was as bad as any.

46

At tea, Dr. Sebastian commanded the other three Houses—Henri's, the Flea's, and the Eagle's—to attend their Housemasters after the meal. The announcement deflated all but Grieves's House, who deduced that the others would soon be joining them in their unjustly gated condition. Grieves's absence from the masters' table, though unusual, worried no one but Gray, but the Lenten fare of cat's head and grass was so revolting that no one questioned his lack of appetite. After tea, they repaired to their own houseroom, where talk continued of the other Houses, of the barn, of what Trevor and Gray had seen there (multiplying each hour), of what Trevor reckoned they'd find when it was searched:

—Pious Pearce's penny dreadfuls and his cheap, foreign smokes.

This suggestion, as patently ludicrous as Pearce's supposed designs on the Third, built new steam in the gossip machine, which had chugged almost to a halt after laboring all day.

—Why else do you imagine he was out there? Leslie cried. Why do you think the fags got six?

—Ar-agh Patsy, mind the baby!

—Ar-agh Patsy, mind the child!

The Remove took up the rest of the song, their anthem of Stalkiness.

—Therefore the tale has stayed untold until today! a voice cried triumphantly.

Halton.

—I beg your damn pardon? Trevor said.

—I wanted to ask . . .

Heads turned to cheeky Halton. He dried up.

—What? Trevor scoffed. Can't you see we've got more important biznai than sodding around with a beast like you?

Therefore the tale has stayed untold. Gray knew the line, had just read it, as recently as this week. Halton was near, but stepped nearer.

—Could we go somewhere else? he said.

The last line of the chapter called "Stalky."

—Listen, you little sod, Trevor said quietly, boxing Halton against the fireplace.

Won't you tell us? Not by a heap, said Stalky Corcoran. Therefore the tale has stayed untold—

—If you think you're going to blackmail us, you're bloody well mistaken, and if you dog us again, you'll be *very* sorry.

Halton looked . . . Would he blub? Or fly at Trevor? Trevor turned and spoke so the room could hear:

—How is Pious today? Still the arm of the law? Has it weakened, would you say, since yesterday?

It wasn't funny, but everyone laughed. Halton elbowed past, catching Gray in the ribs, hissing a curse in a foreign tongue.

In the washroom afterwards, Trevor swaggered before the urinal.

—When are you going to stop gloating? Gray demanded.

—Why should I?

—Because it's sickening.

Someone was being seized, dragged down the room, held upside down over a toilet bowl.

—I'll tell you what's sickening, Trevor retorted, it's you in a twist. You're a genius at messes, but you can't take—

—I don't see the point in showing off to Grieves so you can humiliate him in front of Burton ten minutes later.

—You wouldn't.

Swinton bellowed from the door about Prep.

—So now he's going to search the barn—

—And *find nothing*. Drop it! I told you—

Toilet diver released, the captors rumbled past Swinton.

—Grieves wasn't at tea, Gray said. Why do you think that was?

—Wasn't hungry? Had an assignation?

—He's at the barn!

Trevor buttoned his flies:

—To search it himself before the actual search?

—It's possible.

—You're becoming boring about this, Brains. Either shut up and let me deal with Grievous or go and deal with him yourself. But spare us the embarrassing chat.

Trevor sucked water from the tap and then wiped his mouth on Gray's sleeve:

—And you can stop feeling sorry for beastly Halton.

—I don't.

—You do. It's wet. He thinks he knows something about our Keep. You should thank me for nipping it in the bud.

The corridor outside their form room buzzed. The other Houses had indeed been gated, and their oppressed citizens proposed every sort of rash action until the Flea hurtled into their midst, extinguishing sound with presence alone. As they found their seats, he let it be known that his patience was short, exceeding short. If the Flea's peace was disturbed with even so much as a cleared throat, he would fall upon the offender with teeth and umbrella.

—And what do you call this? he demanded when Gray presented his lines.

—Lines. From last night.

The Flea raised his brow.

—Sir.

—This is unspeakable. Do it again.

The Flea used a ruler to push the foolscap across the desk, stinking meat returned to its owner.

—But . . . I did them.

—I am well aware, Riding, that you believe cleverness excuses everything, but allow me to suggest other qualities you'd do well to cultivate—humility, prudence, civility even. High marks do not repair poor penmanship, slipshod impositions, petulance, arrogance, or any of your numerous faults.

Gray bit his tongue and returned to his seat.

—If you intend to sulk, the Flea called, you can add another fifty.

The first thing he had to do was to stop whatever was happening to his legs, and then he had to stop what was happening to his hands because the perfect revenge had just occurred to him, one so Stalky that it would kill Trevor not to have thought of it himself. He would redo the lines, and the extra fifty, using the bit from Martial the Flea detested, the passage the man had spent a whole lesson vilifying last week. He would have to write slowly, so that what was happening to his hands wouldn't happen to the letters on the page. Making things smaller would help. So would taking time to decorate the capital letters. Each line he began with a flourish and ended with a swash, each word etched with hatred. This man wanted him to suffer? He would make the Flea suffer. He copied the stanza the man hated most and then copied it again three times. The Flea wanted tears to push against his eyeballs, but it was mirth he suppressed! Soon, too soon, the document drew to its close. He blotted the paper, jotted the pages together, and carried them on palms like a salver to the Flea's desk.

—Sir.

He put his heels together with a faint click. Glancing over his spectacles, the Flea swept Gray's pages into the wastepaper basket, dismissed him, and then returned to his marking.

He'd done what the Flea wanted him to do. He'd written the lines twice, for an audience of no one. Mirth and hope fell before him as the papers settled in the bin. He returned to his seat.

This was what happened when guards were let down. This was what happened when things were left to molder.

He'd been intending to read his father's birthday letters again, intending for months, perhaps more than a year. This term he certainly intended to face the box, if only to take the letter marked for his fourteenth birthday. But it had rained, and they'd been gated, and then it had rained again and they hadn't been able to go to the Keep. Yesterday should have brought an end to his dithering. He meant to slip the fourteenth-birthday envelope into his pocket and read it later when he'd worked up the nerve. He would have done, too, if not for beastly Halton. He couldn't remember the exact words of the earlier letters, but he knew his father had included advice. Surely, if he'd memorized the advice, he wouldn't have erred as he had just now, getting carried away with cheeky lines when he ought to have guarded against the Flea's wrath, his boot.

Valarious, too, had run into a humiliating difficulty upon arrival at Thorn Keep, where his half brother, the Elf Rider, was being held captive by Morvella the Virulent. Valarious's companion, Master Shadow, had warned him against direct assault upon the Keep, so Valarious had led them not to the front gates but to the rear entrance. Master Shadow deplored the plan, and indeed the dungeon guards spotted them the instant they broke cover. The two had only escaped the ensuing melee with the rapid fall of night. Back in the forest, Valarious tended to his companion, binding his wounds, reviving him with an elixir. It had been wrong, he concluded, to bring Master Shadow on his fatal errand. The Elf Rider was his own half brother. He was, in short, Valarious's responsibility—

—How do you spell *responsibility*? he whispered to Trevor.

—Riding!

The Remove stirred.

—Talking, again? the Flea demanded.

—I wasn't talking.

—The second night in a row.

—I wasn't!

—Don't answer me, boy. Stand up.

—Shut up, Trevor breathed, just *shut up.*

He stood. The Flea lowered his glasses.

—What was it, Riding, that I said at the beginning of Prep?

Gray stared at the desktop.

—I asked a question, boy.

—Don't know, sir.

—Leslie!

—Sir?

—Refresh Riding's memory.

Leslie stood reluctantly:

—You said, sir, that if anyone cleared his throat you would fall upon him with your teeth and umbrella.

—Thank you, Leslie. Fifty lines for impudence.

Leslie sat back down.

—Do me the decency of looking at me when I'm speaking to you, Riding.

If looks could kill, this man would be dead.

—How dare you crib in my Prep room?

—I wasn't cribbing!

—You were asking Mainwaring for an answer. Don't lie to me, boy.

—I only asked how to spell *responsibility*!

—Why do you need to spell *responsibility* to do mathematics?

It was happening again, the thing with his legs and hands.

—Bring your book here.

He reached for Trig, any Trig, but the Flea swooped down from the dais and sureyed the papers littering his desktop.

—We *have* been busy! A hundred lines and now these? Your powers astound us.

The Flea opened Gray's first exercise book (Latin) and then set it down. The second (Trig), he scanned with relish.

—Ah, yes! The responsibilities of the algebra. Indecipherable to these poor eyes.

Expounding his utter ignorance of the Modern Side, the Flea begged Leslie to enlighten him as to the evening's prep. Leslie read out the assignment. The Flea leafed through Gray's pages and, arriving at the back, professed himself mystified. Gray's prep, it seemed, had vanished.

—Nay, the Flea continued, we spoke too soon! Here is yet another volume.

It was a performance, a drama starring the Flea, its purpose to humiliate. If the Flea read Valarious, he could claim the passage was satire.

—Surely *this* tome bears responsibility for numbers eight through eighteen, if not thirty-six through . . . Leslie?

—Forty, sir.

Unless they liked it, in which case the Flea's tactic would backfire, exquisitely.

—Thank you, Leslie. Now, before you repose yourself to complete those lines, and I believe ten will do after all—

—Thank you, sir.

—Will you satisfy us with the spelling of *responsibility*?

Leslie gave it.

—We are indebted. Sit.

Reading glasses back on his nose, the Flea opened Valarious, first page, second, riffling through to the end.

The Flea couldn't hurt him. Not truly. He could give more lines, he could jaw and jaw, but he couldn't touch him. He wasn't his Housemaster, and any docket he wrote would land Gray on Grieves's carpet, invited to explain how he had irked Grieves's sworn enemy.

—I see we must apologize, Riding. It is plain that you were not in thought or in deed cribbing.

The Flea composed the face he carted out for elegiacs:

—*Valarious knelt before Master Shadow. The thief's ashen counte-nence alar-umed him. Master Shadow, confided the knight, I cannot per-mit you to continue with me. The thief grasped Valarious's ste-a-ly arm.*

The form twittered. The thespian king played to the gallery with phonetic literalism.

—*But nay, my le-ige. I will not abandon you to the dung-on. You will have need of me, my lock picking. But the band of henchmen have already wo-onded you. My brother is my respon-sa-bility.*

Bows, curtain, finis. The Remove would have leapt in ovation, if they'd dared.

—Young Riding hath spoke true! He is in need of the spelling of *re-sponsibility*, not to mention one or two other words.

52

Chuckles, *hear-hear*.

—But once he acquires them, certain it is that Tennyson shall beckon him to the Laureate and shuffle aside to make room in the Abbey.

—Which is more than they'll do for your teeth and umbrella.

Stillness, like a grave. Except in graves things did move, worms, maggots, creatures reveling in their feast. Water tables rose, lifting coffins, and then drained, letting them down again. Grass grew up, roots down. The grave teemed with more labor than shipyards.

The Flea abandoned Gray's book, and now his shoes were clicking in the aisle, past the silent, captivated body, to the wall at the back, where he released a panel and exposed a cupboard.

Some things once done could not be called back. Most could be stepped away from and denied, as one denied breaking wind, but some changed everything. Even God, all-powerful in the garden, saw that nothing could be the same after the man and the woman had done what they did.

The Flea was coming back, carrying the thing outlawed in the classroom. It was a threat, an object in the stage show, meant to frighten him into submission. Not that he'd meant to say the words that had been said, but now they couldn't be pulled back or joked off, not here before an audience of—

—Put out your hand.

When he did, the man took hold of his wrist. He'd never touched him before, not even an elbow, but now warm hands, almost meaty, examined his fingers, stained with ink. He gestured for the other hand, no ink there, and turned it palm-up, exposed in the middle of the room.

He wouldn't, not really, not here, to him, like this. Players, drama meant to— Gust, crack, hand recoiled, something hot, electric—

Hand on wrist, lifting, straightening, guiding his right hand to brace his elbow. Digits curling back into that cup of feeling—

—Don't.

The Flea's voice for his ears only, the way they talked when they wanted you to stick it (if they were decent; he wasn't, but if he were), bidding courage and a vile kind of trust.

—Don't move.

Thunderbolts, two, before breath, thought, blood—

—That will do.

Fire. A glance bid him take hand away. Another glace prompting . . .

—Thank you, sir.

A nod (if they were decent, most weren't, but—).

—I'll see you in my study after Prayers, young Riding.

One thing—fire—at a time. Turning, stepping, sitting. Leafing one-handed to a page like Trevor's. Beneath the desk, hand pressed between his knees. It couldn't be as bad as it felt, scorched, blistered. Couldn't bear to look.

Minutes gone and still inferno. Were they maiming the Elf Rider at the Keep? If they branded his hand or cut it off, it would all be very well for a scene of wicked torture, but the Elf Rider was going to have to live with it the rest of his life (and his author for the rest of the story) (or stories!). If he were reduced to one hand, bow and arrow would be out. Heavy swords, out. Fisticuffs out. How could he even ride? No. What-ever the torturers inflicted on his body, it couldn't be permanent. Even the elixir in Valarious's pouch couldn't un-maim a person.

Trevor nudged his exercise book over, sines, cosines, a soothing, senseless abstraction. He unscrewed his pen and began to copy.

They were supposed to give a docket. In the days before Dr. Sebas-tian, they could do anything to you and did (though Wilberforce never told of maiming), but then came Dr. Sebastian and his dockets so noth-ing would be done in heat, nothing would be personal, at least not *that* personal. But then Burton—and for what? Burton had probably mis-heard, probably thought he'd said . . . he hadn't said much of anything, a joke. All right, maybe umbrellas, but Burton surely misheard even that, he'd been mumbling after all, because he'd given him lines, and then given them again, and then read— So what if he wasn't a perfect speller? Who said it was even a fair copy? He came top in Latin. He did his prep. Still lines, lines again, then—

It should have happened to the writing hand, the one that caused so much trouble. If only it had happened years ago, before that hand had written what it wrote about Wilberforce and what he did. Years ago it had seemed like a purgative cure, expelling the parasite, drawing it out to be sealed away beneath the floor of the box, the secret compartment beneath his father's letters. But once threads of ink touched threads of cotton rag, things expelled became visible. Writing them down was the worst thing he'd ever done. The stupidest, blindest—

He needed to institute a new regime, and he needed wherewithal to do the things he'd left undone. Once he could recover the box, remove his father's letters, and burn the rest, then the New Regime would be-gin: *no more writing*. The bards of yore never wrote, they couldn't, it was all done by heart, and if someone took exception to a song, the bard could leave town.

A scrap of paper the size of a coin slipped under his elbow: letters majuscule and minuscule, a cypher known long from use. The cypher deemed him brainless. He was to speak no more, at any provocation. Under pain of kicking, he was to refrain from drawing the Flea. (*I'll see you in my study*—one thing at a time.) Box room number four, there they two would meet again. When he'd finished reading the code, Trevor drew across it until the majuscule and minuscule vanished in a storm of scribble.

They surrounded him on the way to Prayers, wanting to see and to spread the thing like Spanish influenza. The trenches killed more than they could count, his father said, maimed others, addled the rest, and then came a fire racing through the bodies of the living. It happened in days, sometimes hours, an avenger more mighty than all the Kaiser's guns.

> *Savior, breathe an evening blessing,*
> *Ere repose our spirits seal;*
> *Sin and want we come confessing,*
> *Thou canst save and thou canst heal.*

Never had he sung a more putrid load of tosh.

> *Though destruction walk around us,*
> *Though the arrows past us fly,*
> *Angel guards from thee surround us,*
> *We are safe if thou art nigh.*

Grieves wasn't nigh, in his seat or anywhere, which at least brought the dismal relief that Grieves wouldn't hear of his shame. His prayers had never been answered, not the ones that mattered. Only fools pined for sentimental blessings. He had to put armor *on*, not take it off. Battle now in a foreign House with a potent foe, one gone too far, and not far enough.

◆

Had he known what he was doing back then? It was all embarrassingly obvious to him now, but Moss had no memory of deliberate thought that first year. He and Pearce were natural enemies even without Morgan. Pearce was brittle, pretentious, odd. No one liked him. You had to be blatantly offensive for people not to like you. It wasn't that hard to get along.

Moss's ginger hair was the first thing people noticed in Shanghai, but in England it was less freakish. Along with it he had the skin, pale and easily bruised. Marks always looked vivid on him. Pearce had the faint lines on his back he wouldn't talk about, the only thing that bought him respect until people learned he could fight, and would at the slightest provocation. Being punished always made Pearce angry. He wasn't a coward, but the experience always incensed him. Moss could have told him it was only the cane; it wasn't worth blowing one's top. But Pearce invariably took against any opinion Moss held. If Moss had told him not to throw himself off Tower Bridge, Pearce would have leapt instantly to his death.

The angling for Morgan's attention must have been obvious when Moss would provoke Pearce, especially when he did it in the changing room, everyone coming in and out of the showers, Morgan Wilberforce as undressed as any. Moss would make a rogue streak, pretending to be chased, so transparent he couldn't believe he'd been able to do it with a straight face. There was the time he'd taken Pearce's jacket and run with it—himself undressed, Pearce in vest and pants—into the showers where Morgan stood covered in soap. He'd dropped the jacket into a puddle, and Pearce had charged in murderous fury. Only Morgan would separate them, Morgan's hands wet on his arm, his hair, picking him up and carting him away under an arm. He fought against Morgan just to do it, soap in his eyes from Morgan's body, as Morgan hauled him into the drying room.

Electric confrontation, no words, Morgan's intoxicating determination and strength, down payment for official punishment later, the fear and excitement, the knee, what he could feel and had wanted to feel beneath him. Then Morgan would set him on his feet: *Had enough?* Moss would nod, smarting from Morgan's smacks, beginning to throb wherever Pearce had got him. Morgan would take him out, hand on the back of his neck, give him a towel if Pearce had drawn blood, then he'd go to Pearce, snap his fingers, and Pearce would sit like a puppy. He'd speak to Pearce, privily, and when they'd done, Morgan would finish his shower to deliberate silence from the rest of the room.

Later, of course, the inevitable JCR summons, the look, the moves, the wait. Then the slam and the bite and the ache and knowing Morgan was on the other side of the cane, giving it on purpose; knowing all Morgan's attention was on him; knowing that later at bedtime when everyone wanted to see, even Morgan would look; knowing that his marks would be better than anything Pearce could show. Moss always would have the more vivid, lurid, red-and-purple marks, and they'd last longer, deeper yellow and green.

They said it passed, the tendency to mark, if you got it enough. Lydon said he used to mark like that. Not, Lydon said, that they'd ever get half of what had been dealt in his day. Take the Prank War—but Morgan would tell Lydon to gas off, and he'd tell Moss he'd only himself to blame and he hoped it hurt as bad as it looked. And when he said that, Moss knew he was still thinking of him and remembering what had passed, and Moss would remember the feeling of being picked up, hauled over the knee, disciplined by Morgan's hand, and later his arm.

Carter and Swinton remembered Morgan, too; he'd been their Captain of Games for one year. They respected him, but warily, like a stepfather. Moss never understood their reserve, but he attributed it to whatever had happened the year before he came. Those boys had secrets he'd never touch, and they possessed a part of Morgan he'd never know, no matter what transpired between them in the years that followed.

For a boy making his first visit to the JCR, Halton stuck six like someone familiar with what he was getting. Now in the dorm he was marked, but not as bad as Malcolm minor. Moss knew that Halton, too, had come from the colonies, but Nairobi rather than Shanghai. He was smaller than the others, target for their spite, but when faced with more than any of the Third had taken, Halton had only blanched. He'd trembled as they all did, but he'd held still better than Malcolm minor, who'd flinched twice and had to be held in place.

Halton wasn't wild, he wasn't a comedian, he didn't start fights in the showers. A colonial upbringing was the start and end of anything between them.

◆

—Kept you long enough.

Gray groped for the box-room light. Trevor was perched atop the highest trunk:

—Well?

—Well, what? The Flea thinks his arse is ice cream and everyone wants a lick.

—Don't be that way, Trevor said severely. I'm on *your* side.

It was one thing to be dressed down by the Flea, but another to be reproached by a friend, and justly. Trevor jumped to the ground:

—What did he say? What did *you* say?

—The usual, and nothing.

Trevor looked at him, wary and wolfish.

—Oh, *you know*, intelligence, idleness, insolence, provocateur. I didn't say anything, not even when he tried it on about the barn. I only said what you said, exactly.

—*What?*

—That we told Grieves what we knew, and it wasn't fair to be carpeted right and left when we'd only gone to—

—Did I or did I not say *not* to draw him?

—I'd like to see you in his study, being played with like—

Trevor thumped him.

—Ow! He *dropped* it. He didn't care about the barn. He just wanted to sing through his repertoire.

—You, my dear Brains, are hopeless.

Trevor straddled a trunk and extended his hands:

—Let's see.

—It's nothing.

The wolfish look. He gave his hand. Trevor whistled:

—Flea's got an infernal good eye. Never know there was more than one except for the purple bit.

He snatched his fist out of sight, not that he'd looked.

—He's a puffed-up, underhanded, white-arsed . . . *arse*.

—Oh, Hipponax! Trevor laughed. What'd you expect after that cheek?

—A docket! What he did was entirely, absolutely—

—Inside the box.

Gray boggled at him.

—Come on. Emergencies of order?

Gray demanded he explain himself. Trevor spouted nonsense about exceptions to the docket rule, one being so-called emergencies of order. Everyone knew it. In everyone's fag test.

—Except, Trevor said realizing, you didn't have a fag test.

—*So?*

Trevor rolled his eyes:

—So you can thank the Great Wilberforce for leaving you in the dark. The point is you need to keep your eye on the ball.

—My eye is on the—

—Provoking him, letting him needle you, then rinding off that way? Have you learned nothing?

Hand into fist, heat faded, though surely something was broken?

—It was crude, Trevor said, amateur and unnecessary. It certainly wasn't Stalky, and for all that, moron, you got off easy.

Gray shut up and let Trevor lecture, how to act in the dorm, how to avoid attention as they launched the campaign to rescue his box; *yes*, there was a plan; *yes*, for tonight; Trevor wouldn't hear a syllable of protest; while Gray had been getting himself caned for no purpose, Stalky had studied the field; a single raid would begin and end before the enemy rolled out of bed. In the morning, Gray could thank him, but tonight he was to follow orders: what to do with his clothes, where to hide them, what to listen for, when to wake and how.

Under the covers, other words clamored in his head, words that made his skin hot, that he'd never have heard if Grieves had been there. If Grieves had been there, Prep would have gone as usual. Burton would never have summoned him to the study, as if he were his, as if there were something between them. He fought to stay awake as the Tower bell tolled later, always later, and the words played as if by wireless: *You deserve, young Riding, rather more than that. You know it, I know it. We understand one another, I think.*

—Wake up, England.

Hand on his mouth, voice in his ear, he opened his eyes. Trevor, in moonlight. Barefoot, they slipped from the dorm.

There was a drainpipe out the window of box room number four, all arranged for a penny dreadful lark: moon rising almost full, drainpipe dry, wind dead as the school. They were down in moments, catlike onto the grass, playing fields, poacher's tunnel. He'd never come through at night, but Wilberforce used to, Saturdays, smelling of—

—Steady on, Trevor said.

He shined the torch where Gray bent retching and stood beside him until it stopped.

—Brains, Trevor said, you mustn't worry.

Gray spat, blew his nose.

—This is the Stalkiest night of our lives. We're going to get what we've come for, in, out, safe for good.

Trevor said nothing of the pillows filling their beds, of climbing back up the drain, of the thousand and one ways it all could go wrong.

—We need to burn the box when we get it, Gray said.

—We will burn it. We can burn the whole barn!

—Right.

—We could, Trevor said. It'd flame in a second.

Old timber, ground wet, fire nowhere to go but up.

—We'd be doing McKay a favor, Trevor continued. That place is one good wind from falling down. Can you see it?

Trevor began to laugh:

—Head rousts a pack of prefects, Pious in the lead, off they tramp, torches blazing, and find . . .

The image of Pearce's despair was too much. It was some time before they regained their breath to proceed through the woods.

A screech owl swooped past, but nothing could dispel the luck that now ringed them. At last things would come right, slate wiped clean. When he was small, Gray had thought of life as an always rising staircase. You got older, he thought, and each month and year you knew more, did more, had more to enjoy. Perhaps they *should* light the barn on fire. But first he had to get the letters. He could put them in his pockets and then hurl the box on the fire. Would the nameplate melt, or would it survive, a witness against him? He'd have to pry it off while Trevor prepared the blaze.

—How fast can you make the fire? he asked.

They'd passed the crest and begun down the slope where pheasants nested.

—We can't burn down the barn, Trevor scoffed.

—But you said . . .

—What'll we do for a Keep?

—The Keep is finished! Gray cried. They'll be watching it, and every sodding cad will want to go there now.

—They'll forget it by next term.

Trevor kicked at the underbrush. A burst of pheasant.

—And one day, Trevor continued, you'll write a book about it and we'll be famous. They'll give tours.

The wall was ahead, the barn just beyond, already polluted, his inheritance from Hermes, gone.

—I thought this was the Stalkiest night of our lives, Gray said.

—Yes!

—So what'll it be: nick a few things from a barn, or raze the place in brilliant inferno?

—It *would* be brilliant, Trevor said, wouldn't it?

—And then they'd crucify the fags for tarting around in a firetrap. Trevor laughed:

—You're learning, Brains. You might not be hopeless after all.

They peered over the wall to the barn below.

—Why is the door open? Gray asked.

—You were supposed to close it after they came out.

—I did close it.

—Not properly.

—I put the latch down, Gray insisted.

They crouched, scouts at post, the night silent and still.

—Stay here, Trevor said.

Over the wall he went, skidding down the grass. Gray leapt over, too, following Trevor's line to beat him to the box, but then Trevor was waving at him, scrambling back up the slope and over the wall, crouching breathless behind it.

—What . . . ?

—Pearce . . .

—*What* . . . ?

—In there . . .

Pearce was in the barn.

At this moment?

Even now.

At times of catastrophe, a cold calm always filled him. This was no exception. He asked placid questions, asked them again, but Trevor couldn't explain Pearce's purpose, only that the sub-prefect was sitting just inside the door, his head in his arms, awake or not, impossible to say.

—But . . . *why?*

Who could tell the ways of the loon? Not the prophet's bones, and not Trevor Maxwell Mainwaring. Their only option was to wait.

Wait here, beyond the wall? Indefinitely through the night? As their mortal enemy held the holy of holies?

Trevor saw no alternative. But not to fear! Hours remained before they must needs turn back. And Trevor had a bag of sweets.

—We'll be like the passengers in the mail coach, Trevor said, bound for France to recall the prisoner to life.

Or burn him to death.

—Wonder if we'll be robbed by the Captain.

These and other now bland enactments trickled from Trevor's mouth as they worked through the bag of licorice. Jacques even now guarded the prisoner, Trevor confided, but soon he would be freed. Madame Defarge would not knit their names into her register; they would ride, un-pursued, back to England. They would mount the steps of Whitby and plunge a stake in the vampire's heart. They would, like Sikes and Oliver, rob the house and escape.

—But didn't Sikes—

Gray was not to take a gloomy line. Such was not the night. Such was a night like the night Trevor had once run away to sea. Gray had never heard of such a night, but he heard of it now. Trevor's tale had more than a whiff of fiction—absconding from his prep school, trekking out to Dodman Point, receiving news from the heavens in the form of a comet that his venture would succeed, scouring the horizon for the vessel that would take him to the treasured high seas . . .

The ground was damp, his seat soaked, his teeth coated in licorice. If they could make it back intact in every sense, Gray silently vowed to devote himself to ordinary life and stop confusing it with stories. In stories, you didn't risk your life and your arse waiting in a field to perform your heroics. In stories, no one left stupid things to rot for years. In stories, a coherent hand guided the plot; there was no tumble of make-believe just when you needed to think clearly. Friends in stories never lied to one another.

—I have a confession, Gray said.

—Speak.

The truth dried before he could get it off his tongue—the box not a record of their campaigns but a record of Wilberforce's . . .

—I confess, Gray said, that I'm freezing my balls off.

—Maybe we'll get frostbite! M'pater lost a finger in the war.

—To frostbite, in *Egypt*?

—It got cold.

—Which finger?

Trevor wasn't sure, but he felt his father's admiration would be enhanced if he himself were to lose a digit, or at least part of an ear. Trevor had every confidence that upon hearing their adventure, his father would at last give up talking about his subaltern, Lieutenant Victor. How many letters had been taken up with vile Victor? Victor, who'd been thrown out of three public schools in his day, on the bill every week, the vexation of timid officers, always taking his exploits too far, now in Palestine enjoying wider scope, fulfilling the Colonel's wishes without having to be told how, inventive, fearless, brazen. Now, this summer, when Trevor would see his father for the first time in over a year, Trevor's curriculum vitae would at last be up to snuff. Perhaps his father could arrange a place in his unit? Once he'd passed his Remove, naturally.

—Naturally.

Trevor stopped chattering and cocked his head as the barn door whined below. A figure staggered out, hugging itself, surveying the horizon, and then stalked down the track to the road.

It was happening before he realized: Trevor over the wall, Gray scrambling after, slipping, fall broken by a hand that should have been too cold for bruises. More noise as Trevor dashed into the barn and a figure scurried round the other side—Pearce circling back? Someone else entirely? Gray froze in place. Time was never his friend. The figure darted into the barn, and before Gray could work out what to do, a crash rang out and the figure burst forth, barreling down the track like a fox flushed from cover.

Whatever the figure had seen inside the barn, the clock had begun on their return: thirty minutes by the road, shorter if you ran, longer in the dark; by the night woods, forty at least. Gray bounded to the source of the crash and found Trevor on the grass, debris around him.

The exchange as such made not enough sense. Pearce had come back as Trevor was in the loft searching vainly for *Stalky*.

—Are you sure it was Pearce?

—Who else would it be?

As the invader flashed his torch up the ladder, Trevor had taken to the window.

—You jumped?

Had to. Wasn't hurt, not much, hopefully something to show for it, but— Gray helped him sit up.

—Bloody hell!

63

—Shh, Trevor hissed, Pearce!

—He's gone, and you're bleeding all over the place!

It was wet on his neck, Trevor mumbled. Somewhere in his head was a sound, and a taste, and a— Gray shone the torch on his scalp, took a handkerchief—

—Don't touch me! Trevor cried.

A boot caught him in the knee. Gray backed out of reach:

—Stay there.

Inside the barn, torch to the wall, to the back, very back. Like a fist to the gut. Like the diagnosis you never wanted to hear. Royal tomb robbed.

Up the ladder, nothing. All the straw kicked overboard, bare boards brazen. How many ways could you spell disaster?

Outside, Trevor's face was damp with sweat.

—I'm going to touch your chin. Don't hit me.

Garbled curse.

—I'm going to turn on the torch. Follow it with your eyes.

—Ow, you bastard—

—Hold still!

—Where's your box?

Torch off. Silence thick as fear.

—Did you look?

—I looked.

The patient struggled to his feet:

—We'll get it back.

The physician turned his patient towards the road, but the patient wrenched away:

—Pearce went that way, so we're going *this* way.

Trevor weaved up the slope, scrambled over the wall, and staggered through the pheasant nests, slipping—

—Careful!

—If you touch me, I'll knock your lights out.

He fell again, got up again.

—This is all your fault.

At the poacher's tunnel, Trevor sat down on the old fallen tree. His trousers were torn. Everything was gray. So many things could be stopped. People could be murdered, cities burned, nations destroyed, but dawn came every day, never rushed nor slowed by anything.

—This, Trevor cried, was a lark! The larkiest lark ever.

—It's late, Gray said. We've got to—

—I'm not going anywhere, Brains, until you admit it was the best night of your life.

—We got nothing from the barn, you bashed your head open, and every second we're sitting here is one second closer to getting caught.

Trevor laughed disconcertingly:

—It's always doom and gloom with you! Eye on your Uncle Stalky.

They wriggled down the tunnel and up the other side, where the silhouette of the school brightened against the sky. Squelching fields, drainpipe. The patient began to climb but then lost his grip and fell to the grass.

—I'm done for, he gasped. Save yourself.

—Don't be absurd!

—When they find me, I'll say I did it.

—Did *what?*

—I was never going to make it.

He sounded delirious. Was this how it was when shells hit the front?

—I wanted to do this thing, you see? One good thing, before the end.

—This isn't the end!

It wasn't the front, and the wound wasn't fatal.

—This is the best thing I've ever had, Trevor said. Good things always end.

—Not *now.*

—When they find me, there'll be a flap, and—listen, Brains—while everyone's off their heads, you go to Pearce's study and get your box. And if he ever says anything, tell him it's *his* fault, what happened to me.

—I'm not leaving you here on the ground.

—If they haven't found me by second bell, send someone, won't you? It's beastly cold.

Trevor was shuddering, incapable of climbing anywhere, heat draining every second they stood there. The amateur physician did the only thing he could: drainpipe, inside, stocking feet down the back stairs. If only hearts pumped ideas with the blood. What doors gave outside? The gates would be chained until Farley unlocked them. Wilberforce had told of a window in the Tower. Through it he'd climb when bunking off at night. Trevor couldn't climb through windows; he might not even be able to climb stairs.

Light glared across the passage. He no longer needed the torch.

Wasn't there another way Wilberforce told of one time, when Gray had been ill and he'd come to the Tower to see him? He told the story of the Fags' Rebellion, of going out that night and coming in another way, through a French window, in his Housemaster's study, whose door had no key.

 The birds had a lot to say, and they'd risen early to say it. John had never been a heavy sleeper, but to be wrenched from dreams by their song seemed symbolic somehow. *Come o'er the eastern hills, and let our winds kiss thy perfumed garments.* The days were getting longer, and better now. His goddaughter's voice played in his head as it had chattered in the carriage, broad and frank, *Let us taste thy morn and evening breath,* as they tasted in Eden.

The birds were pecking at the slate and bickering in the gutter, a morning for rivals and wooing. John poked the studs through his collar and reminded himself to remind Mrs. Firth to make him get a haircut. One day, when gray streaked, he'd let his hair have its way, like a nineteenth-century poet, neckerchief and all. *O deck her forth with thy fair fingers; pour thy soft kisses—* Tapping inside now, rapping actually, at the door? He checked his flies and shouldered his braces, expecting—

—Pearce?

—Sir—

—What on earth?

Fire?

—It's Mainwaring and Riding, sir. They aren't in their beds.

Things were racing, crawling his scalp.

—I'm sorry, sir—they're made up to look—I thought you ought to—

He told Pearce to show him. It was one thing to have emergencies during waking hours, or perhaps someone ill in the night, but quite another to be assaulted before he'd fully dressed and led upstairs like a rough customer, which brought out a distressing click in his knee.

Light through the long windows, all fourteen beds piled with blankets. John looked to Pearce for explanation.

—They weren't there, Pearce whispered, five minutes ago they *weren't.*

John sent him away to finish dressing. No, he should not wake his fellow prefects, or anyone else for that matter. John thanked him. He would handle this.

John's slippers clapped across the floor, loud enough to wake the whole room if they hadn't been sleeping the drugged sleep of youth. At the far end, Mainwaring and Riding huddled under covers, backs to him. He cleared his throat. The covers rose and fell. Could Pearce have come unhinged under the pressures of his new post? They were rising and falling just like the others . . . except faster. The thing that had crawled his scalp now clamped his temples. He stepped around the beds. Their eyes were closed, their faces flushed.

—Get up, both of you.

Mainwaring opened his eyes. The mound that was Riding froze.

—*Now.*

Riding stretched as if from a long winter's nap.

—Stop *messing* about. You're making it worse.

He spoke in an undertone but still managed the voice that could instill fear. Riding sat up first, and now it was obvious. They were dressed and filthy. Mrs. Firth would tear strips off them both, though that was the least of their problems. Riding kept his eyes on Mainwaring, who stumbled out of bed. John caught his arm:

—What on *earth* happened?

—Nothing, Mainwaring mumbled.

—None of that!

—He fell and hit his head, said Riding. I stopped the bleeding. He was sick twice, but he's not hurt anywhere else. I checked.

John realized his mouth was open. Who was this child physician standing before him in stocking feet and the deepest trouble, reporting as at a Battalion Aid Post?

—Can he walk? John asked.

—He shouldn't.

—I can . . . walk.

He should never have sent Pearce away, but there wasn't time to rouse another prefect.

—Riding, he said, dressing gown, slippers, wait in my study. I'll see Mainwaring to the Tower.

He took the boy's arm, but Mainwaring pulled away:

—I can on my own!

—All right.

—To Timbuktu or Tipper-gally or—

The boy actually pushed John aside and strode down the dorm with a lopsided gait. The room was beginning to stir. Riding fumbled with his slippers:

—He really shouldn't, sir.

John went to the corridor, bright with bulbs. At the step by the linen cupboard, Mainwaring stumbled, caught himself on the door, and then slipped down the wall. John caught him under the arms and lifted him as he'd lifted other fallen men, when he was young and strong and the world was coming down in shells.

✦

They had gone for a walk. Trevor couldn't sleep. They'd been walking in the cloisters, places such as that. They'd walked, he'd slipped. You could slip on flat ground. Dark, tired, puddle. They shouldn't have done it, but they were sorry. He was sorry. He was young and stupid but he wasn't bad. He'd done a foolish thing, but he'd only been trying to help. He would never do it again. Exams soon, he'd even study Trig. He'd try at football. He'd answer properly at call-over. Of course he deserved gating. He knew that. Accepted it.

He stopped at Pearce's study, but the box wasn't there. Pearce must have given it to Grieves, which was why Grieves had come up . . . Oh, that box? Stolen from him, terms ago. Third Form? Fourth? No idea what that paper was. No idea there was a bottom that came up. Not his handwriting, not *much* like, he could give a sample, no notion why anyone would steal, and write, and hide—

✦

John's arms had stopped shaking, but if he had to lift anything else, he was sure they'd shake again. He was not as young as he'd been.

In his study, he opened the drapes and closed the French windows where they had come loose. Turning, he startled; Riding had been standing in the dark, hands tucked monastically into the sleeves of his dressing gown.

—Whatever possessed you, Thomas?

The boy flinched. John began again. Bade him sit, sat beside him, asked if he wanted a glass of water. The boy kept his gaze on the cold grate.

—What's going to happen, sir?

Voice rough, unused.

—You'll have to tell me everything, John replied.

—I mean Trevor. Is he . . . ?

The boy still didn't look at him but turned instead to the door, as if his friend stood just outside.

—Kardleigh's with him. He said you'd done a commendable job with the first aid.

The boy scowled.

—Thomas, John continued, please start at the beginning. I can't help until I know the facts.

A deeper scowl. John thought he heard teeth grinding.

He could wait. Not long, but some. He would sit beside this boy and wait on the light. He would use the Christian name, which he hadn't used with this one in years. This bone-crushing person beside him bore little resemblance to the child who had first entered his study, too young for the school but enrapt nearly as much as John had been by the woman accompanying him. John remembered thinking the mother was too young to be a widow. The war had produced a nation of them, but even though ten years had passed since then, this woman, girl, wore black head to toe, looking lost and fierce, as if she, not the boy, were being dispatched. He remembered thinking she needed a governess. He remembered, when she spoke, how much it seemed like playacting, as if she'd raided the dressing-up box. He remembered the monologue she embarked upon, concerning the boy's hair, its streaks of yellow and brown, yellow from her, brown from his father, neither color winning the battle but flecking side by side in brindle—as if she were describing a stray dog. John remembered thinking her prattle a charming form of hysteria, and he remembered inviting the two to sit and drink the tea Mrs. Firth had provided while he stepped across the quad. Jamie was in his study with his secretary, and John unleashed in front of them both. Lewis had tried to wheel himself from the room, but Jamie had told the man to stay as he was. He told John that since Riding was here now, he couldn't be put out at the gates. End of discussion, good day, where were we, Lewis?

John knew he'd left the boy and his mother alone too long, and as he strode across the cloisters, he remembered thinking, *She's too young to manage*; he remembered thinking, *They'll eat him alive*. And then he remembered Morgan Wilberforce.

Then as now, the boy sat hunched forward, as if balancing something at the base of his neck. Then as now, his gaze darted, grasshopper eyes someone had said, looking everywhere but at John. Then as now, he mumbled, and John had to ask him to repeat.

—He couldn't sleep.

Mainwaring, he meant. They'd gone for a walk.

—Where did you go?

Grasshoppers.

—You weren't at McKay's barn, were you?

If the boy pulled himself in any more tightly, he'd break. It was killing John to watch.

—I can't go to Dr. Sebastian and simply tell him you were walking, John said. Surely you can see.

—Will we be disposed?

The boy looked to him for the first time, oddly trusting.

—It depends.

Then looked away. Fear was easy to see, up close.

—You can trust me, Thomas. I'm your Housemaster. I'm—I don't want to see you disposed.

Fear, and now something else. Resentment? Distrust? A captured soldier who'd never speak, no matter the torture.

—Nothing? You're breaking my heart!

The boy stayed mute, but his eyelids began to droop, his head to nod. Incredible, here, fighting sleep.

✦

Ear tugged to make him stand and follow. Pulled down the corridor, shoved inside a bright and freezing room. Door locked, bed, mattress, table, blanket, he made a tent against the cold, the kind he'd make those times when he'd hide inside the window seat, making Morgan look for him. He'd almost spoken the truth before Grieves. The urge had come physically upon him, but— *You weren't at McKay's barn, were you?* Grieves said he wanted the truth, but he didn't want *that* truth. Then it was finger-ear-neck, hating him as they all did when they saw what he really was. *Have mercy upon us miserable . . .*

Riding, T. G. it had said on his trunk, tuckbox, mattress. Dorm empty around him, his mother's scent replaced by laundered sheets. No longer *Gray* but *Riding, T. G.,* like a sequel to Dr. Riding with a *G* tacked on, *G* for Gray, for Grieves, for grievous, green, griffon, grove, gravel, grammar, grandiloquence, ginger-haired boy in the door of the dorm, stick and ball in his cheek.

—There you are! Where have you been?

—Sorry?

Stick plucked out, a lurid green lump:

—Name, grasshopper. Chop-chop.

—Gray.

—Name, not color. What's this?

Label, brown.

—That's me. Riding. Thomas Gray—

—God in heaven. Are you *honest*?

—Yes.

—Rhetorical. Where are you from?

Rhetorical? A stinging—

—Oh!

—Shut up, that wasn't—shut up.

—Why'd you—

—Have you never had a clip round the ear? God in heaven.

Where did he come from? What was his father?

—Physician. Was.

—Dead?

Yes, dead, except he didn't like that word.

—Sorry. Look, *sorry*. When?

Five months, one week, six days.

—Bugger me.

Stick to other cheek and from a pocket, wristwatch. Ginger head mounted the bed, folded mattress, king of—

—Listen to me, grasshopper—

—Why do you keep calling—

—I am going to be your crammer, and you are going to swot harder than you've ever swotted in your life, understand?

Not at all.

—If you don't, you won't last a day. Repeat after me, *I know nothing. My mind is empty.* You're *ten years old*? Are you insane?

—Eleven next—

—Shut up. You know nothing. Your mind is empty. Which prepper?

Words?

—Before here.

71

Oh, school. Witchell's Gate at the end of the lane.

—Are you *honest?*

He *was* honest, and since he was eight, his father had taught him, laboratory, study, enough Latin to read the dispensary.

—The Flea is going to *crucify* you.

But he knew things, lots of things!

—Listen, grasshopper, people spend *years* at prepper specifically training for public school. This isn't your Witchell's Gate Jam and Jerusalem.

Words!

—Can you fight?

He was good at gin rummy.

—God in heaven. You'll have to learn to swear. Repeat: Bloody.

—Bloody.

—Bugger.

—Bugger.

—Sod.

— . . . Sod.

—Wank . . . Say it!

Said.

—Sod off, you bloody wank.

He was to say it like he meant it. With vitriol. That meant contempt.

—I know what it means.

Another blow.

—If you blub, I'll thump you black and blue.

Air in, tears in, in-in—

—Better.

There was Fox, their old corgi, lying on the bed, except he wasn't dead, not even old, just rub my tummy and jump to the floor. She'd even let them play ball in the parlor because he wasn't ill, wasn't dead, was back to his self, tracking mud indoors to sit at your—

—Never blub. Never peach. Never be caught alone with another chap.

—What if you happen to be somewhere, and another chap happens to be there, too?

—Never mind. Burton-Lee's House are good at?

—Rugby—rugger.

—The Eagle's are good at?

—Jokes.

—Henri's?

—French letters.

—Don't unknot your tie.

Faster next morning. Jacket here, not there. Waistcoat like this. Laundry there Thursdays.

—What do you think you're doing? Pajamas *over pants*?

—But I always—ow!

—Strip off.

In front of . . . ?

—God in heaven, it's come from the convent.

Everything off, hand in front of—

—Don't. And you can't blush.

Can't help it.

—You can stay like that until you've pulled yourself together.

Naked, both of them, washroom, changing room, dorm.

—Don't look at people. Not unless you mean it.

—Mean what?

—Never mind.

He'd get a Keeper, who'd teach him everything.

—You?

—Please God, no. You'll get me whacked here to Christmas.

In a fortnight the fag test—the who, the what, the where, words used and not used, rules, customs, notions. But until tomorrow, crammer:

—Never?

Blub, peach, blush, look.

—Where were you at prep?

—America.

—Where in America?

—Alabammy.

—Liar.

—Sod off!

—Better.

His old father, lying on the bed, not ill, not dead, back from where he'd been, wearing his suit and reading *The Lancet*. Back for days, or was it weeks? He needed to see him for a serious talk. He was sorry, so sorry, if he'd only hear him say it. *You're back, and surely, surely . . .* He would be the son he wanted, the son he knew, he hadn't meant the things he'd said that awful day, he'd do anything, anything, half a chance, quarter—

—Bring me another. Please?

Wilberforce M., window seat, moon. Ale bottle opened, made to drink it.

—I suppose we'll have to sort you out.

Dressing gown off. Underneath nothing, all.

—The moon shines bright, and on such a night, from yonder window above the earth, Wilberforce, methinks, stands full of mirth, waiting at last the lustrous birth, of thee, thou ravished bride of—

Arm grabbed, twisted tight.

—You'll thank me. Gets it out of the way. Lets you know what to expect.

Eyes, look, sleep has things, grant this day we fall into nothing, ride away, devil in chase, nameplate—look—marshes!

—*Across vale, across fen, over crag, over ben . . .*

Come back!

—*Like a wave on the sea you come riding to me, riding over the moors . . .*

Home? Dorm? Room.

—*Like a hawk, like a tern, like the falcon's return . . .*

Recalled to light. To rumbling, tumbrils? Feet to floor, window thrown open, voice in his throat:

—People are sleeping!

Crash mechanical. Mess on the ground. Flagstones, person. *Wheels?*

—What's the *matter* with you?

Voice from below, under his window, voice of a girl shouting:

—You almost gave me a heart attack!

Awake, not asleep. Her stockings, black, torn at the knee.

—You can't simply go round shouting out windows!

Navy frock, plaits, wheels on her feet.

—Well? she said.

—Sorry.

—I *certainly* hope so! This pavement is full of weeds. Couldn't have more if you *cultivated* them.

Crab-like, standing, wheels clicking.

—Oh, my flowers!

Scattered yellow and white. Wobbling, she gathered them:

—What are you *doing* there?

—Sorry?

—Hanging out the window. Everyone else is at lessons.

His body returned to him, stiff, drugged, thirsty. And desperate need of a—

—I've botched it, she said. Shall we try again?

Arm reached up, daffodil palms:

—Cordelia Light.

Warm, sticky, gripping as if she could wrench off his fingers.

—Riding.

—Skating.

—I mean me. That's my name.

—Is that what they *call* you? What's your proper name?

He was called so many things.

—It's Riding. Thomas Gray Riding.

Hand finally unclenched. He had dirt on his palms, under nails, and . . . blood?

—Pleased to meet you, Thomas Gray.

Whose blood?

—Why aren't you at lessons?

His kingdom for some water. Or at least a chamber pot.

—I've botched it again, she said. Cancel transmission.

—Aye aye.

When she grinned, you saw her teeth, crooked beneath her eyes. Laughter and zeal and chaos and juice.

—I like you, she said. You're funny.

There was a chamber pot, right under the bed, but he couldn't while she . . .

—*Why yes the lady said as he interrupted her stroll I have only just arrived.*

—Yes?

—Come in last night on the Orient Express. We're bound for Paris, of course.

—So says the popular intelligence.

Eyes, teeth, heart-slaying grin:

—You *can* say more! I knew it.

—More?

—More than *yes, no,* and *sorry.*

—It is rumored.

—The swain licked his pencil and applied it to his tablet. Shorthand was beyond him, but—

—Tell us, Miss . . . ?

—Light. That's L-I accent aigu-O-H-T.

—Hungarian?

—Irish. Her mother was English and her father was Irish, but he already knew that.

—It explained everything.

—How could he perceive so much about her when they'd met only moments before?

—*The great Gaels of Ireland are the men that God made mad, for all their wars are merry, and all their songs are sad.*

—Marry me! she said.

She had the kind of laughter that made him want to cry. Girls were supposed to be wet, but she looked as though she could win a hare and hounds, a scrap in the courtyard, or any game of cards you'd care to play.

—I smelled summer this morning. Did you? Like the sea.

He didn't, but he'd try later. He wouldn't smell it, she confided, because of those clouds. Cold weather was headed their way, the mistral, borasco, williwaw.

—German Bight, Humber.

—West backing four or five.

—Increasing six at times.

He wasn't the sort to play along, or the sort people looked at with eyeteeth like that.

—Miss Líoht, our readers are burning to know.

He needed her to leave and he needed her to stay.

—You are the first to attempt a female journey to these parts.

—If not me, then who?

—Indeed. But can you tell our readers why these wilds? Wherefore these tribes?

—These tribes! When I was but a girl, my godfather—you know him of course?

—His name is legendary.

—My legendary godfather, returned from his expeditions, would tell of these tribes, his conquests, his close shaves.

—What a knee to learn from, Miss Líoht!

—So you see why I was compelled to make the trek, to search out Uncle John in the wild.

—Uncle John?

—My godfather. I told you.

—You didn't.

—He's a teacher here, in these wilds.

Things so good could never be real.

—A Housemaster.

Honest trifles to win us to our harm.

—John Grieves.

This was what happens to ones as bad as he.

—Are you going to be sick?

—He's my Housemaster.

The teeth, the smile, the dagger.

—Oh, do you mean it? I'm so envious I could pinch you. What's he *like*?

Words were harlots, gone when you'd paid them.

—It's so queer to see him wearing a gown and ordering people about. Last night on the train he was funny, like himself. But this morning I haven't seen him properly at all. He's been dashing about like a rabbit over those boys.

—Boys?

—From last night. Meetings, wires, bolting here, ringing there.

—What's going to happen?

—Oh, they'll sack 'em, obviously, though Uncle John has the idea he can save them. That's what he's been doing all day. He didn't even come to lunch!

—What do you mean, *obviously*?

—They must have done something terribly wicked. Everyone's furious.

—It wasn't wicked!

—Pardon?

—They didn't do anything!

—Wait—

—They only took a walk!

—Are you one of them?

—No.

—Don't lie. You are!

—I . . .

—Your friend's frightfully ill, you know, raving like a lunatic. He could have died on your *walk*. Goodbye, Thomas Gray.

—Wait!

Wheels rumbling, flowers pumping fist, a thousand cuts left behind.

✦

—It isn't like that, John protested.

—But surely you can see, Jamie said.

Jamie lit into the sandwiches, but John couldn't eat even though he'd missed both breakfast and lunch.

—I gave Riding plenty of chances to confide, and he maintains they were taking a walk.

—They'd no business taking a walk, Jamie said.

—Of course not, but—

—We can't have boys *taking walks*, day or night.

—They aren't that way.

—And how am I supposed to take it when only this week they were out at McKay's barn?

—They went to help.

—I'm sure.

—We've got to be rational, John told him. Factual. Some juniors were caught at that barn. Now duly punished. Mainwaring and Riding have been caught being idiots. The affairs have nothing to do with one another, and neither has anything to do with that other godforsaken—

—That isn't Burton's view.

—Damn Burton! Is he Headmaster or are you?

—Or the Board's.

—What on *earth* has this got to do with them?

—John. Don't be naive.

✦

Mrs. Firth brought him sandwiches and let him use the toilet, not the regular one but some bathroom down the corridor. The door separating the corridor from the House was brown, not green baize, but it nevertheless marked the frontier between private and public. No boys went beyond it any more than they penetrated Soviet Russia, yet here he was on the other side. Wilberforce had told him of a room called the Chamber of Death. They put you there before disposing you, he said. No one had been disposed from their House in Gray's time, but Wilberforce said it happened regularly in Dr. Sebastian's first term, during the Great Clear-Out. If you were in trouble, you went to lessons until summoned. If you were ill, you went to the Tower and they brought your prep to you. The Chamber of Death meant quarantine absolute. Here in the room, no paper, no books. Games were over, and still no one came.

✦

—Word's got round, John admitted. The Remove were all a-twitter last lesson.

—It's inevitable, Jamie said. But I've managed to put out the fire with the Board.

—How?

—Riding's uncle, chums with Overall.

—With the Chairman of the Board? Why didn't I know this?

—Didn't you? It's how we wound up with Riding in the first place.

—And you didn't see fit to mention it this morning?

—Lewis found the letter in a file. I take back everything I've ever said about his fanatical methods.

—He's a miracle on two wheels.

—John, whatever you do, don't take this tone with Burton.

—I'm not taking a tone. This is a matter of *House discipline*. If Burton insists on being present even though it's nothing to do with his House, even though Riding and Mainwaring aren't even *in* the Upper School, then—

—Yes, thank you. And another thing.

—*What?*

—However this mess ends, I'm going to have to deal firmly with them. And with Mainwaring in his current state, I thought to rusticate them for the rest of term.

—I wouldn't object.

—But I've been doing some telephoning—

—Oh God, the Colonel.

79

—Still in Palestine. I spoke to Mrs. Mainwaring.

—Small mercies.

—But I haven't been able to raise a soul at the home of Riding's mother.

—She's traveling. Letter here somewhere.

John was used to being reproached by his basket of correspondence, but it was embarrassing to negotiate it in front of Jamie, and as someone pounded his door.

—Come!

Door nudged, but not by Mrs. Firth or a prefect.

—It's five o'clock, Uncle John. You said—

—Won't be a moment, darling.

—Is this the illustrious goddaughter?

John abandoned his basket and stepped into the breech:

—Headmaster, may I present Cordelia Líoht. Cordelia, Dr. Sebastian.

Jamie took her hand, and she took his, this life touching that one.

—How do you do? she said.

—Much better now I've made *your* acquaintance.

She broke into a grin, which spread to Jamie, flagrant sunshine. John cleared his throat.

—I'll find you in your room, darling.

Mock seriousness wiped the grin from her face, and from Jamie's; she wished him good evening and bounced from the room.

—I'd no idea, Jamie said when the door had shut. This is what you've been keeping from us all these years?

—I wasn't—

—She's charming, John. But it's awful timing.

—I told you, she won't—

—Not her. Your boys. My train's at eight tonight. The conference?

—Can't you go tomorrow?

—My address is tomorrow.

—Bollocks!

—It isn't bollocks. I'm chairman of the hymnbook—

—I didn't mean— Here it is. Shetlands from the fifteenth. Met by aunt in London. School train on the twenty-eighth.

—What?

—Riding. No names, no forwarding address. Beastly woman.

12 The food was appalling. The mutton looked like something Mrs. K's cat had thrown up. The cabbage was gray. The forks weren't clean. The other masters looked too cross to care. They put things in their mouths and washed it down with claret. Except Uncle John, of course, who'd drink tea if he were there. The whole room smelled of a steamy, sweaty toilet.

But Dr. Sebastian said grace as if he meant it, a prayer that rhymed about bread and fishes, his voice, his accent, not like the grown-ups she knew, almost like Uncle John, but brighter. He made announcements about bedtimes, and then he introduced her, his hand on her shoulder as if picking her for Games. They all stopped rustling and gawped. They didn't look like the boys at her school. Their hair was shorter, more cruel.

The air outdoors cleared her nose with the smell of coal. The little man was closing the gates and lighting the lamp. The doorknob of the House, when she touched it, was sticky, handled by all those boys.

◆

—Half the common room just buttonholed me at tea, Jamie complained.

—I thought you said it was inevitable.

—The point, John, is they're right. Goings-on at that barn almost destroyed the school before.

—Amongst other things!

—And being asked to speak at the Headmasters' conference is a vote of confidence for the school, rebuilding from the ash, living it down.

—*Jamie.*

—Maudlin?

—This time isn't that time. These boys aren't those boys.

—What if you're wrong?

—I give you my word.

◆

Mrs. Firth let him into the changing room while everyone was at tea. The Headmaster would see him during Prep. Gray had better eat the sandwiches. He'd get nothing else, and she wouldn't do with wasting.

He got under the showers. Night, mud, blood, drain. *We acknowledge and bewail our manifold sins and wickedness.* He hated the Sunday

Confession. It was overdone. He might have broken rules, but wicked? *Provoking most justly thy wrath and indignation against us.* If they disposed him, he'd be gone in the morning. No goodbyes, not even to Trevor. Mrs. Firth called from the door, told him not to dawdle. Towel, toothbrush, comb. Shirt, collar. There was no later to think things through. It was now or naked. *Think.*

If they believed the walk, why Chamber of Death? He could insist the walk was true, but what else did they know?

If they had the box: stolen, from his cupboard oh terms ago, not his hand, not even much like.

No time to polish the shoes, only spit and rubbing.

If they didn't have it: walking. Who got disposed for walking? You got disposed for . . . they didn't even say why those chaps were sacked last year. Henri of his two had said *il faut mieux*, and Burton of his had said nothing. Trevor declared they were beasts all along and the Academy was better off without them.

So what if they expelled him? He'd be free! No more fists in the scrum, no more puke-on-toast, snot-and-jam, JCR. Home, free, and peace. But they'd drag her back from Shetland. Tell her some, tell her all. Morning and night, her tears hidden and shown. *The remembrance of them is grievous unto us—* A *walk*. Just a walk. Uncle John working to save. He'd been first in his form nearly three years. A walk, Uncle John, slipped on flat ground.

His handkerchief needed folding, his pockets vetting: broken pencil, rubber, nib, stone (amulet, Valarious), paper torn, paper inked, paper . . . blue, unknown. *LOOK IN YOUR PIGONHOLE.*

◆

Cordelia had promised to ring the hospital at half past five, but when her call reached the ward, they said her mother was taking a bath: call at seven and ask for the Sister.

Uncle John had said she could ring from his study. He had his hands full and would be in the Headmaster's study, but she should sit herself at his desk and speak as long as she wished, even as long as ten minutes. But now, at almost seven, he said she'd have to wait. The hands-full matter had been moved to his study. Dr. Sebastian was due and Mr. Burton-Lee. Yes, with the moustache, but he wouldn't call it noodley. She'd promised on the train to obey him when he asked, and now he asked that she go to her room. Here was a book. Here was another. He would fetch her shortly, as soon as he could. He knew the ward hours just as well as she did, and they'd reach her mother before the night was done. The corridor was warmer than his study, and its smell brooked no compromise, orange, nearly brown, like things smelled in other times. The books he'd put in her hand were dry, almost as bad as touching day-old newsprint. The clock there started clanging like an out-of-tune gong. She never thought before how much a clock looked like a coffin. The glass was fogged, and the time was off. The bell outside had just tolled seven as this one finished its three-quarter tune.

✦

Mrs. Firth walked like his mother, footsteps full of blame. Outside Grieves's study, she began to scold someone else. Which might allow a moment for his pigeonhole . . .

—What do you think you're doing, boy? Get on!

He turned and there was the girl, books in hand, wearing shoes, not skates. He looked at her and she looked back straight. Mrs. Firth behind him, he mouthed his prayer: *Help*. Secret ally, secret friend, her eyes went wide, heart, chin, *yes*.

✦

John knew he needed to pull himself together. He hadn't eaten much solid food (had he eaten any?), and the tea was making his thoughts go too fast. He needed to breathe to a deeper depth and slower.

He cleared his desk to the letter table. There, wedged in the blotter, was the bill from his tailor he'd sworn he didn't have. There wasn't time to get Mrs. Firth in with a cloth, so he used his handkerchief on the desk and then arranged the chairs. The window he pulled closed, wondering where the piece of twine that held it had got to.

He was mentally reciting a jeremiad against Burton, and if pushed to it later, he would stop proceedings in their track, dispatch the boy to the corridor, and speak unbridled. Yes, in a general sense history could repeat itself, but this wasn't history. If Burton raged, John would not care. If Jamie raged, damn him. John would speak the truth. But he had to stop rehearsing or he'd sound like some trade-union firebrand.

He checked the glasses on the mantel for dust. Would it be too much to pour out their drinks ahead of time? He decided that it would. The soda was charged, the coasters in their place.

It was impossible not to think of the outcome. The penalty was Jamie's to dispense, John's to negotiate. Jamie flogged less than average. Still, a caning from the Headmaster was always a salutary affair, even if the JCR hit harder, which John supposed they did. The previous Headmaster, S-K, had occasionally caned boys before the whole school, but it was a risky tactic. Even John could see (though he despised the whole thing) that unless you could visibly discompose the culprits, you'd turn them into heroes. Wisely, Jamie had never attempted it. Burton was known periodically to cane his own boys before the House, but as for Riding, his fate was oddly straightforward: expulsion, rustication, or six from the Headmaster's arm.

There were canes in every Housemaster's study, and John's predecessor had left three. If he'd become Housemaster under the old Head, he would have taken the things immediately to S-K and refused, but under Jamie—why bother with gestures?—he'd put them away in the back of the cupboard. Now, with Jamie whimsically deciding to conduct the interview in John's study while also leaving it until the last possible moment before departing for his conference, why not be blunt? Six was the most favorable outcome for Riding, and Jamie could use what was in the cupboard. No, Burton would not have to do it in Jamie's stead. No, they wouldn't have to send for one. The object on the hook by the filing cabinets would serve perfectly well. It was possible John had once tried it—on cushions only—in the interests of research: Had his predecessor used poor tools? Too heavy or too rigid, apt to injure or break? Or too whippy, apt to go every place except where you aimed it? No. Length average, weight average, give average, it did just what he told it—at least to judge by the lines on the cushions. If it came to it, they wouldn't need palaver. A matter of one minute, and Jamie could catch his train.

There was nothing else in the room to prepare. He took the key from his desk and went to fetch Riding.

✦

Cordelia had climbed out her window and now stood below his. His hair was combed, his clothes were neat, the light in the room made his eyes look bruised. He bit his lip, as he had bitten it when he pretended to interview her. He, more than any cloud bank, was bringing new weather.

—Miss Líoht, he said, *please.*

The sick feeling he'd given her this morning, butter turned bitter, seemed only a mistake. She asked what he needed. He showed her a slip of airmail paper.

—What are the pigeonholes?

✦

Jamie and Burton were in the corridor when John emerged.

—Ah, good, Burton said, there you are.

He shouldered past John into the study, and Jamie followed. The Headmaster took a seat at John's desk, and Burton installed himself in the chair John had planned for himself.

—I was just fetching Riding.

—Let him wait, Jamie said.

✦

Fourth hole from the left, top row. Boys clomped like barbarians down the stairs. She hung back until they finished rifling the mailboxes, and then she stood on the bottom shelf to reach. Wood, dust, an envelope sealed without writing or stamp. She held it up to the light. There wasn't even a letter inside.

✦

—We've been through all this, John said.

—Go through it again. Beginning with Mainwaring.

✦

Opening a letter with shaking hands was harder than he imagined, and then it turned out to be empty.

—Is it a joke? the girl asked.

But there, she pointed, even there, inside the flap.

Box is safe. Will return when cost is clear. No one knows. T.

—They want a ransom? she said.

Safe.

—What box?

No one knows.

—What do they mean, *cost is clear?*

—Miss Líoht, he said, about the other chap—

—Or do they mean *coast?*

—You said he was—

—In the sanitarium. Uncle John's just been to see him.

Trevor still in Tower, no way to put notes in trousers or pigeon-holes.

—Then who the . . . bally heck is T?

✦

Twenty past seven, twentieth March, nineteen thirty-one year of our Lord, his study now crown court, judge at desk, king's council in chair, John as defense exiled to the land of French windows. In dock, the boy who wouldn't speak. Jamie let him stand there as he pretended to examine a file. Evidence: one cracked skull, two empty beds, three years good conduct, four years passed since the Great Clear-Out.

—We haven't much time, Jamie said, and I intend to get to the bottom of this.

✦

The Head folded his hands and turned needle-eyes upon him:

—What were you doing out of bed last night?

Standing behind the desk, Mr. Grieves nodded at him.

—Walking, sir.

—Walking?

—Yes, sir.

And they were. First rule of lying, hew close to the truth.

Burton thunked his glass on the desk:

—This won't do, Riding. It won't do at all. Just where were you walking that you found yourselves barely back in bed at six o'clock this morning, filthy dirty, Mainwaring with a concussion of the skull?

Careful. *Careful.* Second rule, remember everything.

—In the quad.

—Are you sure? asked the Head.

—Yes, sir.

Pictured in his mind. Should have started picturing before, but better late than—

—You're aware, the Head continued, that it's forbidden to leave your bed after lights-out, except in an emergency?

—Yes, sir.

—So?

—Mainwaring couldn't sleep, sir.

Quad, cloisters, dogged insomnia.

—I advise you to speak plainly, the Flea snapped. We are not, as you suppose, buffoons in the dark. If you fail to be frank, we shall draw our own conclusions.

—But he couldn't!

Mr. Grieves raised a hand:

—No one doubts you. But it would help, Riding, if this weren't so much like pulling teeth.

Eyes like the classroom, when he knew you could explain and wanted you to try.

—He couldn't sleep . . . Mainwaring, that is . . . he *hadn't* slept. Not in nights and nights. And you know what they say.

—I'm afraid we don't.

—At least my father used to say, with patients who couldn't sleep . . .

Mr. Grieves urging, not doubting.

—Sleepless for five, hard to survive.

And he was a genius. It even rhymed.

—Oh, yes? said the Head.

—Mainwaring knew he had to walk it off, and he asked me to come with him, because it's dangerous to walk insomnia off alone. You could fall asleep on your feet and knock yourself unconscious.

—And is that what he did?

—Sir?

—Fall asleep on his feet and knock himself—

—Oh, no, sir! He slipped climbing the drainpipe.

—You were climbing a *drainpipe*?

—Fascinating, said the Flea.

✦

Burton went to the mantel and poured himself another drink as Jamie led Riding back through his testimony, which was preposterous enough

87

to be true. Unvarying, irritating, unreasonable, it had the ring of adolescent stupidity. Riding described the quadrangle, the cloisters, the moonlight, Mainwaring's manic exhaustion, the game they played with quotations, *Glamis hath murdered sleep*—

—And what has been the cause of this insomnia? Jamie interrupted.

Mainwaring hadn't given a reason, and Riding hadn't a clue. Apparently Mainwaring was prone to it.

—Has there been anything irregular about the past few days?

—No, sir.

—Quite sure about that?

Jamie had always been ruthless, and now, before John could intervene, he went on the attack. Nothing had occurred, had it? Except a foray out-of-bounds to McKay's barn? Riding tried to explain, but Jamie peppered him with questions and sarcasm. Assaulted by mistrust, Riding grew flustered. He was a boy too inept to connive, and too innocent, John saw, to defend himself against doubt.

—But other than that, Jamie concluded, nothing out of the ordinary?

Riding's face had turned red. He was trying to pull himself together.

—*No*, sir.

—And yet, Burton interjected, he had to be disciplined in Prep last night.

—Is it ordinary for you to disrupt Prep in such a manner?

—All I did was ask how to spell *responsibility*!

—*What* happened? John broke in.

Riding scowled at the floor.

—He had to be caned, Jamie said. He didn't tell you?

✦

To have it said baldly about him, as if urgent: *he had to be anesthetized, had to be restrained, had to be locked up for his own protection.* There was a feeling like water and like lava. Mr. Grieves retreated behind the desk and fiddled with a letter opener. The other two wanted him dead. They thought the worst, worse than he'd ever done. But bully though they might, he didn't have to crumble. They could bait him all night long and he wouldn't surrender. If they intended to dispose him, he wouldn't help. They'd have to do it unjustly.

—One wonders what else he hasn't told you, the Flea droned. About McKay's barn, for instance, and how the cries for help—

—Can we keep to the subject, please? the Head urged. We've been through this barn business. I shall be meeting with McKay the day I return.

The Flea looked sour. If they were going to turn against each other, perhaps it would even be worth it. Trevor, when he told him, would—

—I must say, Riding, this is not what I was led to expect.

The Head touched the dossier before him.

—You've been first in your form the last three years. Your record is exemplary.

—Thank you, sir.

—But don't imagine that I believe one word of your story. You're a transparent liar, and it's abundantly clear that the truth lies elsewhere.

✦

John's heart slipped. He put down the letter opener before he stabbed himself.

—It can't be that bad, Burton was saying. We've all done things we regret.

Riding looked defiant. Burton plied the technique. John felt the breathless panic of envy.

—Mistakes are a part of growing up, Burton said. Mistakes can be corrected. But only if we're brave enough to face them.

The boy nearly bared his teeth. John had caught boys lying. He knew the expression. Was it possible that nothing this boy had said was true?

—You walked, Burton was saying, around the quadrangle? Fine. The cloisters? Where else? The changing rooms, perhaps? You smoked, perhaps. It was late. You weren't yourself. You did things you regret.

—Really! John cried.

Jamie seized his arm to silence him. He had given Jamie his word. He'd believed what this one said. Had he been so blinded by pique towards Burton that he'd missed what was obviously true? The simplest explanation was usually correct, even if it monotonously cribbed from the past. People weren't original. All sins, in the end, banal.

✦

The girl had told him what Mr. Grieves had said of him: *If only he would trust me. If only he could see he isn't alone.* If Mr. Grieves would turn to

89

him and show his face, he'd know where he stood. If the face hated: battle lost, forever and always. But if there was a chance, a sliver, that he was mistaken, that Mr. Grieves could ever be rashly on his side . . .

—Thomas.

Mr. Grieves stepped away from the Head, his voice like the arm that pulled him from the window seat when he'd been hiding: *Come on, you, that's enough of that.*

—The cab's here, Mrs. Firth announced at the door.

—It seems you'll have to leave undone more than your meeting with Farmer McKay, Burton said.

—I *really* do implore you, the Head said to Burton, as a personal favor—

—Think before you speak, Mr. Grieves said like a code he should know.

The Head pushed back his chair:

—Have you nothing to say to Mr. Burton-Lee?

The Head looked at him like filth, like a beast who did things without names, things to make a mother sick.

—*Qui tacet consentit*, the Flea said.

—Tell the truth, Thomas!

—Enough, said the Head. Riding, go and wait in the—

—We were looking for something!

—What? said the Head.

Mr. Grieves looking, urging, knowing?

—A box, he said. A box.

✦

There was a way his heart worked when he bowled hard and forced it to pump, except now it strained without his leave.

—Let me get this straight.

Burton's voice distant from the rush in his ears. Like that dream of the school on fire, when he woke himself up hurling out of bed and was fumbling with the doorknob before he realized it wasn't true.

—Your walk last night was to McKay's barn?

The liar, having ringed them in confusion, now took his blade and slaughtered them with the truth.

—To fetch a box full of stories?

Made-up stories, invented, not true. Left there years ago. The barn

90

their Keep. They'd been going there for three years. Reading, talking, smoking. Of course, that's what Pearce had smelled, but only because they'd just finished. Nothing was on fire. They always took care.

John had fought for this boy from the day that woman left him in the study. He'd given him Moss and then Morgan. He took time over his compositions. What if the boy never meant anything he'd written?

The box that night was nowhere to be found. Riding didn't have it. They could search him and his realm. It had been there on the afternoon, but last night the barn was empty.

—And Mainwaring?

—He did fall, but it was an accident jumping out of the loft.

—Mainwaring jumped from the loft of the barn?

Cold and sharp, sour in his throat like that other time, with Wilberforce and Spaulding, that time he couldn't bear to recall but would never be able to forget.

—He'd done it before and never been hurt.

History was like that. People feasted over fields of the dead, never knowing or suspecting the ruin humans suffered.

—We weren't drinking or . . . or anything else. We only went for the box. I promise.

Not drunkenness, not beastliness. Just the godforsaken barn. How could a shack bring so much devastation?

—It's my father's. It's all I've got.

The voice trailed off. Was this, then, the heart? All this for a father's—

—I'll never . . . I'm sorry.

The adamant liar, turned penitent, turned supplicant, spoke now in a flood, tightening the vise on their teeth.

—I could do a double holiday task.

He would learn whatever they told him to learn. Learn it by heart. Anything, he'd do it if they please would not dispose him.

—I didn't mean to cause trouble.

Didn't mean to be bad. Wasn't that sort of person.

An urgent knock sent John's heart working faster.

—Fardley says you must leave if you want any chance for the train, Mrs. Firth called.

—Yes, I know, Jamie snapped.

Burton stood and leaned over the desk:

—I can ring Overall. I'll go and see McKay, and then I'll let Overall know we're—

—Don't do anything.

Jamie stepped away from Burton, brushing John into the curtains.

—But Overall will expect—

—I shall answer, Jamie said, for this and everything.

✦

As the Head rounded the desk, Gray braced himself for a blow.

—Riding.

The man came to stand beside him, voice like honey.

—You have been sorely dishonest.

Words said to beasts, but here softly, so near he could smell his aftershave.

—You have been shamefully self-willed. And you've been abominably . . . naive.

Sunburn, heartburn.

—I hope you're ashamed of yourself.

Nowhere to hide.

—Consider yourself on notice. If I should ever have to speak to you like this again . . .

On notice. Not death, but life. Axe put aside, prison door flung—

—Meantime, you are on tic for the remainder of term.

His throat whispered thanks. The Head touched his shoulder, as Morgan did when—

—Robert, would you kindly see to Mainwaring as we discussed?

—Certainly, said Burton-Lee.

—And give my apologies to the Colonel.

Hand on shoulder still, pressing as though he were his.

—And, John, since you've taken such a personal interest, you can see to the rest.

The stain on the carpet looked like a snail.

—Will you do me the honor of twelve of the best?

Mr. Grieves made a noise.

—A dozen of the finest, tonight please.

—Headmaster, if you wish—

—Thank you, Robert, but Grieves has this in hand. Please tell the cab I'm on my way.

Burton-Lee looked at them, gave a nod, left. The Head stepped away, disowning him.

—If only you'd warned me, John.

Twelve of the best?

—Why didn't you tell me it was that *wretched* barn?

Not the same kind of best that came in sixes?

—I'd no idea.

He meant something else. Mr. Grieves had never, would never.

—I think I see, said the Head. I think I finally see.

✦

They were coming for him, the whole host he'd escaped. No Greek out-ran his fate, and no man avoided judgment. It might wait years, through wars, deaths, across miles or even seas, but eventually, one hour, it would find you.

—You're on quicksand, John.

Too far from shore, and the whole horde, everything renounced, every-thing sidestepped and parried since Jamie came, everything he wasn't, everything he wouldn't, everything he tried with every moment to undo, all arrived. His punishment, now.

—We'll speak after Easter, Jamie said. This, your word, things req-uisite and necessary.

Those eyes saw and remembered: John knew very well how to do what he'd been ordered.

The door closed on Jamie, leaving him alone with the one who lied. Someone spoke, maybe it was he. The liar moved for the first time, looked at him with a stupid half grin, as if he'd known something secret all along.

He wasn't a person luck followed. If things could go wrong, they al-ways did with him. There in the cupboard, on the hook where he'd left it, there it waited, a patience colder than Hell. It had waited this long, all these years, but no longer. Fingers knew what they gripped.

Quick, certain, hard. Sixty seconds to the other side. But then, once there, he could never go back. Never again be this man, the man he'd labored to become. It would be done, but so would he.

—What are you waiting for? You know the drill.

He was done with this one. Damn Jamie, and damn him. Who re-fused? Who lied? Who started fire and fed it as it grew? He would never forgive him. If this one had something to say, he could say it to the cush-ions. After everything he'd lost, everything that had been taken, to have to give up this, and for such a one as that.

It was too drastic to happen, even though he was standing there, holding it, having spoken to him as if they both knew what they were doing.

—Feet there, stay down.

It was a charade for ears outside the door. The Head had said it to placate Burton-Lee. No one got more than six, and never from Mr. Grieves. The Head knew. Had to.

Mr. Grieves hadn't said where to put his jacket, so he set it on the desk with his spectacles. He could play his part for form's sake. The settee where they'd sat that morning scratched his face, dust like a library centuries old. He could say he was sorry. He could explain. He hadn't meant to lie to Mr. Grieves, who never had, never would, even Morgan said—

Light. Breath. Not charade, not the first. All right, he deserved that, but—light, light, hard as he'd ever—harder. All his will to keep from moving. Breathe in then out—fast, faster even than—not enough time to—this, this—

A sound beyond his command, but sound only, not tears, never further. Something professional had intervened. He was cool, eyes dead, self snatched away before this thing could maim. Six, now seven, eight, who cared? They could trick him and trap him, but they had no idea what he could do and what he was doing—not one drop of this would ever touch him. He'd never been calmer. It was like that, after murder.

✦

After nine, the boy flinched and started to choke. Or so he tried to make it seem, gasping and hacking, on what? Did he actually believe he could rook him into—

—You can stop that right now. I wasn't born yesterday.

✦

Breath regained from spit like spite to drown him. Back down for the last. Could not care any less what this man thought of him. Almost disappointment when told to get up. Espionage? Easy. Torture? Nothing. Cupboard door slammed so hard he felt it in his feet. Somehow the handshake was being omitted. The man stood, back to him still, hands on the mantel as if he could faint.

—Go to bed.

 She was working up the nerve to knock. Dr. Sebastian and the other man had left. That meant she could go in. There were sounds, but she didn't think she could say what they were. Coughing. Was he shouting down the telephone? On the count of three . . . the count of ten . . . when the hand on the clock reached the blue square . . . But the door was opening and he was there, her yes-no-sorry boy, the heat of him, face red and wet, handkerchief in one fist, spectacles in the other. He looked at her like an enemy, and the electrics went wrong. There across the room, his back to them both, Uncle John stood at the grate, a likeness of her father, decanter in one hand, glass in the other, the way it always smelled when things turned real.

✦

She stood in the doorway, weeping. The other gone.

—Darling, what's the matter?

He went and drew her into the room. Wherever he put her, tears streamed down her face. Should he offer her something against the shock?

—Now, now, it isn't too late to ring the hospital. We'll do it straight-away. Sit here.

She wouldn't sit. She had a splinter, she said. He asked to see it, held her hand under the lamp. It was deep in her palm, and she'd dug until it bled. Kardleigh would have to get it out.

He put his arms around her as he always did, but she stood ramrod, hand held out before her alien and rigid. Wouldn't she sit down? Here in his chair. They'd ring this moment if she'd dry her eyes. He'd speak to whoever answered. He'd insist they fetch her mother even if she'd gone to sleep. And then, once they spoke to her, and she really must dry her eyes, once they'd seen everything was fine as wine, then they'd see about the splinter.

She jerked away as he bent to kiss the top of her head. She didn't want to ring now. Better, she said, to ring in the morning.

If that's what she wanted, of course they could ring in the waking up, but about the splinter—

Mrs. Firth said she'd help. She wanted Mrs. Firth. He wasn't to touch it.

She was overtired. It was no surprise. She'd had a long journey and a long drink of worry. Tomorrow in the daytime he'd make her feel at home.

She wanted to go to bed. She wanted to go. She turned and rushed from him, wrenching the door open despite the splinter. The back of his mouth throbbed. The brandy was better than he'd realized. Mrs. Firth got it in. She knew things, things to get, and got them. It was touching the back of his mouth and doing something inside the flesh of him and to the bell in his head or the hall. The shaking all over was starting to slow. Another dose—there was the piece of twine! Caught in the latch of the windows. He tore it off and swung them open and stepped onto the bricks and then the grass, where the water rushed in his shoes as he dashed across the field. Under the goalposts, a knife in his side, but he didn't want to bring everything up because it was good and if he brought it up he'd need more and Mrs. Firth would know he needed things sooner than he should. A bell was ringing into his head, to kneel, to sink, ice-mud-trench, if only the shells would fall.

✦

Under no circumstances would she let that person speak to her mother. Forget her own feelings. She was used to words said strangely, to breath you could set alight, to talking as if she were six. She knew what to do with people possessed of spirits.

Mrs. Firth she found bustling down the stairs. She couldn't help just now, telephone or splinter. She should go to the Tower. Like a prisoner, self-arresting? She should like any boy go across the quadrangle and in those doors, they looked closed but weren't, and climb the staircase all the way to the top. Dr. Kardleigh could help her. He'd see to the splinter. He had a telephone.

Boys didn't wear ankle socks or a hem that ended at the knees. They crossed gravel like men, looking as though they used their fists every day. Anyone who used his fists at her school was sent home. Ditto fingernails or even cruel words. The staircase was stone and dark, smooth from prisoners, princes at the top?

The doctor looked aghast when she came into his room, but when she explained, he had her sit beside the lamp. Alcohol stung, and he told her to look away. He asked about her mother and the hospital where she was. It smarted and throbbed and ached deep inside, but he wrapped it in a bandage and told her to keep it dry. Then he jangled the telephone and made them ring the hospital, where he knew someone, he thought. He made them fetch her mother even though it was after hours, and while they went to look, he made her tell him the story of her parents, her mother a child of Saffron Walden, the town that lived on crocuses, a town of Friends, that meant Quakers, she met him at Cambridge, he'd come to speak on the Irish Question, and she'd heard him and loved him and he'd loved her. There had been a price when he'd asked her father for her hand, but he had not blinked. He'd taken her to the maze, there was one in the center of the village green, no not hedges, just grass paths, of course you could cheat but who would?, he took her there and got down on his knee. *If I must give up Rome to have you, Margaret Drayton, then so be it, let me quake.*

—Darling?

Her feeling-ill voice, but brighter than she'd left it. Oh, better, much better, everyone so kind, skies cleared just this afternoon and she knew what a difference that could make. Eating? Doctors pleased, right as rain soon. She got her to laugh by describing St. Stephen's food and the dull things they said at the masters' table. Uncle John, oh, yes, excellent, boys kept him running like a rabbit, oh, yes, like one caught with clover in its mouth, springing here, spronging there, yes, boing!, she hadn't gone in the chapel but it looked ever so stern, of course Paris was just what he needed before he turned Puritan hare. They'd drink French coffee and eat pastries but she wouldn't eat frog legs no matter what they said, oh, yes, it would be beautiful and gay, she would ring again tomorrow, all right the day after, but she must work hard at her resting so she'd be ready when they came next week. Why, that man had been the school physician, name of Dr. Kardleigh, why, yes, he was handsome, nearly as tall as Uncle John and dark as well, with an army moustache, was it an army moustache? He said it was to cover the scar on his lip, yes, he was here, right beside her, of course—

He was so pleased to hear she'd improved, her daughter was delightful, no, she hadn't bothered the boys, so far as he was aware!, certainly he'd keep an eye, he advised her to rest, to put all worries from her mind, wrap her troubles in dreams, dream her troubles away, hey . . . He put down the telephone laughing.

—Your mother is charming.

—Yes.

—And you were brave about that splinter.

—Not really.

 The bell fag was clanging down the corridor, but still Riding hadn't stirred. It was to him, Timothy Halton, to ensure everyone was out of bed, but Riding had ignored him the first time and was ignoring him now. The last thing he needed was a docket for failing to do what he was trying to do.

—Riding, he said, second bell.

There were still the basins to do. He resorted to shaking. Riding growled. The shoulder felt hot. If someone was ill, you had to fetch a prefect. He fetched Pearce.

—Riding, Pearce barked, get up.

Riding squinted. Pearce whipped back the covers.

—What on earth . . . ?

Halton nearly gasped. Riding had gone to bed in pajama top and school trousers, as if he'd fallen asleep half-changed. But Pearce, rather than jawing, touched his forehead. Riding flinched away.

—Halton, Pearce said, wait here and take Riding to the Tower.

Then he spun off to harangue someone else without saying who would do the basins if Halton waited.

No one knew what happened to Riding. He'd been in bed when they came up last night, and when they'd tried to speak with him, he'd cursed a blue streak. This morning he moved like an old man. He was sore, that much was obvious, but had he been injured, too, as Mainwaring had? Halton had heard the crash outside the barn when he dashed in to get what he got, but he hadn't seen what happened after.

He was still tired even after a full night's sleep. Detecting took it out of you. No one ever told him that fagging for a tyrant would sharpen his instincts, but he'd started winning at last. Pearce and Mac made sure he knew where every one of their wretched things belonged: ink pots that shelf, not this; this end, not that; letter paper under envelopes not on top or beside; cricket bat this angle, photo bracket Hobbs at Lords not one speck of dust; these and a thousand other painful offenses had etched a memory of their little pit of hell, and nowhere in that picture were football boots. Football boots went beneath bench in changer, not wrapped in muffler under envelopes, left drawer.

They hadn't been smoking at McKay's barn—though they'd smoked earlier, which Pearce might have discovered if he'd made them empty their pockets—but Halton had admitted, when pressed by the JCR, that the place had smelled of cigarettes. Next day, his own ledger cleared by the cane, he could afford to torment Pearce: What if the smell had been Farmer McKay's pipe? What if someone else had been at the barn before them?

The school had been gated. A search was planned. Football boots did not belong in desk drawers. His bed was near the dormitory door. When Pearce went, he followed.

There was a window below the Tower that got them past the gates. On that moonlit night, not a soul awake besides the sheep, Pearce, bless him, took to the road. You'd never cut across Abbot's Common during the day, Malcolm said, unless you wanted five sightings by local busybodies forwarded to the Head by teatime, but in the middle of the night, only someone entirely lacking imagination would slog the longer way of the road. Unless Pearce was headed elsewhere—tryst? contraband?—which Halton briefly hoped he was. When they arrived at the barn, he'd felt hot disappointment, and a racing fear that Pearce had come to take the thing he himself had glimpsed. But Pearce, after some rustling, had sat inside doing nothing. The barn's shadow had drifted across the track, and eventually, hours later, Pearce departed. Halton had dashed inside, admonishing himself against hope, but there, when he trained his torch on the place—how long had it been since luck was on his side?—not only was there something, but the thing he thought he'd seen: a nameplate, *T. Riding*, tarnished but legible. Nameplates did not float in midair or affix themselves to a rotting beam; they marked, and this one gilded the latch of a varnished box.

Pearce had gone by the road, so he took to the Common. A wooden box could not simply be tucked under arm for cross-country trots, but with luck on his side, he'd got it and himself through the hedge and back in the window; then he'd stashed it under the towels in the changer and regained his bed before Pearce came crashing back to the dorm.

The drawback of luck, real luck, was that you couldn't tell anyone. That morning Malcolm was as shirty with him as ever, Fletcher treated him as a moron, and White remarked that he looked wearish and that he mustn't overdo it on the wanking front. *Moderation in all things, Infant.* Everyone had found this the peak of wit.

Riding wasn't at breakfast, and neither was Mainwaring. Someone said Grieves had hauled them out of their dorm in a fury. Someone else said they'd been sick in the night. He cut French to take care of the box. There was a place by the choir room, an alcove no one knew. As the Third drilled verbs, he, Timothy Halton, surveyed his prize.

He hated reading and did it as little as possible, but once he'd glimpsed the treasure, he couldn't stop. It gave him a headache and made him hungry. He read the letters to envy, for a father like that, and like Wilberforce. If any letter to him had ever said a hair of what these said in manes, and to Riding, that ill-tempered, stuck-up swot, sidekick to the horrible Mainwaring, one who toyed publicly with Pearce and got away with it—it defied fairness. But luck, gorgeous luck, had turned her face to him. She, with her lily-of-the-valley scent, showed him the true treasure. Grieves had told them of pharaohs' tombs, filled with cheap display to throw robbers off the hoard. This wasn't a hoard, but once he'd pried up the bottom and read what was beneath, he saw with panicked excitement why the whole thing had been stashed in a broken barn.

He intended blackmail, but real luck took such things off the table. When the bell rang the end of French, he hid the box where no one would find it. He didn't have words for what it did to him. He was stiff and rattled, and a tantalizing dread breathed down his collar.

He put a note in Riding's pigeonhole, and then later, Riding and Mainwaring still missing, he realized more was needed. Espionage was harder than detecting. He detected Riding's uniform hanging in the changer. It was easy to stay behind cleaning basins, but putting the second note in the trouser pocket felt more indecent than anything he'd done. Real luck brought power all at once; if you wanted her to stay, you had to use her gift wisely, bold but cool, ruthless and impartial.

✦

It had been a late night and an early morning. Kardleigh was not on form. Stanford in G needed two of the three broken stops, and although he'd found a way around it, yesterday a different stop failed. The so-called organ was being held together with string and sticking plaster. He'd been warning the Headmaster for years, but it would probably take a complete collapse before the Board would agree to professional repairs. At least Halton would be ready with the solo, provided Kardleigh could rehearse him this afternoon. The boy knew the piece, but he needed to stop pushing and let the note release like the expression of joy it was meant to be.

Mainwaring was finally packed off with his uncle and aunt— cousins?—so the commotion could end, too. Burton-Lee, for unexplained reasons, had taken charge of arrangements. There had been a telephone call to Mainwaring's mother, who sounded resentful and helpless, and then at some point a string of relations had telephoned, and one way or another, a man and a woman had roared up at dawn in their Oxford Six, disturbing God's good earth with their Klaxon, until Fardley emerged and opened the gates to them. Mainwaring was still unsteady, but he went with them willingly enough. When Kardleigh offered to telephone the family physician, the couple had looked as though he'd said something déclassé.

Burton had also briefed him on Riding's fate: remaining and dealt with. The explanation had seemed complete at the time, but once Mainwaring had left, Kardleigh wondered what was meant by it. Why had Burton taken it under authority when both boys were in Grieves's House? And why, after pestering him all day about Mainwaring, had Grieves gone A.W.O.L., to the point of saddling Kardleigh with his goddaughter?

Doubtless in time all would be revealed. But now, before he'd even made himself a cup of tea to take the edge off the night and the couple in the Oxford Six, now young Halton was careening into the exam room, having evidently taken the stairs three at a time.

—If you've bad news, Timothy, I don't want to hear it.

The boy gulped breath and struggled with Kardleigh's tone.

—If you've come to tell me you've lost your voice, you've got a lot of explaining to do.

The boy finally cracked a grin.

—Not me, sir, Riding.

—Oh?

—Can't say a word. Pearce told me to bring him, but there's still the basins to do, sir, and—

—Off you go, then. I'll see you at one. At the organ, I think, not the choir room.

Riding was taking his time on the stairs. If he intended to malinger after landing himself in hot water, he could think again, but the sight of him put lie to the idea. He had a fever, and efforts to speak yielded only whispers. Throat red but not spotted. Kardleigh examined him for concussion: negative. Attempts to be jocular about the medicines of justice were met with red silence. It was too early in the morning for this. He gave the boy aspirin and told him to lie down in the dayroom. Anxiety crossed his face, and he craned to see the ward.

—You've missed Mainwaring, I'm afraid.

—What happened? the boy whispered.

—Invalided back to Blighty. Don't look so stricken. You did fine with the stretcher bearing, Lieutenant.

Not a glimmer. He handed the boy a nightshirt, but the look of anxiety only sharpened. The whole affair was irregular.

✦

Uncle John missed breakfast again, but one of the masters, with the thick-bottle spectacles, told her it wasn't unusual. *Lives on air and the Hundred Years' War, does our Grievous.* She didn't know what the man meant by it, but she felt it was probably true.

After breakfast, Mrs. Firth let her read the paper in her sitting room. Her mother disapproved of newspapers, but here they took *The Times, The Daily Telegraph*, and even the *Daily Mail*. Mrs. F brought her all three from the staff room, yesterday's date, along with a fresh copy of *The Times*. Mr. Grieves would want it, she said, and there wasn't time to iron it again, so she was to take care to fold it up when she was finished.

The Times teemed with debates about widows and orphans, which she supposed ought to stir her sympathies. It claimed that the first test of a long-distance telephone had occurred between Japan and the United States, but who in America even spoke Japanese? There was a photograph of a new railway station in Milan and a story about the Fascist Clock, a contraption that marked not only hour, minute, and second, but also phases of the moon and day of the week and month. The word *fascist* came from the word for *face*, she deduced, for when the clock struck, pictures of Signor Mussolini and the King appeared. She could speak French well enough to navigate Paris, she thought, and everyone said that Italian was nearly the same. Perhaps in the summer they could go to Rome!

She'd had to take the bandage off her hand to wash in the morning. There wasn't much to see, but there was a feeling inside her palm, an ache and a buzz, memory of the wood that had lodged there. It was her writing hand, the wound personal and wrong.

Perhaps Uncle John had fallen ill last night. Some people took spirits as medicine. It might explain everything.

The NUT at Yarmouth did not concern walnuts but rather lady teachers and some unsightly disputes over pensions and the leaving age. She was beginning to see why her mother avoided the papers, but then at the end of another boring column, this on the Thirty-ninth Annual Conference of the Incorporated Association of Head Masters, Dr. Sebastian's name leapt from the page, as thrilling as the time Miss Pankhurst came to her school. *J.A.S. Sebastian, Head Master of St. Stephen's Academy, will be speaking at Charterhouse this evening about the Public School Hymn Book.* Their own Dr. Sebastian, who had touched her shoulder that way, black and white in the columns of *The Times*!

She folded the paper to put that part on top. Mrs. F had told her to leave it on Uncle John's desk, and the door needed shoving to open. The room smelled carmine as it did before. Unlike in their own sitting room, the mantel had been tidied, glasses cleaned and returned to their spots. She heard a door in the corridor close. The walls were not thick. Last night the other men had already gone, which left Uncle John alone with that boy, and though she'd never heard such sounds before, they did seem . . . But her newspaper swain! Her prisoner in the tower! He was not at breakfast either. When Mrs. F came to stir the grate, she asked her if those boys had been sacked. Mrs. F looked affronted, which meant that they weren't, and then she said to mind her knitting, which meant no one could speak of it.

✦

There was a wireless in the dayroom and Kardleigh left it playing. Some kind of music, slow and old, soft and lost, like the marshes at night. *Are you going to die?—We all die someday.*

Say it isn't true. Say all this will last and be always and ever and the ground that doesn't move. Say it won't be wasted. Say dying is for other

103

people. Say we aren't alone. Even in the marsh, fireflies! Say of the sweet and the sad and the still-remembered, they will one day come back, ocean crossed, curtain torn bottom to top, and all that looked broken will stand and rise and be there to touch.

Later, even after that sword had cut his father away, even then he didn't seem lost forever. He would wait in the window seat, curled like this, to hide and be found by whomever wishes could call. Footsteps would come, scuff to a stop, lights ping, rush of air, and Morgan would be there, window seat in one hand, cushion in another. If he didn't move, he'd pull him out, and whatever it had been that had driven him there, Morgan would find it out, and when he was finished, things would be warm and brave and put back together.

Say it isn't true. Say it only seems that way . . .

Last night, ambush, just when he thought he'd escaped. More than he'd expected, more than anyone got, unsparing . . . but unjust? He had gone to the barn, not once but habit. He had lied as if virtue. And he'd written—only words, but words could take on life—written, kept, festered, by his own grievous fault. He'd imagined he could turn those men to his will. *Dishonest, self-willed, naive.* It would need something daunting to restore him. This had been daunting, but nothing was restored.

Perhaps if it hadn't been an ambush, he would have acted better. One minute, he was lying and getting away with it, and then Dr. Sebastian was denouncing him as a liar and other things, things people only whispered, and suddenly he was on the verge of dismissal for those things, so he started telling the truth, and then things were falling around him, he wasn't being disposed, he was surging with gratitude and relief, and before he was ready to think of the restoring, the Head was leaving and the cane had come out and that man, like some backwards dream, was speaking as he'd never done, and he was in the middle of something new, a ruthless, bitter disdain, and all the ways he knew to cope were failing until they stole him away and locked him underground, in the dungeon below the dungeon, and the man in the room was dead in his heart.

Except, on the way out she'd seen him. She'd blocked his path with the horror good people felt for wicked things. She saw not a person to joke with, to smile at or climb through windows for, but a beast, *dishonest, self-willed, naive.* There had been water on his face—though from choking, not blubbing!—but she would have thought him a coward. A lying, selfish funk.

She was the first good thing to happen, good in a way he couldn't explain, but now she was gone, knowing full well how bad he was. Like that day in the changing room: *Wilberforce is leaving. When? At the weekend.* Two days? *Called up early to bat for the dark blues!* He didn't want to be like the other people Morgan paid attention to. Morgan was the only one who had seen all the wounds and would look, for them and at them. *What are we going to do with you, boyo?* Almost a father, but (he'd blurted it once through tears) better. He'd even begun to believe this was the window after the closed door, but then, before it was time, news came through the changing room, told as if good news and he the last to know. In its way worse than when his mother told him it was over, because at least he'd known that was coming and even secretly wished for it because the gray face and sounds behind the door were too much, and he was scarcely there in the end. But to hear about Morgan, the worst news brought forward, leaving for Oxford almost a whole term early, and then going to Morgan to demand the lies be squashed, only to find out they were true, and that Morgan was happy.

 She didn't know any prayers, not real ones like they said. At her school, there was Meeting every morning, a quarter of an hour when they sat waiting on the Light. Sometimes people stood up and spoke, trembling with the Spirit. When a person had troubles, you Held them in the Light, which meant you imagined them surrounded by rays, like when you opened your eyes after sleeping in the sunshine. Here in their chapel they spoke to God the Almighty and Everlasting. There was no place for silence, no time for waiting.

Her mother's letter arrived Monday morning. It filled two sides and chatted of characters in the hospital, but the handwriting faltered, more like Grandmama Drayton's had been than the script that filled her mother's letters for the starving German children. But writing in the hospital must be slapdash at best. Hospitals weren't peaceful, and they were never silent.

Mrs. Kneesworth had been visiting every day, but now that she'd gone on holiday, there was no one to check or ask or soothe. No one to hear if he had come home, if he'd written, if he was asking for her. No one to open his letters if her mother wouldn't, to coax her into hearing, to tell him where she was.

They called their God the author of peace and lover of concord. Could it be so wrong to speak to him, even if she had to kneel like a slave?

✦

The throat looked normal, the fever faded, but Riding still couldn't speak. Kardleigh didn't think he was shamming exactly, but his sneezes revealed a voice. Patient's demeanor obedient but withdrawn. Liked wireless, declined reading, the last abnormal for a constitutional bookworm.

The boy's friend had gone home, and his Housemaster did not visit. While ordinarily Kardleigh would not expect a Housemaster to slog to the Tower over someone's sore throat, given the melodrama surrounding Riding and Mainwaring and given Grieves's demonstrated concern, Kardleigh kept expecting to hear the man's shuffle on the stairs. But the only visitor was Moss, Grieves's Prefect of Chapel, who stopped by Sunday night. Riding was asleep (or pretending to be), so Moss left the paperback he had brought. There was a bizarre coda in which Moss returned with a handkerchief full of boiled sweets, which he claimed he'd forgotten to leave before, sent by a friend of Riding's, which one, he couldn't recall. When Kardleigh asked Moss point-blank what was going on in his House, Moss flushed down to the collar and declared himself ignorant of any goings-on. The House, like the rest of the school, had seen its gating lifted after tea that evening. The search of McKay's barn had proved unremarkable, or so the four JCRs had been told by Burton-Lee, who'd overseen the expedition that snowy afternoon. Kardleigh confessed it hard to imagine Burton-Lee stomping through snowdrifts, but Moss reported that Fardley had driven all four House-masters to the site and waited while they trekked, alpine fashion (though possibly without ropes and axes), on their errand. In any case, the matter had officially been closed, and the school had turned its attention to hourlies, due to afflict them in three days' time.

The patient showed no interest in the paperback. Whether from illness or perversity, he left the sweets uneaten.

✦

She knelt but didn't know what to say. The chapel was dark except for the colors through the windows. Off in a corner, a candle flickered in a red glass. She wanted to picture her mother surrounded by light, but who could do it in this crypt?

Her yes-no-sorry boy had grown up here, with his round face and his eyes full of play. This cold, smoky wreck of a school, he called home. And Uncle John! She'd always thought of their home as his, his holidays with them as his true life and the leaving an interruption. But in reality he spent more months here than he spent with them and his maiden aunts combined. He had no piles of papers in Saffron Walden, only a few items of clothing and some books. Perhaps most shocking, now that she realized, he had no friends there besides them, whereas here every person knew him. They called him nicknames and spoke of his habits as if he were part of their family. He swept through these corridors snapping and cajoling. He looked at home.

The light she was seeing around her mother turned to rust. She opened her eyes and left the pew. The red candle taunted her from behind the wrought-iron gate, but she faced it down. There was no call for it to pulse like an unsteady heart or to splash its lurid color across the stone column and the painting there of a man. He sat before a background of gold, his face looking forward but his eyes to the side, as if he'd been called by someone just behind her. Her scalp prickled and her eyes prickled. Sometimes people looked to the side when they wanted to tell you something awful.

She didn't run, but she walked quickly away. Outside, icicles dripped from the roof. The air was warmer than it had been in there.

◆

—I treated a man at the end of the war, Kardleigh said apropos of nothing.

He had brought Gray a cooked breakfast, Sunday meal for a Tuesday, and now he was drawing a chair to the bedside and fetching his own teacup.

—He'd been released from a German prison camp at the Armistice, fit enough if hungry, but he wound up in hospital some weeks later after a collapse in Oxford Circus.

Gray cut the white away and lifted the yolk onto a piece of toast. He would eat this slice only and leave the rest. Tea he would limit to one cup.

The man, Kardleigh continued, was known to him. He'd treated him earlier in the war for gas, but this collapse, Kardleigh determined, had been brought on by hard living and a species of shell shock.

—It wasn't noise that set this fellow off, but crowds. The crush of Christmas shopping made him feel he was drowning in gas.

As Gray dipped a sausage into the yolk, Kardleigh told of the man's slow recovery. Restoring the body was straightforward enough, particularly as it was all in one piece. The mind took longer.

—This was Ashurst. After the war, we were being absorbed into Littlemore, and our patients, those who couldn't be discharged, were having their records transferred to the asylum.

The black pudding was salty, the marmalade bitter.

—This man had recovered by all measures. He no longer suffered tremors. He ate well, slept well, even became something of a legend at croquet, but when the time came to leave, he refused. He insisted that he was not cured and called for papers to have himself committed.

—That's mad.

—Quite. Though not in a technical sense. I managed to stall the papers and somehow got the man to agree to an outing. I promised him a picnic by the river, but it was a bank holiday, the weather fine, and all of Oxford turned out with the same idea in mind.

Kardleigh refilled their cups.

—Did he have a fit?

—Not exactly, Kardleigh said. At first I thought we'd had a breakthrough. He ate the sandwiches, drank the lemonade, even picked a handful of flowers for one of the nurses. I was packing up the basket, thinking about the conversation we might have on the walk back, when I heard a commotion behind me. He'd fallen into an argument with a man some years his senior, the volume rose, and the next thing I knew, my patient was pummeling the man on the riverbank.

Kardleigh described the man's wife and children bursting into tears. It had taken two passersby to remove Kardleigh's patient from the scene. Back at the hospital, Kardleigh received a blistering tick-off from his superior officer. He was to provide his patient commitment papers that evening and omit from his report the slightest whiff of unauthorized outings.

—Finished?

The tray was empty. Kardleigh took it away. A slab of snow slid off the roof and landed with a splat in the courtyard. Protest erupted from the birds in the gutter, as though one of their number had been swept to its death. The ward was empty. Gray felt suddenly ashamed.

A faucet ran and stopped, and Kardleigh returned, drying his hands on a tea towel. There was the dreadful feeling of having ruined things through inattention. Kardleigh sat down again, opened a pocket watch, and took hold of his wrist with cold fingers.

—Did you do it? Gray asked.

—Do what?

—Give him papers for the asylum.

—I meant to. I had to obey my CO, of course, but as I was preparing the papers, a kind of obstinacy came over me.

He let go of Gray's wrist.

—I went to the man's room—he had gone to bed—opened the windows, and tore off the blankets. Then, to my surprise as much as his, I sat down on the floor, my head even with his. He was well, I said, in body and in mind. He was not afraid that the world would be like the front, but that life would carry on. After everything he'd seen, everything he'd suffered and done, he now had to face the ultimate obscenity, that the world had not ended.

Kardleigh crossed his legs:

—Life *was* obscene, I told him, and I knew why he wanted nothing to do with it. But I told him he was needed, to stand in its face. If not us, then who?

—Us?

—I told him I wasn't leaving, his room or the floor, until he dressed, packed his case, and took up arms beside me.

—He went back to the army?

—He went to university.

—And then he joined the army?

—He joined the revolution.

—What *revolution*?

—Oh, said Kardleigh lightly, you know the one I mean.

The Remove were at History, bent over books in grudging fealty to hourlies on the morrow. Gray's uniform chafed, but a stubbornness came across him. The hunchback at the front was nothing to him. He opened the door, took his seat, and barricaded himself behind the Deuxième Empire. Revolutions killed people, usually more than they meant to at the start.

When the bell rang lesson's end, the hunchback threw out his grappling hook:

—Riding. Your composition.

He had to go and take it.

—Fine, as usual.

A thank-you rolled up his tongue, but he bit it down and turned to leave.

—Just a minute.

Claw.

—Here is the tic. I'll sign it now. You can see Moss for the rest.

He took the chit, to be signed by school authority six times in the day, a penance designed to entangle you in restriction, to remind you that you were still being punished.

◆

There was absolutely nothing to do there. Newspapers consumed only so much time. Lessons kept Uncle John captive by day and paperwork by night. The snow had melted, but mud remained. She couldn't use her roller skates, and she didn't have boots to muck about the grounds.

She wasn't supposed to wander from the House, but during lessons, who would know? Passages burrowed beneath the school, connecting servants' quarters and giving onto places she'd never be allowed. The smell of the changing rooms defied description, and the sight of their clothing, all the bits in every state, made her stomach beat.

Uncle John's House was not the largest (that was Burton-Lee's), nor the most ornate (Lockett-Egan's), nor even filled with the strangest objects (Henri's). Still, it was home, and its passages and corners smelled of the past, as if every legend had grown up there.

The stone stairs by the chapel led to a paneled corridor. At the far end, she found a music room, and in the interval before tea she heard the choir practicing there. Two of the panels had keyholes in them.

One opened easily to her hairpin, and she spent a heady half hour exploring narrow ladders and planks between pipes of the organ. The other panel required two hairpins but delivered the greater prize: an abandoned balcony overlooking the chapel, airy and silent, piled with broken chairs.

✦

They treated him as one returned from the dead. Not disposed, not sent home raving, had he been half-killed, or what? He confirmed nothing, contradicted nothing, but as he had no note off Games, in the changing room they saw what they wanted. By tea, wild rumors had worn themselves out, and his tale ceased to be notable. Only one splinter remained.

He forced his pen to the sickening note and left it in his pocket after changing for bed. *T: Destroy box and contents. On pain of death, do not read. Exoriare aliquis nostris ex ossibus ultor.* In the morning when he dressed, the thing was gone, murder accomplished.

✦

Wuthering Heights was supposed to be the ultimate love story, but she put it down after they were horrid to the dogs. *White Shadows in the South Seas* proved better and kept her from pondering the boy returned from exile. *There is in the nature of every man, I firmly believe, a longing to see and know the strange places of the world.* She glimpsed him at lunch Wednesday, poking at the horrible meat and making the odd remark to his fellows. *Life imprisons us all in its coil of circumstance, and the dreams of romance that color boyhood are forgotten.* The boys at his table turned to him repeatedly with questions. *But they do not die. They stir at the sight of a white-sailed ship beating out to the wide sea.* He replied with an air of bored authority. *Somewhere over the rim of the world lies romance, and every heart yearns to go and find it.*

✦

He refrained from looking at her since she sat beside the hunchback, but he couldn't avoid thought of her, since she was all anyone talked about. Interloper, goddess, tart. It was indecent, they said, for Grieves to bring such a piece into their midst. She was haughty. She was randy.

She was fresh. She needed to be kissed, or spanked. There was nothing for it but to ravish her.

The afternoon was a half holiday, and he had nowhere to go but his form room. When everyone else dispersed outdoors, he began to track the girl. Having lingered at the masters' table with her godfather, she kissed the hunchback on the cheek and made for the cloisters. There she darted up the staircase by the chapel. Running was strictly banned, but he took the stairs two at a time. At the top, an empty corridor mocked him. He felt along one side, and suddenly the panel gave way, hinging in, spilling light and an audible gasp:

—You!

Revolutions outran their instigators.

—Do you go around *everywhere* giving people heart attacks?

—Sorry!

—Sit down before someone sees you.

There was no one to see him, but he dropped to the floor.

—Lemon?

She thrust a packet towards him. Would accepting her sweets mean accepting her conquest, she who had made a keep in corners of his country no one knew existed?

—If you don't want one, simply say no thank you.

She had an evil eye and used it. He put a lemon drop on his tongue.

✦

He fit there, and he didn't mind the dust. He looked at her as though they were friends, or had once been. With friends you didn't always have to explain. He sucked on the sweet and eyed her newspaper. She peeled off the Special Section and passed him the rest.

✦

Electricity Schemes, the Miners' Welfare Fund, he scanned the words but didn't absorb them. She lay on her stomach and kicked her heels together, as if they always passed half holidays reading in silence. Minutes passed, and she continued to pore over photographs of motor-cars. The paper told of the crocuses at Hampton Court bit by frost, and of a play called *The Messenger. Mr. Audsley has done it again. Never has a more delightful marriage of allegory and whimsy graced the stage of the Gaiety Arts.* She'd done her hair in plaits and the parting was crooked.

✦

John had marked his hourlies long into the night, and he continued the next morning while invigilating the Third at their Latin paper. The Remove acquitted themselves more or less as expected, with the exception of Riding, whose exam was a disaster. He'd left several answers blank, and other plain facts he'd conflated or confused. John slashed through the errors, irate and betrayed. Had the boy been cribbing from Mainwaring all along? Or were the answers intended as a form of vengeance, aimed straight at his heart?

Results went up before tea. John perused the lists for the status of boys in his House. Halton, no surprise, came last everywhere but French. As for Riding, John stared dumbfounded at the singularly miserable results.

✦

On the floor of the chair loft, she gasped. Neck sweaty, side cramping, she couldn't laugh anymore. He'd been relentless in making her laugh, and now he did it again by whispering the word that first set her off:

—Bumf.

Her whole body strained. She hit his leg to signal surrender. He composed himself and waited for her to recover before pronouncing the word yet again.

These boys had a language more exotic than Chinese, everything shortened and removed from its source. He tutored her in Stephenese, terms absurd, terms profane. Dead Man's Leg, Maggots in Milk, Boiled Baby, Grass; soccer, saccer, footer, changer; the Eagle, the Flea, Fardles, Ennui; rag, chaff, pong, swiz; top-hole, dribble-tank, lose your rat, bumf.

She begged him to stop, but he didn't. It was like being tickled, when you pleaded for mercy but didn't mean it, really.

17 Saturday morning, last of term, the usual chaos before they crammed into chapel. The school's hymn, "Love Unknown," felt to John like tradition even though they'd adopted it only four years before. Burton read a message from the Headmaster and then announced a closing hymn they didn't know. As they flipped through hymn books, Kardleigh's choir took the first verse a cappella.

Souls of men, why will ye scatter
Like a crowd of frightened sheep?
Foolish hearts, why will ye wander
From a love so true and deep?

Why, indeed? And what if his didn't, anymore? They were bound, after all, for the City of Light, or would be once he could extract Meg from the hospital. Let everything not be ruined! Let her recover, and in time for Paris, that balm he'd longed for these cold, dark months. Let these miasmas stay far away from her. And let her daughter, his god-daughter still, let her be as she was, untouched and unchanged. Let all specters be shed with his term-time clothing when they boarded the train tomorrow.

✦

Riding's note got under his skin. Halton had to ask the Flea what the Latin words meant, and the man had waxed tragic on Queen Dido of Carthage, who after falling helplessly in love with Aeneas contrived to curse his descendants: *May an avenger one day arise from my bones!* The Flea said the avenger referred to Hannibal, which didn't make Riding's message any less offensive. Halton scraped his imagination for a clever reply; he even leafed through Kennedy for a suitable line of Latin. In the end he took inspiration from the story his sister had read him when they took that boat through the Suez Canal. He left a map in Riding's pigeonhole, X in red and three brief words: *Destroy it yourself!*

✦

Pearce had procrastinated, and now time had run out. He stood in the queue outside his Housemaster's study, doing his best to organize the madness, sending those, like himself, who had the early train forward and telling the others to wait, all the while steeling himself to say what must be said. The whole end-of-term queue problem could be eliminated if Housemasters would let prefects distribute the journey money, but that wasn't what he had to say to Mr. Grieves.

—Next!

He entered the study:

—Sir, if you don't mind, a word?

Mr. Grieves looked up from his ledger, and after a glance at the clock, beckoned him closer. He wasn't ready. He forgot his words.

—Well?

He should have come another time.

—It's Austin, sir.

Mr. Grieves set down his pen.

—Of course. I've been meaning to thank you, Pearce, for your fine work this term stepping in when Austin was taken from his duties.

—You're welcome, sir, and thank you, but that wasn't what I . . .

Mr. Grieves raised his brow.

—I mean, I've been writing to Austin, sir, and he's been writing me, advice and so forth, and he said he wouldn't . . . I mean he might not be back next term.

—Oh, no?

—He thought it likely, I mean *un*likely. He said his pater might send him to a crammer.

—Indeed?

—And what I wanted to say, sir, and I know it's only on the off chance, you see my people want me to go up to Christ Church, and read law . . .

Mr. Grieves stood. People were waiting, trains going.

—My pater knows someone there, you see, one of the dons, and he knows the Head, and he says the docket system is the best preparation there is for—

—I see.

—You do, sir? I didn't know how to say it.

—Obviously you'll have the next available JCR post.

—Oh, thank you, sir, but it isn't exactly that.

Mr. Grieves stepped around the desk.

—I mean it is, but, sir, Austin was Prefect of Hall, and if he should leave—

—Yes?

The clock raced. He should have written out what he had to say.

—I wanted to tell you, sir, that I believe in the truth, and I believe in the truth being told, and it seems to me that most of the time we're more interested in avoiding awkwardness, but if we don't tell the truth then we're wandering in the dark, like what you say about those who don't know their history.

—Pearce—

—And I should like to help the Academy that way, sir. I should like to help people see the truth and find the nerve to—

—For heaven's sake, Pearce, you'll be a prefect!

—But—

—As soon as possible, I promise. Stop fretting.

—It's only—

—We can discuss it after the holidays. There's no time now.

He passed him the journey money and shook his hand.

—Safe travels, happy Easter. Next!

He stumbled over the fringe of the rug. Outside, the queue glared.

—Must've been quite a tick-off, Moss said. Old Grievous read you the riot act?

Laughs, mock horror, *Pious got a docket!* And his hand was at Moss's throat, and they were flailing, fists and feet, crashing together against the pigeonholes, and his arm was pinned, and Moss was landing blows, and pictures were flashing as they fell: Island, Green, Shepherd, Sheep. Like the voice in a whirlwind, the pictures told the truth. He was meant to read law, but they said something else. A shepherd of sheep on an island of green. If anyone should be Prefect of Chapel, it was he, not Moss.

—Pax!

The blows stopped, defeat his. Moss hauled him to his feet:

—Next time you get an attack of berserk, Pious, leave the pigeon-holes out of it.

✦

He couldn't find her to say goodbye, but even if he could, there wouldn't be a point. Good things always ended, bad things only paused. The school hymn was maudlin and the other song worse. He hated Lent. He hated Easter. Macabre, guilty, cloying, like the half-sweet smell of a sickroom.

The hunchback ignored him when he stepped into the room. *Ultor, ultoris, ultori, ultorem.* He took the journey money and put it in his pocket. *Ultore—*

—And this.

A letter addressed to his mother.

—Something to say, Riding?

Ultores, ultorum, ultoribus—

—What on *earth?*

Crash in the corridor, man to the door, he escaped the room and the House. The man had not concealed his disgust. He had seen the vileness inside him, pus no crucifixion could cure, and now he'd committed the fact to paper, sealed and addressed for the eyes of his mother. This world touched that one, and once she knew—*ultores, ultoribus.*

EASTER

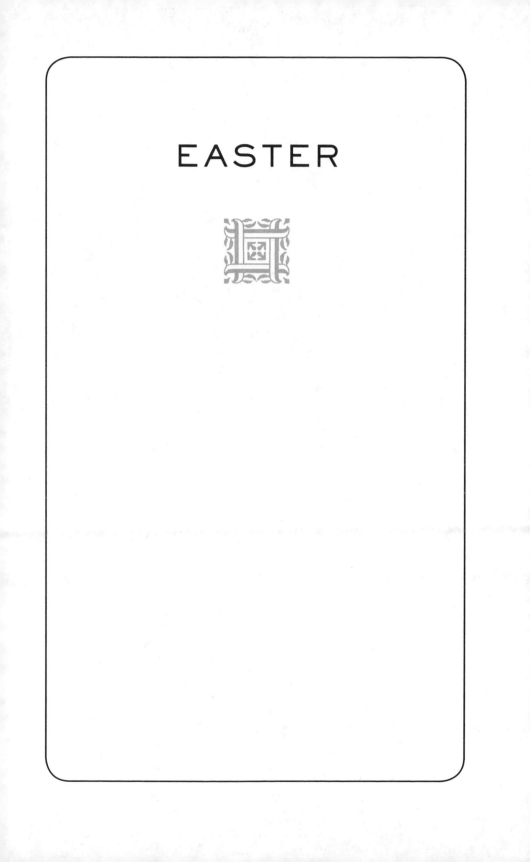

He would never give her the letter. A solution so simple, Gray was astonished it took him so long to think of it. On the train, he had stuck it in the lining of his tuck box; for all anyone knew, it had gone missing in the tempest of the Woodling household.

Nearly a week he had been with his London cousins, tumbled around their somersault world. Uncle Alec and Aunt Beatrice presided over their menagerie with subdued calm and amiable chatter, respectively. Gray's youngest cousins, Arabella and Rory, escaped their nanny more often than not and employed their freedom bickering or pestering the others to play with them. The eldest, Nick, had that term been appointed monitor at Harrow; he made it clear that he was a man with cricket to follow and couldn't be expected to play with them as he used to. Tony, still at prep school, stuck to Gray like a limpet, plying him with one game after another, chiefly their old trope of Herr Wagner and Herr Schumann, secret agents whose business was to uncover treason and conspiracy. Gray's mother had been lured from them by a nefarious romantic association, Herr Wagner judged, and there could be no doubt that Tony's sister, Claire, was likewise engaged in subterfuge given the number of letters she wrote, received, and read surreptitiously at the table each day.

Claire was a year older than Gray but seemed suddenly older. She'd begun wearing stockings, her blouse swelled at the front, and although last summer in Norway she had climbed through windows, Gray couldn't imagine her doing it now. During the outing to the British Museum, Gray had fallen into an argument with her over Egyptian relics and the girls' school myths she had plied re. Howard Carter. Grieves had taught them everything about Carter's expeditions and everything about the specious tales that surrounded him. When Gray peppered her with facts, Claire had accused him of arrogance:

—Boys always think they know better than girls.

—We do if *that's* what you've been learning.

—You look down on everyone, you public school boys, but you don't know the first thing about *real* girls. You swagger about in your cricket flannels and think you can make us melt like a pretty bunch of ninnies, nothing between our ears.

He didn't tell her about the real girl he knew, the one with everything between her ears, a girl who could, if she tried, melt not only him but the snows of deep midwinter.

His mother arrived on Good Friday. He went with Aunt Bea to the station, but the train was late, and when she got down from the carriage, she looked drawn. As Bea organized the porter, his mother looked him over, as she did each time he returned from school. When he said she looked well, she burst into tears.

—*What?* What's wrong?

Her tears turned to laughter as she realized she had frightened him. She was in perfect health, she said, only happy to see him and surprised at how he'd grown. He let her kiss him, and he wrapped his arms tightly around her as she expected. Usually at the start of holidays she was gay, and usually they spent Easter at home. This year everything was being handled by Bea and Alec. There was no reason for her to look strained. Her journey inspecting hospitals in Shetland (whatever that entailed) ought to have been good for her, but she felt thinner; he was going to have to see that she ate.

Everyone said his mother should marry again, but mercifully she'd always found their suggestions obnoxious. Widows did remarry—he knew several boys at the Academy with stepfathers, some of them even decent—but so long as she didn't, they could avoid a second alteration, one perhaps more violent than the first. They had a tacit agreement, he thought, that so long as he looked after her and caused her no distress, she would not resort to it.

On the heels of his father's funeral, she had been besieged by suit-ors; *besieged* was perhaps too strong a word, but she'd received three proposals, two from childhood sweethearts and one from an acquain-tance. The very idea revolted her, she confided; she confided everything to him in those days, and he assured her they were entirely of one mind. Some weeks later, Uncle William descended on Swan Cottage and proposed to supply the assistance his sister so plainly required. He had spoken to someone at his former prep school, he said, and they had agreed to take Gray. They would prepare him for the Harrow exam next year even though he hadn't been put down for it when he ought. Har-row wasn't Marlborough, Uncle William told her. Her husband's views against public school were in their way understandable given the kind of place Marlborough had been when he was there, but Harrow was a proper school. Nicholas was happy there. William himself had been happy there. They all missed Tom, but just as she'd wisely rid the house of his unsanitary laboratory experiments, so should she ring down the curtain on her husband's well-meaning but ultimately dangerous exper-iments in education. Uncle William implored her to think of her son. *Keep your mind on the living.* Her shouts had run out to the porch. She wouldn't be steamrolled, she said. She could teach her son as well as Tom, if not better. Gray had traced the swan on the cast-iron bell, feel-ing she was a lion, roaring off those who would throw him in a pit.

She tried all autumn, and he tried to be taught. When she let him alone to read, they fell into fewer arguments and he didn't have to ex-plain all the ways she was wrong. By the end of November, she was spending every morning in bed, and when, mid-December, she an-nounced to the family that the two of them couldn't come to Norfolk for Christmas, Aunt Bea had pitched up at the cottage, followed two days later by Uncle William. They'd closeted themselves with his mother, jointly and in serial, and Aunt Bea had packed their things for Norfolk.

He didn't remember much of that holiday except the morning Uncle William summoned him to the conservatory. The windows dripped, it smelled of mildew, and his uncle told him of St. Stephen's. He would go there next week, his uncle said. *She's worn out. You can see that, can't you?* He'd wept, and his uncle scolded. Did he care for his mother or didn't he? What would his father say if he could see how selfishly he was acting?

—Yoo-hoo!

Aunt Bea called them to the cab, and his mother pestered him about his coat, which wasn't buttoned, and the fog that rolled up from the river, root of every fatal thing. As they rattled over cobblestones, his mother recounted the boat she'd taken back from Shetland:

—Three and a half days unrelenting seasickness.

—But you've never been seasick before, Aunt Bea said. You aren't . . . ?

—Heavens, no!

—Well, how were his parents?

—You met Peter's parents? Gray interjected.

He knew she planned to see his godfather while she was in Shetland, but she hadn't mentioned the parents, whom no one had ever met since they refused to leave their remote island croft.

—How on earth did you find the time to go all the way up to Unst? he asked.

Aunt Bea burst out laughing:

—Oh, he's the spitting image of Tom! Pitch and word perfect.

A beat of fear, but his mother smiled:

—You mustn't be envious, darling, they're simply fearsome! And anyway Peter's coming to see us once we're home.

—He is?

She took his hand:

—I knew you'd be pleased.

The color had returned to her face. He had to stop seeing threats where none existed. First they had London, and now they would have Peter, too. Things couldn't get worse forever. At a certain point, they had to go in the other direction.

That evening Uncle Alec presented an Easter surprise: theater tickets for the following evening. Gray had never been to the theater before, save pantomimes, and Uncle Alec said they would wear evening clothes. Gray had no such wardrobe, but Aunt Bea said his Sunday uniform would do, and Nick let him use his aftershave and Brylcreem. Claire did something peculiar with her hair, and his mother wore one of Aunt Bea's gowns, striking and alien.

When they arrived at the theater, Uncle Alec led Nick, Claire, Tony, and Gray through a passage to a shop displaying Turkish delights. He purchased four bijoux boxes and presented them as if such sweets were compulsory. They sat in the stalls, the air sharp with cologne and quicklime. On his tongue a lemon square melted, recalling other lemons, other delights, until in a breath, darkness fell . . .

A wail.

A long, wretched tearing sound, curtain flying, lights on a stage filled with fog. A woman keening, soldiers carrying a body wrapped in sheets. Groaning below, thunder above. Lemon, rose, powder, plump.

Lights on a dinner, warm and festive. Restaurant, music, the woman with her son at a table full of friends.

Lights on a wedding. Time moving backwards. Wedding not of the son, but someone important. The woman indebted to the hostess, talk of husbands dead and husbands untrue, barbed repartee now the point of the play? The son won't ask anyone to dance. His mother embarrassed, unpleasant scene, but interrupted by a messenger—Gray's age? Nick's?—riding a bicycle across the stage. Hair golden, uniform navy, cap red, cape silky white. He jingles his bell and they freeze, save the woman, who opens the telegram in fear. Another jingle and they move, chatter filling the stage, messenger boy riding away as if he's never been. A servant appears and says they're out of wine.

Back and back, the woman's son is younger. She has a husband. They go on holiday, always worrying about their child. The boy himself is disobedient and cold, but the bicycle messenger warms the stage, never changing though the others do. He wheels each time from somewhere new—back of the stage, down the aisle, balcony—ring, ring!—folding her telegram into a paper airplane. Last square melting down his throat, time spinning faster, scenes shorter, something coming, good or bad?, something so big it could recast their life. Back and back, the woman as a girl, hair in plaits, reading. Again a rumble, and above, dust like snow. Still reading, rumble louder, dust into debris—the Messenger! climbing down a rope, raiment white, cloak flowing as he leaps. Through the noise, the golden boy speaks for the first time: *Fear not, lady!*

Silence. Sawdust settles. He whispers to the girl. She whispers back, then he, and she again until at last he rises—straight into the air!—only the hem of his cape in view: *With God, nothing shall be impossible!*

Valarious as an enterprise was wooden and dead, he saw. The real Valarious walked as vividly as any, but his creator lacked the power to draw him out where others could see. Would he ever become the kind of writer worthy of his subject, someone who could set Valarious on a stage with lights and ropes and make him live before thousands? The Messenger would make a perfect Valarious, his white cape swapped for green, a living steed in place of the bicycle. How long, O Lord, until other people could know him as Gray did?

In the wake of *The Messenger*, Tony had begun petitioning for a bicycle, Claire had sent and received several telegrams, and Nick had fallen under a spell, wishing nothing besides a romantic association with the actress who'd played the mother, or such was Tony's interpretation of his brother's new penchant for poring over theater reviews, even purchasing a magazine devoted to the stage. *The Messenger* played every evening the following week, Nick confided to Gray. They could get seats for pennies up in the gods on the day. When Gray proposed going a second time, his mother looked scandalized.

—See it *again?*

—With Nick. I'd use my own money.

She protested against their going alone and at night, but Gray reminded her that Nick would be eighteen next month. He appealed to his aunt and uncle. Neither of them could imagine why anyone would see a play more than once, but they conceded that Gray would be safe with his cousin and that the Audsleys drew a decent audience, even perhaps in the gods.

—I don't know what that means, said the volunteer nurse starchily.

—The high gallery, Bea explained, though you'll more likely find nosebleed there than divine inspiration.

Gray thought she'd recoil at the mention of nosebleeds, but something arrived in their midst, changing his luck and reconciling his mother to the idea.

Tony wanted to join them, but Nick pointed out that Tony was skint. When Tony applied for an advance on his birthday money, Aunt Bea reminded him that his birthday wasn't until August and that he still had another week without pocket money because of his Housemaster's letter. Tony turned his efforts towards Nick and Claire but came up empty-handed, as he evidently owed each and had for some time. Undeterred, he petitioned Gray.

—You've got enough for two tickets, Tony said.

—But there's the cab and the tax.

—And something to drink in the interval, Nick added.

—You could ask Aunt Elsa for the extra, Tony said. She never says no to you.

His mother frequently said no to him, though Tony refused to believe it. He continued to pester as they dressed, but when they put on their coats to leave, a bitterness descended and Tony declared that he hated them both.

In the cab, Nick passed him a cigarette, which settled his nerves. Gray asked about the actress playing the mother and how old she was.

—Ancient, Nick said.

—I thought you fancied her.

—God, no. She's the manager's wife!

—Tony thinks you're eloping.

—Wrong end of the stick, as usual.

Nick's crush was the young woman playing the actress, a certain Miss Worthington, known as the Nightingale of Shaftesbury on account of her singing. When Gray asked about the Messenger, Nick reported that he was the son of the manager. Played Romeo last season. Critics keenly disappointed with his small role in this.

—But he's the title character, Gray said.

—He's only got two lines.

Their seats in the gods gave a dizzying view, but Nick produced a pair of opera glasses and let him use them. In the orchestra pit, musicians practiced and smoked. A stagehand consulted the conductor, and then a man, the one who played the father—*The manager*, Nick whispered—emerged and begged their patience. Nothing was amiss, he told them, no players taken ill, not even dear Mr. Brazille after a *heroic* stint at the Queen's Arms last night. The tuba trumped, and the orchestra laughed.

—But I forget myself. Your servant, J. S. Audsley.

Mr. Audsley welcomed them in the name of the Gaiety Arts and of their patron, Lord Huntington—the orchestra broke into a tune, and a boy in the ceiling swung a spotlight on a gentleman in a box. Yes, he welcomed them all on this night, the hundredth anniversary of the theater's foundation. The Gaiety Arts had been under continuous management by the Audsley family since that time. The ceiling, he said, stood twenty-five feet higher than in his grandfather's day. They now boasted electricity throughout, though they still favored the gentle glow of lime at the foot—tinkle of triangle, murmur of flute—and now there were stalls where they in the gods used to stand. And gracious, what a lot of standing there had been for his grandfather's *Lear*. Five hours and a happy ending. Oh, yes, Cordelia lived! Violins from the pit, more laughter. But Mr. Audsley's purpose before them was not to boast but to invite them all—including they in Mount Olympus—to join the players upon the stage after the performance and lift a glass in thanksgiving for the century that had blessed the Audsley family. Stomping, cheers. *God Save the King.*

—There was a cake, and Guilford Audsley—
   —Chap with the bicycle.
   —gave Nick and me our own tour!
   —Gracious! said Bea.
   —He showed us all the cranks and gears. The stage gets moved underneath by five men walking around a treadmill, and the footlights have to be lit in the trap—that's what they call it under the stage because all the trapdoors open into it—and then they crank them up through a slot onto the deck—that's what they call the stage—
   —Really, darling, his mother said, I'm exhausted just hearing about it.
   —And he let us turn the rain machine and rattle the thunder sheets—
   —We can hear the rest in the morning.
   —But I don't want to forget anything! We got to stand on the *stage* and look at the house—that's what they call the audience. And he asked us to come back tomorrow and watch the play from backstage!
   —We're going home tomorrow, his mother scolded. Don't you remember?
   —We won't even have to pay.
   —You know it's impossible.
   —*Why?* Please!
   —Enough, Gray. You're behaving like a child.
   He slept poorly, rehearsing tirades against her, and spent the next morning sullen and morose. As he was shoving clothes into his trunk, Tony dropped an opened letter into the pile:
   —There's proof, you swine.
   —Of *what?*
   —Read it, Herr Schumann. And don't ever forget Herr Wagner gets his man.

Merchant Street, King's Lynn, 29 Feb, Dearest Bea. Could Gray come to London for Easter straight from school? Great favor, extremely so. His mother wished to extend her stay in Shetland and to take a ferry with

Peter Andersen to the northernmost island, called Unst. *I've a feeling Peter has invited me to meet his parents for a reason, and I hope the reason will prove a happy one.* And if he were to ask her a certain question . . . *I feel so agitated, and my heart flutters so absurdly whenever I see Peter that I feel like a girl, not a matron of thirty-nine!* Never had she betrayed the slightest hint of feelings for his godfather, not before and not during these days in London. *Crashing relief, not being on my own . . . William's insufferable purse strings.* He had attended to her, played cards when she wanted, taken pains to portray the recent term as jolly. *Must ask you not to mention . . . loves his godfather dearly . . . may take time . . .* But she, without once confiding, had drowned their understanding and gone tarting around with Peter, his own godfather and his father's oldest friend. *If matters develop, I shall tell Gray once we're home, and spend the rest of the holidays just us two, to show I love him just the same.*

 The drive from the station always gnawed at her, and as they bumped through the awful lanes, Elsa wondered what she'd find at home. The last Swan Cottage had seen of human company had been the boy, eyes bloodshot, and her, two days into the curse, dragging their cases through January fog. Now, as they rounded the bend, her shoulders eased to see the place still standing. Swans floated in the brook, willows dragged around them, the ivy had overrun the lattice, and dried holly clung to the door.

Spring cleaning was the first order of business. Curtains dusty, windows dim, the cloths she used to line the sills against hoarfrost now mildewed. No one had prepared the way for spring bulbs, but they'd forged a channel through the weeds and dead leaves. The patio chairs needed a new coat of paint. Two summers of black had to be the limit, but could she bear anything else? She went to lay down in the guest room; she'd thought that all she needed was her own home, but salt was stinging the pimple on her cheek.

✦

He was finally tall enough to ride his father's bicycle, but the gears rubbed and the tires wouldn't hold air. He wheeled it down the lane to old Jack, who with spit, tar, scraps, and grease restored it to use. The bicycle had been known in its day, and when he rode it through the village, people stared. Though he had no messenger's cape, he sped around the marshes, and at night he shut it in the toolshed, checking the floor for flowerpot shards.

The surgery stayed closed. Behind the door by the disused bell, objects waited like a sleeping kingdom—vials, stethoscope, doctor's bag—lying as they'd been when the clock stopped. If the door were opened, would the place come to life as if no time had passed, or would it be as in his dreams where he went to tell his father everything that had happened while he was away?

✦

Elsa knew a cold shoulder when she saw one, and while normally it was best to ignore it, Peter's train was due. She'd planned to tell him gently, side by side on the settee, but now she had to say it over an unmade bed, wrinkled sheets piled between them.

—You know I've seen quite a bit of Peter this winter.

The linen billowed like a parachute, helping no one.

—And you might as well know, I've grown quite fond of him.

He mashed the pillows into the cases.

—Don't do that.

Dropping them pointedly, he stood at mock attention as she presumed they did at his school.

—I haven't known how to say it.

—How about, *we're to be married.*

Did he take this tone with his schoolmasters? Who could stand it?

—Peter is your godfather, after all. You get along famously. I thought you'd be glad to have him about.

She tucked in the quilt.

—In any case, we'll have a few days with him and then we'll spend the rest of the holidays just us two.

—To show you love me just the same?

✦

For some people life changed constantly. Peter knew men who were always turning over new leaves, embarking on new ventures, meeting another girl of their dreams. They told him there were plenty of fish in the sea, even more than the apostles caught when Jesus bade them let down their nets. But Peter didn't want nets of women, even if by some estimations they outnumbered eligible men ten to one. He wanted— but he tried to repress melancholy thoughts as they bloomed, rather as one plucked strangling vines from the garden.

He'd known Elsa since she met Tom, and while he'd never actively disliked her, for years there had been a rivalry between them, or so he thought. She'd won, of course, but losing Tom to her had stung less than he'd expected because by that time he'd met Masha, who eclipsed every sun.

He'd been a widower far longer than Elsa, and when Tom died, he'd tried to treat her as he wished people had treated him. He worked beside her in kitchen or garden. He was calm when tears overcame her. He talked of Tom to her and around her. This winter he'd been in Norfolk on survey and had visited her in King's Lynn, where it seemed she lived out the school terms in her brother's house, filling her time as some un-paid nurse at a charity hospital. They took to walking together, and he found it was like having a head cold clear up so he could taste things again. She seemed more awake than he remembered, perhaps the set-ting, or perhaps something brought out by her brother, whom she de-spised. Peter had extended his stay and convinced her to look for paying work. She was an experienced nurse. She oughtn't to slave for nothing in peacetime.

How his twenty-year-old self would laugh to see him stepping off the train to meet the woman he'd once wished would drown in the Isis. Clouds banked across the marshes, skies the color of a bruise. She col-lected him in Tom's motorcar, and when he put his arms around her, it felt different than in Norfolk.

—I've told him, she said.

✦

There was a map amongst the books, and he took it out with the bicy-cle, staying away longer than he'd ever before dared. It showed him all the roads, how they tangled and bent back. He'd lived in the Isle of Thanet all his life. He knew the footpaths to Witchell's Gate, the way to St. Nicholas-at-Wade, but now he could see how they all connected, how far, how up and down. His legs grew harder, his arms stronger.

Peter did not leave after the promised couple of days but installed himself for the holidays entire. He and Peter had a tradition of long walks through woods or sands. From Peter, he'd learned the difference between a gannet and a gull, between bonxies and hawks. He could tell a mockingbird from a nightingale. He knew why crickets cricked fast in the heat, and what happened to ducklings when they hatched without a mother. His chief complaint in the past had been that Peter didn't stay long enough. Now, like Russia, alliances had changed.

◆

He hadn't expected it to be so difficult to return to Swan Cottage as a fiancé. Tom haunted it less each year, but still Peter slept in the guest room. He knew he mustn't think of her bed as Tom's; he must think of it simply as the larger bed, though how could he ever sleep there without divorcing himself from human feeling? Could they not sell the cottage and leave Kent altogether? If he broached the subject, she'd surely recoil, though what if she herself yearned to go somewhere new, perhaps even to stay with him until a place could be found for them in Scarborough? It had a hospital, didn't it, sea cliffs, and a train? No matter where they lived, though, he'd have to give up the bothy, his refuge in grief.

He'd decided recently to start telling himself the truth: he was no longer recovering. Thirteen years he'd spent crippled, a visitor in other people's homes, whether nests or cottages. The bothy in Boggle Hole, the only place he could call his, could never hold a family. His parents were almost seventy, but he was not. To live under a shadow was to waste life, and however long or short, you only got one whack at it.

◆

Peter refused to let her call in the sweep. He would investigate the chimney himself; there might be nests. Meantime, he suggested, Gray could assist her in the kitchen. She realized Peter was trying to help by forcing them together, but the way the boy chopped carrots, as if with an axe, sent her straight to hostilities:

—Your term report came today. Do you mind telling me what happened?

He swept the carrots into a bowl and began shelling the peas.

—Don't you ignore me! I'm well aware you've never failed an examination before.

He flinched but didn't break his rhythm.

—If you want to spite me, kindly find a less wasteful way to do it. It costs a great deal to send you to that school.

She snatched the bowl from him, but her fingers slipped and peas scattered across the flagstones.

—Why does everything come down to you? he cried.

—Why else would you do *this*?

She took the report from her apron and slapped it on the table. He spoke with disdain, the sort Tom could cart out when he chose, the sort they learned in their schools to bend the world to their will:

—You've no idea. You've no *bloody* idea.

The first and last time he'd used that word to her, she'd washed out his mouth and his father had read him a lecture. He used it now on purpose, a weapon of two syllables, to show he wasn't hers anymore.

—You've lost your father, she said, but have you ever considered how it feels to lose your husband, the person you've pledged your *life* to?

—Clearly not so bad that you can't find another.

—You spiteful—

He tore off his apron and hurled it at her. She drew her breath and bent to pick up the shards of the bowl.

—Your Housemaster mentioned another letter, she said. One he'd sent home with you?

◆

—We knew it wouldn't be easy, Peter told her.

—Left this on the table before running off on that bicycle.

Elsa passed him an envelope: *Mrs. T. Riding—by hand.* Script fast, ink brown. *Recommend sitting for the Remove at the beginning of term . . . might arrange with your permission . . . difficulty do him good . . .*

—He fails his exams and this man wants to push him ahead? Peter balked.

—There's something I like about that Housemaster of his, Elsa said. He always signs himself *John Grieves* when the rest use surname and initials.

—*Intricate to handle,* eh? The man has a touch with mothers, I'll say that for him.

—In person he has a certain sternness, not at all like his letters.

Peter avoided writing letters as much as possible, but now he felt a stab of envy, that this man had filled the page, and through it her kitchen, with his cause, one he fought alongside the boys, becoming to them both father and king.

—Is the lady in love?

—Don't be absurd. He's far too brooding.

—Miss Ousley doth protest too much methinks.

For an instant she was flustered, but then she laughed:

—You needn't worry. I'm not in love with the man. I'm in love with his goodness.

He rounded the table and took her in his arms, his mouth on hers like a man with his wife. Peter had always considered it the prerogative of manhood to choose his contests, but he was learning that real contests always chose you. When the boy returned, Peter announced an outing to the woods. He had sandwiches and flask already in a rucksack. The boy, perhaps relieved to avoid his mother, changed his shoes and accepted the binoculars.

—Made a go of the cutthroat? Peter asked as they set off down the drive.

The boy couldn't deny it, as his face was nicked, but with the admission, Peter realized he had lost ground. Early in the visit, when he'd presented the shaving accouterments Elsa had contrived for him to give the boy, his godson had informed him that he knew perfectly well how to shave; when occasion demanded, he borrowed safety razor and soap from a friend at school. Peter was hardly surprised. Safety razors made shaving so easy anyone could do it, but since the box from Taylor's had included a straight razor, and since he had to make it look as though he'd procured the box himself, Peter had enlarged upon the advantages of classic shaving. Now the boy had defeated his argument, demonstrating his need for a safety by sacrificing his own face.

When they finally settled down in the woods, Peter offered a cigarette, which the boy refused, whether from habit or spite, Peter couldn't say.

—About your mother and me, he began.

—It doesn't matter.

He was only a boy, emotions outsize, convictions overfirm.

—It matters very much. I know how difficult it's been, for you both.

And, you know, being a godfather means I promised to look after you if your father should ever—

—I know.

Was it this brutal if you raised them from the start? If ducklings imprinted on you at birth, they'd follow anywhere. What did it take with boys?

—I don't intend to replace him.

—Because you can't.

He was used to going where his subjects flew.

—You can still call me Uncle Peter. Plain Peter if you like. I'll still be your old godfather.

If looks could strangle.

—What did you make of *The Complete Stalky*, by the way?

The boy made to pack their things away even though they'd just arrived.

—I think you'd be surprised how well I'd understand. I went to public school, too, you know.

A fleeting expression, like disgust crossbred with boredom. Thunder rumbled, and they abandoned their position. The boy strode ahead, but Peter paced him:

—It wasn't Marlborough like your father. Our Headmaster had a certain sense of humor, even when dishing out the hidings.

He angled his face against the wind, sleet pricking his cheeks like shards of glass.

—I do wish you'd speak up about whatever's on your mind. Your Housemaster said there'd been some sort of awkwardness?

The boy stopped, fists clenched:

—If you ever speak to me again, I'll kill you.

Was Paris everything it was cracked up to be? John supposed it was. The coffee satisfied a place in his throat that he'd never known before. The bread, cool on the tongue, bore little resemblance to the slabs they slung onto plates at the Academy. The butter tanged. John paid little attention to wardrobe, but it was clear by the way Parisians looked at him that even his good suit fell short of standard. Their easy manners, their broad avenues, and their bright skies all testified to enlightenment.

Cordelia had been grave and silent in Yorkshire, but once they had, as she put it, *sprung* her mother from the hospital, she had become gregarious. Crossing the Channel, she'd stood on the deck, gripped the wet handrail, and scanned the approaching coastline like a general surveying a battlefield. She begged to be allowed to present her own passport at the border, and on the train to Paris, she examined the stamp as if she feared it had disappeared. Once they'd established themselves at their pension, she fell into an acquaintance with an American couple, also resident, a Mr. and Mrs. Vandam, whom she would have called by their Christian names (*Everyone does it in America!*) if John had not intervened. This pair of soi-disant artists were clearly flattered by the girl's hero worship, and soon they were inviting her to join them for a *chocolat chaud*, lunch, museums, walks, each outing the result of intricate negotiations on John's part between her freewheeling ambitions, her mother's aversion to conflict, and his own sense of propriety.

Under the original holiday plan, Owain was to join them after the first fortnight, but since Meg didn't mention him, John felt it was safe to assume he wasn't coming. She didn't explain what happened between them, and John didn't ask. The subject was bound to be bad for her health, and in any case, he decided, it would be a perverse waste of their holiday to spend even one hour of it puzzling over that père Karamazov.

John's own timetable revolved around Meg's need for rest and her appointments with her physician. The attending in Cambridge had provided introduction to a colleague in Paris, an eminent man of medicine by the name of Monsieur Chose, premises rue Pascal. For the first consultation, they had gone all three together. M. Chose had taken Meg into his consulting room, and John had spent the hour trying not to snap at his goddaughter, who was behaving like a third former who had eaten too many sweets, pacing the waiting room, examining every object, peppering John with senseless questions about said objects, riffling through French magazines and leaflets, interrupting his own reading with requests for definitions, opening and closing the window, inventing stories about those she observed in the street below, and otherwise continuing her ongoing campaign of *Uncle John? When you were in France did you . . . ?* (eat coq au vin, ride a tram, try marmalade like this, have a duvet . . .). When Meg emerged from the examination, her daughter dashed to her side. The doctor, Meg announced, had requested that she return tomorrow at the same time. When John weighed the strain of sitting with the girl again against the moral peril of her lunching with the Americans, he chose the latter, which had the benefit of cheering the girl up and making her cling less to her mother.

After the second consultation, Meg announced that she would be returning regularly for the next fortnight.

—But what's the treatment? John asked, baffled.

Meg could only say that Monsieur Chose employed a variety of modern techniques and was firm in his conviction that he could diagnose her condition after a rigorous program of observation. Thus, she had agreed to a fixed schedule of bedtimes, meals, light exercise, and resting. Each day, she was to write in her *petit carnet,* a folded grid with details penciled in, less like a notebook than the tic boys had to have signed—*Ça suffit!*— Even more paramount than his decision not to ponder Owain was John's resolution to leave the Academy on the other side of the Channel. He had not looked forward to this holiday so long, so secretly, and with so much yearning to waste it mentally imprisoned at St. Stephen's. He would be remanded there soon enough, but until then . . . *liberté, égalité, fraternité!*

Three mornings out of seven, he accompanied Meg on the metro to rue Pascal. Her skirts and blouses hung looser than before, and when she took his arm, he could feel her bones. The skin beneath her eyes looked paper-thin and dark where once it had crinkled with wit. At the hospital in Cambridge, she had declared everything overblown; she had only been tired, she said. Her physician, a young man trying to look older by growing out his beard, had disagreed sternly. She had frowned to show she was listening, but once the lecture finished, she began to joke with him, and John saw that she had taken the man in as she did them all.

The Frenchman's consulting room was inviolable, but one morning as John made to hold the door for her, he saw that the room where he'd glimpsed her buttoning her blouse at the end of the first visit was dim and that she was passing through a sliding door to a chamber that seemed more furnished drawing room than physician's premises. John tried not to let his imagination run away with him, but before the next patient arrived to the waiting room, he removed his shoes and approached the sliding door.

—*Je vous vois venir, Monsieur Chose.*

She spoke with impeccable accent. She was no stranger to medicine, she said. She had seen a man in Harley Street, and he had been mistaken about everything. She had come to the Continent for a modern diagnosis. She had put herself in his hands, and she had perfect faith that together they could solve the mystery. John could not make out the man's reply, but he could hear the tone, which said he'd been conquered.

She'd never told John about Harley Street, and he didn't know if she'd been keeping things from him or if she was lying to the Frenchman. Each day he asked how the appointment had gone, and each time she declared it satisfactory, even when she emerged with red eyes. If he ever asked what M. Chose had said, she would beg him not to speak of it.

If he were her husband, things would be different. He would demand an audience with the Frenchman. He would accompany her, pay the bills, and insist she tell him everything. They would keep nothing from one another, and under the covers there would be no pretending; they could undress against the world, know and be known, defend each other against every threat to body and soul. If he were her husband, Cordelia would be his. She would listen to him and flush when he summoned her, as boys did when he called their names across the cloisters. Of course, she'd never fear him—why the need?—but she would feel for him the kind of awe she felt for her mother, but more so because he would be her father. Unlike her real father, John would never abandon her. He would never rage against her mother or wound her with dalliances. If John made a promise, he would keep it.

Twice something came over Meg—her eyes flickered, and for a time she couldn't hear him. When it stopped, she couldn't remember what had happened, and her head ached, and she had to lie down. But aside from those episodes—which sent his mind to desperate prayers—she was either abstracted or gay. When they visited Versailles, the day was warm and bright, and Meg sat on the terrace while John and Cordelia toured the palace. She couldn't imagine a more perfect day, she said. To do just as she pleased, and to see the two of them so happy. Such declarations had the contrary effect of making John feel irrelevant, as if he were in Paris solely for a holiday whose chief aim was pleasure.

An outside observer might accuse him of making believe their life was his own, that they were blood kin rather than friends. Such an observer might advise him to tend to his own family, though what was that? His own father had married and seen eight children buried by his age; John was a widower in name only, lacking even grief.

When John was honest, as the middle of the night forced him to be, he could confess that he'd only married Delia to please Meg. He'd lost

Meg the moment Owain arrived in Cambridge, though it had taken nearly a year to realize it, but Meg loved John, she said, and wanted him happy, as happy as she was. Who could make him happier—and whom could he make happier—than her oldest friend, practically sister? John supposed he should have realized then that Meg called people family too freely. Delia, when he married her, proved less joined to Meg than he supposed. She counted Meg a friend to be sure, but she let Meg call her sister, it transpired, out of pity that Meg had none of her own.

Still, Delia fell into quick infatuation with him. At the time, he'd considered her enthusiasm a sign that fate approved the scheme. In retrospect, he realized she would have been a fool not to pounce. As the war dragged on, the shortage of intact men grew worse than the shortage of margarine. John was healthy, tall, educated, and Convinced. Delia, whatever you might say about her, was practical.

Despite a quick courtship, she never fully warmed to him, or (3:00 a.m.) he to her. She was unenthusiastic about the carnal side of things, and secretly (4:00 a.m.) so was he. They'd consummated the marriage, but did it count when he'd only been able to achieve . . . the achievement . . . thinking of—

God, he was ashamed. God, it was wrong. God, he'd deserved to lose her, Spanish influenza raging through a weekend. He'd deserved to wake and find her dead, and he deserved the shame of resilient health. He deserved all that and worse, but dear Lord, had she?

Nights in Paris had become purgatorial. He would fall asleep exhausted at a sane hour but then wake as people traipsed home in their cups, every voice and language paraded below his window. He took to closing his eyes when Meg was resting, a bulwark against foggy thinking, though of course he should have been taking his goddaughter sightseeing rather than let her tag along with the Vandams to their salons and their picnics and their whatever-else he hoped he'd never have to know about. Meg, meantime, slept well, a side effect supposedly of the tablets M. Chose had prescribed. John half-jokingly suggested she let him try them, but she insisted he wouldn't like the way they made one's fingers tingle. Oh, but he mustn't be distressed. She was recording every sensation in her *carnet*, and M. Chose had assured her that tingling was perfectly normal for her condition.

—Do you mean to say he's discovered what's wrong? John asked.

—Of course, darling. He wouldn't begin treatment without a diagnosis!

John couldn't quite believe he had to ask her what it was.

—I told you, darling, *la spasmophilie*.

—You told me nothing.

—Oh, she laughed, I'm a perfect scatterbrain.

And what was *la spasmophilie* when it was at home? Spasmophilia, she told him, though wasn't the name absurd? John said he'd never heard of it.

—Exactly, darling. The medical profession here is head and shoulders above the charlatans at home.

Quarter past three in the night, the direst thoughts had their way with him. *Je vous vois venir, Monsieur Chose.* I see what you're getting at. She did not have the disease he'd suggested. That disease did not afflict her, she'd said. Was this diagnosis truly the product of medical reasoning, or was it an ersatz diagnosis offered after she refused the real one?

His own mother, so far as he'd been aware, had suffered no symptoms, though seven-year-old boys were aware of so little. When his mother had fallen asleep in the middle of the Easter egg hunt, he'd believed she was only tired, but then the aunts came and stayed, and everyone was cross. His father never left his mother's bedroom, and when they finally allowed John in, he was told to kiss her and say goodbye. He'd kissed her, but it hadn't felt like her; he'd screamed and the aunts had boxed his ears.

Once, after the aunts had come permanently to stay and his father had returned from a lengthy journey, John had announced over supper that he was feeling poorly. It was a lie, but he'd said it hoping his father would stay on. He was coming down with the French disease, he said. Everyone had looked at him, and he realized he'd made a mistake, that they knew he was fibbing. His father had asked where he'd heard such a thing, and then one of the aunts had dragged him into the corridor and struck him across the face so hard his ear rang. He'd been sent to bed and made to stay there the next day, only let out once his father had departed.

It was a grim time, shameful and suffocating. That summer his father had taken him walking in Yorkshire and then to the Bishop's in Wiltshire; in the autumn he'd been sent to school, where the shamefulness lessened. They said his mother had been worn out. Eleven children and only one to show for it. Whenever people asked how his mother had died, John launched into the explanation like an exotic tale, death by wearing out.

When John became a pacifist, his father had turned from him, even, according to the blue-crossed letter, cutting John from his will. But although John pitied himself (and accepted pity from others), was it not a delicious tragedy? Did it not prove his stance valiant and vital? And did it not bind him even closer to his comrades-in-white-feathers and even closer to the one who'd seduced him to the cause? Meg had shed tears for him at his father's rejection, but—2:00 a.m., 2:30—did he not savor the injustice? Freshly exiled but not yet supplanted by the Irishman, was it not the best year of his life?

When conscription began, the ambulance service took him to France, and what savaged him there—3:05, 3:10—was not horror or even shrapnel, but Graves, MRCS, LRCP, surgeon at the hospital where John first served. John was his aide, and the jokes began at once—Graves and Grieves—all the grim humor war could sprout. He and Graves always smoked together, and one slow night the subject of their families arose. John carted out the usual narrative—orphaned, disowned—but when he presented the Worn Out diagnosis, Graves had chuckled. John had felt a swirl of confusion but insisted that it wasn't as far-fetched as the homespun term made it sound. His mother had given birth to ten children before John had finally survived. That, along with running a household and raising a child when her husband was required to travel so far and so often, would weaken anyone. Graves at first had been ironic, as if playing along, but once he perceived that John was not joking, he disabused him. Never had enlightenment felt more like assault: euphemisms did not make syphilis less deadly, to her or her children. It was sheer luck, and possibly time elapsed since infection, that John had not been born with it. John could not have conjured the term *French disease* from thin air. His father was not honorable. His father was not chaste. There were bombs and there were bombs.

The war changed everyone, so when, home on leave, John had attacked Owain in the street, breaking his nose and a rib, everyone thought it shell shock. When he refused to hear his father mentioned, everyone believed it the fruits of a father's rejection. He supposed everyone harbored scars that couldn't be seen, and if he had in essence been formed as a man by the beastly revelation, was he so different from those thousands matured in a matter of days by the front?

Spasmophilia didn't sound like syphilis, but if you added up all her symptoms, subtracting the ones that might be caused by the tablets or by strife . . . Wasn't there a library where he could consult some medical books? In ordinary life, if one was still awake at four o'clock in the morning, one left one's bed and warmed milk on the hob. Their landlady had given them leave to use the kitchen, and while John didn't think hot milk would solve anything, he chose it as a respite from his bed. The house smelled of his landlady's perfume and, near the kitchen, of cigarettes. He found Mrs. Vandam at the table, smoking and drinking coffee sans dressing gown.

—I beg your pardon, John said, averting his eyes.

—Don't tell me you're afraid of a woman, she said.

He would have left, but now he couldn't. Her voice was gravelly. She blew smoke in his direction.

—Is it true what they say about English boys?

—I beg your pardon?

—What they like.

John tightened his dressing gown and refused to flinch as he passed her to fetch the milk that sat covered on the sill. She offered him a cigarette. He declined and lit the stove. She drained her demitasse and produced a flask from under her nightgown:

—Drink?

Again he declined, filling his saucepan with milk as she filled her demitasse from the flask. Her lips were un-rouged, her hair fallen loose across her shoulders. The gown she wore looked silk, a bilious green, displaying firm arms and décolletage. If she'd had any bosom, it would have fallen out. Her eyes smiled but at the same time looked sad.

He sat beside her with his milk, helping himself after all to the Gauloises she'd propped against the sugar bowl. She tapped one against the table, and when he lit it for her, she looked at him with the kind of confidence one turned towards a friend.

—Isn't Paris a darned old town? she said. Breaks your heart and throws it in the gutter.

The smoke warmed the space inside his throat. It had been twelve years, but he didn't cough.

—That kid of yours is a piece of work, she continued.

John explained that Cordelia wasn't his daughter, but Mrs. Vandam seemed under the impression that Cordelia was his niece, and Meg his sister.

—You know the kid's crazy for Randall, don't you?

He set down the cigarette. She wasn't *crazy for* anyone, he explained, least of all Mr. Vandam. She was simply affectionate and naive.

—Come on, honey. I know girls. I am one.

She used the end of one cigarette to light another and began to talk about Claude, her psychoanalyst. Claude had turned on any number of lights. Randall, she said, had seemed reliable—

—Steady, you know, like a ship.

A ship in good repair on calm seas, but now . . . Tears rolled down her cheeks.

—It's a complex, Claude says.

John wasn't clear about the aims of psychoanalysis, but this Claude seemed to have drawn out and fed the woman's suffering.

—Your kid, she said, follows Randy like a dog. She begged him to teach her to dance. You should've seen her, hanging on his arm like a jungle gym.

John had no idea what a *jungle gym* was, but the woman's jealousy was blooming. She whined in imitation of his goddaughter, mangling the accent but capturing the desperation:

—*Please, Randall, teach me the Philadelphia Swing. For my birthday.*

—Birthday?

—Oh, Randy can't resist an *occasion*. You only turn thirteen once, he said. I could've told him, *hang crepe on your nose, your brains are dead,* but forget it. He taught it to her. Our dance, to *her.*

She was twelve years old, her birthday not for six weeks.

—Electra complex. Girls fall in love with their fathers. Not you, don't worry, but her dad must be something.

It hurt, more than he ever thought it could.

—Rat bastard, must be. Smooth as satin and just as cold.

There were twelve ends in the ashtray, and only two were his.

—She's a nice kid, but can she ever vamp. Oh, if you could see your face!

She laughed as if it were all a nauseous joke.

—Don't look like that, honey, she's not his type. Randy likes 'em dumb, like me.

Then she leaned across the table and kissed him on the mouth— breathing smoke into his throat and leaving gin on his tongue.

—*Non, non, et non!* the Frenchman cried.

Meg had fallen from her chair at breakfast and shuddered on the floor. John had carried her to the bedroom, and she'd made him draw the curtains against the splitting pain in her head. M. Chose had been sent for, but only now, three hours later, had the man arrived and examined her. Evidently she'd revealed that John had been questioning his diagnosis, for the Frenchman stomped downstairs and assailed John in the parlor.

—*C'est incroyable!* the man was exclaiming. *Incroyable!*

—*Mais*, John stammered, I only said that an incorrect diagnosis risked—

—*Incroyable!*

—Sir, it's . . . *c'est le vérité.*

—*Monsieur, la vérité n'importe pas* if you will insist upon indisposing my patient.

—But if you let her carry on thinking . . .

—If Madame Lumière is pleased with our *discours*, she will follow the orders I suggest for her. The *médicaments* she is employing she thinks to be a course for *la spasmophilie*, but naturally it is the treatment *moderne* for her . . . *affection.*

The room turned hot and the air pressed his skin. Monsieur Chose picked lint from his jacket.

—*Et pourvue que* Madame Lumière concedes with my instructions, *le Salvarsan* is, I can assure you, the very best there is to provide her.

—So you know her . . . *affection?*

—Monsieur, I do not know what the kind of *médecins* you have in your nation, *mais en France nous connaissons nos affaires.* Madame suffers from *le mal de Naples.*

Seeing John's bewilderment, the man relented:

—You can know it as *le mal français*, but this is not a true name.

There was heat inside his eyes, but his mind reached for—

—Monsieur Chose, you. . . . you say this medicine—

—*Le Salvarsan.*

—Salvarsan . . . is . . . will cure it?

—I must warn you, Monsieur, of two things. *Premier*, Madame must continue to follow the course to my instructions, and she has a certain habit to *désobéir*. Second, if you insist upon indisposing her as you have, you will simply cause more *les crises* and she will be having even more *la résistance.*

He wasn't her husband. He couldn't control her. And when her husband returned, the *crises* would explode to another continent entirely.

—Finalement, Monsieur, you must know that her *affection* is already advanced.

He deserved so much punishment, more than he knew, but God, God! *Grind me to dust, but leave her, leave her . . .*

He went to the travel agent's after lunch and changed his ticket to stay for the remainder of their holiday. In another week, they'd make the crossing together, and he'd see them home to Saffron Walden and ensure her physician was apprised of her treatment. Mrs. K would also require briefing, in confidence, for it would be up to her to intercept Owain whenever he returned and convince him of the mortal need for calm.

John took charge of his goddaughter, escorting her three times to the Louvre while Meg rested. She had a penchant for nudes, and he tried to strike a balance between speaking objectively of them and moving along before she became entranced. How the Bishop had raised four daughters on his own (not to mention Jamie), John could not fathom. If it had been possible, John would have liked to visit the man, to ask him any number of things about girls. The task before him was far more advanced than telling her stories of sea fairies, as he had done when she was small. She'd developed a habit of assailing him with questions he couldn't easily answer. Did he not consider Mrs. Vandam the height of chic? Was he not burning to see her next talking picture? Did he know when her father would return? Did he trust her mother's physician?

There was the night she came to his room after midnight, as if it were natural, to ask where her father was. John, not knowing what to tell her, embraced her as he used to, but she wriggled from his arms and scowled:

—I'm not a child. She's *my* mother. I deserve to know.

He wasn't sure anymore what she was asking, but before he could protest, she ducked away to put on the light, surveying in its glare his room's disarray.

—You're always together, she said, the two of you, telling secrets or talking to that horrible Monsieur Chose.

As if in continuation of her argument, she began to tidy his things. Socks paired, dirty shirts folded, drawers emptied and refilled. He stood in his pajamas as if in a dream.

—Did you tell the Vandams it was your birthday? he asked.

She plumped his pillows and arranged them on the bed:

—Yes.

—Did you say I was your uncle?

She met his gaze:

—I've seen things. I'm not naive.

Her voice quavered, but she was nowhere near tears.

—Don't *protect* me.

There was no splinter in her hand.

—Your father is in America, he said.

She took in his statement, looking sobered but not surprised.

—I know, she said at last.

—You *what*?

She began to arrange his museum leaflets by color.

—Have you been snooping? he demanded.

Her silence gave the answer, and John realized that they were now united in their crimes. She as well as he had discovered the letters from Owain hidden in the lining of her mother's case. The previous day when John had been waiting in Meg's room for her return from the bath, he had . . . well, the boys would have said *nosed*. He'd rifled her drawers, her cases and handbag. He'd pulled back the curiously loose lining and seen the airmail letters. He'd know Owain's script anywhere, as unruly as the man himself. The stamps were American, the frank from New York City. Meg hadn't opened them, but neither had she thrown them away.

—Why did he go to America?

Her bold tone of voice rankled.

—He came to her in hospital, John replied. She wouldn't see him.

He was sorry as soon as he'd said it, but the girl took it without flinching and then straightened his hairbrush and comb.

The next morning, their last full day in Paris, he let her tour the catacombs with the Vandams (as recompense for his words or simply to ensure her silence?), and he took Meg for coffee at their favorite place, lingering over *Le Figaro* as a shower swept through. John had just ordered more coffee when Meg set down the paper and sighed:

—You know, darling, Monsieur Chose says I mustn't think of returning to England now.

He wasn't sure what she was saying. Their passage was booked for the following afternoon.

—The damp and the cold, she said. You understand, don't you, darling?

He tried to order his thoughts and ward off the feeling of panic. She wanted to stay longer. He was due at the Academy in three days, but if his matron and JCR could—

—Monsieur Chose has got us into a spa in Vichy.

—I'll wire Sebastian.

She put her hand on his wrist. The air was heavy.

—Darling. The arrangements aren't for you.

She spoke as if she were already gone. The spa was well regarded. Its staff included three specialists in spasmophilia.

—How long will you be there?

—Cures can't be rushed, darling!

Her sudden larkiness made him frantic.

—What about Cordelia? Her school?

All, apparently, arranged. Letter written, reply received. Travel broadened the mind, her Headmaster agreed, and she was learning so much on the continent that she'd likely return ahead of her class.

John, with effort, set aside his pedagogical protest. He flagged the garçon and bought a packet of Gauloises. Meg laughed at first, but when he lit one, she frowned:

—Stop it at once. You don't even smoke.

He inhaled, gazing through the open windows at the boulevard. She'd made her plans, had been making them for days. She'd rebooked tickets. There would be no changing her mind.

The street was wet and brightening. He did not extinguish the cigarette, but he put his hand back beneath hers. She wasn't dead. *Le Salvarsan* was the treatment *modern*, and a stay in Vichy under the supervision of doctors (even French ones) was probably better than Saffron Walden with Owain.

Back at the pension, John found his goddaughter in the parlor. She sprang up guiltily when he called her name, looking as though she'd been crying; when he asked if anything was the matter, she denied it with so much vigor that he knew the opposite was true. He told her he was sorry not to be coming to Vichy, and when she began to quote Baedeker at him, he announced that he wanted her to write and tell him everything.

—Every day, darling. You must keep me *entirely* abreast.

—Like a foreign correspondent?

—Exactly.

He suggested they go to the stationers directly so he could buy her airmail paper and stamps.

—You know I won't get a night's sleep, he said, unless I hear from you every *single* day.

The idea cheered her and seemed to wipe out memory of his bluntness in the night. She began to prattle about foreign postage, and he suggested they buy as many kinds of stamps as they could find. She put on her coat, took his arm, and sang him a song as they walked, something about rainbows and coffee and pieces of pie. When they entered the park with the statue of Balzac, she switched to something violently upbeat. *If you have nine sons in a row.* It had a dance routine. *Baseball teams make money, you know!*

He proposed an early supper at a place near the pension they'd made their *endroit préferé*. Meg and Cordelia were leaving *demain dès l'aube*—before *l'aube* actually. A cab was called for 5:00 a.m. Why it was necessary to depart so early for a simple train to Vichy, John could not ascertain. His own train didn't leave until eleven, and Meg insisted that he not get up to see them off. He promised not to, but he didn't mean it.

At the start of the meal, Cordelia was subdued, but once the conversation flagged, and then sagged, she sprang to questioning John's recollections. Did he remember the time she had the mumps? Did he remember her chicken pox? Did he remember her grandparents' dog? The tooth she swallowed? The hut they made? Did he remember the Christmas she had German measles? (John remembered vividly; her parents had rowed and broken three plates.) Did he remember the story of Speckle? Did he remember—to stanch the flow of her chatter, John feigned ignorance. He'd never heard such a story, but perhaps she would tell it to them now.

—But it's your story.

—You tell it, darling, Meg said. You're so good at telling.

Meg had eaten little, but the girl had finished her *plat* and *salade*. John urged her again, and she relented, clearing her throat and adopting a tone:

—George Fox wasn't looking for a wife.

She invoked the setting, making Lancaster sound curiously like the fens.

—The tide came in faster than a galloping horse.

He'd told her many stories about George Fox, and now she threaded them together, heedless of facts but responsive to her audience. She gave her characters absurd accents and voices, but they amused her mother, particularly the girl who owned the horse called Speckle, which had carried Fox over Lancaster Sands to the home of Margaret Fell, his future wife. His goddaughter was a born performer, and the more her mother smiled, the bolder she grew, embroidering details, pursuing tangents, returning abruptly to where she'd left off, all the while insisting this was the real and true history of Quakers, untold to this day. And as she chronicled the love between Fox and Fell, Meg's face glowed, and John felt the truth of it. This girl, not yet thirteen, had conjured two people who would never have met but through grace. Two by mercy joined, truth served across a table: in jail, under sword, through the years, secretly upon the face of the waters, love moved.

TRINITY

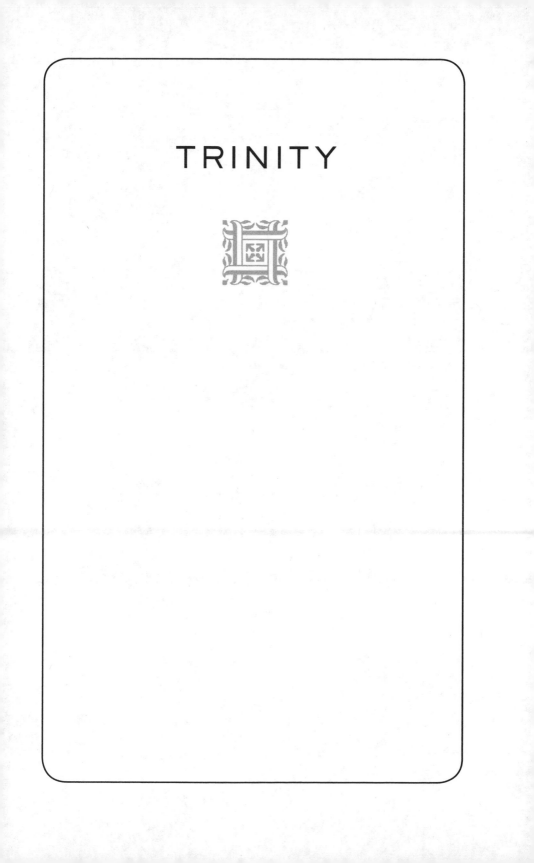

21 Marion's curse had come again. Despite rigorous calendar keeping and even more rigorous effort, Jamie had not been able to give his wife the thing she wanted. The thing they both wanted. At first neither of them had admitted to worry. They weren't in a hurry (though his sisters thought they'd already left it too long). But she was turning thirty, so last year he arranged for her to see a man in Harley Street, someone Beth found while promising not to tell Jamie's other sisters or their father. After a thorough examination, the man had declared there was nothing wrong with Marion; later, he declared there was nothing wrong with Jamie. No reason whatsoever they couldn't conceive. It was simply bad luck. They were to keep trying. She was to eat a healthful diet. They were both of them to be calm.

Still, every month blood, relentless as the Furies. They'd spent Easter at the Rectory with the horde and not one person asked them about it, leaving Jamie with the impression that his father had ordered them not to. Their silence had the perverse effect of making Marion despair; obviously, she said, they'd realized she was incapable. They'd always despised her, and now they knew she couldn't do what every other woman could. Jamie responded with increased ardor in his childhood bedroom. She wasn't incapable, neither of them was, they simply needed to persevere.

This time—the hope of Easter?—Marion had felt different. Something had stuck, she said. Her appetites changed, and her mood. But then his father had cornered him in the summerhouse:

—Everything waits on him, the man began.

Jamie had tensed but made no verbal reply.

—You can't make a child by your own will.

—I know that!

His temper had risen, his mind a tangle of unvoiced accusations.

—What about John Grieves? his father said.

Jamie had to ask him to repeat himself.

—Why have you never had him down in the holidays?

Jamie hurled his pipe across the lawn:

—I don't see what he has to do with anything!

—It's been wrong to leave it so long, his father said.

If Jamie had been younger, he would have stormed up to his room and packed his things. Instead, he took himself for a stiff walk.

When he first took the post at St. Stephen's, his father had agreed not to press him about John. The school needed John in good order, Jamie had insisted, more than anyone in the Sebastian family needed rapprochement about whatever-you-wanted-to-call-it. Since then, the Bishop had confined himself to the occasional query after John's health, which Jamie always reported as excellent. But that was the *thing* with his father: he might seem reasonable, he might even behave reasonably for years on end, but one day, when you were least defended, the old devil would pounce. The very last thing Jamie intended to do was invite John to the Rectory. Even if John and Marion got on, which they never would, John didn't deserve the Bishop uncut, not to mention Jamie's sisters. The very suggestion, Jamie decided halfway through his walk, could only be a maneuver to undermine his marriage and recall him to the time of childhood.

He and Marion were due to leave the next day, so he was spared the fight with his urge to flee. They had a weekend in London, went to the theater, organized a new suit for him (Marion claimed the right to approve his wardrobe), and then returned to a spell of mild weather, a true breath of spring, new things rising unstoppably from the earth.

When her curse started again, Jamie did his best to act as though it didn't matter. He wrote twelve letters pleading for funds for the school library, but what they really needed was a new organ. The recent patch job wouldn't last long.

Gray's relief at escaping Swan Cottage was soon eclipsed. There were the usual nerves on returning to school, but now he had to confront the problem of the holiday task, which he had forgotten in the macabre commotion at the end of last term. Arriving without one's holiday task was the quickest way to a docket, but he had reckoned that he could seclude himself in the form room that first evening if the train arrived to schedule. The bigger *if* was Trevor, who would not easily allow him to swot on a night without prep. Add to that the elaborate exchange of information Trevor would demand, and the chances of completing the hol tak decreased; however, Gray thought it possible, at least as a backup plan, that he might escape a docket given his mother's late and unwelcome interference. According to her, he was to sit for his Remove at the start of term rather than the end. Evidently his Housemaster had suggested it and she had consented, all without consulting him. Was the whole thing a plot to separate him from Trevor, who would stay behind in the Remove? Sickeningly, he realized such a plot could succeed.

✦

JCR—Trinity Term, 1931

Carter	Head of House
Swinton	Captain of Games
Moss	Prefect of Chapel
Pearce	Prefect of Hall

Halton checked the notice board personally to make sure the rumors were true. Pearce's appointment to full prefect didn't make his plan any more or less necessary, but it did increase the chances of success. Fags weren't required to report for duty the first night, but after Pearce's studymate decamped, Halton came to the study. Pearce informed him that he did not belong there; he belonged in the dorm. When Halton reclined on the window seat, Pearce asked if he thought he was clever.

—I was only wondering, Halton replied, if you'll be keeping football boots in the drawer this term.

Pearce froze. He begged Halton's pardon.

—For late-night excursions.

Pearce began to stutter:

—I've n-no idea what you're on about, but as they s-say in Scotland *nemo me impune lacessit.*

—They s-say that in Scotland, do they?

—And in case your Cicero's gone rusty, it means no one messes me about and gets away with it!

Pearce wrenched open a desk drawer and produced a slipper, which he slammed across the desk in demonstration.

—I was wondering, though, Halton continued.

—You, Pearce said, are on my last nerve.

—*Quis custodiet ipsos custodes.* That means—

—I know what it means.

Pearce was still, like he got before snapping. If he hauled off and hit him, it would hurt, but he'd still win.

—Just what is your *beastly* point?

White flag. The thrill of holding secrets and making them pay. Pearce had got away with following Mainwaring and Riding to the barn in the middle of the night, and now Halton had made it plain he knew. But his decisive advantage, greater even than knowing Pearce's night prowling, was knowing Pearce's character. Any other person would have called his bluff: if he actually were to peach on Pearce, not only would he be sent to Coventry, but the accessory hell would make Pearce's knockings-about look like love taps. But Pearce, and only Pearce, was straight enough to fear him. Pearce was too stupid for deviousness, so he never detected it in others, and he was too beholden to the goodwill of authorities to risk a fall from grace.

Pearce watched silently as he departed, and when he slammed the door, Pearce didn't follow. His joints felt loose, like eating too much icing. Everyone talked about revenge served cold, but no one said it could rack your nerves.

✦

Trinity term was the best term, in Moss's view. The weather was good. The sport was cricket. They had Patron's Day in June and fruit in season. The days were long, the bounds wide.

Pearce, as usual, tried to spoil it the very first night by lurching into Moss and Crighton's study when he should have been at dorm rounds. Moss sent Crighton to the dorms and told Pearce to relax. Pearce refused. He was in a bait with Halton though fagging hadn't even started. Despite a torrent of words, Moss couldn't follow.

Pearce wasn't usually this bad. True, he'd gone berserk in the final moments of last term, but Moss had supposed it the looming prospect of home. Had he always been worst at the start and end of terms? Moss had no idea what had transpired during Pearce's holiday (and the thought of Pearce's home life made him shudder), but he felt sure it involved hours on his knees. Too much religion was as bad as too little, though Morgan always said it wasn't that simple with Pearce. Still, Morgan wasn't here, and Pearce had never opened his heart to Moss.

✦

Moss hauled him out of bed and into the corridor:

—I don't know *what* you've been playing at, young Halton, but you can leave Pearce alone.

He would be fagging for Moss and Crighton this term. It was all settled with Pearce. He was to take the innocent expression off his face.

—And if word gets around, that we're soft for example, you'll get something to remember. Understand?

Was it necessary to thank God when good fortune arose from your own maneuvers? Their ayah in Mombasa had practiced witchcraft but always prayed as well to her own gods and to the Virgin Mary. Halton wasn't sure the witchcraft had ever worked, but his sister believed in it. They'd been in England six months, and still Miranda wore that charm under her clothing. It was her luck and her blessing, she said, and without it, she would never have won a single competition. The holidays had not brought them closer, as he'd hoped, and he saw that in his absence she had become wed to the piano as never before. When he accused her of loving it more than she loved him, her reply was unconsoling: *You are my brother. Piano is my soul!*

✦

Dear Mr. Grieves, Thank you for your letter and advice about taking the Remove exam early. A challenge would indeed do the boy good and give him something to focus his mind. (Heaven knows, he needs it.) Can I infer from your vagueness that my son is being a nuisance?

Mrs. Riding's script was neat but boyish, sharper than most mothers' and written in a turquoise ink. His letter had cheered her mother's heart, she said, particularly his expectations for the Scholarship Sixth.

If it isn't too forward, I'd take the liberty to say that there's no other man I'd better trust with the boy than you.

He didn't think she was speaking in code.

I hope the Remove will effect a change of manner in the boy, but in any case I'm confident you'll guide him as only you can. Sincere Regards, Mrs. E. Riding.

And by *change of manner*, she meant . . . ?

p.s. Incidentally, I've made plans to remarry. News not received as well as hoped. Work cut out for you, sorry to say.

He'd been delayed in France by stormy seas. His throat was sore during the crossing, and by the time he got back to the Academy, he was fevered and frantic. Jamie had postponed the staff meeting on his behalf, and his matron had taken care of study assignments, dorms, and other notices according to what he'd been able to shout down the telephone before the line dropped in Dieppe. He sat up that first night, preparing hasty lessons, attending to correspondence, and fielding a stack of memoranda from Jamie.

Choir 7–8 p.m. Sat., 8–9 a.m. Sun.
Austin withdrawn, cramming for Sandhurst.
Sunday timetable, rev . . .
Tea Saturday 5 o'clock?
Mainwaring withdrawn. Explain later.
Tea <u>Sunday</u> 4.30. Marion out.

The final letter had been discovered near dawn stuck to a bill from his booksellers.

Hôtel des Deux-Mondes, Vichy—Dear Uncle John, you mustn't be agitated. It's only been three days, and we didn't get any of your letters

158

until this morning. It was Hôtel des Sources, not Hôtel des Souris, but never mind now 'cause we've moved (see above). Mum has recovered some strength. The three doctors haven't agreed on a scheme, but they have her taking the waters day and night. She says to tell you she's doing splendidly and please forgive her being slack, she doesn't feel much like letter writing. Now she's telling me to say there's no need, with a sweet secretary like me. Help! (Only joking.) (About the Help, I mean.) They say the weather in the Channel is clearing, so I expect you'll soon be home and back to proper tea. Love, Cordelia.

 Trevor wasn't on the train. He wasn't waiting at the Academy, he wasn't at tea, and he didn't arrive with the late train. Though somewhat unnerved, Gray determined to take advantage of his late arrival to tackle the holiday task; it was more involved than he expected, and though he didn't do it well, at least he'd have something to pass in to the Flea. His relief evaporated when he tramped up to the dorms and learned not only that Trevor had still not arrived but that everyone else expected him to know why. What's more, he'd been moved to Moss's dorm, presumably another effort to separate him from Trevor. When he asked Moss for explanation, Moss had none. Moss did, however, report that their Housemaster had been looking for him, though Moss hadn't the first idea why. No, Gray could not go now. Grieves would send for him tomorrow. Meantime, Gray could meditate on this: He, Moss, would not tolerate carrying on in his dorm. Gray could just reconcile himself to ordinary conduct. He was to stay in his bed from lights-out tonight until first bell tomorrow, and he was to do the same every night thereafter.

At breakfast Sunday morning, still no Trevor, and no Grieves either. The notice boards bore no summons. Leslie reported that there had been no bed for Trevor in the old dorm. Was Mainwaring in hospital? Leslie asked. Was he expelled? Surely Trevor had written him in the holidays? Gray assured him Trevor had not. Trevor's view of letter writing was like his view of lady voters—suffered under compulsion.

—Well, Leslie declared, he didn't vanish.

Of course, he didn't vanish. He was probably motoring up with his pater, who'd returned from Palestine at Easter. The Colonel was a nerve-racking driver, Gray could attest. They might have had a puncture, or a wreck. The dormitory matter was obviously some balls-up, like the conspiracy to make him sit the Remove early.

This last disclosure proved red meat to hyenas. Leslie and the others tore into the idea, amplifying its idiocy (*What's the point when we're all sitting it in July?*), unfairness (*You'll have to swot your skin off to keep up with the Fifth*), and moral hazard (*If you do this, Brains, you'll prove yourself forever a swot*). The verdict of the breakfast table was firm:

—Shirk it. Grievous be damned.

✦

John was too old to scrape by with only two hours' sleep, or so his body declared as he lowered himself into the bath. His throat felt like blood, and his first deep breath brought on an extended bout of coughing. A cup of tea would tip the balance, though, and Mrs. Firth had one waiting in his study. It tortured his throat, and when Fletcher knocked on his door with three pieces of post that had been misdelivered to Burton-Lee, John discovered he was losing his voice. Two were bills. The third he opened immediately:

> *Hôtel Beauparlant, Vichy*—*Dear Uncle John, you're going to give yourself a heart attack. We have only now received the <u>sixth</u> of your letters. Please, it unsettles Mum when people worry. I think you'd better write us Poste Restante from now on. We've moved again (above) and for all I know we'll move another time if Mum gets tired of this place. Les trois médecins have agreed to disagree. Monsieur Flagorneur says she has biliary dyskinesia (bile duct hypercinétique). M. Bétise puts it down to a fragile liver, while M. Miteux stands firm with spasmophilia. The only thing they can agree is she must build up her terrain (get stronger, generally), which involves drinking buckets of horrible water from Les Halles Sources.*
>
> *You'll be satisfied to hear she's engaged a sort of a governess. (You needn't have gone behind my back. I read out all her letters, you know.) Her name is Miss Murgatroyd, she's from Dorset, and she's just finished governessing in Gascogne. We are studying French. I'm learning to say things ever so practical. "I like this country and admire its institutions." "The strike is at its worst." Love, Cordelia.*

At least they'd got a governess. He would write the woman this afternoon, though at the rate he was going . . .

✦

Trevor had not arrived for the opening service, and Pearce didn't read his name at call-over, a detail which would have rekindled gossip had the JCR not summoned them for a House meeting. Gray crowded into the houseroom and was forced to wait there, assaulted by everyone's curiosity, until Carter, Swinton, Moss, and Pearce filed in ten minutes later.

Their Housemaster had come down with the flu, Carter reported. Kardleigh had consigned him to bed, but before collapsing thither, he had enjoined Carter to welcome them back. Important term ahead, cricket cup, Patron's Day, bounds, et cetera. Changes in the JCR: Austin withdrawn to cram for Sandhurst, Pearce into the breach. Withdrawal also in the Remove, Mainwaring, wish him well. Next week's innovation, rolling two courts for lawn tennis—yes, thank you, it wasn't just for girls, Swinton's serve was lethal and he'd take all comers. Timetables, Prep, and to review again summer bounds—

—Leslie, do shut up.

—Sorry, Carter, but everyone's wondering about Mainwaring. We heard he broke his head.

Carter warned them against rumor mongering. Mainwaring had broken nothing. Carter had no details for the withdrawal, but potential reasons were limitless. To repeat, they wished him well, and now a cheer for the various XIs and for the best Trinity term yet.

Gray batted poorly and stood useless at long off as the heavy truth bloomed: Trevor was not coming back. Trevor had said the Academy was the best thing he ever had, but that night he had risked everything for the sake of Gray's shame and neglect; he had climbed, jumped, and fallen, not in ignorance but courage. In some real way, he had laid down his life for his friend.

The cricket continued far away, and a mole emerged from the ditch behind him, unruffled by his presence. This, he realized, was the new reality without Trevor at his side, like the term after Wilberforce but lacking the distractions that disaster had afforded. Later, as he stood with the Remove and watched Grieves's First XI, a fag from Burton-Lee's assaulted him: the Flea requested his presence. Stomach dropped, he snaked through the sidelines and met Burton-Lee at the door of his House.

—Sir, Gray said as they came indoors.

The Flea bustled into his study. Gray stood where bid as the man splashed gin in a glass, hissed it full of tonic, and began to orate. The subject, it appeared, was Gray's Housemaster. Seeing that Mr. Grieves had collapsed at his post, taking voiceless to his bed before term had even begun, it was up to Mr. Burton-Lee, as usual, to sort out the resultant messes, chief amongst them Mr. Grieves's fancy that Gray sit his Remove early. The Flea dilated upon the folly, disruption, and bad precedent such a maneuver would produce, particularly for a boy who had already been streamed too far ahead of his years, not to mention his maturity.

—You can just take that unwholesome smirk off your face, young man.

The Flea disliked Grieves's plan, he disliked the cheek of it, he disliked the Headmaster's approval, and he most especially disliked the gross inconvenience to the SCR, who would have to organize it at the drop of a hat. Gray himself would suffer inconvenience, let him not imagine otherwise, for if he were promoted, he would be expected to learn on his own time everything the Fifth had covered since September. If he were promoted, he would be excused Mathematics and Natural Science—

—An attractive prospect, I grant, given that your crib has also quit the field.

He held his tongue.

In exchange, he would have Greek and rhetoric, all in advance of his current attainment. But if, perchance, Gray wished to delay his Remove until the proper time, then the Flea would take it upon himself to speak with the Headmaster and smooth things over on Gray's behalf. This, it emerged, was the point of the interview.

—I've half a notion you were never keen on the idea yourself. Am I right?

—No, sir.

—I beg your pardon?

—Crammed in the hols, sir. I'm ready. And I have the holiday task.

The Flea looked like a child whose ice cream had fallen to the sand, but he quickly recovered. The Flea cared nothing for holiday tasks. The Flea cared only about the intemperate nuisance now facing the SCR. Gray could depart his sight until Primus Tuesday, at which time he could report to the Head's study, where Captain Lewis would direct him. Until then, he could swot in his houseroom during lessons.

—One must hope, at least, that the Upper School will curb your more obnoxious forms of disobedience.

The Flea let that sink in.

—*Fas est et ab hoste doceri.*

It is right to learn, even from an enemy.

He was late changing, of course, and his studs were not in his shirt where he had left them. By the time he got to chapel, Moss had already sent latecomers in.

—You're pushing the boat out, Moss said.

Everything he did turned out for the worst. Just as he'd warmed to the idea of shirking the exam, the Flea had cornered him into declaring himself ready. Now he had a black mark on the first day of term. The narthex bench screeched when he sat.

—Don't you give me the Sullen and Resentful, Moss said.

He smarted at the wielding of one of Morgan's phrases.

—You're a brute to bring him into everything!

—Did you see the papers? Moss asked. The Dark Blues' Great Hope!

The last thing he was prepared to discuss was Morgan Wilberforce. He closed his eyes as the Magnificat hummed through the doors.

—It's this vile Remove, he said at last.

—Ah, that.

Rumors, it seemed, had reached Moss.

—What are you going to do? Moss asked.

—What *can* I do? Shirk.

—Like hell you will! Grievous went to all this trouble. If you throw it away, it'll break his heart!

—What do I care about his putrid heart?

—I'll pretend I didn't hear that.

—Well, really, sod him.

Moss clicked his tongue:

—What would Morgan say?

—Stop harping on him!

Moss gazed at the woodwork:

—You know, it's because of the Flea that Grieves made Wilberforce Captain of Games.

—What the *hell* are you talking about?

—In the beginning. He told Grievous not to.

✦

The matron of John's house did her best to send Jamie packing. Mr. Grieves was ill, she reported, not to be disturbed, Kardleigh's orders. Matrons everywhere were dragons, which was why one engaged them in the first place, but the woman behaved as if everything were Jamie's fault. And as he returned to his study, he could feel someone inside his mind telling him he'd been reckless and self-centered and ought not to have put John in a pincer last term. Perhaps, he conceded. But he had been well within his rights; John had compromised *him*, not the other way round. And now for John to arrive back days late with only mis-spelled wires for explanation, for him to ignore Jamie's communiqués, skip Sunday lunch, skip the cricket, skip evensong and Jamie's invitation to tea, which he had taken such pains to arrange around Marion's evening with her poetry society, for John to do all this and then take to his bed? The last thing Jamie ought to feel was remorse.

He sat up late with Lewis, slicing through correspondence so he could take John's lessons for him in the morning. When he came to bed, Marion was already asleep. The crucial period wouldn't come for another week, but Jamie felt it essential to appear game at any hour. She was curled like a child, so he knew she'd been crying. More than the fail-ure, he hated the cruel taint of the enterprise. This thing, which had been life and hope and everything good, now felt like facing down a lion. They had to do it, religiously and with calm, but the more they failed, the more he dreaded it. He could only imagine how she felt. Procreation was a depraved scheme for putting one off lust.

✦

John was too ill to sleep, but he couldn't think in a single strand. He wanted French coffee. He wanted a croque madame from their *endroit préféré*. If only someone would bring him that *plat*, he could work out how to face Jamie and the things Jamie wanted to discuss. The curtain had been rung down on the barn business, he'd assert, and this was a new term, new slate, and here was Riding, passing his Remove with flying colors, or so he'd shortly be, or had he already? And what about the choir! Hadn't young Halton sounded fine with the solo? Oh, who existed to haul him from this suffocation, hacking up his lungs every time he lay prone? When he was young, he used to soothe himself to sleep thinking of the pond near Jamie's house, where he'd dive through the reeds and find creatures in the mud. When his father had taken him to the Rectory the first time, John had thought it a savage sort of Eden. The Bishop had five children, the son close to his own age, barbarians all. Their mother, too, had died, but so long ago that they didn't remember her. They seemed not to suffer, as if one could get along without a mother. They did frightful things with magnifying glasses and insects. There was a vivisection of a squirrel he still begged God to forgive him for watching. On his first visit, Jamie tried to get him to go bathing, but John refused. Yes, he could swim. No, he wasn't afraid. He didn't mind whether the girls were coming or not, nor did he care to see the wild beehive. No thank you was his answer, now and forever.

Jamie wore him down, of course. If John had been older or wiser, he might have seen it coming. It was a crying shame you couldn't see things coming until they'd happened over and over.

As they crossed the lawn carrying towels, the Bishop had opened his study window and asked them where they were going. When Jamie told him, the Bishop narrowed his eyes:

—Do not climb that tree, or I'll lick you.

Jamie had stared at the corner of his towel.

—Do you hear me?

—Yes, sir.

—And you?

John had felt naked, ashamed, already erring even though he had no idea what was being discussed.

—Yes, sir, he said.

The Bishop released them, and when Jamie turned his face away, John saw an expression he didn't know then but came to know soon: the love of hazard. And he knew that Jamie would indeed climb the tree, and that he would have to climb it, too. They'd both climb it, and they'd both be punished. The friendship had already begun.

✦

165

Pearce woke frozen with fear—that God wasn't real, that he had been inventing him to feel important, different, not a failure, that it was all an empty nothing.

The blankets wrapped him, but he was cold, like the dark wall of ice in the story about Van Vandalson. Had there been a book, or had someone merely invented the story? Van Vandalson trekking across the ice farther from Vandalhaven than any man had trod. Through a world-ending blizzard, through that snow and ice and wind and teeth, Van Vandalson had come to a wall whose top he could not see, whose breadth he could not spy, even after the snow stopped falling and the polar sun squinted on the horizon. An adamantine wall of ice. Except there was a chink that led to an arch and finally to a hall, more vast than the great hall of Vandalhaven. The vestibule of hell. He seemed to remember the wall closing behind Van Vandalson, drawing him inside to fire that burned but melted no ice, lava that boiled but chased no chill, and although Van Vandalson knew how crowded hell must be, he found it was growing vaster and vaster, lonelier and lonelier, and would one day consume creation, because it was so strong and heavy and prolific.

 After years of contention, diplomacy, and bribes, Farmer McKay tore down his barn. The news was received with the muted tones due the dead, but for Moss and the other prefects, it called for raising a glass. Carter and Swinton and those of their year went beyond relief to a puzzling form of rancor. The Head should have made him tear it down years ago, they said. The place was a crime (or at least a crime scene). Moss refilled their glasses and tried to emphasize the positive. No longer would they be plagued by bounds-breaking there. They could rest easy that the summer's bunking off would be limited to nearby hills, streams, and at worst run-ins with the keeper of Grindalythe Woods. Sanity was reigning at last. Even Grievous had risen from his sickbed.

Happy days are here again . . . It wasn't just a song; it was reality. Halton was a more careless fag than his predecessor, but Moss and Crighton found him infinitely more amusing. It wasn't hard to trim his leash: short enough to avoid anarchy, long enough to enjoy life.

Moss himself had never minded fagging; secretly, he'd rather enjoyed it, though Crighton and others in their year still bore the scars. Lydon had been a laissez-faire fag-master. Provided Moss did the basics—and this included a butler-like responsibility for keeping Lydon on the rails, making sure his shoes were in order, that he ate, that he had things he could eat, that he kept general track of time—if Moss did these things, he'd be given some of the things Lydon had to eat, and Lydon would make him feel that the Academy wasn't such a bad place, and that living across the globe from parents had a certain charm to it, that amusements could be had if one found the places to pursue them, and the discretion, the style. He had Lydon to thank for his nickname, too. Lydon called him Bastable and made everyone else do the same, giving coherence to the initials H. O. without his having to reveal what they really stood for. The nickname didn't stick beyond that first year, lacking the ring and the sense of good nicknames, but it had bestowed favor and belonging at the start, an unearned gift that cemented Moss's loyalty to Lydon. Moss hadn't yet been able to think of a satisfactory nickname for Halton. Last term the fags had called him Infant, but it was a dull name Halton had already outgrown. The way things were going, though, something sensational was bound to present itself.

✦

6 Mai, Vichy—Dear Thomas Gray, you said your father was a physician. I'm wondering, that is I'm writing to ask if he was ever unable to diagnose something. If a diagnosis is correct, then different doctors must agree on it, mustn't they? If not, then isn't it a question of finding the right doctor or waiting for enough evidence? Do you know anything about the French medical profession? Are they renowned? It's hard to take someone seriously when he doesn't speak English very well. I know, I'm a snob. You won't hold it against me, will you? I hear her waking. Must stop. Amitié, Cordelia (Líoht).

Letters fixed times and places together. The words she'd put on the page Wednesday week were still there when he read them this Friday and would be a hundred Fridays from now. She wrote them in Vichy, and he held them here in Yorkshire. *Verba volant, littera scripta manet.* Her manuscript, as individual as a fingerprint, grazed him as her chatter never had. The envelope flap had been licked by her tongue, the paper folded with her fingers. Yet, as outrageous as the sudden missive was, what he felt most keenly was her failure—by oversight or design?—

to include a return address. Sometimes eating something small made you hungrier. He asked Monsieur Henri about Vichy, and the Frenchman lent him a copy of Baedeker:

The town of Vichy is prettily situated on the right bank of the Allier and has a healthy and temperate climate. Except its old quarter, which dates only from the middle ages, the town is modern. It is easily reached from Paris in 5 hrs. (by the Vichy–Royat Express, p. xiii) to 7 hrs. 25 min.

—What's this, you brownnosing little sod?

McCandless snatched the book from his hands. After a glance at the fraying red cover, the form's beefy leader hurled it to Tighe, who caught and opened it to the title page.

Gray had been a fortnight in the Fifth and was no less hated than when he arrived. Nearly three years their junior, he could not hope for friendship. His former companions in the Remove had even less sympathy for him; not only had he set himself above them, but he'd had the indecency to place into the Top Fifth, rather than the Bottom or possible Middle Fifth, as any self-respecting cad would have done. Tighe, known as Legs due to his enthusiasm for cycling, was the most sympathetic of the lot, but Gray did not expect his visible support. He would have let them punt Baedeker around until they tired of it except that he'd promised it would come to no harm.

—It's Ennui's, he said.

—Taking you on holiday? McCandless sneered.

Legs twirled the book on a finger.

—Don't bugger it about.

—Golly, he's fierce! McCandless cried.

He gave Gray's desk a hearty kick as the Fifth responded with mock fear.

—He's far too clever for us, isn't he, Tighe?

—Too clever by half, Legs replied.

—Him and his stonking great cerebellum.

Gray lifted the ink as McCandless dumped his desk and its contents onto the floor and Legs slammed the book over his head.

He'd suffered resentment before, but not recently and not alone. Now at meals, he sat in Coventry, at Games he received boots and elbows, at Prep he worked alone in the empty form room while the rest of the Fifth repaired to their studies. He'd made an attempt at ruin, twice submitting juvenile efforts in lieu of prep, but the tongue lashings he endured from offended masters did nothing to improve his standing amongst the Fifth, who considered his poor performance a type of mockery.

✦

Hôtel du Globe, Vichy, 14 Mai—Dear Uncle John, You'll never believe I got my very first French manicure! Mum got un soin des ongles, too, and now we're ready for the Season (which opens tomorrow, in case you didn't know). I've told her I'll need proper shoes, too. Mum says I'm too young for court shoes, but I can't keep dressing like a child, especially when I'm expected to toujours discuter nos affaires comme une jeune fille française. You probably won't believe me, but Miss Murgatroyd agrees. In case you didn't know, le subjonctif is beastly. Miss you heaps. Love, Cordelia.

John dispatched letters daily to the Continent and hovered by the pigeonholes each morning and night as Fardley sorted the post. He emptied the library of medical volumes and was working his way through the stack of journals Kardleigh had given him. His first exercise book (marked *France*) soon gave way to others, as off-hours reading became single-minded research. A German called Ehrlich had created Salvarsan. He called it a magic bullet. The medicine was neither magic nor applied by firearm, but it was made of arsenic and appeared especially toxic to the microbe causing *morbus gallicus*, or so *The Lancet* claimed.

No, she isn't taking M. Chose's tablets anymore. Messrs. F, M, and B stopped them because of what they were doing to her digestion. I thought I'd explained all this! M. Bêtise was particularly concerned about the effect of le médicament on her liver. Of course, Miss Murgatroyd says the French are morbidly obsessed with their livers, but it never hurts to be careful, does it?

The doctor in Paris had said Salvarsan was the modern treatment, but the three warlocks in Vichy seemed to have lost track of essentials. John could not, through letters, make sense of their views, but he could see that their bickering blended perfectly with Meg's parade of complaints, and presumably with the fog of charlatanism in Vichy, to the point that the treatment had devolved into lethal whimsy. Even if Meg refused to hear reason, he ought to be able to influence matters through her daughter, but letters were a vexing medium. If John had been present with the girl, he would have been able to educate her on this matter as he educated the boys on others, step by step, not overwhelming with what they couldn't understand, but leading them inexorably to an appreciation of the truth—in her case, not the precise truth but at least an understanding of the appropriate treatment. As it was, the ambiguity of the written word on top of the exasperating postal delays rendered him nearly helpless. Nevertheless, he persevered, editing each of his letters into a potent, persuasive document (perhaps not a magic bullet, but what kind of image was that anyway?). Meantime, his research expanded as much as Kardleigh's periodicals would permit, which at least allowed him to feel he was making progress somewhere.

✦

Dear Tommy Gray, What would your father say to a patient who couldn't cope on her own but refused to be helped?

✦

The Fifth were more restless than usual, even for a Saturday morning in summer. John was hoping he could ignore it, but since it was only Primus, he knew the disorder would gain steam if left unchecked. He wished he could speak to them man to man. *Just relax*, he'd say, *and we can pass a pleasant morning with the Third Messenian War*. He had a few jokes in hand, and if they would stop being so very juvenile, he could deploy them. But before he could do anything but prepare the blackboard, his peripheral vision caught sight of Riding, pariah of the Fifth, rolling down the aisle an object that resembled a sausage from the breakfast table.

—Riding and Tighe!

The two boys slouched to their feet, the first defiant, the second incredulous. John was not born yesterday. He had every intention of giving Riding the notoriety he sought, but he knew that misery loved company and that multiple casualties improved esprit de corps. Thus he treated them both to a florid harangue on the subject of the lower-thirdery to which they had sunk and, remembering that a little unfairness went a long way, gave them both late-school stretching into the next hot week. When Riding protested, claiming sole responsibility, John delivered the coup de grâce:

—Very well. Tighe, *vade in pace*. Riding, my study after Games.

✦

This was why he hated his Housemaster, and why every right-thinking cad did as well. Five days of late-school was a suitably oppressive penalty that also gave him somewhere to be during the afternoon break, but having bestowed the boon, the beast took it back and lowered the hammer with *my study after Games*. In the changer, he had to listen to sardonic remarks and sound effects, and by the time he arrived to the study, his courage had decamped. Dr. Sebastian said God heard every prayer but answered them according to his wisdom. If that was so, he thought, checking his fingernails, the divine wisdom was grievous. He knocked. *Hark, you tyrant! Almighty and indifferent, who gave your servant into the hands of the accuser, who saw his family slaughtered, who covered him in boils and never said sorry . . .*

✦

Dear Uncle John, Thank you! Thank you! We've just returned from the shops with the most gorgeous pair of shoes you've ever seen in your whole long life! They're navy blue, with a very sensible heel (Miss M says), and they're made of the softest leather you've ever felt. Thank you milles fois for everything you said. Mum says to write that it's beautiful here and that we ought to come back soon all together. I prefer Paris moi-même but il n'importe pas where we go so long as we're together. Love love love, C.

P.S. I didn't mean to imply you were old when I said that about your long life. In fact, Mum says you're a dashing gentilhomme, so there.

John startled at the knock on his door. There wasn't time to brace himself, but he called the boy in and opened with his gambit:

—Ah, Riding, good of you to drop by.

John had a line in surprises and normally could direct all the sections of the orchestra: the public appearance of strictness, the private admonishment, either appealing to better nature or threatening more stringent tactics, and finally the chord, unexpected but perfectly tuned, of allegiance. Sometimes he gave lines when they deserved the JCR, sometimes he omitted punishment altogether, other times he imposed it but not as they expected. He'd never intended to go through with the late-school, but Riding didn't know that. By the end of the interview, he would believe he'd had a lucky escape, and at long last relations between them would be restored to something like normal. John was prepared to forget about the past; one way or another, this boy must be made to realize it.

John sorted mail at the table as if Riding had merely dropped by to banter, but the boy stood rigidly on the rug. John tried it all, from *How are you getting along?* to *What shall we do about the study?* Riding returned monosyllables. The stonewall provoked John to chatter, and he ran again through the options before them, all of which involved Riding joining a previously established Fifth Form study. Riding behaved as if facing an executioner. Even when John suggested that he might be able to do his prep in the library if a key could be found, the boy stared resentfully at the floor. The interview was a failure. If he reprimanded Riding or punished him now, it would only harden his sense of opposition; if he let the boy off, he'd be rewarding bad manners.

—Well, Riding, what have you to say?

Hostility and blame came off the boy in waves, even as he refused to reply; John's blood was rising.

—Out, he said. And stay out until you can behave decently.

✦

21 Mai, encore en Vichy—Dear Thomas Gray, What do you know about the major diseases and their cures? Monsieur Miteux has Mum on magnesium tablets to treat spasmophilia. The trouble is they're making her hands tingly. Try telling him and he shouts "Impossible!"

—Blubbing, Cerebellum?

Gray crushed the paper before they took it from him. He tried bravado, calling McCandless a fool-born maggot-pie, but this only enraged the henchmen. They seized him, dragged him down the row of toilets, and upon threat of *Noah's Flood* made him admit what had not happened in Grieves's study. He may as well kill himself now, they opined, unless he meant to enlist as Grieves's pet and sleep in a basket at his feet. Only the announcement, relayed from the corridor, of a wireless program in the Eagle's houseroom diverted them from bodily revenge.

Gray had avoided the chair loft that term, lest someone see him and follow, but now as the Fifth tramped away, he returned and sprang again the latch.

> I've been thinking perhaps she has a disease of the nerves, or a parasite. When I suggested this to M. Miteux, he treated me to his best French disdain: "Mlle Lumière, vous lisez encore de toute évidence." The beast. We can rule out Malaria because she hasn't had chills, but I've been wondering if it might not be the Kala-azar. I'm looking into things as well as I can, and my reading is improving, at least. I'm doing lessons in the afternoons with a rather dusty English lady named Miss Murgatroyd. (Need I say more?) Mum met her here in Vichy. She says she was recovering from a crise de foie she got during her last appointment, but j'ai mes soupçons!

He'd been keeping her letters in the lining of his tuck box, but the stash was nearly full and the Fifth were bound to turn their ire upon it, now sooner rather than later. McKay's barn had been torn down, not that he'd have taken them there. As foolish as he was, he had no intention of repeating —

✦

—Ah, John! Where have you been hiding?

Jamie arrested him on the way out of the SCR. Startled, John tried to untangle his words. They hadn't expected Jamie back so soon from . . . where had he been?

—The mice have been playing, I see.

John allowed himself to be led into the Cloisters.

—You've missed both of my Friday teas, Jamie said. If I can't keep my SCR in tea, they'll start asking for decent wages, and then where will we be?

John fell into step beside the Headmaster. He was being teased, which he supposed was better than being ticked off, or being reminded of the chat Jamie had promised but thus far failed to inflict.

—Edinburgh was dreary, Jamie said, London even worse. No one ever tells you that running a school means begging across the country like some overgrown Oliver Twist.

They made a fifth circuit and then a sixth as Jamie narrated his efforts to raise money for the new organ. It would take a miracle, but if they could pull it off, they'd secure Kardleigh long term and then be in a position to develop a music program, a proper one, not like the cathedral schools, obviously, but worth the while, and who knew if the Academy might not become a desirable public school for boys who'd trained as choristers.

—Which reminds me, Jamie continued, Father has been pestering.

John froze in shame and surprise.

—He wants you to come down this summer.

Flustered, John laughed.

—I'm glad you can laugh. Three letters. He's determined.

John uttered something about Meg and being needed, his goddaughter and—

—Don't worry. I've put him off for now. Who knows what will happen by summer?

—Just what do you mean?

—Don't take that tone, Jamie said. Makes one feel like a third former, rather.

✦

He was polishing the floor as he had when a fag, and the floor was the floor of study number six, Wilberforce sprawled across the window seat, and he wore an Eton jacket and Wilberforce wore rugby kit and he could feel the girl's letters crunching in his trouser pocket.

—What about that box of yours? Wilberforce was saying. Isn't it where you left it?

Cold with fear, he shouted: It was gone, burnt up, and so was the barn.

—I told you not to go there, Morgan said.

He wasn't a slave, he went where he wanted! Many things had happened since Morgan had left, many and many, and he told them until his throat hurt, and seawater flooded the floor, and he mopped it and Morgan mopped it, but still it rose to their ankles. He explained faster—

someone had taken the box, had hidden it, and then on Gray's orders had destroyed it and everything inside.

—Sure about that?

—Of course, I'm sure.

The water rose higher, to their waists, chests.

—Oh, boyo, Morgan said.

They bobbed, freezing.

—What proof do you have?

He woke, ill rested, to Whitsunday. It was a red-letter day, so the vicar came and talked at them through his nose. *Your young men shall see visions and your old men shall dream dreams.* The Holy Ghost came over the apostles like fire, and like wind, and they began to speak in tongues, telling everything to everyone, spreading the word across the earth.

Come, Holy Ghost, our souls inspire
And lighten with perpetual fire
Thou the anointing Spirit art
Who dost thy sevenfold gifts impart

What proof *did* he have that T had obeyed his command to destroy box and contents? In sane times, he would simply ask T, but he had no more idea who T was now than he had the very first night.

Enable with perpetual light
The dullness of our blinded sight

Like when Guilford Audsley, the Messenger, had climbed down through the rubble to the girl, whom now he imagined as his saffron haired correspondent, smudging ink across her paper at some wrought-iron table beside a pool of Vichy water. He couldn't reach T. He couldn't reach her. He was at the mercy of each, and within it.

✦

King's Lynn, Norfolk—Dear Mr. Grieves, You flatter me with your lines, which I have read many times since first opening them. I am, you must know, merely a volunteer nurse, occupying the hours doing what I can for the unfortunates my brother labels the Destitute and

Deranged. To his mind, medicine comes dressed in expensive clothes, dispensing high-priced concoctions to a wife whose chief ailments are overeating, lack of charity, and boredom, and whose chief requirement is a swift smack across both cheeks.

I almost began to apologize, as you have asked me not to, and to chide myself for writing so spitefully (if not untruthfully) to a person I scarcely know. Everyone here sees a crisp if quickly aging exterior, no hint of the thoughts within, yet something in your lines has let me believe that you will not be repulsed, entirely, and that you might even, a widower, find familiar this madness.

I really must stop before I write things I regret. I remain, Your Correspondent, Elsa Riding.

◆

Grieves would have the girl's address, of course. In a way it was that simple, yet never more out of reach. *Good afternoon, sir, I was wondering if you could let me know your goddaughter's whereabouts as we've fallen into a correspondence.* One might as well confess perversion.

Dear Tommy Gray, I hope you don't mind that I call you that. I know it's bad for Mum to have all these arguments, but she keeps trying to get ~~rid~~ me to go home. Whenever she catches me feeling sour or under strain, she threatens to send me to stay with Mrs. Kneesworth, our neighbor in Saffron Walden. She isn't even cross, she just goes weepy and limp. I can't make her believe that I <u>want</u> to help.

Still, Miss M improves things. She's taken Mum under her ~~fathers~~ feathers, and I suppose it relieves Mum's conscience that I've learned to say things like "Are you a princess? I am." She's waking. Must stop.

Monday first bell tore him from sleep. The morning was damp, as it had been in his dream where Valarious had dismounted in fog, arrested by a goshawk that pinched his shoulder like dread. The lamp above the Academy gates barely penetrated the quad, veil between worlds so thin that it seemed not impossible to wander by accident into a green grove.

He'd hardly thought of Valarious since Easter, but now he took a new exercise book and began a new telling though the old was not complete.

176

He wrote through English, through French, and even through the Flea's Latin Unseen. The goshawk didn't speak in words, but as Valarious questioned it, its talons gripped and loosened in response. The bird pecked at his chin, and when he mentioned Castle Noire, it bated. Valarious examined its jesses; their leather, finely tooled, gave no hint to the owner. A breeze rushed through the greenwood then, but rather than dispel the mist, it blew thicker, and suddenly he knew—had the goshawk purred?— knew the source, who had trained and loved this bird—

—Sit down, McCandless, you philistine swine.

The Unseen had ended, and McCandless had read his translation.

—It is insulting enough, the Flea complained, that you propose to crib your way through last night's prep, but to do so without understanding a single word—

McCandless scanned the room for support, but his aides had faded into schoolboys before the Flea.

—and then to employ your ignorance, shamelessly, with the apparent expectation that we would not notice—

The Flea tore a docket from the book.

—is an affront too far, even for ears as long-suffering as these.

He abandoned the dais, cast the docket on McCandless's desk, and then commenced a tour of the room, dilating on matters of consequence: the form's ignorance, Seneca's wisdom, Dante's error, Cardano's libel. *A maiden most fair, and long golden hair.* The goshawk had begun to sing, and Valarious knew the words and knew the bird was singing of his mistress, trapped not in a tower, but in a hall without window (*find window rhyme*). How had the hawk escaped? And how—

—Riding! Perhaps you would be so good as to join us and continue.

He set down his pen and scanned Auden's *Unseens*.

—Where from, sir?

—Just where we are.

He flipped to the correct page and began translating.

—Riding, the Flea interrupted, do I look to you a man who appreciates showing off?

His stomach dropped.

—No, sir.

Like Valarious felt as the hawk flew away.

—Then indulge us, please, by leaving Auden alone and reading out whatever you managed to scrawl into that exercise book of yours.

Come back, come back!

177

—Don't stand there staring, boy. *Tempus fugit.*

Beyond the fog, in the bracken, wolves moved.

Burton-Lee took his book and drifted to the front of the room reading, though not aloud. Valarious stood at the mercy of men whose property was to have none. The soldiers had pierced the fog, ringing him with steel. The Flea set his book on the chalkboard ledge.

—I am aware, the Flea began, from painful experience, that it would be useless—nay, folly—nay, a desecration of the God-given hour to waste my ink and my dockets complaining to your Housemaster.

The form snickered.

—For if I am not mistaken, Riding, your singular talent, besides translating Seneca ex tempore, appears to be eluding the arm of the law at every juncture.

He looked to the form for confirmation and got it.

—And carrying on with your pursuits in complete disregard of ordinary society.

McCandless brightened.

—You will therefore write me three hundred lines.

A wave of consternation flooded the form.

—You may take up where we have left off and deliver them to my study by half past five this afternoon.

But quickly gave way to glee as they realized that it would be impossible for anyone, even the pariah of the Fifth, to complete the Flea's imposition in the break between lunch and Quintus; his only option was to cut Games. The Flea knew it, they knew it, and now Gray knew it: six from his Captain of Games lay in his certain future, and Swinton was formidable both on and off the cricket pitch.

Things have gone from bad to worse. She found my diary and then got furious with me for lying to her. When I told her I don't lie, she said, How can you pretend to be happy when it's clear you hate me so? I don't pretend! I love her more than anything in the world. I told her I'd been feeling unwell and had just got out of balance. This was partly true, I had the sniffles, and in the end the whole row made me sicker. Then Miss M got into it, saying it was my own fault for sitting up late catching a chill. I burned my diary in the grate when they went out. You're my only recourse now. Thirteen today. Must stop.

He departed the JCR dry-eyed, and without comment to those waiting in the corridor, he proceeded across the quad to a foreign study, foreign realm.

—Ah, Riding.

The Flea continued writing as Gray set the lines on the blotter.

—Seen your JCR, have you?

—Yes, sir.

—Good.

The man looked up, and he was pinned, held by that gaze which
pierced his thin defense with an acute kind of knowing.

—Then this should be an end to the matter.

He held out Gray's exercise book.

—Take, write. Keep it out of my lesson.

He folded it away.

—*Fama volat et crescit eundo*, the Flea said. Or so one should hope
in this case.

—Sir?

The man sighed but did not drop his gaze.

—Don't play the naïf with me, Riding. By now, if you're fortunate,
news of your six should have spread through your House and form, likely
amplified in the telling.

On the rack, pained for thrill and relish.

—You can thank me another time, the Flea said placidly, but for now
indulge me, please, with a touch of recitation.

He pointed to a place in the sloppily copied lines.

—*Haec ego non multis, sed tibi: satis enim magnun alter alteri the-
atrum sumus.*

—Yes? the Flea prompted.

—I, er . . .

—*Scripto*, you'll find, is understood.

—I write . . . this . . . not to the many, but to you only . . . ?

—Go on.

—For you and I are . . . surely . . . enough of a . . . an audience . . .
for each other.

—Very like your translation, but the point. Elegant there, don't you
think?

He wasn't blubbing, but his eyes informed against him.

—Which reminds me . . .

He squeezed them straight as the man dressed as his enemy rifled through a drawer.

—Your Housemaster has been pestering me, and you know how I dislike being pestered.

And held out a key.

—You may tell him this is my only copy. If it gets lost, on his head be it.

Whose tag read *Library*.

The library was out-of-bounds and locked, except during the morning break when the library prefect checked books in and out. Now, he opened it free and clear and pushed the switch for the chandeliers. Never before had he liberty to browse, to roam and see what fate put before him. He finished his prep and then drifted amongst the shelves, which sagged with books misplaced and others that had lost their labels or even bindings. One such tome, on a shelf up a ladder, offered its pages as sanctuary for her letters; he leafed her blue envelopes between its brittle sheets, and when the bell rang for Prayers, he locked the door on his keep, vast, booked, licit.

No one elbowed him on the way to Prayers, and on the way out, Legs asked about something in the English prep and then relayed Gray's answer to another of the Fifth, who agreed. In the washroom, the House admired Swinton's efforts and asked, more than once, how much it had hurt. (*Not much.—Go on.—Well, a bit.*) And when Swinton put his head around the door to rustle them along and admire his handiwork, he had the charity to say *Well stuck* so all could hear.

Still, his eyes defied him, and even though he went to bed with a key to the library and the kind of soreness that makes schoolboys heroes, they revolted in the dark, soaking his pillow. The time, they said, was out of joint, and no one was who he had been anymore.

 Dear Mr. Grieves, the shrewdness is in your imagination, I'm sorry to say. Anything beyond the most common medical cases are quite beyond my ken. I'm sure there's nothing I can tell you that you don't know already, but ask away and if I don't know, I can make inquiries on the ward. A poor sort of Man Friday, I'm afraid. Your correspondent, Elsa.

John had drafted an article about his research, and one rash morning he posted it to *The Lancet*. He regretted it by teatime but consoled himself with the certainty that nothing would come of it. When, a fortnight later, he received a letter from the editor and a modest cheque, fear seized him. "Disease in History—History in Disease" was to appear in the August number, the editor informed him, but meantime, he had taken the liberty of forwarding John's work to a colleague, who soon wrote John to inquire if he was writing a book on the subject. John, in a spirit of rebellious absurdity, replied that he was, the manuscript nearly complete. His flippancy ended when the man replied by return post with an offer of publication.

—Of course you must accept, Jamie told him. I can let you off Games the rest of term.

It was a serious concession, one due a scholar, not a charlatan who'd merely gone along with the conceit because it was so ridiculous.

—I haven't actually begun anything, John said. I'm not even certain—

—Well, chop-chop! Jamie replied.

Jamie was joking, partly, but when John dropped the idea into a letter to France, it was met with an even stronger Amen:

Bien sur, Mum says, tout de suite! Imagine if we had a book with your name on our very own shelf!

He began a new notebook and filled two pages with questions. What if his nursing correspondent could act as his assistant? Hadn't she more or less offered by calling herself his Man Friday? Scholars pursued knowledge by correspondence. His tutor at Cambridge had devoted each morning to letter writing, and John realized he had held it as an ideal all these years: rise at six to tea; bathe and then sit down to his correspondence by seven, with toast and more tea brought inconspicuously to him midmorning; letters to the midday post, luncheon, tutorials, lectures, walks with students or colleagues along the backs, evensong, supper, then evenings spent with colleagues or reading. He still longed for such a life, though it was a bachelor's life, no room for family meals or for one who fed him as—as she would if she were free.

John generally did his personal writing after the boys went to bed. His goddaughter's letters arrived after lunch, Elsa Riding's with the evening meal; he would contemplate both as he addressed the ordinary demands of classroom and House. When everyone else was asleep, it was easier to give his ideas full range, which seemed to inspire a corresponding boldness in his Nurse Friday:

The ill, I sometimes think, are like hostages abducted by disease. The body remains in the bed, but the essential person has gone missing. The struggle for health, then, is a sort of battle waged over the battlefield of the body. A nurse, even a good one, which I am not, is no general or even foot soldier, but rather a kind of officer of the telegraph. All patients send messages. A nurse's lot is to receive and, if possible, translate.

What happened, he wondered, to messages misunderstood or ignored?

Dear Uncle John, Les trois medicins have increased the mercury, so at least they agree on something. And, yes, I did ask them about the headaches, and I asked their mademoiselle, too. The trouble with headaches is they can mean almost anything. I interviewed seventeen people at the baths yesterday, and every one of them complained of headaches! Miss Murgatroyd said my research was poppycock, and that la plupart de gens aren't ill at all but attend the spas as they used to attend the court, in the time before the Revolution. So there's an idea for your book!

Sometimes, when night lightened to morning, it seemed reasonable to imagine his Nurse Friday in Vichy, or his goddaughter roaming the corridors of the King's Lynn charity hospital. He made it a rule not to seal his envelopes until he had vetted the contents in the light of day.

It's an amusing verse you send, "A Code of Morals." I'm afraid my husband so loathed Kipling that he refused to allow one jingoistic page inside our home, though he did, after his year in India, speak of the heliograph and its unreliability. But to answer your question, no. I only wish he'd "taught his wife the working of the code that sets the miles at naught." Forgive the smudge. I haven't time to write this out again. You know, don't you, what it is to await the flash of the heliograph at "even's end," and then to watch them slip away before—forgive me. I ought to use a different ink.

His throat tightened at her blots. They showed him, he fancied, the woman behind the turquoise ink, the young wife in love with a brilliant man, one who'd traveled the empire and then brought his medicine home to their wildish patch of Kent. The man had known how to raise their son, how to cultivate him and train him into a singular mold. John saw how her courage had been tested as her husband, her love—a man John vicariously hated and admired—slipped without warning into a shell, and then—

It was a mercy, you must believe, that your wife went quickly. It's worse when they disappear into the labyrinth and make no effort to return.

What had failed Dr. Riding? Had the remedy come too late? Was the pathogen misidentified? Incurable? Or did he, as she seemed to think, cede the field?

At any rate, I must, as my brother continually reminds me, refer to him properly as my late husband. If I don't "chasten my nomenclature," I'll find myself, I fear, in the most frightful confusions. Your Nurse Friday.

✦

Dear Tommy Gray, What do you know of the tropical diseases? I had an illuminating conversation with a lady whose husband had been stationed all over the world, including India, Ceylon, and Jamaica. I wish there was a proper English physician here to consult. (Actually, there is one, but he's always tight.)

Gray supposed he should be angry to be asked questions and never permitted to answer, but when he imagined writing back to her, truly imagined it, he realized he had nothing to offer. His father had been a physician and had tutored him in what he realized now was a wildly miscellaneous curriculum. He knew the workings of his father's laboratory but nothing of diseases, tropical or otherwise.

She isn't improving. It feels like murder to write that. This morning I pulled out a handful of her hair while brushing it, and she didn't feel anything. I put it in my pocket and when I looked later, it was really and truly a lot. What could that mean?

Whatever she meant by writing to him, his feelings of duty and protection grew with each installment, as if he were her Keep, silent and secure.

✦

It was wet in the sheets and the dorm was getting light. The dream was nothing he could say or even think in daylight, but it had made him a man. So what if his sister never answered his letters? He, Timothy Halton, was a man at a public school. Tomorrow he had a solo, and he would conquer it as he'd conquered . . . as he'd conquered in his dream.

He'd read the T. Riding box only once, and while the contents disturbed him at the time, now he wished there had been more. They'd put a picture into his mind, and at night he would think of it, animated beyond the original, to the point that it seemed his own. Now it intruded into his dreams more strongly than he had dared imagine while awake.

Wilberforce appeared in two photographs that hung in Long Corridor, albeit indistinctly. Moss said he'd never come for Patron's Day, occupied as he was every June with cricket. Still, Wilberforce did exist out in the world. He *could* come to Patron's Day if someone would persuade him.

✦

The Fifth tolerated him now, so congress with Legs was permitted. As long as Gray showed interest in cycling (hours on the bicycle over Easter had strained his knee; Legs advised him to raise the seat) Legs was content to help him with Greek. When Gray asked how he could pay him back, Legs said he wanted nothing.

—Unless you're headed to the poacher's tunnel.

—Pardon?

Legs spoke casually, wadding up scrap paper and bowling it across the library:

—Wilberforce was the heir of Hermes. You were his fag. Who else would he tell?

—He could have told anyone.

184

Legs took a run-up:

—The only other person he would have told was me.

The paper bounced off the window, toothless.

—Or Pearce, of course. And neither of us know.

His thoughts were out of hand. Everyone knew that Pearce had been Wilberforce's first fag, but he'd never known—correction, he'd forgot—that Legs had fagged the next year until he himself arrived.

—Why don't you hate me? Gray said. You could have been the heir.

Legs snorted:

—Got me off fagging two terms early. If anything, I owe you.

Gray could remember much, too much, of that sickening era, but he didn't remember Legs dropping by study number six, as Pearce had done regularly to consult Morgan. He remembered how the quadrangle had smelled of fire when he first arrived, how the button on his new trousers had come off, how he'd thought, at first, that Grieves was the Headmaster. He remembered his first sight of Wilberforce, in the dorm. He remembered the hush that had fallen over the hostile mob that surrounded him. He remembered the crowd parting, confidence draining from their faces, and he remembered a giant towering over them, arms crossed, sleeves turned up, head tilted at an attitude he'd come to know well.

—What's all this?

He remembered how slowly Wilberforce said it and how the others squirmed, they who had seemed invincible until then. And he remembered Wilberforce's voice as he said his name for the first time.

—This must be Riding.

Until then he'd been a freak mistake, but when Wilberforce said his name, he belonged. Wilberforce had told the crowd to clear off but had plucked Legs from the midst of them.

—That'll do, Tiger.

Legs looked at the floor, and Morgan summoned Gray with a finger.

—Riding, this is Tighe. Do as he says.

—Am I his Keeper? Legs protested.

—I am, so just you see he turns up where he belongs.

Legs said he'd try.

—Not try. Do. And a bit less cheek, Tiger. Near wore me out last term.

Legs had smiled, and then Morgan had smiled, and the severity Gray thought he'd understood was gone. He felt hopeless all over again, that he'd ever understand the place, who was who, what they meant, what they were called. Legs cornered him and bade him on pain of pain never to call him Tiger. He was Tighe, Legs to his friends, full stop.

He was going down the stairs and his foot slipped and he was falling, jerked awake, moon on his pillow. Legs, Tiger, Tighe. *Tighe* began with *T.*

✦

—Young Halton's becoming quite the tart, Crighton said.

It was the first rainy day of June. The study smelled of wet wool and toast as Moss scraped the jam pot:

—Told you he'd blossom once he got away from Pious.

Theirs was study number six, one of the larger, given on account of Moss's being a prefect and opting to stay with his studymate. Once it had belonged to Wilberforce, but any trace of Morgan had long vanished. Even the cushions on the window seat were new.

—What's the odds, Crighton asked, on getting those trousers down?

Moss's wager was three weeks, hypothetically.

—If you can make him forget about that sister of his, Crighton said.

Moss knew that Morgan wouldn't approve. He'd refused Moss his entire first year, no matter how outlandish Moss had behaved. Lydon, too, refused to seduce Third Formers, even ones Moss knew had caught his notice. Occasionally, Lydon would stand beside him on the sidelines of the football, trading judgments. When Moss had pointed out a new boy in the House, Lydon had declared him off-limits until the following year, *the new dispensation.* As far as Moss could see, *the new dispensation* meant Morgan's rules, and crossing Morgan invariably meant beans. Moss never knew what had happened with Darke, a boy in Morgan's year, and Lydon wouldn't say, but one night, Darke had turned up to the dorm as if from a back-alley brawl, and the next day, Nichols minor had been let off fagging for him. This, Moss supposed, was the beans.

—He's tragic about her, Crighton continued, *Miranda* night and day. Someone's got to save him from incest.

Morgan's rules were one thing, but there were plenty of ways to pass the time without crossing the line.

—Never fear, Crikey.

And Halton was no innocent.

—There's nothing like cricket to unleash desire.

♦

Dear Uncle John, You say I don't give enough detail, but what do you want to know? Today she ate less than yesterday but more than the day before. We walked the same distance in the parc and she was more tired. The tingling is less since they stopped the magnesium. Her constitution is regular, her color the same as yesterday. Her mood this morning was bright, last night withdrawn, yesterday afternoon cheerful, then irritable, then contrite. She wears her hair the same.

He ought to have more rules for himself, or better ones. He ought not to reread his goddaughter's letters as the boys scratched away at the compositions he set them. Rereading bound him to the cinema of his mind: there was Meg, bathing, strolling; there she was cheerful, irritable, contrite; there her fingers tingled; there her hair tumbled down.

To know loneliness, one had to know its opposite. Paris had not gone as he'd hoped, but there Meg had depended on him. They joked, and she laughed at the madcap punning that sometimes overcame him when he was hungry. The last night, after she'd exploded her grenade, after dinner and packing, he had sat with her in her room, he in the Louis XIV armchair, she stretched upon the chaise longue, drifting to sleep he thought. The lamplight struck the underside of her chin and he saw the veins in her throat. Her eyelids fluttered. He whispered: *Leave him. Come back with me.* Half a minute later—less?—she sighed and shifted, her eyes opened, and she smiled as if he were her husband upon the pillow. *What a time we've had,* she said. John wondered whether he really had spoken or whether he had only dropped off for an instant and dreamed it.

We have been hearing from Da, since last month. I thought you knew. He even sent her a tiny pastel (I don't think he did it himself) in lieu of anniversary present. Fifteenth anniversaries are for timepieces, you know, so he sent her a pastel of a clock. It really is the sweetest thing. Before you ask, she hasn't relented, and at any rate he's abroad, so she couldn't see him even if she wanted.

The refectory smelled of onions again, and the sound of his colleagues droning on about politics made John want to deliver an uppercut. There truly was no creature on the earth before whom he could take off all his clothing—figuratively speaking—no one to whom he could show his un-bound self. Who could stand it without turning to salt? He wasn't fit for human fellowship, not as other people were.

◆

Behind the closed door of study number six, Halton asked how well they'd known Wilberforce.

—Well enough, kid, Moss said.

No one called him Infant now.

—What was Wilberforce like, he asked. I mean really?

—Well, to start, Crighton said, he had the most magnificent member.

Moss told Crighton to dry up.

—But he did. Had to strap it round his ankle!

Halton laughed; they all laughed.

—It was hand-reared, a real python.

—If you're going to be crude, Crikey dear, you can jolly well go do it in the lavs.

—Oh, I shall.

Crighton raked back his hair:

—But don't imagine yours is half as majestic.

Halton pretended to dust the bookshelf as Crighton's baritone boomed away down the corridor:

—This is my body, which is given for you; do this in remembrance of me.

Moss produced a packet of Silk Cuts, and Halton lit two.

—Wilberforce coached your Lower School rugger, didn't he?

—He did.

—But he's a cricketer.

—Morgan Wilberforce, Moss pronounced, was a great man.

They smoked out the window as the sun slipped behind the woods.

—It happened that he got famous for batting, but he loved sport, any sport. The older chaps weren't interested in what he had to say, but he took our Lower School rugger and worked us till we were half dead.

—A real *pumbafu*?

—P-what?

—Bastard.

—No, Moss said, you don't understand.

Moss wedged a chair under the doorknob and poked the panel in the bookcase for their hip flask.

—The Cad had never even beat Bootham until he came. Soon we had the Junior Second Cup, and by the time he left, we'd played Sedbergh twice and won.

The flask was cool, the drink smoky.

—How'd he do it?

Moss shrugged:

—Made us love working, I suppose. People would dive after balls, hurl themselves into the scrum like it was a lifeboat, break ribs, that sort of thing.

Moss rubbed his nose:

—It was the best thing I ever did, playing for him. Before each match, he'd explain the difficulties, give each boy a task, and we'd go out there and try to kill ourselves.

—But why?

Moss took a swig and sighed.

—The highest compliment you could get was when he nodded at you and said, *I can see you've learned how to suffer.*

Halton laughed:

—The Flea says that.

—*Pain passes, but giving up lasts forever.*

Halton put his feet on the table.

—He took the slipper to anyone who slacked. *I've taken an interest in you,* he'd say, whack, whack, whack. *I'm not going to let you disappoint yourself.* Made you feel . . .

—Looked after?

◆

He had to lock the library door behind himself and use only the light in the alcove. Legs was Tighe, and Tighe began with—letters and books were all he could trust.

There's a German doctor here, a Dr. Heimenflinger (Murgie befriended him). He came to lunch "on the sly," meaning he came to look at Mum and she didn't know it, but then he got on her good side and she agreed to an examination. He's convinced that she has vagovegenative dystonia, and he says the surefire remedy is

Kneipping, which I gather is a water cure they do in Bad Wörishofen. He gave us some literature. I'm so relieved. It all makes perfect sense! Must stop.

Sometimes, he opened the lead-paned windows and leaned out as the sky turned dark. The trees of Grindalythe Woods stood like the forest around Valarious, roots growing where he couldn't follow. Valarious heard that twilight cacophony, and his goshawk followed the trees' perfume deep into the woods and to the hand of its mistress. Alone in the glade, Valarious heard the forest's sorrow, like the merman in the poem that the girl's blue paper described.

She likes me to read it to her, I suppose because the heroine has her name. Do you know it? It's in a book for children, but some of the poems inside, if you <u>actually</u> read them, are desperately unsuitable, not least her "Forsaken Merman." If she doesn't get onto another poem soon, I shall have to spill something across the page.

Whatever she read, he sought. If he couldn't write back, he could open her books.

◆

Dear Uncle John, I don't know what you mean about Les Fleurs du Mal, but we've finished so the damage is done. In any case, we've started on German, which Miss M says is like clearing your throat. Mum begins her Kneipping today. Here is her schedule for Phase 1 (6 days): Rise 6.30 a.m., Cold immersion, Lukewarm sponge bath, Breakfast, Rest, 200 meter walk, Hot immersion, 600 meter brisk walk, Ice immersion, Rest, Steam bath, Morning snack.

John's book had begun as a history of epidemics, but now it veered into esoteric realms of metaphor as he grappled with the idea of disease as a reflection of human politics. Did tyranny not plague mankind constantly, like viruses? Did corruption and incompetence not waste them like parasites? And weren't urgent cures at times required once other therapies failed to save the body politic? Put inside such a metaphor, pacifism did not fare well. Pacifistic medicine (and this was merely a conceit) would diagnose diplomacy with the Black Death, or the rallying of natural resistance. But how could buboes be persuaded to abate? After devouring one body, did the disease not pass to another carrier? (*Follow up later*, John noted, *re. the war.*)

> *Rest, cold, tepid, cold, hot, cold, reading or other Restful Occupation, pine water immersion— Oh, I'm out of space but etc. all day long. Mum doesn't like the puckered fingertips, but I told her she'll have to suffer it up to be really and truly cured.*

Even if his research proved too eccentric for scholarship, at least it enlivened the Fifth's study of the Peloponnesian War. They derived a keen pleasure from Thucydides' gruesome eyewitness accounts, readings that led, indirectly, to a gradual opening of channels with the son of Nurse Friday. John almost laughed when he read Riding's first Crit; the boy's analysis was as astute as his background knowledge was imaginary, and John recognized, with a charmed sort of surprise, the swath of ancient civilization that had been ignored in the boy's early education. Extra tuition was clearly required, the sooner the better, but since the boy rebuffed every gesture of reconciliation, adopting the Sullen & Resentful each time John addressed him, John resorted to the one form of communication he knew Riding would absorb: *Neatly said, but I'm not sure it adds up. cf. Assyrian conquests of Egypt and reconsider.* The margins of the boy's work provided only one-way correspondence, but John usually detected a reply in the next composition, if only in the form of incorporated suggestions. *Don't overuse commas; respect the full stop.* That June the marginalia multiplied as John found himself setting the Fifth more compositions than usual. The boys, of course, complained, but the marking of them, in addition to his continued correspondences at home and abroad, filled the after-dinner hours and kept him from the brandy decanter. *Try thesis at the end, might give it more punch.* Sometimes he took a sip or two, medicinally with a spoon, but not enough to be called a drink.

> *My Dear Nurse Friday, No, I don't believe that marrying again can pain them or reduce the devotion we had for them. A second love does not make the first less precious. The years expire, as we historians can never forget. We are all, in the end, dust, and if love should cross our path a second time, who are we to refuse?*

✦

Anyone could bring a petition to Parliament. It was their right as free-born Englishmen. Wilberforce wasn't Parliament, but he had to feel the weight of signatures summoning him to Patron's Day. The Lower School had been easy enough to persuade, and once Halton had earned a docket—for courageously refusing to show Mr. Grieves just what he had been passing around the form—and endured the penalty, he was in a position to confide in Moss.

—He'll never come, Moss said.

—Lots of Old Boys come.

—He doesn't even know any of you.

—He knows you, though. And if you passed it round, the Sixth would sign.

—Ha-*ha*.

—I already got whacked for it. Shame to spoil it now.

◆

Uncle John, You must stop circumventing me! Today Dr. Highman-flinger read me a lecture on German medicine. He thought I had written to you to complain and gave me the third degree. You must send all correspondence through me. It's what Mum wants and it's the only way.

In any case his theory boils down to this: the body and its cells are like city-states. Disease is a conflict amongst the citizens, some-times provoked by external forces. Most diseases can be attributed to an imbalance between the Nerve-Sense (Cold) Pole and the Met-abolic (Hot) Pole. Kneipping tries to right the balance by stimulat-ing the body with different temperatures. He also vouched for the healing powers of a beautiful setting, and for the peace of mind that comes from submitting to the authority of one's physician (hint, hint). Of course, if you ask Miss Murgatroyd, all disease can be attributed to sluggish bowels, and everything else to French novels and Ger-man political theories. So there you are.

◆

Dear Tommy Gray, I'll never be able to list all the things I've learned since coming to the Continent. The French are the most fastidious about their language, but the Germans have the most frightful nouns. In music and art, the French are tops. They've got all the best painters, and in Paris there's jazz music everywhere. Even in Vichy the orchestras played gay tunes. Here we have to listen to the most dreadful Wagner from the sanatorium's gramophone each morning. The staff hum along with tears in their eyes! Everyone says the Germans are severe, but they're actually terribly romantic. They care ever so much about their hearts, and doctors listen to your chest as if it's the only thing that matters. There's a book about sanatoriums everyone's discussing. Miss M says it's nothing but morbid German philosophy, but I don't think she's actually read it.

—Der Zauberberg?

Gray's French master pronounced the title as if tasting wine that was foreign, but good.

—*L'auteur s'appelle Thomas Mann, mais le titre Anglais* . . .

Henri searched the ceiling for translation but then dismissed the effort:

—*À quoi bon?* You will never find it in our pitiful excuse for a bibliothèque.

—*Vous croyez que non, monsieur?* Gray said.

There was more in the library than anyone suspected. He'd found a case with books double stacked, many of them foreign.

—*Alors,* Henri softened, *demande à ton tuteur. Il a plus d'une corde à son arc et une mémoire d'ange.*

The last thing Gray desired was an encounter with his Housemaster's bow, or his memory. He thanked Henri and resolved to scour the library for anything by Thomas Mann. But mention of Grieves had, like black magic, summoned the man, and as Gray made to leave the French room, Grieves appeared with a question about lantern slides.

—*Bien sur, je l'ai entendu parler,* Grieves said when Henri relayed Gray's question. *Suis-moi.*

He had to follow, but at the study door, he balked:

—Sir, I can come back another time.

Grieves pushed him, and he was there, in the dungeon he'd never meant to enter.

—I've got it somewhere, Grieves said.

He had to keep facts and times distinct. The past was not the present.

Grieves had forgotten the past, surely, at least he wrote on his prep as if he'd forgotten. *Thompson makes a similar argument in* The Ziggurat of Ur. *You take it further, though.* There, on the desk lay the broad-nibbed pen that wrote to him. *Rev. para. 2–6. You've missed an important point.* When he read the words, he heard Grieves's accent. *See pp. 26–40 of attached. Return when done.* When he thought of things his father used to say, he couldn't remember the sound of his voice.

—Here it is, Grieves said. *The Magic Mountain.* Wherever did you hear of it?

There was an airmail envelope also on the dish, its writing hidden from view.

—A friend? he stammered. Traveling in . . .

Grieves handed him the book, heavy and thick, its dust jacket new:

—You needn't explain. I was only surprised, *pleased,* to see someone taking an interest in contemporary—

Grieves was touching his shoulder, steering him past the desk and the pen and the airmail to the door.

◆

Crusoe, The pages you send are very fine, and I've marked out a few phrases that seemed particularly apt. As you ask, I've included the odd query and one or two points which mystified this simple mind. You say your audience is General, but I do hope you're consulting better readers than this volunteer nurse.

The book had swollen over two hundred pages, but now, after her eminently tactful but no less poison darts, he watched it deflate. Under her gaze, the concept bared all its senseless fixations. John emptied a cardboard box and heaved the loathsome pages into it, kicking the cupboard door shut on everything he despised.

◆

Dear Tommy Gray, I've done some detectivism on a man called Zoltan Zarday, who's supposed to be the wunderkind of modern medicine. Well, I suppose he's too old to be a wunderkind, but it's a rattling good word all the same. Even my father has heard of him in America. I got a postcard from Santa Fe, New Mexico, with a

*picture of a real Indian totem pole on it. Da rode on the Atchison,
Topeka and Santa Fe Railway, and he says he has lots of presents
for his two little girls.*

✦

Once Moss had got the Sixth to sign, Halton had little trouble convincing the Fifth. They, too, had known Wilberforce, and many considered it a rotten shame that he'd never bothered to come for Patron's Day. With the Upper School's imprimatur, the Remove signed as well. The envelope was addressed and stamped when Halton tracked his final quarry to the Library that hot summer half hol.

—What do you want? Riding snarled.

—It's about the petition.

—I've already said no.

—You're the only person who hasn't signed that Wilberforce actually knew.

Riding tore the pages from his hand and strew them down the stairs:

—If you speak to me again, *ever*, I'll kill you.

 Jamie broke into his lesson and dropped a black-edged notice on his desk. The form stood up as John twigged the Marlborough letterhead.

—Cab at quarter to three, Jamie said.

John told the class to sit back down as he stepped into the corridor to absorb the news: their former Housemaster at Marlborough had died, the man who had later recruited Jamie to the staff.

—I've rung the supply agency, Jamie said. They're sending Johnson.

—But—

—He was fine last month for Henri.

Lessons, John explained, were the least of his concerns. He was never quite coherent when put on the spot, but he tried to get across to Jamie that joining him for the funeral was out of the question.

—We'll be gone two days, Jamie said. Nothing is going to happen to the woman in forty-eight hours.

At the mention of Meg, John's words tumbled: of course nothing would happen to her, but . . . Jamie gave him the expression he used with boys digging themselves into craters. When he dried up, Jamie revealed that he'd already rung Marlborough and said they were both coming.

—If you don't turn up, people will wonder.

John hadn't set foot on Salisbury Plain since leaving it for Cambridge, and by design. Now he'd been ambushed by death, which always got you from behind.

◆

Of course, Marlborough wasn't something they discussed, but attending a funeral did not mean discussing anything. Jamie had taken John's excuses as the usual blathering, or at worse a sulk at being diverted from his correspondence with a woman who would be the death of him. John hadn't been as close to their Housemaster as Jamie had been, but the man—Ali as everyone called him, after his penchant for quoting Dante—had been as fond of John as a Housemaster could be of a Games captain who'd also won the scholarships John had won. Since John had not kept in touch after leaving, he'd no notion of the way Ali had later hauled Jamie into line, how he'd helped secure his commission, how, ages later, he'd stood by him in his disputes with his father over ordination and his degree, or how he'd moved behind the scenes to get him the post at Marlborough. John probably considered Ali a tedious figure of the previous generation, views outmoded, prejudices unsavory, a stumbling block to progress.

It was unwise to dwell on Ali while sharing a railway carriage with John. They had a long journey ahead—hours on the train, a room at the club tonight, more railway tomorrow—and plainly they couldn't speak of Ali, any more than they could speak of Marion.

◆

John didn't see the point of having come to the funeral itself. Most people had arrived for the luncheon, which spilled out of the Master's garden into the quadrangle. As John predicted, Jamie was quickly surrounded. The staff knew him and greeted him fondly, half as former colleague and half as protégé made good. John left him surrounded by Sixth Formers who plainly knew and adored him.

Out on the lawn, Old Boys—now old men—squinted in the sunshine and gulped stiff drinks. John didn't recognize anyone. Those who'd survived the war would be balding, paunchy, or maimed, and they would expect a war story from him. Perhaps it would be easiest simply to invent one? He felt ashamed as soon as he thought it; he hadn't stood white feathers to crumble before these people.

—Grieves?

A man in a crisp linen suit was standing before him. John froze.

Plenty of people had accused him of shirking. He was a pacifist out of cowardice, they said, or at best for the love of a girl. How could he claim conscience, they asked, when nine months earlier he'd won his school's shooting plaque?

—Grievous! the man said. It *is* you!

The man's neck had thickened, but John suddenly knew him: Merewether, fellow prefect 1913–14, Head Boy to John's Captain of Games. Could he say a heart murmur had kept him off the lines?

—What are you drinking? Merewether asked.

John finished his lemonade:

—Scotch.

Merewether snagged a servant, John's glass was replaced, and Merewether was not asking about the war but was taking his arm and leading him through the arches to the House that had been theirs. John hadn't imagined he could remember how it smelled, but stepping inside, he did. The current pupils were outdoors in the fine weather, leaving the House eerily empty.

—Do you remember, Merewether asked, when we were fags and Malpass told me to stand still and have my face slapped?

It had been a classic phrase.

—Then I ducked and he broke his wrist on the doorframe.

They were standing, John realized, before that very door. Despite himself, he smiled, as he had then.

—They came down on you like a ton of bricks.

—Oh, but it was worth it, Merewether said. Brute couldn't bowl straight all summer. This is still, to my mind, the perfect door. Do you think they'll let me have it when they tear the place down?

John and Merewether had gone up the school together, Jamie a year behind them, and it seemed natural to fall back into the friendship, as if seventeen years hadn't passed in silence. When other people approached, Merewether peeled John away as if he meant to monopolize him for the day. To his relief, John found that his former companion had grown into a stylish version of his better traits. He struck a certain figure. Unlike other acquaintances, amusing as children, insufferable as adults, Merewether appeared to John as someone he ought to have maintained. Merewether remembered sport, pranks, their late Housemaster in his comical prime. He kept up a monologue as they roamed the corridors, one that would never comprise or admit the darts silently stabbing John.

Back on the lawn, his thirst had grown.

—Double, thank you, neat.

Jamie looked brilliant across the quad, like the sun reflected off tea trays, and John felt the old urgency. Jamie chattered effortlessly, making friends at will, as if he actually were the cast-off from Heaven John had always imagined. How else to explain the way things never marred him, whereas John always emerged more damaged than before, diminished and compromised. Worse.

✦

Ali's widow looked better than Jamie expected. She sought him out and made him sit with her. She asked after Marion, knew her name although they'd never met. She asked if they had children. Children were essential, she said. It wasn't life without them.

✦

John walked with Merewether to the station, where Jamie promised to meet him later.

—So, Merewether said, you're up at the Bastion's college.

John hadn't heard that nickname since school, and despite a day rehearsing those times, Merewether hadn't mentioned Jamie, any more than he'd mentioned the war. Now, outside school bounds, Merewether was showing that he knew things.

—Housemaster there, yes, John said.

—Always thought it would be the other way round.

The lilacs were drooping like fruit along a fence.

—Still, Merewether said, Sebastian always had face, even if he was too much of a scoundrel to make prefect.

—Top face and plenty. Turned the place around, John said, like a top.

—Went religious, did he?

John tugged at the blossoms, but they wouldn't come. Magic Merewether conjured a penknife.

—Tell me, Grievous, you married?

Presented them, laurels, to John.

—Passed away, in the flu, just after—

—I am sorry.

His arm was being touched, but not as in the House. Then as fellow tourist, now a touch that meant a feeling.

—And you?

—Confirmed bachelor, Merewether laughed. Too much fun in the FO, you know. Females, children, no idea how you stand them.

The flowers were bopping him in the face. He tried to explain, his boys were hardly children.

—Never mind, Merewether said. It only seems a waste of you, an usher, for Sebastian of all people.

They were thirsty again at the station, but when five o'clock came, Jamie had not arrived.

—Come down with me, Merewether suggested. I can give you a bed for the night.

But Jamie had the tickets for a sleeper, and he had books to mark—

—Keep in touch this time, won't you, Grievous?

Merewether handed him a card and then boarded the train. A harpy screamed. Down came the window:

—When you're ready for proper work, let me know.

The whistle had stopped, but his ears still hurt.

—There's a group I've got. Clever, like you.

Steam fogged around.

—You'd find it amusing.

◆

He was late to meet John, and it was all because of that man: once a pupil of Ali's and, it emerged, later protégé of Jamie's godfather, so of course acquaintance of Overall, the Chairman of the Academy's Board. Jamie supposed he shouldn't be surprised by the tangle of associations between men at gatherings such as these. This man, name of Arents, had funded a chapel for the prep school where Ali had once taught. He knew the firm that had built the Academy's organ. He knew a firm that would build them another.

The cab dropped Jamie at the station with only minutes to spare. He clipped up the stairs, bursting to tell John about the organ. No John. On the platform were cases but still no John. Inside, slouched at the bar, aha, John, looking as though he'd be lucky to stagger out on two feet. Bill, porter, cases, John's unwieldy bouquet.

—I'm never going back there, John moaned.

—Don't be silly. Was Merewether a bore?

John crossed his legs as if he would curl up in the seat:

—He tried to seduce me, away from you.

—I thought you didn't drink anymore.

John snorted:

—I've given up abstaining. Filthy habit.

—Quite.

—Wouldn't want to be a Puritan!

Jamie decided to unfold the newspaper. The man came for their tickets.

—I just wonder what it's all for! John resumed when the man had left.

—Don't confuse drink with a philosophical turn of mind.

Jamie said it lightly, but John leaned forward, clutching Jamie's actual knee:

—I'm being realistic. Facing things in the face.

Jamie shaded his eyes against the sun, which was pouring into the carriage. Reunions were strong drink generally, but one couldn't take them seriously, which John would know if he'd had any practice. As a first outing, had reunion plus funeral been too much? Jamie had probably known it was, but time had been too short to reconsider. Now, before him, the fruits of his carelessness: more than a flap, John had been drinking, who knew how much, but given that he didn't, enough to unfasten latches.

—You're the last person I'd expect to get jaded, Jamie said consolingly.

But John lurched to his feet and yanked down the sash. A sooty wind pounded the carriage and knocked John's flowers off the shelf, scratching Jamie in the face.

—Watch it!

Newspaper was flapping everywhere. Jamie shut the window. His temple stung.

—You'll have someone's eye out!

John crushed the wretched flowers into the rack, the smell of lilacs thick about them.

—You've always been at war with the world, Jamie said, exactly like your father.

He wanted to shut up and stop making things worse.

—If you can't stop unclipping grenades, at least don't lob them at friends, he said.

John dug at his temples as if pressure were building inside his skull and only knuckles would open a vent, and then, before Jamie could collect himself, John had collapsed across the seat dead asleep, a casualty to Jamie's rashness.

✦

Box room, cherries, scotch. Heartbeat, heartburn, had it always been so, even in the beginning, watching Jamie climb the tree and leap down into the pond? Or did it happen years later, three weeks before the end, war waiting to strike like a fever you didn't know you had? Peak of their careers, Merewether said, but was he joking? Did the prince of darkness really wait, looking for his chance when you thought yourself strongest? Or was that a story you told to make things not your fault?

He was getting all the prizes and winning back the cricket cup. That day he bowled Harrow off the field, took eight of their wickets and sent them home cowed. The XI celebrated all evening in John's study. But as they broke up for dorm rounds, there was Jamie, who didn't belong, offering a bag of cherries fresh from home. Somehow, later, they wound up in a box room like juniors, smoking cheap cigarettes. They had the scotch his father had sent, saved for prize day but begun and finished that night. Out the dormer window sky faded to ink. Jamie's breath, smoky and sweet: *Don't be a Puritan.*

Sixteen days, seventeen nights, better than he'd known anything could be. Glances across the cricket pitch. Fear and thrill. Box-room swelter-welter, mind overthrown, heart held for the first time, hands of a friend yet new; had the treasure been there all along, waiting only to be opened? Eyes flowed, when they'd long forgotten how. No one said good things could hurt so much.

Was it weakness or joy that gave the prince his chance? His heart, unschooled, never saw it coming. Day seventeen, John bowled the House to victory against their bitter rivals. The House cheered the First XI even as they repaired to the changing room, John carried by the other ten. No one told him he ought to beware. No one told him joy would be so short. The changing room should have been empty, but it wasn't. There, even there, Jamie with another, all eleven players seeing everything on view, two boys naked to their socks, flaunting every article of their common code. John didn't even know the other boy's name.

Gods of the school convened, and since he was one, he had to sit in judgment of Sebastian and his Ganymede. His heart was punching him everywhere at once, but Jamie's face lacked disgrace or even fear. Sixth form library, outraged prefects, sentence handed down: a Marlborough flogging of the first degree. Execution fell to Merewether, who dispatched the Ganymede forcibly enough but then called for a pause and drew John into the corridor.

Sweat down his collar, mind full of lies, John closed the door against the library, but Merewether, it seemed, knew nothing of his guilt or even his shabby delusions. Merewether wanted only the arm of his fastest bowler to deal young Sebastian a lesson exemplary.

There was no way to refuse, and his arm didn't want to. There was a hip flask with enough to silence thought. Detached, resolute, but when it came to it, Jamie's face turned spark to flame—*Down with it, down with it, unto the ground*—until Merewether grabbed him and made him stop. Cane clattered to floor. Person—*thing*—dead. Library faces all turned to him in awe and recoil.

Clock tower. Roof. Down below, the grass. Smooth, far away. Exit quick, over the edge—like his mother when she'd swing him up in her arms, *whoosh*, and set him down again. *More!* No one picked him up and no one set him down, but his shoes, when he looked, were new. Not his shoes, but others, other shoes on other feet. New feet, new man. New wine, new skin. New heart.

✦

In London, John was nearly sick in the cab. It seemed to be a case of getting drunker after stopping. At King's Cross, Jamie paid to get onto the train early so John could collapse in the berth.

Jamie tried to sleep, too, as they rattled past tenements, fields, and finally dark, but indigestion kept him awake, and then they were hissing into York and John required waking.

—You look like hell, Jamie said. How much did you drink?

John seemed to consider the question rhetorical, and once they'd changed trains for the final leg, John closed his eyes again. When the

202

sun broke in at the end of the Burdale tunnel, he howled as if he'd been suffering all along and couldn't stand it anymore.

—Dog bit hard?

—I'm done! John declared. I quit.

—That's the spirit.

—I mean I resign.

—This again?

—I'm serious! Put both of us out of our misery. Don't know how you've stood me so long.

Not pique, but self-pity. John was prone to both. Jamie mentally rehearsed the standard lines, but nothing sounded right.

—Who else can I trust? he said.

John tugged at his hair, for all the world like a madman on the heath:

—Trust? How could you trust me after—

His voice broke into a sob. Jamie froze.

—That? Don't tell me you're—

—It's killing me!

—It wasn't—

—No, John cried, my head! Someone's drilling like . . .

The train slowed, and their platform slid into view. John had begun to sob. In the cab Jamie practiced detachment, and when they pulled up to the gates, Jamie helped John to the Tower, where Kardleigh gave an injection that quieted him.

—He had a bit to drink, Jamie told Kardleigh, but I haven't seen him like this since we were boys.

—Oh?

—He used to get headaches. They were the only thing that could make him blub.

—Brought back old times, this funeral of yours?

—Something like that.

 The Magic Mountain was macabre. Its hero, Hans Castorp as the translator regularly called him (never Hans or Herr Castorp), was a loathsome specimen. Although the author evinced a certain sympathy for him, Gray couldn't bear the man's dilettante passivity, his hypochondria, the way he let life blow him about. Gray longed to tell Hans Castorp to pull

203

himself together. If he felt odd and tired upon arrival at the sanatorium, it was likely the altitude, something Uncle Peter had described at length—light-headedness, nausea, breathlessness, from flying in the war. His father, too, once told how he awoke in the night suffocating in the highlands of India. And if Hans Castorp felt heat in his cheeks and chill in his body, it was sunburn, surely, not fever. Yet, Hans Castorp, the ninny, seemed determined to waste his young life (not that his career as engineer sounded like much) at that mountaintop retreat, courting illness and occupying himself with what was morbid. Gray wasn't sure what analysis entailed, but he inferred a treatment at once risqué, shameful, and dangerous, likely to drive one mad if mismanaged. Yes, he loathed Hans Castorp, the self-indulgent nothing. The book was as heavy as the mood that overtook him when he thought of it, as if the figures carved in the choir stalls were shaking their heads at him, murmuring *beware*.

✦

By the time John came through the other side of the headache, Jamie had departed on a fund-raising tour. John felt only relief at his absence, a lungful reprieve. He didn't trust his memory of their journey; at least he decided that he shouldn't trust it. If he'd had to face Jamie at breakfast, lunch, and tea, the shame might have been paralyzing; as it was, it only burned like low-grade fever and a comfortable reproach. *Turn thou us, O good Lord, and so shall we be turned*. He always felt safer in Lent, contained by its disciplines. It wasn't Lent now, but wasn't it always the season to turn back? Back to his lessons, to marking done on time. Back to his correspondence. He resumed writing to Meg, determined to overcome her silence. When she began to send replies through her amanuensis, he persisted as charmingly as possible—*I fancy you'll tell me, when you can, what they're saying there about MacDonald's cabinet*. She could never resist politics, and her daughter hadn't the first idea of them. He persevered, and by grace she replied:

> We aren't supposed to take notice of the world, of course, but I've cultivated one or two of the servants. The stories they tell would dry out your ears.

Her hand was weak, but he'd know it anywhere; he knew it in his dreams, where letter upon letter came to him. *Blessed be the Lord God of Israel: for he hath visited, and redeemed his people.* He opened the cupboard and hauled out his manuscript. *That we, being delivered out of the hands of our enemies, might serve him without fear.* It wasn't as bad as he'd imagined, some passages actually good. Who had written them? He dashed off an update to Nurse Riding, and she returned encouragement.

It's always darkest before the dawn, they say (though presumably they speak of a night with no moon). Now, in answer to your question about "Patron's Day," I'm afraid I must send regrets.

He had the impression, from her inverted commas, that she'd never before heard of Patron's Day, and her curt refusal brought him up short. It was not his place to invite her when her son had plainly neglected the duty. Did the boy not want her, or did he consider the day frivolous? John had a mind to ask him, but before he could work out an angle, the boy waylaid him in the corridor, bearing the book John had loaned him.
—So soon? John said. Did you finish?
The boy scowled:
—I've read all I mean to read. Sir.
John was left feeling he'd trafficked pornography.
—And what did you think?
Riding clearly wanted to leave, but John stood his ground. The boy could learn to converse, as a sign of good manners if he couldn't manage gratitude.
—I think, sir . . .
He looked as in the classroom when put on the spot and resenting it.
—that sanatoriums are a rum business. Ordinary people go there to get ill, and ill people go there to die. They're run by charlatans and are full of chocolate soldiers.
John had never felt so told off in his life. He suppressed the urge to hide the book behind his back.
—Oh, don't hold back, Riding. What did you really think?
Riding recoiled, and a spike went through John's head.
—Cut along, he said. And I'd better see proper spelling in that prep of yours. You can jolly well make an effort for once.

◆

TG, Something terrible has happened. Zoltan Zarday the wunderkind writes that vagovegenative dystonia is what they call a

205

verlegenheitsdiagnose, a polite diagnosis for people who have nothing wrong with them. When I think of the time we've wasted Kneipping, and we're back where we started only Mum is weaker! We must leave Bad Wörishofen, that much is clear, but it might mean taking Murgie into my confidence.

✦

The drops were bitter and Kardleigh wasn't liberal with them, but the spike eased, the lights stopped flashing, and John's temper cooled. He was just drifting down the Tower stairs when Jamie burst from the porter's room.

—What are you doing here? I thought you were away.

—Good to see you, too, Jamie said.

That smile should have stabbed, but the drops had enrobed him in calm.

—Don't look like that, Jamie said. I hope you aren't going to insult me by trying to apologize or some such nonsense.

—I . . .

—Just do me a favor and go easy on the Pims.

Pims?

—Need you in good nick Wednesday. That man Arents is coming.

Was he speaking of Patron's Day? John was failing to follow.

—Arents, organ, I told you. No? Got to take his wicket.

Jamie was rushing off. Was *wicket* metaphor?

—Big day! he called. Counting on you!

John resolved to leave Jamie for the morrow. His study was peaceful, and Mrs. Firth had left him tea. Was that a wire beside—he tore the envelope, fearful, though it didn't look foreign.

Corpus Christi Oxford—GRIEVES SAHIB GOT LETTER STOP ARRIVE 24TH 1002 STOP BUNK IN DORM QUERY DEPART 25TH 0718 STOP WILBERFORCE M

Not blow, but reprieve, one he'd never expected. Morgan Wilberforce after three long years. Not only coming to Patron's Day, but asking to stay the night. They could sit as they used to, in John's study after lights out. They could speak of books, boys, everything, and put the world to rights.

27 —He's here!

The cry rang through the school as Halton strode from the cloisters. He'd convinced himself that the letter hadn't worked, but then, in an instant, miracle: the Great Wilberforce in their very quad. Surrounded already, Wilberforce shook hands, clapped arms, threw mock punches. He was taller than he'd expected, taller than Crighton or Mr. Grieves, face suntanned, hair cut short, a laugh that made his stomach wave.

Halton edged around the crowd and dashed up the Tower stairs to complete his errand.

—Just coming, Kardleigh told him. Have you warmed up?

Someone was retching in the other room.

—Note from the Head, sir.

Kardleigh read it and brightened.

—Time to sing your socks off, Timothy. Could be an organ in it for us.

—We've got an organ, sir.

—One that works, cheeky.

The sound of violent heaving was making him gag.

—Not you, too, Kardleigh said. Take this.

He handed him a sheaf of music and his gown.

—Start the others warming up. I'll be there directly.

—Yes, sir.

Kardleigh turned back to the ward:

—God's blood, Riding, what are we going to do with you?

✦

God gave them an English idyll, even better than Jamie could have hoped. Neither too hot nor too cold, the sun reigned from dawn to midsummer dusk. Parents, Old Boys, the full Board, distinguished guests, all crammed into the chapel where the choir sang as angels. Luncheon al fresco, refectory tables lugged out to the quad, shrouded in linen, and laden with the best food of the year. Afterwards, cheered by hock, they repaired to the refectory for a charitable auction to benefit the parish school in Thixendale. (Who will say the great are not also good?) As the crowd drifted outside to find chairs for the cricket, Jamie and Kardleigh showed Arents around the chapel. Stained glass by Whitefriars; icon from Moravia; Conacher organ, once very fine but crippled by a flood in

'13. By the time the innings had begun, Arents had used Jamie's telephone to arrange a visit to Rushworth and Dreaper, organ builders. It was all bluff, of course, but one never knew when bluff might turn. Jamie saw Arents settled in a lawn chair beside Kardleigh and then began to work the sidelines. On the pitch, the Old Boys, led by Morgan Wilberforce, batted the First XI into a corner and took their first victory since the war. The day could literally not have gone better.

By seven o'clock all had departed, leaving the Academy to its annual nature walk, led traditionally by the Headmaster. Jamie escorted wildlife lovers, botany enthusiasts, and anyone else who cared to venture out-of-bounds on a two-hour stroll through the fragrant, hazy wolds. And he could hear, somewhere in his ears, the school's hymn as it had been sung that morning. Having been released from their mouths in harmonies too beautiful to bear, the sound lingered like a soul unwilling to leave the body. *Love to the loveless shown that they might lovely be.* He had dreamed of the hymn the night he'd first visited the Academy, that Patron's Day five years before when the Board had courted him and then pressed him into the post. He'd dreamed that night of the Good Friday hymn, of hearing it in the Academy courtyard as he addressed the school, promising to rebuild the chapel.

The chapel hadn't needed rebuilding, but the school had, and now here he was, leading them down the leafy lane, back to strawberries and cream, to a place where they could grow and thrive, where music lived and would continue to live, where boys who once wrecked on the rocks became men who turned and returned, giants and heroes.

Yet, these boys were not his, not in the final sense. Marion had played her part all day, hair blazing fraise-blond in the sun, but what if it was all a beautiful, false feast? St. Stephen's Day wasn't until December. Then, the day after Christmas, when no one roamed the Academy but ghosts, it would be a different celebration, martyrdom in the wintry ground. Were they being formed for fruitfulness or for desolation? It was folly, of course, to identify too closely with the institutions one served, though Jamie thought in his case the warning had come too late.

✦

—That choir, Morgan said, has got half-decent.

He sat where he used to, in the red armchair before the grate, John in the brown. Morgan was expected in the dorms, but John had him for a little while yet.

—Who was that soloist? Morgan asked. And when did we get soloist material?

—The name's Halton, and as it happens, he's one of mine.

—So it's to be musical prodigies as well, Grieves Sahib?

His chest tightened at the old nickname, the thing Morgan began calling him once they entered the second age. After Jamie had come and Morgan became a prefect, they'd sit at night in John's study speaking of the boys, their disasters and conquests, the levers to their affection, the medicines for their faults. Morgan began calling him Grieves Sahib after the Headmaster in Kipling, an unmerited tribute, John always thought. Still, it was a name Morgan used only with him, which meant there was a part of Morgan reserved for him, too.

—Kardleigh discovered him, John continued.

—Is he as much trouble as . . . our former project?

—Perhaps, John said. In time!

Morgan grinned as if in gratitude and relief, and John saw that Morgan was as shy of the subject as he was, the subject of Riding. They'd sat in the same chairs that day, the day John presented the newest in their series of projects: Riding, TG, aged eleven almost; father dead; too young, too small, too clever by half. Orders of magnitude, Morgan used to joke. He'd stride into the study, dressing gown over shirtsleeves, pour himself a brandy, and plop into the chair: *About our project, Grieves Sahib.*

—And Pearce? Moss?

—They're half my JCR, John said.

—So I hear. How's Pearce taking it?

—Oh . . .

John rolled his eyes.

—Comes in here and burbles? Morgan said.

—Moss curbs the excess.

—And I suppose Pearce keeps him from *complete* frivolity?

It was easier then to speak, of the school and other things. When they came round to John, his efforts to manage family abroad, his manuscript and the offer of publication, Morgan understood, or seemed to.

—Don't do it, he said of the book. You'll work yourself into the grave if you're not careful. I know you, sir.

John finished his soda, wondering idly if that wouldn't be the worst thing. As the clock tolled midnight, Morgan, too, drained his glass and stared past John into the night.

—How is he? Morgan asked when the bells fell silent. Our former project?

John rubbed his eyes:

—Sat his Remove this term, placed into the top Fifth.

—Bless me.

—Otherwise . . .

John's voice trailed off, until he realized he was holding his breath. Morgan stood and brushed his trousers.

—So soon?

—I'm expected, Grieves Sahib, and if I don't go soon there won't be a lick of sleep.

John found him a torch and walked him to the dormitory stairs.

—I meant to ask, John said as Morgan started up, in your wire you mentioned a letter?

—Yes, sir.

—I was wondering what you meant by it.

Morgan turned:

—You mean you didn't . . . ?

John knit his brow, and Morgan groaned. Switching off the torch, Morgan reached into his jacket for the letter in question. John scanned the contents.

—Well!

—Ye-es, Morgan said.

—All these signatures, but who on earth sent it? Handwriting's odd. Masked.

—I've been wondering all month, Morgan said. I don't know most of this lot, but I can't help notice one signature missing.

John scoured the columns:

—But why would Riding . . . ?

—I wish I knew, sir. I wish to God . . . there are so many things I wish I knew.

John didn't tell him that the wish would persist, no matter how wise he grew.

—And I haven't seen him all day, Morgan complained.

—In the Tower. Go see him in the morning.

Morgan rubbed knuckles through his hair:

—Fifth aside, how is he? Honestly.

John's eyes flittered.

—It hasn't been an easy—but did I tell you? His mother is remarrying.

Morgan frowned:

—First sensible thing the woman's ever done.

✦

Moss let the other dorms crowd in to see Wilberforce. He captivated them, of course. Oxford, cricket, the ancien régime. The atmosphere was light, but for Moss, strained. Was it so much to ask that Morgan sit there always, pajamas wrinkled, banter flowing? It had gone one o'clock before Moss could peel him away. Down in the study, he uncapped the stout Morgan liked.

—What's this rubbish you've pinned on the walls? Morgan said.

It was only banter, but there was no escaping the sense that the study belonged to Morgan and always would. Morgan's eyes looked tired, and Moss wondered, with a sudden alarm, if Morgan would propose sleep after one drink. Morgan hadn't warned him he was coming—not that he should, they didn't write—but yesterday Grieves had told him and said Wilberforce wanted to sleep in the dorms. To Moss the message was clear enough: Morgan didn't intend to sleep at all. It would be one of those nights. Now, Moss wondered if he'd jumped to conclusions.

It was hotter indoors than out. Moss shed his pajama jacket, and Morgan lounged on the window seat, pressing a bottle against the back of his neck, talking of Corpus, his tutor, the kinds of friends he'd found. A girl, who was vexed with him for coming to Yorkshire instead of to her fête.

—Dodged a bullet, I'd have thought, Moss said.

But Morgan's expression said the opposite was true, though he didn't, it seemed, want to talk about the girl. What he wanted, it seemed, was to defend himself against the accusation, voiced by no one, that he'd shirked duty and loyalty by failing until now to come for Patron's Day. It always fell at the peak of the cricket, he explained, but he knew he'd been a cad not to come, which was why certain people had been reduced to such gestures.

—What are you on about?

When Morgan produced Halton's petition, Moss laughed:

—That wasn't desperation. It was cheek!

Seeing Morgan's confusion, he explained: Riding had not sent the letter. Another boy had, name of Halton.

—Halton? Morgan balked. The pretty thing who sang today?

—The very one.

—Whatever for?

—Do you know, Moss said, I've no earthly idea. Shall we fetch him and see?

Morgan set down the bottle and gave him that grin that always made him—

—You're a piece of work, Morgan said. And madder than ever, Bastable.

◆

Pearce switched on his torch to find the catch in the panel. It knew his penknife as people knew him back home, no matter how long it had been or how much he'd grown. The balcony above the chapel was full of broken chairs, but it knew him, too, kept a place for him, asked him how he'd been. How went the world? How went his project? He aimed to memorize the Bible and had begun last term with Jonah. This term, Malachi, wasn't much longer, but it lacked plot and made him afraid.

They rise and needs will have my dear Lord made away. When they came to that part of the hymn today, there had been a different arrangement that made his chest hurt. Why an execution so gruesome and so shameful? Why crucifixion and not some other death? His slippers were covered in dust after only minutes in the balcony, as if they were made to draw dust to themselves. Was that what God had been doing, drawing out the worst of them, the very worst of their cruel and shabby selves, drawing it out, from the shadows into light, so he could defeat it?

He hadn't been able to talk with Morgan that day beyond the formal put-and-take in front of other people. Lifetimes since they had their little chats. He was not even remotely the same person, and Morgan had never been one for theology. Still, the thought, the hymn, the vision behind his eyes when he'd knocked Moss into the pigeonholes—vision of a priest on a little green island, shepherding its people—it was acting inside him like fizzy drinks in bottles. *Start at the top, Simon. Don't burble.* Morgan would listen, arms crossed in the armchair, and by the time he'd finished explaining, Morgan would be sitting forward, elbows on knees, making it clear he was with him and he wasn't alone anymore. Morgan never said much. He'd nod, repeat a phrase, nod again. By the time the little chat ended, traditionally or not, he'd be calmer, sure.

◆

They'd been at him, two on one, but Halton stood his ground, sweating into his dressing gown.

—Listen here, you little nit.

Wilberforce was annoyed.

—Do you expect me to believe you organized all these signatures—

—I had help—

—Thank you, I'm doing the talking—without discussing it with Grieves or the Head? Then you posted them on and whistled me up here because you *read things and thought I sounded interesting*? Are you completely off your nut?

—Took a JCR whacking for it, Moss said.

—Did he, indeed?

His throat was crammed with rocks. Wilberforce got up from the window seat.

—Listen to what I'm saying, boyo, because I'll only say it once.

His stomach dropped at the name. Wilberforce brought bare toes against his slippers, pajama top tickling his nose:

—I don't think you're telling the truth.

He smelled of sweat, beer, and somehow of Mr. Grieves.

—And you aren't leaving until I hear it. Understand?

He nodded.

—Good.

Wilberforce scraped a chair across the floor and placed it where he'd stood.

—Bastable, drink.

As Wilberforce straddled the chair, eye to eye with him, Moss popped open two bottles. Without releasing his gaze, Wilberforce took a long swig from one and then handed it to him:

—Go on. Guinness is good for you.

A gust blew in the window, and moonlight flooded the room. Wilberforce's eyes looked dark blue. His nose was sunburned. Halton drank, and his voice came in a whisper:

—The moon shines bright, and on such a nightly night—

—What's that?

—from yonder window above the earth, Wilberforce, methinks—

Wilberforce touched the bottle, but didn't take.

—stands full of mirth, awaiting at last the lustrous birth of thee—

Hand on top of his.

—thou ravished bride of quietness.

—You *have* been reading, Wilberforce said.

A noise, and Moss had his arm:

—Where did you hear that?

Squeezing hard, but he was silent.

—You were asked a question, Wilberforce said.

To hold such a one in his power, in his silence.

—Answer, Moss hissed, or so help me I'll—

—What?

—I'll make you wish you never—

Wilberforce pulled Moss away:

—Keep it down.

But then took up Halton's arm and twisted it behind his back:

—D'you know, boyo, there's not a string of muscle in your body? I could squash you like a bug.

The words sounded different spoken out loud.

—I could kill you.

Real.

—One squeeze around that neck, one blow in the right place, you'd be dead. We'd tell them you went mad and killed yourself.

Not a joke.

—They'd believe us.

—They'd want to believe you, he whispered.

Then Moss was on him and he was on the floor. Fists.

—That hurts!

—It'll hurt a lot more, you sneaking bloody cunt!

He yelped. More fists, feet, but then—

—Cunt!

—Keep it down!

Wilberforce dragged Moss to the window seat:

—You may be a prefect, but you aren't too old to have a licking off me. Understand?

Something about the way he said it took all the air away, and Moss put his head in his hands.

—Now . . .

Wilberforce turned and scooped him from the floor:

—No one's going to hurt you. We were only ragging.

Blood poured warm down his chin. He tried to turn away, but Wilberforce took his own pajama jacket and held it against his nose.

—All right, boyo. You're all right.

And something about the way he said that, the softness of his voice, the softness of his arm pressing his head back, fingers pinching his nose, the way they answered every wish—down came the stilts, pier crashed into the sea.

—Steady on.

Clinging, face against his chest, tears and blood, allowed to be the wreck he was, out in the open, blubbing like a fool.

Afterwards, Wilberforce sent Moss to put his things to soak, and when the study door had shut again, Wilberforce picked him up and set him in a chair beside the armchair.

—Now, he said, we're going to have a chat.

He pulled the chair closer and tucked the dressing gown cords around his waist.

—About what you've been reading, and where you've been reading it.

Knowledge reserved for gods only, but once asked, he spoke, changing in a breath from guard to destroyer. Things written, things hidden, he told them all to the one they concerned. Wilberforce said nothing. After, he still said nothing.

Halton had known bullies and confronted a few. They were never silent. Moss's reaction proved the box was as damning as it seemed, but Wilberforce . . . Proved, not proved. All this and clear as mud.

✦

The potted tongue yesterday had looked dubious. It might also have tasted dubious, but Gray had been too hungry to care. As soon as he awoke, he knew what was wrong. Kardleigh probably thought he was malingering; in the afternoon, he'd tried to get him to come down for the cricket, but Gray had mumbled in the negative and clutched the mattress. That bottom-of-a-well feeling when everyone else was having fun, but all you cared about was when your guts would come up again.

Poor Gracey Pissant, whatever shall she do?
Her parents were devoured by a rhino in the zoo.
He ate her mum, he ate her dad, he quaffed her sisters three
But Gracey followed after crying, What was wrong with me?

The wooden bed, its pillars and roof, closed around his father, the Lord's anointed temple broke ope', life of the building stolen. He looked as he had looked when sleeping, but his cheek, when Gray touched it, felt wrong.

People crowded to see him, crushing Gray in their embrace as if death canceled manners. They wept over what the doctor Riding had done for them. Cotton headed, like sitting up all night but lasting the week until they put him in the ground.

They'd get by, his mother said. He could get by without a father, he supposed, people did. (But this was not other fathers! He was not other men!) The truth, he explained to himself in the lane outside the church- yard, was that he'd been doing without him all summer. All summer his father had lain in that bed, waging war, they said, against the thing in- side him. The truth: it tore him down, day by day.

The sun did not stop rising. Breakfasts appeared. He lived without the father. Later, he began to realize everything he'd lost.

—This says late for call-over.

—I was getting the biscuits you asked for.

—We all have duties, boyo. I, for one, have the thankless duty of doing something about your docket. Third this week.

—But—

—Let's just get it over with.

Stabs turned violent, stomach pouring onto study floor, deus ex machina night in the Tower.

—

Ordinary people got buried where they lived. Instead, funeral grotesque: loading the box onto a train, further trains, cart, to mis-locate it north. She said the Ridings were all buried at Sledmere, but they'd never mentioned it, let alone brought him to see. They lowered the box into mud, vicar alien, umbrellas useless against the gale. A wicked place to leave him, all alone with strangers.

—Failure to wipe basins properly, this says.
　—They were wiped properly when I left.
　—And is the House now to be run on your satisfaction?
　Never peach. Moss's rules.
　—What if you did the basins . . . but then someone came along and mucked them on purpose? And you couldn't do them again or you'd be late?
　—Easy.
　Peasy?
　—Take the late, do 'em again, scrub the bogs with his toothbrush.
　—Ha!
　—You're welcome. Now touch your toes.
　Laughter turning again to sick—
　—Bloody hell, boyo.
　Safe again in the ribs of the Tower.

Later, trains and further trains dragged him to banishment. When they pulled alongside the same platform, he shivered. A bitter joke? Only four months since they'd come there with the box.
　—Are we going to . . .
　How to put it, visiting the grave?
　—We're late, his mother said. Another time.
　Facts were catching up with him: they'd come to Sledmere and Fimber not for the churchyard in Sledmere, but for the Academy near Fimber.
　—Did you pick it on purpose?
　—Stop being unpleasant.
　In the cab:
　—It's an excellent school. You'll get on. Thank your uncle.
　Who selected schools for their proximity to graves?

Once there was a little funk who couldn't tie his shoes.
He had no mum or dad to write him an excuse.

—Wherever, Riding, did you learn how to spell?
—Not my forte, sir, I'm afraid.
—Why didn't you look the words out? the Eagle asked.
He didn't dare admit that he'd thought they were correct.
—They call me the Eagle not merely for the spectacles, but also, I believe, for a certain predatory drive.
—Sir?
—Spelling test, tomorrow. Page six and onwards, every half holiday until further notice.

—There's a rat in *separate*. Say it.
He did.
—Emma faced a dilemma.
—Poor Emma.
—You'll scratch through, boyo.
Morgan set aside the spelling primer:
—Now, about the other thing.

There once was a sod called Elf Rider
Who guzzled a gallon of cider
He farted some brass, right out of his arse
And said, I'm my own best provider!

—You have to face it sometime.
—I'll be more careful. Try harder.
Morgan pulled up a chair.
—Listen to me, boyo.
Straddling, eye to eye.
—No one gets through this place without getting whacked. It isn't possible.
So far . . . ?
—It isn't that bad. Not as bad as you think.
He wasn't that bad. That was why he'd never had it. Mistakes, yes. Unpleasant at worst, sent away until nicer. He wasn't bad. Not like other children.

—

The broth made him gag, and his guts turned again.

—That must have been some potted tongue.

Kardleigh held the pan, but mention of it prolonged the heaving, until his eyes flooded down his face. Kardleigh took the pan away and returned with something milky:

—Try to swallow that. Nothing for it but time.

Orders of magnitude more severe, Grieves's arm. Given without quarter. Smiting, not ministry. To think of what he wasted fighting Morgan as long as he did. So long dodging a paper sword, so long refusing what later left too soon. The first time—Morgan's patience expired, dragged to the study, given with the palm of his hand—he'd been shocked more than hurt, yet he kept fighting even as Morgan pulled him up by the elbow:

—Something to say?

—Sod off, you bloody wank!

Morgan kept holding, with a look that saw all, gave all:

—Thank you. You say, thank you.

◆

The clock in the Tower hauled them forward gear by gear. It tolled four, and blood came into the sky. He and Morgan mounted the stone stairs to the passage above the chapel and then, iron ladder, untangled the chain to the hatch. Moss hadn't been up on the roof in years, not since the last time with Morgan. Inside him was an ache, a craving still, and he felt how much he missed what they did, how habit-forming it had always been. Then came the blade, the realization that this would be the last time, last hungry good. And the last chance, on this roof, to say what he owed Morgan to say:

—I've never, you know. Not to anyone.

So much that was real had no words to describe it.

—I know, Morgan said.

—Never spoken, much less written.

—I know.

—So, how did Halton . . . ?

Morgan flicked his cigarette over the edge:

—He read something.

It fell to the walk; they'd have to fetch it back.

—Of Riding's, Morgan said.

—Riding? You and *Riding*?

—Please.

—I knew you were close, but—

—What do you take me for? Morgan said.

—Then how on earth could Riding . . . ?

Morgan lay back and covered his face:

—And he got it all wrong!

—Halton?

—*Riding*. A misunderstanding. A ludicrous, logical misunderstanding. If only the life, if only the cake . . .

—And now it all makes terrible sense.

If only it all were dough again.

✦

She was awake when Jamie opened his eyes, and she put her mouth on him. If every waking could be like this, he'd get her children until they had nowhere to put them. It felt like those times, lost behind the veil, when they could have devoured each other all the day and still be left hungry.

✦

—Why don't you go see Riding in the Tower, Moss said.

—Wouldn't know where to start.

—Suit yourself.

—Besides which, do you know what else your friend Halton told me?

—I've had about enough of that cunt.

Morgan gave him a clip for old time's sake:

—He reminds me of you.

—I wasn't that pretty.

His arm itched. He unbuckled his wristwatch and scratched until it was raw.

—I suppose I might have been almost as much trouble.

Morgan took his wrist and rubbed away the marks:

—Halton said that Riding wasn't really ill. Said he makes himself sick, does it on purpose.

Moss suppressed a curse. He was sick of Halton, sick of Riding, too. Both were spoiled and deserved what they got.

—How does Halton know so bloody much anyhow? Does he peep through keyholes, or what?

They climbed up the leads and negotiated the hatch. He tied up the chain, and at the bottom of the ladder, Morgan took his arm:

—Wait.

They couldn't do it there, but in the study, once more, if they hurried?

—What if, Morgan said, young Halton's not the only one at keyholes?

The picture bloomed, in all its idiocy.

—Riding? Through a *keyhole*?

—He saw, he heard, but he got it all wrong. Completely arse-over-elbows wrong.

 Fünfundzwanzig Juni, Bavaria—Dear Uncle John, We're leaving Bad Wörishofen for Budapest tomorrow. Hymanfinger has arranged for Mum to be treated by Dr. Zoltan Zarday. Perhaps you've heard of him, the celebrated Persuasionist? His remedy consists of a series of talks with the patient. He asks questions and then explains the cause of the disease. The force of his logic is said to persuade people back to health. It sounds unmedical, I admit, but the results speak for themselves. Mum feels certain he can cure her. In any case we can learn Hungarian. I'm getting perfectly tired of Wie lange sind Sie schon hier? Also, I believe Zoltan Zarday is a Friend.

◆

It was five days before food stayed down. Kardleigh insisted there had been no post for him, though of course there was prep. Moss brought him books from his cupboard, things he'd tracked down on her mention but not yet read. The Ash Wednesday poem made no sense, but it caused him to shed tears, such was his weakness. As for Miss Sayers, he'd never heard of the woman, but if her Lord Peter could turn a jailhouse interview to seduction, what could really be impossible?

Upon release from the Tower, he found only one letter in his pigeonhole, from his mother. Three days were the longest he'd gone without hearing from the girl; now six? Stepping on the bottom row, he reached for the back of his pigeonhole. There had always been a gap, but was it wider? He sought out Fardley. There was a chink, he explained, between his pigeonhole and the wall. Was it possible anything had fallen? Fardley stiffened: There was nothing skew-whiff about pigeonholes. Attached to wall. Wouldn't move until the Day of Judgment. The end of time. Fardley had a line in repetitions, but just as the man searched for another apocalypse, inspiration struck and he shifted his fish and chips, revealing the tray for Grieves's evening post. If the young master had exercised a bit of patience, Fardley said, he would have found his pigeonhole full in less than an hour, for here were three, correction four, letters to his name.

The library stairs taxed his strength. He sat by the window, breathless.

The first two were dated four days earlier, the third and fourth afterwards. She'd changed to envelopes bearing a stripe. Both of the earliest began in medias res—which the first? All postmarked Budapest and concerning, it seemed, the fabled Zoltan Zarday.

He said he was leaving in ten days' time for a lecturing tour, but the treatment takes two months, at minimum.

It took persuasion to get past his secretary, a young man with some French. (If the girl had unleashed a fraction of the whirlwind she'd been at the Academy, Gray reckoned the lad had little chance.)

My mother would be a quick patient, Dr. Zarday. She has experience with persuasion.

(Asterisk, to her correspondent: Friends were called Quakers, which was what her family were. They operated by persuasion.)

Can you see, now, why I knew Zoltan Zarday was the one?

The Hungarian resisted, but she was up to the challenge. If he could not accept her mother, she asked that he refer them to another persuasionist. Alas, he replied, he was unique, which was why his schedule did not permit—

222

*She could come anytime, I said, day or night. I confessed I'd taken
a horrible gamble, that when Mum had learned the Kneipping was
a failure, she wanted to go home, and the only way I could get her
to try Budapest was to tell a little (well, substantial) lie and say my
godfather had written him and that he'd agreed to take her on.*

The next envelope picked up with descriptions of a consulting room,
a high-ceilinged apartment on the first floor, oil paintings, a tiled stove
diffusing the last of the day's heat. She described the man's inscrutable
response to her throwing down the gauntlet and more or less insulting
him (in another post?); their adjournment to a *cukrászda* (meaning?) that
overlooked the Danube; crimson chairs in wrought-iron, a table covered
in crumbs (café?).

Have you ever tasted Hungarian kavet, Miss Líoht?

She asked him to call her Cordelia. His closest friends, he said, called
him Zarday. (Where were her mother and governess at the time?) He
smoked a pipe: description, accouterments. He discoursed: *we Magyars*
this, *we Magyars* that; a castle that withstood Tartars, Turks, and even
the feeble plot of Bela Kun (cracking name for a villain, noted); Matyas
Cathedral made mosque by the Ottomans (Had she taken notes or
was this from memory?), now finally restored. There, statue of Saint
Stephen—martyr? No, king. Coffee, pastries (names, she confessed,
copied later from a menu); how to drink *kavet*: in tiny glasses, all at once,
with a toast, Eggy-Sah-Gara.
Letter three broke off there. She couldn't have teased him more if
she tried. The tea bell rang. He ignored it. Letter four:

*There's a constant ache in my ribs. You'd laugh if you saw me. Here
she is finally being treated by Zoltan Zarday, we're in the most beautiful city, and all I can think of is my grandparents' cottage in Drayton Fen where we lived when I was small. There was a smell in the
air a few nights ago, near the river, that reminded me, and now all
I want is England.*

They were doing bits of *The Odyssey* in Greek. *Nostos*, homecoming;
nostalgia, longing for same.

223

The way I see it, we'll be home before summer's end, I'll go back to school, and Da will have been frightened enough that he'll come home and be good to her. He loves her better when he's been away, and if she would only believe in him, everything would work out.

Up the side margin:

I think there's a good chance I can make this happen.

Page two, dated next morning:

I keep imagining you reaching into your pigeonholes and taking down my letters. You hide them in those secret pockets of your jacket until you can sneak up to our Chair Loft. Sometimes I read my horrible script and try to imagine you looking at it. Deciphering? Scornful of its mess? Can you smell the sausages they make in the restaurant downstairs? What about my mother's verbena toilet water? What becomes of my letters once you've read them? I suppose they start to smell of mildew and cabbage. I still haven't been able to eat cabbage (was it called chin flab??) since. And I haven't laughed like that.

The papers she touched could escape Budapest; for the price of a stamp, they chugged to the sea, boarded a packet across the Channel and the night mail to Yorkshire, where Fardley's stained fingers sorted them by House. The words her pen had scraped into the page, thoughts captured by the swirl of her ink, these alone had a passport to *nostos*.

✦

Uncle John, You're making my work more difficult than ever. I've stopped showing her the articles you send. The Lancet put her into tears most of the evening! She already has Miss Murgatroyd pestering her. (I can tell you've been writing her, too, though she won't admit it.) Whatever it is that you're trying to accomplish, please stop, if only for my sake.

John had written his publisher and negotiated terms for delivery: excerpt in September, finished manuscript by April. Arguments could be revived, new evidence sought, fresh avenues explored. Chaos might drive war, politics, and human intercourse, but it need not prevail everywhere.

You mustn't believe a thing Miss M says. She distrusts Zoltan Zarday because Mum is usually in a delicate state when she returns from her treatment, but it's helping her. You must trust me. She has more energy than she's had in weeks and most importantly, she adores him.

He had never tolerated drivel from his students, even from the thickest of the Third, and he would not tolerate it elsewhere. If necessary, he would begin the book over from scratch. If necessary, he would write ten letters a day across the Channel. If necessary, he would forgo sleep entirely.

I can't believe you'd take Miss M's word over mine! Zoltan Zarday is a gifted physician. He has not "exerted unfair influence over an infirm woman." And he most certainly never "brainwashed" me in our first meeting!

Term finished in less than three weeks. He would prepare his reports in advance and take the first train south.

I know Miss Murgatroyd is respectable and well meaning, but if only you could see the change in Mum since we've come to Budapest, you'd believe in Zoltan Zarday. He's a good man. I mean a man actually filled with goodness. He wears a thick beard like a Viking. She likes to tease him about it, and today she told him she was going to bring soap and razor to shave it herself. Apparently his reply was, "You like boyish men, Margaret?"

He would leave behind the pitiful reserve that had shackled him, the pigeonhearted tact, the failure of nerve. He'd arrive on their doorstep and set down his bags. He would speak, and they would listen!

◆

I suppose it was inevitable, Tommy Gray.

225

It had become habit—letters daily, begun any which place.

Miss M unveiled <u>her</u> diagnosis today: auto-intoxication, brought on by a weak colon. She and my mother are so churlish with one another. My mother wouldn't care a fig for M's opinion if it didn't include criticism of ZZ, who we all know is holier than St. Matyas.

Miss M had called the girl naive and deluded. He nearly gasped reading it. Who would dare?

"Cordelia, dear, philosophies like those of Zoltan Zarday are the product of unhealthy dissipations. What those people call Internal Consciousness is nothing more than a gruesome and abnormal self-absorption."

Even his mother would loathe this old trout. He burned to give her a piece of his mind.

✦

Uncle John, There is no need to <u>think</u> of coming to Budapest! What does it matter whether Hymanfinger recommended Dr. Zarday or not? Mum's eating more than ever, and in three days we'll be moving on to Switzerland, where she'll be under the <u>constant</u> supervision of a <u>renowned</u> medical staff. In the third place, it would give her a desperate scare if you dropped everything and came here. She'd think she was dying!

✦

A bargain had been struck with the Hungarian, or so he gathered (lost lacuna?). Zoltan Zarday had made arrangements for them to take the Cure at a sanatorium convenient to his lecture tour (not, please God, near Hans Castorp). He had promised to pass by and see his patient, but now, it seemed, the indomitable Miss Murgatroyd had made her last stand. Mrs. Líoht must be told the truth about the Hungarian's qualifications, Miss M insisted. She must be told that dear Mr. Grieves had not recommended him. If necessary, Miss M would summon Mr. Grieves herself.

The installment ended abruptly, and he had to wait two days for a short page, backdated, describing not her clash with the governess, but her tour of local houses of worship. *I went to three churches today, even a Jewish one.* She didn't explain what she'd done in those places except to say she was listening for messages. Three churches that day, two the day before, but no Almighty wire.

The envelopes lost their stripe and acquired Swiss postage. *Would you know, Tommy Gray, it happened just as it always does when you most need help.* At the Gellert Baths (Budapest), she'd discovered a leaflet in English. The governess, in turn, read it with relish, and its essay by an English physician expressed her views to a T. With it, Miss M approached her employer. *"For example, Margaret dear, here is some literature about a simple home remedy, Carmola, recommended by a Dr. Light, guaranteed to resolve digestive ripples within two days."* The mother thought it a cruel joke and responded in kind. *Elle a reçu leur congé.* (Footnote, in pencil—Carmola Ltd her father's business, Carmola his product though he'd never touch it himself; of course he wasn't a physician, but you had to say so in the medicine business.) The governess was bewildered. *Elle a fondu en larmes.* She never understood the bait she'd taken. *Elle était mise au vert.* She failed to recognize English spellings of Irish surnames. *Elle est maintenant hors de page.* She failed to recognize the assassin's knife when wielded by a girl she thought innocent. *J'en ai fait mon deuil.* The mother's position, Gray thought, was like Hans Castorp's sled. *Il n'y a si bonne compagnie qui ne se quitte.* High on a slope skidding down to a grave.

◆

The Gimmelwald Heilanstalt, John gathered, was the genuine article. His goddaughter's handwriting had come under control, and Meg wrote him three lines daily. Their calm prose calmed him in turn: The establishment perched on a cliff in the Alps. From any window, gray-and-white granite reared into the clouds. At night, the air hissed with waterfalls. A godly, righteous, and sober life after all the mess. Absent the governess, recalled home by family crisis, his goddaughter had become her mother's companion, more sister, she claimed, than daughter. She was on hand during the indoctrination. She took notes at lectures on Right Living. She reminded her mother how long to inhale, how quickly to exhale, what position to assume while breathing, how many layers of rug to maintain around which limbs. She chided her for sitting indoors, a vice apparently known as Being Unfaithful to the Cure. The hours were the hours of childhood in that regime whose sole aim appeared to be the pacification of the physical machine.

> *The weather here is splendid. Everything is tidy and correct. We have hopes for a rapid recovery. The San director has a fondness for maxims, but even if il m'agace les dents, it's a small sacrifice for so great a cure. Until tomorrow, Uncle John, chew your food.*

✦

> *July 13, night—Sometimes I'm afraid that I don't quite love her. Sometimes I want to strike her, or cut her, though <u>of course</u> I love her, more than myself!*

Script small as a whisper:

> *Today I thought what a relief it will be to stay in one place when she dies.*

Large and shouting:

> *I can't believe I even wrote those words. I deserve not to have a mother.*

The yellow Swiss letters seemed too poisonous to keep, but what could be done with them? If he burned them, their ash would drift into the air, and if caught by a wind, return to her. If he buried them like a mummy, protected them with a curse, who could say some enterprising robber wouldn't dig them up again? What chemistry made dynamite inert?

> *July 17, dawn—There's an American doctor everyone whispers about, a man called Felix Rush, just as notorious as you'd imagine. Dr. Himenflingher once said he's no better than an exterminator. He has a new treatment called Penicillin, which has cured many things but which Himenflingher said has a 98 percent chance of killing you first. You can see Dr. Rush on the front of this month's Journal de Médecine. Khaki trousers, wilderness, caption: Aux grands maux les grands remèdes.*

Great ills, great remedies.

4pm east wing toilet—This morning she had another attack, brought on by her first evaluation. They said she'd made no progress and that it was her fault for resisting the Cure. She made me wire Zoltan Zarday, but there's been no reply. After lunch, she announced we were leaving, and then, while she was arranging the train, the San director called me into his office and said if she didn't commit to perfect rest she would be dead in six weeks! She says if she doesn't hear from Zoltan Zarday by suppertime, we'll go to Felix Rush in Paris. She's a young woman!

✦

King's Lynn, Norfolk, 22 July—My dear Crusoe, The enclosed parcel should address some of your questions. The volumes belong to one of our junior surgeons, but there's no rush to return. You may be vexed that I've taken the liberty, but as my son likes to say, hard cheese. You can pay me back by finishing your book.

Will you be at the same address during the holidays? Our own will be sadly curtailed this year. We've always gone with my family to Norway for the month of August, but this year my father (having retired from work and left the family business in my brother's unreliable hands) has insisted on taking my mother around the Aegean. Thus, we'll be spending the holidays at home, the boy no doubt brooding, but I within reach of my husband's library, which may well contain materials of use. (Don't bother protesting, I shall send what I see fit.) Perhaps you'd come down and cheer us up for a time, or at least sort the boy out?

I was sorry not to be able to come north for your Patron's Day celebrations, and your descriptions of the day have only increased my regret. The Wilberforce you mention, is he the same whose exploits on the cricket pitch are peppering the newspapers? I do recall that my son was very fond of him. He must have written to Wilberforce every day of his first holiday home. I remember thinking how absurd it was that, after all the fuss about wanting to be removed, he then couldn't seem to tear himself away. Wilberforce wrote to him a good deal as well, if I recall, but by the summer holidays the friendship had faded. I do hope his studies this term have improved him.

A repetition of Easter would be more than I could bear. I've no idea how you tolerate boys of this age, though I suppose men have their methods unknown to mothers, and rightly so. Whatever the case, and whatever the temper, I await your next and remain, your faithful, Friday.

John finished his coffee both pleased and uneasy at this first of two morning letters. Her parcel contained three books and several journals, all of which he'd have to skim and return before his departure tomorrow. His term reports lay finished on the desk. Tomorrow night he would board the train and travel to wherever this latest envelope detailed. He'd thought to save it for later, but perhaps before lessons there was just enough time . . .

Uncle John, Of course, there was a telephone at the San, but patients weren't allowed to use it. At any rate, we've left Switzerland and are sightseeing on the Continent. We're quite fed up with doctors, and before you say it, Mum hasn't resigned herself to anything. We've decided to travel "impromptu" for a time, so I can't give you an address beyond the poste restante below. Sorry we can't join up with you next week, but Mum is in good hands. Please don't worry. Cordelia.

p.s. John, darling, everything is well. Will write in a few weeks. Try to be cheerful and enjoy the summer holidays. Love, Meg.

He shoved the letter under the blotter as if leather could silence its contents. Could she really slip again from his—a dose was needed, something from the decanter on a spoon to see him through the morning. It wasn't his practice, but desperate times . . .

The day stretched before him, a tiresome, severe suspense. The headache threatened again as John began his last lesson, a presentation with photographs to the Fifth on recent excavations in Minos. He had looked forward to it for some time, but when the hour came, the material felt as dry and irrelevant as Ozymandias. He mentally indexed, as boys asked questions, through his diary in search of someone he could ring, wire, write, some tendril he could send out to retrieve them. After lessons he jostled through the crowds to his study, bargaining with the Almighty if he still existed. If he would deliver them both safely to John's hands, John would remain forever faithful—to the woman, to the girl. He would break off all other correspondences. He would dedicate himself to their protection, expecting nothing in return. He would embrace the life of an ascetic, if only, if only . . .

✦

The end-of-term speeches were interminable, so Moss stood with Carter in the narthex, scrounging breeze as it came. Carter and Swinton were leaving, and Moss had been promoted to Head Boy.

—You're a natural, Carter said. They'll follow you. But when you're Head of House you can't have grudges.

Moss knew he was blushing; it never looked good on him.

—I gave you dorms last night, Carter said, because of your—

—I'd've volunteered anyway—

—your *thing* with him.

—Please.

Halton had landed himself in hot water on the very last evening of term. Crighton claimed it was deliberate, a transparent plea for the attention Moss had denied him since Patron's Day.

—You weren't there, Carter said. You didn't see how desperate he—

—Don't tell me.

—Halton's a good egg. He could do a lot for the House. But if you don't throw him a bone, I reckon he'll make your life hell.

✦

—And so I charge you, Jamie was saying, to recall Whitman's words as you leave us, some for a short while, some for longer, and go the unknown ways, O Pioneers, our Pioneers!

*Hear-hear*s flooded the chapel as John watched from the alcove. Jamie looked as he always did, radiant and easy. The organ began, and the back of his throat yearned for the drop that would calm it. How was it that love should settle in him so fiercely and unsuitably? To be sure, the life of a monk—bachelor schoolmaster, what difference?—was his only recourse now.

✦

Gray set his tuck box in the quad to await the next fleet of station cabs. *All the pulses of the world, all the joyous, all the sorrowing, these are of us,*

231

they are with us; we to-day's procession heading, we the route for travel clearing. He would be clearing no routes. Norway, steamships, midnight sun with the London cousins—canceled. His procession headed only to Swan Cottage and the woman marrying his godfather, the woman whose vapid correspondence was an offense to real letters. Six weeks without one? Six weeks of purgatory, and at such a juncture! It was like reading three-quarters of a Dickens novel and then having it snatched away just as the plot had begun to unwind.

Fardley emerged from the House—carrying an empty mail tray. Hermes! Good Hermes did not forget his heir, but winged on the last breath with one final gift . . . Pigeonholes, envelope—France! He ran for the cab, and at the station boarded a carriage with boys he knew lived north. They got off at Selby, and at last he ran his knife beneath the blessed blue flap:

Paris—TG, If ever you were my friend, you'll do as I ask and tell no one. The train leaves soon which will take us to Le Havre, and from there to New York, America. Dr. Felix Rush has a clinic in Asheville, North Carolina, where my mother will begin treatment at once. If only Zoltan Zarday had answered our wire! I'd thought, once, that he was different, and for a while he actually seemed it, but when I think of him now with his kavet, his beard, his old-fashioned bowler hat, I almost—oh, forget it, he doesn't matter anymore.

Be on the lookout for a parcel I posted through the morning mail. I rescued the contents from a rubbish bin and cannot keep them, for obvious reasons. If I have any favors left with you, I ask this: write to my neighbor Mrs. Kneesworth (The Grange, Museum Street, Saffron Walden, Essex) and tell her what has occurred. In case you are tempted to speak to my godfather, don't. I will write him once we arrive safely in America. If I had the time, I would write a book to you, my truest, most trusted friend, but as the cab is here, goodbye will have to do. My best wishes and most sincere thanks. With love.

SUMMER

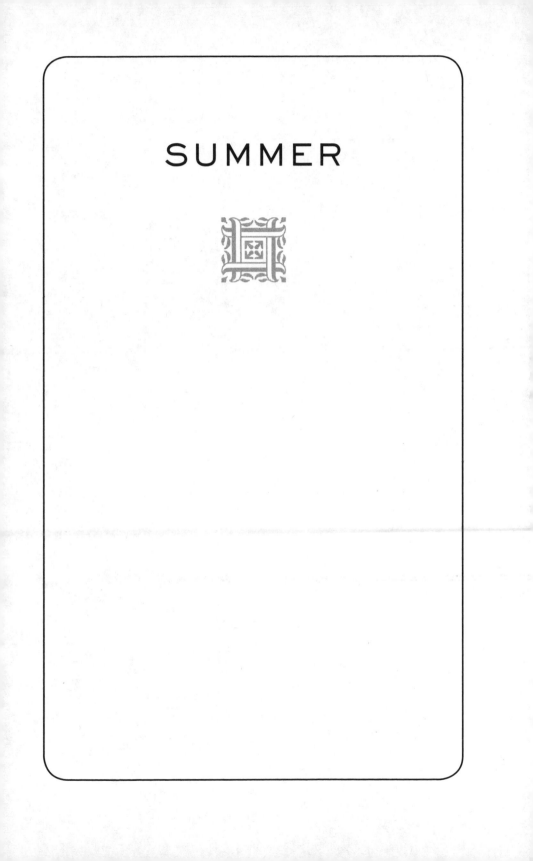

29 Jamie had promised to take Marion away as soon as the boys had gone. *Nowhere foreign*, she'd said. *Surprise me.* He longed for something like the holidays they'd had in the beginning, and though he couldn't exactly take her back to those places, he settled on the Lakes for its scenery and novelty. On Lockett-Egan's advice, Jamie booked them into the Swan Hotel, Grasmere. They must try the gingerbread, the Eagle said. He himself still longed for it.

After a first night spent passed out from exhaustion, they woke to a misty July morning, like the kind they'd had on their first holiday years ago, and just as cold. Marion seemed as attuned to it as he was, and later, in the privacy of the room, it almost seemed that they could go back to the start. Once, he thought he saw in the squint of her eye the girl she had been when he first met her, and he had to fight against the urge to call her by the name she had used then. He wondered if it was too much to hope that he would get a second chance, a chance to get right all the things he had got wrong. Seeing that girl clearly now in her eyes across the pillow, he was cold afraid, even as his mouth watered.

That night he awoke in the dark and she was there, calling him by the name she used to have for him. He put his mouth on her and had her, and she had him, letting out a sound that made him harder even as he wondered if they'd hear across the corridor. She was shuddering still when he'd done, and they lay there, clinging to each other. He didn't want that girl to vanish, but he couldn't hold his tongue: *They*

235

said you were dead. She pulled his arm around her, only he could feel it was Marion now in his arms. He asked her what had happened just then, and she drew him tighter. *It was a dream,* she whispered, *only a dream.* He had spoiled it, his words no less destructive than spells that made kingdoms vanish with a breath.

Still, something in Marion was awake. She laughed and was more daring—the stray remark, the feel-around beneath the counter as they waited for the gingerbread, and then outdoors on the banks of the tarn, she unbuttoned him and teased him until people appeared and they had to arrange themselves. Later, as they lay together on top of the sheets, afternoon sunshine baking the room, she said she wished it could always be this way. *It could!* he said, running his fingers over her. They should make a pact, he said, never to do it from duty again. If things happened, then they happened, but if they didn't, what would stop them from adopting? Thousands of children this very day wanted a home. Why should they— She stopped him talking with her mouth and then went to have a bath.

Later, when he himself returned from the bath, having shaved in anticipation of their dinner in the good restaurant, he found the bedroom empty. A note had been propped on his pillow: *Arthur's Seat, sunset. Ask and I shall answer.*

He rang the restaurant to cancel the booking and asked his landlord for a flask of tea. He got to the top of the fell just before sunset and waited there more than an hour, but she never came. Miraculously he did not turn his ankle descending in the dark, but by the time he'd got back and roused the landlord, his nerves were bad. The landlord seemed to think he was drunk; he said Marion had left with her case not long after Jamie had gone out. She had claimed he'd be joining her at the weekend.

The next stretch was better forgotten. By the time he arrived at his father's house two days later, having driven all the way to Oxford and turned the town upside down looking for her, he'd never felt more deranged, at least not in the present era, and had been forced to confide in his father. He couldn't tell him everything, of course, but the confession was difficult to control once it began. They seemed to sit in the summerhouse an age, and he was on the verge of tears from the start, as much for Marion's present flight as for the one it resembled. His father seemed to understand his terror, and unlike other times, the man did not scold. He brought Jamie back several times to the subject of adoption, a dis-

236

cussion the Bishop did not disapprove but one he seemed to think germane. When Jamie asked point-blank if he had chased her away with his suggestion, his father insisted he extinguish such thoughts. Her flight had little to do with Jamie, the Bishop thought, and much to do with things he couldn't understand. He must be patient. It was no good looking for people who didn't want to be found.

Jamie didn't know how long he could carry on, and the cruel part of holidays was their endless leisure. A fortnight passed, but at last the Lord took pity. Jamie was summoned to the study, where his father was mercifully blunt: she was in Oxford, had been there all along. His father—no explanation—had sent flowers to the print shop. Once they'd been accepted, he had rung. She wouldn't come to the telephone, but on the second call she did. There was nothing physically wrong with her. Her mind was sound enough. She simply couldn't speak with her husband. No, he hadn't mistreated her. No, she didn't mean to leave him. No, he mustn't come or she would find it imperative to flee. Jamie had sat flabbergasted in his father's spindle chair: Why should the Bishop have thought to send flowers, and send them there? Jamie's father deflected every question, handling him gently, as an injured animal, but when Jamie's temper returned and he made to bolt for Oxford and confront her, his father unwrapped the steel fist: He would not go there. He would not pursue her. He would get into his motorcar and return to Yorkshire. If, after a week, he had heard nothing, he would write her a simple letter. No dramatics. Like an ordinary holiday. That was the Bishop's word.

◆

The assignment in the girl's final missive was harder than it had appeared. *Write to my neighbor Mrs. Kneesworth and tell her what has occurred.* Why, Gray wondered, should this woman need telling? Why, second, could the girl not write herself? Third, how was Gray to introduce himself to the woman? The more he thought of it, the more traps he saw. He intended to write on his first day home, but he'd come down with a cold, and as he reread her letter to the point of memory, he could not escape its essential humiliation. People who went to America never returned; therefore, she considered him finished, a pawn to be disposed in a final maneuver—write this neighbor, say this thing, then adieu, my dearest friend. Once America had its claws in her, she would forget he ever existed, just as she would forget their little island. Poor old England-land! Its pebble shores, its heartsick fields, its Kentish lanes full of holes.

◆

Her son went out on the bicycle rain or shine, packing things for a lunch and not returning until tea. It spared them mutual vexation and left time for the project she determined to conquer that summer. She'd kept the surgery closed all these years, and although it had taken time to work up the nerve to unlock it, she now adhered to a firm routine for its clearing out. Tom's library proved useful, and having posted two volumes to her correspondent, she developed an appetite for sending things away. Other items she marked for donation to the hospital in King's Lynn. Tom's handwriting, when she encountered it, took the strength from her, and at the end of her shifts, she had to lie down. The weeds in the garden, too, were getting out of hand, but she was only one person.

◆

John smoked out the library window, watching the puddles steam. The shower had only made the heat more oppressive. The trestle tables behind him were littered with his work and with things he'd left off eating. No one tidied the library, and no piece of mess moved unless he moved it, except now—a bang, and a gust—

—There you are!

Jamie's voice echoed down the gallery. He stood in the doorway, suntanned and brimming with vigor. John looked for somewhere to conceal his cigarette.

—You're coming with me, Jamie declared. I won't take no for an answer.

The weather was perfect for a walking tour, Jamie said, not far, just locally. When John said he'd have to take no for an answer, Jamie bounded down the room:

—Up you get. Do you the world of good. Enough living on tea and tinned herring.

He was seizing him by the collar:

—Back in a few days. Plenty of time then for your book.

At the stairs, John extracted himself from Jamie's grip. The air was thick. There was a glare. He tried to think of another way to refuse.

238

—What's the word from your goddaughter? Jamie asked.

John had to admit there had been none. A look of pain came across Jamie's face, and he touched John's hand, which John realized was still holding the cigarette.

—Nothing's going to happen to her in a few short days, Jamie said. Perhaps when we get back there will even be news.

Jamie took a drag on John's cigarette and coughed.

—You don't mess about. These'll kill you.

John replied by lighting another.

—Father asked after you again, Jamie continued.

—He what?

—Gave me a dressing down for having left you here alone. Oh, do come walking. Just the two of us.

They were alone in the cloisters, the school vacant, Jamie's wife absent. With each breath John felt the wall of words between them, unspoken yet known.

The next morning, they took the train to Scarborough and set off by foot up the coast, turning inland at Robin Hood's Bay to follow the northern edge of the moors. They found accommodation in cottages, usually sharing a bed. Jamie slept in what Mrs. Firth would have called his all-together, which made John feel prudish in his pajamas. Added to that, Jamie slept in a contorted position and thrashed in his sleep, once waking John by poking him in the chest like some sleepwalking grim reaper. When John told him about it the next day, Jamie refused to believe it had happened.

The few days' jaunt turned to several. There was leisure in conversation they hadn't felt in years, the freedom to talk or be silent, time to discuss the school, politics, the careers of former pupils, including their protégé Morgan Wilberforce. John's account of his research and his book prompted Jamie to rehash his own doctorate, and great stretches of Eskdale were taken up with casuistry. Jamie did not dwell on his stay at the Rectory, a delicacy John appreciated. It seemed Marion was stopping with her people, and on his way back to the Academy, Jamie had paid a visit to Arents, the geezer he'd met at Ali's funeral and charmed into buying the Academy a new organ. Arents had shown Jamie sketches for the instrument, but after raising Jamie's spirits, he had subsequently dashed them by revealing just how long the installation would take and how much disruption the chapel would have to endure. John hoped the scheme would die a quiet death and save the old organ the indignity of being stripped out, its case left empty for months as if a troop of Round-heads had sacked it.

Each day, John made a point of finding a post office and placing a call to the Academy. His matron, now returned, reported no letters from abroad, and her tone made it clear she disapproved of profligate telephone calls. On the sixth evening, though, she announced a postcard, photograph of a cathedral, edge chewed, May the fourteenth: *Thinking of you, love Cordelia.*

—That's it? he asked.

She cursed foreigners and their foreign post.

As John emerged into the road, he found Jamie leaning against the wall and penciling a postcard himself.

—News? Jamie asked.

—Yes. That is, no . . .

John described the damaged postcard, sent months before. They traversed a stile and at the top of the field stopped to catch their breath.

—It's no good, Jamie said, looking for people who don't want to be found.

Heat rushed through him.

—I'd have thought that was more your friend Merewether's line, Jamie continued. Wouldn't you?

With this, Jamie set off across the ridge. John followed, crushing a fistful of rebuttals. It was easy for Jamie to say, who had a wife that clung to him like a limpet and behaved like a bull terrier to anyone who came near; whose mother died before he was old enough to remember; whose place in the world had been carved in oak since birth; who waltzed from post to post, including Headmaster before he'd managed so much as a dorm round; who'd never been compelled to pursue an infernally elusive cure.

—You probably don't want to hear this, Jamie said.

The air blew warm across the tops as they picked their way through the spongy ground.

—She's right as rain, Jamie said. Otherwise, you'd have heard from her.

The peat looked firm, but John's boot sank.

—You're the first person she turns to when things go wrong, Jamie continued. And when the sun is shining, she forgets you exist.

Cold peat was running into his socks.

—It's much more complicated than that.

—It isn't, Jamie said. Honestly, it isn't.

He took off down the track, and John let him go. The ground was treacherous, his temper in his throat. He needed to pay attention before he broke a leg or Jamie's nose. Later, at the bottom, he found Jamie puzzling over the route and dribbling tea down his shirt. John snatched the map before he spilled the whole flask across it. It was the wrong way round, per usual. John refolded it and headed for the woods.

—I'm only saying it as a friend, Jamie called.

John pretended not to hear, but Jamie caught up as he was crossing the stream.

—How much of your life are you going to waste loving someone you can't . . . ?

The river roared. On the far bank, John tripped and Jamie caught him.

—How dare you? John snarled.

Jamie smiled.

—He's left her, John said, for good this time.

Jamie searched his face with more pity than he could stand.

—Is it so wrong to love a friend? he blurted.

Jamie's chin froze for an instant, but then he clapped John on the back:

—Don't listen to me. I'm an upstart who thinks the world is his to play with on a string, at least that's what Burton's always telling me. Come on. Last one to the pub pays.

John won the footrace, such as it was in rucksacks, and when he tried to order his usual lemonade, Jamie shot him the kind of look you'd give a child trying out rude language in public. The drink at the pub was porter, it seemed, and no one was having anything else. John let Jamie bring him a pint and took a sip for form's sake—thick, smooth, bitter, you could chew it. Jamie's face broke into gratitude:

—I can't drink alone, not tonight.

They were brought sandwiches on country bread and more porter, but a hot meal never appeared. The stairs, when they climbed them, were uneven. John returned from the bathroom to find Jamie's clothes strewn across the floor and Jamie snoring on the bed. He managed to shift Jamie and pull the coverlet over him, but when he lay down himself, the mattress sagged and they rolled to the middle, peas in a napkin. Heat came off Jamie, sweat, beer, moors. The bed spun like a fairground ride, and when he moved the pillow, Jamie's arm fell against his cheek. Smooth, cool, tasting like the smell but even more, like something you

241

could never have enough of even if you started having it years before, his teeth like a snare, and if he bit . . . ?

Snore, snort—his tongue froze where it was, and Jamie moved again, breathing on his shoulder and then resting there. But Jamie's hand cast about beneath the covers, grazing, reaching, fishing into his pajamas, fingers cold, drawing him out as if they knew where to find him. Softer than handling himself, acutely different from his sorry old hand—he gripped the sheet and his toes gripped the air, and it rushed in his ears and rinsed his skin, taking him, making him, killing him, saving him.

Morning cold and damp, head the size of Lichtenstein. Jamie relished the eggs and kipper, but John had to excuse himself and vomit. When he returned, the landlady had removed his breakfast and left a brackish potion in its place.

—Cure for what ails you, Jamie explained. She says drink it all.

He choked it down for penance sake.

—Strange night, Jamie said.

His stomach seized.

—Strange dreams. Can't remember a thing, as usual.

The rain streaked the windows. They delayed their departure, reading the newspaper and asking for an extra pot of tea, but the storm did not abate. John was just beginning to feel less vile when Jamie rapped the table:

—Come on, Grievous, enough procrastination.

They secured their rucksacks, mackintoshes, caps.

—It can't be helped, it must be done, so down with—

—Yes, thank you, John interrupted and led the way into the down-pour.

They pressed on without stopping until they reached their lodgings for the night, a sprawling farmhouse whose room had twin beds. Their hostess made a fuss of them and insisted on hanging their wet things across the sitting room while they huddled before the fire. John sneezed and wondered, a bit hopefully, if he wasn't coming down with something. Mrs. M, as the two called her, not having quite caught her name, pressed John with hot drinks and a scalding footbath. His body, entire, began to throb.

242

—I've got it, Jamie exclaimed.

He'd received a letter at the post office and slapped it against his knee:

—It's the twenty-sixth of August. Your father's birthday, isn't it?

John blew his nose. He hadn't remembered, but now he did.

—And tomorrow the day he died. I knew something was on your mind.

He coughed violently, and his eyes watered.

—I've always thought, Jamie continued, there's something quite your father's son about this book of yours.

—There's no similarity, John said. He was a showman who spent his life doing parlor tricks with measuring tape and forceps. He cared more about that than anything else, and I mean anything.

Jamie looked knowingly at Mrs. M.

—I'm nothing like him! John snapped.

—Nothing at all.

—I mean it!

—Oh, so do I, Jamie replied. It's only that you've always taken everything so seriously.

John blew his nose again. On examination, he did not feel well. He retreated to bed, where Mrs. M brought him a hot-water bottle and turned out the lights against the long, gray evening.

He awoke later, disoriented and feeling the residue of childhood, as if he weren't old enough to be alone in a strange room, in the farmhouse where he realized eventually he was. He closed his eyes again and felt the boat rocking beneath him, the punt he shared with Meg and Delia. White feathers drifted down like the moltings of angels, and back at college the porter gave him a letter, addressed in his father's handwriting. He popped the sealing wax knowing that the letter had finally come that would take back the disowning. He'd admit John was right: not cowardice but courage to refuse murder in the name of war. This time forgiveness would not come too late, his father wouldn't die with everything between them, and if that could happen . . .

When he woke again, it was dark and the bed beside him creaked.

—Awake?

Jamie's whisper. John coughed. Outside sheep bleated, and Jamie spoke again:

—That letter.

He could still see the dream letter from his father, but that wasn't what Jamie meant.

—Marion's motoring up tomorrow, Jamie said. This morning.

—What? Why?

—You didn't look well. I thought you'd want to go home, and she—

—Doesn't want you spending time alone with me.

Because it was dark, he could say these things.

—No! Jamie said. No. You always do that!

He felt oddly calm, a storm almost upon them.

—You always take the wrong end of the stick and run away with it, Jamie said.

—Do I?

—Just like you did that time.

—What *time*?

—You know perfectly well what time.

The statement flashed in the dark. John thought of counting seconds in the silence that followed.

—Do you imagine it wasn't on purpose? Jamie said. That I'd let myself be caught—like that, in the changing room where anyone could see—and not have it be intentional?

The whirlwind had arrived, winding them both back there and showing John the scene from Jamie's side of the room, the fixed past now blown apart.

—I only did it to get a reaction, and you . . . you did what you always do.

A searing light.

—Do you think I didn't know what I'd get? Do you think I didn't plan that, too?

Riving roots, flesh from bone.

—I had the marks more than a month. You should be proud of that.

How to speak without air?

—I know, Jamie said. I'm the one who should apologize.

—You should have told me, he said at last.

—I know.

The windows were graying, their time passing away. He bowled a last ball in the vanishing dark.

—Why on earth would you do that knowing . . . ?

A creak in the bed as Jamie turned away:

—You wouldn't understand. You've never seen yourself when you're . . .

—*What?*

—Like that. It's . . .

The unsaid poised, sword deserved, aiming its fall.

— . . . it's irresistible.

 He had begun to hear the girl's voice as he rode across the Isle of Thanet. The August sun burned, and he imagined her in a boater hat writing new American letters. *New York is beyond your strongest dreams, Tommy Gray. We watched a parade for Charles Lindbergh and then went up in a dirigible.* By now perhaps her mother would be thriving, restored by *grand remèdes* and Dr. Felix Rush. *We've booked passage to the Kingdom of Peru, where we will visit Mr. Bingham's excavations at Matchu Peetchu.* As he rode against the wind, her phantom letters teased—*The tombs of Deir-al-Bahri simply beggar belief, Tommy Gray*—but also punished his greedy heart—*If only you could see the colors of the Congo!*—the one that made wishes that no one could hear. He wished no ill upon her, but did he not long, just a little, for the girl who wrote him in need? And did he not, if he touched the selfish truth, want her entirely back? Even so far as the storm? Even then.

✦

The roof was leaking again, and when Elsa said in vexation that it might be time to sell the cottage, the boy had cursed her—not in words, but good as—and ridden off in temper, leaving her alone with bucket and mop. She lifted the telephone, that black contraption that used to wake them in the night, and as she negotiated the exchange, her nerves untangled. Peter wasn't at the first place she tried, but she found him at the third. They could marry at Christmas, she told him. Something private, in Shetland with his parents.

✦

The cathedral bells tolled, and the sands and airplane engines of Gray's book dropped him onto a lawn too low and too ordinary. The bookseller he'd been patronizing all summer had given him the French book that

245

afternoon, *a gift from one book lover to another*, and as soon as he sat down with it, time had slipped its bounds, lifting him into the skies with the pilot Saint-Exupéry as he delivered the mail across the Sahara. Now the afternoon had vanished, and given the distance from Canterbury to Swan Cottage, he would certainly be late for tea. His mother would hit the ceiling, but since it was falling in—*ha*. It would serve her right if he ran away and joined the aeroposte. He mounted the bike, but as he passed the gardens, a painted sign made him squeeze the brakes: *Mid-Summer Night's Dr. One Nt only! 1/—*

On a bench near the front he plunged back to the Sahara, but when he looked up again, the seats had filled and children were ringing hand bells. Players were emerging from the bushes, from trees, from beneath the very benches, a small, dark people, their voices like bells in his ears . . . And then it was dark, and Puck stood on the stone ledge, the others melting into the night with its fireflies, as many as the stars. Lantern in hand, Puck spoke as if waking a child: *If we shadows have offended*. A fluttering inside, wings beating in his veins. *Give me your hands, if we be friends*. His throat strained and there were tears on his face, but the shame that should have been there had vanished with the sun.

He walked the bicycle through the crowd, out of the garden, and past a row of tents, their canvas glowing and flapping against the ropes. A plane's propellers could make enough wind to flay your skin, but even planes obeyed the air. The voice caught him like crosswind, *Come, dear*, jingle of bracelets, drawing him in from the night, voice male, voice female—

—Bring that machine, dear, before it wanders off.

Skirts everywhere, costume from another drama, a tiny figure with the hands of a man:

—I don't bite, dear. If you could see your face . . .

She sat on a stool that looked made for a child. Fingers like leather took his and smoothed them, palms up, across the tablecloth.

—Ah. Ah, yes . . .

Pencil, scrap, she told him to write his name. *Don't show it*. Fold in three, tear in six, set beneath a three-fish bowl. She asked for a tanner and he gave it. Her face creased like a contour map, goldfish drifting sluggish before them.

—You've lost a friend, dear, in the . . . you know, dear . . . stable. You think it's your fault, but it isn't, you know.

When he pedaled home, the moon lit the lanes.

—When he closes a door, he opens a French window.

He tried to memorize what she said, but already it was crumbling, like a dream after dressing.

—And her, dear . . . you know the one I mean, be kind, dear, no matter what.

Around him, hedgerow hoots and cries.

—You mustn't give up on him, dear. Not your friend—the other.

She hadn't always made sense.

—Be careful with those tires, dear.

She'd muddled things, places, people.

—Messages, dear, heading to you, but not straight.

Some words stuck.

—You think you've lost something, but it isn't lost, dear.

Hidden in a cleft, covered by a hand.

—Not truly, not for good.

And from the rock they burned.

—Use your eyes, dear. Look.

◆

Not one of her real prayers had ever been answered, but when he didn't come and the clocks passed midnight and there was nobody to telephone, she was back beneath that heel that crushed.

Mercy, mercy. Name the price, name it.

His headlamp came like a will-o'-the-wisp through the marshes. She waited in the door, letting the gnats inside, as he scraped to a stop and dropped the bicycle on the grass.

—Don't start, he said, storming past as if it were all her fault.

—Don't you dare! she cried. Do you have any idea how worried—

—I said I'm sorry.

He hadn't.

—How do you think it feels to sit in this cottage, all night long, waiting for the only person you've got left—

—Leave off!

She shut the door hard, and he startled, fumbling the books he was carrying.

—I've never laid a hand on you.

Relief, nearly joy, of saying what she felt.

—But now I think I've made a mistake.

—Go on, he retorted. I dare you!

She turned and mounted the stairs, but he followed.

—I know you despise me!

At the top, he cut her off:

—You wouldn't care a toss if something happened to me. You wish I'd died instead of him.

She clung to the wall.

—You, she said, are to pack your trunk.

—Out on my ear, is it?

She stared at her bedroom door, that wall of despair:

—This house is falling to bits. Peter has a place we can stay.

The boy stood rigid.

—We leave tomorrow.

—You married the wrong chap, he said.

Calm but as ruthless as a full-grown man:

—If you'd taken Uncle Alec, you'd have a *petit château* in Normandy. Instead, you picked a selfish bugger who left you high and dry with a falling-down cottage and a bastard for a son—

His spectacles clattered across the landing. Her breath came short, hand needles and fire.

✦

He waited on the platform with their luggage while his mother stopped in the post office to give their forwarding address. On the train she offered him a guinea pocket money and a tin of licorice from the shop.

—Thank you, Mother.

—You're welcome, dear.

She leafed through the post and passed him a tattered envelope. The address in Norway had been crossed out, as had the next, his grandparents' in Norfolk. The original handwriting seemed familiar, but it wasn't the girl's, and in any case, he'd never told her about Norway. He put it away until they'd checked in to the hotel round the back of King's Cross, until they'd retired to the twin beds, until she'd fallen asleep and he'd crept along the passage to the toilet and its unshaded bulb:

Markham Square, Chelsea, 31 July—Riding, Sorry to have missed you on Patron's Day. Still malingering? It's time to bury the hatchet, don't you think? I've never been one to mince words, so here it is: You got the wrong end of the stick. Things aren't always as they seem, through keyholes, and you're too clever by half to be hanging on to such a bloomer after all this time. I daresay you've grown frightfully since last we crossed paths, and perhaps you'll find these lines irrelevant. Still, your tactics last month led me to believe otherwise and have since plagued my conscience, rather. So listen, boyo, for what it's worth, you'll always have a friend in me. I know perfectly well you'll do as you like, but at least have the nerve to consider, in that brain of yours, that you may have been wrong about me.

Went down this summer (managed a third in History somehow—won't Grievous crow?) and have been keeping busy otherwise, as you're perhaps aware. If there's a change in that stubborn heart of yours, you can reach me at home (above). Perhaps when you return from abroad you'd come down and see a match for old time's sake? Suit yourself, as always. Wilberforce, M.

Marion had the front to arrive for breakfast. Jamie treated her with scrupulous care, as if she were a Dresden doll and not a brawler who disturbed their peace. Given the chance, John felt he'd go a round with her, and he gave odds on her blackening his eye before he could scratch. Still, she and Jamie behaved like bashful newlyweds, and before the cooked breakfast had even come out, John announced his plan to continue walking solo. Jamie gratified him by looking surprised, and John improvised enthusiasm: Fresh air had done him a world of good, what he needed now was a stretch of days, alone on the moors, to sort through his book. If he could walk for hours without being disturbed, he was sure he could overcome the treacherous bogs that lay, metaphorically, ahead in his manuscript. Marion approved the plan, and Jamie let his discomfort show—that John and Marion had somehow taken up sides together. Swept along in the role he'd set for himself, John bid them farewell there in the parlor and departed with his rucksack before they'd buttered their toast.

A hay cart gave him a lift to Clay Bank Top, but instead of continuing westwards from there, he headed east, penetrating Urra Moor and Bloworth Crossing into the very heart of the plateau. He was led, as if by ley lines, to the Rosedale Ironside Railway, which he found closed and dismantled. He followed the cinderpath of the old line, coming in the end to High Blakey, as he supposed he would. It was too late to go farther, so he inquired at the Lion Inn, the only structure, beside some sheds, on the ridge. The man looked like any man in those parts, but as he began to speak, John was flooded with memories. The man still spoke like a whale through its blowhole, oh aye, they like as had summat for him, or would once Our Ann come down. When John asked what had happened to the railway, the man said it had recently closed.

—Shameful! Near had to close last winter, and us not shut doors since—

—The Civil War?

The man paused, momentum interrupted, but he allowed that John was generally correct, saving the months they'd had to close in the recent war.

The taproom was full of farming types who took no notice of John. He ordered food, and while he was nursing his tea, three walkers blew in the door, lugged off their boots, and spilled into the lounge, stopping to greet everyone as a vital acquaintance. John took out his notebook and attempted to sketch the fireplace, his pencil taking him back to when the railway had run, when the landlord's hair had been black, when the carved lion on the hearth had frightened him.

—What's that you're drawing?

He looked up to one of the walking trio, a boy of some fifteen years, though he could have been as young as thirteen, or possibly a smooth-cheeked eighteen.

—Don't read over shoulders, a deeper voice replied. It's intrusive.

John craned his neck to see what was sweating behind him.

—Excuse my son, said the man.

—There's nothing to excuse.

John turned back to his notebook.

—Are you staying the night? the boy asked.

John admitted he was.

—Marvelous! the man exclaimed. More the happier.

The notebook was not doing its job.

—I'm Joe.

The man extended his hand, and John had to take it, fleshy and damp. The boy was his son, name of Gill, and just there, his wife, Catherine.

—Here, Cathy!

A full-figured woman looked up from her conversation, gave a care-less wave, and then weaved through crowded tables towards them. John stood to greet her.

—Pleased to meet you, Mrs. . . . ?

—Call me Cathy.

John cleared his throat. He couldn't place their accent.

—We were speculating about you, the man said. I said you were only passing, but Gill here spied out your rucksack under the table.

—Shrewd concealment, my good sir.

John had never been called *my good sir* by any boy, or indeed by any person who wasn't trying to argue him out of his ideas. They were well spoken, accent more or less proper London, though it slipped, when they addressed the barman, into shades of the local. Before he'd quite real-ized what was happening, the three had installed themselves at his table, elicited his Christian name, partaken of his tea, and ordered supper.

—We were told this place was peculiar, the man said. People haven't been building crosses up on the moor for nothing.

—Have you seen the crosses, John? the woman asked.

He stammered as he absorbed the intimate address and her touch on his arm.

—You'll come with us, the man announced. We'll have our summer, I mean *supper*—

He parried his son's response:

—That's three, *three*, my boy. Still miles ahead of you!

—We've been plagued by malapropisms, the woman explained.

—Those two have scarcely said a proper word all day.

—He exaggerates, the boy protested. I've only had nine, and Mother seven.

—Do come to the crosses, the woman said. It's a red-banner evening, and you look as though you could use it.

They were not his kind of people, not his *tea*, as the Eagle would have said, but it was easier to go along than to refuse. Their chatter, at least, distracted. They asked nothing about him and volunteered little about their circumstances save that they were visiting Whitby and had come to the Lion Inn to take in the moors. Clearly not country folk, they had nevertheless costumed themselves for the occasion with knee breeches, boots, oilskins, and rucksacks.

The boy carried a map though the crosses were plain enough to see. The cross called Old Ralph was person-size, and when John put his arms around it, he wondered whom he was embracing. All the moors spread out before him, heather rippling like the sea.

—There you are!

The boy came over the top and consulted his map:

—You've found Old Ralph. You went off as though you knew where he was.

He hoped the boy hadn't seen him handling the cross.

—Are you sure you haven't been here before?

—As a matter of fact, I was once.

—When?

—Before you were born.

Gill plopped down at the foot of Old Ralph and looked up at John as if eager for a history lesson. Rather than peppering John with questions, he offered the flask from his belt. The water tasted of steel, as it had tasted from his father's flask in that time that seemed attached to another person.

—Cathy! Cathy!

The man appeared over the rise, distraught. He thundered across the heath, threw his arms around Old Ralph, and keened:

—Oh, my heart's darling! Hear me this time, Catherine, at last!

A disembodied voice:

—It's twenty years! I've been a waif for twenty years!

The man howled anew. John raised an eyebrow at Gill, who sniggered. Then the woman appeared, hand on hip, a scolding wife:

—Who's this you've taken up?

The man unhanded the cross:

—Only my cousin Ralph, but now you're here . . .

He swept her up, and she pretended to fight off his advances. John wanted to laugh—it seemed the thing—but embarrassment rinsed over him. He was suddenly exhausted. The day had begun before dawn with ghastliness that had no place amongst these people; he'd walked all day, wolfed down a shepherd's pie, and then come out walking again. He needed a bed.

The wind howled, and he washed between sleep and life, between now and then, not knowing which shore was nearer.

Oysters were slimy, like swallowing what you sniffed. Sand stung your face so you had to squint. Scarborough rock was not stone but a sweet, and inside were letters that spelled out the place. Overcoats, even in July.

Why would a man like his father come to the moors? And why should he bring his son, not even out of milk teeth?

Shoes had a tongue, like your mouth, but no teeth except when they pinched your heel and made blisters.

Perhaps at the start, his father had planned on Scarborough, holiday to escape a house full of lilies. Had it been the seaside, mournful and freezing, or some cryptic whim that had driven him here, farther up and farther in, to a place so remote that the truth could be unwrapped?

The grate roared and crackled, like the growl the lion would make. If you left your bed in the night, things in the stone would come down and get you.

The pillow was flat, and the muscles in his legs crawled. He needed to run a hare and hounds, even in this sheep-baying limbo. Oh, why was he awake, and why here revisiting? How would it look to a neutral observer, one capable of insight—the Eagle, say? A man revisits a spot, the Eagle would say, to come to grips with the thing his father had confessed upon that spot.

Come to grips, why, though? His mother was dead a quarter of a century; he barely even remembered her.

In that case, the Eagle might posit, what about a pilgrimage? Not to holy ground per se, but to a place where the dead truth was told.

To what end, exactly?

Ah, the Eagle construed, why not a quasi-religious effort to ward off death in the present?

Magical wishing, in other words, re. Meg?

The Eagle wouldn't have put it so bluntly.

But this hypothesis, however neat, could not stand scrutiny. First, unlike his mother, Meg had lost no children. She had one child, his goddaughter, and had never even been pregnant again.

That he knew?

There were no graves.

Had she and her husband never wanted more children? Hot and cold, after all, did not make lukewarm in matters of the flesh. Merely following the laws of nature, the Eagle argued, she ought to have fallen pregnant since then.

John made it a rule not to dwell on her intimate life, and in any case, his father claimed to have caused his mother's death. Was he himself causing Meg's?

Certainly not.

Not medically, at any rate.

Oh?

Oh, where could all of his errors be charged? Had he fought for her as hard as he could, before she married? Had he refused to marry her friend when she suggested it? Had he even been faithful to his wife, who sickened for her death and deserved only love? He'd made love to her with his body, but with his mind . . . Biologically speaking, he hadn't caused Meg's ailment, but not everything had a material cause.

The back of his hand prickled, and the sun came out. He swallowed a fly, and his tooth fell out.

Was he tramping these hills to demonstrate he was his father's son, or to prove, with logic, that he wasn't? He hadn't believed his father's claims of guilt, had taken them as grief too fearful to ponder, had forgotten them, in fact. But his father had been truthful, at least in that window, which was more than he would have managed in the same position. But he *wasn't* in the same position, and if anyone should be compared to his father—roving, unchaste—it was Owain! Though, where did that leave him in the picture?

Irrelevant? Even more so than as a child, when at least he could claim to be the product of the two.

Enough, Eagle, back to your aerie. Whom did it profit to reason round and round? There was no sidestepping the bitter conclusion: If those one loved could not be saved, why bother with them in the first place?

Ah, John—said a voice not the Eagle's. *You bother because you were made for it. Made as in created. It is not good that the man should be alone. I will make him a helpmeet.*

Men of his father's generation saw women as one saw one's matron, essential but subsidiary. But helpmeet wasn't the same as trusted servant. *Meet* meaning fitting; it meant making the man a help *like him*. Helpmeet was what he longed for, one to meet in the garden in the heat of the day, standing in parity, equal but distinct. Man had been whole, but then God took his rib, and from then he wasn't whole except with the woman.

He arose when the sun shone onto his pillow, feeling feeble but alive. The walking family had also risen early and joined his table. A mild air breathed in the windows, bright with the scent of heather. John wondered if human breath had once been so sweet, and whether it ever would be again.

The boy Gill chattered easily, as if he had taken John as a pupil and was tutoring him in what the region had to offer. He had large, wide-set eyes, which made him look constantly surprised. He often laughed, and his hair fell across his eyes in waves more indulgent than the crop-and-slick style of John's pupils. He stood several inches shorter than John yet towered over his father. The man Joe was a compact person, and dark like a man from the west. The woman was fair, like her son, but John could not match any features.

—I can't work it out, he confided. Whom you most resemble, your mother or your father.

Gill spoke with his mouth full:

—Neither, I should think.

—We adopted him, the woman said.

—I'm a foundling.

John couldn't think what to say, and he wasn't completely sure they meant it.

—They found me in an enormous hat on the steps of the—

—John doesn't want to hear all that, the father said.

The tone fell just this side of severe. John stiffened to hear it, but then the man clapped his son on the back:

—Remember, my boy, a story is only as good as its mystery.

Gill had clearly heard this before.

—He's awfully proud of it, the woman said.

—I am, Gill agreed. But not proud as in I take credit for it, proud as in I'm glad of it. And anyway—

He offered John the last piece of toast.

—Foundlings are good luck.

—Good luck to have or good luck to meet?

—Both.

Gill spoke as if they four were a unit. The day was fine; where would they ramble? John suggested Glaisdale. On the way they'd find ruins from the mining days. Mention of mining excited Gill, who proceeded to pump their landlord for stories. They set off midmorning, John leading the way.

The air was calm and warm, but with the stillness came flies, which no swatting could disperse. Even on the tops, they found no relief. They rushed on, waving handkerchiefs, but the flies tickled and buzzed, spoiling any enjoyment. John apologized repeatedly, and eventually the woman Cathy began to tease him: who'd imagined he was lord of the flies? Joe made comparisons with Africa while Gill called him Flymaster. During the long descent to lunch, his cheeks began to sting as the sun burned his face and the sweat bit.

To their relief, the flies had not made it to the Sun and Rose, so they were able to sit beside an open window overlooking the river. Cathy admired the baskets of flowers, and Joe declared the ploughman's lunch the best he'd ever tasted. Gill stayed silent through the meal, but when he'd finished, he sat up in his seat as a Headmaster about to address a refectory.

—I believe I've found a suitable weapon, he said gravely. To repel *them*.

His parents gave him their full attention. The boy hummed a note and then sang:

—*I hate flies.*

He sang the words soberly in three descending notes. The other two hummed his final note in response. The boy sat straighter:

—*They are not grand.*

Same three notes, echoed again. He went up a step:

—*I hate flies. I swat them with my hand.*

This time his father repeated the last phrase, roving up and down the scale, in some strange monastic inspiration. When he finished, the three began again, as if it was something they always did. The tune was "Three Blind Mice," but the pace quickened, and Gill sang stridently:

—*They swarm around till you have a fit, they even sit on your upper lip, they make you feel like a walking gob of*—

—Gill!

—Spit, Father, *spit.*

They laughed.

—*And all you can do is sit and grit your teeth if you're wise.*

The song was absurd, but they sang in harmony, John joining along as they resumed the walk. Gill led them in other songs, too—"Rule Britannia," "Keep the Home Fires Burning"—to which they seemed to know all the words, even ones John had never heard. By the time they returned to the inn, John's throat was sore from singing, and his stomach from laughing.

—You can't go! Gill declared. The wind's picked up and the flies have packed off.

John groped for a joke, or at least a pun, but his mind was spent.

—Besides, Gill said, you promised to teach me to use a compass.

—You did promise that, said Cathy.

—You can leave Tuesday, Gill pleaded. What's one more day, Flymaster?

John tried to be serious but wound up laughing instead.

—You see, he doesn't want to go!

That night Joe took to the piano as Gill and Cathy gave an elaborate rendition of "The Fly Song," followed by favorites that had the entire room singing (rogue wish: that Cordelia and Meg could join him here, with these people), but then "The Old Kent Road" was finishing, and the music was changing into something plaintive, Gill and Cathy in duet, *How shall I my true love know*, sending shivers through him, *which bewept to the grave did go, with true-love showers . . .*

The next day, fine and breezy, they took a picnic up Hasty Bank Top and sat amongst the Wainstones. After lunch they dozed in the sunshine, and John felt he'd been stolen away, not by pirates or even fairies, but by the real kind of life other people lived, people who rejoiced in the day and laughed at flies even as they sang of sorrow and love and the end that awaited them all. The rot at the heart of his sojourn there—whether memorial or magic wishing—now seemed antique, turned under leaves to make humus. If Gill could turn abandonment (in a hat or otherwise) into reason for good luck, surely John could refuse to bow down before a memory.

They drifted down from the tops with the reluctance due a last holiday, but by evening, they were suffering.

—I am going to die, Gill moaned. I've never been so sunburnt in my *life*.

They sat far from the fireplace and cooled their skin with damp cloths, and as they complained, the pain came to seem both validation of their pleasure and a final trial they would endure as one. After supper, Gill revived sufficiently to demand a game. He called it Definitions, evidently a family favorite. It involved writing definitions for unfamiliar words and then reading them out along with the true definition while the others tried to guess which was which. One accumulated points by guessing correctly, but also by writing definitions others believed. It was difficult to find words John didn't know, but after a while he feigned ignorance and voted for definitions that would even the score.

—I'll take number two, a tomb in Egypt containing mummified flies.

The point, of course, wasn't vocabulary, but humor, and on this John trounced them, too. Gill would grin and vow to beat him in the next round. He was like Jamie at that age, the same golden air and irrepressible smile, but more unruly than Jamie, more frank, less cruel.

The next morning it rained. They drove him to Scarborough in their motorcar even though it was miles out of their way. Soon, too, his boys would be evicted from home to the sharp crush of term. He supposed there were people in the world, perhaps even these, who did not arrange their lives around school. In some parts of the earth, one didn't even have to worry about winter.

He made a halfhearted stab at conversation, and Gill responded with a cheerfulness that seemed forced. His favorite site in Whitby? Doubtless the abbey. One could sit in its churchyard and pretend to be Lucy, staring out to sea and thinking of Jonathan. Or the wishbone! What would it take to break the wishbone of a whale?

—Time? John offered.

Centuries of salt water and all the creatures too small to perceive, eating away at the bone, until it, like everything, crumbled.

—At least you can be sure of beating anyone at Definitions, Gill said. Unless you're a poet, or a philosopher.

Joe glanced at his son in the rearview mirror.

—You aren't, are you?

—Don't pry, his father warned.

—I only—

—People should be free on their holiday. Don't spoil it.

—I don't mind, John said.

He didn't mind, and more, he wanted, suddenly, to tell them everything. Not that he'd been concealing, but the way the man spoke made him feel that they were strangers who'd passed an agreeable spell side by side, not like a band, a household.

—As it happens, I'm a schoolmaster.

It sounded alien on his lips. Gill breathed in sharply.

—What? John said.

They began to speak at once. Probably, it was only half a minute, but

258

he felt that they gabbled for ages before he understood. They were sending Gill to school for the first time. Their holiday had been taken en route. In a few days they'd be delivering him . . .

There was a way time got heavy, everything extraneous crushed. St. Stephen's Academy had never sounded more foreign. To them, it was exotic, and they spoke as though the pages of literature were about to become real. Gill described the uniform, gray suit weekdays, tailcoat Sunday, two different ties, a cap. Shut in the back of a motorcar winding up to Scarborough station, Gill would not stop talking.

—The purple-and-white tie matches the cap. Those are the colors of the House.

—Purple and white? John croaked.

It had always seemed penitential, but now it reminded him of bruises.

—The school's colors are red and black, but the House is purple and white.

—How many Houses are there?

—Four, Mother, I told you! Of course Grieves will be the best House. At least we all must say it is.

They laughed. The car had come to a halt. He had to tell them. It was too barbaric to learn as a surprise.

MICHAELMAS

Michaelmas Term, pigeonholes reassigned. His new one was empty and so was the old. He went so far as to examine them all, but there were no airmail letters, no parcel promised through the morning post. On top of that, the notice boards: *Studies—Riding, No. 6.*

—Where have you been? The train was two hours ago.

Pious Pearce, badgering already.

—I was driven. What business is it of yours?

But Pearce was about their Housemaster's business, and their Housemaster wanted him, posthaste. In the study, Grieves wore a sunburned smile:

—Ah, Riding, welcome back. How is your mother?

His *mother?* He said she was well.

—Glad to hear it.

The smile had vanished and the lips were being pressed, as if Grieves had heard how he'd behaved, heard of the things he'd said to her.

—You may have noticed I've given you number six.

Study number six belonged to Wilberforce—punishment?

—It's a prefect study, sir.

Mr. Grieves's face softened, the look he used to crave—

—Moss and Crighton moved to number one, and I thought you deserved some consolation for slogging it out in the library all summer.

Sarcastic?

—I've also given you a new boy. He'll be in the Fifth, but I thought you two might suit.

Thought he deserved Coventry, or that he needed a friend?

—Thought you'd prefer it to being thrown in with another study. Can I count on you to help him about? It's his first time boarding, astonishing as that sounds.

Sounded like suicide, but who was he to say?

—This makes you his Keeper, I suppose.

The irony grated, that he should be assigned Keeper to a new boy in the study where Morgan had been Keeper to him. He was lost in the woods of this viperous conversation, and now Grieves had sprung from his chair and was shaking his hand.

—Thank you, Thomas.

Grieves shook firmly, but never let the center of their palms touch. His hand felt as though it should throb, and his ribs as though they'd been tickled without pity. He couldn't say what had just happened, but the list of objections, when he made it, would be long. Time never went backwards; you only got second chances with prep, and then only sometimes.

Moss was rifling the pigeonholes as he emerged:

—Ah, Riding, in trouble already?

—No!

Moss grinned:

—Cut along, Easy Draw. You know what Morgan would say if he caught us slacking.

These people! He barked his shin dragging his tuck box upstairs. The study key hung in the lock. The room smelled wrong. On the table, parcels.

Two parcels, and a stack of blue envelopes tied with twine. Promises delayed but paid sevenfold? Madness couldn't reign forever!

On the floor of the chair loft he sat and trained his torch on the parcels. One was dated July. The other, last week! Inside each parcel were brown envelopes, opened, addressed to her mother and written by the father. Contents rescued from a rubbish bin? Opened by whom? Did she expect him to read? Who sent opened letters and expected you not to?

He arranged them by postmark and did the same with the blue envelopes, which were addressed to himself from the girl. The first set of brown bore postmarks foreign and domestic, dating back to April. Her

264

blue letters picked up in July, just after they'd broken up for the hols, and continued in tandem with the second set of brown. The floor looked like an elaborate game of Patience. Should the decks be shuffled together or read through separately?

There was a delicious torture in studying the envelopes, resisting the urge, greater than Christmas morning, to open them all at once. A detective, someone worthy of such a puzzle—such a *story*—would proceed chronologically. You could always read a book again, but nothing compared to the first time when you didn't know the people or what became of them.

The father's April letters had been posted from America, but the rest had come from England. He'd written Mrs. Líoht in Paris, Vichy, and Bad Wörishofen, but the letters had not followed them to Budapest or beyond. The second batch, beginning mid-July, were posted to and from various locations in France, and the last were addressed to her simply by name, delivered who-knew-where, presumably by hand. The girl's to him had also been posted from France, but her last few came from a place with stamps he couldn't read.

She had thought of him in these far-flung places. She'd written his name time and again, *Thomas Gray Riding, St. Stephen's Academy, nr. Fridaythorpe, Yorkshire, England*. He should wait until he was calmer. *Like a wave on the sea you come riding to me*. He should savor them, stretched across the long days of term.

Dear Tommy Gray,

The page full of her hand.

You'll be horrified, I know, to hear what I've done.

The world was full of secrets. In or out of order, these belonged to him.

My Darling Little Girl, I'm home at last, but where are you?

The man addressed his wife in a way Gray supposed was typical of the Irish.

It's horrible, I admit, but you must understand.

I've found a clue. A little bird told me.

One, my father loves her, no matter what she says. He's been writing since April. At first she refused to open his post and hid them in the lining of her trunk. Two days ago, I found them in the wastepaper basket, opened not by me!

I know you're reading my letters, even if you don't reply.

Hopefully, you've got the parcel by now. Proof, you'll agree, of his love.

I'm a sorry old fool, you know, always have been, weak, so weak!

Second, doctors will say anything to keep you under their thumb. Whatever your problem, they have a cure! If you keep putting yourself in their grubby old hands, you'll keep getting the same old grubby results.

I know you'll forgive me, my <u>darling girl</u>. You always have, and you mustn't stop now.

Third, penicillin is almost guaranteed to kill you. Americans carry rifles and knives; they sing stupid songs and don't care who they hurt.

America, my girl, is every man's dream.

All right, I confess: I wired him from Paris.

The grandest land you've ever seen.

Mais c'était un cas de force majeure.

The size of it is enough to humble any man.

He arrived in Le Havre the night before our sailing and left a letter at our hotel.

The people haven't two pennies to rub together,

She drew the shades and made me keep the lights off.

but they haven't forgotten how to laugh, my girl.

The garçon came and said a gentleman was waiting.

We'll go there together, start a new life.

She said she'd been Struck. That means she had a message about what she must do. She was Struck last year about the charity fête for the German children, and last month about Zoltan Zarday. The fête was a wild success, and so was ZZ, until he had to leave.

Fear in his blood as he watched the mother improvise: the escape out the back of the hotel, the retreat south to Lourdes.

Even if it was wicked of me to wire him originally, it was all for the best, you have to agree. At least we've escaped death by Penicillin.

Gascony, at the foot of the Pyrenees, beautiful mountains, she said, full of brown bears and eagles.

As soon as we arrived, she was filled with energy, like Budapest, but brighter.

Beautiful, really? If eagles, then vultures.

Lourdes, you know, is a holy site. She is sure it will cure her.

My darling little girl,

The father wrote to Lourdes, to a place called Hôtel du Fin. Couldn't she see it was macabre?

Every doctor has made her worse, but this morning she ate more than she has in months!

I cannot sleep anymore for thinking what I can do to win you back.

I've never seen a miracle, but then I've never seen a lot of things—99 percent of the globe, for example!

      If it weren't for the hope that we one day will be together,

Physicians are bunk! That's our new motto.

      I'd have done myself mischief a hundred times over.

Did you know, Tommy Gray, that in 1858 a girl my age named Bernadette received eighteen apparitions of the Virgin Mary? Now pilgrims come from everywhere to see Bernadette's cave. Its healing powers are fully documented, they say.

      You could go to farthest Mongolia,

She's taken the waters six days in a row.

      and I'd send you a letter. If I knew no address I'd write it the same, and the angels would find you and bring you my love.

Da was asking for us at the hotel this morning.

      If you crossed the Styx to the underworld, I'd pay my coin and board the boat.

She's shut herself in the bath the last two hours. If she doesn't come out soon, I'll get Monsieur to break the door!

      And I'd bring a gilded mirror to see what was keeping you,

She made me pack our bags, but she won't say for where.

      and the mightiest sword to sever its head.

He arrived at the station as our train pulled away.

And I'd play on my whistle the saddest of songs,

Lourdes is full of frauds.

to win your release from that jealous gaoler.

She's been Struck again.

And if you hired an aeroplane to take you to heaven,

The ship at the harbor leaves with the tide.

I'd write to you there.

A page and a half to make him understand:

Being Struck isn't a joke, and it isn't a fraud. I met a girl in Lourdes who said Jesus had lain in her bed, asked her to be his bride, and filled her with his love and other disgusting things. My mother said this girl needed to eat some bread and butter and stop reading Catholic leaflets, which is to say, my mother is levelheaded. When she's Struck, she doesn't go into a trance or imagine things. It just happens. Think of it this way, sometimes you're wondering what you should do, or maybe you aren't even wondering, maybe you're thinking about how muddeningly awful your hair is, and a separate idea just jumps into your head. Being Struck is like that, except the idea is unexpected and not like what you'd think yourself, and most important, it is <u>very loud</u>.

Her next letter, from the foreign postage place, began again in medias res.

It wasn't wrong to cross the Channel either!

They'd come somewhere new, somewhere fresh, the last port, her mother promised, before home.

The Emerald Isle! County Clare!

The one place her father had vowed never to return.

There's a story about the Burren. Do you know it, Tommy Gray? Finn McCool and his warrior friends, the Fianna, are told by King Angus to fetch some eels for a feast he's having. On their way to Doolin, they're stopped by some bandits who've taken over Ballykinvarga Castle. The two groups get into a quarrel and start throwing rocks. The Fianna collect boulders from all over Ireland and throw them at the castle, hoping the bandits will start tearing down the walls for ammunition. To make a long story short, the Fianna defeat the bandits and then chuck the boulders across all of northwest Clare, which tells you everything you need to know about what it looks like here.

Limestone, boulders, underground rivers.

The Burren is a peculiar spot, and Kilfenora is full of crosses.

Orchids, forts, ferns in clefts of rocks.

Lisdoonvarna is a spa town, but they say it's famous for matchmaking. I don't know whether they mean matches you light or marriages.

A wild, stony place where the Atlantic crashed into Galway Bay.

The Cliffs of Moher drop straight to the sea. Mum hates going there. She thinks I'll fall off.

Rain all the year, ivy and holly and moss.

The high roads pass by dolmens and wells.

And everywhere music, reels sliding into each other, notes pattering on like the rain.

There's a lady chapel at the top of the road.

Open for petitions. Candles in alcoves, veiled heads, a Quaker girl kneeling down.

The only Mary prayers I know are in French.

Could prayer cure her mother? If it were so easy, who would die?

She met a woman, older than Moses with no teeth, and the lady told her about a well. Not like Lourdes! There weren't even any people there, just pure and true water from the heart of the Burren.

There she took her mother, up and out to an X on a map, six limestone steps down to a spring. She bathed her mother's hands, and her mother said,

I am healed.

The last parcel, posted from Dublin, contained the brown letters addressed only *Mrs. Líoht.* On the back of the parcel, she'd whispered in pencil:

She told me to burn these, and I said I did. But still, it's proof of what I always said was true.

Her letter to him was seven pages long, divided up by days like a secret journal. (*Like?*) After the well, her mother went to bed so the cure could take. Next day, he rolled in with the tide:

My darling little girl, how proud I am to call you my wife.

He came, Tommy Gray, just like I wished he would!

The man would be shot if he showed his face there again, but show his face he did.

I gave up Rome to have you. I'll give up my <u>life</u> if it lets me have you back.

He came while we were finishing lunch, just as I always imagined.

I'm so happy, my girl, I'm sure my heart will break.

He gave us kisses and presents, and soon he had her laughing so hard she got the hiccoughs. He looked so debonair in a flannel shirt and Irish cap, acting the suitor with her.

Sometimes I think I'll have to start a quarrel with you just to remember how forgiveness feels.

There in their chair loft, like an avalanche, he saw. Not what the girl wanted him to see, but the players behind the curtain, a man and a woman who loved battle more than anything. Fighting, running, chasing, catching.

What could be sweeter than forgiveness from my love? Ecstasy, my girl, worth any pain at all.

Could she not see what was so plain to him? The woman's mad dash to Lourdes, and then, madder, Ireland, reading his letters all the while.

I'll come for you at seven. The shore is at its finest then.

Her flight a gauntlet, thrown down by a woman wanting capture, before a man who couldn't refuse.

He brought us turquoise, a necklace for her, and for me a bracelet carved like a goddess.

I never want to leave my little girls again.

We went bathing and Mum got in for the first time. They kissed in the waves, and he stayed here tonight. He says he's going to buy her—

A fine new house.

In Ely, near Cambridge on the Great River Ouse.

A beautiful place for my dearest one, my onliest heart.

By Drayton Fen, where I was born.

We'll start again, no hurting, no lies.

He wanted to shout at her letter and shake it.

We've booked passage to England.

     I'll never let you be unhappy again.

Day after tomorrow we'll actually be <u>home</u>.

     I'm bringing the ring!

It's a play! Can't you see?

I've wished on every candle,

     My cup is flooding over.

every cake, every wishbone.

     It's growing.

I've wished

     It's bursting

every eyelash,

     me open,

every penny,

     my heart,

every star,

     my mind, all this

clover,

     all this

candle,

all this

horseshoe,

all this

What do you do when your wishes come—

True? He thought the jangling was a charm.

My truest, my best, my—

Only the tea bell, ruthless and sharp, yanking him back into—

Love.

Letters under floorboards: hers, the father's, the one in his pocket from Wilberforce. He set a chair to mark the place, keep it down. Outside: the school, its crowds and clamor. He'd left his jacket in the study and had to run and fetch it.

What do you do when your life is given back?

If life was restored, why send him the letters? Would she want them back one day?

Adieu, my friend, my friend indeed . . .

Adieu meant forever. Could this be her final . . . ? *No*, God, *no*! Study door ajar, someone perched on the table, swinging his legs and whistling.
—You?
—You!
—Riding?
—*Audsley?*

Rank by rank again we stand,
From the four winds gathered hither:
Loud the hallowed walls demand
Whence we come, and how, and whither.

Well might they demand, but John wasn't sure he could answer if asked. Sunday morning, squeezed into chapel, he felt as though he were swirling on a raft somewhere, sans rudder, land in the distance, but which?

His House had been altered by Audsley, and the past by Jamie. At least that was how it seemed to him the first full day of term. When he'd been with the Audsleys, there had been no space in his mind for Jamie, but when he left them to return to the Academy, strife broke out in his head like snarling cats loosed from a cage. At first, he'd been furious with Jamie for having failed to warn him about the Audsleys. He had spent the train journey composing his resignation in strident, superlative vocabulary, but by the time Sledmere and Fimber rolled into view, the cold truth leaked down his collar: Jamie had neither duped him nor sprung the Audsleys on him. Their walking tour—before the part he refused to think of—had been full of shoptalk: staff news, pupil news, which new boys might be up John's street. Jamie had indeed told him of Audsley, son of thespians. The family were one of the theater's dynasties, Jamie had said. In certain circles, Jamie claimed, they were the ones to know, and imagine if the Academy were to become known amongst such people. Jamie had met the family over Easter and found the boy apt. His education had been vibrant but eccentric, which was why Jamie knew John was the one to handle him. At that time, early in their trek, John had been flattered, but in the cab returning from the station, he felt ready to curse Jamie a blue streak, if not for this then for something. Back at the Academy, John had gone straight to his rooms, unpacked his rucksack, and sent every stitch of clothing to the laundry. By teatime, he had passed into a state of detachment, almost as if he had taken one of Kardleigh's drops.

Jamie appeared the next morning at breakfast, looking more well than a person had a right to look. Obviously, his marriage agreed with him again. John prepared himself for Jamie's apology—the charming fog that would envelop everything that happened between them, everything done, said, and not said—but Jamie made no attempt to waylay him as they assembled for Housemasters' meeting, and then after a quarter of an hour, Jamie dashed off, leaving his secretary to address the rest. The other three Housemasters had pelted Captain Lewis with items of business, but John had been so surprised by how embarrassed he felt that he forgot to tell the Captain what he had to tell him. Jamie behaved similarly at the staff meeting, and midweek John received a note from Lewis saying Jamie would forgo beginning-of-term staff interviews unless requested.

He had no firm idea of what he expected Jamie to say to him, or what he himself might wish to say back. No words were equal to the occasion. That entire phase of his life—from when he first met the Sebastian family until the war broke out—had been drawn violently into the present, its most important points of reference altered. Events were not as he had understood them; therefore, neither was he. How exactly Jamie had pulled the centerboard up and set the craft adrift, John could not understand, but he had dug up and reinterpreted everything between them, as Woolley did to the Ziggurat of Ur.

Mercifully, the days before term oppressed him with practical demands. When the Audsleys arrived, John greeted them correctly. He sent Gill away with Moss and made small talk in the quad until Joe pulled his wife away, having noticed that other parents were not lingering. John had not spoken to Gill again that night, but he'd told Crighton to make sure the boy got a haircut. At breakfast Sunday morning, John had been gratified to observe Audsley properly turned out and taking direction from Riding. Now, though, several boys were sniggering at Gill's confident hymn singing, and John was back to yearning, illicitly, for the Lion Inn.

> *Ours the years' memorial store,*
> *Hero days and names we reckon,*
> *Days of brethren gone before,*
> *Lives that speak and deeds that beckon.*

At least his JCR were also singing loudly, setting the example expected of them. They, too, had come up during shoptalk. At the end of the last term, John had accepted Moss's recommendations for the JCR, adding his and Pearce's studymates to the roster: Moss as Head Boy, Pearce as Prefect of Hall, MacCready as Captain of Games, and Crighton as Prefect of Chapel. During shoptalk, Jamie had raised an eyebrow at the last assignment, but John had defended it—in the first place, this year's Upper Sixth was the smallest they'd ever had (thanks to the depredations of the ancien régime), so John hadn't much choice. Second, he didn't think Crighton's bawdy humor disqualified him from supervising attendance at Prayers and organizing lectors for the three services each week allocated to John's House. But Jamie, it emerged, had new ambitions for the Prefects of Chapel, and these were linked to his new ambitions for the confirmation class. The Headmaster considered the present program (twelve lessons in Lenten Term) inadequate; he envisioned taking them through the full catechism over two terms, and supplementing his own theology lessons with informal discussions once a fortnight in House, led by Prefects of Chapel.

—In that case, no to Crighton, John conceded. But Pearce can do it.

—Isn't he rather irritating? Jamie had said. And concrete.

When John suggested Jamie take Pearce under his wing, make him show his discussion topics ahead of time and report back afterwards, Jamie had accused John of flogging his difficult cases off on him. Still, it had been clear that Jamie liked the idea, and when, later, John had presented the revised assignments to his prefects—Pearce as Chapel, Crighton as Hall—Pearce's joy had been matched only by Crighton's relief. John wished he could make everyone as happy.

From the dreaming of the night
To the labors of the day,

Now, though not unhappy, his JCR looked young. In fact, the whole Upper Sixth looked callow, not like senior boys in years past, the Morgan Wilberforces, the others whose names now escaped him. It was only last year, surely, that Morgan sat in those same pews with John's band of brothers, his first JCR, which had turned the tide on the old school; wasn't it only last year that Morgan was coaching the Colts XV, taking young Pearce in hand, smoothing the edges, bending him to the mold, only last week that Elsa Riding arrived with her son, the youngest he'd had? When had Riding grown out of Eton jackets? Surely he wasn't long above five foot two, yet here he stood, in the Lower Sixth, wearing tails.

Brother, if with lure unblest
Tempter-wise the past betrayed thee.

And young Halton, was that a tremor as he sang the solo? Surely his voice wasn't breaking already? And yet, John calculated, Halton would be fourteen now, or soon. When John had first come to the Academy, someone—Burton?—had told him he'd lose track of time, living only for the rhythms of school, terms beginning and terms passing on. John was sure that he'd never be the type of schoolmaster to have trouble recalling a boy's age, or his form, or when he'd left the school. Now, though, he realized that he couldn't be sure of anything without consulting his files, and even then memory might deceive him.

◆

Malcolm minor had been his Keeper when he arrived, and now the notice boards declared that he, Halton, was Keeper to Malcolm tertius. He found his charge in Moss and Crighton's new study puffing over kindling that refused to light.

—You must be the Turtle.

He'd heard about the Turtle. Malcolm minor had complained heavily of his younger brother last term. Halton couldn't understand why anyone would undermine a brother, but now that he saw the youngest Malcolm boy—good-looking and confident, even in his Cinderella state—he realized that his friend possessed a talent for survival, riding the coattails of a talented elder brother while suppressing the popularity of the younger.

The Turtle looked him up and down:

—I'm also called Nipper, Cod-eyes, and Oliver. Take your pick.

Halton stifled the urge to cuff him round the ear.

—Stand up when your Keeper comes into the room.

The Turtle rubbed his eyes:

—Are you Halton? Infant Halton?

His blood raced, first at the insult and then with shame.

—I'd think a bit less about my name and a bit more about your fag test in a fortnight's time.

—That's all right, the boy said breezily. I know it all.

His arrogance was staggering, and dangerous.

—If you get a docket, Halton said, *I* get whacked. And you can be sure I'll pay it back to you with interest.

—I know.

He tried to collect himself. Of course Malcolm tertius would have learned from his brothers. Of course they had given him the one fag who didn't need a Keeper.

—You're in the choir, the Turtle said.

—So?

He was going to thump him, damn the consequences.

—That solo was jolly hard.

He kicked him instead, though not as hard as he could:

—We didn't get to practice.

Brat wouldn't know a major third if it tripped him down the stairs.

—You're better than anyone at my old school, the Turtle said.

Halton bit the inside of his cheek. The Turtle was covered in soot.

—You've got to use paper, he said, for the fire.

—There wasn't any.

Halton took a piece of impot paper from the drawer. Twisted, lit, heigh presto.

—Tomorrow there'll be newspapers in the boot room.

—Thanks.

He moved towards the door:

—If you burn Crighton's toast, don't scrape it. He can't abide scraped toast.

—Right.

—And careful with the sugar. Anything more than a spoonful gives Moss a headache.

—Right.

—They're decent, but you've got to complain about them or you'll catch it from the other fags.

—I know.

—Stop speaking. Really.

The Turtle made a salute.

—And wash your face. You look like hell.

✦

Guilford Audsley changed the light and filled the furniture. Under his eye, the study became a stage. The Messenger stenciled vines over the window seat, fashioned a Chinese lantern for the ceiling bulb, and plastered the walls with pin-ups of film stars called Greta, Marlene, and Bela. Above the fireplace, he mounted a sun-and-moon mask that smelled of glue, and when he saw the flight goggles Gray always kept in his tuck

279

box, he begged to be allowed to fasten them on the mask, and then he begged for their story (his godmother's, lady pilot shot by Bolsheviks, saga would take all term to relate).

Gray found the task of Keeper quickly daunting as he discovered Guilford's understanding of school life. He seemed aware of some customs, such as call-over and capping, but he employed a bizarre array of slang. Gray had to explain that no one at the Academy would ever use the word *rotter* and that there had never been a singing test on tabletops, all while imparting the standard Notions every new boy had to learn. Even he himself had not been such a disaster when he'd landed in Morgan's hands. He may have been more green, but at least he wasn't misinformed. Guilford, by contrast, seemed to have swotted from a dismal syllabus of *Boy's Own Paper* and *Tom Brown's School Days*. Gray felt he would need every hour of the next fortnight to hammer his charge into shape. Recalling Gill's earlier confusion in chapel, he left him in the study with instructions to rule out his exercise books, but when he returned with a prayerbook, he found Gill laughing in the corridor, ensconced in three conversations at once.

What would Morgan do?

—Oi, you, swot up, he said, rapping Gill on the head with the book.

Gill took it amiably:

—All of it?

—Just the usual.

Gill turned to the table of contents.

—Haven't been to church much, have you?

—Not at all, Gill admitted.

—You're not a . . . ?

—Father calls me a heathen sometimes.

Doubt and mistake disarranged him.

—What? Gill said.

—Pater.

—*What?*

—Not father. Pater. *M'Pater calls me a heathen.* Say it.

He did; the second time sounded natural.

—Don't worry, Gill said. I'm a quick study.

✦

That night when the washroom was at its most crowded, Halton took the towel from around his waist and used it to dry his face.

—Bloody hell! Leslie exclaimed. What happened to you?

The washroom instantly suspended its business to pay attention to the marks he'd been waiting to show. Imagining Moss at his most unfazed, Halton flicked the towel across his shoulder, wet his toothbrush, and began to clean his teeth. When they pressed for details, he spat into the basin:

—M'pater took a dim view of last term's report.

As he finished his teeth, word spread, and by the time he found it necessary to put on his pajamas, everyone who was anyone had seen.

Reputation established, he repaired to the dorm. Perversely, he'd been put in Pearce's dorm with the fags. He'd complained loudly and bitterly about it, but it dawned on him that he may have drawn a long straw after all; the rest of the Fourth were in Mac's dorm, and Mac promised to be not only a fanatical Captain of Games, but also, already, an aficionado of the slipper.

—Hear you got the high jump, Pearce said upon entering the dorm.

Halton pretended not to notice the fear and fascination on the younger boys' faces.

—*Disce aut discede*, or as m'pater says, the third option.

—Scorchy?

—Good tennis arm.

Malcolm tertius went pale.

—I suppose, said Pearce, he didn't think much of your JCR Report?

The fact burned through the dorm, *Halton got a JCR Report!*, but as Pearce switched off the lights, Halton got into bed less triumphant than he expected, as if his pockets were empty when he had expected them to be full.

His throat had betrayed him with the solo, jumping places it didn't belong and refusing to obey his command. Worse, his birthday was next month, fourteen damning years. He was going to have to speak as little as possible from now on unless he could force his voice into submission.

And then there was Guilford Audsley, materializing as if by power of his own imagination within the gates of the Academy. His parents had taken him and Miranda to see *The Messenger* at Easter, and at the end of July, they'd returned to the Gaiety Arts for *The Lady from the Sea*. He knew nothing of what the play ought to be, but he found the production romantic and unnerving, especially the Lieder songs they had inserted into the script, according to the program. He knew one from a gramophone record he had received last Christmas. Mr. Gershwin played the piano as a girl crooned along, much as the young lady playing Bolette had done at the end of the fourth act. The boy who had played the bicycle messenger at Easter had a larger role this time, that of the artist Lyngstrand. It was alluring, if somehow wrong, that the actor, who couldn't be any older than Moss, should be playing such a troubled and wasting young man.

When Halton first saw Audsley across the House tables, he thought his mind was playing tricks, that the new boy only *looked* like Lyngstrand, but soon he'd learned that it was the actor, though no one else seemed to know who he was. He hadn't been able to speak to Audsley directly, of course. Aside from the fact that the Fourth did not address the Upper School—a convention they in the Fourth scrupulously followed so as to impress it on the fags—Audsley remained firmly attached to Riding's side. Evidently, they were studymates. Halton knew better than to expect fairness from life, but what sort of justice was it for everything worthwhile to end up in Riding's ungrateful lap? The brute was arrogant, surly, and came top in everything without even trying.

Of course his father had taken a dim view of his reports, though he evinced no surprise. Schoolmasters in Nairobi had been complaining of him for years. He'd listened impatiently to his father's lecture, wishing he'd reach the end of it and get the thrashing over with. He'd never be able to explain to anyone besides Miranda the way letters and numbers refused to stay put, how they migrated like butterflies, making reading arduous, arithmetic absurd. If she had stood beside him, she might have argued his case, explaining to their father how he *had* read that summer—and without her help—a book called *The Riddle of the Sands*. Instead, she had accused him of sabotaging her piano practice, sounding as rigid and serious as the horrible Lyngstrand in the scene with Bolette. Guilford Audsley had delivered the lines like a spoiled boy, making Lyngstrand pathetic as he declared himself an artist who required a wife to Think of him as he Became an Artist, intending with this speech to seduce Bolette, who all the while was laughing at him. *I suppose*, he'd told Miranda, *that you expect me to occupy myself Thinking of you while you go off and Become a Musician.* She'd stared at him as if at a freak, and he realized not only that the joke was a failure but also that their days together had been left in Africa with the murram that used to stick in the treads of his sand shoes, and with everything else that had once been hopeful and beautiful, true and good.

✦

John sat down almost giddy to the paperwork appointed to his freshly tidied desk. Her letter pulsed in his pocket, but he waited until he'd blotted his last page before taking it out and casting his eyes across it again: her very own hand, the swash of her *M* enough to give him heat. She wrote directly to him, two full pages. He couldn't even be unhappy that she'd taken Owain back, so staggered was he by the news that she was home and thriving. The letter had been misdirected to Henri's House, but this afternoon a prefect had brought it by, transforming life in an instant. John had gone straight to Jamie and demanded an exeat, and while Jamie was not in the habit of permitting his staff to leave the premises during term time, under the circumstances . . . Date set, letter sent. He would leave the second of October after morning lessons and return in time for Primus four days later. His JCR and his matron would manage. If only time would go faster.

 —We'll give a play.

It was the third day of term. Gill had not memorized the timetable. He hadn't mastered what was to be worn when and how, who could be addressed and in what manner. He hadn't even purged his vocabulary of bogus slang. The moratorium on dockets would end in a week.

—We'll do no such thing, Gray replied.

—An historical drama about the Wright brothers. You write it, I'll do the rest. We'll use the goggles!

His head spun with objections.

—We don't have a theater.

—We don't need a theater!

They'd give a play in two acts, Gill declared, Act One in the woodshop, Act Two on the playing fields. Gray explained that the Academy had never even had a dramatic society, let alone a play. What's more, clubs were required to apply a term in advance for permission. The more impediments he presented, the more determined Gill became. Gray realized too late that he should have stopped at *no*, that once debate began, the battle had been lost. Still, he couldn't stop explaining—habit? desperation?—the stupidity of getting on the wrong side of authorities and the sorrow that a reputation for keenness would bring them both. Never was a discourse delivered more in vain. Trevor had listened to warnings when they mattered, but Gill remained impervious to reason and indifferent to disapproval. Was this what it meant to be Struck, Gill incapable of rest until the idea worked its purpose out?

To Gray's dismay, their Housemaster thought it a fine idea. Gray stared at the chevrons on the carpet as Grieves and Audsley discussed it. Gill claimed to have met their Housemaster in the holidays, a tale too far-fetched to take literally. Guilford didn't strike him as an outright liar, so it was possible that he'd encountered Grieves at the seaside somewhere, but as to the claim that Grieves had played games and laughed to tears . . . he supposed absurd exaggeration had to be expected from actors.

Grieves having failed to kill off the idea, Gray resigned himself to short-term humiliation. Obviously the play would never happen, but in the meantime, as Gill tried and failed to roust up a company, they would be pariahs. Gray refused to perform, but Gill assured him they'd be flooded by hopefuls once word got out. Only a painful collision with re-ality would change Gill's mind, so Gray decided to leave him to it and meantime to conserve his energies for the other trials of term, such as this evening's unwelcome errand, parley with the Flea.

Burton-Lee had invited each boy in the Lower Sixth to his study by appointment to retrieve their holiday tasks. There, according to Legs, who had gone after lunch, they received their Virgil translations, scarred bloody with markings, and were subjected to a harangue on the subject of the Sixth Form. Gray braced himself, but instead of the promised assault, Burton-Lee launched into a tirade about Gray's studymate, whose acquaintance he had already made. The Flea thought very little of Audsley's skill in Latin—

—If such gross ignorance could be called skill!

And he entertained himself detailing Gill's shortcomings. Gray saw that his studymate had already become known to the Common Room in a way it was never good to be known.

—Kindly remove that expression from your face, Riding. Audsley is your responsibility, is he not?

He was, but what Gill's attainment in Latin had to do with his Keeper was a matter beyond Gray's comprehension. Did the Flea expect him to tutor the Messenger? Or had he bored himself with the usual diatribes and turned to Gray's studymate as a sort of novelty?

—And now I hear the rumor, surely false, that you and Audsley propose to mount some sort of music hall extravaganza?

There it was.

—A play, sir.

Why hadn't he seen it coming?

—I beg your pardon, a *play*. A comedy?

—Drama, sir.

The Flea received the information like a box of chocolates.

—A *drama*. Fascinating!

The Flea occupied the remaining minutes before Prep in florid contemplation of the scheme. (Would he never learn? Though, should he have denied it?) The man's tactics were calibrated to perfection; he'd used them for years, on Gray and everyone. Each twinge felt idiotically familiar, and as he stood on the Flea's carpet, his mind regarded the scene from a distance. This man knew nothing of who he really was, of who wrote to him and what she wrote, of who shared his study and where he came from. Grieves had given permission for the play, so this man had no power to stop it. His barbs fell to the floor like needles hurled at granite. He, Gray, was bigger than this man. He would leave the school one day, and he would write what he would, stories, plays, even poems if Struck. Tonight the Flea laughed him to scorn, but every word fueled a resolve newly lit: to do what this man hoped to shame him from doing, to write this play, to stage it, and even, if necessary, to play a role himself.

The Prep bell rang, and he departed. There were urgent things to discuss with Gill: scenes, casting, lists material. He found him by the chapel in conversation with cheeky Halton. Gray told Halton to bog off and reminded Gill not to speak to the Lower School. More important was the play. He knew how it should start. He knew who to recruit and how.

—I'll tell you what! Gill exclaimed. That boy is perfect for Icarus.

—No!

—Yes! You know it's true . . . *Yes.*

✦

—Tread the boards? Crighton balked. What's that supposed to mean?

Moss explained Audsley's proposal. Their Housemaster had, ludicrously and without taking his JCR's advice, given Audsley and Riding permission to stage a play. This much Crighton knew, and his views on the folly had been aired. Nevertheless, Moss noted that Audsley had already persuaded thirteen boys to join the project, thirteen from diverse years and Houses. The only thing Audsley lacked was two men of their stature to play Orville Wright and Daedalus.

—I hope you didn't encourage him, Crighton said.

—You've got to admit it'd be a lark.

Crighton set aside the rota he was drafting and fixed his attention on Moss.

—Oh, don't start, Moss said.

But Crighton began to lecture, in the way they'd always lectured one another in the firm loyalty of friendship: Moss was not to consider touching Audsley's play. In the first place, his duty as Head Boy forbade it.

—Don't see how. It's licit.

—It's vulgar.

And in the second place, there was the dignity of office.

—Audsley promised the parts would be dignified.

In the third place, Moss should on no account entangle himself in anything that might later become awkward in a personal sense.

—Don't be pi. I'm only looking.

Crighton had nothing against looking, and no one denied Audsley was worth looking at, but looking could be done from a distance, a distance Moss would do well to keep. Especially given the alleged enrollment of Halton, T.

—Is *that* what this is about? It's finished, Crikey, done and dusted.

—That's what you said last term, and then we had the pot-mess with Wilberforce.

—Shut up.

—After which he tried for dockets every day.

—And this term? Not one.

—Yet, Crighton said.

Moss fetched their flask:

—All right, yet.

They drank and spoke of other things, of others worth the look, of Mac and his tiresome fervor, of their Housemaster and his unwonted good cheer, of their rivals and enemies, of every wicked force impeding life's enjoyment. The school was different that term, they agreed. Not as different as it had been when Dr. Sebastian came, yet different nonetheless. Crighton discoursed on borrowed robes not cleaved to their mold, but Moss thought the change went beyond their new posts and belonged to the atmosphere general. They had a pretty fag who knew how to make toast. Grieves had begun to smile as though he meant it. And now the creature Audsley wanted to stage a play. Something in their midst, or in the flask, gave force to the truth, that a play would be a winsome diversion and furthermore that it would offend those they both enjoyed offending. For example, the Flea. For example, Mac, who resented anything that took time from Games.

At the bottom of the flask, Crighton wavered: Everything Moss had said was true, but could they really afford to partake?

How could they not? Moss retorted. It was the only way to stop Audsley and Riding from going overboard with the thing. The reputation of the House was at stake.

—Oh, all right, Crighton said, I'll do it. But don't think you can have Audsley all to yourself.

—Where would be the fun in that?

But Audsley, as it happened, seemed impervious to lust, so fervent was his devotion to the play. He spoke of Rehearsal as Pearce spoke of the Mass. Not satisfied with the mere memorization of parts, Audsley demanded that they respond to unexpected provocations in the manner of their characters. This he termed Improvisation, and at this they labored, almost as Morgan had taught them on the Colt's XV— rigorous practice and anticipation of any play, all put out of mind for the actual match. Moss felt Morgan and Audsley would see eye to eye on many things, not least that practice tilled the ground for something new.

Audsley illustrated the point—if reports could be believed—on the night of the Fourteens' Health Lecture. Tradition dictated every boy at the Academy spend one gruesome hour per annum listening to Kardleigh explain the facts of life. Tradition also dictated they be segregated by age, not form, a point Riding protested bitterly, if vainly, each year. Thus, Audsley had attended the lecture with the Fifteens on Tuesday, while Riding, who was still fourteen, had to wait until Thursday. That night without his Keeper, Audsley had come under attack. (Moss was surprised it hadn't happened sooner; Audsley's eccentricity and lack of shame were two sins the Academy never failed to punish.) Several of the

House XV had swarmed Audsley, boxing him into a storage cupboard and going at him with a cricket stump.

—But then, Leslie said, he wriggled free with some double-jointed mumbo jumbo, coveted another stump, and whacked his way out to the gym.

It sounded flamboyant, leaping across benches with arcane exclamations, but not only did it beat off the XV, it seemed also to have won the House and the entire Fifth to Audsley's side.

—Prout's always thought a lot of his fencing, Leslie said, but Audsley showed him a thing or two.

It was a crying shame the Wright brothers had no swords . . . But now that the play had become chic, the only difficulty was when to rehearse. Audsley squeezed minor characters into their breaks, but as the performance neared, it became clear that the principals needed more time, a problem Moss had been asked to consider.

—God only knows what Wilberforce would say, Crighton quipped.

—He'd have everyone down to the study after lights-out.

Crighton laughed. Moss didn't.

—I dare you! Crighton said.

He was Head Boy; he could hardly dare. But Audsley and Riding were in his dorm, so no one would object if they came to bed late. The only difficulty was Pearce, who had Halton and the Turtle in his.

—If you do it, Crighton said, I'll get us a bottle of Usher's next exeat.

It would take dedication to convert Pious Pearce, but an easy dare was no dare at all, and the stuff in their flask tasted like turpentine.

The first obstacle, Moss determined, was Mac. In his first days as Captain of Games, Mac had unveiled an elaborate scheme for extra practices, and he'd been infuriated when neither the JCR nor Grieves would support it. Moss had tried a range of tactics—flattery, misdirection, humor—but nothing had soothed him. Mac had even requested an audience with the Head, a meeting Moss had attended as much to bridle Mac as to hear for himself what the Head would say. Dr. Sebastian had offered them tea and allowed Mac to make his case. He then delivered a firm and final No. The Academy was not Marlborough or Rugby or even Sedbergh, he explained; it was a small school, and while Games were essential—*mens sana*—it also valued study, prayer, and fellowship. Too much of one, the Head informed them, was unhealthy, and furthermore damaging to other concerns. *Aurea mediocritas* led not, the Head assured them, to mediocrity but to greatness.

Unfortunately for their peace, the interview only fired Mac's zeal. Now, a fortnight later, the First XV were returning from practice exhausted and grim, rumblings of discontent could be heard in the changer, and Mac increasingly invoked the Great Wilberforce: Oh, people had listened to the Captain of Games then! Wilberforce had cared! Moss left the room when Mac began to rant. Mac harped endlessly about the honor of the House, but Moss felt sure that the only honor Mac cared about was his own. Wilberforce's caring was never about himself and not even especially about Games. It was about the boys and what they could become. Even Pearce understood this.

All of which was why Mac could never know of illicit play practices and why Moss had to persuade Pearce—who loved rules as much as the Bible—not only to overlook lateness in Halton and Malcolm tertius, but also to engage in a bit of *suppressio veri* with his studymate.

Moss used his lightest touch: praise for confirmation lessons, mention of Wilberforce, a chummy promise to keep Halton in line. Did Pearce have more sense than Moss gave him credit for, or was the atmosphere general smiling on their venture, bringing them life abundant? Moss had no idea how it happened, but Pearce agreed, Mac remained ignorant, and rehearsals proceeded apace.

✦

Rehearsals were the first good thing to happen in a dog's age, like the rains that followed the African drought. In rehearsal, Audsley would get the look Miranda got, but unlike Halton's sister, Audsley had an ear for other people's ideas. It was important to offer your suggestion lightly, as if it meant nothing. If Audsley approved, he'd absorb it with *Yes, exactly!* If not, he'd let it fade away with a gentle *Perhaps*.

First you learn to spell a little bit . . . That tune Audsley sang stuck in his mind like tar on a shoe, playing like a wireless when he ought to be giving his attention to prep. *Though the process may be slow to you, knowledge of the world will flow to you . . .* What use were sums and parsings when Guilford Audsley walked amongst them? During rehearsals, Moss became Orville to Audsley's Wilbur, brothers, rivals, egging each other on, Moss grinning through Audsley's soft-shoe in the workshop scene.

They'd flown in a biplane one time across the Rift Valley, and now he was zooming over the grasses like the pilot Riding played. The pilot was French, lines gibberish, but he could hear the whole speech. He was speaking perfect French, and he was singing and composing, the whole like Stanford sung by the soloist at St. Paul's.

He awoke drenched in sweat. It was dark, Pearce asleep. He gulped water from the tap and then stole downstairs, out of the House, and up to the choir room. There by torchlight, he tapped the upright piano and drew notes for words he didn't know.

He was skittish the next day and earned fifty lines from the Flea for inattention. He almost welcomed the three-mile run they were forced to undergo that muggy afternoon, but once he'd recovered, queasiness set in. Prep passed too quickly, Prayers even faster. He got ready for bed and lingered in the toilet, but there was no avoiding it. He steeled himself for study number six.

✦

Halton looked ill, and Gray hoped it wasn't catching. As they set the furniture for the workshop scene, Halton's manner grew furtive; this suggested a scheme, or perhaps guilt as it had lately emerged that Halton was one step away from extra-tu, which would remove him from afternoon rehearsals and thus seriously compromise the lakeshore scene. There wasn't time to find out since Gill declared the flying scene needed more dialogue to cover the costume change, and he packed Gray off to Moss's study to write it. When Gray returned with the requested lines, he found Gill, Moss, Crighton, and the Turtle crammed into the window seat, staring at Halton, who looked as though he was about to blub.

—It was only a joke, Halton said.

Gray couldn't recall ever seeing Guilford dumbstruck, but there was a first, he supposed, for everything.

—Where, Gill finally managed, did you get that?

Halton now looked light-headed.

—You wrote that?

—Has Kardleigh heard it? the Turtle asked.

—I didn't mean it—

—Shut up!

—Sing it again.

—But—

—Shut up and sing.

Halton ran a sleeve across his face and with a waver began:

Ici le ciel est clair
Jamais l'aquarium
Ne fut si lumineux
Ne fut si vaste, si vaste

He pressed air through his throat as through the finest instrument, the muscles in his mouth and chest working perfect control, perfect resolve. He was singing the pilot's part, *his* part, from *Courrier Sud*, and Gray knew what was coming, the precious mail, more precious than life itself to thirty thousand lovers. Patience, lovers! In the fires of sunset we come to you! How had Halton made this, from a book found by fluke? They stared as the boy chewed a hangnail.

—Who'll sing it? Gill asked. You or Riding?

—Riding has to, Crighton said. He's *le pilote*.

—I don't sing.

—You sing in church.

—Not like *that*.

—I know! Gill said. Can you write a second part? A harmony?

—Well, Halton said, there's a descant.

—There's a bloody descant!

—I was only joking—

—Sing.

When Halton finished, Gill threw his hands in the air:

—There's our closing.

—What do you call this thing? Moss asked.

Halton mumbled until Crighton clipped him round the ear.

—Only Darwall's 148th with a few adaptations.

—F'what? Crighton said. Speak English.

And so Halton rattled on about hymn tunes, a subject that had never crossed Gray's mind, how the tunes themselves had names and could be used with more than one text, depending on line lengths and meter and—

—So you recut Riding's monologue, forced the meter, found a tune that fit, and composed around it?

Halton nodded.

—He's a freak of nature, Crighton declared.

—Our freak, Moss replied.

—Listen, Gill said gravely. Do you have any more of these?

—What?

—Songs, in your head?

Halton swallowed and Gill stared at him, *feux du soir.*

—Write them, he said. Write them.

She had come home from her wild lurches. This very fact signaled to John a return to soundness. Meg had not in the summer's torturous silence become incapacitated or died. She had not even, by her own account or the girl's, declined but rather improved, to the point of alleged recovery.

Honestly—and wasn't he getting too old to toy with lies?—he didn't quite believe it. How could she have been as gravely ill as she had seemed—so ill that fear had made his scalp break out in spots—and then out of the blue recovered? Not only recovered but reconciled with the scoundrel? There were countless explanations beyond the obvious angle of self-delusion. Perhaps one of the charlatans had offered a cure that worked. This possibility John rated low. It was also possible that the illness had gone into remission. Much of disease could never be cured, yet people carried on with it for a full life span. His own father, for instance. His grandfather, even. John had never known the latter, but the maiden aunts attested to his relentless smoking, drinking, and carousing; he'd been given a year to live when he was sixty yet carried on hale and hearty until the age of eighty-five, when he'd died falling down some stairs. It was further possible—at least John had to consider it if he were honest—that her condition had not been as dire as it had seemed. It was possible that, in his fear of losing her, he had mistaken it for the bane of his family. If he'd had a shred of sense, he would have taken notes in Paris, of her symptoms, of his conversation with the French physician. The one or two fits had stuck prominently in his mind, but had she really been so weakened overall? He'd read his goddaughter's letters many times over the summer, but—honestly—had he not read them with the aim of confirming his own fears, or at least bolstering the thesis of his book?

He knew her. Honestly, he *knew* her. She was often unwell, but *how* unwell? Had it not all begun when Owain ran off with the piece from his office? The cad humiliates her, cue collapse, cue hospital, cue retreat to Paris in the arms of her friend (man-in-waiting?), and then after he leaves, cue lurch across the continent, lurching and lurching, one lark after another (a Hungarian persuasionist?), until now, months later, she lurches back home, having recalled the scoundrel, having punished him and punished him and finally brought him to heel.

It was possible.

But John couldn't know until he saw her for himself. In the meantime, he had her on the line, answering his letters, as long as he didn't spoil it. All calculations rested on axioms, and his with Meg were and must be the principles of friendship. Paris was a distant dream; they were friends, longtime family friends, best friends. When it came to correspondence, friends did not pester or take silence as a slight, but neither did friends calculate their candor, holding back for fear of appearing excessive. At first, he wrote her every day, describing his walking tour and the new business of term. She replied with droll remarks and enchanting descriptions of the house they had bought in Ely. His letters the next week earned only brief reply, but she was occupied moving house. Not wishing to be a burden, he scaled back to three times a week, but even then she blew hot and cold. Mention of his book seemed to inspire silence, whereas sharp remarks on affairs of the day—Dr. Pfrimer's failed coup in Austria, naval mutinies at Invergordon, a dirigible moored to the Empire State Building—received bright replies. The most effective tactic seemed to be a period of silence followed by a couple of sentences or fragments, like a wire cheaply sent. One such dispatch gave rise to her longest reply yet, three pages describing a cast of new neighbors, after which she'd gone silent for another week. The cycle of expectation, disappointment, calculation, and surprise was straining his nerves. But, in less than a week, he would see her in the flesh and sort everything out for himself, and for good.

✦

Gill led them through the usual tongue twisters and physical stretches before going out to supervise the seating. Despite his past solos, Halton felt on edge, and it only got worse when Gill told them to break a leg. They protested vigorously, but Gill explained that in the theater, everything was reversed. Good luck was bad luck. Bad luck was good.

—So say break a leg, and it's all understood.

◆

The atmosphere in the woodshop had all the excitement of a public execution. John had been dreading it, and of course the Common Room had come en masse to witness the train wreck and record it for all eternity. Jamie sat in the front row next to John while Burton-Lee skulked in the back. A handbill announced six titled scenes, demanding some round-the-houses change of seating halfway through. John had been expecting a pageant or perhaps an extended tableau vivant, but as someone flickered the light switch, he realized he'd been hoping secretly for something else, something that would take him back to the Lion Inn and to the bountiful pleasure and invention he'd found there.

Lights out. Guffaws from the crowd. Insults, some profane, hurled under cover of darkness. Then a low, humming whistle, like wind on the moor, growing louder than the catcalls, until—click—a phalanx of torches trained on the audience, blinding them, silencing them, and then swooping around in mad kaleidoscope until they settled on Audsley and Moss, who were turning by hand the pedals of a bicycle, already breathless, already perspiring.

The Wright brothers' bicycle shop. Inventors' dreams. A star-crossed romance with a girl far away. The scene progressed, and though the jeers continued, they never found a foothold. There wasn't time to examine what was happening; Audsley's sheer conviction overwhelmed them. They listened, they laughed when they were meant to laugh, and when Audsley began—insanely!—to sing, they fell silent. Even when Halton and Malcolm tertius began from the sidelines to whistle along and then to make sounds in imitation of instruments, the enchantment only deepened. Audsley could sing, and he could dance; even Moss looked as if he, too, could dance if he chose.

Fifty perhaps had squeezed into the woodshop, but when they moved outdoors, the crowd seemed to double. John had no idea what da Vinci was doing speaking to the Wright brothers at Kitty Hawk, or whether the second scene (*In a Labyrinth*) was intended as a dream or something else. And Riding's role, the French pilot with his *courrier précieux*, why did his speech bring a strain to the throat, his song even more? The crowd whistled during the bows, and before the cheers had ended, Audsley and Co. had been carried off like football heroes. Burton had the grace to congratulate John (as if any of it had been his doing). Jamie beamed, and for a moment it seemed they had stepped into the future, where the

294

school had become what Jamie had always wanted, where Jamie was fully and completely happy and John was part of it, aiding, believing, standing firm.

Afterwards, as he tried to explain the play in his letter to Meg, he realized it was beyond his power to describe. Everything he wrote sounded cloying or outré. The whole thing was a mess, structurally speaking—*Fantasia on Flight*, he would have called it. He'd been their age when he'd first heard the *Fantasia on Christmas Carols*. He tried to express to Meg the link in his mind between *Flight* and the Vaughan Williams composition. Had she ever heard the latter? It had been September, like now. He and his father had been with the maiden aunts in Herefordshire, and the aunts had insisted they attend a certain festival. John had expected candy floss, but instead they crammed into the cathedral for a concert. John had known little of music beyond what he heard in the Marlborough chapel, but the *Fantasia* had knocked him down. He couldn't remember all the parts, but the piece had begun in the Beginning, man's first disobedience, and then it had swept on through every sad and beautiful, half-forgotten but still longed-for good. *God bless the ruler of this house and long may he reign. And many happy Christmases he live to see again.* He set down his pen and pressed the place between his eyes. It seemed impossible that he would live to see another truly happy Christmas, and now, as he remembered his troupe of boys singing, his heart strained again, and he could feel the breath of memory on his neck, of a life before this life, a life they all once had together, before the world began to forget, before they'd fallen captive, before the noise and the machines and this endlessly confused day.

He'd said the truth in Paris, said it out loud. She'd pretended not to hear, and then she'd run away—to escape what, if not her heart's desire? Now she'd stopped running, and he was going to her and she was letting him. Owain might behave, but the one constant with the man was inconstancy. He'd stray again, hurt her again. And then—perhaps not the next time or the time after that—but one time—

✦

Gill said there were always celebrations with plays, when they opened and when they closed, all the more so when they did both at once. Sunday night there had been no time; they only just got the woodshop set to rights and everything else back where it belonged before tea-Prep-Prayers

295

and bed, into which Gray collapsed as if he'd been bicycling for a week. The next day, however, was Gill's birthday, and festivities began by tradition at first bell. Gray had warned Gill what to expect, so he met the ritual with grace. Gray had also warned Gill's parents, by letter, of their responsibilities. They'd obeyed his command, and a hamper arrived after breakfast. Gill shared the whole thing out at morning break, using the occasion to thank everyone who'd helped with the play, and anyone else who claimed to have seen it. This, Gray did not need to tell him, was not done, but it seemed to improve Gill's stock rather than degrade it.

The play had been all the talk and continued so. Birthday rituals continued also, beyond the usual cold bath, seeming actually to intensify as the day wore on. Gill took the kicks, trips, and punches with a smile, though he was reduced to calling Pax at the business in the changing room. Gray wasn't entirely sure if they were accepting him, through it, or punishing him. So long as Gray joined the throng, none of it turned towards him, but he felt that in a breath it could, and that he and Gill both occupied the dangerous shadowland between approval and shame.

At Prep, Gill collapsed across the window seat and fell promptly to sleep. The color was coming up around his left eye, and his shirt was torn. Gray took the flight goggles from the mantel and wrapped them in newspaper. He hadn't been sure, and he wasn't now, but if ever a person deserved them . . .

—What? Who?

Gill startled awake. Someone was kicking the study door, not the horde, but Fardley, who dropped a heavy crate on the table.

—My prep!

—My back, Fardley grumbled.

Gray palmed over sixpence to get rid of him and helped Gill move the crate to the floor. It had been sent from London. They pried the lid off, and Gill began to unpack it, strewing straw across the floor and removing bottles of ginger beer, bags of sweets, tins of sausages, and not one, but two differently iced cakes.

—It's for the feast, Gill explained, after lights-out.

—Oh, come on!

But it quickly became clear that the day had only been a prelude to the main event Gill had been anticipating all along. The dormitory feast was a set piece in school literature and therefore, Gill felt, compulsory for the Full Experience.

—You'll have the full experience all right if you try this on in the dorm!

—Have a little faith, Gill scolded. Moss and Crikey are sorting it out.

—*What?*

—Don't look that way. It's going to be enormous!

The idea was excessive, not to mention embarrassing, but if Moss and Crighton knew, it was up to them to stop it. In the meantime, Gray applied himself to repairing his English prep.

—Dear Mater and Pater! Gill cried from atop a chair. I can no answer make but thanks, and thanks and ever thanks, and oft good turns are shuffled off with such uncurrent pay!

—Switch off, can't you?

—My birthday at the Cad has excelled in every way. Before first bell I was abducted from bed, relieved of my pajamas, and submerged in a bath, one I might add that was covered in ice until it met my arse.

—Life's perilous, Pauline.

—Your first hamper was enjoyed by all, and chaps showed their appreciation with sundry love taps and pranks, in really bang-up style.

—No pun intended?

—Things came to a pretty pass after Games, I must say, when I was debagged and given the Academy version of a birthday spanking, which I don't mind telling you hurt like bloody hell.

—When you've finished your clamorous whining, your present's on the table.

Gill jumped down, alert with anticipation, and opened the newspaper.

—Oh! he said. But, oh . . .

Gray began to sweep up the straw. Gill sat down at the table:

—Are you sure?

—So you'll remember us in your future ca-re-ah.

Gill folded the newspaper into an airplane and threw it into the fire:

—Thanks and thanks and ever thanks.

—It's nothing.

—It's enormous.

◆

Audsley's so-called feast was a ludicrous success, like everything else he touched. The whole House crowded into Moss's dorm, and even Mac enjoyed himself once Audsley had toasted the House's victory over Lockett-Egan's. They'd never done such a thing at the Academy, or, so far as Moss knew, at any school outside the pages of fiction, but in Audsley's hands, it was made to seem natural. His glamour bewitched them into a make-believe school life, one played by torchlight with first-rate food shared like loaves and fishes. As costume, Audsley wore the goggles from the play. They sat on his forehead except when he was proposing toasts, at which time he put them over his eyes. A fag had been set to keep *cave*, the volume remained under control, and the food disappeared before it got late:

—Three cheers for Goggles, Moss said before dispersing them. Hip-hip—

✦

The next day was Michaelmas, which meant goose at luncheon, early evensong, and shortened Prep. Gray was still thinking of new lines for the lakeshore scene, but it was all like a hedgerow full of berries no one would eat. Guilford, meanwhile, had acquired a nickname. Corridors rang with Goggles-this and Goggles-that. Gray couldn't remember the last time he'd slept enough, and as the afternoon dimmed and his head began to ache, he wondered if he was on the verge of the Tower. No harm if he were. His work as Keeper was finished. Gill was better liked than he, Gray, would ever be. As they jostled into chapel, his skin felt raw and his stomach overfull from two days' feasting.

Crighton read the first lesson, his voice rich and confident: Jacob falling asleep with the rock for his pillow, the angels in his dream ascending and descending a ladder to heaven. Then the Eagle, bright tympani, told of war in Heaven and the fight against the Dragon, and then the organ began to blast the pilot's song, only it wasn't quite the pilot's song.

Ye Holy angels bright
Who wait at God's right hand
Or through the realms of light
Fly at your Lord's command

Gray looked to Gill, who grinned and sang: *Trente mille amants!* The pilot's words didn't scan exactly, and the choir sang a different harmony.

My soul bear thou thy part
Rejoice in God above.
And with a well-tuned heart
Sing thou the songs of love!

They could have used these words if he'd known. It would have been finer. More beautiful and better. Jesus saw Nathaniel under a fig tree. *Ye shall see Heaven open, and the angels of God ascending and descending on the Son of Man.* The greatest stories had already been told. No concoctions of a schoolboy could be more than a speck on that eternal face.

Fairies in Heaven . . . The choir was singing again, blowing over them with sound. *Where happy souls have play* . . . That giant breath from the firmament, where everything enjoyed its perfect place, where everything was good and loved by its creator, where Halton sang, open and pure, plunged wholly into making it and giving it. It ended with a whisper, and he didn't want it to end at all. If he were a girl, he might have fallen into tears.

Dr. Sebastian dismissed them to what remained of Prep, but in the cloisters Gray turned back, telling Gill he'd left his pen behind. The mere sight of those blue envelopes pulled from their hiding spot brought promise and hunger again. Rehearsing for the play, he thought that he'd outgrown her, but now, legs crossed in the chair loft, envelopes piled before him . . . what harm would come of opening one, say this, opening and reading again . . . *My dearest and best, my onliest friend. Adieu.*

If he could fly to her new and perfect home, he would stand outside her window looking in. She would sit at a table with her mother and father and the man who was her godfather while he huddled in the snow and wept—like this—and she would open the window, not to climb out but only to ask him what was wrong. *You haven't written!* he'd sob—like this—and she'd laugh gold: *What on earth would I say?*

In the study, Gray repeated the excuse he'd given Pearce—sudden retching brought on by goose—but Gill stared as if he could see how his face had looked before he washed it. They sat down to prep, which was slight and easily finished, and afterwards Gill shared the new praise the play had received.

—The Eagle said he knew the Coward song. Saw it in a review, *This Year of Grace*.

—Good for him.

—Don't be that way.

—I'm not any way, Gray said. I'm only sick to the back teeth of this play of yours.

—Mine?

—No one will shut up about it, even now it's finished.

—How can you call it *my* play when the whole thing's down to you?

—Right.

—You wrote it, Gill said. The idea came from your goggles.

—*Your* goggles.

The bell rang, but Gill held his chair where it was:

—Do you have any more?

—Complaints?

—Stories. In your head that you think about at night.

Hot, the air, and heavy.

—Write them, Gill said.

 Everything is lovely in the town full of eels. It was the first thing she thought to herself every morning, as soon as she remembered to think it. Their house smelled of paint, and the walls of her bedroom were yellow. *Optimisy-May regarde par la fenêtre jaune.* Ely's cathedral had a labyrinth in the floor and an eight-sided tower. When you looked up, the glass and angels were like a kaleidoscope that might sing if someone twisted it. She rode the train to school in Saffron Walden. There had been talk of her boarding, or of Mrs. Kneesworth's keeping her during the week, but she'd begged to stay at home. Every night after tea, she got on with her project—*Improving the Common Weal*—stenciling the bathroom, arranging the bookshelves, tidying the garden. If you turned your back on weeds, they conquered like a Moslem horde. Same with bad thoughts. You couldn't give them a red inch.

Their old house had been bought by a man who'd come to Saffron Walden to kit out the museum in natural history. Taxonomy was not the study of taxes. Through the living room windows, she could see crates heaped against the wallpaper. Something had gouged a streak where the piano used to be. She felt embarrassed for the wall, showing its welts to whoever passed by. Dead animals lay on a table like a macabre doll hospital.

Everything is lovely in the town full of eels. The cathedral was the Ship of the Fens, and nothing could harm them unless they let it. There were candles at dinner, and on Saturday nights her parents went out together. She had found the dearest present for her mother's birthday, and at school they'd learned to pipe fancy icing. Uncle John was coming down, and she would sleep in the sewing room and give him her bed. She didn't mind! The house was different than their old one, but ever so much sweeter. He'd never come for her mother's birthday before, and everyone said it was grand. The cold, sick fear couldn't be allowed a drop of earth to root in. Everything was lovely; nothing horrid, nothing ill.

✦

He'd prepared everything in advance, but when the afternoon arrived, John was rushed. His small case strained and the stitching frayed in one of the corners. The short jaunt seemed to require nearly as much paraphernalia as the holidays. Pajamas, slippers, sponge bag, reading, dress suit. Also, running kit. Since the walking tour, he'd developed a habit of rising at five to take stiff exercise. His routine took him around Abbot's Common before bathing and dressing for Prayers. It also kept him off the cigarettes, but if he skipped a run, sleep became a battle and the decanter more credible. He made room in his case for the books he'd purchased as gifts as well as sixty-three exercise books, which he would mark on the train, mitigating as much as possible the absence Jamie obviously begrudged him.

His neck felt stiff, and as he lugged his things to the gate, the lights began at the edge of his vision. He left Fardley to watch for the cab while he staggered up the stairs to the Tower.

—Ah, Grieves, said Kardleigh. Who's broken what?

—Oh, John panted. No, it's—I'm off, cab's—

—Now don't worry. I'll make the rounds. Everything will be fine.

A yawn overcame him:

—The thing is my head. It's . . .

He yawned again.

—Like before?

John nodded:

—It took Heaven and Earth to get Sebastian to agree to this, and if something were to stop me . . .

Kardleigh felt his forehead, looked in his eyes, and then unlocked the dispensary. John's pulse skipped as Kardleigh emerged with a vial and drew a sip into the dropper.

—Open.

John stuck out his tongue and stifled the urge to yawn again.

—Take this now, Kardleigh was saying, and if necessary another drop in an hour.

It fell bitter in his throat, then warm, blooming—

—Don't take more than three drops in twenty-four hours.

Melting—

—Don't take a drop more than is necessary.

Everything would be well. Meg was well!

—I don't have a smaller vial.

—That's all right! John said.

—So I'll need that back from you.

—Of course.

Not that he was going to take anything further. He hadn't planned to take any, but Kardleigh had insisted. And of course he wouldn't touch anything else in her house, even medicinally. He hadn't, even with soda, since the pints after the footrace. As for the vial, he'd return it untouched, and Kardleigh would see he hadn't needed it after all and the exercise books would be marked and the House would be well and he'd see how well Meg was, how like her old self, and Cordelia, how darling, how all the things she'd always been, and even Owain, all was forgiven and it could be even perhaps a little like the old days, except they were all wiser, and history was progressing with trains, rapid trains like the Flying Scotsman, wonders like that and who knew what else, and things with Jamie were not as they had always seemed and he himself was not as he'd been and so many things, *Flight*, Audsley, the books on his floor from Nurse Friday, time was on the move and so was he, speeding south to that town full of . . . wasn't it something to do with Oliver Cromwell? It would come to him . . . the cathedral tower rising above the fens like a ladder. He'd run three miles every day for more than a month, he hadn't smoked in forty-two days or taken a drink in forty-five nights, things could *change*. Not only could, but plainly were, and although he was older—he'd found six gray hairs the day before—it wasn't too late. He had boarded a train during term time. The sunshine was brisk, the fields green, and the

302

leaves on the trees flamed before his freedom. Life surged through his rejuvenated lungs, the smoothest, warmest spirit he had ever swallowed.

He was awakened the next morning by a vampire bat falling across his face. He jolted upright to find an oversize map of Indochine across the bed, its back heavy with blue globs of putty, which had presumably held it above in an ominous sort of canopy.

He swallowed four tooth-glasses of water and took himself for a run. Halfway around the cricket grounds, the water came back up and he remembered about Cromwell—house in Ely, open for tours? On the way back, he encountered his goddaughter rushing to school. His damp appearance kept her from embracing him, but she let him walk her to the station. Her satchel cut into the shoulder of her coat, but she insisted it wasn't heavy. She carried crates full of books up and down the stairs all the time, she said. She described an attic with a pull-down ladder, a lumber room she called it, where only she could crawl and where lived heirlooms only she had catalogued. For instance, the bed that had been his in the old spare room? That was in the lumber room, but soon, hopefully by Christmas when they had got the men in to knock the wall of the sewing room through to the linen cupboard and make a new spare room that would fit it, the bed would return to regular service and he would have his own room again.

At breakfast he could hear himself being cold to Owain though Meg seemed not to notice. It was her birthday; she ate with pleasure, and her cheeks glowed. As if to make a point, Owain kept reaching across the table to kiss her. Of course, it was his right, but to break off conversation repeatedly and murmur *My darling little girl* was overdoing it, surely.

—Now, John, Owain was saying, you mustn't hurry this afternoon, not in the slightest.

John and Meg had planned an afternoon in Saffron Walden, to visit the graveyard and to collect Cordelia after school for tea with Mrs. Kneesworth.

—You three have a grand old natter with Mrs. K, the old battle-axe. Another kiss.

—My darling girl.

It would be sickening if it weren't so transparent: husbands only overdid it when they had something to hide. Likely Owain had not so much started over with her as he had moved the wife to a different town so he could carry on with his pieces in the first. More obvious was Owain's hostile maneuver in buying a house without a spare room. By many measures the new house was better than the old, but there was no place for John in it. Cordelia had decamped to a cupboard-cum-sewing room and given him her bed, but his neck had begun to ache as soon as he arrived, necessitating another drop.

As they left for the station, Meg put her arm through his. She had been chattering about the new house and town, and now she began to describe the Meeting in Ely, though it sounded as though she'd gone only once. Tradesmen where shouting across the road, and the unsaid pressed like the weight of the scrum.

—Darling, she said, closing her hand around his. Let's not speak of it. Let's agree, shall we, not to?

He tried to stop, but she pulled him along.

—You know, don't you, darling, how grateful I am?

She used the voice that repelled every protest.

—We're all grateful, for everything you did and are doing.

—I can't think what you mean.

—Darling.

Sweet, shaming. He sounded like a child and knew it.

—We've such a beautiful day. Don't let's spoil it.

He followed her, chastened, into the carriage and smiled as she, through a stray association, began to reminisce about the production of *Patience* they'd both been part of at Cambridge. He'd almost forgotten it, but she conjured every detail.

—Knee breeches vermillion!

A man such as Jamie would simply insist. *I'm afraid this won't do. I'm afraid we must speak of it. It being the madcap string of*—what to call them even? Travels? Consultations? Dramatics?—*adventures you followed from the moment I left you until the end of August, one hundred and twenty-five interminable days later, when you wrote from Liverpool that We were coming home All of Us, that Everything Was Splendid, that you were, no explanation, Cured. And as for the Splendid New House, it's plain our holiday arrangements will have to change.* But if he said those things, her eyes would overflow, she'd begin coughing, and it would all come around to his spoiling things again.

In Saffron Walden, Meg bought chrysanthemums to put on Delia's grave. It was something they did every holiday, but this time they found weeds grown up around the headstone. Meg pulled them out with hor-

304

ror and apology, and John realized she was treating him as if he required consolation, presumably for the distress of seeing his wife's grave untended, this woman dead ten times longer than he'd even known her. Meg was acting as if she were the one whose life was satisfactory, whereas he—wife in the ground, life held hostage by some wretched school—were the one deserving solace. For a moment he froze in fear that she might suggest, obscenely, he marry again.

—It doesn't seem so long ago, she was saying, does it?

—On the contrary.

—Oh, darling!

He had always believed Delia was pregnant when she died. He'd found markings in her diary that suggested it, and to his shame, rather than grieve at the notion, John had felt only relief that the child had died with her. What sort of creature would it have been, he'd told himself, a child conceived while in his heart he made love to another? He'd always believed it had been a boy, who would now be Cordelia's age, just old enough to come to the Academy. Now as he carried the grave weeds over to the rough, it occurred to him that the child, if it had indeed existed, would exist still in this very grave, inside her, without name or headstone or even a prayer. Was it wrong to pray for a child you'd no proof existed? Perhaps it was even sacrilegious. This was the kind of question Jamie's father could answer. You could ask, and he'd listen, and all the embarrassment would vanish as he told you decisively: *Yes, pray this*; or *No, and here is why*. Was writing the man so far out of the question? Yet if the Bishop's portcullis were to raise again for him, Meg would accuse him of backsliding to the superstitions of his childhood.

Did it go against the point of love to keep chambers of one's self sealed from one's beloved? Of course it was all hypothetical, wildly so, but if it ever ceased to be hypothetical, he vowed he would renounce the church and conform himself to the Testimonies they affirmed. As they left the cemetery by the far side, he drew a cross in his hand with his middle finger, *This is my solemn vow.*

The hockey match at the Friends' school disconcerted him. The mixed environment for a start, and the sight of his goddaughter whacking things with a stick. He'd never seen her in Games kit before and rarely even seen her amongst other children. She seldom spoke of school, her friends there, her masters and mistresses—teachers, they called themselves.

Also, the pupils' conduct on the sidelines repelled him. They seemed the worst of modern children, though not quite so poorly behaved as the barbarians he'd once observed in a brief, ill-advised episode of holiday training at that progressive school whose name escaped him. The nonsense that was being written about education was enough to drive decent people to violence. At least he and Jamie agreed on that. John supposed the people clustered around the hockey field believed children ought never to be punished, that at root they wanted only to please and that wrongdoing was the product of misunderstandings. Surely no child had ever done a wicked thing for the pleasure of it? Surely actual sin had passed from their world with the establishment of the League of Nations? He was working himself up. A long afternoon beckoned, Mrs. Kneesworth followed by dinner with Owain. The light was glaring, his neck stiff. He'd seen toilets when they'd arrived, and now, as Meg chatted with Cordelia's form mistress, he excused himself. One drop, a small one, in defense of the headache that prowled . . .

◆

She'd always wanted her godfather to come to her school, but he'd never been free during term time. If only he could see it at work, he would realize what she'd been telling him all these years, that he should leave his school and come teach here. Now that he'd finally come, she saw with shame how wrong she had been. He looked pained and disapproving, and he greeted her teacher with a chill lack of interest. Like a green cloud snuffing out the sun, he scowled at them all, even slipping away early as if the place were too uncouth to bear.

She had gone into her bedroom that morning to fetch a hair ribbon and found her bed unmade, one of her maps fallen down, and piles of drab exercise books littering the dresser. Inside one was a boy's labored script, and in the margin Uncle John's broad brown ink. She found the book of her yes-no-sorry boy: *The Arrow War in China*, coolie trade, transit duties, serious topics she'd never heard of. Comments filled the margins top to toe, scolding inaccuracies and praising things that eluded her. This was how he treated his own pupils, strict, unsentimental, unsparing. He lavished time on them, even when he'd left them to come see her.

◆

John had always been a favorite with Mrs. Kneesworth, and he realized as she welcomed them that he'd neglected her. After everything she'd done to help in March, he'd sent her updates from Paris, but since then not a word. She appeared not to hold it against him and kissed them all repeatedly. Since the Líohts returned, she had seen them only once, when the removers came. Since then she had been trying to get them to pay her a visit, but ah, she understood how very busy they'd been. And Mr. Grieves, dear Mr. Grieves, he knew he was always welcome in her spare room should he ever need accommodation in Saffron Walden. Of course, her room would be nothing to the rooms in the grand new house in Ely. John glanced at Cordelia, who returned an expression roughly equivalent to boys kicking one another under the table.

Mrs. K had made a tower of sandwiches, and although she obviously had a tower of questions, she allowed the conversation to unfold in the customary way: what John was getting up to (a book; an intriguing new boy in his House), how Meg was keeping in Ely (splendidly; plans for next spring's garden; service with the housebound), how Cordelia was finding the long journey to school (quite short, actually), whether she didn't after all fancy Mrs. Kneesworth's spare bedroom (so kind, but no), just how churchy was Ely (rather), how in any case it wasn't Saffron Walden (never), what the bachelor who'd bought their house was getting up to (travesties).

—And you still haven't told me about your Grand Tour.

Meg glanced at the clock:

—Your da will be wondering where we've got to.

—It's only five, Cordelia replied. He said not to hurry.

—You mustn't dash off yet.

And so a monologue was undertaken about their Grand Tour, first by Meg, who put quite a gloss on it, and then by Cordelia. To hear the two of them tell it, the whole thing had been one lark after another, *ridiculous* foreigners alternating with *marvelous* foreigners, the account peppered with quaint foreign phrases and their confident assessments of The Germans, The Hungarians, The Swiss, The French, The Italians, The Americans, The Irish.

—And how is Mr. Líoht?

John thought Mrs. K's voice had turned sour. Shouldn't she try harder to conceal it? But Mr. Líoht, Meg assured her, had never been better. Business was thriving, and he was compelled to travel less than previously, scarcely at all. In short, there was nothing under the sun that could be judged unsatisfactory.

Mrs. K turned to Cordelia:

—And whatever became of your correspondent, dear?

Cordelia blanched, and John saw her gaze flit to the clock.

—Pardon?

—The person who wrote to me in the summer, Mrs. K said. I always assumed it was a young man, but I was never certain.

The girl's face was flushing, her cup was being set on the table, and a polite smile was forming, one plainly false, yet one John realized he had seen before and taken as true.

—The one you *asked* to write to me, dear.

—I feel queer.

John had never seen his goddaughter be rude, yet here she was not only interrupting Mrs. K but refusing her mother's help and now actually pulling Mrs. K into the kitchen.

—Whatever was that? Meg asked.

They'd closed the door, and John could glean nothing through it. The mantel clock ticked louder than a galloping horse and then commenced an elaborate chiming.

—I ought to stay with Mrs. K next time, he said.

—Darling. Don't be that way.

She flexed her fingers as if they were stiff. He set his cup on the table and took her hand in his. The edge left her face. She sat back on the settee and closed her eyes.

His lips beat. He could see the pulse in her throat.

It wasn't too late, couldn't be. If Christ were to be believed, it never was, not until the end, and that wasn't yet.

✦

—It was only a young man I met in Budapest, a medical student.

Mrs. K raised her brow.

—It was *entirely* gallant, but you can understand, can't you, why I didn't want to bother my mother with it?

Mrs. K could certainly understand. She'd had a German suitor herself once. This Cordelia had heard many times, but she smiled as if she hadn't. (Had Tommy Gray not received the update telling him *not* to write Mrs. K? She'd written it right after the first, at least she'd thought

308

of writing it . . . had she really lost the thread once her father had . . . train, Lourdes—)

—But, Cordelia dear, why would you ask this man to write to me rather than writing yourself?

She pretended to cough again, and Mrs. K fetched some water.

—It's *such* a tedious story.

Mrs. K settled into a chair.

Oh, dear, the truth was that they'd been in a rush. Their train was earlier than they thought, and this boy—the medical student?—yes, this *poor* boy was simply in love with her, and she felt ever so sorry for him and so she'd tried to make him feel useful and asked him to write to Mrs. K for her. But she hadn't said America! She'd said *Austria*.

But what about the rest? Mrs. K persisted. He mentioned a doctor, Mr. Felix Rush in Asheville, North Carolina? She took down a tin and produced a letter.

Oh, dear!—she snatched it—What a misunderstanding! There had been an *article* in a *journal* about such a man. The boy must have somehow confused it with Austria. He was foreign and tearful and she needed to be rid of him. It had been unwise, she knew, but no harm had come of it.

But what if the young man turned up at her door? He sounded unstable.

But Mrs. K needn't worry! He was Hungarian and penniless and couldn't afford to leave Budapest.

Then why had the letter been postmarked Kent? It was an English letter from an English correspondent. It didn't look foreign and neither did the penmanship.

Was that so? Could she see the envelope? How curious. How *entirely* curious! But . . . ah, now see, she knew *exactly* what had happened. What a circus! This penniless Hungarian doctor-in-training had a friend, a kind older doctor from England who was in Budapest at the time lecturing at the medical school. They had spent time together. No, he hadn't examined her mother, he was a dental doctor. *But* . . . what must have happened was that her Hungarian—his name was Stefan—Stefan must have been *overwhelmed* by the prospect of writing in English, even though he so desperately wanted to help, and so he must have got the English dentist to write it *for* him. And to save the postage, the dentist must have taken it back with him to England and sent it from there. What an adventure! Wasn't life funny?

The birthday, after all, was delightful. Owain's insistence that they not rush back had been, it emerged, so that he could decorate the house with flowers and candles. There was dinner and a cake and a new record for the gramophone, which was playing when they arrived.

After the meal John presented his gifts: for Meg a book of poems by Elizabeth Barrett Browning, and for Cordelia, though it wasn't her birthday, a dictionary of geographical places. His goddaughter kissed both his cheeks in continental style. At least she'd lost the strain of earlier, the ugly, cheerful falseness she'd maintained all the way back from Mrs. K's—some tea cake had gone down the wrong way, Mrs. K had a remedy, and as for the woman's remark about a correspondent, sadly she was becoming confused, more than ever, muddling their journey to Budapest and Bad Wherever with Mrs. K's own childhood suitor from Germany. The girl had tried to correct her memory but in the end decided to humor her. *C'est la vie!*

—Darling, Meg said as the gramophone reached the end.

Cordelia sprang up to turn the record.

—Isn't it grand? she said to John. Da made it my birthday present. It's an *electric* gramophone!

Must have cost a fortune.

—And it's portable!

—Are you planning another Grand Tour?

Her face froze, and he realized the humor had failed. But then Owain had returned from upstairs, where he'd gone to fetch Meg's gift. After numerous *my darling little girl*'s and nearly as many *my onliest heart*'s, he presented an envelope.

—Oh, darling! Meg cried. *The Barretts of Wimpole Street*! I've so wanted to see it.

—There's a ticket for you, too, angel child.

John got up to clear the table, his own gift now striking him as second-rate.

—Oh, Da! When?

—Ah, well . . .

Owain flushed as he did when in a pinch, a blush John had just seen, actually, on the face of his—

—You see, it's a bit intricate.

By which he meant desperately awkward. Meg examined the tickets:

—This Monday? How splendid!

—But that's Uncle John's last night with us.

At least someone remembered. But Owain was spinning an explanation about tickets bought well in advance of John's proposing a visit, and when the visit had emerged, Owain naturally had rung the box office to arrange a fourth seat, but alas the performance was by then sold out. An intricate situation to be sure, but one Owain was sure they could sort out somehow.

—Uncle John should have my ticket. I've got school in the morning, after all.

—I won't hear of it, John said.

The last thing he intended to do was attend *The Barretts of Wimpole Street* with Meg and her husband.

—There's someone I must see in London, he continued. I've been wondering how I was going to fit it in, but now . . .

Meg was looking quizzical, Cordelia was trying to conceal her relief, and Owain was beaming.

—So you see, John said, it's all very convenient. We can ride down together—

—And have an early tea, Owain added. I'll ring right up and change the booking.

—And I'll see my friend.

—Who is this friend, darling?

—Come to think of it—

Improvising wildly now.

—isn't there a night express from King's Cross?

If he took it, he could get back much faster.

—Oh, but darling—

—We could pop over to the station right now, Owain was saying. Just see what they know.

He and Owain went together, and it was concluded that leaving from London rather than Ely would be a boon, a convenience, and a perfect idea.

Back at the house John excavated a card from the pocket in his case, where it had sat since the last time he used it. F. P. Merewether, LVO, CMG. The Boltons, Kensington.

Sometimes you had a spot, and you squeezed it and squeezed it but it wouldn't burst. She said she had prep and went upstairs. Her father had put candles everywhere, so it wasn't anything to take one and to open the window and to feed Mrs. K's letter to the flame. Mollifying the woman had been harder than the most vicious hockey match, the kind where you came away with cut shins, but she had fought and fought and eventually won.

He had no reason to write Mrs. K again, but if he did, the things she could imagine were more tangled than morning glory. It had seemed the best thing to send those parcels to him, to treat him as some underground library, open only to monks who knew the password, monks who could say spells and turn people into fishes—like when St. Dunstan turned Ely's monks into eels—but he was not a monk, her yes-no-sorry boy, he was more like a secret agent behind enemy lines, and you never told agents a word more than necessary in case they were captured, because then they would be tortured and forced to tell whatever they knew, which was why she had to do this thing, no matter what it cost.

Dear Tommy Gray, If you are honorable, you will do as I ask.

She had to make him obey no matter what he thought.

You must swear an unbreakable oath never to write me or anyone I know (most especially Uncle J and Mrs. K).

To guard against the worst.

Take everything I've ever sent you and put it in the fire, completely all the way.

Batten the Hatches.

And then forget I ever existed.

Luck Turn.

If you are a gentleman, if you have a heart, you'll do these things. It's desperate, life and death. I am not exaggerating.

Blood Sacrifice.

My truest and best and onliest friend.

She had a stamp, and after they'd gone to bed, she went down the road and dropped it in the pillar box. Disaster stopped, nearly, or would be after blood had been given. Her penknife had cut her once by mistake, but now . . . three down, one across, behind her ankle where no one could see. Iodine like a train's brakes, trumpet pumping, sparkly sound, *my stardust melody, the memory of . . .*

 John forced his sponge bag into the horrible case, but the exercise books would have to be arranged more scientifically in his satchel. If he'd known how slack he would be marking only ten on the train and none during the visit, if he'd known how abominable his head would be, as abominable as the Remove on the Ottomans or the Fifth on the Punic Wars . . . Failure flooded him, swarmed him, persecuted him, like a murder of crows. Though why not detected him like a sleuth of bears? Worried him like a troubling of goldfish? Upbraided him like a scold of jays? He was being flippant and it was unwise. (Chilled him like a shiver of sharks?) He could hear the gramophone being cranked up—switched on?—the needle lowered onto another record. (Lay in wait for him like a skulk of foxes?) His goddaughter had developed a mania for popular music, which, if this weekend's sampling was anything to judge by, concerned itself exclusively with love: love lost, love found, love longed for, love soured, love in every state including neat. He couldn't follow the currents of modern culture; he knew his Beethoven from his Bach, his Elgar from his Gilbert and Sullivan, but that was about it. And these cursed exercise books, an unkindness of ravens, he'd simply have to sit up on the night express and finish them. Hopefully his supper with Merewether would finish early and he'd be able to make a start—finally, the tongue caught and the wretched books shut up. (Ye pandemonium of parrots!)

He scanned the room for forgotten items. The suffocating map of Indochine lay across the armchair. If the spare room wasn't finished by his next visit, he would insist on staying with Mrs. K. Sleeping in his goddaughter's bed felt indecent, and the patchwork of maps were reminiscent of the pin-ups he was sometimes forced to confiscate from boys' cupboards, as if she'd lain in bed at night thinking rash thoughts about them, an infestation of cockroaches.

The vial rolled out from the quilt. He slipped it into his pocket and went downstairs.

She was dancing with her father, her head resting against his chest, hair pulled back with a red ribbon. Owain looked dashing, far better than John in his evening suit, and he could dance, rocking her gently and stepping into a turn. *Stars fading but I linger on, dear . . .* John was at the bottom of the stairs, but he couldn't bear to interrupt, not when she looked so happy, as happy as a girl could be, in the arms of her father, French shoes on her feet.

—You look smart.

Meg's voice at his elbow, her scent not what he knew, but something complicated and floral.

—Miss Drayton?

She took his hand, and they danced in the corridor, and even though he couldn't dance, they fit together, beat by beat.

—May I? said Owain, stepping in beside them. Mrs. Líoht?

Her smile stabbed worse than the orchestra's strings. She was happy in the arms of her husband.

But his goddaughter was tugging him back to the parlor, arranging his hands at her shoulder and waist, steering him around like the turntable, like the years. And then the orchestra was sighing, and her arms encircled him, her face against the front of his jacket inhaling the dust of a wasted life, fatal and acute.

The Travellers Club inspired awe, and John supposed it was meant to. Merewether was waiting in the cocktail bar, looking even crisper and more native than he'd seemed wandering Marlborough's corridors in June.

—Grieves!

He took John's hand and leaned into his ear:

—I was afraid you wouldn't come.

—Why?

Merewether pressed his lips together, as he used to at the preposterous but lovable aspects of school life.

—What can I get you? I've people for you to meet.

John realized it would be gauche to refuse a drink at a club.

—Scotch, isn't it? Merewether said.

In some ways, Merewether was like the Marlborough boy John remembered, the one who'd run the House with him, employing more charm and discretion than any Head Boy John had known before or since. In other regards, Merewether was a stranger, one who nevertheless fêted John around the club as a man of note, a man they all would want to know despite his schoolmaster's shoes and provincial suit.

He'd eaten already, but it seemed a meal was planned. They sat in the dining room with three other men, intimates of Merewether—Pursey, Hamilton, and Swann—or was it Purdey, Hamlin, and Swann? John had lost track during the introductions, and he couldn't ask now. Despite the fact that Merewether treated everyone there as a friend, John thought there was something different about these three, the Three Swans as he came to think of them. It was as if Merewether were hosting a party with him as the guest of honor and them as fellow hosts, even though they'd never met him before.

The Three Swans had been in Egypt with Merewether during the war, and before that had been at Winchester and Charterhouse, or was it Westminster and Charterhouse? One of them had known Jamie at Oxford, but otherwise there appeared no clear connection between them and John. Their looks and their talk, peppered as it was with references to everything à la mode, made them seem younger than Merewether, but John also thought they must be older since two held posts of some influence in government, and Swann himself was something to do with art, or so John supposed given his references to the Museum. John thought Merewether was with the Foreign Office, but now he couldn't recall where he'd heard that, or even if he'd heard it.

After dinner they retired to the smoking room, where brandy was ordered and cigarettes produced.

—What is it your people are seeing tonight? Merewether inquired.

John told him. Swan One poured scorn upon the play:

—Invalid lady takes up with poet. Papa forbids. I ask you.

—Not our sort of thing, Swan Two agreed.

—Now *Salome*, that would be the ticket.

—It's being staged? John asked.

—Opening night, my dear!

—But not for the family, perhaps.

Merewether passed the cigarette case, and John vowed to take a double run at the next opportunity. The cigarettes were opening his veins, his blood was flowing more freely, the brandy like a warm remembrance, but he wouldn't have more than this glass.

—Well, Grievous, what do you think? Merewether asked.

John smiled. Merewether and the Swans smiled back. John wondered if something had been decided. He fished out his watch.

—It's early, Merewether said. We aren't letting you go that easily.

John wasn't sure if it was the brandy or something else, but he felt content. He accepted a second cigarette as they launched into a debate about the relative demerits of the Soviets and the Germans. The Germans were schemers, according to Swan One. They'd no more secured relief for reparations than they'd turned around and given the Soviets discounted credits. John couldn't follow beyond the general, but their discourse made a change from the ill-informed bloviating he was forced to endure in the SCR. Swan Two thought the Soviets were worse. They accepted German loans knowing full well they could never repay them, and meantime they sat on the jolly side of what John inferred was a significant trade imbalance with England, taking full advantage of the fracas with the gold standard and favoring the Germans because they could barter with them like Arabs rather than pay cash like decent people.

—But if the Soviets skin the Germans, then won't the Germans skin us? John asked.

—You see, Merewether said, I told you he'd suit us.

The Swans nodded and tapped their cigarettes. Were they moving in unison, or had his mind drifted off? Something was eluding him. He had to make an effort. This was something to do with Merewether's group. The Swans were the group, surely? Had anything explicit been said? He hoped he wasn't making a reckless inference. Certainly the Swans were clever, and between them appeared to have information on every topic under the sun, but the group itself, had Merewether said what it was about? John wondered what a more clever man would do in his place. Merewether had called himself a confirmed bachelor, but was it possible that the Swans, clearly so eligible, could be unmarried?

—I can't imagine how a widowed old schoolmaster could have anything to offer, he said.

There was a commotion at the far end of the room. Merewether and the Swans seemed not to notice it.

—We don't mind widowers, said Swan One.

The other two sucked their cigarettes as if someone had uttered a pleasantry.

—I think we might do something with you, Merewether said, schoolmaster and all.

The brouhaha grew louder, drowning conversation.

—Oh, for pity's sake! Merewether exclaimed. Excuse me.

He got up from the table and approached the quarreling group:

—Colonel Mainwaring, good evening, sir.

The ruckus ebbed as Merewether engaged the man who had been doing most of the shouting.

—Dreary old bore, said Swan One.

—Club only puts up with him, Swan Two explained, because he was right about Suez when no one else was.

John's mouth was dry.

—What did you say his name was?

They told him. The repetition didn't make it any better.

—His son, John stammered. In my House at St. Stephen's, until this Easter.

—Yes, said Swan Two as if he knew it already.

But Swan One was opening a panel in the wall and whisking them through it to a corridor.

—Billiards? Swann asked.

John asked for the cloakroom, his neck an ambush of tigers. The cloakroom servant refused to leave his side even when he'd accepted the proffered towel. He feigned dizziness.

—Please, could you fetch Merewether?

Door shut, vial, tongue, sun, blood utopia . . .

Coffee, black, at the club, at the club at the club at the station. Cordelia's head in his arms, hearty thanks from his mouth, Meg's cheek cool and hot then gone to their own train. He had to sit down on his case and close his eyes, heart in every point, descent of woodpeckers.

—You haven't any idea what we've been talking about, have you? Merewether had asked.

They'd walked alone out to the street where Merewether had fetched

317

a cab. John didn't know what he'd said in reply, but it had made Mere-wether laugh:

—It's what comes of too many clever people in close quarters.

—A shrewdness of apes?

—Oh, Grievous!

John opened his eyes. A figure that looked like Meg was weaving towards him. *Sweet dreams hmm-hmm-hmm-humm-you* . . .

Merewether had held on to his hand after he'd got in the cab:

—If you leave Sebastian's place, be in touch, won't you? You can join us. Do something for the country.

Mischief of mice.

—No one understands. Practically no one.

—No?

Merewether had glanced at the driver, who ignored them.

—One can't fight the old wars again, or make the new ones vanish by wishing them away.

Deceit of lapwings.

—It will be amusing.

Sweet dreams . . . It was Meg, really, after all. She was waving. He stood:

—I thought your train was going.

—It is, she gasped. I didn't want to leave without saying goodbye properly.

She took his hand, both of them.

—You know, don't you, darling, you're my oldest, my best—

His mouth was on hers and it was soft, pressing, open, all the longed-for, impossible—tongue, teeth—

—Darling, she said.

She put her lips back on his, and it was real, flocking around him like the feathers in the war, love become act, wish become true, rescue as never—never to now.

 Halton knew strange forces were afoot. First *Flight* and now the latest, *Not Far to Castle Noire*. The day after Michaelmas, Audsley had pinned an announce-ment to the study door, and the page had quickly filled with names of hopefuls. There wasn't room for his, but Audsley had summoned him at break, as if everything had been long ago decided and he, Halton, were only pretending not to know it. His part would be larger than before, with more lines to learn. Master Shadow was a conjurer, an acrobat, a thief without peer. He wasn't sure about the acrobatics, but Audsley promised to teach him. Audsley himself would play the lead role, a knight called Valarious. The plot concerned the quest of said Valarious to rescue his brother, the Elf Rider (played by Riding), from the evil clutches of Perspicacious (Crighton). The Turtle would be playing a girl (ha), Kahrid of Langstephen, while Moss would portray a rival magician called Flash. Everyone else on the list was given brief roles or else thinking parts, Audsley's term for people who walked on and said nothing. The main rehearsals continued as before in study number six, and every morning before breakfast, Audsley took him through exercises in the gym. Already he could walk on his hands and turn three kinds of cartwheel.

The new play was more dramatic, and rehearsals had teeth. When, in his long speech (two pages!) he denounced Moss's character—Who was this *Flash*? This magician soi-disant (that meant so-called), this fraud who trafficked in electricity? He stole sparks from their fire. He was vulgar, his name too short. Master Shadow had never heard of him!—when he recited this tirade, Moss colored with true emotion. It was better than eating a whole cake. Everything in the study made him hungry, the decoration, the smell, the pink glow when Audsley put the lantern over the bulb, and even though something scratched his throat and made him sneeze—perhaps dust from the great number of books Audsley and Riding had borrowed from the library—still he craved it. Even as he languished in extra-tu Monday afternoon, laboring hopelessly under Burton-Lee's hand, his true self was turning somersaults, fingers restless for the next lock to pick.

—If you don't apply yourself, Halton, you'll become a regular fixture here.

—Laubadamar, sir?

Clip round the ear.

—Lau . . . lau . . . ba . . . I mean da . . . ba . . . mur?

Gibberish, surely?

—Continue.

Deep in the uncharted passages of Castle Noire, the party confronted traps and guards. Swordplay, backflips, spells sung and chanted, they

worked their way through the servants of Perspicacious, the most intelligent and evil man in the land.

—What are we going to do with you, Halton?

If only the letters would keep to their place. If only Flash could stick
them still.

—Do you think you're the only one?

—Sir?

—To find things difficult the way you do?

If only time would skip to the evening, to rehearsal, that hardening,
mouthwatering—

—Empty your pockets.

—Sir?

—You heard me.

Nothing contraband, thank God, just the usual stores and supplies.
The Flea sifted through it, pausing only over the tin of Nigroids for Throat
and Voice, which he opened and sniffed.

—How many of these vile confections have you eaten today, boy?

—Today, sir?

The glare.

—Not more than half a tin, sir.

The Flea poured them into the bin.

—Oh, sir . . .

—Since your Housemaster appears to have strayed from the hearth,
young Halton, it appears that a docket issued this evening would benefit no one.

—Yes, sir. I mean . . .

He wasn't sure he could stand another earnest jaw from Grieves.

—It appears, then, that we have no choice. You shall have to pop by
my study instead of his, this evening after tea, and we shall have to see
if we can find a way to enhance your concentration, one way or another.

—Yes, sir.

—Fewer sweets, more sleep, I think.

◆

They were developing terrible habits during their Housemaster's absence.
Moss knew it couldn't continue, but if for the moment rehearsals happened to stretch past lights-out, and if they afterwards lingered over

320

Audsley's game of Definitions, and if Mac slept like death, well, where was the harm?

—Thou detestable maw! Audsley groaned as Riding swept the round for the fourth time running. Thou womb of death!

There might be little hope of getting into Audsley's trousers, but the Billingsgate that flowed from his mouth was consolation enough.

—Riding's almost as infernal as Grieves, Audsley said, but he shan't prevail.

Moss announced bed, but Audsley brandished his pencil at Riding:

—Draw thy tool. My naked weapon is out!

Crighton snuffed the candle, and Moss retreated to their study for a fortifying nip, enough to calm seas and the ships upon them.

—Leave some for me, Crighton said, closing the door.

Moss surrendered the flask and sighed.

—Everyone's turnable, Crighton said. Eventually.

He meant it consolingly, but it only stirred the embers. They'd been discussing it for weeks, could Audsley be turned? In Moss's experience most boys could, but Audsley met temptation as one who never hungered.

—I don't think he even wanks.

—Bollocks, Crighton said. Everyone wanks.

Audsley broke so many laws of nature, why not this? He seemed to care for nothing truly beyond his enormous ideas. Ordinary things—washing, eating, even sleeping—he seemed to perform with only a fraction of himself until he could return to rehearsal, a term Audsley used to encompass anything that served the play. Even now, back in the dormitory, Audsley sprang from bed:

—You won't forget to talk to Grieves tomorrow?

—Please.

—You're sure he won't say no?

—Go to bed.

—It's the only place that will hold everyone and—

—If you're not in bed in ten seconds, you're getting a docket.

The only thing better than hearing Audsley swear was pulling rank and then watching his reaction:

—You are a fishmonger.

✦

John tore through the exercise books as the night express churned north. He hadn't taken any drops since the club. He didn't need them. Perhaps he'd never need them again. He was learning something surprising enough to change the color of air: mercy hurt, and the breaking didn't stop with the chains. It was real between them, unmistakably and radically; everything else would change without his help.

A calm had come upon him, and a deep vitality. Here he was charging through the countryside at speeds unknown, and with him this procession of humanity and their luggage. And the mail. The blessed night mail! In what other country could one post a letter on the Monday and have it delivered a hundred miles away the next morning? The world was awash with sensational activity. He could spare a thought for it because the other thing was taking care of itself. Here was *The Times*, left on the seat by the previous passenger. It simply teemed with activity: marriages, deaths, situations wanted, bungalows for rent, automobiles of 1932; cycling results, boxing results, rugby football club and school (Dulwich beat Merchant Taylors' by a goal and a try to nothing); cinema news, literature news, opera news, theater news (*Salome* at the Savoy, *The Good Companions* at His Majesty's, *Jane Eyre* at the Kingsway); air-mail schedules, shipping schedules, national radio schedules; *Ovaltine Builds-up Brain, Nerve, and Body*; and Sanatogen. Sanatogen! *Three months ago I started taking Sanatogen on the advice of my doctor. My system had been undermined by years of neurotic strain and mental debility and I could not expect miracles to happen. But a miracle did happen, and in a few short weeks I found myself acquiring a new sense of well-being. Now after three months of regular treatment of Sanatogen I am reborn. Sanatogen has instilled new life into me. It is amazing.* Where, God, could Sanatogen be found? And Jaeger, not for his eyes, surely, but nevertheless printed here beside discussions of MacDonald's Cabinet. *The new line is touchingly dependent on the lingerie beneath. The little more and one is a bundle; the little less and one is a void. Jaeger, with superhuman cunning, contrives to blend firmness and flexibility in the most diplomatic way in these austere little two-piece sets. The most sustaining and secretive vest that will not gatecrash the frankest décolletage.* The underscoring made the paragraph a gem. *Tiny panties that furl the hips and waist in the most etherealising sheaf, yet remain utterly plastic and benevolent.* Seriously, though, how could they print such things in a family newspaper? But here was Selby, and so to Driffield and then Sledmere and Fimber, where he'd find Fardley, who would convey him to the gates of his home, where he had his own rooms and space enough besides; where he could bring her; where no one, not even Jamie, could make him deny what he knew. He was needed there and wanted, and now as the light came into the sky, his boys would be rising, intent on the day, eager, hungry, waiting for him to show them the way through this godforsaken mess of living to the future that waited, just beyond the crest, for them to seize, to mold, to possess.

✦

Mr. Grieves had been back a day already without giving them his answer on *Castle Noire*. Now the unnerving message from Crighton:

—Grievous wants you, start of Prep.

—Us? Gill asked.

—You, Crighton said to Gray.

—But why?

—Buggered if I know.

Gray scoured his memory. He hadn't received a single docket that term, not even the threat of one. If Grieves wanted to discuss the play, he would have included Gill; likewise if he'd found out about late rehearsals. By seven o'clock he'd checked his uniform so many times that Gill threw him out of the study. He went to wait outside Grieves's door.

The pigeonholes mocked him. They brought post to other people, but not to him, unless you counted his mother's turgid reports. His godfather neglected him, despite the week they'd spent cheek by jowl in Boggle Hole at the end of the holidays, and despite the fact that Gray had written Peter three times with news of Guilford Audsley and *Flight*. He used to check his pigeonhole twice a day, but now he avoided it. The other pigeonholes had been ransacked already, though Mac's still contained a letter, as did Halton's, and Audsley's a parcel, likely delivered late and containing, he could tell by the size, a shipment of Nigroids, now all the rage amongst the cast. His mother would not approve. She ought to send him something, though, anything to fill this void that reached back into the deepest—wait . . . He scraped something forward. Not blue, but—the hair stood up on his scalp—her script across an English envelope, no return address but a postmark—Ely!—torn, shaking— 3 October—four days ago!—*If you are honorable* . . .

His breath was stuck in a pipe at the right side of his chest, pressing like a boil about to burst, but as he read, he grew more vital, more defiant.

When he came to the end, his answer was sure: *Like hell I will. Burn them yourself!*

—Ah, Thomas, sorry to startle.

Grieves, books in arm, escorted him through the door. Light, dust, carpet.

—Hope I haven't kept you waiting.

Her letter bulged in his jacket.

—Sit.

He pressed it as flat as he could.

—I expect you're wondering why you're here.

There was no reason on the earth to make him empty his pockets.

—I wanted to speak with you alone.

About the letter? *Pull yourself together.*

—Please, Riding, sit.

Let him not have gone there. Let him not have made her write—

—You needn't look so stricken. Unless you've something to confess?

Pull yourself together! Grieves was *joking* about the confession. How did a person with a clear conscience look?

—I wanted to speak to you about this.

Grieves slid an exercise book across the desk. It was Guilford's. *Results of the Punic Wars*, 3/20. That wasn't good. Gray didn't remember the composition. If Grieves was going to put Gill in extra-tu, why not tell him directly?

The man leafed through another book and, after finding the desired page, placed it beside the first. Also Guilford's. *Causes of the Punic Wars*, 18/20. Better. It ought to have been since Gray himself had written the draft, a draft that appeared little changed, to judge by the first page. Why had it earned only eighteen marks?

—So you see, Grieves was saying. It's one thing to offer friendly advice, but to actually write the composition for him . . .

Surely this wasn't all about *that*? Everyone cribbed. Who was Grieves suddenly to take offense?

—You can wipe that expression off your face. Don't bother denying it.

What expression?

—You're a terrible liar, and at any rate it's obvious when you compare this essay written in class with these others, submitted as prep.

He'd have to be more circumspect in his assistance, but how on earth did Grieves imagine Gill would avoid academic ruin if someone didn't do his prep for him?

—And you can drop that expression as well. Do you think we masters don't know everything that goes on here?

Of course, they didn't.

—Of course, we do. Just because we choose not to remark upon a thing does not mean it goes unnoticed.

Madness.

—For example, Audsley's last four assignments were written by you. Of course, he copied them over, corrected a few of your spelling errors, sadly not all, fudged a date the wrong way, and put his name to it.

What spelling errors?

—And from the look of his English and Latin preps . . .

Here Grieves produced more exercise books, bearing the unlikely remarks of the Eagle and the Flea.

—Oh, yes, we do speak to one another. It seems the same is true everywhere, with the conspicuous exception—

He riffled backwards through one of them.

—of the two nights you were in the Tower with a throat infection.

Laryngitis.

—Let me see if I have this straight: Audsley under threat of extratu. Rehearsals jeopardized. You assist, which on top of your own work keeps you awake until Heaven knows what hour—

The pipe in his chest!

—Of course, Moss knew nothing about it—leaving you exhausted, hence the throat infection, and today falling asleep in Lockett-Egan's Chaucer lecture. Am I wrong?

Wherever Grieves had gone, it had transformed him into a freak of nature. There was absolutely nothing to say to the man, which was just as well since he'd launched into the Earnest Rebuke and showed no sign of stopping.

It was unfair, and cruel besides, to terrify him halfway into the grave with invitations to the study and then proceed to jaw him about something as inconsequential as Guilford Audsley's prep. Obviously, Gill was destined to be one of those boys who languished his entire career at the bottom of the form, a reliable measure of rock bottom. Every school needed such people, surely, and where was the harm so long as Gill offered something else, which he so plainly did, like Halton with the choir or any number of boys with Games? Take Mac, for instance: he hadn't made it beyond the Fifth and probably never would.

—Are you listening to me, Riding?

—Yes, sir.

The only difference between them was that Halton and Mac actually did their prep, whereas Gill would have turned up empty-handed any number of times if Gray hadn't intervened. They'd have to discuss that. Guilford had to be seen to try.

—Now, before you go—

It was coming to an end, though not soon enough. He had a hundred things to do before bed.

—I'm hoping you can convey a message to your studymate.

Do your own prep. He could write the script. He could write any script!

—I've spoken with Dr. Sebastian—

About this? Was he cracked?

—about your newest play, and I'm afraid he isn't amenable to your performing it in the chapel.

Ah . . . that. Gray hadn't thought he would be, but Gill had insisted.

—However, I've managed to secure the gymnasium for the upcoming Sunday. It isn't as spacious, but I'm sure you can sort something out.

—Thank you, sir. The eighteenth?

—The eleventh, after the Sedbergh match.

Four days away? Impossible! Worse than impossible. Disaster!

—And, Grieves continued, it might interest you to know that I shall be making a tour of the dorms tonight, and in future whenever it seems necessary. I shall expect to find the entire House asleep, and I shall look unkindly upon any somnambulists I encounter.

Nail in the godforsaken coffin!

—Do I make myself clear?

As death. How had this interview gone so wrong?

✦

A clear success, as interviews with Riding were wont to go. John knew he shouldn't have favorites, or their opposite, but Riding he had to class one of the latter—keen mind, a way with words, but outside the classroom, deliberately infuriating. What was it Morgan used to say? Anxious and pleasing, or sullen and resentful. Now the boy had got his categories crossed, anxious and resentful, of *what* even? And the lying! Not that he'd actually said anything untrue this time, but his expression screamed untruth. For a boy with little need, he lied often and unconvincingly. He had to be the world's worst liar, which, John supposed, might be a kind of achievement.

◆

Gill called the news a minor snag and started twirling pencils in and out of his fingers, his usual technique for solving problems. They'd only rehearsed the first two scenes. They could shorten the others, but how much? And they hadn't even begun with the costumes or the setting or—

Gill stopped twirling:

—A serial!

—What?

—Like *Tarzan the Tiger*, but live and talking!

Objections were already clogging the pipe.

—We'll give the first two scenes Sunday, then one or two more each Sunday after that!

What was the point in objecting? He knew they'd do it. They always did it. He even wanted to do it. Why should his be the voice of reason? If saffron-haired girls could emerge from the void to write such arrant trash . . .

 John ransacked his medicine cabinet for a suitable container. Kardleigh had asked for the vial back, and a difficult patch lay ahead. Jamie had asked to see him after lights-out, and while he hadn't said why, John suspected the Headmaster hadn't appreciated the witty advertisement Audsley and Riding had staged at the end of Evening Prayers. Pearce had already given them fifty lines apiece, so as far as John was concerned, justice had been dealt, a fact he would convey to Jamie in no uncertain terms.

Also pressing, letters. He'd already sent Meg a note of thanks, simple and neutral, for the visit. Her reply would show him where things stood. He had written Tuesday night, and now it was Saturday; nothing would come tomorrow, so . . . He rinsed out the iodine bottle and poured Kardleigh's solution into it. A drop rolled down the side; he licked it—prophylactic—before refilling Kardleigh's vial with water.

Dorms, Kardleigh, Jamie. Then work, to repel thoughts of Monday's post.

—Sir, to what do we owe the honor?

Moss greeted him outside the washroom.

—Making sure everyone finds his way to bed.

—Of course, sir.

—I'll be through later.

—That won't be necessary, sir.

—Nevertheless!

He left them to their noise. Outside, the wind had teeth. He bounded up the stairs to the Tower.

—Maestro?

—Be right there, Kardleigh called.

His heart slammed. The morning runs had improved his stamina, and he wouldn't expect the stairs to wind him, even taken two at a time. Perhaps he ought to try Ovaltine? Tonight alone he had the Fourth, Remove, and Upper Sixth to mark in addition to the day's correspondence. What was taking Kardleigh so long? It was spoiling the illusion of spontaneity.

—I've no idea how—

Kardleigh returned, wiping his hands with a towel.

—But Fletcher has made a pig's dinner of his knee.

—He was all right at Prep, John said.

—Some sort of mucking about on Burton's stairs.

—I only popped by, John said, to return your little drops.

He removed the vial from his pocket.

—Didn't need them after all, luckily.

And dropped it on the floor.

—Oh, no!

Where it broke.

—I am sorry. What frightful butterfingers!

He stooped to collect the pieces.

—I'll clean this up. It's the least I can do.

Burton was in Jamie's study when John arrived. Jamie was refilling their drinks and wearing that look: Headmaster displeased with his school.

John refused the brandy and was forced to sit on the settee since Burton was occupying John's usual seat.

—There's method in Audsley's insolence, Burton was saying, as if he's laughing at us.

Jamie murmured in agreement.

—Tradition is tradition because it *works*, Burton continued. We must maneuver *within* it. We must find ways *around* one another.

Heavily, John realized he ought to have tackled this sooner, before Burton had worked himself up and before Audsley had worn out his welcome with Jamie. He poured himself a glass of soda as Burton waxed lyrical.

—Think of the original Academy.

The garden made by Academius for Plato, to think, to work, to teach. What would have become of the Academy, Burton asked, if each pupil had taken Academius to task for the shape of the walks, the choice of flowers?

—People like your Guilford Audsley—

Burton waved at John.

—Are blind to the delicate equilibrium we labor, yes *labor*, to maintain here, one garden at a time.

Jamie was agreeing with him.

—Peace is fragile.

Even John was beginning to agree with him.

—I'd thought, Jamie was saying, that it would only be the one play. But now we have another, not to mention these disruptions.

—Work is suffering, Burton said. Look at young Halton. Look at Audsley himself. You can't deny it, Grieves. *Ordinary life* is suffering.

The days of excess were past, Burton reminded them. Their mandate was balance, decency, discipline. Without these things, one element could overpower the rest, like aggressive weeds or bullies. Too much study led to dullness, too much sport to brutishness, too much prayer to zealotry, too much diversion to shallowness, too much food to gluttony, too much desire to wantonness, too much of anything, in short, led to corruption and the flight of reason.

—I'm not sure what we're arguing about, John said. The performance is tomorrow, and then it will all be over.

✦

A fag came to him halfway through the Sedbergh match to announce Uncle Peter, waiting at the gates. Gray left the sidelines, walking briskly, nausea rising. To run would make real what he feared. That was how disasters worked. They hacked down everything you took for granted just to show you how powerless you were. He hadn't answered his mother's last letter, the one asking about Christmas, and now it would haunt him to the end of his days. Though, perhaps Peter had come to say she was only ill. Had his knowledge of the girl's mother brought a sword upon his own? Or was this punishment for his refusal to obey the girl's final command?

—What's happened? he demanded.

Peter's face was cheerful, not grave. He opened his arms to Gray:

—Unexpected change of plan.

—Is she . . . ?

—Well! She's very well. Oh, no, look at you.

✦

As usual, he'd made a mess of it. First, he'd frightened the boy half to death arriving unannounced for his first visit ever without considering how it would look. Once the boy recovered himself, he began to babble, and Peter saw how foolish he had been to assume the boy would be grateful for a spontaneous exeat. It seemed a football match was in progress, attendance compulsory, and after that . . . The boy's letters had described a play he had written, and now it emerged that he'd written another, to be performed after the match. Exeat therefore impossible. Chastened by his ignorance, Peter accompanied the boy back to the pitch, determined to see the school at least.

The playing fields, hacked out of moorland, looked as though they might revert to wilderness in the holidays. The school was smaller than he expected, only four houses, which helped explain why attendance at the match was compulsory. After the visitors had humiliated the First XV, the boy introduced him to his Housemaster, and Peter accompanied the man to the gymnasium for the promised performance. Grieves, too, was nothing like he'd imagined. Young, bright, charming, and possessing a sense of humor, he bore no resemblance to the dire tyrant his godson seemed to think him or the austere saint Elsa portrayed. There was an awkward moment when Grieves asked after Elsa and her fiancé, and Peter had to report that she was well and that the fiancé was he, or had been. Grieves had grown flustered, and Peter had been forced to reveal his purpose, which was to explain to his godson why the engagement had been suspended.

—Say no more, Grieves stuttered. Forgive me.

—Only suspended, not called off.

Something about the man compelled him to explain himself. She needed more time. The engagement had been too swift. They hadn't called it off, but they weren't going forward presently. It was all frightfully intricate, and the last thing Peter wanted was for his godson to get the wrong end of the stick.

—He's good at that, Grieves said.

—Isn't he though?

Grieves offered the exeat before Peter could ask. He'd need the boy back for Prep, but the Cross Keys in Fridaythorpe did a first-rate steak and kidney. Grieves also recommended the spotted dick, if they had it.

Peter liked the man and felt they might have been friends in another setting, not rivals, as he realized he had always imagined. Grieves was a Cambridge man, hadn't Elsa said? What was he doing at a drab little school in the middle of nowhere with a First XV hardly worth the name?

—Are you married? he asked.

Grieves froze, and he saw that again he'd said the wrong thing.

—Good evening, ladies and honorable gentlemen!

Mercifully, the play was beginning. Two boys stepped to the front.

—*Not Far to Castle Noire*! the first boy announced.

—A serial in nine parts!

The play was most peculiar, some combination of penny dreadful, matinee romance, and *Idylls of the King*. His godson worked a variety of contraptions on the sidelines, another boy sang and turned tumbles, while another entranced them with swordplay. The audience, so half-hearted at the football, now followed the drama with unfeigned enthusiasm. Peter had always taken his godson's reports of the school as a product of the boy's skewed perspective; now he saw the opposite was true and that he knew shamefully little about the heart of the boy or the men who shaped it.

—Ladies and gentlemen, the adventure continues next Sunday!

There'd been only two scenes, and now the cast was assembled for bows.

—Will Flash escape the giant's trap?

—Will Valarious find his brother?

—Will Master Shadow defeat the gruesome guards?

331

—Will Kahrid of Langstephen repel the advances of Perspicacious—

—The most intelligent and evil man in the land!

—Find out here, seven days hence!

✦

Uncle Peter bought them pints to celebrate. It was not Gray's first drink, but it was the first he'd consumed in the open. Gill seemed to think nothing of it and in fact bemoaned the lack of public house at the Academy. It was much easier to resolve differences, he claimed, when one could simply nip round the corner and discuss it over a friendly pint. Gray couldn't imagine resolving anything over a pint. He was more likely to make a fool of himself or say something ill-advised, such as pointing out that the Cross Keys was the place Wilberforce and his cronies used to go, through the poacher's tunnel Saturday evenings. The night Wilberforce had told Gray the legend of the tunnel, he'd called it the Key to the Keys and thought it witty.

By the time the second round arrived, the flavor had improved. They ate five steak and kidney pies between them and ordered the spotted dick. The best thing about exeats was eating until you couldn't anymore. Had Morgan & Co. had the steak and kidney, too? Unlikely, as they were busy downing as many pints as possible between tea and Prayers. Morgan had expected him to use the tunnel to come to the Keys, but he wasn't a slave. He and Trevor had used the tunnel to go to the barn, damn what Morgan said, and even now that he had a study and could, theoretically, cut Prep for the Keys, he wasn't tempted by the prospect of drinking himself sick and then staggering back through the woods.

—Ah, Grindalythe Woods! Peter said. Now there's a place. Have you ever taken the binos around there?

—Out-of-bounds, I'm afraid, sir, Gill replied.

—I know the keeper. Quite a population of redleg partridge he's got.

The spotted dick had arrived, and the irony swirled like smoke from the men's cigarettes: that the fabled keeper knew Peter; that Gray's first visit to the Cross Keys had been accomplished not with the poacher's tunnel but with his godfather's car.

—What poacher's tunnel?

Gill was talking to him, looking at him.

—You said it was ironic you hadn't come through the poacher's tunnel.

He pushed the second pint away, empty.

—School legend.

—Tell!

That was the last thing of course he intended to do, yet he was doing it, spilling not only the legend but the secrets Morgan had told him, the ones he'd sworn to tell only his own fag, if he ever got to the point of having one. Gill looked shocked:

—Why the *hell*—sorry, sir—haven't you mentioned this before?

He hadn't deliberately concealed it, but they'd been busy with rehearsals, and in any case the barn had been leveled that summer. What need had there been to speak of the tunnel?

—Reason not the need!

He'd eaten too much. He excused himself. Careless—excess—ruin. When would he learn simple cause and effect? Peter could be sworn to secrecy, but Gill's eyes had fixed in the middle distance, twirling pencils with his mind, desiring the tunnel for the Full Experience.

◆

His godson returned looking queasy, and Peter realized he should not have got the second round. Audsley could handle it, but he was older. When Audsley at last went to the toilets himself, Peter had only a scant moment under poor conditions to convey what he'd come to convey.

—Only suspended, not called off.

—Oh, said the boy.

—I'm not giving up, on her or you.

—Is that why you came?

He nodded.

—How's she taking it?

There was something incorrect about the way he referred to his mother with pronouns.

—It was your mother's idea.

—Oh.

◆

The dark leaked everywhere. It had glowered when they left the Academy, fallen when they arrived at the Keys, and by the time they emerged, it had spawned a chill rain. Peter's motorcar crawled through the mist

333

and smelled of Boggle Hole, recalling the things Gray had heard through the walls there, walls so thin they barely deserved the name: *He looks so much like Tom it feels like adultery . . .*

Fardley was waiting to lock the gates:

—Headmaster to see you, Audsley. Quite a spectacular this afternoon.

—Thank you, Fardley.

—That Valarious, what a fellow!

—You'll be there next week, I hope?

—Wouldn't miss it for the world, young sir.

Gray reported their return to Crighton and quizzed him on Gill's summons.

—Congratulations, probably.

They'd missed the congratulations going with Peter, and Gray had missed Jottings, his practice of writing down what mistakes he'd noticed so they could be fixed next time. There hadn't been time for anything, not even to remember who he was and wasn't, and now he was opening the door to study number six and the light was off like it used to be when he was smaller. In the dark, rain ticking the panes, was now really so different from then? It didn't look different or even feel it, but he could no more shrink back to that time than he could rebuild the barn or climb through any window of memory. Sometimes change came sudden and drastic. Sometimes time refused to budge. What if he'd been traveling weeks on foreign soil without having perceived the frontier? Had there been signposts? Such as the Keys, where he had gone today after so long refusing. His visit had been licit, to celebrate something he couldn't have imagined two months ago. The Keys had not been sinister, but warm and good. No one said I told you so.

Signpost two, Valarious, who today had stepped forth, escaping his mind and rehearsal's make-believe. Today his people had taken on public bodies, independent and visible. No one had warned him how it would feel.

There was a pain in his chest, hot below his heart, and he had to lie down on the floor. His blood was thumping when it ought to rush. Heart attacks weren't supposed to happen to people his age, but there had been a boy his father knew: fifteen, football, dead. If he himself died, would anyone really mind? The play could go on; the script was complete. He'd passed on the secret of the poacher's tunnel—not meant to, but had. What else was he needed for?

It was too late for games, especially with himself. *You can lie to other people, boyo, but not to yourself.* He'd been telling himself that her last letter was indeed all he could expect. He'd felt bold refusing her command to destroy them all, but in truth, in his floor beneath the floor, did he actually believe she'd stop writing? Didn't he expect, in his secret cell, that any day her retraction would come, and when it did, he could say, *Fear not!* He could say, *Here they are! Here am I.*

His blood was about to stop flowing, and the truth, the *true* truth, was that she meant what she wrote. He would never hear from her again. He knew it now, and he'd known it all along. True truth more grinding than stone.

And to such a hopeless fortress Peter had come like a vandal. He had dropped his news in the final moments, defenses retired, and now the fact burned like mustard gas: after months of laying siege to their engagement, he had defeated it. Time didn't blow backwards, but there they stood, his mother and he, waist deep in the brook, willows pulling past them. Swan Cottage leaked, moths chomped through the books, but year on year they waited for the dead to return, and when she had tried to climb from the river, he had pulled her back, and when Peter had reached out his hand—to take them to a cove where the tide came every day, new sand, new sea—he himself had hacked at the arm and run away into the marsh, into the window seat, sleeping with his arms around things that weren't there. And now death was breathing on his neck even as he galloped through the wind and the rain, his father's arm around his waist, horse warm between his legs, sand stinging, the devil behind them, gaining, gaining with his claw and his staff, *Hold still, boyo, you're not going anywhere* . . .

—What are you doing down there?

Light from the corridor flooded his face.

—And in the dark?

Light switch thunked, and Gill knelt beside him, eyes bright, ears red.

—What? Gray said. What happened?

—Bad news.

He sprang up, heart racing.

—Head gave us the chop.

—What!

Gill took off his jacket and tie before relaying the Head's edict: Two plays, delightful, but more than enough. Apply for club permission next term.

—Next *term?*

—*Aurea mediocritas* leads not to mediocrity, but to greatness.

—*What?*

—The Head says.

Moderation was the worst kind of tyrant. It leached life for arid routine.

—Next term is next *year*!

—Why are you on the floor?

His hand returned to his chest.

—I had a pain.

—Probably cramp, Gill said, after all that pie.

It wasn't a cramp, but that didn't matter now.

—What will we tell people?

—Nothing, Gill said.

The look was back, and he hadn't picked up any pencils.

—We'll be like the people in Paris.

Speaking *French?*

—Uprising crushed. Gutters run with blood. There's only one thing to do.

Die?

—Head for the sewers.

Literally?

—Go underground!

 Meg's letter, when it came, revealed and resolved nothing. Her correspondence had never been as unguarded as Nurse Riding's, John realized as he reviewed the specimens side by side, but given her circumstances, how could it be? Meg returned his thanks, for the visit and for his birthday gift; she was reading the book and promised to share her thoughts soon. John had hope that although she could not state the truth directly, he would understand what she meant when she wrote about the Brownings.

And he saw, as he was filing their letters, that he'd been remiss in his correspondence with Nurse Riding. Had he thanked her for the last volume she'd sent in August? He kept a ledger of correspondences—

date, sent or received, to or from whom, general subject. It was the only way to manage the never-ending stream of professional and personal envelopes that crossed his desk, most promising one unpleasantness or another if not answered promptly. His habit with Nurse Riding had been to thank her within two days, but his ledger delivered the mortifying news that he'd overlooked it thanks to Jamie's walking tour and the disruptions that had ensued.

However, the visit of her fiancé—ex-fiancé—and the presentation of her son's newest play provided a natural excuse to write, and her reply came by return post.

> *"Suspended or called off—what's the difference, I wonder, when it comes to engagements?" You can't know, Crusoe, though perhaps you do, what a breath of air your words are, and how suffocating it is to have one's half-truths routinely taken as fact.*

He hadn't meant to be blunt, but perhaps he'd been exhausted by the exacting calculations required with Meg. Now he wondered what would happen if he were to dispense with half-truths altogether. Perhaps he could get away with telling Nurse Riding that she was well out of the business with her son's godfather, that the so-called second chance had been ill-judged and that she could begin again more prudently now.

He watched the post even though he knew it would take Meg at least a week, if not a fortnight, to finish the Brownings and compose a response. In the meantime, the churn of term demanded his daily attention: Audsley's ignorance of the curriculum, Halton's ignorance full stop, a bitter feud amongst the youngest boys in his House, overweening ambition from his Captain of Games, Jamie's efforts to rewrite the prospectus. The last had put a strain on John's time as Jamie sent him draft after draft for editorial critique. Jamie was not a natural stylist, and every time John untangled his clauses, another version would appear, taking a new and more baroque angle. When they at last had a draft ready for the printers, Jamie asked if they shouldn't include a Theatrical Club.

How's that when you shut them down? John wrote in the margins.

But next term?

If you're prepared to stand by it!

Are you calling me fickle?

Finally, John took the portfolio to Jamie's study and hammered everything out face-to-face.

Oh, Crusoe, you can't know the humiliation of negotiating with tradesmen! They seem to consider a woman on her own as a mental defective or at best an easy mark. I have been assured that the roof of our cottage is easily repaired, reparable for a hefty sum, and beyond hope entirely. My brother advises I sell the place and come to King's Lynn. After everything, I'm inclined to agree with him. Your view?

He outlined his view in seven interlocking arguments (précis: don't move in with brother), and just as he'd regretted sending that off with the postman, he discovered a letter from his publisher asking when the promised article could be expected (deadline, a fortnight past). As consequence, he had had to sit up five nights in a row, which did not—he emphasized to a clucky Mrs. Firth—indicate habit, but rather duty. Evidently he'd failed to convince her, and the old dragon had gone to Jamie about it (or done the next best thing by gossiping to one of his servants), which had let John in for an irritating lecture during the Lower School hare and hounds, which he ran with Jamie as usual.

—I need you at full whack, Jamie scolded. It's breach of contract to run yourself ragged.

John replied by sprinting ahead.

There's no question of moving in with my brother and his wife. How could you think it, Crusoe? But the agent has sold the cottage. You can't know my relief!

The more Nurse Riding enumerated what he couldn't know, the more he wanted to shout, *I do!*

I've no idea how to break the news to the boy. It's bound to bring on every sort of unpleasantness. I don't suppose you could have a word? Though, as I write this, I realize it's asking too much, of a Housemaster or a friend.

Her retracting the request made John want to grant it, but he reminded himself of a lesson he'd learned the hard way, that it never paid to intervene between a mother and her son. How would it be, after all, to summon the boy to the study and treat him to a paternal pi-jaw along the lines of *Your mother has just sold your home, you'll never see it again, and you must behave better towards her, good day.*

On top of everything, Kardleigh's drops were losing their potency, that or they'd reacted badly with some trace of iodine still in the bottle. John had expected the vial to last beyond Christmas, but now he wasn't sure it would make it to Guy Fawkes. He was reduced, after another week of silence from Ely, to digging out his own copy of the Browning and writing a response to the first two poems. He itched to send it but managed, by strenuous self-control, to put it aside in the drawer. She had to fashion her own position without influence from him. If she didn't, how could he ever trust her decision?

Finally, arrangements have been settled with the removers. My brother keeps telling me I ought to go down there myself to sort out Tom's affairs, supervise the removal, and ensure nothing goes missing or ruined, but I've had to take on four more shifts at the hospital as they're paying me something now. My brother naturally does not approve of waged work for ladies, but he isn't a widow, and in any case, he can't know the desperate suffering of our poor unfortunates! Those in the grip of tuberculosis, cancers, laudanum, drink, or the occasional young thing run afoul of Absinthe,

Which reminded John he'd quite like to try that . . .

people in such circumstances have needs far greater than some vague desire to wrap china just so or to see the old house "one last time."

The way she wrote of her patients provoked an irrational urge to fall ill under her care. The pain in his head had become general malaise, and his entire body yearned for the release the drops used to bring when they were strong enough to soothe him singly. He approached Kardleigh once more with an array of new symptoms (aching Achilles tendon, raw throat, rash inside the elbow, boil on the back of the knee, dyspepsia), but the doctor had given him only aspirin and advised him to apply a poultice to the boil and get more sleep. The drops, he'd said, were not to be employed except as a last resort.

*I'm certain half an hour's consultation with a physician would ad-
dress your research questions better than I can, but given the "baying
hounds" (your publisher?) we shall have to make do, Crusoe. Generally speaking, our unfortunates are ordinary members of society.
Many have been carrying on quite happily for years in the grip of
one daemon or another, their families never the wiser. There are
thousands who can quite comfortably drink themselves into a stu-
por on a daily basis and suffer little harm. The trouble comes when
they vary their routine, for instance by combining their drink with
laudanum, or with any of the great number of "patent" medicines
hocked by charlatans to a gullible public.*

Sometimes a dose of brandy would take the edge off his complaints
and calm the sensation of dread. Sometimes he lay in bed until the boys'
second morning bell, imagining a sanatorium at the top of an Alp. If only
the right doctor existed, one who knew him and could prescribe just the
right regimen . . . instead he had Mrs. Firth pounding his door, forcing
him to stir, to wash, to dress.

*As to where my patients acquire their "poisons," there are always un-
scrupulous persons who for a price will provide what they so ear-
nestly desire.*

Merewether would know such people, or would know someone who
knew them, surely?

*I discussed your question with a boy on the ward, and he reports
that here in King's Lynn there is at least one public house where,
upon making discreet inquiries, one might be shown into a room
where an individual known as "the doctor" will procure whatever
one requires. I'm confident he tells the truth—before coming to us,
he was in the habit of injecting a shocking amount of morphine
each day.*

He had forgotten that it could be injected. He'd seen it in the war, of
course, even administered the injections on occasion. Until now, though,
that substance, which had delivered such mercy to those on the brink
of death, had been nothing to do with the bitter drops Kardleigh kept in
his dispensary. Was there in fact a difference between them? She hadn't

said why the boy on the ward had resorted to injections, but it was possible that he'd first required them in a field hospital. John didn't think Captain Lewis took anything. He got around the Academy well enough in his chair, never complained, was a paragon of efficiency. True, there were days he failed to appear, and occasionally Jamie's affairs would fall into disarray when, they understood, his secretary was under the weather. John had in those cases assumed a cold, but what if Lewis's condition were more fragile than it appeared? Why else would Kardleigh keep ready vials in the dispensary?

This boy tolerated the morphine well enough. His trouble was gin. He was barely alive when he arrived. I can't tell you how they revived him.

Her accounts, after all, were a relief. Her patients could not teach history lessons, run a House, or conduct correspondence. They could not travel with colleagues to the polls and vote in the general election. They could not vote contrary to their colleagues and contrary to the nation, casting their ballot for the opposition, however doomed it may be. The fact that John had no convincing reason to vote for the Labour Party other than a vague sentimental support for the underdog was neither here nor there; he, unlike those who'd abandoned ordinary life, could still exercise his native-born right as an Englishman without having to explain himself to his friends, his colleagues, or his employer.

The city of York always induced in John a mild claustrophobia, made worse by the city walls, which closed around the crowded, twisting streets. Still, he reminded himself, it was a half holiday, and he was at liberty, or would be once he'd finished Jamie's errand and then fetched the book for his aunt's birthday next week. The proprietor of the Crooked Staff greeted him warmly and behaved as if he hadn't been waiting seven months for John to collect the novel he'd ordered. John let him wrap it up but realized with shame that he could never send his aunt a book called *Vile Bodies*, no matter how entertaining Mr. Waugh's previous novels had been. Pretending he'd ordered it for someone else, he solicited the man's advice for his aunt and then settled on a book of stories by Mrs. Mansfield, which he asked the man to post on for him. Freed from the weight of a long procrastination, he tramped around to four different printers before settling on one he felt confident would produce the new prospectus in a tasteful, timely, and frugal manner.

More than an hour yet until his train, and all he wanted was to lie down and close his eyes. His stomach felt off, though he couldn't think how his usual breakfast of toast and tea could have gone awry. A wind was whipping papers off the ground and penetrating his insufficient suit. The Hanged Man possessed a large fire, so he worked his way inside, the crowd much larger than reasonable for four o'clock of a Wednesday afternoon. Huddling by the hearth, he could feel the muscles in his back shuddering, like butterflies drying their wings. He downed one medicinal scotch and ordered another, but despite the fire and the smoke and the red faces of the workmen around him, his skin crawled, and the chill bored deeper. A wall of voices: Labour lost York, Burgess out, Lumley in, foreigners and their blethering cheek. John had skimmed *The Times* and its columns on *The Belgian Reaction, Opinion in Denmark, The Soviet Explanation*, but he didn't think the Hanged Man would appreciate his treatise on foreign affairs. In any case, the twitch had disappeared, and perspiration was trickling under his collar. He returned his glass to the bar and strained to think of how to say to the barman what Nurse Riding's patient had told her he said. His shoe caught the flagstone, he stumbled, someone laughed, and the barman told him to mind himself or be upskelled.

—I . . .

He groped for words. The barman pulled his head back like a goose. Was it a doctor he was wanting?

—I understood there was a man called the doctor here.

Chatter, chatter, muscles on his back.

—Oh, aye?

—Aye.

The man wiped his hands and lifted the counter. John followed him out the back to an alleyway. *Tap door end of snicket, look frinit*, and he was gone.

On the Alp, he'd be summoned by bells, told when to sleep, walk, eat. Wrapped in the knowing arms of the place, he'd give in and the pain would cease and the longing subside and the mountain air would cleanse him. The door scraped open to his knock, and he tripped inside down a dark flight of stairs. Cots, couches, curtains, the room went back and back. He waited for his eyes to adjust. It was cold inside, the temperature of vice.

He was not there, not truly. He was watching a man like himself ask for the doctor. People shuffled aimlessly, and there was smoke, sweet, flowery, like roasted chicken. A man with one eye asked him what he needed. He hadn't got so far as planning what to say, but he babbled about the front and what they did for dying men. The doctor brought out a vial, brought out a strap, brought out a needle, led him to a cot, wrote a price on a piece of newsprint. Wrote it with a pencil stub. John could pay the price. He did not fear the needle. But he knew all at once that he must leave, the cellar and the city. Upstairs in the alley, it was milder, wetter. How curious that Hell should be colder than the night.

A cab took him to the station, and the train took him away, Warthill, Holtby, Stamford Bridge, away from the flowers and the chicken and the man who left his eye behind, to another cab and the Wetwang road, its holes, its concealment. Mistake averted was no mistake at all. She need never see, in word or in fact, what he'd become—only *nearly* become. His problem was a late-October flu, nothing a bowl of soup and a good night's sleep wouldn't cure. He could taste her mouth as it tasted on the platform, filling him with the fire of all the holy spirits—oranges and lemons, farthings.

Morning, rain, Mrs. Firth at his door.

—Chapel twenty minutes, she said.

Where, God, had the rising bells gone? He forced himself to move, if only to turn his head to the wall.

—Wire come, last night.

—Wire?

—On your desk.

His feet were on the floor, every pain gone. She had answered his kiss, not in a letter but in the brevity of a wire, mercy like an arrow, swift and sharp. Mustn't rush it. Must remember, recall for the future every moment of this day: this clock in the hall, this corridor of his House, boys tramping down the stairs. What would he tell them once he could tell? He had some money from the maiden aunts, enough to live simply, plainly, with goodness. How would she say it? What words would mark his history, correcting its course from now to its end?

The drapes had been opened, and rain was tickling the French windows, perfect counterpoint to the pool of lamplight that ringed the holy wire. Origin, Ely. Inside—not yet. Take a second to recall what was passing, the years of longing—suddenly tender—and Jamie, the Bishop, the boys, the Common Room, yes and even Nurse Riding, her son and her unfortunates and her spoiled second chance. He nudged the point of his knife against the flap. Don't rush, don't rush. Remember everything, hold it in your heart, remember every moment of this blessed . . . bless . . .

When God made agreements with people in the Bible, his contract was clear. Even if the terms could make your skin crawl—a whopping great lamp moving by itself between animal parts—even then, nobody doubted what had happened, and no one got confused later. In Meeting they mostly talked about the Light when they meant God. This Light didn't act like the Lord in the Bible, but then real people didn't act like books and the Bible was only a book.

Her mother was cured. She herself had done her bit, as well as she could do. She'd swept up the mess and sent it away in two parcels. Done, dusted, past. But then came the harrowing weekend. To harrow meant to dig with a plow, to crush and to break and basically to plunder. She'd been expecting something good that weekend; her mother was turning thirty-five, and now there were years more to come. The harrowing started at Mrs. K's, when her mistake came snarling out of the ground. She thought it had been wise to send all the letters away, but in Mrs. K's kitchen she saw how close she had come to ruining everything. History was full of blood sacrifices, and if killing off a friend—could she call him one?—if such a killing didn't count as sacrifice, what would? It wasn't like a lamp moving in the night, but that was the contract: her mother or the boy.

Of course, that was only the beginning. After you killed things on an altar, you had to amend your life and be serious about your duty. *Sleepers, wake, for night is flying! The watchmen on the high are crying.* People sang it in the streets at Christmastime. She had been asleep, but from this point forward, she would watch.

When Uncle John left, the incursions began. Had they been happening before without her noticing? Her mother's face, often flushed. Eyes unrested, attention like gnats. She said she had hay fever, but did she really? Watchmen's leave, canceled. Effort doubled: arranging books according to the color of their names, and then when her father couldn't find the one he wanted, sorting them back alphabetically; preparing dinner; stopping by her father's premises after school and waiting until he came home; early one morning finding a glass on the mantel, the first in Ely, washing it, replacing it, half emptying whiskey bottle and refilling with water. All this, then one night a skirmish on the walls.

In the old house, you could hear everything; here only a tune, though one no watchman could ignore. In the bathroom was an airing cupboard, and in the back of the cupboard some plaster had come away and you could touch the lathe and if you put your face close . . . The back of their radiator had cobwebs, but you could see the bed. It had sounded bad, but now it seemed he was only teasing her; she was wearing her shift and laughing as he complained of her secret lovers. But then she walked past and he stopped her, taking her wrists and pulling clips from her hair, dings on the floorboards as she pulled away and fell to him, hairbrush sliding towards the bed and disappearing beneath it. Sounds were cries and not cries, words and not words.

Watchmen, attention, your Prince and Captain cometh.

Report, men?

Something, my lord, against the walls. But the night is dark, the moon snuffed, may chance it was no enemy. May chance it was . . .

Understood. Return to posts.

Days and weeks learned by heart: eyes good, color good, appetite good then quite good. Post fetched every day from the door to the table. Fetched that day, too, reviewed that day, too. Three pieces for her mother about the German children; one from Mrs. K, infallible Wednesday letter; a notice from her school; the last—*hark, men.* Postmark Paris. Pocket, not table. This was not filching. Review then return, no one the wiser.

On the train she examined it. Their old address had been struck out and the new one written by a different hand. The penmanship looked foreign, but the numbers weren't French.

My dear Margaret . . .

This, watchmen, *this.* This was what they were *for.* Notebook, pencil, six minutes to their stop—this, men, concerned tomorrow, and if they replied and posted it before school, he would receive it today at the London address here. Makeshift letter, yes, no time for frills: Oh, dear

Dr. Zarday! Her mother was overjoyed to receive his letter. Truly, she was cured, as they realized soon after leaving the sanatorium. Her father had returned, and so her mother could not correspond, as Dr. Zarday must understand. But *she* would come, in her mother's stead, tomorrow to his lecture. *À bientôt!*

Watchmen didn't lie, but watchmen did as duty required: French shoes and skirt to be exchanged for school uniform after lunch. The stop in Cambridge was on her way home, Wednesday half holiday not hard to explain. The lecture was free. She wouldn't speak to anyone.

In the lecture hall, two young men sat down to her right, and a third came to her left who was their friend. When she offered to swap seats with the one, they refused, treating her as if she'd been part of their clique all along. They puzzled over the lecture title, *The Power of Persuasion in Modern Medicine*, and asked if the speaker was Austrian.

—Magyar, she blurted.

They smiled, curious.

—He's Hungarian, she explained.

They weren't much older than the boys at her school, but they sported colorful blazers and cologne. They peppered her with questions and made her laugh, like the boy in the chair loft but more confident. They didn't give their names, but soon she was addressing them as they addressed each other, Toad, Van Gogh, and the Comrade. The one called Toad sat at her right hand, and once the lecture began, he drew comments in a pocket notebook, which he passed with his silver pencil so she might sketch a response. Zoltan Zarday's talk went over her head, but the Toad's silent banter made her sides hurt from holding in laughter.

When his uppercase told her—not invited, but informed—that she would join them afterwards at a place called the Foot and Fungus, the watchmen recalled her appointment with Dr. Zarday. Lecture adjourned, she snaked through the crowd, rousing the watchmen to their duty. *Give the thing to say that will snuff his questions forever. Send the shot true for your Captain and your Prince.*

He had trimmed his beard and looked as though he'd spent time in the sun. His voice cut—

—Cordelia Líoht!

Familiar, shushing, warm, as if her chest held a half-cooked egg that oozed from a hairline crack. Then his arms were around her and with them the smell of his tobacco and the prickle of his jacket. He squeezed her hard and planted a kiss on the crown of her head, and the flood rose, stinging behind her eyes, the temptation to tell him everything. *Watchmen, watchmen!* She said her mother was cured. His face dimmed, and he took her hands: she must take tea with him, very dear girl, tell him all from the very beginning. Show him the *cukrászda* in this English town of hers.

People were pressing round, but he kept a hand on her shoulder as he spoke to them, as if she were under his protection and he could hear a secret and keep it. Across the hall the doors stood open, her boys smoking on the pavement. As he went to fetch a paper for a man, she stepped back and then along the aisle, breaking outside to the boys.

The Heel and Toe public house was full in every nook, but the Comrade led them to a cellar that was dim and full of smoke. The Toad put his hand in the small of her back and steered her to a table where other boys welcomed them. She couldn't join their jokes about men they were studying, but when the Toad said she knew Zoltan Zarday, they addressed her as an equal. The Comrade had been to Paris in the summer, and his talk of its rues and cafés concerts gave way to her descriptions of salons, the spas of Vichy, the glaciers of Italy, the mouths of the Volga. Van Gogh brought a tray with long glasses and slotted spoons, and Toad showed her how to put a sugar cube on the spoon and hold it over the glass while Van Gogh poured water. The sugar dissolved through the spoon and mixed with the green cordial, swirling and clouding like potions in children's stories, and they were lifting the glasses to their lips, smelling sharp and—

— Is it spirits?

They all laughed.

—The Green Fairy!

They laughed again, and Toad's breath warmed her ear as she tipped the cordial onto her tongue. Licorice like the cakes her grandmother made at Christmas, and something else—lemon? coriander?—smoothing, soothing laughter. Toad's fingers were twiddling with her sleeve, swishing the cuff buttons in and out of their holes, and they called for more fairy, and the light smelled green, and his fingers stretched like vapor from a bottle, swirling around with the cigarette smoke, warm at her ear a licorice lip, and her spine rose and it was at her mouth and in it, tongue soft and sweet—first kiss, with a Toad, not frightful but fair—warm ears, warm throat, spreading, spreading, Christmas-cakey-lemon-balm of mother's love, mother's arms, mother's—

Shot, dart and spike. And her coat was in her hand and her satchel

347

on her arm and she was falling up the stairs and through the people to the street. She ran but the moon said, *Late, too late.* Bounding for the train, she knew something clung to the carriage, like things she couldn't draw. *Watchmen, watchmen! Gates open on their hinges!* Train screeched in—run for home. Mustn't, mustn't panic. Level head, faithful heart. *Mercy, Captain. Mercy, Prince.* Light bled from their windows, such light, rays. Knowing, then, like shrapnel.

The contract was not what she had thought. She had been deceived by the oldest of swindlers, the one who'd delivered her heart's desire— cure to perfection, instant and complete—while wearing the mask of the Captain she trusted. *Watchmen! Watchmen! The Prince has come for his price.*

Prickly heat. Ice-in-bone. Door. People. Da kneeling, floor, settee, across her mother, who . . .

Nothing made sense. Everything was clear. Her satchel fell. The light smelled like eggs. She would never wear these clothes again.

 O *God, forasmuch as without thee we are not able to please thee, mercifully grant that thy Holy Spirit may in all things direct and rule our hearts, through Jesus Christ our Lord.* That had been the collect a fortnight ago, and Pearce was still praying it. He didn't know if his prayer had failed or if he was simply too stupid and stiff-necked to pray well, but his heart in no way felt ruled. Dramatic choices were the province of literature, not life. People always said to do what was right, but they never explained how to work out what that was if the circumstances were messy, which they invariably were. His most recent interview with Dr. Sebastian had been awkward. After discussing confirmation lessons, Pearce had asked how to know what the Holy Spirit intended him to do. Dr. Sebastian advised him to begin with the truth and then to take counsel. All far easier said than done without Morgan.

Truth: the Headmaster had forbidden Audsley to stage his plays. Yet, how could brief recitals absent scenery and formal trappings be called plays? Also truth: they were the King's free subjects whose free time was their own. He took counsel with Moss, and Moss's view was clear. So long as no one was breaking any rules—and Moss challenged him to cite one regulation being violated—who were they to interfere? This view had satisfied Pearce for a fortnight, but this week, Audsley informed them, the location for the so-called scenes would be tight, requiring multiple performances; hence, some of their own House would have to wait for what Audsley called the Late Showing.

Pearce took counsel again, but bedtimes, Moss argued, could at best be classed convention. Hours were pushed and pulled all the time, officially and unofficially. It wasn't as though ten-fifteen had been carved on the tablets at Sinai. Pearce was perfectly aware of that, but if bedtimes were so fluid, why not secure Grieves's blessing? Moss asked how he proposed doing that when their Housemaster had vanished overnight. The Head had said Mr. Grieves attended urgent family business, so urgent in fact that he'd not even been able to brief his Head Boy. Under the circumstances, hand-wringing over bedtimes was beneath them.

Nevertheless, Pearce argued, Mr. Grieves trusted them to look after the House. How could they trample that trust by permitting clandestine theatricals in the tunnels Saturday night? At this point, Moss lost his patience. What, he asked, did Pearce imagine prefects were *for* if not to govern the school while letting masters believe that *they* did? There was much masters did not and could not understand about harmonious existence, and if prefects were to start confiding in them, chaos would ensue. Furthermore, it was perfectly clear to Moss, and should be to Pearce as well, that the Head had merely shut down the play to avoid contradicting himself.

—Contradicting himself how?

—Come on, try. He's already told Mac he can't have his blasted extra practices, so he can't very well allow Audsley extra performances, now, can he?

But, Moss continued, just as the Head's edict had not stopped Mac from holding Voluntary Exercise and oppressing them daily with his thirst for victory, so, too, was it perfectly acceptable for performances of *Castle Noire* to continue on a discreet and unofficial basis.

—Yes, but lights-out—

If Pearce was going to harp on the letter of the law, any number of inconvenient consequences might arise. One might, for instance, argue that Pearce ought not, strictly, to have trespassed in McKay's barn even as a sub-prefect in pursuit of miscreants; he ought not, strictly, to have wielded the cane until a fully fledged prefect; and while they were on the subject, Morgan Wilberforce ought not, strictly, to have done the majority of things that he did, things they both knew were in the best interests of the boys, the House, the school, and probably the nation. Everything worthwhile was done unofficially, and the sooner Pearce made peace with that fact, the sooner he'd get on.

—Honestly, Simon, what would Morgan say?

✦

Audsley's position in the Upper School, his amiable nature, and his Housemaster's aversion to corporal punishment had thus far kept him from experiencing the cane, but Moss calculated it was only a matter of time. No one as unorthodox as Audsley would ever make it through the term without running afoul of the JCR. The play and their late-night gatherings notwithstanding, Moss knew he'd have no trouble dispensing justice if (when) the occasion presented itself.

And the occasion looked as though it might present itself sooner rather than later if the signs were as they seemed. Audsley, like every boy Moss had ever known, was developing the keen curiosity of the un-whacked. His studymate, who ought to be nurturing that curiosity, was no fun at all. As far as Riding was concerned, the less said on the subject the better. Audsley was therefore reduced to wondering, out of Riding's earshot, what the cane must feel like.

—Does it hurt like buggery? he asked one night after rehearsal.

—That depends, Crighton said.

—On what?

—On how much you think buggery hurts.

Audsley hadn't seen the humor and had left thinking much too hard. Entertaining though it was, Moss felt it wasn't fair to toy with Audsley. He'd already read enough *Boy's Own Paper* to thoroughly warp his mind; the last thing he needed was Crighton egging him on.

Next day in the changing room, Audsley resumed:

—Is it really like a red-hot poker pressed against your backside?

—Oh, grow up! Moss said.

—It isn't, then?

It was so tempting, but someone had to draw the line:

—Cut Games and you'll find out.

Audsley bit his lip in a way that tempted Moss all over again.

—Ask the Turtle, Halton chimed in. He got his first off Mac yesterday.

Now was that or was that not a smirk across the changing room? If the Turtle couldn't make it to Games on time, that was his lookout. What it had to do with Halton was a matter Moss thought best unexplored.

—Pearce has a better eye, Halton opined.

—Expert, now, are you? Moss retorted.

—Had the slipper off Mac enough to know. He works himself up and gets off the mark. Pearce at least has the sense to wait.

Whatever Halton intended with his treatise, it was uncalled-for. Moss clipped him round the ear:

—Cut along, before Kardleigh starts to fret about his primo castrato.

✦

—Something isn't right in Grieves's House, Burton began.

It was All Hallow's Eve, a night for the dead to torment the living, but Jamie thought it was steep for Burton to turn up and inflict the torture himself.

—Please tell me you haven't come to get your licks while Grieves is away.

—Nothing of the sort, Burton said, but I've had Pearce in my study the last half an hour, burbling.

—Whatever for?

—Heaven knows. He couldn't bring himself to point fingers, but there's something afoot, and it's distressed him enough to come to me.

—Why should he bring it to *you*? Jamie asked.

Burton stared, and he felt ten years old before the man, as he often felt when he let down his guard.

✦

They'd been waiting weeks for the scene to arrive. Only Audsley and Riding appeared in it, and Audsley had maintained strict secrecy even from the rest of the cast. It was being staged in a crevice of the tunnels, so the audience had to crowd together to see. This was Riding's first appearance in *Castle Noire*, and Moss was astonished by the performance. Riding's sullenness, normally so irritating, now conveyed a sense of derangement, as from an ordeal. While Audsley produced stage tears, Riding grew increasingly remote, as if suffering shell shock, or so Moss supposed. The effect was a heartbreaking futility; for ten long scenes Valarious had sought his brother, only to discover this icy wreck.

—What's all this?

They startled and turned. Moss was near the back, so nothing obscured his view as their lights revealed not a dungeon guard but Dr. Sebastian, torch in one hand, the Turtle's collar in the other.

After commanding them to lower their torches, the Headmaster turned his own upon each of them:

—I can't imagine Mr. Grieves has given permission for this . . . gathering.

He stepped forward and the crowd parted.

—Audsley, Riding, surely my eyes deceive me, for it does appear from your costume that I've interrupted a reprise of your dramatics.

Moss glanced to Pearce, but he stood frozen, staring at the middle distance.

—It's much too late to discuss this now, the Head continued, for if I am not mistaken, lights-out is still quarter past ten, is it not?

Moss didn't know if the Head was addressing him, or whether answering would make things better, or worse. The audience mumbled vaguely.

—In that case, as I'm sure your Housemaster would look unfavorably upon this assembly, it seems the least I can do to gate his House—

Torch swooping directly on Moss.

—*All* of it. And I'll see you two—

Light on the players—

—tomorrow after tea.

The Head let his edict settle and then turned his spotlight back to Moss:

—Is the JCR capable of seeing everyone to bed?

—Yes, sir.

—Then I shall leave the House in your *capable* hands.

How long had it been since he'd felt so small and wrong?

✦

Gray woke in the morning still feeling ill. He knew it was all part of the punishment, making them wait through the day before learning their fate. He knew they should distract themselves—do work, take exercise, prepare their explanation as much as possible—but knowing and doing were entirely different things.

At breakfast Gill made the rounds of the cast. It was only the two of them, he said. They were all to conform to the story: no one else had anything to do with the play. They agreed without much protest, and Gray couldn't even blame them. No one wanted to risk having Moss and Crighton stripped of their badges, and as for Halton and the Turtle, they had enough on their hands without coming to the Headmaster's notice.

It was a relief, somehow, that they'd been discovered by the Head and not Grieves. Gray knew he should be frightened, and he was; everyone knew the Head's talent for making boys blub. Still, the weight felt lighter because they would not be facing their Housemaster. Perhaps Grieves wouldn't even hear about it. It was far-fetched, of course, but wasn't it possible that the Head would take the gentleman's position— jaw them, thrash them, and then mercifully say, *The matter is closed?*

As for explanation, Gray knew they had none. They'd been caught in flagrante, and the best strategy was to say as little as possible and have the grace to appear repentant. He himself may not actually feel ashamed, but he could act it. Guilford was another matter. All the long, gated afternoon Gray took up the mantle of Keeper, tutoring, or trying to: what to do, what not to do, what to say and not say, how to dress, how to stand.

—Will we be beaten? Guilford wanted to know.

Gray thought it likely, though it was possible that as members of the Upper School they'd be jawed half to death and landed with a gruesome array of impositions. Gill flooded him with questions, but Gray kept his instruction brief:

—If it comes to it, I'll go first. Watch and do the same.

—But—

—Yelp if you have to, but don't move. And when it's over, don't forget the thank-you.

◆

Headmaster's study, seven o'clock, Audsley and Riding at attention before the desk, Jamie pretended to consult a file. He'd been consulting it for several minutes, all part of the technique. He'd begin when their composure started to crack. Riding obviously knew which way was up, but Jamie wasn't sure if Audsley grasped the offense. He looked, in posture and expression, not as distressed as he ought. Perhaps he thought it was merely a question of disobedience, but did he not see that with his underground theatricals he had made a mockery of Jamie's authority, unsettling the equilibrium between past and present, inciting fervent

353

I-told-you-so's from Burton-Lee, and showing up their Housemaster as weak and naive? When he finally asked if they'd anything to say, Riding stepped into the breach:

—No, sir, except that we're sorry.

It was a start. At least they didn't propose to talk their way out of it.

—I most certainly hope so.

The school, Jamie began, Mr. Grieves's House rather, could not be permitted to congregate after lights-out, in his absence, in the tunnels, clogging them dangerously, all because one boy seemed to have difficulty following direct orders.

—No, sir.

And why had Audsley not seen fit to follow a perfectly clear instruction? Riding assured him that they did not know.

—Audsley can speak for himself, can't he?

Riding's face darkened.

—We had to, sir, Audsley said at last.

—You *had* to? Were buccaneers holding your sisters hostage?

—I haven't got any sisters, sir.

—Don't be cheeky. Answer the question.

Audsley hesitated, but his voice remained clear:

—We had to, sir, because people expected it.

Jamie took the sympathetic tone:

—They expected it, did they?

Hook, line, and—

—Yes, sir. If only you'd seen last week.

Sinker.

—We couldn't leave them hanging just as Valarious found the Elf Rider. We simply couldn't!

—I see. And how many installments have you presented thus far?

—Only four, sir.

—Only four?

—Yes, sir. It's a serial—

—In nine parts, I recall.

—Yes, sir!

At this point Riding threw his accomplice a look that convinced Audsley to shut his mouth.

—Might I ask if these performances have been limited to your House, or has the entire school been permitted to partake?

Another murderous glare from Riding answered his question.

—I see.

Worse than he thought. Jamie brought out the silken tone:

—Riding, you appeared in this entertainment.

—Yes, sir.

—And what other business have you with it?

—Well, sir . . .

The inside of the lip probed, hopefully not for lies.

—I wrote it.

He wrote it.

—I see.

Of course, he would have written it. He'd written the one about the Wright brothers, and now that Jamie thought of it, hadn't there been something in the McKay's barn fiasco to do with writing, Riding claiming to have gone there to fetch a box of stories, or some such tripe? How many awkward situations could one boy get himself into? Jamie couldn't deny that Riding had a gift with the pen and, unlike many of his age, could wield it without cloying irony or sentiment. Why couldn't he misbehave like an ordinary boy, break simple rules, pay the price, and go his merry way? Why, with him, was it all overdone? McKay's barn and now clandestine theatricals—this boy was on his last nerve, impossible to warm to, and even more impossible to dismiss. Threats last spring notwithstanding, Jamie did not like expelling pupils. He'd do it if he had to, but in this instance . . .

—What are we going to do with you two?

Technique, and more technique. Make them ask for it and cheerily oblige. Riding took the silent tack, but Audsley screwed up his courage:

—You could let us finish the series, sir. If it was official, everyone could see it together Saturday afternoons.

—I see.

—You do, sir? I knew you would! There're only five more parts to go. Riding and I promise not to let our lessons slip.

Riding looked as though he'd rather be swallowing hornets than standing where he was. Riding understood what Jamie was saying. Audsley, however—

—That will do.

Jamie employed the muted voice he reserved for his greatest displeasure.

—There will be no more theatricals.

—But . . . sir—

—I will not have my instructions disregarded.

He'd let this go on far too long.

—You are both on tic for a fortnight. You will report to me for the first three days, and afterwards to your Head Boy.

They blanched.

—Yes, sir.

A fortnight was a long time, and Jamie rarely had boys report directly to him. It ought to send a message.

—Now, Audsley, if you would please wait outside.

A bold move, one already yielding results: first, the realization that justice had not been fully dealt; next, Riding's expression of naked shock. Likely he'd been expecting the dual execution typical with boys who co-operated in their crimes. What's more, they were studymates; it was an insult to separate them. It also upset the usual order, in which the junior boy by tradition went first. In this case Riding was the younger, but Audsley the junior, convention arguably moot. Last, it was customary to deliver the tick-off before the punishment. Going straight for the cane and making Audsley wait outside was bound to unsettle them both. Good. They deserved to be unsettled.

✦

Jacket off, hands on the desk, he could feel the Head at his side, smell his aftershave.

—You have been disobedient, immoderate, and extremely unwise.

Hand on his shoulder adjusting his posture, tightening the stretch in his legs.

—You are a terribly awkward boy, Riding. In your Housemaster's absence, we shall have to do what we can to encourage common sense, shall we not?

Rhetorical?

—Shall we not?

—Yes, sir.

—I'm glad we agree. Hold still and count these out.

✦

Potholes, Wetwang, John's cab swerved and swayed, sun long set, *Holy Stephen, pray for us.*

✦

Gray returned to the study and made a poor attempt at work. He'd made it through the six, composure intact, and had just begun to feel the surge of relief when the Head fired a final shot: *Mr. Grieves has had a death in the family, unexpected, taken hard, and the last thing he needs, the very last, is to be let down by boys in his House.*

The Head's disgust lingered with the rising fear—*let down, death, unexpected, hard.* Grieves had family besides the girl, surely, but—

Door slammed open and shut. Guilford flung himself across the window seat. Fear cresting, curdling—this wasn't supposed to happen, not to Guilford. Experiences weren't supposed to end in tears.

—It doesn't hurt for long, Gray said.

Guilford turned on him, bloodshot:

—I'm not blubbing because it hurts. I'm not a bloody coward!

Wrongness and blame, from a friend, his only. He should have stayed while Gill went in, even outside the door.

—What did he say?

Had the Head got him, too, parting shot more keen than the rest? Gill turned his face to the wall.

—He called it rubbish. Music hall rubbish.

✦

It was the time of night when the things you'd put behind you woke you up just to kick you in the teeth. By bedtime Moss had regained his equilibrium, but now echoes of his interview with the Head were toying with him like a dog with a rabbit. Mr. Grieves had undergone a personal loss. Having just now returned from the funeral, he needed his Head Boy's help more than ever. Would the good governance they had labored to establish survive and prosper? Surely Moss could remember the miseries of the past? Surely Mr. Grieves's trust, and through him the Academy's, had not been misplaced?

Everyone was defenseless in the middle of the night. Demons could play on you, especially ones you deserved. Grieves had looked like a shell when Moss found him in his study talking with the Head. He'd been nursing a cup of tea and pressing his brow as if he might pluck out his eyes. Moss had brought Riding, who needed his tick signed by the Head but couldn't bring himself to knock on the door, and then he'd hauled Riding away when he'd asked impertinent questions about where Grieves had been. Moss had never let Grieves down, no matter what the Head believed. Though he supposed, from a certain point of view, it might look that way.

Bedsprings creaked across the room, and Riding slipped from the dorm. Moss left the demons on his pillow and went to the toilet where Riding was on his knees being sick, or trying to be.

—Give it a rest, won't you?

Riding pulled his hand away from his mouth.

—Can't you do what you're told just one night of the blessed year?

The boy gripped the toilet as dry heaves racked him. Moss went to him. Face, flushed. Forehead, cool.

—Why can't you stay in your bloody bed, if only as a personal favor to me?

Riding spat, raised himself, spat again:

—Do you know where Grieves went?

—Not that again.

—But do you?

His nose itched.

—Buggered if I can remember. Cambridgeshire somewhere.

Riding gagged, and a gag rose in his own throat.

—Stop it!

Pulling himself together, Riding got up, and rinsed his face and mouth. Shoulders set, he turned back to Moss:

—If you find out who died, I'll do whatever you want.

His sudden desperation was as bizarre as it was embarrassing.

—What I *want*, Moss said, is for you to keep your nose clean.

—*Will* you, though? Find out?

Moss sighed.

—The wire said someone called Margaret.

A cry, ringing off the tiles.

—Shh! Give me strength! Why on *earth* do you care?

Riding bent down, racked again, but not this time with—

—*What?*

—I'm sorry, he gasped.

He pretended he was sick, but his shoulders gave it away. Moss turned off the torch. This was one of those ambushes school could inflict, particularly when you were tired.

—Thank you, Riding whispered.

You never got to choose who saw you at your weakest, or who heard your confession when you couldn't help make it.

The only way to face the day was to think of it as a schedule of doses. In Ely, Owain secured the services of a physician who provided drops to see John through the term as well as a neatly ruled timetable for tapering the doses so that he might by Christmas be free of them. John hadn't begun the tapering yet, but he would as soon as the shrill icebergs left his head. The doses made it possible to move himself through the time in Ely and to tolerate the ghastly sense of relief the funeral produced, not only in himself, but, judging by his conduct, in Owain. The latter followed his usual prescription, which left him vague during the day and maudlin at night. John wished that he hadn't let himself sit up with the man, drinking his whiskey and permitting him to recount, repeatedly, her final moments. Now he couldn't get Owain's sloppy Irish words out of his head—*an she sat herself down right there where you're sitting an she blinked her eyes an then she . . . oh those angel eyes!* At the time, Owain's grief had left him cold, and the more Owain declared that the Holy Ghost had come and tapped his angel on the shoulder, the more numb John felt; now, in unguarded lulls of the day, the image would blossom, and he would imagine her clutching her chest, or racked with pain, even spurting blood inside, all pushing him to the point of sickness until he could substitute the memory of Owain blubbing down his shirtfront.

Despite a macabre curiosity, John had not managed to enter her bedroom, let alone sleep in the bed she'd shared with her husband, as Owain had offered. The man had declared he would never sleep in the bed again and had taken to collapsing, still dressed, across the settee where she had been sitting when it happened. When the time came for John to leave, Owain announced he would sell the house and move back to Saffron Walden in the New Year. Or perhaps he would move to Cambridge. John couldn't care a toss about any of it.

Life now was like unsalted soup. Moss had lost his humor, the school had lost its dramatics, and Halton had lost . . . to say he had lost Audsley would be to suggest that Audsley was gone, but how else to describe the removal of that thing that had made time worthwhile? The Turtle bemoaned the new regime as a personal tragedy, which made Halton want to punch him in the nose. He contented himself with making acid jokes at the Turtle's expense, which at least improved his standing with Malcolm, White, Fletcher, and other rugby-crazed members of the Fourth. Now, having been accepted back into their company, Halton could not afford to be addressed by the Turtle here in the tuck shop queue. He looked away when the Turtle caught his eye, but the Turtle would not be deterred:

—That descant is a stinker!

White and Fletcher sneered. Malcolm minor snickered:

—Still bumming around with fags, Infant?

His hands were prickling.

—Is Malc's baby brovver your special fwend now? White mocked.

—We'd no idea the choir could be so *stimulating*.

—Run along, Infant, and play with baby Malc.

—Unless you're letting him play with you, saucy tart.

Halton left the queue and went to the chapel to think. That night after Prayers, he set to the remedy. When he'd finished, the Turtle was in tears.

—It's only a joke. Don't be a girl.

The Turtle looked at him, rubbing the sore spots, his red eyes uncomprehending:

—I thought we were friends.

✦

Bonfire night came and went. Tics were filled, prep submitted, rugby football played. The Lower Sixth began *Paradise Lost*, which Gray considered a slog. Even more of a slog were the bizarre articles Grieves was making them read, in French, from a French magazine called *Annales*. What *La potasse en Allemagne* had to do with medieval kings who cured scrofula by royal touch, Grieves did not deign to explain.

Gill did his own prep, but the results seemed a matter of indifference to him. Gray tried to rekindle morale by talking about the plays they would stage once they had a proper dramatics club.

—The Head'll relent once he sees we're sorry, Gray assured him. No punishment lasts more than a term.

—Bugger that, Gill said. Look at *this*.

He slapped down the paper, but it contained only dry announcements of London productions.

—The Classical Players!

—Are rehearsing *Hamlet*. And?

—Theodore Rhys-Mills is playing Hamlet!

—Who's he?

—Who's *he*? Vain, untalented, almost thirty years old! We gave *Hamlet* two years ago, but my father said I had to be at least sixteen to play him. Now the Players are giving it, and I'm sixteen, and they've cast Rhys-Mills of all people!

It hurt to hear Guilford speak this way. He seemed to regard Gray as shallow, concerned only with lessons and prep, while London held the strings to his heart. Gray came close to telling him about the girl, but each time, the volume of what there was to tell prevented him. In one way, it was a relief that her mother was dead. The thing she'd long dreaded—the thing he realized he had dreaded with her—could no longer be feared. But if he let himself stand inside with her, imagining how she must have felt and how she must be feeling now, a snuffing terror closed in, and he could feel death breathing down his neck again. He did not, for any reason, want to recall how his father had looked in the bed. The memory had battered him for years, and only recently had he realized the battering had stopped. Now, thinking of her took him back again, but this time he imagined her standing beside him, her arm brushing his as they looked at the four-poster thing.

One wet afternoon while Gill was in extra-tu, Gray ventured to the chapel and stood in the nave. From below, the chair loft looked like nothing, a railing, no more. The choir were rehearsing, and he felt the sound in his teeth.

—Stop! Kardleigh was calling. Stop, stop, stop.

Voices tapered off.

—Breathe, Halton, after *day*.

In his mouth, an aching weakness.

—No, you cannot. The edge is coming off *pride*. Again, alone please.

Halton's voice piped through the dark:

—I loved the garish day . . . and spite of fears, pride ruled my will.
—Breathe!

Grieves disappeared again the day before their tic finished, and when they reported to Moss at tea, he signed each twice, freeing them from the final reporting that night:

—Cut along, and don't say I never did anything for you.

They stopped at the pigeonholes, where Gill collected the late *Times*, its headlines surely of interest to someone. *Labour Amendment Defeated. Marked Improvement in Textiles. Air Defences of London: Interceptor Theory from Our Aeronautical Correspondent.* Saturday evening, free and empty, they drifted back to the study. Gray scanned the bookshelf, but there was nothing he wanted to read.

—We could go round to Moss and Crighton, Gray suggested. They might let us listen to the gramophone.

—I've a better idea.

Gill let the paper fall to the floor:

—The Cross Keys.

Gray told him to forget it.

—To be, or not to be, Gill proclaimed, that is the question!

The eyes were back, that Messenger who brought so much disorder and so much joy.

—Who would fardels bear, to grunt and sweat under a weary life, but that the dread of something after death—

—It'll be death all right if the Head finds out.

—The undiscover'd country, from whose bourn no traveler returns—

—Not to mention the JCR. They'll make the Head's six feel like pattycakes.

—And makes us rather bear those ills we have, than fly to others that we know not of!

They emerged from the tunnel to darkness, Grindalythe Woods cut only by the beams of their torches. Everything about the woods delighted Gill. Trevor had appreciated it as a shortcut to the barn, but he'd never seen it as Gill did now—evocative, creature-filled, alive. At the fork, Gray searched for the path to Fridaythorpe. He'd never taken it before, and while it might have been straightforward in the daytime, now they were forced to double back and recover the way.

At the Keys, Gill treated the woman behind the bar as an old friend. The place was even more crowded than when they'd come with Peter, the only seats far from the fire. Gill bought their pints and chatted to three young women on the way. When Gray asked who they were, Gill claimed to have met them last time.

—What do you mean you met them? Where was I?

—Puking?

As the evening wore on, Gray found it easy to believe Gill had befriended three girls; he began conversations easily, and just as easily had people laughing. Steak and kidney pies came and went, the first pints were followed by more, and at last Gill succeeded in convincing the barmaid to let him stand her a pint. She came out from the bar and squeezed beside Gill, treating him half as a lovesick puppy, half as a daring new craze. Gill's accent had altered to blend with those around him, mimicking their expressions and even getting the barmaid to teach him Yorkshire sayings.

—'Ear all, see all, say nowt, she recited. Eat all, sup all, pay nowt.

—And if ever thou does owt fer nowt, Gill answered, allus do it for thyself.

—For thissen, love.

—For thissen, flower.

The barmaid returned to the pumps, and Gill collected another round.

—We've got to go, Gray told him.

They could slip in Grieves's French windows, but bedtime was less than an hour away.

—In a minute.

Gill took a sip and then set the glass aside as if clearing the table for business.

—Now, he said, about Valarious.

Gray grinned despite himself; Gill was staring like Mr. Grieves with a point to make.

—It's time you faced facts. The play is dead, but Valarious isn't.

Gray tried to order his thoughts. Valarious had been with him for years, but the play had effected alchemy upon the tale. Now it was inseparable from their performances, and from Guilford, who embodied his hero.

—What have you been doing these past two weeks? Gill demanded. You could've had the story written.

—Why would I do that?

—He stopped us performing it, but he can't stop you writing the book.

Valarious wasn't a book. It wasn't even a complete story.

—You've got to finish it.

Even if he went back to the notebook and put into prose the scenes of the play, the story would not have reached its end. He didn't know when it would.

Gill was squeezing his wrist:

—Once you've started a thing, you can't stop. You've got to finish and publish and then write something else. If you don't, you'll be like those people in Exodus who tried to store things overnight.

—Manna?

—It'll breed worms and stink.

—It already stinks!

—You can't keep hold of precious things.

Gray laid his head on his arm:

—What about love?

—Love most of all.

The table started to spin. She had given away precious things, terrible and precious, and if he didn't keep them, who would? Keeper of a hundred secrets, all concealed beneath the planks of the loft, infused with dust and incense, held above their heads as they prayed. How many radiant secrets were hidden all around them?

Gill leaned close:

—The trick with secrets is knowing who to tell, and how to tell them.

They got up to leave, but heat rushed through him.

—I'm going to be sick.

Gill pulled him down the street and over the stile; inside the woods, it all came up, disappearing into the dark. Gill had his elbow and kept them to the path, kept their way within the light of his torch.

—There are things I haven't told you.

—I know.

The darkness closed behind them and before them, protecting them from the day, from its wrecking and reproof. Here Morgan had walked, and here had walked all the keepers before him, in darkness, in light, *thou knowest, woods, the secrets of our hearts,* and words were spilling out like eggs from a basket, and Gill was catching each before it hit the ground, hiding it in his pocket, which never filled.

—You love her.

—I despise her!

—Write her.

—I would if I knew where!

Guilford sighed:

—I don't think you've been trying very hard.

—*What?*

—And the same for him. You must write to him as well.

—Morgan?

Naked on his tongue, ten years old again.

—Everything I touch gets ruined.

—Nothing's ruined.

—When people leave, you don't have them anymore!

—Don't you?

They reached the old log, and the truth fell down, like the rock in the rack where they found the Elf Rider: Guilford Audsley did not understand. He had seemed sage, even Delphian, but he had never watched everything struck down before him. The worst he'd ever suffered was the Head's cane and insult. His wisdom was shallow, and his pockets couldn't hold a robin's egg.

Gray plunged into the tunnel, upsetting up and down, dirt, stone, head and teeth pounding. Then Gill was crawling out and telling him to hurry, steering him around the playing fields to Grieves's windows, Grieves's study, corridor. In the changing room, Gray lay across the bench to keep from being sick again.

—What time is it?

—Curtain time.

They changed their shoes, Gill rehearsed their alibi—library, reading—and they staggered up to the dorms, which were empty save for the dorm fag, who gassed about the Empire Film in the gym, North American prairies, everyone watching a second time through. In the washroom, Gill seemed to supervise him, as Morgan sometimes had, taking a flannel to the back of his neck and hanging up his dressing gown in the dorm.

—Good night, sweet Prince.

Gill's voice was benevolent, as if it were true what he had said, that nothing was ruined, like the kindly light amidst the gloom that encircled but never quite consumed.

John couldn't see why Owain refused to use the telephone, though on reflection it was obvious: telegrams were more dramatic. COME AT ONCE SHE NEEDS YOU STOP was designed to instill panic even before John picked up the apparatus to ring for an explanation. This time he didn't bother asking Jamie, who was in any case away with Kardleigh. John informed his matron and then departed for the station just in time to make the night express.

When he arrived in Ely Saturday morning, no one met him. He walked to the house in the dark. It took repeated hangings on the bell to rouse Owain, and when the door finally opened, John's alarm surged.

—Thank Jesus you're here, Owain muttered.

The man's voice and appearance were rough. John followed him into the kitchen, where Owain poured a drink from a near-empty bottle and offered it to him.

—Let's start with some tea, John replied.

Owain fell into a kitchen chair and cradled his head. Questions swarmed, but John concentrated on the tea and then on washing the dishes piled in the sink. Owain seemed to have fallen back to sleep, but once the tea was ready and the whiskey removed, John jostled his chair.

—You look awful, he said.

Owain blew his nose into a dirty handkerchief:

—You've no idea, no earthly idea.

John resisted the urge to roll his eyes. Instead he stirred sugar into Owain's tea and pushed it across the table.

—Jesus, man! Owain said as the tea sloshed and burned him.

John wanted to tell him not to take the Lord's name in vain.

—Where is she?

—Upstairs!

Having delivered himself of this, Owain began to weep. John decamped to the corridor. The jaws of family had closed with the front door and were pressing with all their undressed knowing. He called to

his goddaughter, and, receiving no answer, went up and announced himself at her door. It was locked, the corridor frigid and drafty.

—Cordelia?

—It's no good, Owain called.

John peered down the stairs, but Owain merely gestured for him to
descend. John did, impatience growing. He hadn't come all this way to
indulge an Irishman.

—She'll not answer, Owain said. Locked herself in three days now.

—Surely she comes out sometimes.

Owain denied it. She'd taken neither food nor drink. Owain had
heard her moving about, and her wireless played loudly whenever the
programs were on.

—So you see, Owain concluded, why I sent for you.

John took his tea into the parlor to think. He knew he mustn't be
drawn in, to the dramatics or Owain's tears, but, good Lord, how many
children would he have to sort out? He asked Owain for the key, but
Owain claimed not to have it.

—You mean she has the only one?

—What d'you think I've been telling you?

His head was hurting now. He retrieved the drops from his case and
took them with his tea as Owain raised a smeary glass. An idea sailed
over the wall . . . and Owain's collar was in his hands, and he was shoving him against the table.

—If you've laid one finger on her, God help me, I'll—

His hands were doing it, closing on that throat to end the odious
breath.

—Jesus! Never!

—Swear it.

—I swear.

—On her mother's grave.

—On her mother's godforsaken grave!

Owain sobbed again, this time with rage:

—Black-and-tan bastard!

His fist connected with John's face, and they yelled together, John's
knuckles hitting bone and flesh, and they were falling to the floor
cursing.

—Dirty mick!

He was saying things he'd never said aloud, and they were scrapping
with the strength of lifelong rivals.

—Blow-bottle!

Then Owain was rolling away and sobbing, or was it laughter, and something was dripping down John's face, and he realized he was laughing, too.

—If she could see us now, he gasped.

Owain's laughter mixed again with tears:

—Hooligans.

Later, after each of them had bathed and changed, Owain announced his intention to pop round his offices. John began to object but then realized the wisdom of it. Perhaps the upstairs door would open if Owain were out of the house, and if it wouldn't open willingly, John would be free to try stronger measures.

First things first: old tea discarded, fresh prepared. Next: renewed knocking, feeble beside the blaring wireless. Then torch, cellar, fuse box . . . silence already down the long stairs. He let his feet fall heavily on the steps. Time for the man who could make boys quake.

—Open this door, Cordelia Líoht. Your father has gone out.

Silence. Jamie's father always claimed that boys were a walk-over compared to girls. Right again, John realized grimly.

—Enough nonsense, young lady!

Sounds of movement in the opposite direction.

—If I have to dismantle this door, I shall, but you won't like the consequences.

To complete the performance, he banged with the butt of his torch. He was just wondering if the ladder in the cellar was long enough to reach her window when the key turned. He pushed into the room and into its cold draft. She huddled on the bed, blankets tentlike around her, eyes sunken like a consumptive, the room's every surface covered with maps.

Words failed him. He lifted her and carried her squirming from the scene. She was bigger than the last time he'd carried her, but he made it to the bathroom and set her on the stool. Breath labored, he stood there, one hand on the door, one on his hip, waiting for something, from himself or from her. She hugged herself and avoided the gaze he was deploying, the one that always drew from boys stammered explanations. When she darted for the window sash, he caught her:

—Oh, no you don't.

He secured the latch, put the plug in the bath, and turned on the taps. She flopped down on the floor, suddenly deflated, and when the tub had filled, he told her to get in. Her expression sent a splinter through his eye.

—Oh, very well, he said turning his back, though I don't see what the fuss is about. I've been giving you baths since you were born.

He waited, arms crossed, until he heard her settle beneath the bubbles. It was too soon to get her to talk, so he sat down on the stool and occupied himself skimming back issues of *The Friend*, which he found in a basket beside the toilet. She stared at the walls, and when the steam stopped rising, he added more hot water. He wet her hair, and she let him wash it as he used to when she was small. Finally, he set out a towel, gathered up her clothes and told her to wash properly. Taking the key from the bathroom door, he went down the corridor to her room.

The draft, he discovered, was coming from the window, which was open behind the map of Suez. The whole chamber deserved to be burned, but first, key to his pocket, hairbrush from bureau, clothes from the press, he gathered it all and locked the door. The bath was draining, and she stood at the sink cleaning her teeth, cloaked in the towel like some Indian chief. He set down her clothes and stepped into the corridor— but then returned: What was that on the back of her legs, like the scratches of a cat but more vivid and regular?

—What's happened?

She dropped to a crouch, covering herself, but her arm revealed more. He took her wrist and then her other arm, pulling her up to see her legs and the backs of her knees.

—How *could* he?

His arms were around her, tears at his throat.

—How could *he*? she croaked. Is that what you think?

He reached for her, but she pushed him away.

—He isn't here, darling. He can't—

—Don't be daft!

She drew the towel tight.

—I always knew you were green, Uncle John, but this takes the cake.

He recoiled as if struck—by her, and by a thought.

Corridor, key, stripping the bed of its morbid covers, pencil case, nibs, penknife, handkerchief, spotted red.

He made her eat toast and an egg and then come for a walk. At the cathedral, she led him to a place off the transept where there were chairs and prie-dieux. Someone was practicing the organ, and the low notes filled his throat. She slipped her hands into the sleeves of her coat, like a cold monk.

—If I tell you, she said, do you promise not to speak of it? Ever to anyone, even me.

How could he promise? But how could he not?

She knelt and put her head in her hands. He imitated her, the organ a force field of sound, like a labyrinth raised around them. Between the blasts, she whispered, not many words but enough to make his skin prickle. Her words issued from a grief-filled mind, but what if they also were true?

✦

Someone shook his shoulder, the Turtle's voice like a hurricane in his ear.

—Second bell, Riding.

He turned his head but then laid it down again.

—Moss wants you in your study, ten minutes.

He groaned.

—He says you're not to tell anyone, and you're not to think of skiving off to the Tower.

He sat up, but the maddening messenger had gone.

His head was pounding like an overzealous organ. He was parched, but anything more than sips from the tap made his stomach turn. Evidently, Gill was not suffering, as he'd already gone down to breakfast. Gray couldn't remember Morgan's face ever looking the way his looked now. Probably he was coming down with something.

No sign of Moss at the study. He tidied the table and floor. The newspaper lay where Gill had let it fall, open this time to an item of sensation: *Actress's Death from Burns*. A lady had died from burns received in an accident at her lodgings. She had come to London to rehearse with the Classical Players. Authorities believed that the lady was alone in her rooms when her nightdress came into contact with a candle. The article did not explain why the lady should be running about with candles when an electric torch would do, but Gray supposed it was the kind of thing actresses did. *Mrs. Ward acted under her maiden name of Muriel Rhys-Mills. Her brother, Theodore, will accompany her body to Edinburgh, where the funeral will be held.* Rhys-Mills, Theodore? Vain, untalented, thirty *years old? The Classical Players have confirmed that Mr. Rhys-Mills has resigned his role. There is no word yet as to how or whether the Players will proceed with the production.*

Here was a bright spot in an unpromising day. At least Gill could rest easy that Theodore Rhys-Mills would not profane *Hamlet*, this season at any rate.

Moss burst in without knocking:

—There you are.

He was pale.

—What's the matter?

Moss rubbed his nose.

—Don't piss about! Gray said. Tell me.

—Did you see Audsley last night?

If this were about last night, they'd be standing before the JCR, their fate already decided.

—We went to bed early.

Moss looked pained:

—There's no good way to say this, and after chapel everyone will know.

—What? For God's sake!

✦

Everything had passed over into the absurd, John thought. Here he was Sunday morning, stuck in Nowhere, Lincolnshire, waiting for an accident up the line to be cleared. His goddaughter stretched across the seats, asleep at last. Against his better judgment, he'd given her one of his drops, but then so much in the previous twenty-four hours had been against his better judgment. Had it been good judgment to grant her request, issued hoarse beneath folded hands:

—Take me away from here, Uncle John. *Please.*

As if he alone could save her. John had sent her to the shop so he could snatch a few words with her father. Alone with Owain, John had rambled. He had no qualms about breaking her confidence, but how to avoid appearing out of his mind?

—Been seein' ghosts, has she? Owain replied to the winding introduction.

John felt the hair stand up on his arms.

—How did you . . . ?

371

—You can laugh.

John wasn't laughing.

—In my country we know to be careful of the dead.

His eyes pricked in fear.

—She never seemed to notice until a few nights ago, Owain continued. I was frying an egg, like her mother used, trying to get her to eat, and the room came over cold, and the smell . . .

She'd whispered as much in the back of the church: lemon all around but like fruit gone off; chill like snow when the windows were closed. There in the kitchen, John smelled nothing besides Owain's drink, and felt nothing beyond the heat of the stove. It was little wonder the girl was losing her grip, shut up with a man who slept in shirtsleeves and armchair, a man who hadn't seen twenty-four sober hours since—

—You must take her, Owain said as her key turned in the door. Take her away from here.

—Take her?

—Love her, Owain whispered, like she was your own. Can you do that, for her mother's sake?

He hadn't asked Jamie. This was bigger than Jamie. Orders of magnitude couldn't be refused.

✦

Gray refused to believe it. Why would Guilford have crept from the dorm after midnight? Why would he have broken into Mr. Grieves's study, drunk his brandy, and then raised the alarm by knocking over a table? And why, having done these incredible things, hadn't he escaped before Mrs. Firth appeared in dressing gown and dismay? Why had Guilford—master of improvisation, master of drink—offered no excuse beyond a drunken blathering?

—The Head didn't elaborate, Moss said. Put him on the early train and told Matron to send his things on.

—Did you see him before he left?

Moss hadn't, but he took a note from his pocket:

—Matron gave me this.

Torn from an envelope, the girl's script unmistakable: 27 *Willow Walk, Ely.*

—Audsley asked Matron to give it to you.

On the reverse, Gill's hand, small and clear: *Write!*

He'd written her so many times in his mind, but now that he tried, everything sounded wrong. Chapel passed, luncheon, football. He tackled the weekly letter home, a task made more turgid by the fact that he couldn't mention the week's extraordinary events. At three o'clock, Divinity lesson cast him into the company of the Sixth, who, rather than interrogate him as the Fifth had done at luncheon, regarded him with an embarrassed kind of awe. Dr. Sebastian thankfully ignored him as they swept through the day's scriptures and hymn. Source for the latter was a poem by Newman, the Head informed them, written nearly one hundred years ago while Newman's ship home to England was becalmed by fog in the Strait of Bonifacio. The hymn was known as "Lead, Kindly Light," but the poem was called "The Pillar of the Cloud."

—An allusion to what, Riding?

So much for slouching in the back of the room.

—Exodus, sir?

—Go on. And stand up straight.

Had Guilford told the Head of their excursion to Fridaythorpe, when Gill's torch had led them home like the light in the hymn?

—God uses a pillar of cloud, sir, to guide the Jews out of Egypt, and at night it turns into a pillar of fire.

Dr. Sebastian nodded and called for their hymnals, which they produced for close reading. The poem was beautiful enough to break hearts.

After Divinity, he took paper and pencil to the window seat. Could a letter begin with the poem? *So long thy power hath blessed me, sure it still will lead me on.* Was there a way to link the condolences he had to offer with a glimpse, if she wanted, into his heart and the force her letters exerted on him even now? *O'er moor and fen, o'er crag and torrent till the night is gone. And in the morn—*

A motorcar crunched below. Its engine choked off, doors clicked open. The window was dirty, and the square by his face was cracked, but it couldn't conceal what was on the other side: in twilight and mist, the saffron-haired girl, materialized within the gates of the Academy as if called there by the force of things unsaid. She wore black, not gray, and lugged a heavy case. As Mr. Grieves paid the driver, she set her burden down, cast her eyes upon the barren scene, and coughed.

✦

Lewis was on guard when John arrived:

—He's expecting you. Go straight in.

With this, Jamie's secretary rolled off, as if he'd merely been waiting to admit a boy for his thrashing.

—Thank God! Jamie exclaimed when John entered.

John fumbled the greeting, but Jamie drew him near the fire, offered him a drink and, when he refused, tea.

—Is everything all right? Jamie asked at last.

—Yes, John said. I think it is now.

Jamie looked puzzled, tense.

—I'm sorry to have dashed off like that, John continued, but I think I can promise it won't happen again.

He launched into the story, but it sounded even more inept than when he'd practiced. Jamie listened without interruption, draining one glass and most of another. When John came to the end, he kept talking even though he knew he was repeating himself—his goddaughter would on no account pose a disturbance, Jamie need never meet her, she could take her meals in the kitchen and never be seen in public.

—Don't be silly, Jamie said. I expect her at Prayers this evening.

The color was returning to Jamie's cheeks. He poured himself a third glass:

—Now about her lessons.

John assured him that he would see to her tuition and that the boys would not suffer.

—Don't be silly, Jamie said again. She can come to me for Divinity and Latin. The Eagle can supervise her reading. She does French, doesn't she? I'm sure Henri will chat to her a few times a week.

John felt something scratch his eye, and he blinked to clear it. He'd rehearsed countless scenarios on the journey up, but none matched this.

—Thank you, he managed. It's—

But Jamie dismissed his thanks and began to pace. John felt hungry for the first time in days. Had he actually eaten anything besides a bite of her sandwich since the halfhearted attempt at fish and chips the night before? Jamie's clock chimed, and shortly the tea bell would sound—only soup on Sunday evenings, but Academy broth, brown bread, and a bit of butter would more than satisfy. John felt he wanted nothing in the world beyond warm, honest food, the bonds of friendship, the pleasing burden of his vocation, the asylum of their little world.

Jamie was drawing aside the drapes.

—Looking for something? John asked.

—Nothing.

John got up to leave, but Jamie began to riffle through the items on his desk.

—Is something wrong?

Jamie stopped:

—Not exactly.

—Was there some other reason you wanted to see me?

—I think you had better sit back down.

◆

The knock came halfway through Prep.

—Housemaster to see you, young Riding.

Mrs. Firth had narrowed her eyes as if to say, *You're for it*. Gray's mind, numb with events, offered no advice. *Lead thou me on.* He followed her downstairs, and she abandoned him at the study. When he knocked, the Flea burst out, looking daggers.

—Come in and shut the door, Mr. Grieves called.

He did as he was told. The man pointed to the orange chair:

—Sit.

And they were back: the hunchbacked man and the boy who fought back tears before him.

—Well?

As if he saw every lie, every vice and mistake.

—What do you have to say to me?

What did he have to *say* to him?

—You can take that look off your face.

—What look, sir?

—Don't be cheeky!

His ears stung. It would take only the ash of a cigarette, the jostle of an elbow to ignite—like before, only worse. Yet she had trusted him. Completely, rashly, repeatedly. He had never betrayed her—

—*Well?*

If Grieves thought he could make him now, then he did not know his subject! The girl's address was not on his person, so even if commanded to empty his pockets, he would reveal nothing. The one who had stolen the address was gone. *Guilford* was gone—the fact was hitting him now, here in the chair—but if this man thought he would yield

375

to a scowl, he could think again. He, her confidant, might not be bold, but he was stubborn, Morgan always said. Grieves had no idea how stubborn he could be.

—If that's the way you're going to behave . . .

Grieves spoke slowly, each word a spark.

—Then you'd best go back to Prep.

—Sir?

Thunder upon them.

—You heard me. Get out.

✦

His head was killing him. The boy had just left, and John had just decided to take his next dose early when there came another knock at the door, his goddaughter, sallow and dark-eyed. She pulled her blazer closed:

—Is it always so cold?

He beckoned her into the room and explained about the wind.

—Like in *Wuthering Heights*?

He paused, though he knew he oughtn't to be shocked by her unsuitable choices of reading material.

—I think you'll find it far less dramatic here.

No ghosts, he wanted to say, but no good came of putting ideas in people's heads.

—Aren't you allowed a fire? she asked.

She was wandering around the room, peering at objects on his mantel.

—Of course, we are, but the coal allotments . . .

Fingering the brandy decanter, its stopper now chipped by Audsley's shenanigans.

—Cordelia, sit down.

He nodded at the chair before his desk, and she sat, shivering. He wondered if she was trying to make a point.

—This, he said, is the timetable.

He passed a card across the blotter, and she held it up to the desk lamp.

—I did warn you I'd be busy and that life here would be dull.

—Yes.

What was it about her tone that reminded him of his last, enraging interview with the boy who'd said nothing at all?

—Dr. Sebastian has very kindly made arrangements for you to continue some of your studies here.

She looked up, attentive:

—What form will I be in?

A flash of alarm as he glimpsed her misunderstanding, one that might, he realized, be extensive.

—Cordelia, listen. You are not going to lessons with the boys.

She had misunderstood; disappointment crashed upon her.

—You won't—and this is very important, darling—be having anything to do with them.

She didn't look happy, but he'd never agreed to make her happy.

—We'll talk more tomorrow, John said, but since it's Prep, I think you ought to make a start.

He passed her Auden's *Latin Unseens*.

—Mr. Burton-Lee will be expecting you tomorrow at four o'clock with the first passage prepared.

She opened the book and scanned the page, idly chewing the inside of her lip.

—Now, look at me, please.

She closed the book but kept a finger inside, advertising her intention to return to it as soon as he stopped wittering, so much like her infuriating counterpart that he had to bite back a reprimand. Of course Riding was in no way her counterpart even though both had sat in the same chair, a few minutes apart, and looked at him in ways that made him want to strike. The only face more infuriating, though not by much, was Jamie's when he'd finally coughed up the truth about Guilford Audsley, a ludicrous tale delivered semi-incoherently. Jamie had rattled unsteadily at first—discomposed by guilt, John supposed—but then he seemed to settle into a spiteful kind of confidence. He'd left John dazed, confounded about where even to begin dismantling the mess. The story in its lunacy incensed him, and John was sure Jamie had not got the truth out of Guilford. More offensively, Jamie informed him that he'd already telephoned the Audsleys to explain, a task that John, as Guilford's Housemaster and friend of his parents, ought to have performed. The Audsleys had been surprised, Jamie reported, but accepting. John felt this, too, was suspect, and he knew he must write them as soon as he could gather more information. After everything that had passed between him and the Audsleys, after all their trust, for this grotesque thing to transpire—he felt paralyzed with shame and failure.

Jamie claimed that Audsley had acted alone—the boy had said so and had been discovered on his own—but John did not believe that either. Guilford had never done anything without his studymate, and there was no reason he ought to have started now. Riding had most certainly played a part and would possess information most germane.

John had just dispatched his matron to fetch Riding when Burton had arrived unannounced. He'd treated Burton impatiently and then been mortified when Burton had proposed seeing his goddaughter for Latin. John, dumbfounded, had refused, explaining that Jamie had already offered. Burton had turned to examine his bookshelves:

—You've accepted, then, after recent events?

John wasn't sure just what he'd said in reply, but he knew Burton had considered it burbling.

—Do as you wish, Burton said, but it isn't always best for boys, or girls if you prefer, to have to negotiate other people's awkward situations.

Burton had stood thumbing a book, giving John time to progress through outrage to truth: that he trusted Burton with the girl better than he trusted Jamie.

—I can't honestly say I was sorry to see Audsley go, Burton said, but I do think—

He set a copy of Auden on the desk.

—it wouldn't have made things any worse for Sebastian to wait for your return.

The man gazed at him:

—And, you know, none of us is indifferent—

With subterfuge? Pity?

—to you, and your circumstances.

Compassion was impossible, yet—

—We do worry, you know.

John knew he'd accepted the offer with poor grace, hobbled as he was by pique; by removing the mask of cantankerousness to reveal a face of charity, Burton had destroyed the certainties that made life manageable.

He was just ushering Burton out when Mrs. Firth had delivered Riding—would it never stop? He'd pressed the spot on his eye socket that sometimes gave relief, but the draft from the corridor chilled him, and he'd had to tell Riding to shut the godforsaken door. The boy had stood at the edge of the rug staring at him as if he were the one due an explanation. John knew he'd not handled the interview as well as he might, but the boy was enough to drive a man to violence. When John had asked him for something, anything which might shed light on the preposterous saga of Guilford Audsley, the boy had not only refused to answer but had looked at him with more impertinence, resentment, and arrogance than John had ever imagined possible from a pupil. What he'd ever seen in this boy, what Morgan had seen, what *Guilford* had seen, it was all beyond his withered comprehension. This boy deserved the soundest of thrashings, and a good clip round the ear, as Moss had dealt the other night before hoiking him off to bed.

John had sent the boy away before he murdered him and was just about to fetch his drops, remembering that they lay in the pocket of his overcoat, when his goddaughter had arrived and complained of the cold.

She shivered now as her eyes drifted back to her book. He fetched a spare muffler from his cupboard and gave it to her. She examined the purple and white as if at a Parisian boutique and then, having judged it acceptable, wrapped it around her throat.

—House colors, he said.

Still no smile. He fetched an exercise book and set it before her.

—I shan't bore you with rules. Let's try to keep things simple.

She gazed at him again, world-weary, nearly bored.

—You're expected at meals and Prayers, but you're not to fraternize with the boys.

She nodded.

— You're not to leave school grounds without my permission.

Another nod.

—And bedtimes are to be strictly observed.

The corners of her mouth twitched, and she made him a sort of salute.

—Don't be cheeky.

It came out sharper than he intended, and she pulled her face into a bland mask. He'd saved the worst for last, and he didn't know how to manage it.

—I want you to promise me something. It's very important.

From his desk drawer, he removed her pencil case. Set it before her.

—Will you promise?

She went to take it, but he closed his hand over hers.

—You must promise me you won't . . .

She tried to pull away, but he held her.

—Promise me, darling. For—

—Don't you dare say for her sake!

379

—For *my* sake. For me.

He let her open the case, devoid of penknife.

—How am I meant to sharpen my pencils?

—I'll do it for the time being.

—I'm not a child, Uncle John.

He waited, firm.

—I know you aren't.

◆

Sunday Evening Prayers were always brief, one reading, responses and collects, and a reprise of the day's hymn sung now by the choir. Gray usually enjoyed it, but tonight as the choir prepared to sing, he felt afraid, a feeling that deepened as Dr. Sebastian rose from his seat and cleared his throat.

—I should like to welcome back most warmly a visitor to our midst, Miss Líoht, who is Mr. Grieves's goddaughter.

A flurry in the pews as they strained to see.

—I count on you to show her every courtesy.

The girl sat beside her godfather, gazing up at the dark windows. She looked like a person who had never smiled, a Puritan who wore black the year round, occupying her thoughts with the sins of the world.

◆

The song they were singing rattled her skull, knocking away bone to let the wind through. People at Meeting sometimes began to shake when the Spirit entered them, or so they said. Now, as the singing fell away to two voices, her elbows began to buzz, the words like spears.

I was not ever thus, nor prayed that thou shouldst lead me on.
I loved to choose and see my path, but now lead thou me on.

She didn't belong, in this place or to it.

I loved the garish day, and spite of fears, pride ruled my will

She buried her head in her arms as if she'd received a blow to the back of her knees. She thought she'd been cut all the way to the ground—

380

her mother on one shore, them on the other—but the axe hadn't finished. It was falling still and still.

✦

The choir sounded as it never had before, and it seemed to John that Kardleigh was conjuring the music to destroy what remained of his composure.

So long thy power hath blest me, sure it still will lead me on.

To pulverize his doubt with a thing he couldn't see.

And with the morn those angel faces smile . . .

He was coming apart, savaged by the hand that made him.

Which I have loved . . . long since

Mercy, mercy—

 It snowed there at the drop of a hat. She would wake to their bells, and the pavement would be dusted. The days were shorter, and sometimes the snow fell like a veil across the afternoon, forcing them to switch on the lights before time. No one had weeded the grass from the pavement in the middle of the cloisters, and the snow made a carpet of green and white diamonds until the prefects trampled it with their bossy shoes. She cycled each morning, fingers cold in mittens, to the school in Thixendale where she was supposed to study geography and drawing, but where instead she helped the children with their arithmetic.

The Academy, as she learned to call it, was shabbier than she remembered. The chapel ceiling needed new plaster, and the whole place needed airing. The food was still vile.

Sometimes on the floor of the bathroom it hurt so much she felt sure she would break. If you cried hard enough, would it crack a bone?

Mr. Lockett-Egan was shocked by her reading, whether by what she had read or what she hadn't, he didn't say. Dr. Sebastian was shocked by her religious education, Monsieur Henri was shocked by her knowledge of certain parts of Paris, and young Mr. Palford from Llangollen was shocked that she knew mathematics at all. Only Mr. Burton-Lee, the old man they all feared, seemed perfectly at ease with her. He would quiz her on the prep and demand her quick reply. He would answer her queries with conviction and let her know that they mattered, that he had no intention of taking pity on her for anything. When she burrowed beneath the rough blankets at night, it seemed not impossible that she might one day wake up and find herself a boy. She could change her name to something better, switch her clothes, play football, punch things, and be beaten for her crimes.

That boy never looked at her, which meant he had done what she told him. Not that it mattered. Nothing that mattered could be changed. In the refectory, he sat with his scores of friends, laughed at their jokes, and shoveled the sickening brussels sprouts into his maw like a creature that couldn't taste. He behaved like one who'd never known her, but on the floor of the bathroom she knew the truth: she had ordered him to forget. He was being faithful in the only way he could.

✦

It was worse than he'd imagined, worse than any book described. To read her words on airmail paper was one thing, but to live and breathe within her orbit, to glimpse her out the window as she mounted a bicycle and pedaled through the gates during timetabled lessons, free when they were not, to have to listen to every licentious remark from his fellows, each crude rumor and joke—it was enough to bring on angina.

Was she bewitched or merely cruel to pretend he didn't exist? Grief, he knew, could change people. It had turned his mother into a shade who despised him. Could this other one be the same? She'd no reason to blame him for what happened to her mother, but that didn't mean she wouldn't. Was he, by receiving her letters, supposed somehow to have stopped it? Did she regret her confidences now that the purpose behind them was dead? Or were her refusals meant to be defeated? Had she expected him to track her down months ago, and was her final, amputating letter a sign only of her disgust?

Her wardrobe was a palate of gray and black—woolen stockings, pullovers, hat, and coat. She even tied her hair with black ribbons. The single splash of color came from the purple stripe of the House scarf and tie. He found it strangely indecent for her to wear House colors, as if she might one morning don their uniform entire.

✦

Dr. Sebastian said that Advent meant *coming towards*. Not people coming towards Christmas, but Jesus coming towards all of them. Dr. Sebastian wandered off into the thickets at that point with the first and second coming and the end of times and the meanwhile. It was hopeful, he said, but also terrible.

She had always been afraid of ghosts. When she was small, she had dreams in which ghosts filled her room but her parents refused to believe her. After the funeral, she lay awake, abruptly unafraid. Then there was the night in the kitchen with the smell and the cold, and for a few seconds—she wasn't sure how long, it might have stopped time—she thought her mother was there. She went to call out, but before she could unfreeze her throat, the true freezing came: lemons but rotted, like her but not her. That time with Toad and the Green Fairy, *that* had been her, warm, not cold. In the kitchen was an imposter. She'd been fooled by it once, and was almost fooled this time, but in that frozen instant she had seen through it, smelled through it, *thought* through it, and she knew the only way to keep it away was to make the air so cold that its cold could not be felt, to make the room so loud that nothing could be heard, and to stop the smell—blood.

Uncle John said that there were no ghosts at the Academy, but then Sunday came and Advent, hopeful and terrible, and when darkness fell across the afternoon, she could feel the thing coming, that vile cheat slipping in when she was weak, sliding its rotten old hand up her leg.

✦

It was John's unpleasant duty that month to supervise the Fourth Form at Prep. The Fourth towards the end of Michaelmas were almost as notorious as the Remove in Lent. Having made it through their first year and grown bold at the start of their second, they faced the final weeks of term with brazen hearts. John was particularly vexed by the reunited quartet of White, Fletcher, Malcolm minor, and Halton. He had done what he could with glares, threats, and rearranged seating, but he had hesitated to dispense lines, his usual penalty for mucking about in Prep, because impositions would interfere with Halton's schedule of recreational reading, something John had labored all month to establish. However, to let the four continue in their obnoxious whispering, snickering, and passing of lewd notes was to encourage them, or, worse, to encourage their odious leader, White. White's sidekick, Fletcher, was decent at heart, John believed, but under the sway of White's charisma, he had grown flippant and lazy. Malcolm minor had always gone along with whatever was going, and since Halton seemed determined to egg them on, John saw little hope that any of them would recall his better self.

He fell into discussing the problem with the Common Room, with whom he'd been spending more time lately, in part for the fire and in part to exhibit gratitude for their help with his goddaughter.

—Why don't you simply docket the little devils? the Eagle asked during morning break.

It was difficult to be perfectly frank. Docketing the boys would deliver White and Fletcher to their Housemaster, who would deal sharply with them—not, John knew, because Burton routinely backed him up but because Burton thought very little of White. The trouble, of course, was that what Burton did, John would have to do, or the boys would perceive unfairness and the trouble would continue. John explained his objections to the disciplinary options at his disposal until his colleagues' eyes glazed over.

—But damn it, man, the Eagle exclaimed, this is precisely why your bolshie beliefs are so very unfair on the boys.

—Whack 'em and have done with it, Palford advised.

John had inured himself to the opinions of his elder colleagues, but he was not prepared to take advice from a Welshman of twenty-three. Nevertheless, he could see that his principles did, on this occasion, box him into a corner with options either unfairly burdensome or irrelevantly light.

—I was thinking, John said, that if I were to have a quiet word with Halton or perhaps with Fletcher—

—Don't be inane!

Burton thrust aside his paper:

—Why must you make simple things so infernally difficult?

John poured himself another coffee and retreated to the window seat, but the man had been roused. Burton-Lee was there to tell him that it was a fact, one he'd learned from bitter experience, that it was no use whatsoever to interfere in relations between boys. One could only hope that St. Stephen's would instill enough character to temper the odious ones or at least enable the decent ones to reject them in time. The Third and Fourth Forms were hothouses of tribalism, and it would be folly to try to influence Halton, Fletcher, or any boy away from his unsavory peers. One was more likely, Burton argued, to drive them closer together. Except in cases of flagrant or gross bullying, it was the role of masters to stay out of it.

—But surely, John argued, it's wrong for us to stand by and—

—That is precisely what we must do, Burton declared. Moral guidance is one thing, living their lives another.

As for their insubordination, Burton confirmed that it would only escalate if nothing were done. He assured John that he'd be pleased to deal with White and Fletcher if John could be bothered to write them a docket. He wouldn't take the cane to them, as that would give them too much satisfaction. No, Burton concluded, the only way to injure White's infernal pride would be to put him across the knee like a prep school boy and apply the slipper until he howled.

—Don't look so scandalized, Burton said. It isn't as though you don't know how.

John left the room.

The sense in the Common Room had always been that Jamie had dealt with the Riding-Mainwaring debacle. John had never corrected them, and neither had Burton. At any rate, he had been given no choice that night; he'd protested, yes, but then he had to follow Jamie's orders. His only other option would have been resignation.

Unless, of course, he had simply refused the orders. He might, if he'd thought of it, have sent Riding out of the room and gone bare knuckle, figuratively speaking, with Jamie. There had been the pressure of the train, but he might have refused that, too. If he'd had his wits about him, he might have launched another contest—himself, Jamie, and Burton contending over the future of Riding as they'd contended over Wilberforce when he, too, trespassed at that barn.

The drops soaked into his tongue and melted the pain in his knee. If Morgan were here now, he would sort Halton out in ten minutes. He would perceive that Halton was the hinge in this cohort, and that Halton stood in the greatest danger. He was brighter than he looked, Morgan would see, and if he didn't find a suitable outlet, he would make their lives a misery, including his own.

John stopped pacing the cloisters and went to sound Kardleigh.

—His voice has broken, Kardleigh said. He keeps trying to prove himself, but I can't rely on him anymore. That throat infection over the weekend didn't help either. He's off singing until Friday at least. Please don't let him go off the rails in the meantime.

That afternoon John kept the four boys after History. He was finished, he informed them. If he had to speak with them again, they would not care for the consequences. Halton flushed, which gave John hope that they might pull themselves together enough to keep their mischief beneath notice.

That night at Prep the four behaved worse than ever. They clowned outrageously in the back, and then, once separated, Halton directly below the dais, they had the nerve to pass anatomical diagrams and continue their communication in semaphore until the rest of the form stared at John in disbelief. There was nothing for it; he wrote White and Fletcher dockets and told Halton and Malcolm minor to see him afterwards. The rest of the period he spent uselessly reviewing his options, and when it was over, Halton and Malcolm minor standing before him, he procrastinated further by demanding to see their prep. Malcolm minor's was uninspiring, Halton's a travesty.

—I have just about had it with you!

John lowered his voice and instructed them to report to his study when they were ready for bed. They looked surprised, but not as surprised as he expected. He dismissed Malcolm minor and turned to Halton.

—Please, sir, the boy said. I've got choir.

—Oh no, you haven't!

✦

The Elf Rider was debating with the gaoler's daughter the many, many dangers of attempting an escape, and her keys were jangling and bells were ringing, and by the time he was finished crawling from the dream, the bells had fallen silent and the studies were still and he had slept through Prep and missed the start of Prayers. He could hear the voice

386

of the gaoler's daughter, *two lates already, dangers many and many*, but no, he told her, he knew this dungeon, a winding iron staircase, choir room to sacristy. If he spent the service in the chair loft and came down just in time, he could slip into the recessing crowd, and Pearce would have to say he'd been there all along.

✦

Uncle John wasn't in his seat. He wasn't anywhere in the chapel, though it was hard to see because the candles hadn't been lit. One of the prefects said the choir was going to process. That meant parade around. They were going to carry a big candle and walk in a shape like a knot, and while they walked and sang, the candlelight would spread. It was special, the boy said, for Advent. And then they were lighting the candle and a shadow was rearing, coming towards them like a snake—she told the prefect she'd be back in a jiffy.

✦

Heart in his throat, wild beats. There she stood, and there she sat, having dropped to the floor of the chair loft. The light was growing, brighter even than daytime. She clutched her knees to her chest, rage pulsing, and he felt the hungry excitement of fear. He could touch her if he wanted, the strands of her hair escaping her hair ribbon, the holes in her stockings. She put her head in her arms, and her shoulders were trembling. Was she actually weeping, or preparing to denounce him? Below, the Litany: *Remember not, Lord, our offenses, or the offenses of our forefathers.*
    —I'm sorry! he whispered.
    Spare us, good Lord, spare thy people.
    —You're always sorry!
    She was crying after all, looking like his mother had looked before striking him. He deserved it, and in that breath he craved it, but he was falling forward, pulled by her fist, nose bumped bone, and something dry and warm—her lips on his chin, on his mouth, her hand on the back of his head. She pressed, and he pressed back. When she pulled away, he gasped for breath, but then she had him again, teeth bumping his, flood of lemon drops.

John sat in the back and tried to calm his pulse. *From lightning and tempest; from plague, pestilence, and famine; from battle and murder, and from sudden death*—the world was not unraveling everywhere at once—*Good Lord, deliver us.* The problem at hand was not life and death but simply a pair of boys who believed they had more influence than they deserved. *From hardness of heart, and contempt of thy Word and commandment; Good Lord, deliver us.* How hard was his heart, after all? Too hard to touch them when they needed it? The Eagle had accused him, and now the Litany did, too: Who said pacifism had to be so cold? One could refuse to take life and yet deal with boys as they deserved. What if his long objection was merely a form of contempt, a shield against things that shamed him? And what if it had caused him to set his heart against them, even as he considered himself benign? *That it may please thee to strengthen such as do stand, and to comfort and help the weakhearted.* These boys had asked for the strength of his arm, loudly, repeatedly, over and against everything he had offered. Was he so selfish as to keep it from them now? Uncomplicated, unvarnished, direct, and in that way much closer to the simplicity of the Saffron Walden Meeting House than his usual tactics. Begun and ended quickly, no more maneuvering, no more *words*.

Advent said the world was coming to an end, the world as they knew it to be. A turning, or re-turning, a homecoming after years of flight to truth he had known before he realized it took knowing.

✦

It wasn't the same kind of kiss as the Toad's. Nothing was in it except his lips and his tongue and his teeth, and the place on the edge of his chin where it prickled. Her ribbons fell out, and her hair got tangled in his spectacles. When they stopped, he looked as though he would laugh, and she could tell it was one of those times when explanations could be skipped.

✦

By the time Halton got back to the dorm, the monkeys were chattering. They had heard the news from Malcolm but demanded it again from him. Grievous had deployed the slipper? Against him and Malcolm minor? They'd already seen Malc's marks, and now he showed them his. They unanimously declared it not cricket. Masters had no business changing; it undermined everyone's hard-won understanding of them. Halton heartily agreed. God knew he had spent enough time exploring Grieves's foibles, and despite a variety of provocations, he'd never been able to get more from his Housemaster than lines, sad lectures, or referrals to the JCR. Even in his first term when he'd accompanied White and Co. to McKay's barn with Pearce so blatantly trailing them, even then Grieves had been more interested in Riding and Mainwaring, and in restraining his annoyance at Pearce, than he had in Halton. If being caught at McKay's barn under accusation (sadly false) of smoking could not provoke Mr. Grieves, nothing could. So he had thought. So they'd all thought.

The monkeys condemned the man and his fraudulent pacifism, but their vehemence didn't make the experience any less vexing. He broke free from the dorm to go brush his teeth, but he could feel the Turtle at his heels, bursting with questions. If the brat said one word, he would make him regret it. It was bad enough that Grieves had oppressed him all month with extra-tu, most of it having nothing to do with History, not to mention wasted his time with tedious lectures and empty threats when he could see that Halton had no intention of abandoning his friends; but then for Grieves to make him late to the Advent service with more bloody jaw, so he had to sit in the back instead of with the choir, even if Kardleigh had forbidden him to sing, in fact for Grieves to make it clear that he *knew* Halton couldn't sing; and then for Grieves to have the gall to slipper him and Malcolm, hard, leaving them with the unpleasant sensation of having underestimated him; and then, when he had simply attempted to bring some color back to Malcolm's face by joking about Grieves's reversal, for the man to seize him, to turn him over his actual knee, like a child, and to start whacking all over again until he yelled pax; and, finally, for Grieves to dismiss Malcolm and jaw him yet *again*—this wasn't the playground where Halton might call pax, this was his Housemaster's study, Mr. Grieves was his Housemaster, and he was an impudent boy who had better rearrange his priorities. At this point Halton had actually begun to feel a glimmer of hope despite the embarrassment, but then the man had to spoil it by taking away his morning break the next day so he could return to the study and redo his English prep.

—But, sir! Halton had protested. I've got to pass it in at Primus.

Grieves had actually torn the page from his exercise book, wadded it up, and thrown it at him:

—You're not passing this anywhere!

Halton wanted to shout right back, to tell Grieves to get his own priorities straight. Either he could take up whacking or he could interfere, but to do both, to wield a plimsol like an expert and then to make him work, when everyone knew he was a lost cause—

—I say, said the Turtle.

Halton spat into the sink, elbowed the Turtle down the row of toilets, shoved his head into the last, and flushed.

✦

He'd no idea that a kiss could be so infectious. Something had come inside him, and now it was moving through his head, disordering his thoughts and everything they touched. They'd hardly spoken, but now they didn't need to. She had forgiven him whatever there was to forgive, not only forgiven but reached for him.

Something sensational was being discussed in the dorms, but gossip paled beside this. Not a single one of them would understand, and none, he felt certain, had ever passed a half hour as he had just passed.

In the washroom, Halton was cleaning his teeth. Could he ever clean his own teeth again? He washed his face and swallowed the flavor in his mouth, unlike anything that had been there before. He peered into the glass: his lips looked normal, but wasn't it obvious just to see his face?

Behind him, the Turtle emerged from the toilets as if he'd taken a shower in pajamas.

—What's the idea? Gray said.

The Turtle froze and Halton spun around, their expressions handing him knowledge he neither sought nor wanted.

—It's only a joke, Halton said through his toothbrush. Mind your own bloody business.

Tuesday. Wednesday. Thursday. Friday. Each an eternity, yet gone before he could catch it. They met in the chair loft during free time and talked, and then again at Evening Prayer, when they didn't. She had seemed too grave to laugh, but he discovered the wit that would make her. They spoke of books, newspapers, songs; the Academy's people, places, and customs; everything except the past. He found a moment, the third day, to mumble a condolence, but she instantly changed the subject. Friday evening, she blurted:

—What about Christmas?

He felt it like an elbow in the side, and he knew what she feared, the hollowness of the first one, the half-alive gestures, the attempts to keep things as they'd always been when their hearts lay frozen in the ground.

—Can you spend it somewhere new? he asked.

They stretched across the floorboards as the hymn was sung below.

—Does it ever get better?

He considered lying, but it stuck in his throat.

The next day he woke with new determination, to bring her new air and show her new things. The last thing she ought to do was stew. It was Saturday, a half holiday, and they'd arranged to meet by the ruined lodge after luncheon. He had drawn a map to show her where to go. They would spend the afternoon in Grindalythe Woods, hours to call their own. She promised to bring a tea flask and biscuits; he promised to read her some of Valarious, which he had described but never shown. A day of disclosure, at least on his side. He'd induct her to the poacher's tunnel, and she'd meet his people. In some sense, he thought, it would begin to right the balance between them.

Lessons that morning were purgatorial, and his pigeonhole announced the weekly letter from his mother. He put it unopened into his pocket and entertained himself imagining a strictly truthful reply. *Can you imagine, Mother, the torture of standing in the lunch queue and watching her across the cloisters in conversation with Mr. Lockett-Egan?*

—You can quit lusting, Leslie said.

—I wasn't.

—You were, but it's all for naught, Brains. She's an ice queen.

He groaned as if in agreement and took out his mother's letter to show he had better things to do than think about that girl. The letter was shorter than usual, and its style . . . It only took half a minute to read. She put Vandals to shame.

The queue began to move as he fought to absorb the ambush, delivered in public with everyone's eyes upon him. She had sold their home, sold *his* home. She had contrived the removal behind his back. He would never see Swan Cottage again. They would spend Christmas in let rooms, near Peter's or near the Academy—she was sure of any number of things, but she couldn't be sure of that!—somewhere desolate and godforsaken.

—Riding?

—*What?*

Halton stood before him with his face:

—Grievous wants you in his study.

—It's lunch, idiot.

—He says now.

He was going to punch someone before the day was out because this howling insanity could not continue. Now, on top of everything, he was going to be late to lunch. All right, he couldn't eat, but it was the principle of the thing.

Inside the study, Grieves wore a peculiar expression. He gazed as if waiting for Gray to speak, as if waiting for him to . . . She couldn't have told about the outing they planned, about—*God, really!*

—Something the matter, Riding?

He'd told her everything, the tunnel, the heirs of Hermes. *Admit nothing.*

—You sent for me, sir.

—So I did. You've got an exeat.

—I beg your pardon, sir?

He was expecting no one . . . but he hadn't expected Peter last time.

—Until bedtime.

—*Bedtime*, sir?

—You heard me.

He couldn't go on exeat, not today.

—Sir . . .

Grieves handed him a chit and appraised his uniform:

—You'll have to go as you are.

—But, sir—

—Wash your hands, change your shoes, be at the gates in five minutes.

—*Five minutes?*

Not even enough time to—

—Sir!

—Four minutes, chop-chop, and wear your coat.

He left perilously close to tears and in the changing room let out a stream of curses. Decent people announced visits in advance. They were both of them vandals, Peter and the woman who carried on like a whore. He stormed across the quad, thrust his chit at Fardles, and approached the car, ready to denounce—but the car wasn't Peter's. He'd never seen it before in his life. The door opened without his touching it. At the wheel a face—unknown, known:

—Get in, boyo. You look as though you've seen a ghost.

Morgan Wilberforce gripped the steering wheel with one hand and stretched across the seat with the other. He looked the same, only thicker. His mouth still suppressed a grin, his finger still wore the signet ring with the Wilberforce crest, and the air around him smelled the same, Taylors of Old Bond Street, mixed now with petrol fumes.

—Riding! Moss called from the quad.

—Come on, before we're ambushed.

Gray dove across the seat, the car lurched, and they took off down the lane, swerving to avoid holes and animals. Morgan drove like he played cricket, no-holds-barred. As they approached the Wetwang road, Morgan shifted, something shrieked and fell into place, and the car yanked forward with a sharp burning smell. The hedgerows whipped by, and before Gray could put together a question, they had skidded to a stop in front of the Cross Keys.

—Lunch, Morgan announced. I'm ravenous.

The former Keeper unfolded himself from the motorcar and slammed the door. Gray stayed where he was as Morgan rounded the car, opened the passenger door, and leaned against the frame:

—Aren't you coming?

His teeth rubbed against one another. Morgan sighed, took a silver case from his pocket, and lit a cigarette:

—Why not?

Exacting and frank, the voice struck him as it always had.

—I'm not going anywhere until someone tells me what the hell is going on!

Morgan took a drag and blew into the wind.

—You'll have to forgive me, boyo. It was all rather unexpected. I suppose I got carried away.

He offered the case to Gray, who refused.

—Oh, boyo, if you could see yourself. Daggers!

Morgan held the cigarette between his lips—

—Come on—

Reached into the car, took hold of his arm.

—I'll tell you whatever you want, but inside. It's colder out here than the devil's cock.

And Gray was standing on the pavement with the distinct impression of having been hoiked.

Inside, the barmaid made a fuss over Morgan, and the entire room seemed to think itself entitled to an explanation of his movements over the last three years. Gray stood disregarded, vexation and curiosity sparring within him. Morgan Wilberforce was not as tall as he'd been, but the voice was the same. So were the glances and the clearing of his throat, as if it were nothing to swoop in like the Fates, drag him off in a motorcar, and speak to him like no time had passed.

When the food arrived, Morgan exchanged glances with the barmaid, and she shooed the others away and gave them a table near the fire.

—How've you been keeping, pet? she asked Gray. And where's your friend?

—Been here with friends, has he? Morgan asked.

—Bonny one. Yorkshire lad.

—He wasn't!

—Shut up and eat, Morgan said.

—Gill he were called, weren't he?

—Were he, Polly?

—Right chatty thing he were, too. Almost as canny as you.

She gave Morgan a playful slap, and he pulled a long face:

—You haven't forgotten me, have you, Poll?

—How could we, pet? Been reading about you in paper.

The man behind the bar watched them as he pulled a pint. This was Our Robert, it emerged. She recounted the wedding last year. Her father was glad for the help on account of his lumbago. They never reckoned to see Morgan again after he went foreign, but here he was turned up like a penny.

Morgan shimmied out of his overcoat, revealing a black band on his sleeve:

—Buried Aunt Millie this morning.

Polly clapped a hand to her face and then to his cheek. She was sorry. She called him flower.

—She had a good run, Morgan said. Whole family come up the Minster.

Polly declared he'd need another pint and retreated to the bar to fetch it. Gray cast about for something to say. The pie had burned the roof of his mouth, and the ale made his stomach turn in remembrance of the last time.

—Sorry about your aunt, he managed.

Morgan broke open his own pie:

—Never knew her. Only time I ever saw her was at my mother's funeral.

Gray let the food cool on his fork. He remembered Morgan having told him once about his mother, and he remembered being shocked that Morgan had also lost a parent. Now he was embarrassed for having believed that no one else could have suffered as he did.

—Besides, Morgan continued, Uncle Bertie lent me his car.

Gray didn't think it quite the favor Morgan supposed. Between the drafts, the gear box, and Morgan's driving, Gray thought Morgan was lucky to have made it from York in one piece.

—It was all a bit of a lark, Morgan said. We'd just got back from the churchyard and people were starting to arrive. Hundreds of sisters, girl cousins, great aunts and all their friends, circling, hawk-like, but then Uncle Bertie called me outside, gave me the key, and told me to bugger off.

—You're missing the reception?

—Isn't it brilliant? I swear I'll pray for Uncle Bertie tonight. So you see, boyo, it was all a bit . . .

Morgan grinned.

—But why me? Gray blurted. Why on earth would you come and see *me*?

—Oh, I think you know the answer to that. You're the one with the brains, after all.

Morgan ate without further comment. Picking the burnt pie from the dish, Gray could feel the room growing dimmer and more distant, as if he might awake somewhere else without ever having to finish this scene. He might wake to a second chance: morning, lessons, and escape to the woods with the girl before Morgan could snatch him. Except his mother's letter would eventually arrive, and even if he never opened it, he could not escape its sword because the house had already been sold, Swan Cottage already dead. And the worst part, the most infuriating, was that if there had ever been anyone who would take his side against her madness, it was Morgan.

—Drink up, boyo. It's cold outside.

The second round had arrived, but he'd hardly touched the first. When he tried again to drink, the smell made him gag.

—On second thought, don't. We can't have that stomach of yours.

—It isn't that.

—I know what it is, Morgan said. Bring us a lemonade, would you Poll? Don't worry, boyo. It's happened to the best of us.

The tone of Morgan's voice was destroying his—*not here, not for this*.

—Now, Morgan said, who's this friend, the one that got you so frightfully pissed?

Breathing in and in, wrist shaking, eyes would fail soon if he didn't—

—Fine!

He clacked down his fork. Morgan blinked.

—You want the truth? You can take it and go to hell.

The truth was he'd come to the Keys only once before, last month with his studymate, Gill. He'd never come before because he'd never wanted to, and as for Morgan's parting word—that the Keys was the point of the poacher's tunnel—he, Gray, begged to differ. He was not a slave, and he did as he pleased. His monologue gathered steam, as if it had been written expressly for this moment. Morgan sat silent as he strew before him everything there was to say about Gill, about *Flight*, and about Gill's senseless downfall and disposing.

—Not sure that's such a tragedy, Morgan said at last, not when he planned it.

—He did no such thing!

Morgan chuckled:

—Of *course* he did. Come on, boyo, try. This is Guilford Audsley from *The Messenger*?

—Yes.

—On the bicycle?

—*Yes.*

—The same Guilford Audsley who's opening in *Hamlet* next week at the Shaftsbury?

—He . . . *what?*

—I've got tickets, Morgan said. Thought after their Ophelia got burned to a crisp, it would be canceled, but replacements apparently were found. Still want to tell me he didn't get disposed on purpose?

He'd finished pie, parkin, and lemonade, but now he felt the hungry fear and the thirsty weakness that came with knowing Morgan had him in his sights. When he'd told the saffron-haired girl about Guilford, she had shown only polite interest, but now Morgan was listening as if every word mattered, spurring him to tell more, *Castle Noire*, Moss and Crighton costumed before the school, Halton turned acrobat and composer.

—The Halton who sang on Patron's Day?

Morgan's posture had changed, and Gray recognized the figure arrived before him: the hunter he used to know, Nimrod at your service.

—Just goes to show, boyo, the truth is more cockeyed than the pages of literature.

Gray demanded explanation, but of course, Morgan refused to give it. Nimrod never revealed his paths, and as they left the warmth of the Keys, Gray felt a deeper warmth he had all but forgotten, that uneasy knowledge that there was nothing Morgan did not know, or could not learn given time.

After some tinkering under the bonnet of the motorcar, Morgan gunned the engine and proposed a walk around Flamborough Head:

—Should make it if she holds water.

What Morgan proposes, God disposes, Moss used to say, and in any case it was too late to protest now. Morgan was driving as if they were being chased, scraping the hedgerows and nearly colliding with a cart. Just outside Bridlington, the engine began to smoke, and Morgan had to turn off the engine and coast down to the shore. There the lamps were being lit, the surf was pounding, and the wind was whipping off the sea.

—Come on, Morgan said. Let's go down to the pier at least.

The sand stung their faces and blew into their ears. For the last stretch they sprinted before turning up towards the road.

—Don't know why you insisted on that, Morgan said. It's colder than . . .

—Shackleton's arse?

Morgan clamped his head in an elbow, chaffing his face against his coat.

—Still a foul mouth, I see. What are we going to do with you, boyo?

They blew into the tea shop, and while they awaited their order, the talk returned to the poacher's tunnel, and from there Morgan lured it back to Trevor and the barn.

—I hear they tore it down, Morgan said. And I hear it's your fault.

—Where the *hell* did you hear that?

Morgan cuffed him round the ear.

—Watch your language in company, boyo. And as you know, I have my sources.

A ruddy matron set a tray on the table. Morgan poured the tea, placed a scone on Gray's plate, and gave him the look he'd craved for so long: *Come on, boyo, you can tell it to me.*

There was little excuse to fight it, here in an empty tearoom, and soon the story of the barn was coming out, their first visit through their last. Morgan listened, the wry set of his mouth unchanging until Gray got to the night, Pearce, and Trevor's fall, at which point Morgan stopped chewing. Like Valarious in the sinking marshes, Gray realized he had said too much.

—Don't think you're stopping there, boyo. Spill it.

The barn was ancient history. He couldn't get into more trouble than he already had, surely.

—You won't tell Grieves, will you?

—No bargains, boyo. Talk!

When Nimrod bade you speak, you spoke, but if he omitted certain details about the box, about the girl he'd met through a window, about what happened in Grieves's study, still it made a good story, one Morgan seemed to regard philosophically, emptying the teapot and stretching his legs beneath the table.

—So, Morgan concluded, that's two of your friends got the sack.

He wouldn't have put it that way. And Trevor hadn't been expelled, that he knew.

—You've been giving Mr. Grieves trouble, haven't you?

—Me?

—Oh, save it for someone a bit more credulous, boyo.

The thrill of a hunter who could see through any ruse.

—He looks, I must say, something the worse for wear, does old Grievous.

—That isn't my fault.

—Isn't it?

—Someone was ill in his family. He was worried about her a long time, and he left the Cad almost every weekend this term, but now she's dead after all, and his goddaughter is here, staying in the House, and— and he whacked two chaps this week!

—Grievous don't whack.

—Oh, yes, he bloody does! He's gone do-lally all on his own, and it's nothing whatever to do with me!

Morgan looked stunned. He dipped a finger into the sugar and sucked it, gazing at the next table as if it held a map of trails loved by the hart. Finally, he drained his cup and cleared his throat.

—Back up, boyo, to the part about the goddaughter.

—What about her?

Morgan leaned back and looked at him in the way that had always made him laugh. The laughter, he knew, gave everything away. Morgan knew it, too:

—Oh, boyo. This is going to be good.

The thing with the hunter was he chased you where he would, and before you knew it, you were lost in the marsh. Gray began with her letters, and though the details, which in some cases he could recite verbatim, drew Morgan off for a time, before he knew it, they were back at the chair loft, where at least—he made this decision, when he had a breath to think—he admitted only to talking. Morgan didn't press him, and he escaped down the path of his mother's exploits, her romantic aspirations, her maneuvers with property, her vile temper, her overweening irrationality.

—I despise her!

—Watch it, boyo.

—I do!

Morgan shifted, and that keen, hawkish air swept in, the same that had dragged him first across the threshold he feared. Study number six, undergoing the rebuke, the bands had slipped—*You aren't my father!* A fatal pause, decision. Morgan picked up the gauntlet—*Be that as it may, I'm the closest thing you've got.* Ear seized, across that knee—*Sometimes I find, boyo, this serves better than the rest.* Hand on the back of his neck—*Hold still.* Tears at school were utterly banned, but Morgan let him, behind the door of study number six. They came as though they'd been stored years against the drought and now, with the lightest of touches, released. Afterwards Morgan would escort him back to the slumbering dorm, hang up his dressing gown, and sit on the edge of the bed until he fell asleep.

But those days were in the past, just as unreachable as anything dead, and if he meant to keep his sanity, he had to stop responding to this ghost across the table—all right, not a ghost, but what else to call a person who abided, who made you speak the way you used to when it mattered, but who would be gone again in the morning?

—This is a hobby for you, I suppose, extorting confessions.

—It's no hobby, Morgan said.

—Then why don't you say something instead of sitting there like the cat that ate the songbird?

Morgan smiled:

—I was only thinking how much you've grown.

—Spare me.

—You're in the Lower Sixth, you can talk without stuttering—

—I never stuttered—

—and you've got plucky enough to do things most of the Cad could never dream of.

Morgan paused to let him feel the praise.

—Of course, being you, you've taken it overboard and run headfirst for every tearaway scheme.

—I haven't!

—McKay's barn, clandestine theatricals, and now this girl?

—Just what is your *point*?

Morgan looked as though he were about to say something but then changed his mind. Gray decamped to the toilets, where he turned on the tap and put his face into the ice water. The day had been a swindle. His afternoon with the girl had been ruined, and in exchange he'd allowed himself to be worked on by Morgan Wilberforce, for no reason known to God or man.

It took them two trips back to the shop for water to get the car started. The rain had begun and was turning to ice on the road, but it made no difference to Morgan's driving; if anything it made him more reckless. Being back at school, in Prep, even under the odious supervision of the Flea, would be preferable, Gray thought, to having his life threatened by Morgan Wilberforce behind the wheel of this decrepit motorcar.

—Oi! Morgan cried.

He swerved to avoid a fox, and the car skidded into a ditch. They leapt out to push, but no exertions could budge the vehicle, and once it stalled, no amount of coaxing under the bonnet could bring it back to life. They retreated inside the car, and Morgan lit a cigarette. The rain pinged on the roof. They waited. Gray wormed his aching fingers into his sleeves as a damp fear settled: Morgan had something to say, something he'd been avoiding all afternoon even as Gray demanded he explain himself. *Don't tempt the devil,* Dr. Sebastian always said. *He's stronger than you.* Now in the dark of a Saturday night, he had no escape from what was coming.

Morgan finished one cigarette, lit another, and offered his flask:

—If you want to hear this, boyo.

—I don't want to hear anything.

—Do as you're told.

It tasted of petrol and stung his throat.

—Did you get my letter, then?

Down the wrong pipe.

—I'll take that as a yes.

He conquered the choking. Morgan's cigarette tip gave the only light.

—You wrote something . . .

His voice cut through the clatter of the rain:

—No idea why . . .

The Morgan he knew.

—But we both know nothing like that ever . . .

The Morgan he'd heard in his mind every day since he left.

—I've an idea that you might have seen something . . .

He groped for the cigarettes.

—Something you oughtn't to have seen . . .

Morgan struck a match for him and held it, illuminating that face for a moment.

—Something, at any rate, that wasn't the way it looked.

He choked again as the smoke burned.

—I'll take that as a yes. Easy.

Smoother than roll-your-owns, as smooth as giving in.

—Look, boyo . . . it was just a bit of fun. He made it up. You know Moss.

—Do I?

A sigh.

—I'm not exactly proud of it, but I haven't lied to you yet, and I won't start now.

Under cover of darkness and freezing, slamming rain.

—You've done a bit of drama. You should know what it is to pretend, and to pretend with someone else.

Moon shines bright, beastly words, protest, conquest—

—It was . . .

Moss's arm twisted by an unclothed—

—You didn't see his . . . when we said . . . when we . . . you had to be there.

The rain had soaked them. The windows had clouded, and their breath gathered before their faces. They passed the flask between them until it was empty. Morgan's fingers grazed his own, and as the drink melted the ice in his veins, it also fired the longing, which pressed against his eyes until he was glad for the dark.

—Was it the keyhole, then?

He didn't give an answer, but Morgan read one. The Keeper sighed, at first like relief, but then he shifted in the seat and hunched forward over the steering wheel.

—Is that what *happened*? Morgan demanded. You looked through a keyhole, got the wrong end of the stick, and *that's* why you cut me?

Cigarette punched out.

—That's why you never answered my letters? That's why you haven't spoken to me in three years? After everything—

It sounded spiteful, and it dawned on him that rather than being about to receive an apology, he was in fact on the verge of a rebuke.

—You absolute idiot!

Morgan cuffed him.

—You put that together all by yourself, did you?

Another cuff.

—And what in the devil's name were you doing out of bed peering into keyholes?

Again.

—Sometimes doors are closed for a reason!

—So people can't see what you're up to?

Hand stayed.

—You were too young to see that. You were too young for it all.

And the liquid in the Keeper's voice, the sadness and tenderness, melted what remained behind his eyes.

—Why do you think no one ever bothered you? Who do you think made them leave you alone?

—No one did even after you left.

—Did you ever stop and wonder why? Who do you think told Moss to keep an eye?

—Moss?

Who did he think had been keeping an eye, ever since the day Morgan left?

—But he never said anything . . .

Never paid him any notice, in particular.

—Of course not, boyo. You aren't his type.

—His *type*? What's his *type*, then?

—Girls.

Gray snorted.

—And older boys with dirty minds.

It was true, all of it, he knew in a flood. He'd known it all along, probably. If that night, after Morgan's farewell and the story of the poacher's tunnel and the cut that made him heir of Hermes, if later he had crept from his bed to seek one more hour in Morgan's company, if he'd peered through a keyhole and seen what he did, then Moss's lack of distress the next morning ought to have told him something. But abhorrence was better than longing for people who weren't there. Weren't gargoyles meant to keep evil at bay? And didn't they do as charged, warding off a desolation so acute it would rend the heart if permitted inside?

The rain kept hammering. He could feel his strength crumbling before the cold and before the truth. The car was dead, there were no passersby, the rain wasn't stopping and neither was the clock. Morgan switched on a torch, its weak light showing red in his eyes where Gray didn't expect it.

—Come on, boyo, out.

They emerged into the sleet and its talons. Morgan removed his own muffler and wrapped it around Gray's throat:

—We'll have to hoof it. No backchat! Go.

The running warmed them, and neither one slipped on the ice. Soon, though, Morgan's torch died, and all the forks looked the same in the dark.

—Grieves'll have our heads! Gray panted.

—He will, won't he? Morgan replied. You say he's taken up whacking?

—It isn't funny!

—Oh, not in the slightest! And it's your fault as well.

403

—*My* fault?

—You swindled me into this exeat and then broke poor Uncle Bertie's car. Grieves'll give you the business!

—Shut up.

—Unless you appeal to the lovely Miss Líoht.

—Leave her out of it!

—Absolutely, boyo. Won't mention her again. *Lead, kindly light, amid the encircling gloom*—

He lunged at the voice and landed them both in an ice-water ditch.

—Just shut up!

He flailed out, but Morgan caught his fists. When he staggered to his feet, Morgan stayed where he was, hip-deep in water and laughing.

The clock in the hallway said twenty past eleven. Mrs. Firth treated them as boys who deserved the worst, leaving them to drip in the vestibule while she summoned Mr. Grieves. He burst from his study but stopped short in dismay.

—It's my fault, sir, Morgan said. The beastly car broke down. We've run all the way.

—In *this*?

Morgan grinned sheepishly. Grieves shook his head and then looked Gray up and down:

—You, bath, bed.

To Morgan:

—And you the same, I think.

—Sir, if I might ring my uncle. I don't want him to worry.

—He'll have to, I'm afraid. Telephones went down an hour ago. The lights will go soon if this freezes through. I'm afraid you're stranded.

To Gray:

—Why are you standing there? Chop-chop.

Then Mrs. Firth was upon them with her half-dead-of-cold, her catch-your-death, her Morgan-Wilberforce-you'll-never-change. She herded Gray upstairs, drew him a scalding bath, and ordered him out of his clothes. When he protested, she declared that she had raised five boys of her own and had been giving baths longer than he had anything to hide. Then she confiscated every strip of his clothing and left him alone.

The steam calmed the tickle in his throat, and under the water, the day's carapace dissolved: He wasn't strong. He wasn't sovereign. He was shamefully knit together with people he'd no right to claim. There had been a time when Morgan had stood between him and the world, protecting him even from the worst of himself. Whatever it was that took people away, when they were needed and knit—it was the cruelest thing he could think of.

✦

John left Morgan in his own bathtub, soaking away the chill and hopefully warding off the chest infection that was doing the rounds. It had been plaguing his goddaughter, and he had just finished supervising her inhalation over a steaming bowl when Morgan turned up with Riding, both looking as though they'd swum home. John set out his dressing gown and his clean set of pajamas, made up the bed in the spare room, filled a hot-water bottle, and tried to suppress the envy that had been festering all day. Once Morgan emerged from the bath, he offered him a brandy.

—A toddy it's not, but . . .

Morgan drank it gratefully and followed John into the spare room.

—So it's to be the Chamber of Death, sir?

John hesitated. Morgan smiled slightly, exhaustion upon him:

—It's what we used to call it.

He examined the candles John had produced in case the lights failed and then took off the dressing gown.

—Thank you, sir. Sorry to be a nuisance.

—You're nothing of the sort—

—Uncle John?

His goddaughter appeared at the door, minus dressing gown and slippers, coughing into a handkerchief.

—What are you doing out of bed? he asked. Did you take your medicine?

Her hacking came under control, and her gaze drifted from him to the figure on the bed. Morgan wrapped the dressing gown around himself again, and she ducked behind John's back.

—You needn't hide. This is Morgan Wilberforce—Mr. Wilberforce, an Old Boy of the school.

She began to cough again, and John steered her down the corridor, promising to follow in a minute. Back in the spare room, Morgan wore a curious expression:

—Was that the goddaughter, sir?

—You heard?

Morgan nodded.

—Kardleigh gave her a mixture for that cough, but you've got to stand over her to make sure she takes it.

—A child that won't take its medicine? Never heard of that before, Grieves Sahib.

The remark, so vague and trivial, yet carrying with it the remembrance of so much, made John's chest hurt.

—A shame you rustled her off so quickly, Morgan continued. I'd *quite* like to have chatted to her—

A grin:

—and seen what this newest project is all about.

John managed a smile in return. The lights flickered, and the hall clock tolled midnight. He left Morgan a torch, and by the time he made it to his own bed, the lights had given up the ghost.

◆

Pearce had been awake in the alcove off the choir room reading psalms in the hope they would calm his mind. They hadn't, and now he would be ill-rested for Sunday. He still didn't know how to phrase the letter— how did a son refuse a family's ambition and announce a vision as whimsical as it was shameful? Yet, the figure he had seen when the pigeonholes fell on him—*island-green-shepherd-sheep*—that person was more like Morgan than anyone. Morgan had called him by name, not Jere as he was called at home, but Simon, an apostle. The good shepherd would search all night for one sheep, but what if it was ugly and mean and afraid to be found?

◆

There was nothing more to drink, nothing more to smoke, nothing to eat besides the last of the biscuits crumbling in the tin.

—Bugger me, it's cold, Morgan said. I'd forgot.

There was only enough coal for one more fire in the term, and a meager

406

one at that, but Gray got it burning, and they huddled at the fender as the wind rattled the windows.

He didn't ask why Morgan had come to the study, and Morgan didn't ask him. The itch in his throat, which had begun with the cigarettes, settled deeper with the heat of the bath. He took care to muffle it in his sleeve, but Morgan looked alert, as if they might be discovered.

—That's an interesting bark.

—It's just a tickle.

—I'll bet.

Morgan said nothing else. The last biscuit was dissolving on his tongue just as the night was draining out. Morgan wasn't treating him as a friend, he wasn't talking to him like a Dutch Uncle, and he wasn't doing what he'd always done when sitting in that chair before the fire. He could hear the catechism through the deafening silence: *You haven't done enough, have you? You've left things undone that you ought to have done?* Morgan was looking at him, no longer in pursuit, no longer in anger or regret, but with a growing abstraction, as if he were leaving breath by breath. Now when he most needed his hand—*Have you told the truth?*—Morgan tucked it away, leaving him to stagger under the weight of what he carried.

The truth: he was too old to be helped. Leaving childhood behind meant facing everything on your own.

The armchair creaked. Morgan stood and retreated to the window seat, its arctic wastes preferable to such a one as him.

—I'm sorry.

The words that had choked him sailed across the room. Morgan seemed not to hear but only wrapped the rug around himself.

I'm sorry. I'm sorry!

—For what, exactly?

—Everything.

Morgan turned; his voice, when he spoke again, was thin:

—Did you really put that into a *letter*? To the *Head*?

Too degenerate in words.

—I never—I mean, I never sent it—I—

—I hope not!

—I never showed it to anyone.

—Then *why*?

His ribs jerked.

—It was only a story.

—That's a fine thing to call a lie.

The old sinking feeling, the heavy dread that accompanied his own wrongdoing, when he was made to see the harm that could come from careless acts.

—I still don't see how you could think that of me.

Morgan's voice was hurt.

—It was easier, he said, wasn't it?

—Than *what*?

He put his feet on the fender and reached for the fire:

—How did you find out?

—Patron's Day, Morgan said.

—What! How? *Who* . . . ?

Morgan grunted:

—If you really don't know, boyo, I'm certainly not going to tell you.

To know and not tell?

—Does Grieves know?

—Please!

—You won't tell him about *her*, will you?

Morgan frowned:

—I should.

—What!

—To save you getting yourselves found out.

—But we—we don't—we—

—The balcony by the choir room, you say?

The smiling was happening to his face again.

—Even Pearce'll work it out eventually.

—But—

—Listen, boyo, you've got to think of Grieves.

Grieves?

—You've got to think of how he'd feel if—

There was a limit, he informed Morgan Wilberforce, to all things in nature, and this was well past it. Under no circumstances would he take advice on such a subject. Matters between himself and Grieves were none of Morgan's affair, and his friendship with the girl was nothing to do with either of them.

—What happened between the two of you?

—I told you! We only talk!

—No, you and him.

The tickle seized him:

—N-nothing.

—Nothing?

—Except . . . he can't . . . stand me and he's so bloody . . . temperamental . . .

—Look, Morgan said, just what are your intentions with her?

—Are you *her* father now?

—Don't get stroppy. You know what I mean.

—I don't see why you have to spoil everything!

—What will happen once term is over?

—What do you care? You're buggering off.

Morgan flushed and bit back a reply.

—You think you're important, Gray said, but you aren't.

✦

A jerk ripped Halton from where he had been, where syrup had been flowing down his throat, restoring its power, and into his ears where a melody rang, thick and new and familiar—*Oh, miserable power to dreams allowed, to raise the guilty past*—that poem Dr. Sebastian made them learn—*and back awhile the illumined spirit to cast*—broadcast pitch-perfect, meter reconciled, sung by purest treble—*on its youth's twilight hour*—he fumbled torch, slippers, stairs—*welcome the thorn*—choir room, piano—*its wholesome smart shall pierce thee*—matching sound to keys before him—*and warn thee what thou art, and whence thy wealth has come.*

✦

Morgan propped his bare feet on the grate and accepted the tea John offered. The fire, though usually not lit until evening, had been stirred for Morgan's benefit until Mrs. Firth could rustle up his clothing, hopefully now dry. John took his own cup and sat opposite Morgan on the old, deflated settee:

—He's been giving you grief, I see. Last night.

—Light night, sir?

—I know an un-slept-in bed when I see one.

Morgan looked abashed, and John felt the kind of fondness he'd not been allowed to show in ages.

—I suppose he's told you everything.

409

He could see Morgan waver, flickering between the boy who once laid his burdens at John's feet and the prefect who sat with him dissecting boys in their charge.

—I've made everything worse, sir.

—I'm sure you haven't.

—*Quit rootling around in the entrails of the past*, my father always says.

—Oh, dear.

It was the first Morgan, the one spilling confessions in the middle of the night. John sat back to listen, and Morgan gushed as if he'd never been allowed to confide: the whirlwind of the past months, leaving Oxford, cricket, New Zealanders; his father's patience, cheering him on and introducing him at the club, the New Hope of Middlesex; the position awaiting him at the firm, the welcome in every good circle.

—And yet? John said.

There was no *yet*. Morgan rejoiced in all that. What annoyed Morgan, what he found grossly objectionable, was the unforgiving . . . what to call it? The long line the Academy cast, releasing him—or so he thought when he left for Oxford—only to draw him back when he'd got used to being free. First Patron's Day and now this? What kind of sinister hand took an unplanned lark of a day, beginning with a funeral, and lured him back into business not his own, consigning him for the night to his Housemaster's Chamber of Death?

—I'll try not to take that as an insult, John said.

—I didn't mean that, sir, I . . .

Morgan tried to conceal his distress by devouring a piece of dry toast.

—You know, John said, if you're ever going to join the Common Room, you'll have to stop calling me sir.

Morgan stopped chewing:

—I hope you're joking, sir.

—Life is more than cricket.

—I know.

John managed a smile. He was teasing, but Morgan didn't realize it. Morgan finished the toast and then began to describe his father's firm, its opportunities and influence. His father had given him two years to play cricket, after which they both agreed he would set his feet on the ground.

—Or you could climb into the boat, John said, with us fishers of men.

Morgan sucked in his breath, and John wondered if it was teasing after all. He felt a sudden wild excitement, but before he could say more, Mrs. Firth returned bearing butter and jam, more tea, and news: Fardley was going to Sledmere at half past six. He could give Master Wilberforce a lift in time for the early train. John glanced anxiously at the clock. He'd expected Morgan to stay the morning at least. They were just getting to the heart. But Mrs. Firth reported more weather on the way. Master Wilberforce would want to get out while he could. Fardley would make arrangements for his uncle's car. His clothes were dry. He would find them on his bed.

Morgan dressed and shaved quickly, nicking himself in the process, John noticed. He looked forlorn now, huddled by the fire in mourning clothes, recalling somehow the boy he'd been when John met him, the chirpy Third Former turned bewildered orphan.

—Sir, Morgan said, about Riding.

John added coal to the fire:

—You try your best with them, but it's never enough.

Morgan sighed in agreement:

—Clever mind, broken heart, a dreadful combination I said from the beginning.

The morning's dose had not sufficed, and John realized he should have gone back to his bathroom while Morgan was changing. But on his desk were exercise books—two of them Riding's—and if Morgan would read them, he could slip away for a moment—

—What were these plays of his, sir?

Morgan had set the books aside:

—I couldn't make head or tail of them.

—Who could? John rejoined.

He gave a précis, which seemed to fill the gaps in what Morgan had heard.

—I don't suppose Riding told you what was behind the business with Audsley? John asked.

—Getting sacked, you mean? What a frame-up!

—Pardon?

—Audsley getting himself disposed so he could go and play Hamlet.

His knee was hurting and his tongue itched.

—I thought you knew, sir.

John was losing control of the thread. He knew nothing of the sort, he told Morgan. In fact, he had asked Riding—with super-human patience—what he knew of the affair, but the sullen, contrary,

bloody-minded urchin had refused to explain, had looked at him with—
oh, he'd tell it to Morgan! He'd tell anything to Morgan, but not to him,
not when it was desperate, not when—

—He didn't tell me anything! Morgan protested. I had to explain it
to *him*.

John struggled to keep up.

—It was perfectly obvious. Honestly, the pair of you!

But there was no call to pair him with Riding, for any reason! The
boy was an affliction. In lessons he was fine enough, the Anxious &
Pleasing usually, but whenever one got him alone, full-strength Sullen
& Resentful, nothing he had tried made a lick of difference—

—He needs—

—A better man than me, to be sure!

John flung himself into the swivel chair:

—I hope you dealt with him last night.

Morgan raised his brow at the bald declaration, issued as if part of
their usual chats.

—God knows he needs it, sir, but it's none of my . . . it's only making
things worse, pretending.

An unaccountable sadness descended.

—Anyway, sir, I hear your habits have changed in that regard.

Rogue wave—

—*Habits?* You do a thing twice and it's habit?

—Twice, sir?

—God help me.

Two boys this week, infernal nuisance. One, Malcolm minor.

—You knew his brother.

—Roy Malcolm? Fly-half on my Colts XV?

—First XV now.

As for the other, perhaps Morgan recalled their soloist last summer?

—Why did I know you were going to say that, sir?

—You know him?

—In a way. He was the one behind that petition.

The sun was bursting all across the room, leaving only a cat's eye to
look through.

—Crikey, sir, I hope you aren't giving yourself grief over those two.
If Malcolm minor is anything like his brother, that's the only language
he'll understand. As for young Halton, I'd keep him on a *very* short string.

Eye opening briefly?

—Leave it to Riding to get the wrong end of the stick, Morgan said.

—I beg your pardon?

—The way he tells it, you've gone up the pole.

The floor was pitching. He excused himself.

The light was smoother when he returned, blood looser, Morgan brighter and softer.

—Sir, is everything all right?

—Perfectly.

He poured out the rest of the tea. His mouth was speaking, words proceeding in an order that was right:

—I went to considerable trouble, personal trouble, to persuade Sebastian to keep the boy on.

—Not Riding, sir?

—You know how Sebastian's always been about that barn.

Morgan sat forward:

—You mean McKay's barn, sir? That business with his friend Mainwaring, and Pearce and—

—It did begin with Pearce. He collared some juniors there, the same lot, in fact, I had to deal with this week, but—

—Hold on a second, Grieves Sahib—

—Sebastian was annoyed, and then, bad to worse, night prowling, Mainwaring injured, so on and so forth.

Morgan was setting his cup aside.

—But when it came to it, Riding lied. And when the damage was done, he turned around and told the truth.

Morgan shook his head:

—He's always had a talent for making things worse.

—And I'd interviewed him, petitioned for him, *vouched* for him, convinced Sebastian it was nothing to do with that wretched barn.

Morgan groaned.

—And then, well, Sebastian gave his orders.

—Snails, sir, what did he get for that?

He told him.

—Cri-key. Hard?

—I'm afraid so.

Morgan gave a low whistle:

—So much for the Head saving his strength for the tick-off.

413

The book on the shelf was covered in dust.

—I thought you said he told you everything.

—Sir?

—The Head didn't give it.

He removed the book and blew the dust into the fire.

—If the Head didn't give it, sir, who on earth did?

The whole row needed to come down.

—His Housemaster.

He dumped the books on the floor and went to work with his hand-kerchief. The room needed dusting top to toe.

—Hang on a minute, sir, was there a box involved in this?

—A box?

—Or a letter?

The dust was in his eyes.

—He did mention something in the end, a box of stories? Not that we ever saw it, mind you.

There wasn't a lot of breath to breathe.

—It's all my fault, sir. From beginning to end.

John's handkerchief was ruined; he threw it in the grate, where it blazed and fell to ash. Morgan's declaration, as irrational as it was, had de-stifled the air, leaving behind that close-shave feeling. And then, before anything could spoil it, Mrs. Firth was at the door, and it was time for Morgan to leave.

—Do you have everything? John asked, looking around the room.

Morgan seemed lost, and when John handed him his coat, he took it with an air of one who'd been jilted. The radiators clanked, and outside the cold hit like a scream. At the gates, Morgan stopped short, casting his gaze back at the school, looking almost homesick, as one facing banishment. But the motorcar was belching petrol fumes, and as Fardley swept detritus onto the floor, Morgan fumbled in his pocket:

—Sir, I know you've got your own now to keep an eye on—

Produced a cigarette case, empty. John reached for his own—

—and I know Riding can be infernally—

Offered one, several.

—Thanks. But you'd give me a good night sleep, sir, if you'd—

—Just *what* do you propose I do with him?

Morgan flinched.

—Sorry, sir. I've said too much already.

He knocked one cigarette against the car:

414

—And there probably isn't much you *can* do, unless you're prepared to marry his mother.

John reached for the wall.

—Only, whatever happens, sir, please don't overreact.

—What *can* you mean?

—Nothing that I'm prepared to divulge.

Morgan grinned. John forced himself to grin in return:

—If that's your line, at least promise you won't let another three years go by.

It was still dark, but John thought Morgan looked unwell, his eyes choked, as if he might begin to—

—Whatever is it?

Morgan ducked into the car and ran a sleeve across his face:

—It's this beastly cold, sir, and the soot from this blasted . . .

 The bell fag came through again, dragging him into Sunday, last of the term, last in every way that mattered. His throat felt scoured, and he could still taste Morgan's cigarettes, but the circus of Sunday morning baths washed the night from his skin, and by the time he poked Sunday studs through Sunday shirt, he felt he was landing on the sands of the present, having forgotten how warm they were. Three hours free for the chair loft today, this afternoon before Divinity, and then again this evening. Morgan Wilberforce could never spoil this.

✦

The match against Burton-Lee's was in its death throes. Mac was full of venom, and when Halton dropped the ball, Mac sent him off and put the smallest fag in, on purpose to shame him. That morning Kardleigh had given the solo to the Turtle, and now Halton's humiliation was complete. If he'd slept properly, instead of being forced from bed by feeble ideas, none of this would have happened. He ducked behind the sheds and kicked the siding until it splintered.

—Rotten luck with that knock-on.

The Turtle appeared like a jinn. Some things were better to kick than the sheds.

He read her the opening of Valarious as he'd planned to do yesterday. She begged for more, the whole story, but he said it wasn't finished. He wasn't sure she believed him, but she let it drop and took out the book she'd selected to read to him. It was stripped of its cover, and she said she'd got it from a shop where all the books were stripped. You never knew quite what you were getting, she said, but the books were wonderfully cheap. Upton-on-Severn, Morton Hall, a couple who gave birth to a girl they called Stephen.

—Oh, come on!

—Really! she said. Look for yourself.

She wasn't teasing. The atmosphere of the story was foreboding and full of longing, all the more so as she read on, recounting this girl who dressed sometimes as a boy, who pretended to be Lord Nelson, who hungered for love, the daughter of an Irish mother who didn't quite love her, and a cleft-chinned English father who doted on her although he had wanted a boy.

◆

Halton wasn't always that way. In play rehearsal, he had been sensational. In the dorm, he told filthy jokes, more filthy than the Turtle had ever heard. He knew about Africa, and in a way the Turtle couldn't put his finger on, Halton knew things about people, as if he might be the keeper of a hundred secrets. He had a temper, but also courage. The Turtle had known from the first quip in the dorm about his father's tennis arm that Halton possessed a fortitude that he, the Turtle, could never attain, try as he might when undergoing Halton's brand of humor. Halton was that rare class of person who could sing in the choir, appear in dramas, perform indifferently at Games, and yet never have his mettle questioned. And he was the only person who could understand what was happening in choir, and what had happened with Audsley. Even when Halton went berserk, it was worth it for the aftermath. Sunday behind the sheds, Halton had been scared, and sorry. After sending someone to find Kardleigh, Halton had pressed his own shirt against the Turtle's leg to stanch the bleeding. He'd come with him to the Tower, brought him sweets and a book, and looked at him in a way that made the Turtle wish it had been more than four stitches after all.

What lay beneath his trousers? She'd glimpsed, when he sat cross-legged, the skin above his socks, but what did the rest of him look like? She'd come to know the callus on his right middle finger, where the pen pressed and ink collected. In lessons they used nibs and inkwells, but otherwise he relied on a temperamental hard-rubber Dinkie. The few times he'd written in her presence, he'd required a handkerchief for the blots. If she were ever chained to such a thing, she at least would designate a cloth for its maintenance rather than staining every handkerchief in her possession, not to mention shirt cuffs and trouser knees. And she wouldn't carry it as he did, jumbled in his pocket like a box of matches. If she had the pocket money, she would buy him a proper pen, like her own Parker Duofold from America, and perhaps a bottle of quick-drying ink. Her form teacher in Saffron Walden would have suggested a finer nib to improve his penmanship, but she felt that even then, his hand would still rush urgently across the page, too entranced by what it chased to do more than scrawl the ending of one word before plunging into the next. It was the only time he let himself go, telling her a story or writing it down; otherwise, he held himself in, always warm but never free. She knew that he possessed a secret island and that if she could ever reach it, the volume knob on life could be turned past the thickest mark.

She'd always associated such a hunger with maps. *Yorkshire NE 46* had been her first, purchased for her when she was small so she could see where Uncle John went when he left them. It showed contours, populations, cities and hamlets, but not the Academy. Their chair loft—a place seemingly forgotten in that unmapped school—had the properties of magic. Whether it was invisible because it was insignificant or because it had been protected by the spells that twisted through his stories, the result was the same: it was safe from every vandal, every rule.

✦

Kardleigh was not amused. How had the Turtle lost his music between the beginning and end of choir practice, and the second day in a row? The Turtle scanned his mind for places it might be found—form room, drying cupboard, toilet tank—but Kardleigh was commanding him to search the choir room again, from top to bottom. He picked through the wastepaper basket for form's sake, but it contained only balled-up pages. Uncrumpling one, he found not "Once in Royal David's City," but a staff and notes roughly sketched, and beneath them words broken by syllable: *Nay, hush thee, an-gry heart! An An-gel's grief ill-fits a pen-i-tent.*

—Found it, have you?

Someone had set that poem from confirmation lesson to a wild tune. What key was it, even? He recovered two more pages as Kardleigh scanned the first. *Welcome the thorn, it is divinely sent*—a mad counterpoint—*And with its wholesome smart shall pierce thee in thy virtue's palmy home and warn thee*—where was the breath?—*What thou art*—high C!—*And whence thy wealth has come.*

◆

Halton had finally said something that made White laugh when the Turtle materialized and demanded he return to the choir room. Upstairs, Kardleigh sat at the piano, spectacles on his nose:

—Ah, Halton. I'd like a word with you.

—Please, sir, I don't know where the Turtle's—

—About this.

Kardleigh lifted a wrinkled page. His excuses and confusion resolved into the home key. He said he'd no idea what Kardleigh meant.

—Come, come. *Words, Newman; tune, St. Stephen's?*

Kardleigh couldn't prove a thing. His name was nowhere.

—It's your handwriting, Timothy.

—No, sir.

—It's your spelling. The illumined *sprit? Plamy? Thron?*

One expected it from the Flea, but not from—

—When did you write this?

It was worse than clothing nightmares.

—I found it, sir! cried the Turtle.

He burst in clutching a sheaf of music.

—Well, Kardleigh said, put it away properly, and as penance you can sort out those blue books.

Halton edged towards the door.

—Ash Wednesday, Kardleigh said, turning back to him. We'll rehearse your piece next term.

—Sir!

—It's too difficult to get up just now, and there's something agreeably Lenten about it.

The future swarmed like spiders—if White heard, if *anyone*—

—Please, sir! It was only a joke!

—Meantime, Kardleigh said, we need a descant for "People, Look East." So, Turtle, if you should discover anything else in the wastepaper basket . . .

✦

Choir practice had finished, and Gray could hear them departing. Gone, another hour, one of the few left to them. Her fingers were tickling his ear, where earlier her tongue had—he rolled over, pressing himself against the floor, but she drew close and looked at him searchingly.

—There's literally no more free time, he said, unless you count the middle of the night.

She put her mouth to his ear and whispered:

—I will if you will.

Hunger, ache—crash—she recoiled. Footsteps clattered down the passage. The noise had come from the choir room.

—I thought they'd left, she said.

He put his hand across her mouth, and she kissed it. He felt the kiss there on his hand and also in his root, and then the panel sprang open, sudden and violent like all bad things—the Turtle, eyes wide, his nose streaming blood.

—Do you *mind*? she said.

Gray leapt to his feet, but the Turtle fled. He pursued him across the quad, into the House, and up to the fourth-floor box rooms:

—Just what in hell—

The Turtle cringed before him. The blood was flowing not from his nose but from a gash on his cheek. Gray tackled him and pinned his wrists, but when the Turtle began to blub, he let go. Tossing him a handkerchief, he glared as fiercely as he could:

—If you breathe *one* word, I'll make the person who did that look like your best friend.

✦

Grieves's goddaughter was standing beneath the lightbulb at the end of the corridor. Her mouth was open, and Halton felt her accusation. She looked at that moment ominously like his sister, and he could hear, in

419

the yards that separated them, her chill contempt: Did he fancy himself a composer? Just what sort of drivel had they led him to believe about himself? She coughed into her sleeve and then turned away and clattered down the stairs.

If she weren't a girl, he'd go after her, just to teach her some bloody manners.

✦

At tea, the Turtle was chirpy, but Gray thought his laughter too zealous to be genuine. He'd never been one to interfere in other people's affairs, but something nagging and reproachful was ruining his appetite. Hadn't it gone beyond ragging with the Turtle, even the sort that could be expected in one's first term? If, as Morgan claimed, Moss really was responsible for his own escape from such treatment, why wasn't Moss interfering now with his own fag?

✦

He followed Kardleigh to the Tower after tea to persuade him, to beg him if necessary, not to mention the composition again. If anyone found out that he'd tried writing music—now or ever—his name would be worth less than Pious Pearce. But Kardleigh was repeating his plan to rehearse the piece next term, even going on to suggest that Halton take up organ studies.

—I shall write your father, Kardleigh said, and ask him.

—Please, sir! Don't!

Kardleigh smoothed his beard:

—Wouldn't you like to learn the organ?

—There isn't enough time with the choir.

—No singing next term, Timothy. Perhaps again in a year or so.

Kardleigh put a hand on his shoulder, but a draft cut in the door bringing Grieves, and that girl.

—Ah, Miss Líoht! Kardleigh said. How's the chest today?

Where was the hand to wake him from this hell? He dodged snowballs in the quad and retreated to the form room before anyone could see his eyes and know his shame. *Write them*, be damned. Audsley could take his effeminate advice and—

420

Dr. Kardleigh put a stethoscope to her chest and commanded her to cough. He could tell when she'd sat up late and when she'd gone cycling without hat or muffler.

—Now a nice, deep breath.

That boy knew something, too. He'd pounced into the passage the moment she emerged from the chair loft, staring as if to say, *I know.* In the refectory, he'd followed her with his gaze, and just now he'd been waiting for her, as if to prove that he could find her when he wished.

—You've been naughty, I think, Dr. Kardleigh said. Have you taken that mixture?

—Sometimes.

Uncle John pursed his lips. He was trying to give her the grim look he gave the boys:

—Shall I write her a docket?

He was teasing. She tried to smile. Being a girl was a passport to nothing. Her father once told her about a lady archaeologist who'd traveled solo through Persia. Eventually he revealed the woman's ignominious end, death from an overdose of sleeping tablets, which proved the point exactly.

They were talking now about one of the boys, which was all any of them ever discussed. Her father might be thinking always about the contents of the liquor cabinet, but these men were even more single-minded. Now, for instance, the doctor was blending her cough mixture almost absentmindedly as he asked Uncle John to shed light on some boy's obstreperousness with organ lessons:

—Isn't his sister some sort of awful prodigy?

—Is she? Uncle John replied.

—His twin. She's won a few piano competitions, according to him, and a scholarship to St. Paul's Girls.

—How tiresome.

The doctor gave the mixture to Uncle John, who carried on as if she weren't there:

—Moss says the father is hard on him. Quite hard.

If she were a boy, she'd be punished as a boy. Then he would abandon his cloying concern and talk of her with the same warmth and interest that always gripped him when talking about them.

John peered over Kardleigh's shoulder as they spoke. The dispensary door stood open, revealing neat regiments each containing its own mercy, and as Kardleigh lectured the girl on the importance of steam inhalation, John began to think of burglary, slipping from his quarters in the middle of the night and borrowing the dispensary key Kardleigh had just fetched from the top right drawer.

A violent retching came from the ward.

—That'll be McCandless, Kardleigh said. Just a moment.

He disappeared behind the curtain. Cordelia drifted to the window and pressed her face against it. His feet moved, his fingers snatched a vial, and his body returned to its place before a visible second had passed.

◆

An unnatural quiet hung over the studies. Only coughs, the blowing snow, and the occasional hum of conversation disturbed the ringing in Gray's ears. He huddled under a rug, coal supply exhausted. His eyes scanned passages for the Latin exam in the morning while his mind hearkened to the corridor, where some miscreant was emerging from the JCR, and to the chair loft, where he'd promised to meet her tonight, if he could bear it after the Turtle's invasion.

It wasn't for him to intervene with fags. Or rather, if he truly objected to their treatment, he ought to interfere directly, corner Halton in some unfrequented spot and apply a Stalky-like persuasion. The proposition was absurd, of course—any contest between them was more likely to end in Halton's favor—but the problem of the Turtle remained. Gray didn't peg him for a sneak, but the Turtle had seen them, and he was desperate. *Never peach*, Moss's rules, but what would Moss say about such a sticky stitch? This wasn't the House Moss thought he was running.

That night after Prayers, he followed Moss and Crighton back to their study.

—A word?

—Can't it wait? Moss said. We've got Greek all bloody morning to-morrow.

When he said it couldn't, Moss adjourned with him to study number six:

—Make it quick.

Gray twisted the cap of his fountain pen.

—Riding!

It didn't come out the way he intended:

—When are you going to stop it? That's what I want to know.

Moss boggled.

—The Turtle, Gray said. Don't tell me you haven't noticed.

—He's a careless little boy, that's what I've noticed.

—*Careless?* How?

—Can't make it through a day without losing something, wrecking something, or wrecking himself.

Countless dockets. God-awful bore.

—Ever wonder why? Gray said. Oh, come on, try. Seen him in the changing room lately? He didn't get that banged up at rugger.

—Didn't he?

—Where d'you think he got the gash on his face?

—He walked into the corner of our bookshelf.

—Did you see him before he did it?

—Look, piss off, Riding—

—Because I did, and it didn't happen in your study.

Moss sat down, looked at his ink bottle, looked at him.

—You mean . . . he staged it?

—Looks like he learned something from Audsley after all.

Moss blinked, his mind catching up to the evidence.

—But . . . who's doing it?

—Don't you know?

—Do *you?*

—Of course, I do! Gray said.

—Does everyone?

—I doubt it.

—But . . . ?

—Come on! Whose place has the Turtle taken, in choir, with you and Crighton? Who's back in with that brute White? Who—

Moss raised a hand. He looked ill. Another realization:

—Bugger me, I just gave him three.

The Turtle had been sent out of Prep, Moss said, for allowing, again, his ink pot to spill into his desk and ruin the contents, which tonight included a book belonging to the Flea.

—That's steep.

—I didn't have any choice, Moss protested. Burton knew what he was doing, and I couldn't send him on punishment runs in this.

He gestured to the window. Snow was sticking to the panes.

The bell rang for Upper School lights-out. Moss got up to leave.

—He won't be disposed, Gray said, will he?

The shadow of the Head's edict against bullying passed between them, his declaration since the Great Clear-Out that bullies would be expelled. Not that the Head knew half of it, but still.

—Halton isn't going anywhere, Moss said at last. He won't be able to sit down for a week once the JCR have finished with him, but as for disposing, I think we've had enough of that.

◆

He spent an animated half hour discussing it with Crighton. As Moss's own anger towards Halton grew, so did Crighton's conviction that the JCR should not take the case. If they could do it dispassionately, Crighton argued, that would be one thing, but dispassion was impossible. First, the Turtle was their fag, as Halton had been before. Second, there were the plays. Third, there was Moss's past with Halton. Fourth, well, they could go on all night, but there was a pig of an exam in the morning, and the right thing, Crighton concluded, was for Moss to speak with Grieves posthaste.

Moss took exception; once masters were involved, the Head would have to be told, and Halton's low acts notwithstanding, no one wanted him expelled. Crighton acknowledged the risk, but he reminded Moss that Halton was one of Mr. Grieves's projects; Grieves, therefore, was unlikely to put the boy's career in jeopardy. In all likelihood, he would deliver a blistering pi-jaw and dispatch Halton to the JCR, in which case Crighton would be the first to volunteer for inflicting as much pain as legally possible.

◆

John needed two brandies to get through the interview with Moss. He'd always feared this sort of thing, and here it was a cold reality. He'd been unable to shield Morgan from the likes of Silk Bradley, but now, under his very nose for such a thing to occur? How had he so impossibly misjudged Halton?

Don't overreact—wasn't that what Morgan had said? It was possible, he thought as he undressed for bed, that they were all jumping to conclusions. Perhaps he hadn't misjudged Halton after all. Perhaps a rumor had swirled out of control, exploiting their exhaustion and their fears and making pranks and horseplay look sinister. He splashed water on his face. What were those yellow-and-black streaks beneath his eyes? And when had gray hairs sprouted in his sideburns? What else had Morgan said? *As for young Halton, keep him on a very short string . . . ?*

He had another brandy and resolved to sleep on it. First thing in the morning, he'd consult Kardleigh. He had no idea if he could trust Kardleigh not to go straight to Jamie, but refusing to overact had to start somewhere.

Kardleigh, when he told him, took it like a punch:

—And I believed him. The bookcase, the shin at rugby, that clump of hair he said he'd pulled out in his sleep.

—Do you think it's true, then? John asked.

Kardleigh looked at him pityingly, and John felt the punch himself.

—What does the Headmaster say?

—I haven't even spoken to the boys yet.

—Surely, you don't propose to ask the Turtle for testimony?

—Please, John said. But I do intend to have a close chat with young Halton this morning after exams.

Having said it, he now had to do it. It was the correct first step, of course, but as the Remove sweated over his Reformation exam, his agitation grew, and he rehearsed inquiry after inquiry, one minute feeling full of wrath and another hopeful it could still be a misunderstanding. The Remove groaned for more time when the bell rang, and John groaned along with them, but none of them could stop the tidal force rushing into the courtyard. A fresh powdering of snow had covered the morning's footprints, and John saw smiles for the first time in days. He spotted Halton four-abreast with White, Fletcher, and Malcolm minor. Halton looked dazed from the morning's exertions, yet his eyes were casting around (for prey?).

—I should very much like to speak with you, John said, taking Halton by the shoulder.

—Me, sir?

John shifted his grip to the collar and marched the boy away from his friends. Inside the study, he placed Halton in the straight chair. He could feel himself trembling, his joints weak as when he was a boy on the carpet himself, or when he was a prefect, under pressure to execute a perfectly calibrated maneuver. He poured himself a drink, swallowed it, and then rather than take his place behind the desk, he put one hand on the front of the desk and the other on the back of the boy's chair, boxing him in, invading his air.

—We are going to have a chat, Timothy.

Halton was fidgeting.

—And whatever happens, you are going to tell me the truth. We both deserve that, and if you don't, I shall know it.

Please, Lord, let it be so.

—Is that clear?

A faint nod.

—Do you know why we are here?

No answer. *Take no thought how or what ye shall speak.*

—We are here to discuss a boy in this House. A boy who is being treated abominably.

Halton didn't move.

—He is being treated cruelly, by someone he considers a friend.

Halton began to cast around.

—By someone cowardly.

Pink at the cheeks.

—Someone coldhearted.

At the chin.

—Someone who has behaved in a way, frankly, that sickens me.

—But—

—*Sickens* me.

Flush across the entire face.

—This boy, and let us call him what he is, this *bully*, was new to the school himself not so long ago—look me in the eye—and since then, he has had every interest shown to him, by older boys, by our choirmaster, by me.

Gaze dashed to the floor.

—Look me in the eye! This is a boy I've taken time over, cared over, fought over—

A flicker of surprise, or disbelief.

—How do you imagine he made it into the Lower Fourth after last term's disastrous results?

A wave of understanding received like a toothache.

—And this boy has now taken it upon himself to persecute someone younger and smaller, someone who idolizes him—oh, yes, he does! This bully has caused, to my personal knowledge alone, three dockets for lost prep, one for a spoiled desk—you can take that expression *right* off your face—not to mention the loathsome and utterly callous physical treatment.

A vein pulsed in Halton's forehead.

—This story, I am bound to say, not only sickens me, but has betrayed my trust. When I look at this boy, I am ashamed.

He was about to blub, which John thought would be a relief, but then, instead of crumbling, Halton straightened his spine.

—One question for you, Timothy. Am I mistaken?

The boy swallowed. His head moved.

—I can't hear you.

A whisper:

—No, sir.

The temperature in the room changed. John began to breathe again. He let go of the chair and crossed his arms. He ought to be congratulating the boy on making it through hourlies and on showing some improvement at last, if a straw poll of the Common Room were to be believed, but now, instead, this monstrousness.

—The case is the Head's now, he said.

—The Head, sir?

—He handles such matters personally.

—But, sir . . .

The boy's composure, so fiercely maintained, now began to waver.

—Sir, I thought you . . .

The jaw began to chatter, as if from the cold.

—This is far more serious than a talking-to, Timothy.

—I know, sir, but I thought . . . I thought you'd be the one to . . .

This wasn't going the way John intended. He was out of words. He took Halton by the shoulder and led him to the spare room, the Chamber of Death, Morgan had called it. The boy went in without being pushed, and John locked the door behind him. Sometimes symbolism was best left unexplored.

◆

As a prefect, as supervisor of their dorm, as a Christian, Pearce knew he ought to have noticed something. Halton's arrest was, fundamentally, the result of his own failure to safeguard the common weal. When Halton attempted blackmail last summer, he should never have yielded. Morgan would have seen it for the test it was. He would have found a way with Halton, and not Moss's way either. *By their fruits ye shall know them*—had Halton thrived under Moss's regime? Last term he'd frequented the JCR in a way that was frankly provocative; this term he'd larked about with Audsley, run his lessons into the ground, relentlessly baited their Housemaster, and bullied the fag of two House prefects. If he had seen to Halton properly in the beginning or even along the way, none of this would have happened. Perhaps there was a reason he hadn't been able to write the letter to his parents. Perhaps its errand was vanity, *vanitas et arrogantia*.

✦

The Headmaster was in York until evening, Lewis said. John wasn't sure whether to feel relieved or vexed, but the delay gave him time to organize his arguments and to read the fifty-four compositions that needed marking. Of course, the Common Room had learned of the affair, so his afternoon was interrupted by colleagues coming by to take his opinion and offer their own. A midafternoon dose had been necessary to settle himself to the Remove on the Reformation, and then as darkness fell and he contemplated a preprandial corrective, another knock.

—Uncle John?

A sight for sore eyes. Her hair was falling out of its plaits. He capped his pen and leaned back his head as she rubbed his scalp in the motherly way she'd taken to lately, discharging the day's vice, the stupidity of the Fifth, the dangling participles, fingers now at his hairline, shivers turning warm, bathing him in a kind of love he'd never deserve.

—There's something I ought to have told you, she said. Promise you won't be cross?

He murmured and placed her index fingers against the ridge of his eye socket.

—I've . . .

She pressed, a pain that satisfied like iodine.

—I've invited Da to the caroling service.

His eyes flicked open.

—And he's said yes.

—You what?

428

—Mrs. Firth said lots of parents come.

He sat up.

—Don't be cross. He'll like it.

He got up from the chair and raked back his hair.

—He *is* all alone, she said. I feel sorry for him. Don't you?

She wrapped her arms around him, and he hadn't the strength to re-sist. He hooked his chin over the crown of her head, and beneath his hands, her back vibrated as she hummed and then began to sing a hymn the choir were preparing. *Lo! he comes, with clouds descending, once for our salvation slain.* Strange, powerful strange, to hear this Quaker child sing and know the words as if they were hers. *Thousand thousand saints attending . . .* If only he could be the man she thought she knew.

After Prayers, Jamie summoned him to the study. Evidently, in the hour since his return, Jamie had been deluged by the SCR's opinions of the Halton business. Evidently, he resented the ambush, and evidently he blamed John for leaving him exposed to it, or so John supposed given his blustery diatribe on the evils of bullying and the necessity of cutting the canker out. John tried to return him to a calmer state of mind, but the more he reasoned, the more punctilious Jamie became. Bedtimes came and went, and as the vise tightened on John's head, discussion turned to quarrel, and John lost his patience:

—For Heaven's sake! I never would have told you if I thought you might actually send the boy down!

Jamie was shocked from his petulance:

—You would have kept it from me?

If Jamie imagined he could or should know everything that went on in the school, he was overtired and solipsistic. And if he insisted on cling-ing to an unsuitable solution out of stubbornness, from sheer pique that the matter wasn't proceeding under his control, then it was time some-one stopped humoring him.

—Damn it, Jamie, stop larking about! You aren't going to dispose him and you know it.

A bull-point chisel was chipping at his skull.

—Damn it, yourself! I'm Headmaster here, not you.

—Then punish the boy, John said, by all means. But he stays. Can we drop it now, please?

He got up to leave, but Jamie stood between him and the door.

—Are you quite all right? Jamie asked.

—Except for this wretched headache!

Jamie's expression softened, and John could see moving across it the recollection of his headache that summer.

—It's been a long day, John said, a long term.

Jamie inhaled, and so did John at the thrill of tweaking Jamie where he felt it. He pressed harder, holding Jamie's gaze, refusing to release him.

—Very well, Jamie said, I'll see the boy tomorrow and think on what you've said.

He stepped aside to let John pass, but as John opened the door, Jamie touched the small of his back.

—*Yes?* John said.

—Good night.

Jamie let him go with a look, *that* look, daring and cheeky, and as John reached for a riposte, the chisel resumed, blurring his vision and queering his balance. House, bathroom, cabinet, make it stop, softer, smooth . . .

Another knock—would they never cease, even after midnight in his own bathroom? He emerged as if on an errand and encountered Mrs. Firth, tray in hand. She'd brought him something before bed, she said. As he mulled the unusual gesture, she delivered a report: she had enforced bedtimes on the corridor (said with the air of a wife who'd sorted out ten children while her husband was off on a blind). She had supervised steam inhalation and cough mixture with Miss Líoht. She had escorted young Halton in his preparations for the night. The boy, she informed him, had eaten next to nothing all day even though she'd brought him lunch and tea. She'd taken the liberty of providing a hot-water bottle. She thought Mr. Grieves might not mind, given the terrible cold in that room and the wind that had blown across it all afternoon—John thanked her and excused himself. The dose had not sufficed and he couldn't wait—*with what rapture, with what rapture* . . .

Back in his study he found biscuits and a cup of steaming milk. He ate the biscuits without tasting them and assigned the last two exams the low marks they deserved. Unbuttoning his collar, he drifted up the corridor and saw a light under Halton's door. He ought to have checked on him earlier. He hadn't because he'd dreaded it, but now he had no choice. He fetched the key from his study and opened the door. The room was cold as its moniker and dark now. Halton did not stir.

—You needn't play possum, John said. I saw the light a minute ago.

A pause, during which he found the light switch. Mercifully the boy opened his eyes.

—Have you any idea what time it is? John demanded.

Halton looked away.

—You ought to be asleep.

John stepped closer. The boy's eyes, usually prominent, looked sunken and dark. John wondered if he'd been crying. He looked stretched out, as if he'd been dragged to the Orient and back with only one change of camel and half a flask of tea.

—Please, sir, what's going to happen?

Damn Jamie and his wait-a-day tactics. The boy had been alone since eleven o'clock in the morning, and now he faced a frigid night waiting further. John felt an ache, the wish to put the boy out of his misery, or at least put him through it.

—Wait there, he said.

✦

He had lost his bearings entirely. This morning in the study, he'd almost shed tears, not because he was trapped, but because he'd been suddenly rescued from it all. He had just begun to sense it—not only that he was being delivered but into Grieves's hands—when Grieves had cast him aside, declaring him untouchable and consigning him to the Chamber of Death. No room had ever been colder, and he'd had all day to understand the jaws that held him.

He threw off the blankets and stood at the end of the bed, cold to the marrow, like the man in that story Grieves had made him read, the man who thought of killing his dog (or was it his horse?) just so he could thaw his hands inside its carcass. If he had a dog, he would defend it to the death. He would pick fleas off it and drown them in antiseptic. He would give the dog room in his own bed and food from his own plate. Never would he turn his back on it.

—What are you doing? Grieves said from the door.

He startled, and before he could answer, Grieves handed him a cup of milk and told him to drink it.

—Chop-chop.

Grieves rested his other hand, the one holding the slipper, behind his back. Halton choked down the lukewarm milk, wondering what tortures it held beyond the usual foul taste. Did it contain castor oil or some other purgative chosen to punish him as his ayah used to? Grieves took the empty cup and told him to get into bed.

—Aren't you going to whack me, sir?

Grieves frowned:

—Whack you?

And took the hand from behind his back, revealing a book.

—I'm going to read to you.

Eyes stinging, Grieves's hand on his shoulder, he dove into bed and bit down on his tongue. No one had read to him since Miranda read him that girl's book, under the eucalyptus trees in Victoria Road. It was about a garden and a boy who was ill, and when they sent him to Yorkshire, he'd expected Misselthwaite Manor but encountered only the Academy.

—Head on the pillow, Mr. Grieves said. Close your eyes.

He closed them against the cold and the past.

—*Marley was dead, to begin with* . . .

Grieves's voice surrounded him, not scolding, but drawing him to another place, a place of wraiths and chains, Audsley, Miranda, Wilberforce, the Turtle's face leaping from doorknobs, pursuits and pursuits, accusation, condemnation, an icy ghost grabbing his wrist—

The room was dark, and his hand stuck out in the cold. He lay rigid, unable to stop every dire thought he'd ever had, from his ayah's *chinja-chinja* to the ghosts Fletcher claimed to have seen in the cloisters one night. Oh, the night! How long would it last? With the lions that could savage a grown man, the sorcerers draining your blood, and the jinns that came up through the floor to bite the willies off wicked boys.

✦

Halton looked seasick, Jamie thought. He told him to sit down before he fell down and then poured himself another cup of coffee. When he began the questioning, Halton admitted everything, even volunteering evidence John had never mentioned. He answered briefly but firmly, as if he were testifying against an enemy and not himself. John was right, of course, in what he had said and what he had left unsaid. This boy was not some remnant of the noxious root Jamie had been compelled to dig out when he took charge of the Academy. The dramatic dismissal of boys and staff, with all its collateral injuries, was an action peculiar to that time; the present grew out of the past, of course, but it never emerged a perfect replica. Timothy Halton was not Alex Pearl, nor was he any of the other unsavory characters whose names Jamie would never forget. There was no question Halton had acted despicably, but after only a few minutes' interview, Jamie was convinced he would not be bullying again; more likely he'd be a front guard against it. Whatever John had done with him had turned the tide. Jamie knew he shouldn't be surprised. John had always had that gift, even if he buried it in a field.

Nevertheless, he was glad he'd called for the boy during lessons when John was occupied. He wouldn't have been able to think straight if John had been there, too. He had no intention of expelling the boy, but a case of bullying brought to the Headmaster demanded exemplary response. Young Halton, though repentant, would have to take his medicine; the question was how, and what measure.

Jamie poured another cup of coffee. This boy was stoic, courageous, and, Jamie sensed, lamentably experienced in taking what was dished out, yet his entire body broadcast his misery, one that longed not for clemency but for deliverance. Jamie felt a certain envy and irrelevance as it dawned on him that the justice the boy required could never come from him. The rescue had to be personal.

◆

John had saved the magic lantern slides for these last two days after exams. The Third were excited by the images of mummies in various states of unwrapping and with the views of pyramids and stellae. The knock on the classroom door was unwelcome; so was the intruder. He stepped into the corridor, and Halton handed him a note from Jamie. John read it and told the boy to come to the study after lunch. There wasn't time to see Jamie, to burst into his study and ask what he thought he was playing at, only time to set the Third drawing as he stepped into the washroom—pocket, tongue—and returned before mayhem erupted.

—Turtle, whatever that is, put it away before I notice. Martin, turn your book or you'll never fit the whole coffin in.

As they drew the eyes of Horus, John read the note again: quid pro quo, the boy could stay but . . . orders. And beneath his reflex for outrage, amidst the memory of the last orders he'd received and the travesty that had unfolded—the shame that stung him still—beyond the determination to refuse, something else grew. Even if Jamie did intend to punish him with the command just as he'd punished him with the last, still was there not a secret relief? Oh, why cling to the desiccated shell of his principles and continue to shun what, in truth, he'd always known? He had thrown himself body and soul into everything she believed, her rejection of war, her declaration of friendship with mankind that made killing or even violence impossible. Yet now and for some time, perhaps some long time, these principles—dearly cherished and hotly defended—had left him impotent in the face of serious things. Her pacifism, so romantic in its disrepute, had seemed to answer the cataclysm of war, but had it truly answered anything? He hadn't been on speaking terms with Jamie's father since the war, but he'd long wondered what the Bishop would say about all of it. As for this mess with Halton, he knew with good confidence what the Bishop would say: there was sin in the world, and it shot through every one of them. It was the fashion to reject such a view as both overdone and pat, but wasn't it the only blade that could cut through this thicket? John had once known, and despite it all still knew, that sin was not an old-fashioned term for things society disapproved, but a condition as old as the world, a desolate and willful separation. Across that chapter of his life, the Bishop had revealed to him sin's power, and had shown him the remedy. Why, John had once asked, was suffering necessary to bridge that gap? It was a mystery, Jamie's father had admitted, but the best that could be said was that it had been true throughout the ages, and was yet true now.

An exotic stubbornness came over him as he imagined her reaction to these orders: What did she know of escaping such a prison? Inflicting a measure of pain on this boy, who suffered in exile and required something to release him, this, he felt now, was a kind of mercy. Who was she to condemn it? Hadn't she held herself indifferent to his suffering, scourging him with her pacifism year after year, life after life?

After the Third, the Upper Sixth, and a lunch scarcely eaten, John went to the study, where he found Halton waiting. A dose was needed, but in a rush of solidarity, he refused. If Halton had to face it, then he would give it unaided.

Boy on the carpet, John passed him Jamie's note and asked if he'd anything to say. Halton's eyes widened, but he shook his head.

—Well, John said, I have.

Before the punishment one delivered the jaw, a first-class reproof to prepare the ground and heighten the yearning. John felt strangely impatient, but he steeled himself—

434

—Please, sir!

He turned, half relieved. The boy was digging in his own pocket, extracting another paper, something torn from an exercise book: confession, apology, unreserved and undressed.

— Has Dr. Sebastian seen this?

—No, sir!

The boy looked wounded, and John realized it had been written for his eyes alone.

He hadn't the heart for rebuke, not to that face, one miserable in every sense of the word. There was only one way out, for either of them.

He opened the cupboard. He wasn't there for his manuscript, nor the boxes of letters, the ink bottles, the housekeeping receipts, or the carbon copies of term reports. He was there to step into the fire, sear him though it would.

—Are you ready?

He closed the cupboard door and set the cane on his desk. Halton nodded. John removed his jacket and unfastened a cuff link.

—I shall have to write to your father, of course.

A flash of panic:

—Sir?

It was something John had made Jamie agree, that whatever the outcome, John would deal with the father.

—Write him about what, sir?

—About this.

And the composure, so stoic and resigned, now faltered:

—Please, sir, can't you   ?

The boy's jaw tightened, his fists clenched at his sides:

—Please, sir, please don't.

Jamie's sentence had been willingly accepted, but now, at the mention of the father, this ungoverned pleading?

—If your father has something to say about this, Timothy, then you must face it.

—I know that, sir! I'm not . . .

Breath as if inflating a balloon.

—I'm not afraid, sir.

The chin faltered, feet shifting.

—Stand still.

If Halton didn't want his father written to, then he oughtn't to have done the things he had. But the tears—for they were tears now, leaking down the face and brushed away—surely these were not the tears of a boy afraid of his father, not this boy who feared so little.

—*Please* don't write to them, sir.

The voice had returned to issue this prayer.

—Couldn't you deal with it, sir? You could give it to me twice. Once from you, and once from—

—I'll decide what's to happen, not you.

John could feel it himself, the need for conclusion, and he could sense now what unhinged the boy. *Don't write to them.* Fear not of the father, but of others. The mother? Or was it the sister, the twin, and the thought of the look on her face if she heard? She would not avert her eyes from wickedness in his charge. He would never be the same to her.

—Your father's coming to the carol service, isn't he?

—Yes, sir. They all are.

After the furnace, the slate was to be wiped clean. That was the contract. Not perpetual disgrace in the eyes of those who could never understand.

—Very well, John said, I won't write him.

—Oh, sir!

—But I will speak with him. We shall speak with him together.

—Oh, sir . . .

Tears again, almost.

—Do you trust me, Timothy?

A look of bewilderment.

—Trust me, please.

 The sky behind the chapel looked auspicious, but Cordelia couldn't be sure. The wind cut from the east, and the clouds moved in the opposite direction. Would the two fronts blow past one another, one above, one below? Would they collide in slow motion and brew for days? Or would their encounter produce another storm, even tonight? *Adam lay ybounden, bounden in a bond.* The choir had been practicing after lunch. *Four thousand winter though he not too long.* Not too long if it kept them there, safe in their secrets, making life over wildly in ways she'd never thought she would seek.

By tea the sleet had turned to a vindictive rain that fell heavily and froze. Gray slipped crossing the quad, and when McCandless and Co. laughed at him, they slipped, too. In the study, he burned old papers in the grate and opened a new exercise book. Guilford's Throat and Voice drops didn't stop the coughing, but they calmed it as his hand raced. He had always imagined the romance of the tale would lie between Valarious and Kahrid of Langstephen, but the play had shown him how flawed that notion was. Not only was Valarious too gripped by his quest to have time for anything else, but Kahrid of Langstephen, as she'd been portrayed by the Turtle, was far too intrepid for a romantic lead and had, furthermore, taken up with Master Shadow as a kind of apprentice. Everyone knew that books required planning; Dickens had sketched his enormous plots at the outset and never deviated. Were his own fits and starts the fault of his poor talent, or did they express, as Guilford had always claimed, the voice of the story itself, telling him what it was, rescuing him from error, drawing him nearer to its true heart?

Boyo, the Elf Rider, had been imprisoned in Castle Noire longer than he could precisely remember, and although he had desired freedom, always freedom, his captivity had been marked by his friendship with Aurora of the golden hair, the daughter of his warden, Perspicacious. Now that Valarious and his party had finally found Boyo, won his release from the dungeon cell, and slipped a draught into Perspicacious's cup—now that freedom beckoned—the Elf Rider grieved at the thought of leaving his wonted home, the prison and the girl who had been his companion these many, many years.

◆

—Who wrote this one, Uncle John?

His goddaughter held out an exercise book with exaggerated horror. She'd been feverish again at tea, so he'd made her spend Prep before his fire. Having finished her book, she was amusing herself leafing through his last pile of compositions.

—His name's Halton, John said.

—Which one's he?

John summarized: House, choir, Fourth.

—You mean the one with the frog eyes?

437

John almost laughed.

—It isn't very good, is it? she said of the composition.

—You should have seen what he was writing a month ago.

—Why was he in that room last night?

—Pardon?

—Did he do something wicked?

—I don't think that's any of your concern.

Her chin turned pink, and she took up a different exercise book. The ache in John's head had been there all week playing its tune in a variety of keys. Just now it sat on his forehead with the steady thrum of a double bass.

—Who's your worst student?

—I'm sure I can't say.

—Can't or won't?

He frowned.

—All right, she said, which is the cleverest?

—You're the cleverest.

—Uncle John!

She held out the book she'd been examining:

—How about this one. He seems clever.

Riding, John saw. She certainly could pick them.

—*Is* he clever?

—Quite.

—Is he naughty?

John capped his pen:

—It's time you were in bed.

—But it's only eight o'clock.

He moved the exercise books away and handed her *A Christmas Carol.*

—In that case, he said, you can be quiet.

◆

She watched him around the edge of her book. Hunched, absorbed in their work, he wouldn't have noticed if she'd stuck out her tongue. His lips twitched in a silent conversation with them, and when he uncapped his pen, she could tell which compositions interested him and which tried his patience. She couldn't imagine his reading a letter from her in the same way.

—Uncle John?

—Hmm?

—What can I get you as a Christmas present?

—I'm sure your smile will be enough.

—I'd like a set of pajamas.

He looked up.

—Whatever for?

—Loads of girls wear them. Julia, for example.

—Julia?

—Vandam. From Paris.

He touched the nib to his tongue as if trying to keep his patience. Julia had actually worn a silk gown, but that could only be attempted with a suitable bosom. She longed for pajamas, striped like they wore. For her to prop her feet now against the fire rail, the draft blowing up her bare legs, and then to encounter men and boys in the corridor, not to mention loitering in the chair loft, with nothing above her ankles—it was crippling.

—Were you ever in love, Uncle John?

—I beg your pardon?

—With anyone but your wife, I mean?

He set down pen and book:

—What are these questions?

—Nothing, she said. But were you?

He pressed his thumb to his eye socket in a maneuver she was sure would blind him one day.

—Perhaps, he said at last.

—How did you manage, when you had to part?

—Not very well.

He left the room. Something from the fire went up her nose, and she began to cough, the kind that wouldn't stop until you'd almost retched. He returned presently and caught her like that, gagging into her handkerchief, and that was the end of the evening. She wasn't crying, but it didn't hurt that the tears from coughing made it look as though she were. When he turned out her lamp and felt her cheek, she took his hand and made him sit on the edge of her bed.

—Were you ever naughty, Uncle John?

—Pardon me?

—When you were a boy?

He crossed his legs.

—I'm sure I was.

—Very naughty?

—Perhaps not very.

She poked a foot out of the covers. Light from the door fell across her ankle, and she could see him pretending not to look at it.

—Did you get into trouble at school?

—Certainly.

—And how were you punished?

He covered her foot. She could not see his face.

—In the usual way.

—What about girls?

He got up from the bed.

—Don't go!

—Then close your eyes.

She closed them. He drew up a chair.

—Did you know any girls?

He sighed.

—Not especially, except for Dr. Sebastian's sisters.

She pulled the blankets around her ear to show she was settling down.

—What were they like?

—Oh . . . Amazons. Except Lucy, who was only a few months older than I.

She tried to imagine him as a boy with Dr. Sebastian, perhaps like the youngest boys here and Lucy just her age.

—Was she ever naughty?

—Aren't you asleep yet?

—Was she?

He sighed again, but it was more like a laugh.

—Several of our mishaps were entirely her fault.

—What happened to her?

—Oh, her father made very little distinction between her and her brother, or me for that matter.

—You?

—Enough, now.

She rolled over to face the wall and swallowed against the relentless tickle.

—Was he a terribly strict man, Dr. Sebastian's father?

—Terribly? No.

His chair scraped the floor.

—Reasonably.

—Did you ever sneak out at night, you two, in your pajamas?

—We wore nightgowns.

She turned around. He was standing in the door with the light behind him.

—But you were boys!

—Most boys did, then.

—Like mine?

—I suppose, as far as nightclothes are concerned, you're no different from a boy of thirty years ago.

✦

Moss came to John's study after lights-out to discuss the Christmas tea. For an event that lasted less than an hour, it always required an inordinate amount of preparation. As they reviewed the roster of parents, tallying those who'd sent replies, adding those who were likely to turn up regardless, and considering what kind of handling each was likely to require, John was reminded that Elsa Riding had promised to attend and for the first time. He felt a ripple of hungry fear at the thought of her black garments and sapphire eyes—though surely she no longer wore black?—and grew distracted wondering how she would regard him. Would she embarrass him by addressing him as she had in their correspondence and inquiring after the manuscript that still languished in the cupboard? Or would she be formal, making it clear that she was finished with him since he'd declined to intervene between her and her son? Of course, Owain would be there, too, and would require looking after if only to curtail visits to the punch table.

—Is there anything else, sir? Moss asked.

John collected himself. They hadn't discussed Halton, and they had to.

—I need a few minutes with Halton and his father, in my study.

Moss rubbed his nose:

—Sticky stitch, that one, sir.

—I'm afraid it could be.

John switched off the desk lamp to signal the end of the conversation.

—Still, Moss said, well done today.

The chisel again, or not?

—How is he?

—Sore, Moss said.

John inhaled.

—Whatever you did, I've never seen him so—

—Please—

—*calm*, sir.

John blinked, and Moss began to relate what had happened at Prep, how Burton had sent Halton to the JCR.

—A docket? John balked.

—Of sorts. Said Halton had fallen asleep. Twice.

After everything that had happened, for Burton to persecute the boy!

—What did you do?

—I sent him to bed, sir.

Moss's voice contained a note of outrage, as if he couldn't believe John had asked.

—He groused about it being only a quarter to eight, but when I came back a few minutes later, he was dead to the world.

That night after his last dose, John composed a prayer of thanks for Moss, for Wilberforce, for the others like them, before and to come. And as he lay in the dark—the kind of dark that took root in December when storms smothered all memory of stars—something pressed upon him, there in his chest, something that could not be dislodged by sleep or doses. It hadn't been with him when he woke that morning, but by the time his goddaughter began her questions, it had found a roost in his ribs. Had it been there in the study with Halton, just before it began? He had stood on the carpet feeling at each side an avatar pressing for submission: the pacifist demanding he lay down his weapon, and the other one, cold wrath in his fingers. But John had stood between them and submitted to neither, permitting the furnace its flame and char, standing it, withstanding it, until something else moved his arm.

His foot jerked in the bed, and a knowledge washed across him: it couldn't be taken away, what had passed between him and Timothy Halton. No matter how the boy might grow or how far he might travel from the Academy, this couldn't be erased; there would always be that study and the things they had learned there, the wind rattling down the chimney and the pressure in his own throat as he gave the boy what he needed, not recoiling—from it or him—ministering, administering the suffering required to escape that exile, to relinquish wrongdoing, to bring

442

him again to his fellow man when he was lost, loving him enough to do this.

◆

Pearce knew he'd passed the point of being able to sleep, but getting up was out of the question on a night such as this, black, wild, colder than the cellar of hell. In reality, of course, hell was colder, but who cared when merely taking his head from under the blankets made him shiver. His dressing gown hung at the foot of the bed, and if he could reach it, he'd be warmer. *Rise up, Lord, and help us.* If he had a book of prayers like Dr. Sebastian's, prayers beyond the prayerbook, God might hearken unto his request. Instead, day after day his letter stayed unwritten. Even scripture failed him. Advent was an unending procession of Isaiah, which, however salutary, could not be said to encourage anyone, not even in the upside-down style of Amos, whom Morgan liked to quote as if he were the Lord and they Israel. *You only have I known of all the families of the earth—you see, Simon, God has projects, too.* But God's favoritism of Israel, like the interest Morgan took in him, came dear—*therefore will I punish you for all your iniquities.* Never had he been more secure, more seen and steered. Now he stood alone, vision in one hand, nothing in the other.

A whimsy unfurled of traveling to London in the holidays. He'd use his Christmas money and go to Morgan's house or his club or his flat if he had one. *Need a word. Could you?* Morgan would wire back, *Come, time, place.* He'd wear his uniform, and while he wasn't thirteen years old anymore, would it be so very different? Morgan would untangle his long legs before a fire: *All right, Simon, start at the beginning.* Since the beginning, everyone had said he'd be in government and the law. It had all been assumed, until the collision with Moss—he'd blush admitting this, and Morgan would raise his brow and wrath would be put on the list—the collision with Moss and the pigeonholes, yes when they were both prefects, yes in front of everyone, yes he'd charged him, fists flying, until the pigeonholes came down on them both. Clang in the head, flashes: island-green-shepherd-sheep.

Once Morgan had ticked him off for brawling, he'd turn onto the trail of truth. *Sure it's not a farmer you're meant to be?* But that would be a joke, to ease his true pursuit. *Have you sat the exam yet?* For Christ Church, he meant, where he was to read law. *What makes you think you'll pass?* A syrup seemed to seep into his scalp. *Not to put too fine a point on it, Simon, but nobody will be surprised if you don't.* His father would be let down, though. His mother worse. *But that's the trade, isn't it?* Morgan was handing him a cup of tea and making him sit beside the fire where it was warm. *Don't get too comfortable; there's still the pigeon-holes to deal with.* The tea was sweet and salty, like melted toffee and gravy. *What you need,* Morgan said, *is someone who knows about this shepherding of yours, where to go, how to get sent, who you've got to know.* And the tea was empty and Morgan was punishing him for his wrath and his cowardice and his stubborn pride, and he was weeping, but instead of relief, they were tears of despair: *I can't find out! I don't know anyone!* Morgan touched his shoulder. *Sure about that?*

A shot like a cannon outside the window, and the bed rattled and the air went back inside him and he remembered the time that he'd broken Moss's nose. Morgan was taking Moss home for the holidays because Moss had no people to go to, because his parents were abroad, his father with the Bank and his mother a missionary in the far, Far East.

✦

Gray woke to a crash outside. Through the window he distinguished something—branch of a tree?—across the gate. The lamp lay smoking on the ground, and the branch loomed above it, like some monstrous arm begging admittance. He couldn't see the clock, but he felt his mistake, falling asleep when he'd promised to meet her. The night was dark and the tunnels darker still, but the chair loft glowed with her torch. She wasn't angry, he wasn't too late. She'd brought a rug, and when he showed her the new exercise book, she put the rug over both of them and closed her eyes as he read. It took longer than he expected, and at the end he saw streaks by her ears that could have been tears. In forty-eight hours, her hair would no longer drift into his mouth. Christmas brutal, seven weeks, an age. Seven weeks ago they'd been rehearsing *Castle Noire.* Her mother had been alive, insensible to the sword that would cut her from them.

—Did you do what I told you? she asked.
—Pardon?
—With the letters.
He froze and couldn't answer. She pulled away with the rug:
—You didn't, did you?

He began to cough.

—Where are they?

She fixed him with her stare, the one that always made him feel full and warm in the root, now even more since she'd spoken things they'd silently agreed never to mention. He fought for breath, retorts filling his mind, but when the coughs finally stopped, he found himself smiling. And she was smiling, too, and both of them were laughing, and his reason melted and he pushed aside the chair and up came the floorboard.

He couldn't tell if she was more astonished to see her letters or to discover that they'd been underfoot all the time, but he removed both bundles and set them before her. Her own letters she ignored, but her father's she untied, examining the postmarks. They were hers, her inheritance from her mother. He was right, he saw, to preserve them. She re-tied the bundle and set it behind her.

His hand rested on the other stack, her letters to him. No, he would not relinquish them, no matter what she said. She looked at him—*never*—and then to the floor, where she shined her torch and discovered a stray letter.

—What's this? she asked, plucking it from its envelope.

He snatched it from her, but she'd seen.

—Wilberforce, M.? Is that Morgan Wilberforce?

—*What?*

—The man who was here last weekend? He's very tall, isn't he? And handsome.

He shoved it beyond her reach, through the quick fright and the sharp, twangy shame. When he turned back, his other letters had been captured in her lap.

—Those are *mine*.

The words strained his throat, and he saw in her face how childish he sounded. He tried to imagine Grieves giving a command he knew would be obeyed:

—And I'd like them back, please.

—What will you give me for them?

What would he *give* her!

—It isn't exactly fair, she continued. I wrote all this and you wrote me nothing.

He swelled with indignation, but his retort came out appeasing:

—I'll write to you now.

—It wouldn't be the same, she said.

He groped for an argument but sensed with each moment the hopelessness of recovering them. And he was filled with sudden pity for his father's box, long since destroyed by T, letters long since burned, from his father, from Morgan, all because he had not fought for them.

—What about this? she said, snatching up his exercise book like found money.

—It isn't finished.

—Tomorrow. Do you promise?

Last day of lessons, nothing serious would be asked of them. He might manage if he accelerated the story. She took one letter from her bundle:

—Down payment for the finished manuscript.

—What about the rest? he asked plaintively.

—You'll have to earn them.

By this, it emerged, she meant answer her questions. She asked about Halton, who he was, why he'd been in the Chamber of Death, what had happened after. He tried evasion, but she called it obvious and mean. Too late, he realized he'd been caught in a riptide, one carrying him somewhere foreign, new life and new land, wanted or no.

She peeled off another letter and called it his second payment. The stack was too thick to earn back in one day. He might know her letters mostly by heart, but to face seven weeks without them or her? He told her what he knew, and when he'd finished, she gave him the letter.

—Tell me what it's like.

—What?

—You know.

If he tried, he could take them back by force, but he didn't. He'd lost the strength to resist experiences, just as he was losing the power to forget, and the will to lie.

✦

He shouldn't have taken the last dose. He convinced himself of much nonsense while awake, but now, bed spinning beneath him (around him?), he had to acknowledge that dosing in the middle of the night was a new breach, and that it had been too much when chased with brandy. He had to start reducing or he'd kill himself, though on the subject of honest, he would love, *love* . . . ! Not because he wanted to suffer—he'd watched enough men die and it was terrible in every sense—but wouldn't it stop the merry-go-round? The only reason he didn't was because of his child. She would be savaged twice, and then what might she not do? *Yes, you ears of truth, yes,* her questions threw him off, *yes,* she knew more than she should—yes of her mother and yes of him—but listen, *listen,* she had always been *reasonable,* never caused the slightest problem—all right, the summer she was three, time and again wandering down Drayton Fen stark naked, but all small children were insane to some degree. And all right, *yes,* there was the aftermath of her mother's—it wasn't necessary to review—but the point was that she'd always been curious, so her questions were *in character,* and in any case soon he'd begin looking for a school for her, perhaps boarding at her old school, or perhaps one in the company of only girls and women. When Lucy was that age, on her fourteenth birthday she had drawn him into the cloakroom and kissed him, at length, and he wasn't as surprised as he pretended, and he felt it where he felt things, and Lucy went away for the rest of the summer, and it never happened again, but *you,* you ears, who sit there in the corner of this gray, gray room, pressing through the air from the other side, you who frightened my child in the kitchen that night—come here through the fog, all the way in, I won't flee and I won't fear—come, come back, whatever you are, *come.*

Queer things happened when you sat up all night. Your head was full of cotton wool, and everything ran together like old things down the drain that swirled in the basin and streaked it with their smell. Uncle John knocked on her door and came in with a candle. The electrics had gone, he said. She wasn't to go to Thixendale today. Breakfast would be late.

Tremendous icicles hung from the eaves, and the middle of the cloisters looked like a mirror. She climbed the ladder Mr. Fardley showed her one time and looked out the window in the clock tower, like a crow's nest on a vast, white sea. Boys skidded across the quad, shoes like skates, whoosh! beside the chapel, zing! off the porch as the men groped along the stonework. Mr. Fardley sawed at the tree that kept them behind the gates, the sound orange and achy. From the clock tower, she heard no train whistle, saw no movement on the roads. Marooned, just as she'd pictured when she brushed her hair yesterday, counting backwards from three hundred and three. She went back to bed, and when she woke up again, things seemed less strange, her power less terrible.

After a luncheon served confusingly and cold, Dr. Sebastian silenced the refectory. Afternoon school was canceled, he said, but the forecast was favorable, and he'd every hope that the trains would run as usual in the morning. Meanwhile, without electricity or coal deliveries, fires would be lit in studies and houserooms, the remaining daylight would be devoted to packing, tea would be served early, Evening Prayer canceled, bedtimes moved forward, and the carol service would proceed as planned tomorrow. Dr. Sebastian finished with the tone he used when he was pretending to be too polite to make threats: he was certain they would all lend a hand and that in this last day of term nothing beyond the weather would disturb them.

✦

He loitered by the pigeonholes after lunch as he had promised. She passed without appearing to notice him and then with a hiss called him down the passage towards a shaft of light. He hesitated outside her door, but she pulled him into her bedroom, more forbidden than any corner of Grindalythe Woods. She laughed at his expression and tried to ease his fright: Her godfather and Mrs. Firth were round the bend with packing. No one would be back for ages. Reaching past him, she dragged a wireless across the table.

—It's probably already started, she said.

Latin exercises fluttered to the floor, but she either didn't notice or didn't care. Soon music filled the room, louder than anyone should dare. A man's voice, light and smooth, explained what they had been hearing and then announced the next song and the people who would play it. She took his hand, but he assured her he couldn't dance.

—It's worth two letters. I'll show you how.

She knew the tunes and all their words even though no one sang with the orchestra. Some songs she claimed to have on gramophone discs.

—*Have you seen the well-to-do, up on Lenox Avenue?*

—It's too fast.

—*High hats and colored collars, white spats and fifteen dollars.* Follow me!

She smiled at his missteps and pulled him in a way that made his heart beat in his mouth. His ears drank and his hands held hers and he no longer cared what might happen to the old life.

✦

Turtle and the rest of the fags had been press-ganged into chipping the ice from the walkways. By the time Kardleigh ordered them inside, having dealt with two gashes from so-called snowballs, the Turtle's hands had come out in blisters. As he rounded the cloisters, Halton tackled him as he used to during rehearsals. Wary, excited, he followed Halton to the choir room, but as the door closed behind them, his heart froze—that Halton would speak of what never should be spoken, either to condemn him or apologize, one as ghastly as the other.

But rather than speak, Halton put his foot on the soft pedal and picked out a melody:

—Got that?

He nodded.

—You can't tell anyone.

Halton played the tune again on top of "Besançon."

—For the descant, he said.

The Turtle didn't have Halton's volume, and the highest notes jumped too high for Halton to reach. Together, though, they thought they might achieve an Audsley-like surprise. *Set every peak and valley humming*— beautiful and joyous, ringing in the news.

✦

They met again, after tea in the chair loft. She was waiting with a candle, three letters set out like banknotes. Fear and excitement filled him.

—Let's dress up, she said.

He asked her what she meant.

—Try on clothes.

—What clothes?

—Each other's. Don't worry, I don't want to see you naked.

He blushed, appalled:

—Forget it!

—All right, then, a game.

—No!

—Afraid you'll lose?

The game was called Geography, she said, and as he was clever, he would probably thrash her. He didn't like her turn of phrase, but the thing sounded simple enough, naming places that began with the last letter of the word one's opponent used.

—What happens if I win?

She held up an envelope.

—And if you win?

—I probably won't, she said, but if I should, you've got to let me wear something of yours.

He inhaled sharply.

—*Just* while we play the game, and you can have it back when you win another word.

—It's bedtime soon.

—It's only a game.

It didn't take him long to realize he'd been had. Once the obvious places had been used, the game degenerated into words ending in awkward letters. He'd used every East he could think of, and even though he parried Runnymede with Eureux, she provided Xanthus after only brief hesitation. Soon he'd lost his jacket, his waistcoat, his tie—

—Aylesbury.

—Yap.

—Paraguay.

—Yosemite.

Collar, four studs, shirt. She made him look away as she dressed in his things. When he turned around again, she had pulled back her hair and knotted his tie. A cheeky Fourth Former if you didn't notice the skirt.

—I don't want to play anymore.

—You can't back out now.

She resumed by answering the word he'd lost.

—Yosemite . . . ? Egrafel.

—La Paz!

—Zurich, she deadpanned.

He won his jacket back with Riveaux, but he suspected she let him have it out of pity. After his socks and shoes, how far would she go?

✦

John made a final tour of the cloisters. The chapel was empty as his torch swept across the narthex, and he only had to lend a quick hand in the dorm before—

He froze. A sound like . . . He went down the aisle, scanning the pews. The sound again, this time from above. Heart cold, he mounted the stairs to the choir room.

He knew her cough well enough, and though he couldn't swear it was hers, she was the only person not required elsewhere. He'd no idea what she could be doing up there, but the day had left her idle and he'd not had a second to spare her. The choir room he found empty, but in the upper passage he heard it again, muted, but from . . . ? Wall? Panel? Light beneath, his torch like a sword, balcony, figures, boy with boy, with . . . girl, with—

✦

She gasped, and a hand seized him, dragging him backwards and onto his feet. Tugged down the stairs, no shoes, no words, tripping all the way, socks soaked, gravel sharp, jerked forward by one too tall and too strong to resist. House, corridor, room, *that* room, Grieves jangled in his pocket for a key.

—Please, sir, it's not the way it—

A blow from behind, forcing him into that icy, wicked—stumbling on the threshold, a hand at his elbow to keep him from falling, but then he was being swung, hearing it before he felt it and falling, face afire, against the bed frame and down until something cut through his tongue. Door slammed, floor shivered, metal running down his throat in the dark.

✦

Jamie's homily was failing to find its stride. He had been mentally drafting all week, but this afternoon when Lewis presented him with his notes from last year, he was chagrined to see he'd used the same theme twelve months previous. He'd begun again before tea, but after the meal he'd been forced to scrap that draft and start a third time. This new idea had potential—their longing for salvation as they longed to be free of this ice—but it was forced. If the night was thawing, he couldn't feel it. If the sea at Bridlington lapped at the ice on the pier, if the workmen of the Malton & Driffield Junction worked into the night to clear the line, no one would know it any more than they'd known of the nativity. Fine enough, but Jamie was fed up with silent-night Christmases. The point about Christmas, surely, was not that it was obscure, but that it was cataclysmic. That baby in the manger, as he looked up at the stars and the angels and the shepherds smelling of their sheep, surely he knew, in whatever way God could know when newly born, that this was only the beginning of the fight, that these were only the first breaths towards that final, tearing—

His study door fell open and John tumbled inside.

—He . . . he . . .

Jamie had ink all over his fingers. He fumbled for the blotting paper as John fumbled for words.

—He's done it this time!

John stood in the door as if a barrier kept him from entering. Jamie closed the ink pot with a reeling sensation of error. He gave John a wide berth and poured him a drink.

—Won't you sit down? he said at last.

But John refused. He drained the glass and then began to pace the room, dropping fragments of a manic tale, a lurid, addled account of his goddaughter and . . .

—*Who?*

Alone and in a state of . . .

—*What?*

Jamie's dread overpowered his composure, and the more he heard, the more his outrage grew.

—Dammit, *where?*

And the angrier Jamie got, the less John paced, as if the storm were being passed one to the other, until John finally stopped moving and spoke with all the gravity scotch could produce:

—I don't want to see that boy, ever again.

—John—

Alarm, blaring on his—Jamie dove for the telephone receiver.

—Yes?

A chipper voice at the other end brought news from the outside world. The telephone exchange had come back from the dead. Trains were moving from Driffield and—

He covered the receiver:

—I'll come find you in a moment. Good news!

John spun on his heel and lurched from the room as the lady on the line told her gospel of railways, electricity, and coal wagons from Hull.

✦

He should have gone to her first, John realized as he hurried up the chapel stairs. Jamie could have waited, but she—it stabbed him to think it. She was his first responsibility. His *child*. The upper passage was empty. Ditto foul balcony. His torch was dying. He went back to the House. Should he bring her milk, something stronger, or . . . He forced his thoughts into a line. The first thing she needed was to know that she was safe.

The lamp in his study had been lit, and so had a candle, which made him squint. She hunched before the cold grate, dressing gown like a cloak around her. They said it was a dagger to see your child hurt; this was worse.

—Darling!

He went to her, but she drew back from his arms.

—Darling, he assured her, I'm here now.

She pulled her feet up onto the armchair, and he saw that she had changed back to her own clothes. Her familiar cardigan calmed him slightly, but when he pulled her chair towards him, it rucked up the carpet, and she made a sound like a puppy whose tail was trod.

—I'm sorry, darling. You mustn't be afraid.

There were tears at the back of his throat, but he swallowed them as the words poured out. The boy would never bother her again. He'd be sent away, never to return. She must trust him. He took her hands in his, hot and clammy.

—It's entirely my fault, he said. You'll never have to see that loathsome—

—Stop it!

She pulled back, but he held her.

—Darling.

—Stop *calling* me that!

Her voice pierced the room. She wrenched free and clasped her knees.

—It was *my* fault, not his!

He tried to pull her close, but her foot shot out, making contact and taking his breath away.

453

—Why is it so hard to imagine? she cried.

Like the worst headache there in his root. He swallowed the nausea and tried to breathe.

—It was *my* idea.

She spoke in a new voice, one he didn't know.

—My game.

And yet, he did know it, through the bedroom wall her mother's aimed at her father.

—He didn't even want to play.

It had been a game she'd designed to win his clothes from him. She'd only wanted to try them, and the other times, he would never have come unless—

—Other?

His voice weak and futile.

—We're in love, Uncle John. There's nothing wrong in that.

A hit.

—And you can't say there is because you've been in love.

Palpable now in his chest, like the brutal rush of blood to frozen flesh. He thought he'd been saving her from the world, but now as the melt-water pressed behind his throat, he saw he'd been saving her from this. He'd brought her here, a spot barely on a map, to a school more austere than a monastery, and yet, and *yet*, she had found it even here, and in a heart he'd never . . .

—You should be happy, she whispered.

—*Happy . . . ?*

She took his sleeve:

—*Please* don't be cross. It wasn't clever, I know, the game. But there's nothing wicked in him.

She touched his cuff link and the skin of his wrist:

—You mustn't send him away. For my sake.

A flame branded him from the inside—drag through the school, backhand, malice thrown to the ground with the boy. The fault wasn't hers, and it wasn't the boy's. The poison lay entirely with him, in his heart, his arm, his mouth. The boy was only a poultice drawing venom to the surface, just as he'd done the first time, resurrecting the man he thought he'd killed.

—He worships you, you know.

She had his hands between her own.

—Don't look like that, he does. Are you *blind*, Uncle John?

He deserved this thorn, thrust like a bodkin between his ribs.

✦

He huddled under the blanket like the hedgehog Morgan used to call him, but it was still cold even though he'd done star jumps until it hurt too much to continue. His right sock was torn, and his mouth throbbed where metal had struck it—ring? bed frame? The clock rang ten. *You've got to think of how Grieves will feel—use your eyes, son, use your eyes and—*

Footsteps, rattle, he peeked out to an aching light.

—You can go, it said.

Flame flickered in a glass. His teeth chattered.

—I was wrong, the light said.

—Sir?

—I'm sorry.

—*Please*, sir—

A pile of clothing thrust at him.

—Put on your shoes.

His shoes were there, but his feet were too cold, and the right one wouldn't go . . .

—That'll do.

Shoes snatched away, lamp taken up.

—Follow me.

His studs clattered to the floor, but the light had departed and he had to follow.

—What did you do with that blanket? the man snapped.

The corridor was warmer, but not enough to stop him shaking in his undershirt.

—Oh, never mind!

Study door breached. Pushing him inside, the man set down the lamp and continued across the room. And he understood, like rocks falling, that he was not being let go, that everything before this had only been a rehearsal. *Within an inch of your life* was an expression, but here in this room, tonight, now, he would learn how close an inch could be.

The man turned from the mantel and held out a glass:

—Drink this.

He had to go and take it. The smell went up his nose and made him cough again.

—Oh, very well!

Water splashed in—could he swallow without gagging? Alice drank hers in one gulp, but Alice never stood before one such as this, whose coiled strength could—

—Chop-chop!

It warmed his throat. He finished and wished there were more, but the glass was gone, and the light was on the move, and they were leaving the crypt, up the stairs to the dorm, into another glare:

—It's you, sir.

Moss lowered his torch.

—Just bringing Riding to bed.

They whispered as he fumbled for his nightclothes and sponge bag. In the washroom he stripped off the appalling garments. His foot wasn't cut after all, but when he splashed water on his face, blood ran into the basin.

—What the hell happened? Moss said, coming in the room. If he's at it again, I'll thrash him myself.

Moss took his chin and turned his face to the torchlight:

—Little beast.

And it dawned on him that Moss had misread.

—It wasn't Halton.

—Oh, no?

—An accident.

He spat metal down the drain. Moss let out a sigh.

—Leave it under the tap, Moss advised. Bring down the swelling.

He did, as long as he could stand the ice.

—What happened, then? Moss said as he wiped his face. At bedtime Grieves said not to expect you, but now here you are half-dressed and frozen, looking like you've come from the scrum.

He made for the door, but Moss blocked the way, new suspicion in his voice:

—What did you do?

—Nothing.

—You're an incompetent liar. You know that?

A fit of coughing, stifled in his sleeve. Moss shone the torch in his face.

—It's her, isn't it?

His face responded, and Moss stared. He tried to stop smiling, but—

—God's nails, I knew it! I bloody knew it!

He *knew* it?

—I've seen her look at you, all the time, and you never look back unless you think no one's watching.

He knew from *looking*?

—It's true, isn't it?

He opened his mouth—

—Wait, Moss said. I don't want to know.

Tell, don't tell. Chamber of Death, dorm. These people needed to make up their minds.

—Can I go now?

—No.

Moss had him by the arm:

—What in hell were you thinking?

—I wasn't.

—Obviously!

Moss loosened his grip, trying to control himself:

—Did you get it from Grieves, then, what your friend Halton got?

His eyes, rebel hordes, began to sting.

—No!

—Well, Moss said, you deserve it.

—*What?*

—If Morgan were here, you'd be going to bed sore.

—What are you going to do about it, then?

The words had shot from his mouth. Moss stiffened, and he braced for a blow.

—Thirteen hours, Moss said. Thirteen hours to the carol service. Could you please, for the love of God, for the love of *Christmas*, stay out of trouble until then?

He started to cough again, and Moss took him down to the study, where Moss's case lay open.

—Finish it, he said, handing him a flask.

Fire, more and stronger than the glass, stinging even warmer, burning away the tickle in his lungs.

—Next term, Moss said, things are going to be different.

The last sip was smoothest.

—You've got seven weeks to sort yourself out, and if you don't, the

JCR will do it for you. That is, if you can make it through the night without getting yourself disposed.

✦

Jamie swung his lantern across the entryway of John's House and found John hunched at the bottom of the stairs.

—Are you quite all right? Jamie asked.

John looked startled. A candle flickered beside him, and the light looked as it used to when they were children. Jamie came closer, smelled drink, and sweat. John put his head in his hands.

He had to be as quick and as clinical as possible. John must go to his rooms, and Jamie would take charge of Riding. John must put this entirely from his mind, and later, in the holidays, when John was rested and the rankness had retreated, then Jamie would broach the subject of John's goddaughter, her welfare and how sensibly to proceed once the holidays were done and the new year arrived. Whatever wonders or horrors the world and newspapers delivered, whatever ordeals the holiday inflicted, whatever bloodlettings, quarrels, or tedium Jamie's family meted out, when they were over and the year had turned and the days had begun to lengthen, then he would sit with John, as long as was necessary, and tether him to a scheme for soundness and health.

The candle in John's glass had burned down to the nub, and when he finally looked up, sweat was trickling down his neck.

—Now, Jamie said in his lightest tone, where were we?

—Oh, John said. Never mind.

—I beg your pardon?

—It wasn't . . .

John's candle hissed and went out.

—It seems . . .

—Just tell me where Riding is.

—No! John said too loudly. I've sent him away.

—You *what*?

—To bed, to bed. It wasn't . . . as bad as all that.

Jamie bit back everything he wanted to say. John was standing now but only with the aid of the banister. Jamie put an arm around his waist, helped him to his rooms, and told him to get into bed. John muttered something, and when Jamie returned with a glass of water, John was sprawled across the blankets, dead to the world.

He feigned sleep as Jamie unfastened his collar and his shoes, but as soon as the door shut, he went to his mercy. The dropper fell and rolled away, though there couldn't be much . . . oh, more than he thought, though how much was too much in a final sense? It wasn't killing him, and even if it did . . .

 The feeling was fear, Jamie knew, not the stimulating kind, but the fear that hung around and sapped one's strength. He added a few sentences to the end of his homily and reread the draft. It wasn't his best, but they'd be too eager for the holidays to notice. His father always said Christmas homilies were a gin and tonic on a silver platter. Don't try to be original, just deliver the goods and sit down. Jamie read it one last time, removed the sentences he'd added, and dropped it in the box for Lewis to type in the morning.

The fear still lurked in the corner like a wolf. No one ever told him that he'd sit up nights afraid once he became a Headmaster. No one ever told him how irrelevant the world beyond the Wetwang road would prove to be. Whether Japan abandoned the gold standard or Parliament granted self-government to the Irish Free State, such questions were ultimately trivial, whereas in some obscure but real way, the decisions he faced, the way he used his power and his weakness, these could turn the fundamental battle, one they, each of them, could aid or oppose.

He took the lantern to the grate and covered himself in the rug Lewis used. *Come on, you. Sit here beside me. Put your teeth away, and we'll pour it out drop by drop.*

But no matter what lashes he used upon himself—how he'd handled the Audsley boy, what he'd told John that summer, his indifference to John's troubles with the Líoht woman—no counterirritant dislodged the cold facts: a boy in the Lower Sixth had been caught, by his Housemaster, in a balcony out-of-bounds, in the *chapel*, in a state of undress with a thirteen-year-old girl. It was never pleasant to expel pupils, but the thought of disposing this boy made him feel ill. Riding was one of the rare ones. He'd have a scholarship to Oxford and earn himself at least one first. The theater business, though an infuriating nuisance, had been good for him; it had loosened his joints, revealing a less defended, more generous aspect. And despite the colossal irritation of the boy—the lying, the self-righteousness, the blindness to others—it was impossible not to see to his heart, just as it was impossible not to see John's. St. Stephen's was the best place for both of them, irregular enough to accept them yet austere enough to contain them. Wherever Riding went after this, it would never quite do, as St. Stephen's had. And wherever Riding went, there would be no one the equal of John.

✦

She tried to sleep, but something was sitting on her chest. She tried the breathing trick her mother had taught her, but the something touched her temple and she was out of the room and running down the corridor to the front hall table with the candles and matches. It was dark in the courtyard, but in the cloisters there was a light, and she knew then what she had to do and why she'd been chased from her room.

✦

Jamie had never heard such a thing, but having heard it, he knew it was true. Riding had not taken advantage of her; the coercion had been entirely in the other direction. Until this moment, Jamie had considered girl children beyond his ken, but this girl sitting before him was starkly fathomable. He recognized in her the perennial temptation to stir a boy up and watch him go. The exchange of clothing, though, seemed not as he had supposed. Her aim had not been to see the boy's body but rather, in a sense, to try it on.

—I wanted to see what it was like, she said.

—What precisely?

—To be a boy.

To dress as a boy, to act as a boy, to have everything there was to have as a boy.

Jamie pulled his chair back so that her knee no longer touched him. He felt dizzy, if not physically then in a deeper way. *I know!* he longed to tell her, but he forced himself into the present: this pale girl, resolutely not what her kin supposed her to be, was confiding to him her true, undaunted self.

—What's wrong with being a girl? he asked.

—They're all unhappy, she said, and cruel.

She spit it out like a bottled accusation. The bayonet sunk home to hear it from this time traveler, except she wasn't one. Resemble Marion though she did—and now that Jamie examined her, he could see the pout of Marion's lip and the color in the same places of her cheek—this girl carried a life not only separate from his wife's, but one just now more broken.

—Tell me about your father, he said.

She buried her head in her arms, but he made her sit straight in the chair. He may or may not ever be a good father, but he could refuse to stand nonsense. He repeated his question, and she began to describe her father, his provenance, his profession, his tastes. Jamie redirected: How did her father punish her when she deserved it? She looked appalled.

—He never did!

—Your mother, then?

—I was never naughty!

Jamie snorted, meaning it as humor, but she flinched as if struck.

—But I've been so bad, she blurted, so wicked! And no one, no one knows it!

She looked as though she would cry, but she didn't. He wondered if he would instead. He'd long ago condemned Marion's parents and her whole Irish brood, but this girl testified to a more subtle barbarism. Did modern parents ruin everything they touched? Or was it only the pacifists who murdered truth on the altar of their vanity?

✦

—Headmaster to see you.

Mrs. Firth pulled back the covers and stood over him with a lamp. Gray grappled for his spectacles as she lit the candle on his bedside table. The time, she said, was quarter past six. The Headmaster expected him presently.

Fear, fire, whirlwind, all came and went before he finished washing his face. Steel water, steel truth: term ended today. Whatever the Headmaster said or did, in only eight hours the most brutal punishment would begin.

✦

Riding kept trying to suppress a cough in his sleeve. Jamie lit a second lamp to discharge his aggravation and opened the drapes so they might benefit from daylight should it ever deign to arrive.

—What's happened to your lip?

—Tripped on the ice, sir.

The room was dim, but Jamie could see well enough to know he was being lied to. This point, perhaps, was not germane, but Riding's willingness to tell the truth was. Jamie took his seat behind the desk.

—You know why you're here. Explain yourself.

—Shouldn't we wait for Mr. Grieves, sir?

Jamie hesitated, parsing the question, not long enough to give Riding the upper hand, but . . .

—Mr. Grieves will not be joining us.

Riding seemed to expect him to say more, but Jamie folded his hands and turned his stare upon the boy. Riding's bravado evaporated, and he began to speak, incoherently at first, but when Jamie didn't interrupt, he found his thread and provided an account that essentially tallied with what Jamie already knew. What irked him was the jaded voice the boy affected, as if none of it meant anything. Nerves were one thing, but this? Jamie wasn't having it, not at this hour and not from this boy, who seemed to have nothing better to do than make life difficult for John, and anyone else who came close to him.

—This is becoming a habit, isn't it, Riding?

—Sir?

—You and I being forced to discuss your conduct.

Silence.

—Just last month in this very room, if I am not mistaken.

Sullen.

—And what was the subject of that little chat?

He waited for the answer.

—The play, sir.

—Ah, yes! The play. And what did I give you for that?

Riding mumbled but admitted it.

—And earlier this year, the business with McKay's barn . . . remind me?

Technique, and more technique. Feign senility and make them say it. Riding was beginning to look uncomfortable, but he made his way through the barn debacle without contradicting Jamie's memory.

—And tell me, Riding, was your testimony about that barn entirely truthful at the time?

A cough, into his handkerchief at least.

—Not at first, sir.

—But eventually?

On his face, a chasm.

—Mostly, sir.

—I see. And your account just now?

—The truth, sir.

—Mostly?

—*Entirely*, sir!

He said it with such bitterness that Jamie knew he meant it.

—And yet here you are a third time.

Something very close to a glare. Jamie ignored it.

—It would seem our efforts with you have failed.

Pressing instead for the heart.

—Or perhaps you are simply unsuited to our ways here?

—No, sir!

As if his courage had been questioned.

—In that case, Riding, what will it take to persuade you to use the sense you were born with?

Jamie's voice had risen, and Riding's face was shifting, not to a suitable expression of shame, but to an impossible, defended self-righteousness. Jamie took a breath.

—Listen to me, Riding. Love is not a crime.

He let that sink in. Riding coughed, surprised but adamant. Love, Jamie continued, was not what the Headmaster objected to. What the Headmaster objected to was impropriety. The Headmaster objected to indiscretion. The Headmaster objected to his abject lack of common sense.

Riding did not bother to conceal his disdain. This boy was the limit! How dare he stand there with his tight silence, his stubbornness and indignation? And how had this boy, this *impossible* boy, managed to entangle himself so impossibly with John?

Jamie had sent for John before he'd sent for Riding, but Mrs. Firth had reported that John could not be woken. Jamie had gone over himself and found John breathing but otherwise dead to the world. He'd left the woman with orders to let John sleep as long as possible and to avoid bothering him with the Riding business, which Jamie promised to resolve before breakfast. Breakfast was still a ways off, but they were no closer to resolution.

—Look at me when I'm speaking to you, boy.

How long would John persist with it—this tying himself into knots over people who didn't deserve it, people who made habits of aggravating him with no care for the agony they caused? People like that woman. People like this boy, who also appeared oblivious to how much John cared for him. Jamie might not have been able to intervene with the woman, but he could here.

—But these faults are nothing, Riding, when put beside your selfishness.

Disarming, at last.

—Your callous disregard for the way your acts affect other people.

Truth dawning.

—Your Headmaster, for instance, who permitted Miss Líoht to come to the Academy. The Academy itself, still rebuilding its name.

Gaze cast to the floor.

—And finally, there is your indifference to Mr. Grieves. Have you any idea how you've compromised him?

—He doesn't care what—

—Hold your tongue!

If the boy said another word, he would strike him, hard.

—Your Housemaster has done nothing but advocate for you since the minute you came here.

Mr. Grieves had paired him with Wilberforce. Mr. Grieves had arranged the acceleration of his studies. Mr. Grieves, last March, had petitioned for him, believed in him, exposed himself for him, done everything possible for a boy who didn't deserve it.

—As for your friend Audsley and his precipitous departure—

—I had nothing to do with that, sir!

—I know you didn't! Jamie barked. But it upset Mr. Grieves terribly, and he thought you could explain something. Yet you refused him even that. How do you suppose Mr. Grieves has taken it, being disgraced this way by his own goddaughter and his favorite pupil?

A look of naked shock. At least he'd managed to tell the boy something he didn't know.

—Perhaps you'd be better off in another House.

Jamie didn't know where the idea had come from, but as soon as he said it, the boy turned red to the ears. It wasn't something Jamie had ever done, but it might actually solve the problem. Flogging the boy would do little good, and expelling him would hurt John unbearably. Yet, Jamie had no intention of allowing this boy to torment John any longer.

—Burton-Lee's perhaps.

—No, sir!

—Or Henri's.

—Please, sir!

The less the boy liked it, the more Jamie warmed to the notion. The French master, in fact, would be ideal. Henri took little interest in Sixth Formers who'd dropped French, so the boy was unlikely to get under his skin.

Jamie went to the side table. He poured a cup of coffee. He stirred in cream and sugar, returned to his desk, arranged some papers:

—I shall think on it.

—Oh . . . please, sir . . . *please* don't—

Jamie didn't look up.

—When I require your opinion, Riding, I shall ask for it.

—Yes, sir . . .

Voice breaking at last. Jamie sipped his coffee.

—When I've taken my decision, I shall write to your father. Or is it your mother?

He could see the jaw clenching.

—I think perhaps it would be best for all concerned if, when you return to us in February, you begin again in a new situation.

—Sir—

—That's all, Riding. Good day.

The boy looked as though he'd been struck. He tried to hold his breath as he strode from the room, but Jamie knew he was blubbing. Coffee set aside, brandy poured. It had taken long enough and shot Jamie's nerves in the process, but at last the arrow had found its mark.

 Toothbrush, powder, shaving brush, foam. Were razors really wise? Sting zesty, marshaling thought: Jamie, carols, parents . . . Owain! Lord help them, if the Lord indeed existed on his icy throne, and cared. Aspirin forced down with the muscles he'd been given. The timetable they'd prepared scrolled in his mind: first bell, half past seven; breakfast, quarter past eight; dorm inspection, nine; trunks downstairs, quarter past; choir rehearsal, half past? Studs, tie, hair. What time was it now? Through the window, an unfamiliar sun. Was he truly awake, or was this one of those dreams where you thought it all made sense until you realized it didn't?

He heard the hall clock but lost track of the chimes. Its face, when he arrived, claimed a minute after ten. First train presently, but now, even now, while Kardleigh was rehearsing . . . Tower, desk, key, what regiments! Five vials amongst them wore his colors. Which of you shall we say doth love us most? Hail, friend! And hail, thou friend-in-waiting. You others, holy three, stay until we meet again. Farewell, farewell, one kiss and I'll descend.

◆

Uncle John was not at breakfast and neither was the one she didn't know how to name. She chewed the toast as her thumb rubbed the place that stung beneath her knee socks, chaffing it more sore. The sting relieved nothing, not now and not last night when she'd taken back the tool of her restitution. She found it in his desk amidst other objects she could only assume had been confiscated. Each score bit, but none stopped the iron that stretched her ribs from the inside and the out.

Once, across the Channel, she had etched things onto paper and sent them to that faraway pigeonhole. Her paper now was white, and what she had to write deserved blood, not ink: bargains, green fairies, watchmen, princes; cold air, lemons, what she'd done again just now. There was more she could have said, but the pen ran out. In the morning she couldn't bear to read it, but only to fold it, thrice times three, and take it with the blue stack to their chair loft—she vowed always to think of it so and never to let what happened spoil what it was to her heart. Under the floorboards she buried them again, the old with her new. She hadn't watched when they closed the lid on her mother. It had been open and she had been in it, and then it was closed and only a box. Now she fit the board back in place and knocked it down with her heel.

◆

The clock had just tolled ten, and now it was going eleven. From the library window Gray could see the throng in the quad, his mother cer-

466

tainly amongst them. He'd refilled his pen twice, and his hand cramped. Only a few more lines, a paragraph at most . . .

✦

John caught the Headmaster's eye:
—A word!
—Feeling better?
—Perfectly—
—Mrs. Briggstone-Egge, Jamie cried. Good morning! How is the Major?
Minutes passed before John could pull him aside:
—I'm expecting Mrs. Riding today.
—I've seen him already.
—*What?*
Jamie removed John's hand from his elbow:
—It's been dealt with. Please don't worry. Ah, Fletcher! Is this your father? Canon, an honor.

✦

She showed her father the painting of the boat that hung in the hallway. She suggested it might be famous, and as he examined it, she dropped the note in his pigeonhole. *Look in our place*.

✦

He signed his name and closed the cover on Valarious. It wasn't perfect, parts of it weren't even good, but it was finished. He might have failed to win back her letters; he might have blubbed before Dr. Sebastian; he might even be banished from the House, but he had kept one promise, at least.
Everyone was filing into the chapel. He locked the library door and slipped back to the House. Corridor empty, her room empty. There was her hairbrush, her wireless, her dressing gown. He swapped his fountain pen for hers and left the book on her pillow.
Crighton hailed him in the corridor:
—Where the hell have you been? You missed inspection, and your mater's here.

She stood by the fire in the empty houseroom.

—Darling!

He went to her, and she wrapped her arms around him, his arms above, like embracing his own child.

—What on earth happened to your lip, darling?

Again, he blamed the ice. She adjusted his tie and gave her nurse's smile.

—It has been wretched, hasn't it?

He offered his arm and led her to the chapel, glad for its darkness. His face betrayed nothing, he hoped, but inside a sick weakness spread. She knew nothing, pressed for nothing, yet her touch, her smell, the pitch of her voice all kicked aside his bricks like toys.

She admired the pew candles and the greenery, praised the prefects and the boys she had met. He should never have let her come. With every observation, she penetrated further the fortress that was his, until the hour removed its mask: not a festive visit but hazard, reckless and fatal.

The Turtle began to sing from the back, and light spread up the pews, candle to candle, showing faces where there had been only forms. There near the front, the girl sat with a short and ruddy figure who daubed his eyes with a handkerchief and held her tight beside him. Her father, plainly.

The choir continued in parts, processing up the aisle.

—That poor boy! his mother whispered.

The Turtle was going past, his purple eye set off against his red robe and white surplice. Gray murmured something about football, and his mother shook her head with the kind of happy disapproval she displayed when discussing her Unfortunates.

Christian children all must be
Mild, obedient, good as he

He hated this song, so cloying and didactic, but at least it made a change from people telling him he was a terrible liar.

✦

The crowd adjourned through the smoke of extinguished candles and drifted to the refectory for the Christmas tea. Everywhere John looked was too bright. The light glared off the ice, and their usual palette of black and gray was littered with frocks, hats, and handkerchiefs in every possible color. He'd been obliged to sit with the Common Room, but who could miss Owain's lusty singing and his daughter's averted gaze? Now as John scanned the refectory, he couldn't see either one of them.

—There he is, darling.

He turned towards the voice. A woman extended a gloved hand:

—Crusoe.

A clumsy hesitation, and then his mind caught up. He took her hand, gave a slight bow:

—Mrs. Riding, my pleasure at last.

He saw in her eyes that he'd cut her, but she continued as if he hadn't. Her son had shown her the classrooms. He promised to show her the gymnasium after tea.

—I was certain he was trying to keep me from you, but he's been foiled now, hasn't he?

He suspected she was teasing, but the boy scowled beside her, drawing a hand across his mouth as if to hide a sneer.

—You must tell me everything, Mr. Grieves.

She called him that deliberately, whether in retaliation against his calling her Mrs. Riding or to erase the unseemliness of her initial greeting, he couldn't say. This new address felt strained, yet also somehow wanton.

—The boy is impossible, as you know.

She tucked her arm through her son's.

—I do hope you'll be candid and tell me about these plays of his.

She smiled, and the boy looked away. Jamie had dealt with him? *How?*

—John, man!

Owain burst into the refectory, girl in tow. Several people turned to see the commotion. John needed a dose, but he was being clapped on the back and drowned in Irish chatter, and then Owain was introducing himself to Mrs. Riding and her son, and a ray of sunshine was glinting off the silver. The room was too hot, too close.

—Excuse me, sir?

Another? Moss, into focus beside him:

—Sorry, sir, but Halton and his father are waiting in your study.

—*Now?*

—As you asked, sir.

It was suicide to leave this lot together.

—They're catching the early train, sir.

On the other hand, if he stayed, he might faint.

✦

Grieves considered him dead. The man hadn't even concealed his disgust at meeting his mother. By contrast, the girl's father chattered away, flattering his mother with what Gray supposed to be Irish charm. Gray could tell she found him overdone, but when he revealed that his daughter had been staying at the school, his mother launched into an animated interview. The girl refused to meet anyone's eye. Did she loathe him, too, or did she simply find him mortifying? Would he ever again see those eye teeth or hear her say *Follow me*?

—Riding!

Moss summoned him, and he went, not knowing if it was a mercy or folly to leave the girl alone with his mother. Drawing him into the nearest washroom, Moss revealed an envelope:

—From the Head.

Mrs. T. Riding. By hand. On the back, a glob of wax.

—See she gets it, won't you?

The sick was spreading everywhere.

—Well, *put it away*, Moss said.

He fumbled with his coattails. Moss lingered, turning off a dripping tap:

—I heard about Audsley, *Hamlet* and all that.

The envelope stuck going into his pocket.

—Might go down and see it in the New Year. You?

There was simply nothing to say. Moss gave him a slug:

—Cheer up, Riding. It's Christmas.

✦

—What do you have to say to your father?

His tongue stuck in his mouth, dry as the bush. Mr. Grieves pressed his shoulder:

—Go on.

His mouth spoke as though only learning how, and when it stalled, Mr. Grieves supplied a phrase, until it seemed the outline was covered.

470

—I see, his father said.

He couldn't look any higher than their knees. His father's voice had edge, vague and chancy, as when having things explained to him by African overseers or English housekeepers.

—He's been punished, Mr. Grieves said, by me, and I'm convinced the lesson has been learnt.

—His blushes agree with you, sir, his father said.

—I think you'll see an improvement in his term reports as well.

Grieves let go of his shoulder and handed his father a drink.

—He comes from perfectly good stock, his father was saying, but he's lazy. Isn't that right, boy?

A thwack on his back made his teeth slice his tongue.

—Enough mollycoddling and running wild like heathen, I said to his mother—

—Excuse me, John—

Kardleigh was coming in.

—Moss said I might find you here. Ah, you must be Timothy's father?

Kardleigh was shaking his father's hand and accepting a drink from Grieves.

—That third descant was his own composition.

Ruffling his hair, which he'd labored that morning to shape.

—He kept it a secret, but we have our sources, do we not, Timothy?

—Not bad, this choir of yours, his father said. Not St. Paul's, but—

—And this must be Mrs. Halton!

The door opened farther and they slipped in from the corridor.

—And Miss Halton?

—Not a *bad* service, his father was saying, but whatever possessed you to end with "Little Town of Bethlehem"?

Kardleigh was taking his mother by the arm:

—Are the musical gifts your side of the family, madam?

He glanced to Grieves in vain appeal, but his Housemaster was busy at the mantel.

—Everyone knows you end with "Hark the Herald," his father insisted.

Like a flame, his sister's hand on his wrist:

—You wrote that all on your own, Timmy?

His face laid him bare, and his traitorous eyes.

—It was good, she said. Beautiful and good.

In the toilet stall, he broke the seal. The school crest pressed into the page, speaking for St. Stephen's entire. *My dear Mrs. Riding, It pains me to write this.* He scanned the rest, brief but plain. It omitted nothing—barn, play, loft above the chapel—and proclaimed the Headmaster's sentence, exile to an alien House. He crushed it away without suffering the end. *Eyes, to your posts.* His mother was waiting.

As the call came for the last train, the refectory disgorged its crowd, full of hope and even joy, calling farewells and Happy Christmases. His mother waved to him across the cloisters, and he forced a smile as deep as any lie he'd told.

—Riding!

God! How many—*Pearce* now pushing against the tide:

—Where have you been? Lucky I caught you.

Pearce's hat was askew. He was holding an envelope.

—You dropped this.

Another? This one bore his name.

—Someone found it, Pearce said.

Surname only, but he knew her hand, would know it always.

—Mind yourself, won't you?

This day was making him delirious, so much it seemed that Pearce's face contained a shadow of—

—Happy Christmas, Riding.

◆

Two fresh vials clinked in his pockets, but there hadn't been a moment even to step into an alcove. Now he'd seen off the last cab. The grass beyond the gates held only a few motorcars. He'd lost track of who had gone and who remained, but he'd got through his appointed chats without disaster. The interview with Halton's father had gone better than expected. The parents were awful, of course, but in the sway of Kardleigh's flattery, they softened; why the boy should have left in barely suppressed tears, John couldn't fathom.

—There you are, Mr. Grieves.

This chat wasn't on his list. The worst ones never were. He held the door for Nurse Riding, and she came into the House with her son.

—Do you have a moment to spare us?

Her sapphire eyes pricked him. Her son gazed at the clock.

—Won't you come across to the study? he said.

This was going to be unpleasant.

—Ah, she said, the inner sanctum!

He gestured to the settee. Would it be too much to offer her a drink? She joined him at the fireplace, but Riding slouched by the door. It was obvious he'd been dealt with, and now his mother was perching on the settee awaiting an explanation John was helpless to give. Her gaze roamed as if touching every object and then landed on John before flitting away again. She looked more like her son than John remembered. She wore blue instead of black, and her voice was higher than he'd imagined from her handwriting, more light and girlish, a voice he would have considered flighty if he hadn't known its mind.

✦

Grieves couldn't even bring himself to speak to his mother—that was how much he despised him. Silently, the man held out a glass. She took it, but didn't drink. How long would they all stand there, helpless and held in? Grieves put a piece of coal on the fire. His mother picked something invisible off her frock.

—Excuse me, sir! Fletcher cried, bursting in without knocking. Is Kardleigh here?

Was this what they called being put out of your misery?

—He isn't.

—It's Mrs. Sebastian, Fletcher reported breathlessly. She and the Head were in our houseroom, talking to my pater, and Mrs. Sebastian up and fainted!

If this didn't end soon, Mrs. Sebastian wouldn't be the only one.

—Is she hurt?

—I don't think so, sir, but—

Grieves told him to try Lockett-Egan's, and Fletcher dashed away. Mercifully, his mother got up:

—We really must be off.

Opened her handbag, removed a parcel.

—I hope you won't mind, she said, offering it to Grieves.

The man accepted it gingerly, as if it might bite.

—A small thank-you for all you've done.

Gray retreated from the room and his movement drew her with him,

473

out of the House, across the quad, through the gates to a verge of rucked-up grass, where she approached a motorcar that had his trunk inside. When he opened the door, the smell hit him like a fist—leather, antiseptic, his father's car displaced from home. When he asked where they were going, she said not far. He turned his face to the window. The sun had fallen behind the ridge. The Head's letter crackled beneath him in his tails.

Grieves hadn't said goodbye and neither had the girl whose fountain pen pressed his leg. They hadn't even looked at him. He was poison. Worse.

She stopped across from the post office in Sledmere.

—What's wrong?

—We're there.

He followed her to a cottage, watched her produce keys, open the door, light a candle inside.

—It's cozy enough with the fire going, she said.

A cruel joke? Or punishment? Christmas here, where his father was buried, that place they'd gone once and never again.

He began to cough and was sick, and then they both knew how to behave. She said it would all seem better in the morning. She'd brought the bicycle up and some lovely new books.

Back at the Academy, Kardleigh would be tending to Mrs. Sebastian. The girl and her father would be sitting by the fire, talking with Mr. Grieves, loved by Mr. Grieves. The studies would be empty, his still marked by Guilford's stencils, its window seat empty and abandoned. The pigeonholes of the House would forget his name, forget their sacred office, forget they ever held for him pieces of a heart.

CHRISTMAS

Could time not pause even briefly, stop the earth's whirl and the graying of his hair, the factories, the mines, the omnibuses and trains, hold all his errors in a cellar until he could work out what to do with them, or until they didn't matter anymore? Could grace, which none earned and none commanded, not fall one time on him?

The courtyard outside John's House had the dejected look of a theater after the audience had left, but at least Marion had come round, or such was the word when John arrived at Burton's House. Kardleigh was examining her in the parlor while Jamie and Burton paced the study. When John tried to ask what had happened, Burton silenced him with a look. He collapsed into a chair, but beneath the exhaustion, John felt a certain eager excitement. If she died or was dying, it would be awful, but on the other side Jamie could start fresh. He'd be a widower, of course, not a bachelor, but after a few years, would there be such a difference?

—Headmaster?

Kardleigh was at the parlor door, beckoning Jamie as if to the Colosseum. Burton mentioned going to check with his matron, and John realized they were leaving Jamie to it.

He drifted back to his House ashamed of his thoughts. Darkness had fallen as swiftly as a guillotine, and although the air was warmer, the ice still tried to trip him flat. Inside, a lamp stood sentinel on the table, and more light spilled from the houseroom, and voices.

—John, my boy!

Owain sprang from his seat beside the fire and assaulted John with claps to his person and exclamations of praise for the carol service. He'd clearly found the punch bowl and achieved a state of merriment. His daughter had been showing him her lessons, he said, and they were nothing short of enchanting. The girl herself huddled by the fire until her father brought her to his side, at which point she hid her face as he called her angel child. John asked about the journey, a deflection that inspired Owain to narrate multiple delays along the line, not to mention his acquaintance with the pair of Irish brothers—Jesuits but not bad ones—who shared the carriage from Peterborough.

—Could talk of anything and everything, and did!

The girl looked flushed, and when John felt her brow, it was warm. True, she'd been sitting by the fire, but it was possible, even likely given the past twenty-four hours, that her fever had returned. She belonged in bed with soup brought to her later.

—Christmas at Lindisfarne, now there's a place!

It occurred to John that Owain would be spending the night. They'd never discussed arrangements, but of course Owain would have to stay, presumably until John was ready to leave with them for the holidays. He'd have to be fed, entertained, endured, and without electricity, proper heat, or kitchens.

—Now, Owain said, throwing a heavy arm around his shoulder, about this business.

The girl stared resolutely out the window. John drew Owain into the corridor and cast about for how to begin:

—I . . . that is . . .

Owain grinned:

—Young love! Never forget your first, now do you?

The man gabbled with pride and delight: she had told him everything (everything?), and he'd a notion John would be taking it to heart, but he mustn't because it was a dear thing, and the young were foolhardy but where would the world be without them? As for the young pup, a fair lad if bashful, and something of a poet, by the dear saints.

—Now, John . . .

Owain turned somber, or turned on the somber performance:

—It's been gnawing, it has.

—Yes? John was forced to ask.

—I know you Friends don't go in for the sacraments, but that doesn't mean they're wrong, now does it?

John agreed that it didn't, that they weren't. Owain had included him in *you Friends*, but it struck him like a drowning wave that he didn't see himself as one of them, and hadn't for some time.

—I'm sure as can be that her mother wouldn't mind if she could see the state we're in.

—Mind?

—Having her confirmed. What d'you think I've been saying, man?

John had no idea what Owain had been saying, and in any case, he found the man's scruples forced seeing that Owain was the one who'd insisted on having Cordelia baptized a fortnight after she was born; nevertheless, having confessed his current aim, Owain abandoned the conniving charm and relaxed into a state of ease. John gathered that they'd come to an agreement, though the how, when, and where of it seemed immaterial. John edged back into the houseroom, hoping to leave Owain by the fire while he broke the news to Mrs. Firth that they'd have another guest for tea and for the night, but Owain seemed to have fixed upon the idea of visiting *the local*, for comfort and a meal, all three of them. It would be his treat, he wouldn't hear of John's paying and he wouldn't hear—something banged in the corridor, startling Owain:

—Ho!

John went to see.

—Jamie! What's—

Jamie seemed almost to stagger towards him, swinging a lantern. John took it from him, led him into the houseroom, and made him sit down.

—Is she . . . ?

Jamie's eyes opened wide:

—She's pregnant.

John inhaled but could do no more.

—I'm going to be a father.

With that, the Headmaster burst into tears. John froze with shame, but then Owain began weeping, too, loud and fruity, and Jamie's head fell into the hollow of John's shoulder, pressing against him and shuddering.

—Oh, now! Owain cried.

Unlike Owain's display, Jamie's tears were silent, seeping through John's shirt as if they might through holy orders dissolve whatever they touched. Owain clapped each of them on the back, and John managed the words *study, mantel, brandy,* sending Owain away in a flurry as Jamie gripped his arm.

They were going to have a child. Children sealed a marriage. Children made the future. Yet here was Jamie, clinging as if John were his raft, his tears on John's wrist, his head falling to John's lap, John's hand on the back of Jamie's neck, feeling its heat and the oil from his hair.

—Now! Owain announced, setting down the tray. It's a miracle!

Jamie inhaled sharply and sat up:

—I'm sorry.

Owain handed him a glass.

—I never thought, Jamie stammered.

—Sláinte!

John echoed the toast, and in relief they drank.

—May we see you gray and combing your grandchildren's hair! Owain cried.

They drank again, and a mournful dismay came over John, that Jamie's tears, the first he'd seen since they were boys, had passed and might never return.

—May misfortune follow you the rest of your life . . . and never catch up!

Owain refilled their glasses and called a fourth toast:

—May peace and plenty be the first to lift the latch on your door, and happiness be guided to you by the candle of Christmas!

—You must be Owain, Jamie said.

John tried to rescue the introduction, but Owain raised Jamie to his feet and embraced him as a long-lost relation.

—After all these years! Owain cried.

The girl regarded them from across the room as one peering into a sewer. John set down his glass as memory of the previous night crashed over him. Had he looked anything as mawkish and torrid as this father?

Owain was orating on the blessing of children, and Jamie was beaming and inviting them to supper, overcoming John's objections and even Owain's thoughts of a pub, and before John could collect himself, Jamie had left, Cordelia had vanished, and Owain had collapsed in an armchair and begun to snore.

✦

Her father made a fuss over Mrs. Sebastian, and Mrs. Sebastian liked it more than she should have, given that she was married to the Headmaster and having his baby. Cordelia had never had a long conversation with Mrs. Sebastian, and now she was glad of it. The woman was just the sort to lap up her father's nonsense. Mrs. Riding had not lapped it up. She'd been kind to him but kept a certain distance, as if he were a patient she felt it necessary to humor. Mrs. Sebastian could perhaps be called pretty, but Mrs. Riding was beautiful. Mrs. Riding wore a light scent, like summer in a woodsy glen. She felt sure Mrs. Riding had never been ill a day in her life.

When her father took Mrs. Sebastian's arm for dinner, the Headmaster offered his own:

—Miss Líoht?

He was going to be a father. Soon he'd have no use for other people's children.

—What is it? he asked.

She threaded her arm through his, and they stood alone in the parlor. The words she'd put beneath the chair loft floor rose as if to choke her. He took hold of her chin and narrowed his eyes:

—None of that. It's Christmas.

◆

Marion presided at the table with thinly veiled triumph. Before the meal, John had tried to find out from Jamie what had happened with Riding, but no sooner had they stepped into the corridor—only long enough for Jamie to say what he hadn't done: *I didn't flog him if that's what you're asking, and I didn't dispose him either*—than Marion pounced, wrapping her arm around Jamie's and insisting that he was needed and that surely business could be suspended on this night of all nights.

Talk at the table quickly turned to Christmas, exposing John's lack of planning and leaving him defenseless against Owain's juggernaut.

—We'll go home tomorrow, Owain said to Marion as if it were her concern. The place is temporary, but three bedrooms.

He was speaking of Cambridge, where he'd found a leased flat. He'd told the agent it must have three bedrooms, insisted upon it. One bedroom looked out to the back garden—*for you, angel child*—and another had a cozy nook for a reading chair.

John protested. He couldn't possibly leave in the morning. Mountains of work, term reports, Housemaster's reports . . .

—Oh, now, Owain said, I'll take the child and you follow when it pleases.

He really could not stand the way Owain called her *the child*.

—John can come down with us, Jamie inserted.

They were stopping some days in Oxford—

—My people's place, Marion said to Owain.

They'd carry on to Wilshire for Christmas Eve. The three of them must come to the Rectory in the New Year.

—Oh, now! Owain rejoiced.

Even Cordelia perked up at the suggestion. Obviously, they would do no such thing, but John thought this not the time to discuss it.

◆

Calendars made everything terrifyingly concrete. There was one on Jamie's desk that extended into next year, and it demarcated the finite stretch of days before he would become something other than himself, something other than Headmaster, son, husband. At first, in that window when all restraint failed him, he'd thought John understood the scope of it. Now he wasn't sure. At supper that evening, John had resembled a wraith floating above the sod of life, and last night, Jamie had come by John's study in the hopes of discussing it, only to find John in the grips of procrastination, the room thick with cigarette smoke, John's desk littered with papers and remnants of food. More alarming, he found John had not even begun his term reports but was still marking classwork. Jamie felt a jaw was in order. It was Sunday night, he declared; everything would be posted Tuesday, and the other Housemasters couldn't complete their Housemaster's letters until John had sent them the History reports for their boys—

—I know!

The classwork, surely, could be considered later.

—You *know* these boys, Jamie said. Just write the blasted reports and be done.

But John, rather than be soothed by the suggestion, launched into a tortured and torturous monologue: perhaps he had overdone it assigning compositions that term, but it had done the boys good, Jamie had no notion, and their efforts deserved John's fullest attention. Jamie by necessity saw the school from above, like a soaring eagle, but it fell to foot soldiers such as John to cultivate them day by day, to contend with each mind, and to develop now a detailed critique for each boy so they'd have a launching point for next term. He continued in a flurry of mixed metaphors until Jamie managed to interrupt: Reports for the other Houses would be completed no later than noon on the morrow. The other Housemasters were waiting and would wait no longer.

He left without broaching what he'd come for, but even though his request felt urgent, he knew it could keep until the holidays. John would say yes; who refused the honor of godparent? In the new year he'd have new time, to achieve entente—with Marion, his father, and John—and to exert himself with this girl who had come to him in the night. She'd sought something from him that John could not provide; Jamie hadn't provided it either, but that didn't mean he had to let her down entirely.

✦

Henri stopped by Monday evening, and John, having finished with History and now facing the Matterhorn of Housemaster's letters, greeted him warmly and offered him a drink. Henri declined and announced he'd come in search of two missing History reports. John riffled through the piles and by some miracle found them. Rather than thank him, Henri frowned like a prefect with something unpleasant to impart:

—Is there anything particular I ought to know?
—About what? John said.
—About Riding.

✦

Marion was asleep, so Jamie ushered John through to the study.
—How could you? How bloody could you!
John looked crazed. Not as bad as the other night, but still. When Jamie asked lightly what was the matter, John began to splutter. Jamie's heart beat as it always did when he knew he had it coming:
—I didn't tell you?
—Don't try that! John said. Don't you dare.
—Oh, very well. I did mean to tell you, but you've been so very—
—*What?*
A vein was pulsing in John's throat, and Jamie felt that no one

483

cared for John quite as he did, and that no one could see what he saw, the luster around John like frozen breath.

—You've been through so much this term, Jamie said. I didn't want to—

—What do you call removing a boy from my House and leaving me to hear it from Henri?

—A mistake.

John absorbed the apology, but it didn't calm him.

—How am I to explain to Riding's mother why I said nothing to her?

—She received my letter at the tea.

—*What?*

Jamie touched John's elbow, feeling the wool's scars, the darning that had kept that pullover together since Marlborough:

—I thought it would be best for everyone.

John wrenched away.

—Don't be this way, Jamie pleaded. I can't bear it.

—*You* can't bear it?

—You *know* how much we've wanted a child. And you know perfectly well I'll never be able to get along without you.

—But that's nothing to do with—

—Can't you be happy for it? Or at least for me?

John was seized by sneezes, and his eyes were running. Jamie watched his body have its way with him, but as the sneezing abated and John blew his nose, Jamie wished they could stay there—this pullover, this Advent—forever before the turn of the year.

◆

A god-awful hammering, and John jolted upright at his desk, neck cramped, arm tingling. His fingers righted the vial. He didn't remember finishing it, but could it have spilled? Drapes glowed, clock claimed morning, letters lay unfinished on the blotter. An almighty crash in the corridor. He emerged to find Fardley, hurling oaths at a collapsed . . . wall?

—What on earth? John croaked.

The dust was clearing. It wasn't a wall, but—

—New one January, Fardley declared. This'n cleared today.

The pigeonholes. John remembered that they were to be replaced before they fell again on some boy and killed him. He tried to inquire *why now?*, but Fardley honked about some papers in a basket, and then the front door opened with a gust of December.

—There you are!

And with Jamie, too, speaking louder than necessary.

—Cab in ten minutes. Where're your things?

John began to gabble. He hadn't packed, and his letters—

—Oh, don't! Jamie admonished.

Before John could assert himself, Jamie had dragged him to his rooms and was throwing things carelessly into a case.

—You can finish later, Jamie said of the letters, and post them on.

—Don't crush that!

—If you ever try this nonsense again, I'll—

—What?

Jamie smiled, golden, golden . . .

—You, he said, are impossible. Thoroughly, brilliantly impossible.

✦

Marion clung to Jamie on the train. She looked at moments like a child unwilling to give up its bear and at others like a mistress of the hounds who did not trust this dog's untethered conduct. When Jamie stood to get something down from his case, her hand lingered on the crease of his trousers until it could possess his elbow again.

Everything was too bright and too loud. John was sure he felt just as queasy as Marion, though he did not demand windows be opened and then closed for him, or that Jamie dash down the passage with him so he could be sick between the carriages. The tragedy of it all seemed to squeeze the place around his heart—that Jamie should have made himself one flesh with such an invalid. He closed his eyes and tried to pass out, if only to escape their insufferably shallow conversation.

Owain and Cordelia would meet him in Cambridge, his own people to take him home. It wouldn't be the home he knew, but there would be three bedrooms, one for him, one for Cordelia, one for . . .

What if life was on the edge of revolution, and against all reason she was waiting, kept secret by the other two as the most sensational Christmas present? *Ah, now, here's a thing* . . . and there she would be, her hair twisted on her head as she'd worn it when they met, reduced perhaps but breathing, having only been away, having only got lost, and even if it didn't seem so, the year had turned, the time had turned, and he wouldn't even wish for her to run away with him, he wouldn't think of her kiss or look for another, he would be elated to the point of breaking simply to be the member of the family he had always been, never realizing how good it was, how many gifts had snowed down on him, but now, when they took him home and showed him their surprise, he would fall on his face and worship the one who had given him this second chance, the last chance, the chance where he could get it right—even at the last minute, you could write the answer down and turn your exam to treasure from loss—and if he had that chance, what other chances could he not find and take? He'd got it right with Halton; could he not turn the corner with Riding somehow? Then Morgan would come, perhaps even come *back*, and he could say, *See? See!* and Morgan would grin, and they would know how precious their work had always been, and he could show Morgan everything he had learned, and even if Jamie cleaved to this creature who was unwrapping a peppermint and sucking it like a child with its thumb, even then he could stand it because of what they'd had before, and even though he couldn't go back and change the things he'd done, he could be as he was in the dream last night, a passenger in a motorcar, watching the streets of London full of color and beauty, as the man beside him steered through traffic to the white walls where they were going; if he had been driving, he'd have feared the narrow streets, but the man was driving as one who knew the map like his own creation—

—Here's Peterborough, Jamie said.

—Is this where John leaves us? Marion replied.

There was an obnoxiously cheerful note to her voice. John's back and arms ached, and putting on his overcoat showed how feeble he'd become. When the train slowed, he fell into Marion's lap, and her head slammed against his lip. She yelped, and he apologized even though his mouth was the injured party, and Jamie pulled him into the passage where steam clouded the windows, and Jamie's hand was at his chest, slipping a card into his breast pocket and resting there.

—Telephone, won't you?

John could smell him to taste. Jamie tapped his chest where the card now lay:

—This evening, so we know you arrived?

His feet were on the platform, and the whistle blew. Soot bit the back

486

of his throat, the train ripped away with its jesses, shards began to wet his face, and things that looked like people moved around him.

He'd seen her dead himself. When he'd touched her body, it was cold and firm, the wrong color, but real. There were no rehearsals, no second chances. Time flowed one way, and it never ever turned.

 The recent past flavored his dreams. His mother consigned him to bed until the fever diminished, but the rest of him wandered like Odysseus . . . Euboea, Libya, Trebizond . . . Church bells recalled him to the chill room, the oddly lumped bed . . . Xanadu, Leningrad, Buenos Aires, Guam . . . the strong-smelling plasters she laid across his chest . . . Lasswade, Darwin, Ceylon, Marrakech . . . *my dear Mrs. Riding* . . . Ogygia, Ismaros . . . *I regret the necessity* . . . Lichtenstein, Thrace . . . she made him drink broth and then brandy with hot water . . . Orinoco, Amazon, Volga, Ouse . . . his mouth hit the frame and the floor came up . . . Budapest, Cyprus . . . lemon in her mouth . . . Los Angeles, Peking, Tristan da Cunha . . . *how do you suppose Mr. Grieves has taken it?* . . . his mouth throbbed but when he touched it there was nothing . . . Witchell's Gate, Sledmere, Ithaca, Nostos . . .

✦

Trains were good at going back where they'd started. From York he had issued, to York he returned. He was hot and cold and his nose was running, but Micklegate Bar took him in like a woman. Lamps were light and the sky was dark and still he was a person who remembered his way. Snicket, stairs, cave beneath the street, the one-eyed doctor asked his need. Rule of hell: say it yourself. Cot, ticket, price. He could have charged anything! But that was the way these things became real, a price like a price you could find in a shop, coins you used for stationery, air that smelled of chicken. The man was missing teeth. He tied his arm with a strap and rubbed iodine in his elbow. A flea crossed the pillow. Like an aid post, but quieter.

✦

Breakfast, his mother always said, should be the best meal of the day. She had every nurse's excuse for frying up a nauseous mixture of eggs, fish, and last night's vegetables. She plainly thought him neglected at school, and the more he tried to convince her of the contrary—that he was in fact controlled and interfered with beyond human endurance— the more she undertook to restore him. He felt he'd reached the age where nothing in the holidays ought be compulsory; to have to eat in the manner she expected was enough to drive him back to bed if not for the fact that he was desperate to get up.

She'd let him get dressed, so that was something. The things she'd brought from home didn't fit, so he had to resort to pieces of his uniform. His Sunday clothes had vanished, but he found the tailcoat hanging in the airing cupboard. He felt the tails, and then the other pockets. Panic broadside—he mastered it. He must have put the Head's item in his trouser pockets instead, but the tailcoat hung alone, and the bedroom cupboard was bare. Bedside table, only a vase with holly sprigs, but ahoy, avast! Bureau tray, Captain! Fountain pen (hers), clean handkerchief (his), envelope! *Riding?* Memory a wave, Pearce acting as though he had dropped it, his name in her script but no time to open. Now, he popped the seal on a page from an exercise book. *Seven Ferry Path, Cambridge.*

He unearthed the book for his holiday task. You alphas and epsilons, guard this with your lives, these *e*'s, these *r*'s, fold the page like—Hark! On the back, *Look in your pigeonhole.*

—Found your things, have you?

His mother stood in the door and gave him a clinical look. He put the book in his trunk. He didn't know where to stand.

—Would you go across the street for me and fetch the milk? she said.

He found his coat and fled. The cold outside made him cough, and so did the air in the shop, thick with the cigarettes the postmistress was smoking. She knew who he was even though they'd never met. She was glad to see him about, she said. He looked peaked, but that was it for you. He managed interjections as his mind raced. Head's item, missing or delivered? *Look in your pigeonhole?*

✦

He awoke under a foul rug. Above him, the one-eyed man, like a cyclops but smaller. The man was touching his head . . . something at his mouth . . . back of the ambulance smell . . .

—The fresh air suits you, she said.

He was making an effort with the breakfast.

—Can I take the bicycle out today?

—If that temperature stays down, and if you eat—

He stuffed toast into his mouth.

—properly, she scolded. Then tomorrow, we'll see.

The Academy was only a few miles away. He and Morgan had run it in the rain. He'd no idea whether anyone would be there, but surely he could find a way inside? And surely, surely, the pigeons still guarded . . . ?

✦

Sharps. Tights. Poppy drops. The one-eyed man spoke a language of childhood in which everything sounded benign. *Fastest through sharps. Never sharps without tights. Only one sleep a day, but come back again.* Ticket, price, poppy drops. He thought they should be small and red, nestled in a Christmas stocking. *Poppy drops see you through, take before need, everything smooth.* Door, stair, street, day! Why could his eyes not be reduced to one? Thunder, Harpies, cast onto the platform without a log to hold. Ye shivering carriage, ye Sledmere ye Fimber, cab to the gates of what hell he knew.

Aren't you being a teensy bit overdramatic, darling? He could hear her now, jollying him through the first morning of holidays; he'd think he had influenza, but once she'd gone through two pots of tea with him, it would turn out to be only fatigue. The gates were chained, no soul to be hailed, but the cab had disappeared and wind knifed across the Commons. If everything was hell, then he supposed that nothing was. This stranding, though disagreeable, was not the final word. He could scale the gates or go around.

Grass in flood, shoes ruined, but lo, his window latch had not yet been mended. Three thwacks, heigh presto, welcome to his cave. All right, not cave, but could everyone agree there would be no studying today? No coal for the grate, but—tactician!—pigeonholes, ex-pigeonholes, piled in the corridor. Man makes fire before savage Laestrygonians. Wine in cups of gold, poured out before the hearth, sláinte! So sang the bard illustrious, sing of the past and its luscious pastness. He was captive'd on this island, no logs in the fire to show the one who waited, fending off

489

suitors, and weaving. *Romantic stuff, darling.* But nonsense, of course. That was the problem with life: it was never as beautiful or well-wrought as art. And even if it reached perfection at the Last Day, a fat lot of good it did at Christmastime in their year. He had poppy drops, but even though they stopped the torture, to be brutally honest—when was honesty not brutal?—they did nothing to take him to a better meanwhile. He didn't want to *feel* better, he wanted things to *be* better. Feeling better had ground him to powder because every morning he woke up and knew the better wasn't so; instead, the hollow man, the shame, the fraud of him was so. Every morning it was harder to stand, and this morning in the cave had been so harrowing, though he'd pretended it wasn't, that he wasn't sure he could stand up again. He was bored, more bored than he could remember ever being, and satisfying as it was to turn pigeonholes into heat, the varnish was giving off an odor, though if he died from poison gas in his own study, it would be nothing if not humorous! Nevertheless, *Fainting Fannie,* he cracked the windows and cast about for other fuel, such as boxes in his cupboard full of papers obsolete. The boys they concerned were men, their foolscap and cotton rag such food for fire! More! More and more. Was this the allure of arson? Each a blaze, bright freedom, all too soon to ash.

More food from the cupboard, from the box he dragged across the floor, the pages he used to called manuscript. *A History of Disease; or, The Disease of History.* Fatuous was the only word for such a title. He fed a page to the maw and the maw despised it not. Each leaf he perused begged also for its end. The world was getting better leaf by leaf! Hot work, thirsty work, cups of gold in crystal cut, do this in remembrance . . .

God, was he really as maudlin as he seemed? *Stop larking about,* he'd told Jamie, but ought he not cast the beam from his own eye? *You, yes you, stop moping like a boy who's never known grief. Your mother died when you were small? Welcome to the human race. The girl you loved chose another? How long have you spent pretending otherwise? The war didn't get you and the flu didn't get you and even the one-eyed man didn't get you, yet here you are choking on self-pity? Read a book. Your shelves are heaving. Pick up a newspaper, and if you're too bored by the world, at least have the decency to pretend for form's sake.*

The paper hadn't come in days, of course, but there on the table was the basket Fardley honked about, things left behind in the pigeonholes. There was a magazine, *Man and His Clothes.* There were others, *Shoot-*

ing Times, *Yachting Monthly*, *The Cricketer*. There were letters, not to be opened—though it would certainly provide a few minutes' diversion—but there was a paper folded sans envelope, as public as a post on the notice boards: *Hyde minor, parcel*. The boy had gone home early with mumps, parcel likely collected when he was. *Football Chronicle, Cycling Today*, and another public note, torn from an exercise book: *Look in our place*.

A hand he knew, oh did he know it. Oh heart, oh blood, oh place, *that* place? Addressed to no one, but to whom else? He could feed it to the maw, but he put on his jacket. The age of overreacting was past. He would think before acting.

Finish sorting through the basket, more mail chastely sealed, a paper six days old, and beneath it something wadded, no, folded, puzzle, papyrus, amulet? The larks these boys larked, pretending to be men! Unwrapping easier said than done, but once accomplished, map. Drawn in pencil, star with legend majuscule, *FRIST PANEL ON R*. He knew of only one who spelled that way. The star went with an inset, cryptic symbols save X-marks-the-spot. The back was blank except for three words, written hard and violently underscored: *DESTROY IT YOURSLEF*.

✦

She didn't despise him. Quite the opposite. The new note revived every hope he'd grieved the past week. What was she doing this hour where she was? Had she used his fountain pen as he was using hers? This very pen had written him from abroad, and now at last ink could flow in her direction! The most obvious ideas took the longest to see. He could write her today, this hour even, explain about Valarious, its makeshift status, how unfinished, unreviewed, how half-baked it was. As for whatever she'd left in his pigeonhole, couldn't he simply present this letter as a prelude? *More later! Howzat?* There was no wireless in his exile, but did she dance still, at Seven Ferry Path, to songs whose words she knew by heart? How was it possible for her to be so irresistible when no one watched her?

✦

A cloud began to cover the sun, not enough to stop his eyes from watering, but enough to shade the cloisters until he reached the stone stairs.

First on the right was indeed the place he knew. He never thought a panel could feel so dire.

His goddaughter had seen him possessed by wrath. She'd seen him mishandle the boy, haul him off, throw him in a pit. She hadn't seen the blow, but everyone could see his lip the next day. Behind the panel, nothing now but broken chairs and planks that teetered. The inset showed X in a corner. He tried to shift the clutter, but dust got up his nose. He wasn't cut out for archaeology. Was the notch in that plank like the shape on the map? Perhaps if turned . . . Plank up, hand in. Snakes? Mummies? Only dust as thick as fur, a farce from A to Z.

Except, there, beneath the joists, a corner, four corners, some weight but not too much, no latch, nameplate, tarnished but . . .

✦

—She seemed a pleasant girl, his mother said lightly, Mr. Grieves's goddaughter.

The soup burned his tongue.

—Did you know her at all?

He fought the urge to laugh:

—I wouldn't say so.

Was she merely making conversation? The sky was blue, and the clouds looked like camels, as if magi might arrive carrying gifts no one could ask for or imagine.

✦

The box was partitioned in half. On one side, a uniform stack of brown envelopes, some opened, some sealed. A small spidery hand, almost like a woman's but belonging, apparently, to Dr. Riding. John had never seen a likeness of the man, but the script evoked a fine-boned person, feeling but capricious. Letters written for the occasion of birthdays, three opened (ages eleven, twelve, and thirteen). The one marked for February of that year was inexplicably still sealed. Could it be that the boy was still fourteen, scarcely older than his goddaughter, scarcely older than the one whose misspelled map had led him there? What, God, did Halton and Riding have to do with one another? When Morgan had probed into the business of McKay's barn, hadn't he asked if there'd been a letter involved, or a box? *A box full of made-up stories,* one that had belonged to Riding's father. Jamie's interrogation of Riding returned to him through the fog of time and lies, through the quicksand when John had thought himself betrayed: Riding had gone to the barn to fetch a box, his father's box. All the monstrousness of that day had been in protection of this.

Dr. Riding addressed his offspring as *son* and sometimes as *Gray*, which John had always supposed to be a family surname from the mother's side. The father never addressed him as *Thomas*, and John cringed at the memory of having done so himself. This father wrote of books, of hopes, of memories, all the things he would have liked to say to his son on those birthdays he'd never see. Reading the first letter, a tearstained eleventh birthday a few weeks into the boy's first term at the Academy, John might have wept himself if his eyes remembered how. *I wish with all my strength that I could inhabit more than this page.* What a thing to know your death. *But I haven't gone entirely. You've only to use your eyes, son. Use your eyes, and look.*

◆

The postmistress chattered and sold him a stamp for his letter. He'd never actually written the girl's name before, and as he capped the pen, a bell blared *Halt!* The woman reached beneath the counter and produced not weapon, but telephone receiver.

—Sledmere oh-four.

She held up a finger as if to hold her place.

—This is Mrs. H.

When the connection came through, she turned her chatter to the other party. His alarm faded, and something new began to grow. If there was a telephone at Seven Ferry Walk, he might arrange a time to ring her. He'd no idea what it would cost, but Uncle Peter always gave him a guinea at Christmas. The bigger question was this woman and whether he could trust her to book a call without informing his mother. He'd already sealed the letter and affixed the stamp, but he wrote along the flap with her fine-tipped nib, *Sledmere 04*.

◆

On the other side of the partition, a thicker stack from one Wilberforce, M., written after Morgan's departure for Oxford. Morgan addressed him as *boyo*, a name John had heard Morgan's father use. These, all opened, seemed letters from a different father to an awkward Telemachus, now doubly bereft. He could hear that voice he knew so well, the one that called him Grieves Sahib, trying to look after the boy from afar. It seared merely to read, as if he might return to his study this moment and find Morgan, dressing gown over shirtsleeves, settling down for a late-night chat. Soon it became clear that Riding was not answering the letters. *You, boyo, are out of hand, and I've a mind to ask Mr. Grieves to deal with you from me.* John leaned back against the chairs as fever washed across him. He remembered this. Morgan had begun to write him more frequently, almost like an assistant Housemaster merely away on exeat. He had asked John to take Riding *in hand*. John had invited Riding to the study, given him tea, tried to make sense of how he was faring and why he wasn't doing his prep. Riding had returned only monosyllables and had poured on the Sullen & Resentful as if every ill were John's fault. *You've been giving Mr. Grieves grief, and it won't do, boyo.* John had put him on report for a fortnight, but every evening brought the same frustration. *You don't give Grievous enough credit, boyo. His tastes might run to Cromwell, but I'm quite sure your Elf Rider wouldn't be beyond him. Take this poem that you sent me in the hols, go straight to Mr. Grieves, and show him, from me.* Between the lines, a stranger in their midst, a cold, severe Housemaster, one who awed him, who made him yearn, but who always stood aloof.

Oh, Telemachus! Whither Pallas Athene? Where was her wisdom when needed the most? And what vengeful god kept fathers from home across the seas, across the page, across the years?

✦

His mother believed him: that he'd been posting a letter to Peter, that his throat no longer hurt, that the pen was a gift from Guilford Audsley, who had left school for a command performance in *Hamlet*.

—Can we go down and see it?

She explained all the reasons it was impossible, but he covered his vexation with the kind of jaunty small talk she expected in a son. Michaelmas Term had been first-rate; he was glad for the holidays, charmed by their adventure in the cottage, proud of the position she'd been offered at Scarborough Hospital; he was sure she'd find a house there better than Swan Cottage, a place he never mourned. Such assertions softened her mood and attested to his health. He pretended to believe her, too, about her amusing patients, the endearing letters she had had from Uncle William, the excitement and variety of Scarborough. Her outings each afternoon had been walks in fresh air, and had she mentioned that Peter would arrive in time for Christmas? He acted the boy delighted by a treat, and his cheerfulness made her nicer.

Morgan once called him a professional liar, but what kind of professional was he if everyone but his mother could see right through him? Had his weakness begun with Morgan, who'd demanded the truth, or had it sprung up in answer to the saffron-haired girl who was so true and so real that lies shriveled before her? He lay across the lumpy bed and closed his eyes. Lying took it out of you. He no longer had the strength for it, or the heart.

✦

John folded Morgan's letters back into the box. He'd always dreaded overhearing boys gossiping about him. Their frankness, their criticism, his very visibility sickened him. Now here was this, not even gossip, partitioned from the father's letters by a thin slat, though surely in the realest sense not partitioned at all.

For these Riding had absconded in the night, for these Mainwaring had fallen, for these Riding had lied, but now that John had read them all, he saw less sense than before. Why should a father's letters be hidden in a barn? And why, as to Morgan's, should they mean so very much when the boy had not been able to bring himself to reply? That was the *problem* with archaeology, indeed with the whole disease of history— facts could be recovered, tablets, secrets even from the grave, but possessing them did not guarantee the truth. Another document could emerge—take the business with Richard III—something lost and then found that took everything known and exposed it for a fiction. Even this box felt more substantial than two partitions would suggest, as if it might rattle when shaken—as it rather did, ha! Whatever the truth of this boy— Telemachus loved by Morgan, Bard loved by Guilford, Abelard loved by Eloise—John had drunk enough truth about himself to drown his vanity in gall.

His nose was running and his skin was crawling, medicine overdue. The plank refused to go back down, and when he kicked it, the floor shook as if the balcony would collapse. And the heel that caught him then caught on something else, and he teetered and went down, things collapsing all around, and when he came to rest, he was prone, arm dangling into the floor as if fallen into his grave.

He caught his breath and conducted an inventory: his shin throbbed, but miraculously nothing else hurt beyond the usual. He nearly laughed. If Jamie could see him now, sprawled in this wreckage, sweat soaking his collar, one arm grazing the joists as if groping for buried—paper, twine, tied as if a bundle? Oh, there was absurd and then there was this! Had he missed the part of their fag test that said, *Any private documents, hide them in the chapel?* Dear God, these boys! He pulled himself up, dragged the lantern to his side, hauled out the papers, *All right, miscreants, up you get.*

The blue, the ink, the name that cursive formed . . . just how many letters had this boy received?

✦

The sun outran the clouds, shining low in the sky but promising at least an hour of daylight. He watched out the window until his mother emerged from the post office and slipped into the churchyard. She'd be there until dark, according to habit. He set a note on the table, *Back soon!* The bicycle's tires were firm, its chain newly greased. He wheeled silent past the gate, muffler over mouth, round the bend, though not *round the bend*. If you could laugh, you weren't beyond hope.

His thighs burned to ride again, and his lungs strained. Flying down the lanes, swerving between holes, stamping on the pedals to achieve the tops and then down again, to anywhere, any place she could name. Over the crest, Grindalythe Woods stood in relief, like a cutout forest strung across the hillside. Below, the Academy, dark as a tomb, not even a lamp at the gates. His throat ached suddenly as it did in dreams, not with grief but with affection: here was the Academy, this place where he had been so unhappy and so ecstatic, this place that had grown him and grown into him. Midsummer days in the library, rehearsals in study number six, morning lessons in the dark, clanking radiators, poacher's tunnel, tickling in his ribs when Guilford twirled pencils, when Halton sang, when Morgan rolled up his sleeve, when she pulled him close, when Mr. Grieves pursed his lips, when Pearce, even Pearce, gave passionate badger—it was all passing away, and he wanted urgently to keep it.

◆

How this correspondence had come about, how they had made acquaintance, and how she could have thought such things, never mind commit them to paper and to such a boy . . . He had lost the plot entirely, long before he'd realized there was one.

He had always considered himself a seeker of self-knowledge, but this mirror cut him to the ground. Here was one who wrote with unsparing honesty, nothing like the girl who'd corresponded with him. Through all the letters he'd received, he had never actually known her. But this boy—this boy from the box—he knew her secret heart. Neither one was as callow as he'd flattered himself into thinking. They feared, they grieved, they judged, they loved—and they were both so very ill-served by him. He had taken their feints for cuts, and until this moment he'd been deaf to how muddled they really were. Her final confession, so she called it, did not disclose wrongdoing so much as it testified to ignorance. When it came to right and wrong, she truly did not know her right hand from her left. One could blame the parents, of course, but who had stood at the font and sworn that she, by him, renounced the devil and all his works, and that she, by him, would love and serve the Lord? It was not the custom to speak seriously of the devil, but that didn't mean those works were not still being wrought, through confusion, unholy fear, the twisting of good and the shellacking of evil.

The sun had died behind the walls of the cloisters, and back in his study, the fire had gone out. His arms were full, box and bundles, evidence against him no defense could overcome. This was what one called a cold realization, now literally cold, so at least the scene was apt. This was the moment when men saw their illusions collapse with the tide and then took up their reason to build again on rock. Give up the medicines. Get back on the train and proceed to Cambridge. Take up his duty with his goddaughter. Accept Jamie's invitation, make amends with the Bishop, beg his counsel and help with the girl, and with the boy while they were at it. Here in this box he was shoving under the chair, here was a boy who needed nothing so much as a father, any father who would stand his ground. And here was his Housemaster in loco parentis, put into vexation when the boy was awkward, put into wrath when asked to perform a father's ordinary chastening duty, put into coldness when his vanity for one moment failed to be flattered.

His shoulders were twitching, and he knew that without a dose his legs, too, would begin, and he'd be unmanned, unable to resolve any-thing. Drops and drops, flushed down by something sweeter. Still twitch-ing but softer, he fell into the chair by the dark, dead grate.

It was the twentieth century. He was not Odysseus. He was not even the man he thought himself to be. And the truth—the true truth—was that beginning again would produce nothing better. Hadn't he been kill-ing himself to do his best, only now to see that his best was monstrous? As a scholar he was foolish, as a mentor, dangerously aloof, and as a lover and friend, as essential as a wall hanging. Men employed reason because they believed it would yield a wholesome result. He'd been trying all his life for wholesome results, and not only had he failed, but the field on which to pursue them had vanished. He stood on sterile pavement in a drab, modern street.

Damn reason. Really, damn it. He had never been reasonable despite the lies he told, so why now, after everything, alone in his chair, should he not simply be what he was. Here was medicine, and here was *medi-cine*. He was a drunkard, no better than Owain, who at least had the grace to admit it. He was an addict, a slave to Morpheus, in chains and lustily so. He'd never been allowed to eat an entire bag of sweets at once, but you, pristine poppies, stop pretending, down you go, and you, flask of blood, down with you as well. Oh! What kind of way was that to be-have? Crash-tinkle-splash after only one sip?

She slipped once in stocking feet, grandmother's floor, wrists sliced with the shells of her bracelet. Her mother stopped the flow, arm above head squeezing even as blood dripped. Like or unlike when she did it herself with a common blade? Blood and wine general—hearth, rug, knee, even arm, nothing at all once done (had he done it?), deep, pain-less, blood let out. And the room was thick, heavier than air, *stop the flow, hold him together*, and against his head, the touch of lemon. Could he al-low it now with nothing left to hope? Would it melt the ice that had never been melted, ice in the hand, that instrument of ice? Ice in the hand because torn from somewhere else. From another target, the only target.

✦

The gates were bent where the tree had fallen, so he wriggled through to the courtyard. Some window surely somewhere could be opened, though sometimes secret entrance lay . . . through the front door? Dark, cold, but on the table, candle stub. Matches, light, *wall*? Waves crashed in his ears like a dream. How could the pigeonholes, entire, disappear? And where, flaming angels, were the things they had guarded?

A thump made the hair on his neck stand up. He was too old for ghosts, but his fingers tingled as he reached for that door. If something roared forth, there would be no escape. In his throat, lemon. Stop thinking and go.

 She was paying for the evening paper when a shrill bell intruded, the kind that used to wake them and send Tom out on dark roads. Mrs. H brought up the receiver, an object she regarded like an animal she had never fully trained.

—Sledmere oh-four!

Her expression shifted to insult, then disbelief.

—It's for you.

She extended the receiver like smelly parcel. Elsa put it to her ear as if it might spark. Could wishes without hope come true in a breath, the call from the other side, come through a common wire?

—Yes?

It took her some moments to realize it wasn't Tom, longer to recognize her son and to grasp what he was saying, but even as her equilibrium faltered, her voice held, the firm command of a ward nurse:

—Is he breathing?

Mrs. H offered a stool.

—Does he have a pulse?

Water.

—Does the bottle have a label?

The boy was rattled and confused; her jaw strained with helplessness.

—Is there a doctor? she asked Mrs. H.

—Oh, aye, the postmistress said.

—We need him at once.

—Aye, but you won't have him. Birth up Stockingdale.

She thought the hospital had inured her to crisis, but her hands were starting to shake. It wasn't panic, but something else she knew, the sudden, acute dread that had engulfed them when Tom's numbered days were set before them, beads on a chain short enough to choke.

—Gray, stop talking. You must wake him.

Telephones were the worst inventions. They gave the illusion of nearness without the body of truth.

—Throw cold water on him, slap his face, do whatever is necessary.

In the absence of a doctor, nurses stood in the breech.

—Yes, you can. I'm coming.

Even at the fearsome speed of forty miles an hour, the distance was too far. She had to drive across the playing field to the door the boy described. As he opened the French windows, she took in the scene: the blue-lipped man, the red stains, broken glass. The boy had doused him in water, which he said had provoked momentary sound, but the man had lapsed back into—she pushed the boy aside and felt for a pulse. Her fingers fumbled the buttons then tore the shirt to a chest white and boney, breastbone, knuckles, no pause for pity on that naked spot.

✦

Heart cleaved, weeds about his head, sea—
    —Come on!
    Hook faster than pain, harder than love—
    —Wake—
    Up, wake up, *night is flying*, what bridegroom, what sword—
    —Yes!
    Air, ribs, breaking, broke—

✦

His mother swore. Never in his life—and her face like a washerwoman murdering her laundry, exhorting it with curses to breathe.

✦

She sent the boy for towels. He was laboring to breathe, which meant he could labor, but they could slip away as you watched if the things they swallowed overcame the brain. There was brandy on the floor and a vial without label. Perhaps too late but that should never bar trying.

She turned him on his side, took hold of his head, put a finger to the back of his throat.

✦

When he returned with the towels, the man was propped against the side of the desk. Gray helped her to lift him and haul him into the back seat of the motorcar.

—He's asleep again!

—Be quiet!

Face tight, mouth fierce, she switched on the headlamps and reversed across the playing fields. Back at the cottage, she roused the man enough so they could get him up the stairs to her bed. She sent the boy again for towels and hot water, but she didn't let him back in the room, not that night, and not in the days and nights that followed.

Dishes became his domain. He applied too much soap and too little effort, his mother said, but he took pride in the sight of clean things waiting to be put away. There were people, he supposed, who washed dishes every day of the year. Often he imagined the girl at his side imparting wisdom. Contrary to appearances, he informed her, he had cleaned dishes before, though not many. She would lecture him about the privileges of boarding school, where housekeeping was performed by others.

His mother slept on the chaise longue in the little study off the parlor. She may have also dozed in the bedroom armchair. He didn't think she was getting much sleep. He himself had been disturbed by groans and cries issuing from that bedroom, but it was merely a bad fever, his mother insisted, like the malaria that used to come upon his father. She was immune so risked nothing from contagion. He, however, was to stay clear of the room in every circumstance. She issued her command with such vehemence that he didn't dare disobey. Fear, too, kept him away. He'd never before seen a master incapacitated. What grown man fell so ill unless he was dying?

He asked his mother whether the girl and her father ought to be told what had happened. (Even with a perfect postal service, she wouldn't get his letter before Monday.) What if the man upstairs died?

—He isn't going to die.

When he asked how she knew, she said it wasn't that type of fever. Shouldn't his family be wired anyway, Gray persisted, at least to be told where he was? Certainly, his mother agreed, but there would be nothing assuring to tell them until the fever broke.

The second night passed much like the first, and as he lay awake trying to pretend that the patient was one of his mother's poor unfortunates, arguments with the girl played out behind his eyes. *You'd let me lose him, too, and not give me a chance?*

He tackled his mother again at breakfast, having prepared the eggs and toast himself:

—What if they've been expecting him? he said.

She looked the way she had looked last summer when he'd shown her the roofing that had blown off into the strawberry beds.

When she lay down for a nap, he took coins from her pocketbook and crossed the street to practice charm on Mrs. H. The woman was well and foresaw a busy day. After the shop closed at one, she had mince pies to manufacture, pastry chilling now. Oh, yes, the wire prices were correct, but she could help him, if he needed, trim his message to his coin. Here was paper, pencil. Just what was the thing he most needed to tell?

JG HERE ILL STOP WONT DIE STOP PH SLEDMERE 04 STOP TGRAY

◆

Her mind was blunted by lack of sleep, but she knew the boy was right. The man would be expected by someone, surely frantic now. In the pocket of the man's trousers she had found ticket stubs for Cambridge and York, and in his waistcoat, a card reading *Oxford 67*. She'd never placed a blind telephone call, but her patient had passed a most difficult night. In the parlor, her son was pretending to read. The post office was closing and wouldn't open before Monday. There wasn't time to handle things as she liked.

—Do you recognize this exchange? she asked.

The boy blanched in a way that said it wasn't the card of a stranger.

—It may be his family, she said breezily. I shall place a call directly.

—The post office is closed!

—I don't think so.

—But—but that's Dr. Sebastian's . . .

She'd had enough of this one and his games:

—Bring in some more coal, please.

◆

He waited as long as he could stand before following her. Wind tore down the street, and he could see her speaking into the telephone.

—No, you mustn't come up, she was saying as he entered. I haven't been able to speak with him yet.

The bell on the door tinkled. She snapped around:

—Get out.

—Is that Dr.—

—Now!

◆

Her father said Uncle John had only missed the train, but when Dr. Sebastian rang up to check, she felt a grim vindication; no one missed that many trains. Dr. Sebastian had later telephoned the Academy, but no one answered no matter how long he let it ring.

Friday morning, lunch, supper, dark. *Girls who can't treat people properly don't deserve to have them.* Saturday dark, light, breakfast, lunch. *People who've been happy deserve an equal measure of grief.*

It would be a relief in a way, nothing left to be taken. When the telephone rang, she let her father get it. This blade would never again take her by surprise.

—Are you sure? her father cried. Holy Mother!

She had not arrived late to a house full of people. She knew what she was getting this time, and why.

Another bell, at the door. A boy in a uniform presented a wire, name on the front not her father's, but hers. *This is what happens to girls who—* She tore it, eager, numb with dread. Inside the snake coiled, hissing to show her the landscape of the future.

◆

His mother returned from the post office and made a racket in the kitchen. When he brought more coal for the stove, she brushed past him and disappeared upstairs. His heart pounded in his chest, and then it pounded on the door.

—Thomas Gray?

Mrs. H stood on the mat. He froze.

—Telephone come through for you.

—What's that? his mother called.

Mrs. H repeated herself. His mother darted down the stairs, took him by the wrist, and escorted him like an urchin to the shut-up shop, where Mrs. H passed him the receiver.

—Yes?

Her voice like melting chocolate.

—He's all right, Gray told her.

He'd never heard her cry, not even for her mother, but now came a geyser bubbling in his ear, making him wish that she would cry all afternoon, that he could see her eyes when red and hold her while her shoulders shook.

—It's only a fever, he said at last.

His mother took the receiver from his hands:

—This is Mrs. Riding. To whom am I speaking?

He stood exiled by the magazine rack.

—Cordelia, put your father on the line.

She turned to him:

—Go home.

—No!

—*Now.*

✦

John retched into the chamber pot. There was nothing left, but his stomach still writhed. His chest hurt, too, as if he'd been set upon by professionals. Beneath the covers he shuddered, like something being mauled into life. Had his first birth been as bad? Then, he'd come breathing water, not racked on a feather bed, pain every place that could feel. They were expert at their work. Until this hour, he had never imagined.

✦

He tried to read, but the cries upstairs froze him. They stopped as if on command as she unlatched the front door. Again without a word, she went to the kitchen. He slammed down his book and followed her:

—When are you going to tell me the truth?

Slowly, she turned:

—I *beg* your pardon?

—The truth about what's happening!

He had shouted. She set down a handful of cutlery.

—I can't believe I just heard you say that.

Other times, her tone would have shamed him.

—I'm not a child, to be ordered out of the room when grown-ups want to talk!

She darted forward, but instead of raising her hand, she brushed past him to her workbasket and began to rummage (would she pierce him with a sewing needle?) until she found an envelope, roughly opened.

—When you're prepared to tell me about this, then perhaps we can talk about the *truth*.

An envelope that belonged in his tailcoat.

◆

The symptoms peaked Sunday night. She knew it when she saw it, the body's near-refusal to live without the thing it had come so intensely to need. She sat with him, sponged him, held him down when necessary. This body had little to do with her son's Housemaster, the one she had trusted to guide and to guard him. So many people refused to see the truth when it stood before them, preferring instead to anesthetize themselves with confusion or optimism. Tom had never been that sort of person, and neither was she. But part of being Tom's sort of person was accepting what the facts left behind. If she were to start making excuses for this man—because she wanted him to be trustworthy, and because she wanted him to be as he had seemed through the slant of his script, the pressure of his pen, the daring of his words—if she disregarded facts, she'd be no better than the hospital's patroness, who after touring the ward proclaimed that its patients could be cured if their poverty were eliminated. While not every fact of John Grieves could be known, it was clear that he had fallen into a dependence upon morphine, as the empty vial testified when she put it to her tongue. It was also a fact that he'd failed to reform her son, as the Headmaster's letter attested. She knew she needed to replace her previous idea of John Grieves with the truth of the patient before her. The truth hurt in a part of her breast where she was used to feeling pain, and she recognized the symptoms in herself that she'd endured the first year after Tom, though admittedly not now as acute—sleeping poorly, waking with a curious lightness, remembering the brutal new reality. But even as she urged herself to put feelings aside, she found it impossible to treat this one with the dispassion she showed other patients. He clung to her hand and yelled into his pillow, as if part of him were there with her, waiting on the man who suffered. Sometimes when she bathed his neck, he would reach for her, eyes closed, and rasp a thanks.

The Headmaster's edict alarmed her, but she knew, when she thought coolly, that it needn't be taken as a fixed decision. Much about the future had been thrown into question by her patient's arrival. She'd seen enough cases to know it was futile to be vexed by decisions in the old life. When a person wound up in circumstances such as this, the patient, or the patient's family, would often grasp desperately at details from the life they had just departed—what about the wedding they were to attend? How long could their employer get along without them?—without realizing that the old life was just that; that they stood now at the shore of a new life, and in the process of disembarking, many things would likely be discarded.

There would be time for questions, but not yet. Now she had charge of this body, which belonged to this man, a man who knew her son more than she could ever hope to know him even though he'd come from her and nursed from her and had been known by her before the sea had changed.

◆

If she proposed to flog him with the truth, there were things he could say in return. First, her choice of holiday cottage, across the street from the ground where she'd let them put his father. What kind of person spent Christmas in such a place? Answer, deranged women; *that* was the truth. Second, her expeditions into said churchyard, once and sometimes twice a day. Just what did she imagine? Was she cursing the man or conducting dark rites to raise him from the dead? In either case, letters from his Headmaster faded before such conduct. And if she disapproved of his sitting up late playing Patience, it was a bit steep from one who rarely slept. What did she expect him to do when bedlam noises froze him in the night, when he woke not knowing where he was, Swan Cottage or the Academy, whether his father was dead in the ground across the street or fighting for life in this very house, yards away in another bed.

✦

When the racking stopped long enough to string a thought together, John realized he was naked. He felt a growth of beard on his face. His chest seared when he moved. Of the memories that rinsed through his mind, none seemed to go in a line. Outside a steely sky, dawn or dusk? Too new, too unskinned, his heart strained to have her back, she who had sat beside him, watching, nursing, standing with this wretched man.

✦

He was sitting up in the bed, awake and apparently lucid. She locked the door, set down the tray, and took his pulse. Better. Skin cooler and drier, eyes only bloodshot. When she let go his wrist, he pulled the covers up and looked away, embarrassed. This she expected.

—You needn't. I am a nurse.

He met her gaze with understanding but seemed unable to speak.

—I don't suppose, she said lightly, that anyone expected a few letters would end up like this.

She'd meant it as a quip to put him at ease, but he reddened. The color sharpened his eyes, emphasizing his cheekbones and lips.

—Could . . .

His voice parched and ragged, he asked her what time it was. This, too, she expected.

—It's half past three Tuesday afternoon.

His eyes searched, putting it together. She told him the date, two days before Christmas, and then when his brow still strained, she told him the year.

—I'm not that far gone, he said.

He had a smile that went with his letters. She gave him the tea and then brought him some broth. When he slept again, she departed on her errand, taking bucket and rags in the back of the motorcar. She left the

507

French windows open as she worked, airing the room as she removed remnants of the event. When the school servants returned, they would find only ordinary untidiness, a study whose grate wanted a broom and whose surfaces wanted polish. She explored the nearby rooms until she found one with a suitcase, still packed for a journey. A minor convenience, amidst everything else.

◆

He awoke to a clump—case at the foot of his bed. She was searching the bureau and found a key to open the latch. He gazed at the contents. His case, in fact. She removed his pajamas:

—I suppose you'll be wanting these.

He felt the teasing before he grasped her technique: calm their panic while they face the fear. He peered at the items, clothing, sponge bag, papers—could they actually be term reports? He leaned over the chamber pot, but nothing came up. She closed the case and moved it to the floor.

—Listen, she said.

He mastered himself and sat back in the bed. She straightened the bedclothes and sat beside him, her hip against his, divided only by a sheet.

—The sooner you face it, the easier everything will be.

Pulling back the covers, she exposed his chest, so thin, so sunken, so . . . bruised.

—You can blame me for that.

He shivered.

—That's what it took, waking you. Do you remember?

Did he? A savage hook that had ripped him from the deep.

—I've told him you have a fever. My son.

Her son, the boy—pain flashed through his head.

—He doesn't know about this.

She was gripping his wrist, indicating a dressing where his shirt-cuff ought to be.

—Or this.

The inside of his elbow. That hollow ached, too, and a dark blue line ran the length of it, a river of bruising.

—And he won't know, either, she said.

Command or consolation?

—I've also spoken with your family. Your goddaughter and Mr. Líoht.

Each sentence dispelled an amnesia he hadn't known he had, ringing back curtains on monstrous portraits that had decked his halls all along.

—And to Dr. Sebastian, of course.

He didn't think his heart would survive it, but she took his hand in a way that felt familiar, the friend indeed who'd stood beside him through the torture. Now she answered his questions without his having to ask. She'd told them all enough, she said, enough but not too much. Telephone calls were booked with both parties when the post office reopened after Christmas. He needn't fear their descending in the meantime. They had wanted to come, she said, but they wouldn't. A smile took hold of his face as he imagined Jamie and Owain going up against this woman, this cavalier he longed to call friend.

—Now.

She took hold of his jaw as if she meant to wrench it from his face, turning him to her, eyes dark, voice exquisite:

—Don't you *ever* do anything like that again.

Such orders, from such a vengeful angel. She released his chin and fished in her apron pocket. Vial. Empty. His.

—Never again, she said. Not ever, in your whole long life.

—I'd never imagined that it would be long, he said.

Again the dark stare. He wondered if his jaw was in for another clutching.

—I'm telling you it will, she said.

She placed the vial on the bureau:

—Every time you think of it, you can see it's empty. There will never be any more, not today, not ever.

—My whole long life?

She pursed her lips and told him not to be cheeky. His heart beat everywhere, which showed at least that it still knew how to beat. She brought him broth and bread and instructed him to eat. When he'd finished what he could, she rummaged in his case for a brown-wrapped parcel:

—Why didn't you open it?

Another curtain, portrait.

—It wasn't Christmas, he said feebly.

—It wasn't a Christmas present. It was to say thank you.

Breathing hurt.

—Open it now.

—I . . .

—Consider it part of your treatment, she said.

He took an age over the knot but gained confidence as he unwrapped the paper. He could pull himself together to be gracious with a gift. He was the last person to deserve one, but that didn't excuse bad manners.

It was a slim green volume by a poet he'd heard of but never read. She took it from him and opened to the first page. *Because I do not hope to turn again . . .* How long had it been since anyone had read to him? A lifetime, depending whose life one measured. Meg used to read to him when they'd take a punt down the river. He'd maneuver the pole and she'd read Tennyson or Blake on those long and cruelly short undergraduate afternoons, before everything was lost, time always time, place always only place. He didn't understand the words, but tears were falling from his eyes, dripping into his beard. Would the staircase ever turn, would the leopards leave off feeding, would the lady by the yew trees, spirit of the desert, spirit of the garden, give him water cold enough and deep enough to make a life worth living long?

 The next morning she drew him a bath and let him shave, dress, and come downstairs. Legs weak, head vacant, he felt descending the stairs that he had left something behind, something beyond his vocabulary but in any case unmourned. He sat at a table with his nurse and her son. The boy's attire—half slovenly school uniform, half ill-fitting pullover— jarred him but at the same time sharpened a hunger that had just arisen, almost as he used to get when discovering an author he'd not yet known.

Nurse Riding instructed them both to eat their breakfast and then pestered as if they might disobey. The boy did not meet his eye (whether he would not or could not, John couldn't say), and he resisted his mother in small but persistent ways: dropping a piece of sausage as if by accident onto the floor (not a whole sausage, only a piece); cutting his food into the smallest possible bites and trying her patience with the length of time he proposed to spend eating them; getting up in the middle of the meal to put her pans to soak in the sink; asking her to repeat herself as if he'd been too lost in thought to hear her the first time—a parade of silent dissent.

After breakfast, they sat by the fire in the room she called a parlor. She read him headlines from the morning newspaper but refused to let him peruse it himself: *Sufficient unto the day are the headlines thereof.* The boy took an inordinate time over the dishes and then breezed through the parlor announcing a bicycle outing.

—Sit down and behave, his mother admonished. You aren't going anywhere in this snow.

John was surprised to see flakes blowing past the window and piling up on the gate. His chest ached again, but with pleasure for the simplest details in the living world.

✦

Being forced to sit in a small, close room with one's Housemaster and mother, any concentration for reading broken by their intermittent chatter, would be enough to drive anyone round the bend. Add to that the memory of the girl's voice down the telephone and the picture of her at the Christmas tea, her godfather's arm on her shoulder—his nerves buckled, and he was forced to banish her from his mind as long as this man remained in his presence. No one had said how long that would be, but when he asked his mother when Peter would arrive, she looked up from her knitting in a way that made him feel she'd been biding her time:

—Didn't I tell you, darling? The wire's somewhere.

She rummaged in that sinister workbasket, emphasizing with each rustle that she had her own correspondences and would conduct her affairs without regard to him.

—Ah, here it is.

He took it, jealous and ashamed, wishing he could say he didn't care to read it. BESIEGED BY WEATHER STOP. Stuck in Shetland, no boats out, Peter wished them a happy Christmas and promised to come down in the New Year. He sent Gray his love, and she'd never told him.

—I thought Peter didn't write letters.

—A wire is hardly a letter, darling.

Mr. Grieves was staring at him in a way he didn't recognize, one that made him feel examined. The man sat with his legs crossed on the settee beside his mother; he wore a dressing gown over his shirtsleeves, an unseemly costume that would have been almost scandalous were they not holed up in a let cottage as if on holiday together. Earlier Grieves had drawn a chair up to their table and eaten their breakfast as if it were natural to do so. He had complimented his mother's cookery and now he was chatting with her like some old family friend. At other moments, he behaved as her patient, placid and compliant, as if he might reply *Yes, Matron*. All morning he had bowed to her commands, stirring in Gray the disconcerting feeling of being a fellow subject with him.

✦

Even though the boy couldn't look at him, John could look back, with leisure in the coal-warmed cottage for things he'd lacked the patience or capacity to perceive before. He could see how little the boy resembled his mother after all, and how indifferent he was to her beauty. He could see how tightly the boy held himself, even at leisure, as if a moment's failed vigilance would allow the escape of . . . who knew what? He could see that the Sullen & Resentful he'd experienced at school was merely a restrained version of what the boy performed for his mother. And John could see that the mother didn't understand her son, or that if she had understood him once, she had no notion now of what he'd become, a state of affairs that repulsed and frightened her in equal measure. She didn't recognize the boy's provocations for what they were, and instead took every slight as confirmation of their estrangement. They recoiled, the pair of them, from confrontation or indeed any closeness, clinging instead to a polite armistice, which John found chilly and exhausting. They were lost, these two, like Odysseus at the hands of Poseidon—or were they Penelope and Telemachus, their Odysseus lost to them? His brain was too feeble for analogies, but it was nevertheless obvious that this family, what remained of it, was adrift. The fact that they had no home and had chosen to spend the Christmas holidays in this unlikely cottage in such an unlikely spot seemed to John opaquely symbolic. It was all colley-west and crooked, as Morgan used to say. It could take, John thought, a long time to set right. More time than he possessed even in the long holiday.

But the boy wasn't as impossible as all that, not when John recalled, with an astringent kind of relish, the heart he had discovered in the father's box and the chapel's floor, the one loved by those John loved still.

And as for his mother, John felt almost light-headed contemplating the persons recent hours had grafted onto her—the widow, his correspondent, his nurse, the friend who kept watch and read him back to life. Through it all he could see that a shadow lingered near her, a pain only dimly concealed, and John thought, with a chivalrous indignation, that the shade had overstayed its welcome and that someone ought to show it the door and keep her from following, someone who knew what shadows were but who nevertheless had the bloody-mindedness to lure her into intercourse with the living, as he was doing chatting over newspaper headlines and playing Black Maria. John knew little of cards, but he found her a hawkish player. When the boy pleaded headache after losing four hands, she retired, claiming the game wasn't suited for two. A pity, John thought; he would lose to her all the day if he could.

✦

Mrs. Riding, speaking only through a telephone, had pulled her father together as he'd not been pulled before. Uncle John would not be coming for Christmas, her father reported, but she was not to worry even in the least. Uncle John was in the best of hands and wanted more than anything for her to have the grandest Christmas. They would go and visit him in the New Year with Dr. Sebastian, but meantime, her father told her, they would have a change of scene. She reminded him that she had only arrived in Cambridge the week before; it had scarcely had time to get old. He conceded she was right as always, but was she sure she wouldn't fancy a chalet in Bavaria, sledding, gingerbread houses, a museum of cuckoo clocks? Or perhaps Lapland, reindeer, Father Christmas, Eskimos. Did they have Eskimos in Lapland, or only Laps? He began to hum a tune, and she had to tell him that wasn't how it went.

She purchased an empire map to decorate her empty wall but took it down after one night. Its pink places seemed to suffocate the world, promising journeys arduous and bland.

His first-ever letter had come. It fed and it teased, leaving her more vexed than before. Who was this boy signing himself *Me*? He didn't acknowledge the return of his letters (her letters? theirs?), nor did he allude to her final dispatch, but only wished her a happy Christmas and signed off, *More later, Me*.

✦

She, like her husband, addressed her son as Gray, when she addressed him at all. John couldn't bring himself to follow suit, yet the look on her face when he once called the boy Thomas—as if he'd uttered an obscenity—was enough to scald the name from his vocabulary. He couldn't very well call the boy Riding, not there, so he tried to avoid the direct address altogether.

When the boy retreated upstairs after cards, John picked up the book he'd left behind, a specimen of the penny dreadfuls John was often forced to confiscate. He'd never actually read one, and he spent an absorbed hour with the florid, high-pitched prose. At tea, he tried to make a joke about it, but this only prompted the mother to request that he cure her son of his ghastly taste. When John had said mildly that he'd always found the boy capable of directing his own reading, the boy had scowled as if John had betrayed him.

Yet beneath the scowls, John recognized something else, something he'd seen in the treasure-mapped box: an outsize heart and a mind bewildered by its exertions. The sullenness, he realized, was not insolence but self-recrimination. John watched as bedtime neared and the boy, worn out by the day and its demands, believed himself unobserved. A terrible longing seemed to fill him, but before it could overflow its banks, it was seized in iron fist and turned to imagined accusation.

—Another day wasted! the boy declared.

His mother glanced up from her knitting:

—You needn't take that tone.

—I'm not! he protested. I'll start on the holiday task tomorrow.

The boy hadn't looked at him, but John felt the comment as rebuke.

—I haven't the slightest interest in your holiday task, his mother said icily.

The boy took umbrage and made for the other room:

—All right, I'll start now!

The door closed loudly, knife edge between slamming it and not.

◆

He was stepping out of his bedroom at Swan Cottage. December air drifted along the floorboards, encircling his toes, and he heard the crunch of shovel against snow and glimpsed through the window his mother below, clearing the walk in dressing gown and Wellington boots. Behind the door at the top of the stairs, faintly then louder, his father's voice was singing a Christmas carol. The latch was warm. The door fell open. His father looked up from his work and smiled.

✦

John woke with a gasp. Everything hurt. The vial stood on the dresser, empty his whole long life. His slippers were lost under the bed, but the corridor floor was warmer somehow. He felt his way along it towards the bathroom, but behind the other door, a sound like a howl.

The door was ajar, and moonlight painted the wall. The boy lay on his front, one arm exposed and wrapped around the mattress as if clinging to a raft. His eyes were closed, but there were tears, and a strained sobbing. John sat down on the edge of the bed.

—Gray?

With a cough, the boy turned his face into the pillow. Did he know he was there, or was he weeping out of his sleep? The sound was jagged, throttled, almost—he realized like a blow in the dark—the same as the sound from that other pillow, the cushion in his study where the boy had also cried out, also choked, undergoing something at least as sore and categorically more immediate. He wanted to pull the boy out of his dream, and he wished against all possibility that he could pull him also out of that day, to stop him before it went too far, to shield him from the man he had been.

Another blow then, as sudden as the first but given in the light: What if the fault had not been the orders but the way they had been executed? What if the punishment had wrecked not because it was wicked or because he himself was wicked, but because he had hardened his heart, because he'd hated him, because he'd abandoned the boy when he'd been the most desolate?

Once during a late-night chat, Morgan had been talking of some boy (Pearce?) when he shifted into the confidential tone he used for things he thought John already knew:

—Sometimes it's hard, sir.

—Hard?

—To hurt them.

John remembered the shock of hearing it spoken without the veil of euphemism.

—Or rather, Morgan continued, it's hard to hurt them and not harden your heart.

John remembered his deep unease.

—But that's what it takes, isn't it, sir?

—A strong arm and a soft heart?

John had said it ironically, but Morgan took it straight.

—Better from someone who minds than someone who doesn't, sir. Better than what they do to themselves if left on their own.

—To themselves?

—There are people, Grieves Sahib, who go their whole lives holding on to mistakes, their own cruelest master.

John remembered changing the subject to escape the flood of shame. He felt shame now, but this time he didn't flee. He sat on the bed and withstood it until the boy's tears were replaced by a deep and regular breathing.

This boy had never hated him. This boy had never mocked him. This boy had only needed him, and did even still.

The sun flooded the kitchen window as John lit the stove and made the tea. He was sweeping out the grate when she emerged from the little study, hair loose and tangled.

—You must let me sleep downstairs tonight, he said.

She rubbed the back of her neck and claimed she'd grown fond of the chaise. He wished he could rub it for her, there where she couldn't get purchase.

—Anyway, she continued, someone needs to play Father Christmas.

His mind raced.

—It's Christmas Eve, she said as he realized it.

He had known he would spend Christmas there—she'd told him as much when relating the telephone calls—but it hadn't occurred to him to wonder how it would go, here in this remoteness with these two.

—You'll come with us, I hope?

To church, she explained. Across the road at half past ten. A late supper, she'd thought. He was ready, she judged, to go out.

He poured out the tea as his mind began to fire. They hadn't prepared to have Christmas together, but she had been knitting a stocking cap, and he thought it was almost done. He had nothing to give either of them.

—I need a favor.

—Oh?

She regarded him with hopeful curiosity. He asked if he remembered a motorcar. One that might drive him to the Academy.

—You won't find what you're looking for.

—That isn't what I'm looking for.

He swept snow off the car as she coaxed it to life. Through thick lanes she steered them, undamaged, to the school. He told her to keep the motor running, he wouldn't be long.

French windows he found closed but unlatched, his study smelling carbolic. The whole place seemed reduced in size, like a childhood haunt visited years later. He went to his room and packed a few items of clothing. From the box on his dresser, he removed a pink broach, coral, his father had claimed, carved in a pattern he'd always seen as lace. *Of her bones are coral made, nothing of her that doth fade*—he wrapped it in a handkerchief and put it in his pocket.

From his study, treasure box. And since they needed something to read, he dug through pigeonhole detritus for magazines that had escaped the inferno, amidst which—he wasn't even surprised anymore—yet another letter for Thomas Gray Riding, postmarked the day term ended, hand of Wilberforce, M. Boxes within boxes, secrets within secrets, hearts within minds, and in them all . . . ?

The taps were running upstairs when they came in. Eventually, the boy slouched downstairs, and his mother took in his ill-rested appearance.

—Sat up late with those playing cards, have you?

He shrugged.

—The day's half over, she complained.

The boy's gaze darted to the fireplace, which John had laid but not yet lit. Anxious & Pleasing, John thought, at its peak, though the boy hadn't even spoken. John watched as he bustled, checking the kitchen stove, laying the breakfast table, even tidying the parlor, as if he expected disaster to have ensued in the night.

—Did you sleep well? John asked.

—Yes, sir.

The *sir* stung, though it had been uttered casually enough. It seemed to unsettle the boy, too, and he made for the other room.

—Just sit down, please, John said.

The boy froze.

—I won't bite, not today at any rate.

The boy sat, rigidly, fiddling with a cuff link. John puzzled over something to say, something to put the boy at ease or at least discover whether he recalled his tears in the night, but before anything occurred to him, Elsa called them to breakfast.

At the table, the boy announced that he would forgo church that evening.

—I beg your pardon? she said with lethal calm.

—I think it would be better for me to rest, he continued less confidently.

He produced a yawn and a cough as evidence, but she declared that he could have a nap instead.

As the day wore on and they made an effort to decorate the parlor, such as they could without a tree or, as the boy plaintively reminded her, without their usual ornaments, John saw how much the boy curried her disapproval, yet how her barbs stung him and how her coldness veiled as pleasantry advanced the gears of the A&P until it hardened into the S&R, or something more grim.

—Can't we go to York Minster instead? the boy tried.

—It's much too far.

—We could take the train.

—And how would we get back?

—You brought the motorcar right across the country, yet you can't see a way to get to York tonight?

She plunged her needle into the pincushion, cranberries dangling from the thread:

—I've no idea what I've done to deserve this treatment!

Her eyes brimmed, her voice rose:

—Whatever it is, I'd rather you say it. I'm sure I can't stand any more of your—

She broke off in tears.

John found himself curiously cool, as if he were merely watching a play, one in fact he'd already seen. He felt sure he could write the rest of the script, and indeed the boy was rising silently, taking the coal scuttle, and slipping meekly outside.

How long would it continue, the frankly predictable skirmishing? When both were in the room, the air fairly seethed, but when the boy went upstairs to lie down, a weight seemed to leave his mother, and John's friend returned, the woman he could make laugh. When later he sat alone with the boy, the mother having gone upstairs for a bath, John wordlessly passed him a half-completed crossword. The boy attacked it with zeal, and they passed it between them, silently correcting each other's errors and leaving tentative answers in the margins, until together they mastered it. Were things always this way between the mother and son, or was his presence making things worse? Was he truly a bystander, as he'd been his whole life long?

Sometime after ten, the church bells began to play. John unstuffed his shoes and found them dry enough. He was just taking off his slippers when the boy appeared wearing pajamas and dressing gown.

—Don't, his mother began, don't even—

—I told you I'm not going.

—Thomas Gray Riding, you most certainly—

—I don't believe in it.

—I *beg* your pardon?

—I'm an atheist.

It was all John could do not to laugh. There had been a time, perhaps, when such a declaration might have moved him to ire, but now he found it distinctly ridiculous.

—Atheists are welcome, I'm sure, he said.

She inhaled sharply, and the boy turned on him with a murderous expression. John had meant to diffuse the moment, but now he saw he'd accomplished the opposite.

—Why don't you, the boy said slowly, just shut *up*.

John blinked.

—Gray! his mother cried.

—And *you*! the boy continued in the same venomous tone. If you want to go on worshipping someone who's dead, then please yourself, but I'm not doing it.

She gasped. John almost gasped, but before he could think:

—Apologize to your mother.

—It's true and she knows it.

John got up:

—I said apologize to your mother.

He stood where he was, wondering what he'd do if the boy refused again, but then the boy was turning pink and, inexplicably, grinning.

—It isn't funny.

A smile still, as if he couldn't wipe it from his face.

—Well? John said icily.

Gaze cast to the floor. A graceless apology.

—Thank you, John said. Now you can go in there and wait for me.

He gestured to the small room off the parlor. The boy gaped.

—Go on.

But went, kicking the ottoman on the way. When the door closed, John turned to his mother:

—Go ahead without us. This could take a while.

—But—

—Trust me, this once, please.

◆

He was still smiling even though he knew it was making things worse. When Mr. Grieves came into the room, he tried to compose himself, but Mr. Grieves, too, looked out of character, his face mild and inscrutable. Rather than bark at him, the man busied himself lighting the other lamps in the room, spreading the glow across the whole book-lined chamber.

He felt almost as he used to with Morgan despite the strangeness of the scene. A room that wasn't a study, quite. Housemaster and boy that weren't, quite. His costume the same as he sometimes wore to see Morgan, and Mr. Grieves in his Sunday suit, an outfit Gray knew but not in this way. It was all like a stage set ineptly provided. He threw himself into the armchair in vexation.

—I don't remember telling you to sit down, Mr. Grieves said.

He stood:

—I don't have anything to say to you!

The man turned to face him but said nothing further, leaving him in the middle of the carpet feeling distinctly uneasy, not in the usual way, yet in a way he knew, quite.

◆

John had no plan what to say or do. He trained all his concentration on the lamps. Finally when no more remained to be lit, he sat down in the armchair with a slow deliberation. Each breath brought him further into the scene, the real one they were making together here, and with each breath he admitted another fraction of the truth: he did know what he was doing; it hadn't always been beyond him.

—I have had quite enough, he began mildly, and if you think I'm going to stand by and watch this nonsense, then you're mistaken, I'm afraid.

He let this sink in, for both of them. The boy's frame tightened:

—You're not my father!

Dear God, the gauntlet already?

—And yet, John said, here we are.

The boy gaped:

—It's none of your business!

—And yet, here we are.

—You're not even my Housemaster!

—Yet, here we are.

The calm repetition pushed the boy to his limit.

—I don't have to stand here and listen to you!

—You can leave, of course.

The boy turned furiously and made for the door.

—But I think, somehow, you won't.

Hand on latch:

—Won't I?

—No, John said. Because you know you've been wrong. And you know you deserve it.

—Deserve *what*?

—What I'm going to give you.

He hadn't planned any of it, yet here he was removing his jacket, unfastening a cuff link, and rolling up a sleeve. One did it only for effect, of course, a signal of intent and a first move in the assertion of authority. Now, having done it, he had no choice but to carry it through. Literally, of course, there was always a choice, but despite the boy's petulance, or perhaps because of it, he could see the boy had already joined the pact. He had not left the scene. He was standing at the door, scanning the room—for the customary objects?

—Oh, John said, we can get along perfectly well without that.

The boy looked startled, and John's hands felt unsteady, not in the way they'd been lately, but in the way they used to be before a trial began. He placed a chair in the middle of the rug and took from his foot a carpet slipper.

—Sir . . . !

—We'll have to make do.

His voice sounded bizarrely cheery, and even as part of him was looking for a way out, another part plunged forward with instincts no less keen for having been forgotten.

—I'm too old for that! the boy cried.

—You aren't too old.

He thought the boy might bolt, but he didn't.

—And it isn't too late.

It wasn't like the time with Halton. They were nearly the same size, but with Halton he'd done it to bring him to his senses, done it with vigor, surprise, and a school plimsol that meant business. Now, although the boy was still protesting, John felt strangely relaxed. This would take as long as it took. He told him to hold still, and then he began.

—Your mother doesn't know what to do with you, does she?

He built a certain rhythm that made the words sound natural.

—Does she?

—No, sir.

He continued, reading the breath, the tension, the weight he gave over.

—And your father, what did he do with you?

—Nothing.

—When you'd done wrong?

A gasp, though certainly not from anything he was doing. He sensed the art of it, showing him he wouldn't relent without pushing him over to defiance.

—Gray?

The name sounded as strange as in the night, but judging from the breath, some arrow had gone home.

—I'm waiting.

—He . . .

Don't stop, not yet.

—He wouldn't talk, that's all.

—To anyone?

—To me.

—And when he died?

The boy erupted into coughing. John paused, and the coughing continued, not a performance, though certainly a reaction. John pulled him up and gave him a handkerchief as he fought, as if drowning, for breath. John fetched the wastepaper basket and stood beside him, holding his shoulder and trying to overcome the fear that was rushing in: no one was going to be hurt by a carpet slipper. He'd used it smartly but still, *no one.* This crisis of respiration had to have been conjured by the theater of it, though which part? The assertion of this particular style of authority? The domesticity of it, here in the little book-lined room? The closeness that forced them both into their roles, insisting that he wasn't too old and that it wasn't too late (though, God, for what?). Could it even be the mildness of the act when the boy expected something worse that had unlaced these strings so long knotted shut?

He coughed something into the wastepaper basket, and his breath began to come back under control.

—It's been a long time, hasn't it?

The boy winced, and John let the ambiguity stand. The boy's shoulders had softened, and the impulse to petulance was gone, but he still held something, there in his chest, protected by his arms, which clutched one another.

—Right, John said. Get ready for bed.

—But—

A protest without conviction, issued for form's sake.

—Clean your teeth, wash your face, come back to the kitchen.

This would take, John thought, a long time. More evenings. Many more, perhaps.

He heated water for steam inhalation and prepared the mixture the boy's mother had been giving him. When the boy returned, John administered both.

—It would mean a lot to your mother, I think, if you went to church with her tomorrow.

The boy hacked loudly under the towel.

—I can't.

—Won't, you mean? Have a little charity.

The boy said nothing more, but when it came time for the mixture, he protested. It was vile and useless and he couldn't be forced to take it.

—Don't you think this is wearing a bit thin? John said.

The boy looked caught between cursing and laughing.

—You have my attention, so you can just calm down.

He handed him the mixture. The chin wavered, and he drank it.

—Right, John said, passing him a glass of water. It's time you were asleep before Father Christmas passes us by.

He meant it as a joke in which the boy might play along, but to his dismay it summoned everything he'd labored to repel.

—I wish it weren't Christmas! the boy exclaimed.

—You what?

—I hate Christmas.

Who was he to hate Christmas?

—You aren't too old for presents, surely?

—I don't want them!

—Whyever not?

Eyes threatening tears again, then retracting them, alchemy.

—I don't deserve them.

He took him upstairs, watched as he got into bed. He was too exhausted to read to him, and suddenly too sad. He ought to make him say his prayers, but it seemed too pat and shallow a response. The sorrow that abided in this one answered the same that he carried. He'd been teased about his surname since he was old enough to know what it meant. The old Adam sat on them both. Neither singly nor together did they have the strength to cast it off.

He sat down again on the edge of the bed, and the boy lay with his face turned away. John turned down the lamp and waited for something to say, but his mind was filled with a scouring silence, a limitless nothing when he most needed aid.

The Bishop used to put his hand on John's head, like this. He didn't speak, but he held it this way, fingers on the crown. Sometimes his head seemed to tingle, even like this. Did the Bishop feel it, too, as his fingers were feeling it now, something potent and alien, fierce and good, flowing through him, through the same fingers that tipped the vial that almost stopped his heart, through the same hand that tried to kill this boy, or at least kill him off that day, through the same arm that wrapped around Meg as their lips told silent truth. His hand was touching the top of the boy's head, and the thing that overshadowed was quickening him—real things never happened the way you expected. Cataclysms were all the same that way. You were living a life and then everything was different. The telegram fell, the rock rolled aside, and you were in a cottage as Christmas bells rang, and it was dark, and a star appeared.

Acknowledgments

My thanks to Jennifer Gibbs, Jean Wagner, Wendy Weckwerth, Cameron Henderson-Begg; Jeremy M. Davies, Jonathan Galassi, Alice Tasman, Beth Parker; The Writers Room (NYC), Holy Cross Monastery (NY), and the Hawthornden Literary Retreat (Scotland).